The Faith of Phebe

A NOVEL-OGRAPHY OF A MORMON WOMAN
PHEBE DRAPER PALMER BROWN

The Faith of Phebe

A NOVEL-OGRAPHY OF A MORMON WOMAN
PHEBE DRAPER PALMER BROWN

BEVERLY
THOMPSON

Photo courtesy of Al Rounds
Illustrations by James Cameron Dayton

Distributed by:

Granite Publishing and Distribution, L.L.C.
270 South Mountainlands Drive Suite 7
Orem, UT 84058

(801) 229-9023 • Toll Free (800) 574-5779 • FAX (801) 229-1924

ISBN: 1-57636-040-7
Library of Congress Catalog Card Number: 97-67619

Typeset, layout and cover design by:
SunRise Publishing, Orem, Utah

TABLE OF CONTENTS

DEDICATION

For Jimmy, my husband, who encouraged and helped me with every part of this lengthy project.

For our children; James, Susan, Cynthia, and Kerry and our seventeen grandchildren.

For my mother, Nettie Boulter, who preserved the documents that inspired this work.

For relatives and friends who read and encouraged me to complete the book.

For all the progeny of Phebe.

FOREWORD

Daddy put the old, dusty, wooden box on the oilcloth covered kitchen table. The box was covered with cakes of dust and smelled of musty grain and mice. Mamma, who was always afraid of mice, grabbed the closest towel she could reach and carefully tried to wipe the dust away without loosening the lid. Her nose was wrinkled up from the smell and she stepped back away from it, as Daddy turned the old rusty nails that were bent over to hold the top of the box in place.

I was about seven and very curious about what was in the box. Would a mouse jump out, or maybe a snake? I stayed on the other side of the table, waiting for my parents to reveal the contents of the box. I'm sure my dark brown eyes were as big as saucers and goose bumps as big a gooseberries ran up and down my skinny arms.

"Nettie, I had forgotten about this old box until I found it when I was cleaning out the granary. It has been stuck away in the extra bin with the old furniture and some old trunks I moved to make room for a feed delivery tomorrow." He started to pry the lid up by pushing his big pocket knife down into the dust filled cavity.

As he pried away he continued to tell us about the box while Mamma and I reluctantly watched his progress, not sure we were brave enough to see what was inside. He looked me in the eye and seeing my fright, his blue eyes twinkling, he showed a faked concern for the contents. "I don't know what is in this box but my mother, your Grandmother Boulter, told me I was to always save it. That it was very important to the family."

In those days we listened to mystery stories on the radio. The night before I had heard about some children who confronted a bear in their cellar. Nightmares of the story had haunted my dreams and I was a prime target for another mystery.

"All right, Roy. I think we are ready to see what is inside. Go ahead and lift the lid." Mother's dark eyes were snapping and her mouth started to curve into a smile as she could see Daddy was milking the situation for all it was worth.

"Honest, Nettie. Before Mother died she made me promise that I would always take care of the contents in this box. When we emptied the old house, I put it in the granary with some of the old furniture and I completely forgot about it."

Well, Mamma was convinced now that he wasn't pulling a prank on her. She picked up a kitchen case knife and helped him pry it open.

Mother had been a school teacher before she was married and had always had a very inquisitive nature. Perhaps I had inherited that trait from her, but I think I was just a normal seven-year-old.

She looked into the box and her first words were, "Oh, my goodness."

Well you can imagine that my curiosity was out of control. I climbed up on the kitchen chair by the table so I would be high enough to see into the box.

There were papers, books, old tin type pictures and letters tied together with ribbon or yarn. The papers were quite brown on the edges and, as I recall, some were water stained and it looked like a mouse had found his way into the sealed box and nibbled on some of the contents. Sure enough, Daddy reached in and pulled out the dead carcass of a mouse and I thought mamma would faint on the spot. He walked to the door and threw it out into the back yard.

Mamma bravely picked up the book on top of the pile. It was a Book of Mormon that my Grandfather Boulter had brought from England in the 1850s. There was his name written on the inside cover. The next paper was his citizenship record and then there were blessings, written in beautiful penmanship, that had been given to Grandpa and Grandma. They had died a long time before I was born but suddenly they started to seem like real people, not just the pictures staring out from the bedroom wall.

As mother went deeper into the box, she continued to find more treasures that had belonged to people in our family. There was a picture of an old lady looking rather sad. On the back was written, "Phebe Draper Palmer Brown." There was a picture of another lady but she seemed softer and sweeter. On the back of that picture it said, "Lovina Palmer Munro."

Daddy looked over Mamma's shoulder now. "That is a picture of my Grandmother and the other is of my Great Grandmother. My great Grandmother, Phebe, taught me to read when I was too little to go to school." Then his eyes got all misty like and he took the other picture in his hand. This is my Grandmother Lovina. She had the most beautiful singing voice I have ever heard. She lived with us until she died and even when she was very sick she would sing happy songs to us."

Mother kept taking things from the box until the table was almost covered with the papers. There were cemetery receipts, deeds to property and immigration fund receipts. At the bottom of the box was an old book that almost fell apart as she carefully lifted it out. Holding it with two hands, she asked Daddy to open the cover. I could read the front page that said "Holy Bible." Under that was some writing that was hard to read but I recognized the word "Family."

He turned to the next page where a list of names and dates were written. I could see the same name I had seen on the sad lady's picture: Phebe. As Daddy turned the pages the book fell open to a folded paper. Mother put the book down and unfolded the paper. "Roy, do you know what this is? It is your Great Grandmother's Patriarchal Blessing and it was given to her by the Prophet Joseph's father in Kirtland, Ohio."

Well, that didn't mean a lot to me. I knew who the Prophet

Joseph Smith was because my Primary teacher had been teaching me about the prophets of the church. I decided it must be very important because my mother was reading it and she was crying.

Mamma cleaned up the box, put the treasures back in it and put the box under her bed where we stored most things that we didn't have room for. I could tell that it wasn't going back out in the granary and that Mamma was disappointed that Daddy hadn't taken better care of it.

After that, Mamma wrote a lot of letters to people and some of them came to see the treasures in the box. One lady even took a picture of the Kirtland blessing and the pages in the old Bible and published them in a book.

By the time I was married and had three children, my Daddy passed away. Not long after that Mamma came to live with us. My husband built a special room for her and she had her own drawers for storage in the linen closet. She liked to fill out sheets of her ancestors, and Daddy's also. She wrote histories about their lives and presented them to the Daughter's of Utah Pioneers.

She lived only about eight years after Daddy died. I was so devastated by her death it was all I could do to clean out her room. I didn't touch her drawers of treasures until one day my brother ask to go through them with me. There were the treasures from the old box, carefully put in folders and stacked neatly in the drawer. Now I was old enough to value the contents. I vowed I would take care of them as Mamma had done for these many years.

Last year as I was writing an update of Phebe's history for the Centennial Book on Utah women, I read again the blessing given to my great, great, grandmother by Joseph Smith Sr., the Prophet's father. As I looked at the date written on the blessing and compared it with the 109th section of the Doctrine and Covenants, I realized that it was given the day after the dedication of the Kirtland Temple. From what I had written in the brief history, I could visualize an amazing story here about an amazing lady. It was a story that needed to be written and I was the one to do the writing. My discoveries have spanned a year of research, prayer and inspiration.

PROLOGUE

Phebe climbed down from the wagon, stretched her back and turned her face to the blue Pacific ocean. She was forty-nine years old, thin and browned from the months of travail with the Mormon Battalion. She was the oldest of the four women who had finished the trek, but she may well have been the strongest. With them she had cooked, washed clothes, delivered babies, cared for the sick and encouraged the others with her fervent desire to move on. She had felt the pangs of hunger, the thirst for water and the fear of wild bulls. The heat of the sun had weathered her skin and the cold desert nights had chilled her bones. She was still a thousand miles from her destination but today she could rest and enjoy the warm and comforting sea air. As the waves crashed against the rocks and receded back into the calm waters, they were as a mirror of the happiness and hardships she had and would endure.

Ebenezer left the men under his command and came to her side. His arm encircled her waist and she leaned on his shoulder. They had sent the last of their money north to the main body of the church to help pay for the great migration of saints. The joy of their arrival was dimmed by the stark realization that hard decisions lay ahead of them. They had few options. They could reenlist as Col. Cooke had urged them to do, or they could travel northward to the Great Salt lake Valley with some of the other Battalion members who had been mustered out, which would require them to live off the land and enter the new Zion with nothing to start their new life. They quietly climbed into the back of the wagon where they knelt and ask the Lord to guide them in their decision.

Phebe called to Zemira, her sixteen-year-old son who was an aide to Col. Cooke. He helped her lift down the large pots from the side of the wagon and before leaving to fill them with water, turned to question his mother about their future. Phebe put her hand on his shoulder and said, "We will know tomorrow. The Lord will let us know." Zemira lifted the heavy pot and accepted the answer to his unvoiced question. He could wait until tomorrow. Mother always seemed to know what was best. Hadn't her faith saved them 'til now?

Phebe was a pioneer woman with great faith, fortitude and perseverance. In her eighty-two years she crossed the continent from Canada to Mexico and from New York to California and back to Utah. She traveled by foot, sleigh, wagon, horseback and mule. It appears that each mile and every task answered a call to go beyond her own comfort or personal desire. That same spirit that drove the efforts of her maternal great Grandfather, the noted Reverend John Lathrop (1584-1653) who fought for religious freedom in England, seemed to propel her through life. It was a life of devotion to God, family, and her fellow man.

PART I

FAVORED FROM THE CRADLE
1797—1813
CHAPTER ONE

The early frost had brought the brilliant colors of autumn to upstate New York. Lydia Lathrop Draper looked out the window at the New England array of colors as contractions controlled her body and she knew the time was close for her second birth. She remembered the joy at the birth of her first born son, Charles, who now played at her feet. She wondered if this child she carried could also bring that much more joy and fulfillment to her life. Phebe, her second child, was born later that day of October 9, 1797. As she held her new little daughter, Lydia sensed a special aura and mused over what she would look like, who would she marry, where would she live? Would she choose to stay here in Rome, New York, where the Drapers had been established for the last century or more? Would she become famous and travel to Europe? She kissed the forehead her little newborn daughter, felt the soft brown tuft of hair and counted the tiny fingers and toes. Wrapping her tight in the flannel blanket, she rocked her softly until she heard the rhythmic breathing of a deep, restful sleep.

William came into the room and bent over to kiss his first born daughter, "She is so beautiful, Lydia. Now we have a son and a daughter. The perfect beginning of a wonderful family. Man is that he might have joy and I have it abundantly." He kissed his young wife and saw the glistening of tears in her pale blue eyes.

Lydia looked up at him, "She is beautiful, isn't she. Is

mother still here? I am very tired." She rested her head on the pillow. William took the baby from her, laid it in the cradle and then held Lydia's small, slender hand in his until she fell asleep.

Rome, New York, had been a good farming location and many proud patriots had lived here in the northern part of New York. Two years ago William's family had moved to the southern Ontario area of Canada. His married brothers had joined them and they had homesteaded good tracts of fertile, farming land. They had to live on the land for at least three years and in their last letter to Lydia and William had told of their good crops, hard work and enthusiasm for their future in Canada.

William's father, Thomas Draper, and his mother Lydia Rogers Draper still had unmarried children with them; a daughter Olive and the twins, Joel and Lucretia. The twins were born when their mother was forty-four and she had not been well since. Lucretia was a very small baby but her brother Joel was strong and healthy. They were the same age as their little nephew, Charles. The two Lydias, mother and daughter-in-law, had shared those months of pregnancy together and developed a great love for each other. Lydia missed her mother-in-law now and wished she could share this new little, Phebe, with her.

William, his young wife and child had stayed on in New York to farm the land and harvest the crops. Now the crops of the second year were in and many of them sold. Lydia was glad to stay in Rome to be closer to her Lathrop relatives. She loved it when her mother, Lucy, prodded father, Isaac, to repeat the family genealogy back to the Reverend John Lathrop who maintained his right to religious freedom in old England. Isaac's eyes sparkled as he warmed to the story of the grandfather's capture and imprisonment, and then his exciting escape and migration to the new world. What a strong man he must have been. How proud his progeny were of his history and the influence he had on the people of Massachusetts and the men who had preserved religious freedom as they wrote the laws for this new land.

John Lathrop and his children along with thirty-two members of his congregation arrived in Boston, Massachusetts in 1643. Governor Winthrop commended Lathrop as one who had so "prominently, so ably, and so fearlessly upheld the Puritan faith." Reverend John Lathrop died in 1653 at the age of sixty-eight years after a lifetime of working for the preservation of religious freedom.

The legacy John left to his progeny was one not to be easily forgotten. It was passed on in oral and written history, becoming a force to shape values of those who would carry on the banner of freedom of religion, speech and the press.

Lydia Lathrop Draper had every intention of instilling those inherent precepts in the lives of her children. As the children grew, Lydia taught them letters, sounds and words. She and William daily read excerpts from the Bible and would tell the Bible stories to the children as they taught them about their responsibilities as children of God. The Puritan heritage of both Lydia and William permeated the values they taught their children.

Lydia would smile when she heard the children copying their Grandpa's voice inflections as they recited the family "story" exactly as they had heard it at Grandma Lathrop's home and as she had heard it from her grandfather before. Isaac was the son of Jabes, who was the son of Israel, who was the son of Samuel, who was the son the the Great Reverend John Lathrop. Sometimes the children sang it in a chant as they jumped rope.

William urged the large work horse on along the furrow as he pressed down hard on the handles of the old plow. The roots of the dead stalks hung tenaciously to the dirt and the plow share often found a rock embedded in the soil. The knotted reins hung loosely around his neck, seldom used because the old horse followed the trail of the last turned furrow. The corn stubble would soon be turned under and the field would be ready for spring planting. He had cleared an additional two acres last spring but the drought left him without extra cash at the end of the season. It would be so much easier if he and his brothers could work their farms together. His family had been in Canada for twelve years and he missed them terribly. Olive, his sister, was now married to a Canadian, Pierre D'Honore. His little sister, Lucretia, had not survived her second year. Joel, her twin, was eleven years old. William was thankful for the occasional letter that found its way to them by various sources and brought him news of his family.

The chill in the fall air nipped his ears and the evening shadows lengthened as he headed the horse toward the rustic log barn. His thoughts turned to the happy family that would greet him at the supper table. The babies had come along so fast lately. Carson was already eight, Lucretia was five and Fanny was three. Phebe was a great help to Lydia. He felt some concern that they needed her to accept so much responsibility. She seemed, however, to enjoy mothering the three little ones. He was glad Lydia had found the china tea set for Phebe on their last trip to town.

She was growing so fast and her chubby, childhood characteristics had turned to gangly legs and arms. She was a determined child and often challenged her older brother to spell hard words or add sums faster than she. Her diligence at such a young age puzzled Lydia also. She was as exuberant in her love and loyalty to her family as she was competitive. Just yesterday she had come home from school with disheveled hair and a scraped knee. Charles followed her, insisting that it embarrassed him when she tried to fight his battles. She was quick to remind him that no one was allowed to say unkind things to, or about, a Draper.

It was Phebe's tenth birthday. Lydia brought the birthday cake to the table after the children had finished their supper. Phebe made a wish and blew out the birthday candle. She did not reveal her wish, nor would she ever. After they had eaten the cake, William slipped into the bedroom and came out with a package hidden behind his back. "Happy Birthday, Phebe. We have a special surprise for you." He handed the package still wrapped in the brown store paper to Phebe.

Phebe loosened the string and carefully folded the paper back from the box. The other children crowded around her to see the surprise. She lifted the lid and there was a little china tea set with cups and saucers and a tea pot with a little lid that lifted off and a spout that curved and a handle just like the handles of the cups. A tiny gold line rimmed the top of each cup and the spout of the tea pot. Lavender pansies were painted below the gold trim on the cups with a larger pansy on either side of the tea pot. Carefully, she placed the box containing the precious tea set on the table. Her grey eyes sparkled as she looked up at her mother and father. "Thank you. I will take such good care of it. It is the most beautiful thing I have ever seen."

She placed the little china cups and saucers and tea pot on the window sill by her bed in the loft. It was a wonderful birthday surprise that she would cherish. Yes, it was the best gift she had ever received. If Lucretia and Fanny were very good she would let them play tea party with her but for now she would keep it out of their reach. She knelt down by her bed to say her prayers. She had so much to be thankful for.

The Thanksgiving and Christmas seasons were filled with parties and family fun. The Lathrop clan gathered for all the occasions. The five Draper children were in the midst of it all with goodies to eat and surprises from Grandma and Grandpa

Lathrop. Fanny made them laugh when she said in her three year-old wisdom, "Granny, you make the best tustard pudding." Phebe would be glad when she could pronounce her "c"s.

A hard winter was well established by late December in upstate New York. The Northeasters were unmerciful to the New Englanders. Snow drifts filled the lanes with new storms heaping the white cold frosting higher and higher. As the winter months wore on the children were confined more and more to the cabin. Whenever possible, William would put Phebe and Charles in the sleigh and take them to school in town.

The cold February wind whistled around the house as the children wiped the moisture that had condensed on the window and looked down the drifted lane. The drifts made it impossible for them to go to school that day so Lydia had reviewed their lessons with them and Phebe helped with the house work and meals while her mother rested. A new baby was expected in April and Lydia tired easily as the day wore on. It would soon be time for William to return from the barns for supper. Phebe again, wiped the steam from the window and peered through the growing dusk.

"Mother, a stranger is coming down the lane. He looks like an Indian with leather clothes on and furs hanging from his shoulders." A moment of fear trickled down Phebe's spine and she felt a shiver start from her fingers and move up her arms. Then she heard her father's feet stomp away the heavy snow from his boots on the porch and she felt safer. William threw the door open wide, letting the light and warmth flow out to the lane, and waved the stranger in to the comfort of their fireside. William was like that. No one was a stranger and Lydia could always set an extra plate at the table. William's favorite scripture came to mind as he closed the door, shook hands with the man and moved to Lydia's side in a protective stance. Yes, "even as ye have done it unto the least of these my brethren, ye have done it unto me."

Phebe looked up to the weathered face of an old Indian. As she peered into his eyes she saw warmth and caring. She cocked her little head to the side as if to say, "Why are you here?" Sensing the air of expectancy, the Indian pulled from the buckskin coat a letter addressed to William Draper; Rome, Oneida County, New York. It had been coated with wax to protect it from the weather. William took the letter and held it over the warm fire to soften the wax. It was soon open and as he read it tears glistened in his eyes. He passed it to Lydia who read it quickly. The color drained from her face and she sat down in the chair by the table. The children dared not speak as they saw their parents reaction to the words in the letter. William knelt by Lydia and called the children to him as he read;

> *Dear son,*
> *Come to us as quickly as you can. Your mother is very ill and we fear that she may not last until your arrive. Her greatest wish is to see you and your family before she dies. Our good friend, Okinihah, will deliver this message to you and guide you to us, if it is at all possible. We pray that you can come to us.*
> *Your loving father,*
> *Thomas Draper.*

Okinihah, hearing his name, pointed to himself and smiled. He then sat on the rug by the fire and put his hands out to warm. Phebe put the spoon holder on the table. Lydia ladled up stew from the pot on the stove into bowls which she placed by each cup of milk Phebe had poured. She then opened the oven door and pulled out the warm bread. The aromas of the hot food seemed to soothe the pain of the news. They shared the food with their guest who ate heartily. Lydia wondered if he had eaten since he left Canada. As they ate William talked of plans for the trip north. The winter wind howled outside and the unborn baby turned and kicked as if to remind Lydia that she had yet another soul to care for. Could she make this trip in the dead of winter? William pulled the Bible from the shelf and read to the children before he and Lydia heard their prayers and sent them off to bed.

Okinihah, well fed, curled up by the fire and was soon snoring away in a sleep, long earned from his trip across the ice and snow. William and Lydia lay huddled close to comfort and warm each other. Phebe slipped into their room and gave her mother and father one more kiss and then she said with conviction, "It will be alright, Grandma will wait for us."

The next few days were filled with preparation. Lydia and Phebe baked and prepared food for the coming trip. Clothes were mended, washed, ironed and packed. William arranged with the Clark's on the next farm to take care of the animals. He traded the team of draft horses for a matched team to pull the larger sleigh he received in exchange for the hay wagon. He packed the bottom of the sleigh with hay to feed the horses and also to serve as a barrier to the cold that would permeate the floor. He filled some sacks with oats and tied them to the back of the sleigh.

Lydia came out to survey the progress. She was concerned about her parent's reaction to this untimely trip. "We must see Mother and Father before we leave and tell them the news. Can we try out the new team and see if we can all fit in the larger sleigh?"

Tears rolled down the plump cheeks of Mother Lathrop as they told her the news and their plans to travel to Canada. "My dear friend, Lydia Rogers is at deaths door? You must go to your mother, William, but I worry for our Lydia in her condition. It will be hard on the children traveling north in this terrible weather."

William tenderly laid his hand on her shoulder, "I feel very strongly that we all must go. I promise you, I will take care of them."

"It is your decision. Give Thomas and Lydia our love and come back safe to us." She embraced Lydia and the children, touched William's arm and turned to the house to hide the tears that were glistening on her cheeks below her spectacles. Phebe hugged her Grandpa Lathrop and helped gather the children into the sleigh. "God go with you." Grandpa called to them as they pulled away.

They had said their goodbyes and all was ready for their departure in the morning. One more night of sleep in the warmth of the old log house. William called the family to prayer. They knelt in a circle, holding hands,

> *"Our Father-in-Heaven, we beseech thee to protect us from the elements as we travel north to our dear mother. If it be thy will, allow her to live until we arrive. Bless Lydia and the baby she carries with strength for the journey. Help the children to stay well and be brave as we travel. We thank thee for Okinihah and his safe arrival to us with the letter. Help him to guide us safely to our destination. We put our hand in thy protective care.*
>
> *Thus we pray, Amen."*

CHAPTER TWO

Okinihah and William helped Lydia and the children into the sleigh filled with blankets, clothes and food to last the trip. William jumped in beside them and picked up the reins. "Giddy-up" he called to the horses and they started off at a fast pace. Okinihah rode on the back runner of the sleigh or trotted along side as they traveled north. The drifts were deep in the seldom traveled roads and the horses pulled and jerked the sleigh when the snow was not crusted enough for it to glide over the surface. Lydia held to the side of the sleigh, trying to protect herself as the sleigh jerked forward. It would be a long trip to Richmond, Ontario, Canada.

The first day passed with the excitement of a new adventure for the children. The sun was shining but failed to warm the air much above freezing. They would pull their knitted caps down over their faces when the air chilled their noses. They were making good time and, with the Indian's direction, they hoped to make it to the top of the state before the dark of night crept upon them.

William pulled on the reins and the horses came to a welcome halt as they stopped to prepare some food before the evening light faded. He jumped from the sleigh and gave his swarthy friend a nod of approval, "Okinihah done good."

Okinihah nodded and started a fire with some of the dry hay. The harness was dropped from the horses and they were tethered to the nearby trees and given some hay and oats. They ate the snow for moisture and the children laughed as the horses nosed down into the snow bank and then blew their lips as if to blow the cold away. Charles and Carson imitated the horses and frolicked in the snow after the long confining ride. Phebe and the little girls huddled together by the fire while Lydia and William heated some stew and fed the hungry travelers. A common bed was made under the sleigh. Blankets were draped on the sides for protection from the wind. Okinihah would not join them in the makeshift tent but sat by the fire feeding it with dry twigs he broke from the trees. The children were soon asleep but relaxation came more slowly to Lydia and William. They finally dozed as the bright stars of early morning pierced the blackened sky.

The horses whinnied and shied from the tethers that tied them to the trees. Okinihah was by their side in a flash, calming them with unfamiliar sounds that only the horses understood. William jumped from the bed to help him. Lydia and the children soon followed, pulling on their heavy coats, hats and mittens.

"Wolves near, horses spooked, "Okinihah pointed to the grove of trees to the east where the narrow strips of morning light was just breaking through between the trees. William untied the horses and walked them around for some exercise, watching the grove of trees for signs of the wolves. Okinihah built the fire high and heated some melted snow for a hot drink to warm them. They sipped the warm liquid and folded the bedding, organizing the sleigh for another day of traveling. William threw the harness on the horses and hooked them to the double tree. The family was stowed into the sleigh amid the blankets and they were again on their way.

As the sun neared the arch of the sky, they were approaching the eastern end of Lake Ontario. The ferries were not running because the northern lakes were frozen. The sleigh would have to carry them over the ice and snow to Canada. Okinihah ran by the sleigh as they glided on to the ice covered lake. He watched for soft spots in the ice as it creaked under the weight of the sleigh and horses. He urged the horses on and reassured the family that all was well.

Okinihah guided them carefully across the frozen expanse. He would sometimes kneel down and put his ear to the ice to listen for the special sounds of danger only he could recognize.

The days and nights rolled together for Lydia as she weakened from the rigors of the trip.

Charles and Phebe helped the time to pass with their endless challenges to each other, playing games and singing songs with the little ones. As they snuggled close together in the sleigh the warmth of their bodies blended together to defy the cold and freezing wind.

The second night they heard wolves howling as they reached the Canadian side of the lake. Okinihah built a fire, adding wood until the flames shot high and cinders flew about them. That night the children slept in the sleigh huddled close to Lydia who worried and waited for morning to come. William and Okinihah kept the fire going and quieted the horses when the mournful howls of the wolves cut the black silence of the night. William silently prayed that he could protect his family, that his mother would last until their arrival and that Lydia would be able to survive the trip and give birth to a healthy baby.

Well into the third day, Okinihah let them know they were close as he peered into the woods and watched as they rounded the bends in the narrow, undefined trail they were following. The children were glowing with the cold and anxiety. Just when Lydia thought she could not go on, they came to a fork in the trail and there was Father Draper, waiting for them. Almost frozen stiff, he ran to the sleigh and hugged them all. He had waited for two days at this turn in the trail so they would not miss it. He guided them back along the snow packed path for several miles and finally a wisp of smoke in the distance brought hope to their hearts that the trip was soon to end. Father Draper had assured them that grandmother, though gravely ill, was still alive and waiting for their arrival. She had seen them in a dream crossing the ice in the sleigh, and Phebe, whom she had never seen, was waving to her and calling, "We're coming, Grandma Draper."

The Draper cabin on the Canadian frontier was a welcome

sight to the travelers. Warmed by the fire and love, they were soon settled with a bed for everyone and a place at the table. With the children cared for, Lydia and William went to his mother's bedside. She looked so small and frail lying on the feather tick bed with her head resting on soft down pillows. Lydia recognized the quilt that covered her as one they had pieced and quilted together.

Mother Draper took William's hand. Her voice, barely audible, whispered, "My son. I knew you would come." She reached for Lydia with her other hand. "I love you both and wanted to see you and my grandchildren before I go. I have a message for each of you. Please send the children in one at a time." She looked almost transparent as she lay there but her eyes were clear and it was apparent to Lydia and William that she had something important to tell them.

Lydia leaned over and kissed her mother-in-law's forehead and slipped out, leaving William alone with his mother. She gathered the children together, "Your grandmother has a special message for each of you. I want you to listen carefully to what she tells you so you can always remember it."

William came from his mother's room with brimming eyes, but a look of quiet resolution. He motioned Lydia to go next, and one by one they entered to receive their special blessing.

As Phebe left her grandmother's room she climbed quietly up to the loft and found a secluded corner where she could think of the promises in the blessing. Grandmother Draper promised her, "You have a special work to do for God. Your life will not be easy but you will have protection from opposition. You will have blessings and opportunities come to you. Read and study the Bible so when God is ready for your help you will know what He expects of you. Help your mother with the children and be an influence for good to your brother's and sisters. You are one of God's chosen daughters. Don't ever disappoint Him." Phebe's ten year old mind tried to comprehend what all that meant. She knew if Grandmother Draper said it, it was true and it made her a little afraid. She went over it again, trying to commit it to memory.

The Aunts, Uncles and cousins soon came to the Draper cabin and they each had their time alone with Grandmother Draper. Finally, Grandfather hushed them all and went to her room. He closed the door for his quiet time alone with her. William asked the family to join him in prayer. They knelt by their chairs as their older brother prayed for their mother and grandmother to go peacefully to her maker. Just as he finished, Grandfather came out of the bedroom and tearfully announced that Grandmother Draper had slipped away in her sleep.

The Draper family gathered at the grave side in the grove of trees. The grave had been dug and prepared by the sons of Lydia Rogers Draper; Thomas, William, Carson, David Clark and Joel, who was just twelve. Next to it was the small mound where little Lucretia was buried. The rough hewn casket, also made by the sons, was lowered into the grave and Father Draper released his beloved Lydia back to God and blessed the hallowed ground where she would rest. He wiped the tears from his eyes with the back of his brown gnarled hand. Phebe slipped away from her mother's side and threw her arms around her grandfather. He bent down and kissed the top of her head. How did she know that he felt so alone and that her little arms could comfort him so? She looked up at him and smiled. He smiled back.

Thomas and William stayed to cover the grave. The rest of the aunts, uncles and cousins consoled each other as they walked back through the grove of trees to the house. It was a time of sadness but also a time of rejoicing in being together. The women soon had warm food on the table and were feeding the children while the men filled their plates and found a chair or hearth to sit on.

Bitter sweet feelings welled up in William. It was so good to be with his family again. The hugs, the teasing, and their admiration of his little family. They had always loved Lydia since the day they met her. Sometimes he thought, maybe even more than they loved him. But then, who wouldn't love Lydia. Since his mother's name was Lydia also, they had nicknamed her "Little Lydia" and the name had stuck. She blushed now as they called her, "Little Lydia." She was far from little in the last month of pregnancy. She grinned back and mocked the title, "Little."

"William, fill your plate again and let me tell you how good it is up here." David followed him to the table. The Brothers had a plan for William. He was soon in serious conversation with them as they touted the possibilities for free land and good crops in Canada. They had proved up on their land and purchased more. Father Draper, trying to put his personal sorrow away, joined the men and added his endorsement to the benefits of the Canadian frontier. The fruit crops alone gave them a sizable income and now the trees were mature they were adding other varieties. Why, they could make it so much easier for him because they were all established now.

William and Lydia waited to discuss the possibility of them moving to Canada until the children were asleep. Lydia could see that William's brothers had convinced him that there were great opportunities in Canada. "William, we will need to stay here until after the baby comes. Father Draper needs us to be with him for a while. He will be so lonely." Lydia laid her hand on his arm. "We can decide then about moving."

The children were delighted. They could spend more time with the cousins they had just come to know, and their Uncle Joel, who was the same age as Charles. Every family vied for their company. They had never been so happy. It was like having lots of mothers and fathers who loved you. At least here, Phebe wouldn't have to fight any battles because someone said something bad about a Draper. They were all Drapers.

The air was warming and the buds on the trees were breaking through. The days were getting longer and the pain of losing Grandmother Draper was easing. The men were out working the land while the wives put their efforts into preparing for the new baby. Quilts, dresses, and nappies (diapers) were sewn with loving hands. Bonnets, bibs and sweaters were knitted or crocheted. The hours flew by for Lydia as she added a bit of lace, embroidered a flower or heart, or smocked the sleeve and bodice of a new little dress.

A Midwife in Richmond had agreed to help with the birth and when the pains started, William lifted her into the buggy and took her the few miles to Richmond. It was April 24, 1807. William Draper Jr. was born shortly after their arrival. Though it was never painless, this was one of her easier births. It was a robust little boy with the lungs of a Draper and the stamina to support them. Lydia rested her head against the pillows as the mid-wife, Jenny, placed the baby in her arms and wiped the moisture from her brow. Lydia looked down at him and it was as if she knew he was destined to be an instrument in God's hands as had his grandfathers been before him.

When Lydia was sufficiently recovered, William went again to Richmond to bring her home. Phebe and Charles took turns watching at the window for their parents to return. The other children were asleep. Father had told them they had a baby brother and they were going to name him, William Jr. Phebe was sure she would love him with all her heart and she may let her mother help take care of him. She turned once more to check the stacks of baby clothes she had laid out when Charles called, "I see them coming, they just rounded the bend."

Grandfather Draper stood at the open door with them. His arms around his grandchildren and a lump in his throat. "Oh, that my Lydia could have been here," he thought, and then that sweet peace of understanding encircled him and he felt her presence there.

CHAPTER THREE

Lydia was already homesick for her family. She longed for her old log cabin with the loft for the children, remembering the curtains she had sewed and hung at the windows and that good old stove that baked things just the way she liked them. William seemed so happy here with his family and she knew the children loved it too. Father Draper and Joel would be very lonely without them. She thought to herself, "Lets face it, the farm in New York has not yielded good crops and we have had a bit of a time trying to live on the meager income it generated. I will just pray about it again and this time I won't ask for William to take me home. I'll ask for what is best for all of us."

William saddled the horse and rode to his brother's farms and then back to that of his father. He knew it was time to discuss the move with Lydia. If they weren't staying here he would have to go back to Rome and get the crops planted. He couldn't expect the Clarks to seed his land and take care of his animals indefinitely.

As William came into the frontier farm house, Lydia looked up from the rocking chair where she sat nursing little William. She broke the silence, "I've given it a lot of thought and prayed about it. For some reason I can't understand, I have decided it is best for us to stay here and raise our family. But can I please go to visit my family once in a while?" The words tumbled out before she was aware of what she was saying.

William took two strides and fell to his knees by the rocker. He kissed her tenderly, "Thank you, thank you." He lifted William Draper Jr. from her arms and laid him in the crib and with a twinkle in his eye said, "How often is once in a while?"

William applied for a land grant near that of his brother's and as soon as it was granted to him, the men took their wagons and went south to Rome, New York, for the furniture and personal things he and Lydia had left behind. He was optimistic about his future in Canada and his brothers were so delighted with his decision. Lydia had made a list of things he was to be sure to pack carefully and bring to her. She wrote a long letter to her parents and promised she would come to see them soon.

Phebe made only one request. "Father, please bring my tea set to me, and pack it very carefully. It is so important in my life." William smiled to himself at her urgent request. He hoped he would remember, but if he forgot he could always buy her something even better after the crops were in this fall on his new farm. Each of the other children were allowed one special request. William started south with his list.

The men made good time in their wagons. They had filled them with last winter's apples and sold them along the way. Carson was the salesman with a smile on his face and a glib tongue. Always he carried an apple in one hand and his pocket knife in the other to offer a sample of the juicy fruit. The last of them they saved for Lydia's family.

William and his brothers went to see the Lathrop's and deliver the letter from Lydia. It was difficult to tell them about the decision to live in Canada. They had such strong ties with this new land and had sacrificed so much to be free of the bondage to England. They had serious misgivings about this little family going back to British rule. They respected the Drapers however and knew William would take good care of Lydia and the children. William described the new grandson to them and told them how much the other children had grown. He told them about the trip across the frozen lake and about his mother's death. The brothers began to describe the fertile land of Ontario and the opportunities they saw for their future there.

"And just taste these apples we raise." Carson said as he pulled one from the sack and started to cut it with his knife.

"Enough, enough. We are convinced. But we will never

leave our beloved land. Just you remember to let Lydia and the children come to visit." Grandma Lathrop shook her finger at William and gave him that determined look that only her black, snapping eyes could convey. He gave her a kiss on the forehead and raised his right hand in a formal promise.

He sold his farm, house and animals for little more than he needed to get a start in Canada. He gave what was left of his hay crop to the Clark's for tending to his place while he was away. The men soon had the wagons loaded with everything on the list and then some. They covered them with tarps and tied them down to protect the loads.

William remembered the tea set. He returned once more to the house and climbed to the loft. There, as Phebe had said it would be, was the little tea set waiting on the window sill. He wrapped each piece carefully and packed them between some of the quilts and clothes in a trunk. He smiled to himself, knowing the happiness it would bring to the little girl who had moved to Canada.

Phebe rocked her baby brother, William. She was accused of spoiling him but how could you spoil a baby? He was so perfect. He had fallen asleep with his little hand curled around her finger. As his body relaxed, the grip loosened and his steady breathing told her it was time to lay him in his cradle. The rest of the family was at the new farm where all the uncles were helping William build a house and a barn. It was to be a great house as there was ample wood in the area. A bedroom for the Boys and one for the girls, a sitting room, a large kitchen with room for the big oak table where the family could congregate, and of course, a large bedroom for William and Lydia with room for the baby crib. All the men had put their farming on hold to help William get his family settled.

Every day was like a holiday. After the men had worked

hard all day on the new buildings the wives would bring covered dishes and set the food out on planks supported by saw horses. Roasts of cured meat, hot potatoes, parsnips and carrots, apple pies and cakes and hot bread covered the table. The hungry men ate first, the wives fed the children and then it was time for them to enjoy each other's cooking. "Olive, how do you make that tender pie crust?" Jane asked. She was David's young wife and all these good cooks were quite intimidating to her.

"Yes, I'd like to know too. I haven't made a good pie since I left Rome." Lydia added. "Why don't we get together and you can show us some of your tricks." She put her arm around Jane to let her know that she was one of them.

Olive was a bit embarrassed and still proud that she could do something better than Lydia. She really didn't want to share her pie secrets with anyone, let alone Lydia who seemed to do everything right. "Maybe we can sometime when we aren't so busy." Experience had shown her that they were always busy. "I just use Mother's recipes." As the only surviving daughter she didn't feel compelled to share them with the in-laws.

The children ran through the new buildings on the fresh cut planks. their laughter echoed in the open building. "You're it," Fanny called as she ran to hide in the new game of "Hide-and-seek." Running feet and the quiet that followed attested to the fact that they had all found a hiding place. An occasional squeal revealed that someone had been found and soon the hubbub began again. The men and older children passed by the picnic table again and again to enjoy the left-overs.

Dusk alerted the men to gather the tools and the women picked up their dishes. Lydia had prepared a plate for Phebe who had stayed back to tend the baby.

William put his arms around Joel and Charles, "You boys earned your dinner today. I didn't know you were so good at pounding nails." He laughed at the competition and comradeship that had developed between his son and young brother.

The William Draper family was soon established in their new home and the community. The older children went to school in Richmond and the younger ones were taught by Lydia at home. Phebe spent evening hours reading to her younger siblings and listening to their sums. School Master, John Park, had loaned her a book of poetry to read and she saved some time each night to read the rhyming lines by the Scotsman, Robert Burns.

Sundays found them filing the pews of the little village church. Traveling preachers would expound their interpretations of the Bible, some of them roaring in loud voices as they called them all to repentance whether they had sinned or not. Phebe wondered how good she had to be for God to love her. She probed into her action of the past week. She had helped mother with William, behaved well in school and finished all of her lessons. She had, however, had words with Fanny over the red ribbon for her hair. Fanny's black curly hair looked so pretty. It didn't need a ribbon. Her brown hair, on the other hand, looked much nicer with a red ribbon to brighten it up a bit. She would have to ask forgiveness about her feelings in her prayers. It was very hard not to be a little selfish and vain. What would she have to do to be forgiven?

The Draper clan met together often to dance, sing and play games. They always seemed to find something to celebrate; Spring apple blossom time, finishing the harvest, birthdays, Thanksgiving, Christmas, new babies and marriages. Father Draper was always at the center of the festivities. His joy in this bulging family was evidenced in the sparkle in his eye and his hearty laughter. The little ones would look to him for approval and the teens were at hand to tease each other and mimic their elders in a somewhat disrespectful way. It was all in fun and they all knew that the Drapers were in this life together and that was the way it was.

The one shadow over the family was the brewing war between America and England. William's sister, Olivia, was married to Pierre D'Honore. He was a native Canadian and his allegiances were definitely with the English whereas the Draper's were from Pilgrim stock that fought for freedom from the King's rule. Their migration to the southern frontier of Canada put them right on the battle line of the skirmishes between Indians armed by the English and the American volunteers. Family discussions about allegiances often erupted into heated arguments, the result of which was Olive and Pierre and their children leaving early. More and more young Canadians were showing up in British military attire with the promise of free land to pay for their service.

Phebe was developing into a beautiful young lady, tall and slim. Her brown hair was long and shined from frequent brushing. Her unusual steel grey eyes often snapped as she initiated debates with friends. Her beauty was sometimes overshadowed by her outspoken behavior. She had opinions on many subjects and made sure they were heard. Her interests were broad in that she read everything available to her and often challenged the logic of a traveling preacher or teacher. William and Lydia wondered where she came by her intellectual energy. One of her favorite arguments was about the unjust treatment of American seamen on the oceans by France and England. She also defended President James Madison. She stormed into the house one day with a political cartoon comparing the president to Napoleon. She was furious. Lydia gave a knowing look to the girls and they cleared the path until the rage subsided. Another of her concerns was the current thinking on the Godhead. These preachers were so confusing when they expounded their theories of three but one and being everywhere but nowhere.

Charles and Joel had many friends and often included Phebe in their activities. It was the Harvest Holiday in Loughborough and all the young Drapers were off to the celebration. The crowd was dotted with young men in the uniform of the Glengarry Light Infantry Fencibles. Phebe was invited by several to join the reel lines and as they do-si-doed and swung their partners, her face flushed with excitement. As they completed the set, a tall young soldier who had been in the line, invited her to have some refreshments with him. She was soon into a spirited discussion on the advisability of the conflict between the American forces and the Kings soldiers in Canada. They were well into the debate before her new companion took a breath and ask her name. "I'm Phebe Draper from Richmond but I was born in America and I have strong allegiances to my native land. And who are you?" She said it in such a way that he wondered if she was challenging his worthiness of being here in her presence. He thought to himself, "Who is this snippet who is so sure of herself?"

George straightened his young shoulders, taking on a very military stance. "My name in George Palmer. I just returned from Kingston where I enlisted in the Infantry Fencibles for a three year stint. I leave for York tomorrow."

In spite of her disagreement with the war she thought George seemed very brave and he was handsome in his uniform. He ask her for another dance and swung her into the dance line to the beat of the music. They smiled as their eyes caught across the aisle between the reel lines and caught each other in the crook of the elbow as it was their turn and then holding hands took sliding steps to the head of the line. They held their clasped hands high to form the bridge for the other dancers to go under. Joel and Charles winked at Phebe in a teasing way, as they passed her, but as soon as the reel was over they whisked her away as if to protect her. She remembered the smile, his black curly hair, and the blue eyes that seemed to dare her as they peered out from under the brim of the soldier's hat. Joel winked at Charles and asked, "Did you see Phebe actually speaking to a British Soldier? I think she even danced with one."

"Yeah, its a good thing we rescued her." Charles quipped.

Phebe blushed and poked Charles in the rib.

Chapter Four

Phebe was fifteen that fall and formal school was over for her. The normal school would not be offered another year. Of the seven girls in her class, five had married in summer weddings. Mary Waggoner, her best friend, was going to the states to continue school in Philadelphia at a girls academe. A letter from Grandmother Lathrop had encouraged Phebe to come to New York for an extended visit but Phebe knew her mother needed her. The new Baby, Zemira, was fussy and needed care day and night. Phebe's touch with babies was needed now more than ever.

She was walking the floor with the baby when she heard a knock on the front door. School Master John smiled as she opened the door to him. He removed his hat and walked into the parlor. "Good afternoon, Phebe. May I come in?" He was four or five years older than Phebe. He had dark hair with a very distinctive hair line, parted on the left and always combed neatly back. There was a wisp of a curl on the locks just touching his ears and a slight curl to the short beard he wore. He was not tall, five foot ten, and his soft blue eyes registered a sincerity about him that earned immediate respect from students and parents. He was always neatly dressed with a white shirt and frock coat.

Phebe looked at him with delight. There was no one she admired more or would rather have had come to their home, "Please do come in. How nice to see you. Do you need your book? I apologize for keeping it so long." Phebe moved the baby to the other shoulder and stepped aside for him to enter.

"I would like to discuss the book with you sometime but I have another reason for coming. Is your mother at home?" John glanced through the door to the expanse of the family kitchen. Lydia was lifting the hot bread from the oven. She turned to place the hot pads on the cupboard. She saw this handsome, young man who had become a frequent visitor to their home. She and Master John had often discussed her methods of teaching little children the basic reading and arithmetic skills at home. The success of her children in his school room was evidence of the fundamental learning skills they had received at home.

Lydia came into the parlor and took the baby from Phebe. "Won't you sit down, Master John?" She used the informal way of addressing him that he had encouraged his students to use. She and Phebe sat also.

"Mrs. Draper, I have come to ask you for a special favor. You are aware of how impressed I am with your teaching methods. We have discussed them at great lengths on many occasions. It is my feeling that all of the younger children in the village could benefit from those methods. My time is limited and I am directed to teach only the older children, ages nine to fourteen. I have met with the School Committee and they have authorized me to find someone to help me with the children ages six to eight."

"I have observed that Phebe has a special talent with children. She knows your methods well, having been taught by you personally. Under your tutelage and with some help from me I am sure she could fill this position to which I have referred. Would you and Mr. Draper consider letting her teach at the school as the instructor for the younger children?" John waited for her response.

"Of course they will!" Phebe blurted out and then realized the question had been directed to her mother. She dropped her eyes to her lap but the excitement of the idea sent her heart racing.

"Well, I will have to discuss it with Mr. Draper but we must also consider how Phebe feels about such a great responsibility. I am not sure she would enjoy such an assignment." Lydia was politely teasing her daughter but also knew she must defer the final decision to William.

John stood and shook hands with Lydia, "Let me know of your decision." He nodded and smiled at Phebe with out asking her directly if she would be the teacher of the younger children. He put his hat on and said, "Good-day ladies. I hope to hear from you soon." He closed the door behind him.

Phebe had mixed feelings. She was ecstatic at the idea of teaching the children and working with Master John. At the same time she was furious that her future had been discussed in her presence without including her in the discussion.

"Mother, I would like very much to accept Master John's offer. I would, however, expect him to ask me directly if I would consider the position. Your approval and that of Father are important to me but I think the decision should be mine. I'm going for a walk." Phebe turned and left by the Kitchen door.

A good fast walk through the orchards would do her good. Why were girls treated like possessions when the boys were allowed to make free decisions. Joel and Charles were debating the pros and cons of military enlistment. Just last night Father had told them the decision was theirs. She stomped on between the rows of trees and plucked an apple from a limb. The leaf and stem came with the rough pull. She turned the stem and chanted, "I will, I won't, I will, I won't" until the stem broke loose from the apple. She was relieved that it broke loose on the "I will" part. That silly superstition would not predict her fate, however. She took a bite of the apple and walked slowly back to the house. Perhaps this independent spirit was the part she should consider including in her repentance thinking, "Blessed are the meek."

"Mother, let me know as soon as you discuss the teaching position with Father. I am so excited. I already have some ideas about some teaching games." She skipped upstairs and sat on her bed. She looked at the little tea set on the shelf above her bed. She took down one of the cups and smiled,

"My cup runneth o'er."

John rang the bell and the children lined up in rows according to ages. He introduced the little children to Miss Phebe, who would be their teacher. They followed her into the room and sat on the benches by the tables. She had Charles and Joel come in yesterday and cut the table and bench legs off to make them low enough for the children to put their feet on the floor. She had prepared a box containing a bag of beans, some chalk, and a piece of soft cloth. Under the box was a small slate board.

Phebe wrote in big letters on the chalk board, "Miss Phebe" and then spelled it aloud as she pointed to each letter. She then repeated the process with each child. Soon every name was on the board and all fourteen children were looking at the board and trying to spell their own name. Little William, her brother, was one of her pupils and she had already taught him how to write and spell his name.

She had packed a little sandwich for each of them and brought a pail of milk. After they had eaten a snack she took them out for a game of freeze tag.

At the end of the day she sat at the low table writing each pupils name on a piece of paper. She would test them tomorrow to see if they could recognize their names. They had all counted the beans to ten. Yes, she was going to enjoy this.

John walked in with a newspaper under his arm, "I've read this and I thought you may like to read the editorial. It sounds like this war is going to land right in our laps. How was your day? The first day is always the most tiring. It gets easier after the students get into a routine. By the way, what was that game you were playing with the children?"

Phebe looked up from her printing, "Thanks for the paper. I wish we could get the news more often up here. The game is called, "freeze tag" and the little ones like to play it because they can all run around until they are touched. I have a few variations of it I plan to teach them on other days."

John was treating her as an equal and she felt better about their relationship. He was at least discussing things directly with her and not through her parents as mediators. She must admit, however, they were good mediators. They were actually happy about the teaching position and her mother had helped her block out the teaching plans for the first month.

"What do you have planned for tomorrow?" John asked.

"I plan to review the concepts I introduced today. They should all be able to read and spell their own names very soon and those of the other children also. We will do simple sums tomorrow and practice them with the beans." Phebe wondered if she should ask for suggestions but she felt very sure of what she planned to do.

"It sounds like you have things well in hand, Miss Phebe. See you tomorrow." With that, John left and Phebe picked up her things and started her walk home. There was so much to think about about and also the paper to read. She sighed as she inhaled the fresh autumn air and felt like skipping. She thought better of it and decided she must act more mature if the students were to respect her.

Phebe opened the paper and turned to the editorial. NEW ENGLANDERS HURT MOST BY WAR jumped out at her. She hurriedly read the article and tried to put the war into perspective. Her patriotism had influenced her feeling about the English and French attacking American ships at high sea and she knew the maritime states were war hawks because of the effect of the war on their economy. New Englanders understood little of the intricacies of the conflict between England and France. They saw the war as the second war of independence. As she read down the column she saw the editor's opinion that the "primary battles of the war would be fought on the Canadian border. The Canadian border was where the British were most vulnerable. Land hungry young imperialists dreamed of capturing the whole of Canada. The arming of the Canadian Indians with British guns gave justified defensive reasons for establishing a strong military front on the Northern borders of the states."

The paper was one sent to John from friends in Philadelphia. Other articles talked of the British blockading the American Coast and of troops moving north to join General William Hull at Detroit. A cartoon showed "Old Ironsides", the 44-gun frigate, Constitution, sinking the British frigate, Guerrier. The caption read, "Tally Ho". Headlines of the paper read, "Constitution sinks Java".

"Look at this Father. Will Grandma and Grandpa Lathrop be safe?" Phebe passed the open paper to William and, as he read, the worry lines on his forehead deepened.

"I am concerned about the safety of them and us as well." he replied.

Joel and Charles looked at each other. It had all sounded pretty exciting to join the Canadian Calvary but when it came down to a bloody battle, that was something else. Even the promise of free land didn't make it worth fighting their cousins from the states. Charles nodded toward the door and Joel followed him outside. They still had a lot of thinking to do before they made a commitment.

Phebe changed the mood by sharing the highlights of her first day at school. Lydia was happy for a change of subject. She hated the talk of the war and the news in the paper didn't help at all. "Was Little William well behaved or did he take advantage of you?" she asked.

"He was very good. All of the children were obedient and followed my directions. I think tomorrow I will give them a set of rules so they will know exactly what I expect. I do want them to enjoy school so I won't make too many rules." She made a mental list of the behaviors she would expect and decided she would make the list of things for them 'to do' instead of the things 'not to do'. She started to help Lydia with supper and called Lucretia and Fanny to set the table.

Carson came in from feeding the animals and washed his hands for supper. Little William followed his example. The family was soon around the big oak table. Charles picked up the baby and put him in the high chair. William offered up a prayer of thanks for their bounteous blessings, prayed for their welfare as the war seemed to be escalating, and asked for a special blessing on their loved ones in Rome, New York. After blessing the food the family joined in the "Amen."

The table talk was heightened by the children's first day at school. Carson, Lucretia and Fanny were anxious to share everything Master John had said to them but Little William would not be outdone. "Miss Phebe wrote my name on the board."

Phebe smiled as she realized that her little brother now saw her as the teacher, not the sister. She would still be his sister at home. She loved all of her brothers and sisters but there was something special about Little William.

They were soon off to bed and as Phebe closed her eyes for the night, her plans for the coming day lulled her to sleep.

The daily routines seemed to follow the same pattern. She helped the children get ready for school. They ate the warm cereal and toast for breakfast and then walked to school with Miss Phebe.

Master John rang the bell each morning and school began.

The first three months of school slipped by quickly. The holidays were just around the corner. John ask Phebe to meet with him in his room after school. She straightened up her classroom, picked up her coat and walked into the adjoining room.

"What would you think about us preparing a special Christmas program for the village? Some of my students can write the play and the children from both groups can sing. I wanted to discuss it with you before I talked to the students."

John was so enthusiastic and Phebe was soon caught up in the spirit of the idea.

"I'll help with some costumes and maybe we could get Joel to play his guitar. That would be better than the pitch pipe. They are through with the harvest now so he could probably come over and practice with us during the afternoon school hours. Did you know that "Silent Night" was first performed by Gruber using a guitar for accompaniment? Oh, by the way, I brought your book back. That Robert Burns writes some interesting poems. They are fun to read, once you catch on to the Scottish brogue. My favorite was, "To a Louse on Seeing One on a Lady's Bonnet at Church." My favorite line is:

> *"O wad some power the giftie gie us*
> *To see oursels as ithers see us!*
> *It wad frae mony a blunder free us, An foolish notion*
> *What airs in dress an' gait was lea's us. An' ev'n*
> *devotion."*

I can't decide if he was very religious or just making fun of God or church. What do you think?

John put his chin in his hand in a thoughtful pose. "I think he just understood human nature and used religious settings to help people look more carefully at themselves. He makes us look at human foibles and see them for what they are. For instance, in this other poem, Holy Willie's Prayer. He asks the Lord to judge others without sparing but to have mercy on ourselves."

What fun it was to share things with John. He seemed to know so much about so many things. He was good with the older children too. He listened to them and gave them opportunities to develop opinions about things. He had encouraged her to think for herself. Maybe that was part of this independent spirit she was always worrying about. "May I trade this book for another?"

John went to the bookcase and ran his eyes across the titles. He wished he had more. He pulled another book of poetry from the shelf. "How about William Wordsworth? He is much easier to read than Burns."

Phebe thanked him, tucked the book under her arm and turned to leave. "Oh, I'll be thinking about the songs we need to teach the children for the program. That is such a great idea, John They will have so much fun." She was half way home when she realized she had called him "John" to his face. She must be more careful. She thought of him as John but always addressed him as, Master John Her mind turned to the poem by Burns and she wondered how John saw her. Was she just a former student that was helping him with the young children or was she an intelligent young lady that he may be more interested in some day? She had to admit she hoped it was the latter. She would read this book more quickly so they would have reason to discuss it soon.

The Christmas program night arrived. The school was filled with parents, grandparents, aunts and uncles and the members of the School Committee. When she saw the Committee come in, Phebe was very nervous. What if they decided she wasn't teaching the children enough. What if the children misbehaved or forgot their lines? What it — what if? But she soon regained her composure and motioned for the children to march in. Every head of hair was combed and they all wore their Sunday best. She gave Joel the cue to start and as he strummed on the guitar the children's voices resounded through the room. When the last scene was over and the children sang the last verse of Silent Night the audience sat in silence as if to say "Is that all?" and then they clapped and the children grinned from ear to ear.

The committee congratulated Master John and Miss Phebe for an excellent production. The parents collected their children and the school was quiet except for the broom as Master John swept the bits of red and green paper from the floor.

Phebe was pulling down the paper chains and moving the desks and tables back in place on the clean swept floor. She broke the silence, "Where will you be spending Christmas?"

"I was going back to Philadelphia but I understand the ferries are all confiscated by the Army. I guess I will just take the opportunity to catch up on some reading." John placed the broom in the corner and straightened the papers on his desk.

"Why don't you have Christmas with us? We Drapers have a big time. All the families get together for a party on Christmas Eve and you can't believe the food. Grandpa Draper has a fiddler coming this year. We have the most room so it will be at our house. We will push back all the furniture or put it on the porch so we can dance. Mother and I have been working nights after the children are asleep making Christmas surprises. Father and the boys are going to the woods for a Christmas tree tomorrow." Phebe stood in the door waiting for an answer.

John considered the invitation for a moment and then said, "I would like that. Your family always makes me feel so welcome. Perhaps you should check with your parents."

"They will love having you. We have a tradition at our house you know. We always have room for an extra plate at our table in case a stranger stops by and you are no stranger." Phebe walked out into the night. The snow was starting to fall and she pulled her scarf from her pocket.

John opened his umbrella to protect them from the snow. "I'll walk you home. I can't have my best teacher getting lost in a snow drift." He left her at the porch and promised he would come by on Christmas Eve for part of the party at least.

Phebe hurried in the house. She had never been quite so excited about Christmas before. "Merry Christmas everyone." she shouted as she ran up the stairs.

No lessons to prepare tonight. She pulled the William Wordsworth book from her shelf and started to read but she could not seem to concentrate. She read the line again,

She was a Phantom of delight
When first she gleamed upon my sight;
A lovely apparition, sent
To be a moment's ornament.
She read on to the line:
A perfect woman, nobly planned,
To warn, to comfort, and command;
And yet a spirit still, and bright
With something of angelic light.

Would John ever see her as an Angelic light? Here she was, back to that repentance mood again. She slipped out of bed and knelt in prayer.

CHAPTER FIVE

As spring came to Richmond Canada in 1813 the apple trees blossomed and the new turned soil was covered with seagulls as they gorged on the unearthed insects exposed to the warm air. The war was dragging on, but the fear of conflict in Richmond had subsided. It seemed to be a naval war contested on the Great Lakes more than on land. They occasionally heard of infantry battles but they seemed rather foolish. Neither the Canadians or the Americans had much heart in crossing the border in armed conflict. It seemed that if the American soldiers joined in battle on English soil they were considered professional American soldiers and assumed a five year stint in the army. As in most wars, no one planned on it lasting five years.

Phebe was happy with her first year of teaching. She looked at the little class of children and realized how much they had grown this year. They all knew their letters and sums quite well and could read the stories from the first reader. She often quizzed them and had them write the answers on their slate so she could quickly assess their progress and help those that didn't catch on so easily.

The children were needed to help with the planting and so the school year came to an end. They wished her good-by and ran along home. She would, of course, see them during the summer as they all lived in the village together.

No one had talked to her about a teaching assignment for next year and she hesitated to broach the subject with John. Perhaps he would go to her parents first for their approval. She had cleaned the room and there was little left to do. She picked up some of her personal things and started out.

John met her at the door and thanked her for the excellent progress she had made with the children. "I will be able to start them at a higher level than usual because of the training they have had this year. That is, assuming that I am employed again by the committee. I am to meet with them this evening."

"What of my position?" She had not even considered that John may not be teaching again next year.

"I will come by tonight after the meeting and let you know the decision of the committee. You can be sure you will receive a high commendation from me. You have a natural ability to teach and I would hope that your talents have been noticed by the committee members. Lets hope it will go well for both of us."

Phebe walked slowly home, feeling the soft spring breeze on her face. She tried to imagine what she would do if she did not teach next year. She would be sixteen in the fall and most girls were married by that time or had a serious suitor. She had been so caught up in the excitement of working with John and teaching the children that she just assumed that wonderful things would happen to her. That something wonderful definitely included John but he was just a good friend. Her dreaming of spending her life with John reading poetry and discussing world affairs was just that, a dream. She walked past the house and to her favorite spot in the orchard and sat down in the new green grass under the June Apple tree.

The aroma and beauty of the blossoms reminded her that things change in life, just like the seasons, and sometimes for the better. She would concentrate on the good things in her life and try to improve them. Perhaps John would have good news tonight. It wasn't like her to borrow trouble.

Father greeted him at the door and she could see from the concerned look on John's face that the meeting had not gone well. "The Committee has decided it is not wise for an American to be teaching British subjects while our countries are at war. They are advertising for a new Master to take my place next year. They feel that the new Master should decide if he wants to continue with the Primary School. I am sorry

Phebe. It has gone so well this year. I can't imagine that the parents will not make a request to the committee that it be continued. My only recourse is to go back to Philadelphia and apply for a position in the states."

Phebe bit her lip and held back the tears. She would not let on that her feelings were hurt. "How soon will you be leaving?"Not waiting for an answer she quickly turned, "Oh, I will get your books for you. She walked upstairs, giving her some time to compose her self. She took the last two books he had loaned her, put a smile on her face, tried to bury the disappointment in her heart and walked back downstairs.

He held his hand out for the books, "Thank you, I hope you had time to finish them. Perhaps the new Master will have access to more books than I. I do hope you will continue reading." He thanked William and Lydia for their kindness and hospitality and turned to Phebe. "My best to you, Phebe. I will write you a letter when I know where I will be teaching next year."

Joel and Charles recognized the void in Phebe's life. They tried to keep her busy and happy. They had each found a girl friend in Loughborough and they took Phebe with them to parties and dances. Joel's friend, Eunice, had a cousin, Frank, that came to see Phebe and danced with her at the parties. He was a fair dancer but Phebe described him as "dull". He had a slow wit, was paunchy and his arms seemed to be too long for his body. His blond hair seemed to follow no pattern as if it had never been combed often enough to train it. She was sure he had never read a poem in his life. How could she find someone like John? Would He write to her? Perhaps he would even find a position for her.

It was time for the Harvest festival again and Phebe reluctantly agreed to go with Frank. They were dancing and enjoying the activities when Phebe looked up into the face of that soldier she had danced with last year. He smiled and tapped Frank's shoulder. They finished the dance together. "May I come by to see you? I am on leave for a few weeks? Or does the "turkey" you were dancing with have you all tied up?"

"Frank is actually a very nice person. We are just friends but I did accompany him to the dance. I would be happy to see you again. I'd like to know your views on the war." She smiled and walked away from him, across the hall to where Frank and the rest of their party were chatting. His eyes followed her and he smiled a quizzical smile.

Charles had all their friends mesmerized with his account of his plans to join the American Army. Phebe had no idea he planned to go to America and enlist. She wondered if he had discussed it yet with their parents. Why hadn't he talked to her about it? Joel even seemed surprised. She was sure Joel wouldn't be going because he and Eunice were already talking about getting married. A lump grew in her throat and tears welled up in her eyes. Everything was changing. She, Joel and Charles had been a threesome for so long and it was all falling apart. The music started and she took Frank's hand to enter the dance line. She had to get her composure. Everyone was leaving her; John, Charles, Joel—who would be next?" I wonder if they let girls join the army?" she thought to herself.

"The soldier, what was his name, George Palmer? Was he serious about seeing her?" Phebe was lost in thought as she danced in an automated state. Frank was busy trying to keep up with the beat of the music so he didn't press her for conversation. It was the last dance and as they left the floor she caught the soldier's eye. He tipped his hat in a mock salute and winked.

Lydia turned away and wiped her eyes with the back of her hand as she busied herself with breakfast. Phebe could tell her mother had not slept well. Charles must have dropped the news on them last night. Why had he made such a decision at this time? Her father came in with Carson from doing the morning chores. It was only eight in the morning and he already looked tired. Charles came down the stairs with a bed roll and a pack, full to the brim. They gathered at the old oak table for family prayer, kneeling at their chairs as directed by their father. He led them in the morning prayer and prayed for the safety of Charles, his first born son. A silent sob slipped from Lydias lips. They took their places and avoided facing each other. Two-year-old, Zemira, climbed into the high chair by himself. William cleared his throat and announced, "Charles has decided that his allegiance is to America, since that is the land of his birth. He is going to Rome to visit his grandparents and will then enlist in the American Army."

"We all have an allegiance to America. We cannot forget our heritage even though we have moved across the border into Canada. Grandfather, John Lathrop, would be disappointed if his great grandson had not decided to defend the freedom of America." Lydia had made her speech and defended her son's decision, though her heart was not in it. How do you say good-by to your first born son and send him into dangers way. She ladled up the hot cereal and busied herself with serving the family.

Phebe was still hurting from being excluded from the whole thing. She felt like a rock, unnoticed by the people around her. Lucretia and Fanny were chattering away, giving Charles all kinds of instruction about what to do in America and what to tell the grandparents. Carson was staring at him with admiration. "I wish I was old enough to go with you."

Little William was sitting by Phebe and he took her hand, "I'm glad you will still be here, Miss Phebe." She gave him a reassuring squeeze.

"Your horse is saddled," William hugged his son and passed him the saddle bags Lydia had packed with everything they could possible hold. They all walked to the hitching rail at the front of the house.

Charles put his foot in the stirrup and threw his body up onto the saddle. "Watch out for that red coat soldier, Phebe. I love you all. I'll write when I get to Grandma's." His spirited roan reacted to the nudge of his heel and they watched until he disappeared around the curve.

The emptiness in Phebe's life with Charles gone was greater than she ever imagined it could be. For as long as she could remember they had played together, competed with each other, shared friends and secrets. When you have an older brother like Charles you don't need a lot of other friends but now she needed friends badly. She would go to Grandpa Draper's and talk to Joel. He must be feeling a loss too, even if he did have Eunice to confide in. She took the shortcut through the orchard.

Joel was out working in Grandpa Draper's adjoining orchard. He was attacking the weeds with a vengeance. The shovel hit the dry dirt, hardly penetrating the late summer dry-pan. He kicked at the shovel and loosened the big weed covered with burrs. "I'm glad I'm not a weed," Phebe quipped as she approached him from the back. He wheeled and that familiar grin broke the dusty crust that had formed on his face. He pulled his kerchief from his pocket and wiped the perspiration from his forehead, streaking the dust on his face to muddy smears. Phebe laughed at him. They laughed and felt the relief that comes from laughing when you have been very sad. They each picked an apple and sat in the shade of the tree munching the crisp fruit. They were feeling the absence of Charles and finally talked about his leaving. A part of them wished he was still here and a part of them wished they had gone with him.

That afternoon, Phebe drove the buggy to the general store for supplies. Carson went with her to help load the purchases. She decided while she was there she would spend some of the money she had earned for some material for a dress. She pointed to a bolt on the shelf. Mr. Barnes lifted down the bolt of bright red muslin. She chose a printed calico to trim it and some red thread. The store keeper was itemizing the purchases and adding the column of figures.

"Oh, keep the material and thread separate. I'll pay for that." She opened her handbag and counted out the money.

Mr. Barnes took the money and grinned at her, "I have something else for you, Miss Phebe." He picked up an envelope from the mail shelf and made sure he read the return address again before he passed it to her. She calmly put it in her hand bag as if she received letters every day and helped Carson carry the supplies to the buggy. They said a polite good-by to Mr. Barnes and nodded to some casual friends outside the store. Carson helped Phebe into the buggy and hopped in beside her.

Only after the buggy was unloaded and the supplies put away did Phebe pick up her paper wrapped material and handbag. She walked up the stairs and to the part of the girl's room that was hers. She was so glad Lucretia and Fanny were out picking peas. She looked at the envelope: Miss Phebe Draper, Richmond, Ontario, Canada was printed in the center. The return address was also printed in the neat script Phebe recognized as John's; Mr. John Park, 322 Freedom Road, Philadelphia, Pennsylvania, America. It was postmarked, August 3, 1813.

Phebe opened the letter and read:

> *Dear Miss Phebe,*
>
> *I arrived here in June. There were some difficulties getting on the Ferry but I was able to convince them of my American citizenship. The rest of the trip was uneventful. My family and friends appeared happy to have me back in their company and I have enjoyed being home.*
>
> *As to my future, I have applied at several normal schools in the area as far west as Harrisburg and south to Brandywine. To this point I have not received a permanent position. I am also investigating the possibility of going*

back to the University to study medicine. Doctors are in demand with the many war injuries. Some doctors have been drafted into service, leaving their practices. It is sad that concerns to meet the needs of war overshadow those of teaching the children.

    I had hoped that I would have certain plans by now but as you can see, they are very indefinite. This should be my permanent address for the next several months. It would please me to receive a letter from you with the news of the school and the activities of the village. Have you received a position and is there a new school master?

    Please convey my best wishes to your parents and brothers and sisters. Thank them for their hospitality on so many occasions. I have fond memories of the Christmas party. The Drapers really know how to celebrate. I recall the special glow you had that night. You were as Wordsworth would have said;

    "A perfect Woman, nobly planned,
    To warn, to comfort, and command;
    And yet a Spirit still, and bright
    With something of angelic light."

    Have you read any books this summer? I have been unable to find sufficient time for casual reading and if I choose to study medicine there will be little time for poetry. I await your answer to this letter and wish my best for your future.

    Your friend,
    John Park

Phebe read the letter slowly and then reread it several times. She was then ready to share it with the family. First she would let her mother read it and then perhaps the rest of the family. Carson would tease her about that poetry, especially the "angelic light" part. Maybe she could read it to them and leave out that personal part.

Phebe and George were a stunning couple at the dance. She, in the new red dress and George in his red dress suit adorned with gold braid and gold buttons. Her light brown hair cascaded down her back almost touching her small waistline. The front of her hair was caught up with a red ribbon and tied at a jaunty angle. Her cheeks were flushed, emphasizing the blue grey eyes. He was tall and slim so that she had to look up to him. His chin just clearing the red bow in her hair. His almost black, curly hair and mustache seemed to turn in all the right directions giving him a well groomed appearance. They led the square and as they bowed and turned, George looked at Phebe with adoring eyes. "You are smashing in that red dress. I think every man in the room is lookin' at you."

Phebe blushed and looked around in dismay. Never had she seen herself as a beauty. Now, Fanny was a beauty with her dark hair and snapping eyes like Grandma Lathrop's. Lucretia had a delicate look like mother's with light golden hair and blue eyes. They were both old enough to be at the dance and Phebe measured her beauty against theirs. "Well, the red dress and ribbon did help." she thought.

"We are having a new preacher tomorrow. Would you like to come to church with us and to dinner after?" They had never discussed church before and Phebe wondered if George had any interest in religion.

"Thank you for the invitation. I wondered what you Drapers would be doing on Sunday. I don't go to church often but I'll give it a try again. Guess I need all the help I can get. I go into battle when I get back. At least that was the talk when I left." He was pretty flippant about it.

The new preacher was a dramatic, Protestant orator. His body was as wide as the pulpit topped by a round face with a bushy beard that ballooned out, hiding his ears. The white cleric collar appeared too tight, causing his face to flush a bright red each time the volume of his voice escalated. He called them all to repentance and expanded on all the sins any of the congregation had ever committed or even thought about. His voice rose and fell to emphasize the point he was attempting to make. He would point to one member of the congregation and then another in an accusatory stance and pound on the pulpit. Little William sat beside Phebe and she could see the fear and concern on his face. She took his hand to reassure him.

George leaned over and whispered in her ear, "Now I 'member why I didn't go back to church."

Phebe nudged him and gave a barely audible, "sshh."

The preacher dramatically changed the direction of his sermon to the life of Jesus and his love for little children. "Let the little ones come unto me and forbid them not, for of such is the Kingdom of Heaven." He smiled at the children in the congregation and the Mothers looked at their offspring with adoring eyes and then let that adoration transfer to the pulpit. After a brief supplication to the Lord for forgiveness for all the congregation, he pronounced a loud "Amen" and walked to the door to receive the hand shakes and compliments from the worshipers. His extension of concern to the children with their parents was obviously political.

George lifted Phebe into the buggy he had rented at the livery for the day. "How about a Sunday ride before dinner? I'd like to see more of this town of Richmond."

Phebe was glad to show off their little village. She pointed out the village school, Mr. Barnes General Store, the fruit market where travelers stopped to buy the local fruit, and then out to the farm land. The Draper's farms were well tended and Phebe pointed out Uncle Carson's acreage of orchards and red barn that overshadowed the small cabin where his family lived. Aunt Olive and Uncle Peter's place adjoined it with just a lane between the properties. Uncle Peter raised Tobacco which he sold to the southern tobacco brokers. David Clark and his wife Jane, William's younger brother, had 20 acres east of Grandpa Draper's. Most of his was in fruit orchards of peaches, pears and cherries. Grandpa Draper's was all in apples as was her fathers on the west of Grandpas. The Drapers made up most of the village but other homesteaders, Swensons and Braithwaites, were on lands to the north. The natural valley was surrounded by low hills covered with forest. The Ottawa River was on the other side of the forest.

"This is good land and the people here are hardworking, and God fearing people in spite of what the preacher thinks." Phebe's voice was filled with pride as she looked out over the valley.

"Oh, I wouldn't take much mind to that Holy Rollin' preacher. How does he know what's been goin' on in Richmond? Didn't he just get in to town? Who is he to judge anybody?" George put the reins in one hand and pulled the horse to a slow gait as he put his arm around Phebe's shoulder. He gave her a hug that she somehow felt was more than conciliatory.

"We must get back. Mother will be starting dinner and she needs my help."

George removed his arm and took the reins in both hands. "Oh, I was hoping for a little huggin' out here by ourselves. You look mighty pretty today."

Phebe set her chin, "I'm not the buggy hugging type. Sorry to disappoint you."

"Oh don't get huffy, I was just teasin' ya." He flapped the rein on the horse and urged him into a trot.

George was a perfect gentleman at dinner, using his best traits to win over the family. William and Lydia were asking about family ties and mutual friends. He didn't seem to want to talk about his family but changed the subject to his war experiences. "Did you hear about General Hull runnin' tail at Detroit. We chased him out of their without shootin' a musket. That was last summer before I got there. The first battle I was there to fight was on the Niagara river. It was quite a sight. This row boat's a comin' to us from the south of the river and we're all aimin' our guns at it. A bundle more of 'em are just loadin' up on the other side when the first one turns back. Seems that some dumb private throwed all the oars in the first boat. Van Rensselaer had 'em so fired up they lost their heads a hurryin'. Course, they hit us again but we chased 'em back across the river, us outnumbered too. Come to find out they had a lot o' yellow backs that wouldn't cross the river when they seen things goin' bad. Ole' Van Rensselaer got it pretty bad I hear."

His colorful account fell on deaf ears as William and Lydia pictured Charles in such a battle. It was awkward and Phebe blurted out, "I hope you and Charles don't meet in battle. He has joined the American army and I can assure you he is not a yellow back."

"Oh, I didn't know, I guess I didn't get around to askin' ya where your brother was. I kinda put my foot in my mouth. None of us are in this cause we hate each other. It's all politics and the big spenders. I'm just in it cause they promised me free land. One more year and I'll be turnin' sod on my own place."

"Where do you plan to homestead?" William asked politely, relieved at the change of subject.

"I don't know the area all that well. Maybe you could watch out for a good piece for me. Phebe's sold me on this valley. I'd like to come back here if I make it through the war. I 'poligize fer my war stories." He stood up, shook hands with William and thanked Lydia for the dinner.

Phebe followed him to the door. "When do you go back to war?" They stepped onto the porch and closed the door.

"I leave tomorrow and report on Thursday at Morovian town."

Before she knew it he was kissing her lightly on the lips. "No huggin' OK? I hope you'll be here, when, or if I get back."

He unloosed the reins from the hitching post and jumped into the buggy. He flapped the reins and waved as he drove away.

Phebe stood in amazement. She would have to think about this.

An unfamiliar buggy was coming down the lane from the other direction. A heavy man in a black frock coat and white collar pulled his horse to a stop and got out of the buggy. It was the preacher from church. "Hmm, I wonder what he's doing here?" Phebe hesitated on the porch to greet him.

"Hello, I'm Reverend Black. You must be Miss Phebe. I saw you at church this morning with that handsome soldier. Are your parents at home?" He stepped aside for her to open the door and followed her into the parlor.

"This is Reverend Black, Father. My Father, William Draper and my Mother, Lydia Draper." They welcomed him into the room and offered him a chair.

"I understand the Drapers make up most of the village around here. Thought I should stop by and get acquainted. I have been appointed as the new school master for the coming school year. I like to get to know the families of my students. School will be starting in two weeks when the apple harvest is finished."

Phebe almost held her breath. Would he ask her to teach the primary school? The committee would certainly have discussed it with him. He seemed to know who she was when he saw her on the porch. Did the parents want her to continue?

"I was hoping you would allow Miss Phebe to discuss the wisdom of continuing with the primary school experiment started last year. I am a very traditional teacher and would have to consider this carefully before I gave my approval. I am not sure children ages six through eight should leave their homes for formal instruction. A mother's influence is so important at that age." He nodded to Lydia with a conciliatory smile.

Phebe didn't like him. That was that, she didn't like him. He was obviously a politician that got through life with sugary insincerity She was sure he had never even read Robert Burns or he would see how hypocritical he was. She wondered if he had ever looked himself in the mirror. How could they ask such a pompous person to fill the shoes of Master John Park?

"Miss Phebe, do you have time this afternoon to explain the philosophy behind the Primary School?"

She hoped mother would come to her aid. The thoughts were racing through her head. Of course the children were old enough to learn how to read and work sums. Perhaps he just wanted to teach the basic skills so he wouldn't have to challenge the older children. The mothers had been happy to have their little ones taught last year and had nothing but praise for the school at the end of the year. He would see how advanced the children were because of last years learning experiences

"Mother, perhaps you would join us since I used your teaching methods." Lydia, Phebe and Rev. Black moved to the kitchen and sat at the family table. Lydia explained how she had taught her children the basics of reading and arithmetic before they went to normal school, making it easier for them to move ahead in such classes as geography, literature, Latin, grammar, advanced arithmetic, civics, etc. "Master John Park observed the difference in the students who knew the fundamental skills and thought it wise to give the opportunity to all the children in the village. I helped Phebe the first month or so with her plans and then she continued on pretty much on her own with Master John's supervision."

Phebe added, "All of the children could read simple sentences and solve simple arithmetic problems by the end of the year. We played games to learn the letters and number combinations. We sang songs and the children learned to play games together at recess. Along with the older children, they presented a Christmas program for the village. The parents were very proud of what their children had learned."

"I am concerned about the discipline with an atmosphere of games and songs. I am a very traditional teacher and I expect my students to obey my rules without question. I have written my 'ten commandments of behavior' and part of my curriculum is to have the students memorize those before we move into the regular school subjects. The Bible teaches obedience and so do I. Each commandment starts with, 'Thou shalt not' just like those Moses brought down from Mt. Sinai. I also list resulting punishments. Every parent must sign a document approving my discipline methods before I enroll their child in school."

The color rose in Lydia's face, "You will find the children in the village are easy to discipline. They are used to working, playing and learning together. You may find some resentment to the regimentation you recommend."

"I have discussed it with the Committee and after reading my credentials, they have given me Carte Blanch to determine the needs of the school." Rev. Black was very self assured.

Phebe was torn between what she wanted for the children of the Primary School and her concern about working with Rev. Black. Of course he hadn't ask her yet.

"Miss Phebe, I will observe you for one month and suggest to the committee that you not be paid for that month unless I approve the continuation of the Primary School." He rose to go as if he didn't need an answer to his proposal.

Phebe looked at her mother for a cue. Only those close to Lydia would recognize the slow anger that was rising in her demeanor. "Rev. Black, your offer insults my daughter. She has successfully taught the children and earned every pound she was paid. Her salary was very small but her commitment to the students was not limited by the monetary compensation. We can well afford to provide for her and so do not need her to earn her own money. Mr. Draper and I agreed to the position last year because we saw it as an opportunity for her to extend her learning as well as give service to the village. It is my opinion that she should not accept your offer under the prevailing circumstances. She has already proven her value and is well qualified to conduct the Primary School without your stern evaluation procedures."

He left without a word, pulled his bulky body up into the buggy and sat down hard on the spring seat. The hard slap he gave the horse with the rein belied his composure.

William looked at Lydia for an explanation, "I have never heard you raise your voice to anyone in all the years I have known you. The Rev. Black met his match today. I can hardly wait to hear his sermon next Sunday."

"Mother, thank you for defending me. Now what do we do about school? They made a big mistake when they fired Master John and hired him." Phebe looked out the window, watching the dust clouds raise from the Reverend's horse as he whipped him down the lane.

"Your father and I will visit each committee member tomorrow and the good Reverend Black's methods and discipline program will be carefully scrutinized. I fear that the well documented credentials he claims to have were not come by honestly. No one, who knows anything about children or schools, would recommend him to teach, let alone be a Head Master."

William put his arm around Phebe, "Your mother has spoken. So be it."

PART II

DESIRES IN RIGHTEOUSNESS
1814—1832
CHAPTER SIX

It was the spring of 1815. Phebe erased the day's assignments from the blackboard and contemplated her plans for the following day. Reverend Black had lasted one month to the day and left quietly before the village residents ran him out of town. It took that long to verify his teaching credentials were forged as well as the certification from the Protestant Church he professed to represent. The committee was able to procure the services of, Mr. Joseph Stewart, a former teacher from Loughborough. He had tried his hand at farming but found he preferred teaching. One of the stipulations of his employment was that he include the Primary School concept in the village school. Phebe was invited to discuss the direction of the school with him during his interview with the committee. At the conclusion of the meeting both Mr. Stewart and Miss Phebe were employed for the school year. Mr. Stewart, his wife and children moved to Richmond and became contributing citizens of the village.

Lydia and William Draper became their unofficial sponsors, inviting them to family and village activities until they were well established and felt comfortable with their new neighbors. Mrs. Stewart played the church organ and joined Phebe in teaching music to the children at school. Two of their children were in Phebe's class. The oldest was Little William's age and they became good friends. Confusion abounded since his name was William also. Not to show partiality, they were called William the first and William the second with Little William being the second. Thereafter, he formally became William Draper II. This was fitting because being named after his father he was, in fact, William Draper II. At recess they were dubbed "One" and "Two".

When the school decision was made, Phebe wrote to John Park in Philadelphia to apprise him of the happenings concerning the school. She poured over the letter for a long time before she sealed it in the envelop for postage. Her only reference to the reading she had done was to assure him she was still enjoying books in her spare time and at present was reading, "Love's Labors Lost" by William Shakespeare. She did not tell him about the British soldier, George Palmer. She still didn't know how she felt about his coming back to Richmond, if in fact he would. Every time she was reminded of him she pushed the thoughts back. It bothered her that she thought of him at all.

Phebe threw herself into her school assignment and found many ways to improve her teaching skills. She used the children's slate boards repeatedly to monitor their learning through immediate response to problems she gave them. It was evident that their writing skills improved as they had to write their answers. Hours of making flash cards of simple words and charts of stories written by the group had the students reading earlier in the year than last year. She had made up for the loss of the first month of school by Christmas.

Newspapers were seldom available after John left and she wondered if she could request copies sent to her from the Philadelphia Inquirer. She found the last copy John had given her and located the address. It would be money well spent since Charles was serving somewhere on the American front. In his last letter he had talked about the troops moving to Blandensburg, Maryland.

Charles stood with friends on the board walk outside Bloker's Tavern and watched the stream of humanity pouring over the bridge from Washington to Virginia. They had stood watch the night before and must report to the lines in just a few hours. This was one of the few brief furloughs they had been given in weeks. The army was very small in light of the danger that lurked on the Atlantic coast. A British blockade was tightening from Maine to Mississippi. Word had reached the Virginia troops of skirmishes up and down the coast. Cape Cod had been plundered and Stonington, Connecticut was bombarded into ruins when they failed to surrender to Admiral Thomas Hardy. At Hampton, Virginia the British had landed and because of a weak defense the town had been pillaged, women raped and people murdered in their beds. The peripheral boundaries of New York City closely resembled those of the Revolutionary War. Men were forced to "volunteer." Maryland called out 3, 000 militia and fewer than 300 reported.

Panic prevailed as Charles and his friends watched people fleeing Washington. The booming of the big guns bombarding the city was heard in the not far distance. Puffs of smoke and flames of fire lighted the sky. With each piercing sound the masses on the bridge pushed on faster. A young woman tripped on the hem of her dress and would have been trampled to death if the agile soldiers had not jumped to her rescue. People were scattering over the countryside, finding shelter where ever it was available. Businesses closed and bolted their doors against the pushing intruders. Animals and chickens were shooed from their barns and hen houses to provide hiding places. Government employees carried files from their offices. Valuables had been hurriedly thrown into carts and buggies. The soldiers laughed as they saw velvet dresses and petticoats in an unorganized pile on the seat of a buggy. An ostrich plumed hat was teetering on the top of the heap. The owner sat unashamedly in her petticoat and bloomers beside her clothes, whipping the horse on through the throng. Time was of the essence.

The crowds were still pouring over the bridge when the soldiers left to report to duty. The noncommissioned officers were urging the men to prepare to defend the city but there was a general reluctance to move ahead. Foot soldiers walked at a slow pace along the back roads, trying to avoid the stragglers leaving the city. They bivouacked for the night but few slept even though the guns stopped at midnight. What tomorrow held weighed heavy on their minds as the smoke settled into the dampness of the night. The sweltering August heat denied them the comfort of sleep.

Charles crept to the edge of town with the rest of his troop. They had scattered across the countryside taking cover and waiting for the orders to advance. From his viewpoint, Charles could see the Capitol and the White House still smoldering from being torched. The pungent odor of burning wool carpets and velvet drapes hung heavy in the air. Fresh flames shot into the sky as breezes fanned the embers of yesterday's pillage.

British Admiral, Sir George Cockburn, was riding around the city ordering his foot soldiers to destroy the rest of the buildings. As they approached the newspaper office he shouted, "Destroy the typeset. They've printed their last nasty stories about Admiral Cockburn." As the men approached the building, an earth shaking explosion rocked the crumbling, smoldering city. A British soldier had dropped a torch down a well. To his surprise, and demise, the well was a secret storage of barrels of gunpowder. As explosions followed in static, repeating rhythms, the bodies of the British soldiers were plummeting into the air. Winds raised by the displacement of air from the exploding gun fire pulled at trees and windows. A hurricane like storm hit the city, rolling cannon about like logs and ripping the roofs left from the few standing buildings. The scattered American soldiers moved from their hiding places and to some of the British soldiers looked like a large army encircling the city. A call of retreat sounded and the red coat invaders fell back.

When the British attacked Baltimore the American forces were ready for them. After twenty-five hours of British Bombardment, the American flag was once again raised over the city. The British withdrew to the Caribbean.

Charles would remember those two days of battle whenever he would hear the lines penned by Francis Scott Key, "Oh, say does that Star spangled Banner yet wave?" He would feel that joy and pride once more that he felt that day as the battle ended.

By Christmas, the war seemed to be winding down. There was rumor of peace negotiations going on. There were still shortages of supplies as the British were doggedly blockading the major ports. Prices were high and soldiers were ask to take script for payment that could be exchanged for property or cash at a later date. A decisive battle for the Americans defending the Canadian border at Lake Champlain turned the war to America's advantage. England's, Duke of Wellington, was offered a North American command. London acquiesced to talks of peace. Christmas Eve, 1814 the peace terms were finally signed in Ghent, Belgium. Sadly, the two main causes of the war were not addressed: Free trade and sailor's rights, and a United States-Canadian border, later to be determined by boards of commissioners.

Indian skirmishes still erupted on the frontier. Before the news of the peace terms reached the states the great battle of New Orleans was fought with Andrew Jackson's Tennessee backwoodsmen and Kentucky riflemen leading the defensive assault. It was a rout with the British wounded and killed numbering 2, 036 as opposed to 21 American casualties. When Phebe finally received her Philadelphia Inquirer the headlines read: THE GREAT NATION OF AMERICA DEFEATS BRITAIN AGAIN!!!

Charles was mustered out with most of the volunteers as the states fought forced subscription and wanted to put the war behind them. He went to Rome, New York to see his Lathrop grandparents and then on to Richmond to be reunited with his family. He was lean and tanned from his months on the battle-field. He was a mature man now, no longer the carefree boy that rode away two years before.

The family took a holiday from the spring planting and held a gala celebration in his honor. Away from the festivities, Phebe and Charles walked through the orchard. Phebe took hold of her brother's hand, "I'm so glad you came back safely. We missed you so and prayed for you every day. May I make a request?"

"What is it little sister?" he asked jokingly.

"Next time you make a big decision in your life, will you tell me about it?"

"I was afraid you would talk me out of it. It took all the courage I had to do what I felt I must do." He kicked a clod of dirt, "I'm pretty glad to be back. I missed all of you and was afraid I may never see any of you again. There were times when I thought about the family around the oak table praying for me. You can be sure that gave me courage to go on.

I don't know what I am going to do now. Just stay around here and help Father and Joel for a while until after Joel gets Married. He tells me he is going to take over Grandpa Draper's farm. What are your plans?"

Phebe stopped and pulled a blossom laden branch of the apple tree close enough to smell the sweet aroma. "School will be out soon and now the war is over I was thinking about taking Mother to see her parents in New York. Her trip back to Rome never did seem to materialize. There was always a new baby or the war or something to prevent it. Do you think the two of us could safely travel to up state New York now?"

"Sure. With the ferries and coach travel it would be easy. I'll take you to the ferry. Our Lathrop grandparents aren't getting any younger and they would love to see you. It has been over eight years and that is a long time. Does Mother know about your plans?"

Phebe looked up at him, "I couldn't even think about it until you arrived home safely. Now things are settling down, I'll ask her and Father what they think about the idea. I never remember them being parted. Maybe Father won't let her go."

They walked back to the house discussing Joel's impending wedding to Eunice. Charles smiled as he thought about Joel and Eunice. "They seem so right for each other. Have you noticed how they sort of glow when they are together?"

Phebe nodded her head in agreement. "I'm glad they are going to live with Grandpa Draper. He would be so lonely if they had decided otherwise. I am going to have a party for her and invite all the girls who live here in the village. I have been making some special linens for a wedding present." Phebe started making a mental list of the guests.

Fanny ran from the house to meet them, "Phebe, you have a letter from Master John. Carson just brought it from the store."

Phebe sat at the kitchen table and opened the letter.

April 12, 1815
Dear Miss Phebe,
Much has happened since my last letter to you. You must know by now that the war is over and things are starting to get back to normal. It was amazing how many things we needed that were unavailable because of the British blockade. My favorite tea was no where to be found and new books were out of the question. I found an old edition of Christopher Marlowe's poetry in an old book shop by Independence Square. I like the challenge of reading the old style of poetry. The new poets are easy to read but take little thought to interpret.

I have enrolled in a medical school and have done some work in a clinic. I think I will finish the program but my real love is teaching.

Our mutual friend, Mary Waggoner, and I happened to be attending the same concert in the city. It was such a delight to see her. She is a governess to some children from one of the prominent families here in Philadelphia. They hired her as she finished her year at Bryn Mawr girl's school. We see each other quite regularly when we have free time, she from her position and I from my studies. She inquired about you and your family. I let her read your last letter. We laughed about your description of the Reverend Black. I am so relieved that my former students were not subjected to such as he.

Phebe, I am seriously considering asking Mary to marry me. Since you know us both so well I wanted to ask your advice about the matter. I will not be financially able to support a wife for at least another year, however, so have some time to mull it over. Please write back to me with your thoughts on the matter.

What are your plans for the future? Please write soon. The mail seems to move faster now the war is over and I am anxious to hear of my dear friends in the village of Richmond.

As always, give my regards to your family. I hope Charles is safely home.

Respectfully,

Your friend, John Park.

Phebe reread the letter and slowly walked up the stairs without sharing it with her family. Fanny sensed her sister's mood and turned the attention of the others to Charles and Joel coming in the door.

"I am thinking of asking her to marry me." Phebe read the line again and tried to sort out her feelings. Yes, she and John were just very good friends and anything else that she had imagined was just a fantasy. She took the little tea pot down from the shelf and held it with both hands. If she could read tea leaves and if there were really tea leaves in this little pot, what would they tell her? How would she answer his letter? She had lots to tell him about Charles, Joel and Eunice, the progress of the children at school and... The feeling of emptiness that came over her was indescribable. There was a void in the corner where a little light of hope once flickered. Of course, he should ask Mary to marry him. She would be perfect for him. By now she must be a very refined lady and they could share such a good life together in the society of Philadelphia.

A tear leaked out of the corner of her eye but she willed no more. She could make a good life for herself and so could John. They would just be different. She picked up the letter, pinched her cheeks, forced a smile and took the smile and the letter down to share with the family. "Come and hear the news from Master John, he is going to be a doctor."

Phebe wouldn't allow herself the privilege of wasting her time in self pity. She would keep busy and think of other things. She started immediately to make plans for Eunice's party. She made a list of the girls she would invite and planned the refreshments. If Mother helped her they could make something special. Perhaps some fancy cakes with berry topping. The first berries should be ripe by then. She would invite the guests early enough for them to make Eunice some special gifts for her trousseau. She still had some lace to finish on the pillow shams.

As soon as the wedding was over she and Mother would go to Rome to see the Lathrops. Maybe they should take Little William and Zemira. Yes, they should definitely take the little boys. They hadn't seen their grandparents in Rome and everyone should have the blessing of knowing their grandparents. Little William had learned to read so well. They would be very impressed with how smart he was. Oh, my, there was so much to think about. She would write to John and then get busy with all of her projects. There was certainly no time to sit around and pine over something that never would be. She had plenty to fill her time and thoughts.

Lydia had pieced a beautiful quilt top for Joel and Eunice. She and the girls were preparing to quilt it. The furniture was pushed back in the parlor to make room for the quilting frames. Lucretia, Fanny, Phebe and Lydia each took a corner of the guilt back and stretched it tight to square it to the frames. Then they moved to the center of each side and pulled to the center of the frames and pinned the fabric to the center mark. The sky blue material matched the blue pieces repeated on the pattern of squares and triangles on the quilt top. Lydia rolled out the wool batting she had carefully combed to remove all the burrs. As she unfolded the pressed quilt top over the wool, the girls each took their side and stretched and pinned. Lydia remembered the beautiful quilt Mother Draper had made for her and William. Every stitch of this quilt was a memory and tribute to this woman who had been such a good friend to her. It was the least she could do for her Mother-in-law's youngest son and his new bride. Joel seemed like a son to Lydia. Sometimes when Joel had needed counseling it was as if Mother Draper was by her side, helping her know the right things to say. Yes, this was her gift to Joel and Mother Draper.

The girls threaded their needles and stitched tiny quilting stitches in the ditch of the seams. They chatted as they worked and Lydia looked at her three girls with pride. They were all good cooks, housekeepers, seamstresses and students. Then she contemplated the unique qualities of each of her daughters.

Fanny was the bubbly one of the family with a giggle for every story she told. She was always repeating something funny one of the children had said and had the whole family laughing before she was through with the tale. She made friends with newcomers as fast as she met them and her black shining hair caught the eye of the most casual observer. Every color she wore seemed to be drawn from the rainbow just for her.

Lucretia was quiet, holding her thoughts to herself, unless she was alone with you. Then she would release them as if it was her only time to share those very personal ideas. Her charm was in a reserved demeanor that gave one the impression that there were secrets to be shared, but only with the chosen few. When Fanny giggled, Lucretia would smile and the little wrinkles by her eyes would tell you she was controlling her laughter. Her blond hair, blue eyes, and fair skin gave her the essence of fragility and elegance. She moved gracefully and Lydia envisioned her at a grand ball, bowing to a gentleman with a powdered wig.

Phebe, was an enigma to Lydia. She remembered the day she was born in the old log house in Rome. Even then she seemed to challenge her fate. Phebe was in control. Mature for her age at every stage of life. Her beauty was radiated from an inner soul that seemed to direct her thoughts and decisions in life. Her hair was brown and she also had blue eyes but they were more of a steel blue that conveyed the strength of her convictions. Her religious nature was evidenced in so many ways. It seemed that she was the one who, along with William, had a deep abiding faith that the Lord would take care of them and those they loved. She thought of the blessing Mother Draper had given Phebe when she was only ten years old. The promises of protection through opposition made one wonder what this child would face in her lifetime. Her fine features belied her strength and perhaps it was that very characteristic that surprised people when she expressed her strong convictions. She was the brightest of all of Lydia's children though they were all good students. Phebe accepted learning as a challenge and a God given privilege. Her sense of direction in life was unequaled in the family. Lydia felt the twinges of disappointment for her since her letter from Master John. She mused, "How does one know a real love from an imagined one?"

"I'm ready to roll my side, how about you?" Lydia was pulled back to the task at hand as Fanny stood to release the clamps from the quilting frames.

"Fanny, the fast one, will have us all with pricked fingers. Rest your back and see what Zemira is doing while we catch up to you." Phebe chided.

Lucretia finished her seam and tied off the thread, "I'm ready when you are." She pulled the thread from the spool and directed it through the eye of the needle. Snipped it off and rolled a little knot in the end. She reached in and pushed the needle into the next row, ready to start when the quilt was rolled.

"Yes," Lydia thought, "The Lord has blessed me with lovely girls. I wonder if that soldier will come back to see Phebe this summer. William was supposed to look for land for him. I'll bet he hasn't thought another thing about it. I'll have to ask him if he remembered. Now what was that brash young man's name? George something, I think."

CHAPTER SEVEN

George sat erect in the saddle of the large, strawberry roan steed he had received as part of his reward for service in the Glengarry Infantry. He reined in as he reached the Draper Lane and walked the horse up to the hitching post. It was a warm July day and his horse had worked up a lather on the ride over from Loughborough. He dismounted and looked at the house with some reservation. How often he had thought of that kiss on the porch and his hasty departure. He could hardly hope that a girl like Phebe would still be single. If she wasn't there he could always ask her father about the available home-steading land.

Lucretia answered the door. She hesitated a moment, not remembering him at first. "Oh, please come in. Mr. Palmer isn't it?"

George took his hat off, wiped the dust from his feet on the porch mat and stepped inside. "Lets see, you're Lucretia or is it Fanny?" He walked to where Lucretia had motioned him to sit in the parlor.

"Yes, I'm Lucretia. Are you here to see Phebe? She and Mother and the little boys have gone to New York to visit our grandparents. We are expecting them back next week." she said shyly.

"Well yes, I did come to see Phebe, but I would also like to talk to your father. My, you've grown a piece since I saw you last. You must be fifteen by now."

The color rose in Lucretia's cheeks, "I'm just fourteen." She did not like to talk to strangers and Mr. Palmer was almost a stranger. She had only seen him a few times last summer. She wished Fanny were here. She could chat his leg off and not even have to stop to think of what to say. "Father is out in the orchard if you would like to see him."

He stood and moved to the door, "Thanks, Lucretia. I think I can find him."

"Oh, would you like to stay for supper?" She had almost forgotten the family rule and Father would be disappointed if he knew a visitor had not been invited to a meal in his home. It was so hard to remember all the things mother did. Being the oldest daughter at home was a big responsibility.

"Why, yes, I'd like that. I'll go out and find your Pa."

Lucretia checked the chicken roasting in the oven. She had made bread and some apple pies. Next she should peel some potatoes and shell the green peas she and Fannie had picked that morning. She put a clean white cloth on the oak table and took the dishes down from the cupboard. Let's see, that would be six for supper. The blue and white china dishes sparkled as she placed them on the milk white cloth. The knife and spoon on the right side and the fork on the left with the glass at the tip of the knife, the blade turned in. Some of those bluebells by the back door would be pretty. She would get them when she went to the ice house for the cool milk. She sang softly as she peeled the potatoes and shelled the peas. New potatoes and peas were a family favorite in the summer. She added some wood to the fire box of the cook stove and put the water on to heat. The windows were open to catch what summer breeze came by. The table looked beautiful. "Oh, the napkins. I forgot the napkins."

"Whew, what's the occasion?" Fanny ran in the back door. Without waiting for an answer she was going on and on about all the nice things Eunice had in her trousseau. Eunice had spent the afternoon showing them to her and Fanny had helped her put them away. "I don't think she'll even have to use a bit of Grandma Draper's dishes or linens. That will make Aunt Olive happy. She thinks she owns everything that grandma ever touched. Have you seen how she manages to take one of the pretty dishes home with her every time we are at Grandpa's? Heavens knows what she takes when no one is there. Every time I think about that shocked look on her face when Grandpa gave mother the cake plate with the gold trim, I just start laughing. 'Why Lydia, Mother always said I was to have that.' Mother just smiled and told her she would take good care of it for her." Fanny had imitated the voices so exactly that Lucretia was giggling right along with her.

"So, who's for dinner? The white table cloth and blue dishes? Six plates? Last time I counted there were only five of us at home." Fanny lifted the lid from the pot on the stove, "New peas and potatoes?"

"George Palmer is out in the orchard with Father and the boys. I think he came to see Phebe but when I told him she was in New York he ask for Father. Do you think he is going to ask Father if he can marry her?" She peeked out the window to see if they were coming in.

"He'd better not say yes without Phebe's permission. Remember how upset she was when Master John ask Mother and Father about her teaching the Primary school and didn't ask her. She thought we didn't know but we knew, didn't we? I wonder if she likes George as much as she likes Master John. We girls have hard decisions to make sometimes, don't we?" Lucretia nodded yes to all of Fanny's questions.

After dinner, the men sat in the parlor while the girls washed and dried the dishes and tidied up the kitchen. "I'm not sure where the homestead land is for the next draw out. I heard it would be in the next valley around Northumberland. Maybe in the area they call Cramahe."

"It sounds like Indian country. Have you ever had trouble with the red skins?" George asked.

"No, they have been very peaceful in this area. My father befriended them when he first settled here and they have been friendly ever since. In fact, it was one of his Indian friends that brought our family up in 1807. They come through here occasionally but we usually feed them and send them on their way with some of our fruit. Even during the war, the local Indians didn't seem to get involved in the skirmishes. They travel in families and seem to live off this lush land covered with wild berries and plenty of white tail deer. There is so much water around that they find plenty of fish also." William was concerned that people understand the Indians and appreciate their right to live in the area.

They discussed possible crops to raise in Cramahe and the best trail to follow to get there. Charles offered to ride along with George if it would help and William encouraged him to go. He knew Charles had been restless since he came home from the war and it would do him good to get away for a few days. He marveled at the friendship that had sprung up between the two when they had so recently been on opposite sides of the war.

George thanked the girls for the dinner and complemented Lucretia on the "tasty pie". He and Charles arranged a meeting time for the following day.

"Did he ask for Phebe?" Fanny asked.

"No, we mostly talked about farming and what good land was available. He seems like a nice sort, ambitious and knows what he wants." William picked up the family Bible and started to read where he had left off the night before. It was obvious that Fanny wasn't going to get any more information from Father if there was more to get. He finished the book of Matthew and looked up. "I do miss your mother. How many more days until we go to meet the Ferry? It seems like they've been gone forever. I hope they're having a good time but I will be so glad when they get home. Lucretia, you cooked a mighty good meal tonight. I'm glad you invited George to stay. We never want to send anyone away hungry from our home. Your mother will be proud of you when I tell her."

Lucretia smiled with adoring eyes at her father, appreciating his kindness. Not only to strangers, but to everyone in the family. He was just like Grandpa Draper. She gave him a hug and ran up to bed.

Fanny pressed again, "Didn't George even mention Phebe? I'll bet he really came to see her and just pretended to be interested in homesteading." She didn't wait for an answer but kept chattering to herself as she went upstairs.

Carson and Charles said, "Good night" to their father and left him to his thoughts. He blew out the lamp and sat back in his chair. Basking in the dark and quiet. His thoughts returned to the old log house in Rome and he wondered if Lydia and Phebe would take the boys there to see it. He hoped so. It seemed like just yesterday that they had crossed the icy Ontario with Okinihah. Could it really be eight years ago? Yes, Phebe was only ten then and she would be eighteen this fall. This had been a good move. In spite of the war they had fared well and he had been able to provide the necessities for his family and had saved against a poor year. Lydia had made their home a haven and he was proud of the children. He stood up, stretched and walked slowly to the bedroom. That bed was pretty lonely with out his Lydia.

Phebe took her dresses from the trunk and shook the wrinkles out, hanging them on the hooks in her closet. It was good to be home again and she mulled over the memories of the trip. The Lathrops were so happy to see them and it seemed like one round of parties. Mother glowed as she basked in the joy of being with her family again. They even went to see the old place in Rome. She told Little William and Zemira about the day the Indian came to take them to Canada.

Fanny and Lucretia had filled her in on what had happened while she was away, including George Palmer stopping by and Charles going with him to Cramahe.

"How long have they been back?" Phebe realized she was anxious to see George again.

"Oh, they came back a couple of days before you got

home. He is staying with his aunt in Laughborough. I heard Charles tell father that they found a nice tract of 200 acres that George wanted to file on." Fanny seemed to know everything that went on in this family.

George was at the Draper's that afternoon and when he saw Phebe sitting on the porch shelling peas he jumped from his horse and ran to her. He picked her up and whirled her around. The peas went flying. "I hope you are as glad to see me as I am to see you."

"I am glad to see you. I wondered if you had survived the war. I tried to follow the news of the battles but I was never really sure of your location. I did remember you in my prayers." Phebe felt something more than a casual interest. She did have feelings for George after all but there was a lot more she needed to know about him. She looked at him and started a mental list of her questions.

He picked her up and sat her on the porch railing, "Now, Miss Phebe, I hope you have saved all your dances for me. I can tell you right now that I plan to marry you, so you had better get used to the idea of me being around."

For once in her life Phebe was speechless. She looked at George in a state of shock. She could see that he was dead serious. "Don't you think that is rushing things a little? I don't really know you that well. You have skipped in and out of my life the last three years without stopping long enough for me to know who you really are."

He put his arm around her. "Well, we had better start getting better acquainted. Let me see, what can I tell you about me? My parents and I came from Vermont when I was about ten and we homesteaded in upper Canada. My father had trouble proving up on the land. It was hard on my mother and she died when I was about twelve. My Father and I moved back to Laughborough to live with his sister. I went to school there until I finished Normal school. My father and I both worked for my Uncle. My father found a new wife to marry and tried his hand at homesteading again. I didn't quite fit in with his new wife so I stayed on with my aunt and then I joined the Infantry. That was when I first met you. I've pretty much fared for myself. I have learned to work hard and survive. I could take good care of you and I want to have a family just like your family. I have my eye on a two hundred acre homestead in Cramahe. Charles and I went up to look at it at your father's suggestion. It is so pretty up there, I know you will love it. Charles even looked at a section he would like to file on. The only problem is we need someone to swear an oath for us. Your father offered to do that. Well, what about it?" He waited for Phebe to respond.

The color rose in her cheeks. "I need some time to think about it. I also think we need to talk to Father and Mother about it. Have you talked to Father yet?" Phebe hoped not. It was high time for her to make her own decisions though she did want their opinion.

"I know enough about you not to assume that much before I ask you. I have an idea that if I did that, you would send me down the road. That's what I love about you, your feisty spirit." He took her hand and they walked down the lane together.

"George, do you like to read?"

"I've never had many books around to read but I read the newspapers when I get a hold of them. I liked reading when I was in school but my folks didn't think it was so important. Do I have to pass a reading test or something? That's right, you've been teaching school. I guess you wouldn't want to marry a guy that couldn't read." George looked dejected.

"It's just that I like to read and discuss what I read. I like poetry more than anything. Have you read any books by poets?" Phebe knew she was starting to sound a little uppity and she didn't want to offend him. "I brought back a book from New York. Maybe we could read it together."

"You might have to help me some. I'd like you to be my teacher. I could have you all to myself. But there is a lot to be done to get that homestead going. We'd have long evening's together, just the two of us." George put his arm around her shoulders, "Will you just give me a chance?"

"Lets walk back through the orchard. That is my favorite place on the whole farm" Phebe led the way and they walked between the rows of apple trees. As they walked and talked Phebe relaxed into a casual conversation and George didn't push the subject of marriage. They sat under a tree for a while and George ask her if she made pies as well as Lucretia. He raved on about that apple pie he had for dinner and what a good cook Lucretia was.

Phebe was starting to feel a little pang of jealousy and her natural competitive nature was piqued, "Of course I can cook as well as Lucretia. I taught her how to make pies. You come for supper tomorrow night and I'll show you who can cook in the family." Then she realized he had trapped her into an invitation. She did want to show him she could cook anyway so she let it pass, but she knew he had tricked her.

He grinned at her and leaned over and kissed her on the cheek. "You read, you cook, and what else can you do, Miss Phebe?"

"Let me pass the cooking test first and then you can give me that next assignment. This may take months." Phebe baited.

"We don't have months. I am twenty years old, practically an old man and I need to get movin'. Do you think your Father is close by. I am anxious to talk to him about that land. I was hoping he would sign for me. He doesn't need to put up any money or anything, just verify that I am an honest person. I won't talk to him about us until you give me the word. I hope the word is, 'yes'." He kissed her lightly on the lips and they started to the house.

Phebe was eighteen. Most girls her age were married and had children by now. It had crossed her mind that she may end up being the spinster of the family. She had to be honest with herself and George. She would not marry him unless she felt their was a mutual love and respect between the two of them. She enjoyed being with him, he was a tease and seemed to know just how to get her goat. It wouldn't be dull married to him. He was fun to talk to. Her life would be different than that of the wife of a school teacher. John was still just a fantasy and George was a real live person that wanted to marry her and he was very handsome.

It was a warm July evening and the house was stifling. The family moved out to the north porch after supper. They sang some songs and Fanny started to tell some of her ridiculous stories about her friends. These summer nights were nights to remember. Phebe sat on the porch and hugged her knees. The crickets were chirping and the animals in the barn were making their evening sounds. "Mother, would you take a little walk with me before it gets too dark?"

Lydia stood and walked with Phebe out the gate and down the path. She had been waiting for Phebe to share her thoughts. She had obviously been preoccupied during supper. "Mother, George ask me to marry him this afternoon. I am so confused. I like him a lot and we do have a lot of fun together. As far as I can tell he is a good man, though he likes to tease. I don't think he is very religious though. From what he tells me he hasn't had much of a family to love and teach him like I have. He says he wants to have a family like ours and I think he means it. I want to get married and have children and be a mother like you have been to us. When I think about the good things our family enjoys, I realize that you and Father have done it together. Did you know Father would be the kind of man he is when you married him? You were younger than we are."

Lydia looked at her oldest daughter and prayed silently that she would say the proper thing. "Phebe, I love you very much. I want you to have all that is good in life but I cannot guarantee that for you. George seems like a nice enough young man though he did get off on the wrong foot with us the first time we met. You must study this out in your own heart. You may have many opportunities to marry so I would just warn you not to be too hasty or rush into it because you think it may be your only chance.

I know how much you thought of Master John and I felt your disappointment when you realized he wanted to marry your friend, Mary. There is only one John and there is only one George. Try not to compare them because they are totally different. Look for George's fine points. You owe him that much. In answer to your question about your father, I have to admit I was smitten with him the first time we met. I probably would have married him if he had been the worst person in the world, but the Lord blessed me by guiding the finest man in the world my way.

Phebe, dear, study your heart and pray about it. Only you can know what is best for you. I would suggest you discuss it with your Father also. He is a wise man and he will give you good council. Men sometimes know other men better than we do and we should look to them for advice." She put her arm around her daughter, "I love you and I want your happiness. What ever your decision, I will help you all I can."

The family had gone in. The evening breeze had cooled the air. "Thank you Mother." Phebe walked up the stairs slowly. She slipped her clothes off and pulled the summer nightie on over her head and knelt by her bed.

CHAPTER EIGHT

Phebe was the first of the Draper grandchildren to marry. The Uncles loaded their wagons with tools and supplies. William's wagon was filled with everything Lydia could think of that newlyweds would ever need. One son from each family stayed home to tend the animals and the rest of them migrated to Crahame to build a house and barn for Phebe and George just as they had for William and Lydia. William had signed for George and Charles and the two adjoining tracts of land were ready for these young pioneers. Charles would live with Phebe and George until he could get a cabin built on his place.

The women had worked furiously to get quilts and linens ready for the wedding. Phebe had made her decision in August and the wedding was set for her eighteenth birthday, October 9, 1815. It was a beautiful Indian Summer and the warm air stayed late that year. The apples were harvested and shipped down to the states. Phebe and George were married in the village church where the Rev. Black had preached his fiery sermon. The current minister was a kindly old gentleman who spent several minutes giving them fatherly advice before he finally got to the ceremony. George was afraid Phebe would change her mind before they got to the "I do" part. She looked so beautiful in her white satin gown.

Lydia and William stood proudly at their sides. George had endeared himself to the family the last two months and it was evident that he was in love with Phebe and she with him. The bride and groom kissed and then William and Lydia embraced them. Grandpa Draper, with tears streaming down his face hugged them both and presented them with a new black family Bible. The rice began to rain on them as they left the church and jumped into the buggy to make their escape. The Uncles formed a protective line against the pranksters and the newlyweds were off to their new life in Crahame.

Phebe was undaunted in her determination to set her house
in order. It was a comfortable house with a fireplace in both
ends. The weather would be colder here and the heat from the
fireplaces would keep them warm with the heat rising to the
lofts. It was not as large as her home in Richmond but there
was plenty of room for the two of them and Charles also. She
hung the curtains to the windows and put a fresh towel and
wash cloth on the wash stand. By afternoon the dishes were
unpacked and placed in the cupboard. The last was a small barrel that she had carefully packed herself. She lifted the teapot
and cups and saucers carefully, almost holding her breath for
fear that they might have broken on the way. At the bottom of
the barrel was Grandma Draper's cake plate with the gold rim.
Mother had insisted that she have it. "When you look at this
plate, remember the blessing your grandmother gave you.
There may be some time in your life when you will want to be
reminded of her promise of protection."

The tea set and the plate were arranged on the shelf above
the fireplace where Phebe could see them as she "kept" her
house. She must tell George about them. Now, where to put the
family Bible. On the table by the rocker so it would be close at
hand to read each night. She opened the cover to a page that
was headed: FAMILY and under that BIRTHS. She found the
pen and ink she had packed and carefully wrote at the top of
the page; George Palmer was born July the 13, 1795 and under
it she wrote her new name for the first time; Phebe Palmer
born October 9, 1797. She blew the ink dry and tried to hold
the new cover open so the ink wouldn't smear.

This was a new beginning. The first page of the rest of her
life.

She heard George coming toward the house so she hurriedly put a cloth on the table. Mother had taught her that trick. If
dinner wasn't quite ready it looked like it was ready if you had
started to set the table. She smiled as she remembered her

mother pulling the cloth from the drawer before the men walked in. She had dawdled over the dishes and the Bible but she had put some potatoes in the oven to bake and a small roast. Mother had sent enough food with her to feed them for a month.

George grabbed her in a bear hug and gave her a big kiss. "Did I remember to tell you that I'm glad you married me? You have been working. This place looks just like home. Our home." As he looked around he was overcome with a feeling of belonging that he had never experienced in his life. Phebe was definitely the best thing that had ever happened to him.

"I'll get dinner on while you wash up. Have you decided where to plant the orchard? I hope apple trees grow and pro- duce as well here as they do in Richmond. What other things are you going to plant?"

He wiped his hands on the new towel and carried the wash bowl out the back door to throw the dirty water away. He went to the well and let the bucket down for some fresh water. Those uncles and Father William performed miracles; a house, barn and a well for water built for them in a little over a week. They were a great family. Only Little William and Zemira had withheld their approval of him. They resented him taking their Miss Phebe from them and he couldn't blame them. He would be angry too. Maybe they could come to stay with them for a holiday. Phebe would love it.

He put the pail of water on the wash stand and replaced the wash bowl. Phebe dipped some water from the pail and put it on the stove to heat for washing the dishes later. Supper was on the table and they sat down to their first meal in their new home.

George picked up a piece of the brown packing paper and drew a square with the stub of a pencil. It represented his two hundred acres. He sketched in the house and barn. Then drew the natural water routes that crossed the property. He shaded in the areas that were heavily wooded, they could be cleared last, and then blocked off the rest of the space. Phebe could help him decide which to clear first. They would need to get the Apple Tree Cuttings planted as soon as possible so they could take root before heavy frost.

Phebe sat down on his lap and looked at the drawing. They had a lot of work to do but the enthusiasm of youth was high. She opened the Bible and showed him what she had written on the 'Family' page. He gave her a long tender kiss, picked her up and carried her to the bed covered by the beautiful quilt Lydia and the girls had made for them.

Phebe opened the Bible to the FAMILY Birth page to record the next entry. Lovingly she wrote Lovina Palmer, born July 20, 1816. Her darling little daughter woke from an infant slumber and whimpered for attention. She picked her up and sat in the rocker to nurse her new born. The black curly hair dampened as the baby labored to draw the life sustaining liquid in gulps. Who was she like? "More like Fanny than me" Phebe thought. Her dark hair and coloring was the same as Fanny's. She remembered the argument over the red ribbon and decided then and there that Lovina would have a ribbon of every color of the rainbow. She looked at the smocking on the little dress she wore. It had been a busy year.

George and Phebe had planted the apple trees. She had showed him how to prune the little starts as they put them in the ground. George had cleared another sixty acres and was considering tobacco and cherries. If he planted a variety of crops it would spread the work more evenly through the grow-ing season and give them various sources of income. His only help was Charles and Phebe and he needed to help Charles prove up on his land too.

They worked long days when the weather permitted. Phebe would lead the draft horse as George or Charles pushed the grubbing plow into the virgin soil. She would stop before they did and go to the house to prepare meals. Pregnancy seemed to agree with her and she maintained a high energy level until the last few months. When she could no longer work in the fields with the men she spent her time making clothes for the baby.

It had been hard work but it brought its own rewards. They celebrated when the first apple leaves appeared on the the little trees. They would not bear this year but it was a promise of things to come. George had some savings from his army pay and Phebe from her teaching. It wasn't much, but if they were careful it would get them by until the farm started to produce.

George was learning some carpentry skills and spent the winter days making a cradle for the baby and other furniture for the house. On the long dark evenings Phebe would read aloud to him. Sometimes from the poetry book and sometimes from the Bible. He often fell asleep before she finished. Phebe hoped that he would gain a love for reading as she had.

Charles had spent the fall and spring with them but had gone back home during the cold winter months. George decided to go hunting to get some deer meat to supplement their food reserves. He dressed warm in several layers of clothes, took his army musket, some dried meat, biscuits and an apple with him. He headed north to the woods hoping to find the trail of some white tail deer. He had been on the trail three-to-four hours when he heard some wolves howling in the distance. He took a firm grip on his musket. He had it loaded with a full measure of gunpowder from his powder horn and tamped a ball into place. If a deer or wolf crossed his path he would be ready. Wolves usually traveled in packs. One shot could not protect him from the pack. He felt the hair raise on the back of his neck. He decided to move in a circle away from the howling wolves and head back home.

A heavy cloud cover darkened the sky and snow began to fall. George quickened his pace and tried to verify his location. He was soon in a ground blizzard, unable to see his direction.

The wind was blowing the freezing, wet snow into his face. He pulled his scarf over his face for protection and leaned into the storm. An object loomed up in the distance and appeared to be crouching animal. George found cover behind a tree, readied his musket and waited for any movement. Visibility was almost nil so he watched between gusts. He pulled some dried meat from his pack and chewed on it for energy. Fighting the snow had been exhausting.

Almost an hour passed and the snow storm let up a little. George was tromping his feet to keep them warm and using the tree for protection from the cold. Since no other animals had appeared he decided to approach the crouching object. He pulled the hammer back on his musket and crept slowly forward. The soft snow concealed his foot steps. He neared the object and released the hammer. The flash of gunpowder was blinding as the ball was propelled into the heap. The blast echoed around him. The smell of the burned gunpowder filled his nostrils. He walked up to the target and cleared the snow. It was a rock whose shape was similar to that of a crouching animal. He sat down in the snow and laughed. He laughed until the tears rolled down his cheeks and he contemplated telling Phebe about it when he got home. At first he thought he wouldn't because he would look so foolish to her and then he decided this was the kind of story that would bear telling over and over with varied embellishments. He ate his apple, picked up his musket and started home. He was still chuckling when he walked up to the porch.

Phebe had her own story to tell. Not long after George had left on his hunting trip Phebe was dusting the furniture and sweeping the floor. She opened the door to sweep the dust balls out on the porch. She swept the porch and steps. Light snow had begun to fall so she swept the skiff of snow from the step. When she looked up, two Indians were staring at her. They had moved up so quietly she had not heard them. She walked backwards to the door, keeping her eyes on them but stopped in the door way.

"Foo-Foo" the largest of the Indians put his fingers together and moved them to his mouth. The smaller one nodded and mimicked the first. They moved closer, not pushing her but invading what she felt was her space.

Phebe continued to look them in the eye and then, as she had with Okinihah, she saw sincerity and knew they were just hungry. She thought of her father and his admonition to feed the poor and hungry and she could not turn them away. She stepped aside and motioned for them to enter. They went to the fire and warmed their hands and then turned to let the warmth touch their backs. She watched them carefully and as she did her eyes fell upon Grandma Draper's cake plate leaning on the hearth. Grandma's promise of protection gave her courage and she went to the cupboard and found food for the hungry natives. They ate and when they were warm, walked to the door. She picked two apples from the bowl on the table and gave to them. "Brave Squaw, we go".

Only then did Phebe realize how frightened she had been. Her knees buckled and she fell into the rocking chair. The smell of the Indians hung in the little house. The smell, the fright, the pregnancy or all three caused her suddenly to feel very ill. She hurried out the back door and retched onto the snow. Back in the house she opened both doors until the cool air had cleared it of the offending smells. She closed the doors and fed the fire until the room was warm again. She put a chair back to each door and pulled the curtains closed. "I hope George gets back soon." She muttered to herself and then sat down to read. She was soon lost in thought and dosed off to sleep with the book in her hands.

The scraping sound of a chair being pushed back along the plank floor awakened her with a start. Had the Indians returned? Then she heard, "Phebe, are you in there?" as George burst into the room.

She ran to him and threw her arms around him, weeping out her story.

He held her away from him to make sure she was alright and then held her in his arms until the fright left her body and she relaxed.

"Well, my dear, I have a story to tell too." He sat in the rocking chair with Phebe on his lap as he recounted the story of the big grey wolf that wasn't. They laughed and giggled about how funny George must have looked hiding behind a tree so he wouldn't be attacked by a rock. Then Phebe imitated George creeping up to the rock and more peels of laughter emanated in the little house in Crahame. They giggled until bedtime and then went to sleep still smiling.

Fanny came to stay with Phebe the last few weeks before the baby came and then Lydia brought the Midwife from Richmond to be there for the delivery. They had stayed for a couple of weeks but Phebe had recovered quickly. It had been an easy birth. Phebe was a good mother, caring for her baby with little assistance and Lovina was a relaxed baby that slept and ate at will without much fussing.

Lydia held her and rocked her for the last little while before she had to leave to go home. Her own little granddaughter. It didn't seem possible. Wasn't it just yesterday that she was holding Phebe like this? Then, as mothers and grandmothers do, she contemplated what Lovina's future might be.

CHAPTER NINE

It was Phebe's thirtieth birthday and twelfth anniversary. More settlers had moved into the valley and Charles had married Hanah. They had three children and had proved up on their homestead west of the Palmer's. Phebe and George had long since proved up on their land also. George had cleared and planted all but thirty acres of forest which would act as a buffer between them and the river. It also was a cover for migrating animals and there-by a place to hunt. When ever George picked up his musket Phebe chided: "On your way to hunt rocks again?" He had told the children the story many times with the actual events altered in the telling.

Grandpa, Thomas Draper, had died the year after Lovina was born. That dear old man who had opened his heart and his home to William's family when Phebe was just ten. He had been the key stone of the family for so many years. Now he had gone to be with Grandma Draper. Phebe knew how much he would have enjoyed her little family.

Phebe looked at the Family Bible which had been a gift from her grandfather.

She picked it up, realizing that she had not written in the last entry. She opened to the Birth page and read.

> *George Palmer was born*
> *July 13, 1895*
> *Phebe Palmer*
> *was born Oct. 9, 1797*
> *Lovina Palmer born*
> *July 20, 1816*
> *Asahel Palmer born*
> *January the 26, 1819*
> *William Palmer born*
> *August the 25, 1821*

Eliza Palmer born
May 31, 1824
Lydia Elizabeth Palmer born
Oct. 15, 1826

George had added on to the house to make room for the family. More bedrooms and a kitchen large enough for the new family table. The older part of the house was now the parlor with three rockers and a settee. The plank floor was covered with polished wood and a braided rug lay in front of the fireplace. Side tables held oil lamps sitting on crocheted doilies and by one rocker was the table which held the Family Bible. Phebe was rocking baby Lydia Elizabeth who would soon be one year old. She watched Lovina playing singing games with Eliza. Lovina's voice was so melodious they all listened when she sang.

Lovina was eleven years old and mature for her age. Her long, black curly hair and milky complexion were striking. She looked so fragile and delicate but was as strong willed as her mother. She emulated her mother in many respects. Phebe saw herself mirrored in Lovina since she was a little girl. Sometimes it shocked her as she heard her own words coming from little Lovina's mouth. She was always teaching the little ones something and was firm in her devotion to her family.

Asahel was definitely his father's son. He not only looked like him but had his pension for teasing. The impish glint in his eyes often gave his trickery away and Phebe knew when she must look for a surprise in a drawer or even the water bucket. He idolized his father and was George's shadow. At the age of ten, his legs were growing out of his trousers and his shirt tails were continually slipping out from his belt. He was going to be tall when he had his growth. He had a tendency to be impatient and squirmed in church if the preacher's sermon was lengthy.

William George, who had been named after his father,

grandfather and uncle, was studious already at the age of seven. He learned to read quickly in the Primary School Phebe taught in her home. It seemed that he remembered everything he heard and could repeat it word for word which was sometimes embarrassing. He was very good at repeating the voice inflections of others, which made him somewhat of a comedian. When the other children laughed at his mimics he would hold a straight face and ape another person. George and Phebe tried to dissuade him from making fun of others but would often have to turn their back to conceal their own smiles.

Eliza was the three-year-old darling of the family. She too had impish ways and a bob of auburn hair. Phebe wondered where she came from. No one in the family had hair even close to that color. She had Grandma Draper's snapping black eyes and a personality that melted everyone in the family. Lydia never knew where she would find her in the morning. She would get up in the night and snuggle in bed by one of the other children. They argued about who Eliza loved the most. She and Lovina would spend most of the daylight hours together, usually singing. William would read her stories at night and Asahel would play hide-and-seek with her. Phebe had read a story once about a fairy child touched by the angels and she thought of Eliza as her fairy child.

Lydia Elizabeth was almost a year old. She tottered from one family member to another on her little wobbly legs. When she made it without sitting down they would all clap and she would clap also, delighted with herself. Phebe was glad she named her after her mother. She had those same fine features of Lucretia and Granny Lydia, as the children called their grandmother. Yes, she was definitely a Lathrop. She would have to teach her the jump rope chant about the Lathrop genealogy that she and Charles jumped to when they were children.

The children were a handful now. Even with Lovina's help it was hard to get everyone ready for church on Sunday. They had to start early to get into Loughborough. There wasn't a church in Cramahe and Phebe insisted on her children attending a religious service each week. George was not so concerned about that part of their upbringing. Most of the time he went with them but never seemed to feel the spirit of the meeting. The church was Protestant with traveling preachers most of the time. This rural part of Canada could ill afford a paid clergy, so often had self acclaimed preachers that taught from the Bible and accepted what ever donation the congregation contributed each Sunday. Phebe made sure each of the children had a coin to put on the plate.

It soon became evident to Phebe that the religious training of her children would be her responsibility. Unlike her father who would spend evenings reading to him self and the family from the family Bible, George was not inclined to do so. George was an honest man and a hard worker. He taught his children to be honest, show concern and be helpful to others. He encouraged Phebe to lead the family in prayer but seldom did so himself. In her secret prayers, Phebe asked that George would feel the Spirit and come to know Jesus as she did. Most of the time she read from the New Testament because she felt that it conveyed the message of hope and love.

Phebe used the Old Testament Bible stories, however, to teach the children in Primary school, often writing them in a simplified language so the children could read and understand them. She would help them act out some of the Old Testament stories such as Daniel in the Lions' Den. William George loved to play the part of Daniel and show his bravery. He also wanted to be David slaying Goliath.

Lovina and Asahel were going to Normal School in Loughborough. George let them use his horse and buggy. They would take the other children their age from the valley with them. Because of the long winters they were lucky to get one month of school in the fall after the Harvest and one in the spring before the planting and pruning season. Phebe tried to find books to supplement their education. She wrote to the last address she had for Mary and John Park in Philadelphia. John would have access to the books she would need and know which ones to send her. By the fall of 1828 she hoped to have a small library to use for the valley children so they could keep up with the town students.

The orchard was mature now and the whole family helped pick the ripe apples.

George insisted that the baskets be filled to the brim. The buyers were to get a good measure. Wagons came from villages and nearby towns to purchase the juicy apples that were raised on the Palmer Farm; Banana, Johnathon, Winesap, Blacktwig, Astercan, and Pearmane. George picked the top of the trees, the boys shinnied up the middle and Phebe and the girls picked the lower branches. They were careful not to drop and bruise the fruit.

Phebe loved this orchard as she had her father's. Apple trees were like families, they put their roots down deep to get the sustenance that gave them life and then blossomed. They shared of their nectar with the bees that gently touched each blossom that they might bear fruit. Protected by the leaves until mature enough to be picked and go on to meet their destiny. Adam and Eve and the apple had made families possible. Phebe sat under a tree and closed her eyes, "Thank you, Eve." she said quietly to herself.

The books finally arrived from Philadelphia. Phebe was ecstatic. She pulled them from the crate and caressed each with her hands. The geography book had maps of the old and new world with the names of far away places and stories of what the people were like. A book of mathematics with Algebra equations and, thankfully, the answers in the back. The history book of ancient civilizations and last of all the literature book with a section of Grammar and Sentence Structure. In the bottom of the box was a small book: "To A Nightingale and other Poems" by John Keats. The book opened to a page with a note tucked into it.

> *Dear Phebe,*
> *Mary and I were delighted to hear from you. I enjoyed shopping for the books you requested. The money you sent was more than adequate to pay for them and the shipping charges. This book is a gift to you from your friends, Mary and John.*
> *We have news to share with you. We have five daughters and Mary is expecting our sixth child. I have been given an offer at a University in Tiffen, Ohio. My medical profession keeps me very busy but my love is teaching. I am thinking of taking a position with the University to teach medicine. Mary has not been well of late but I am devoted to caring for her until her health improves. Our move to Ohio will be dependent on her health.*
> *Miss Phebe, enjoy your family and teaching. Give our best regards to your husband George and your children. If you have need of further teaching materials please give us the opportunity to be of assistance to you.*
> *Sincerely,*
> *Your Friends, John and Mary*

Phebe sat down and started to read the titles of the Poems in the book, taking mental note of those she would like to read later. Keats was new to her and she could see that he had a style that would take some studying.

"Phebe, you have another son." She could hear her mother's voice as she fought the mind shadows of the Laudanum. This had been a hard pregnancy and the delivery didn't go as well as the others. Mother had been with her for a month and as the hot July days had worn on to August she thought the baby would never come. George was patient with her and

Lovina, now fifteen, was able to cook for the family and help her grandmother with the other household chores.

Little Lydia would be five soon and Eliza was seven. Phebe didn't think she would have any more children after Lydia. This was a surprise to her and to George. He walked in the room and kissed her forehead, "I guess the Lord knew I needed more help and sent me another son. What shall we name him?"

The cobwebs were clearing and she said, "I've been thinking that if it was a boy I'd like to name him after my brother, Zemira. He would expect that after we named our last boy William. Bring me the Bible and I will write it on the Birth page.

Zemira Palmer born
August 9, 1831

George blew on it to dry the ink. Lydia brought in her new little grandson, freshly washed, bound with a belly band, diapered, dressed in a gown and wrapped loosely in a light flannel blanket. George cradled the baby in his arms, "Well Little Zemira, you had a hard time getting here but it looks like you made it in fine shape. You grow fast because the boys and I need all the help we can get. We'll be hand swathing that field of grain north of the house. Maybe you could be a shocking it." He smiled down proudly at his new little son. With his rough hand he gently touched the delicate, little fingers that were pulled into a tight fist. The little fingers stretched open and as George placed his big, weathered finger in the palm of the babies hand the fingers closed into a tight grip. It was at that moment that father and son formed that invisible, gossamer-like bond.

Phebe looked at this rough hewn man that she had come to adore over the years. He loved his children with a passion and for that she was grateful. It more than made up for the loneliness he had felt as a child. He was good to her and though he didn't enjoy reading and poetry he never resented her spending time with books. Over the years they had each found their own way of fulfillment and happiness; he with his farm and family and she with her home, teaching her children and studying. Together they planned new ways to market their crops, new crops to plant and methods to make the work easier. They laughed together often at funny things the children would say or do. George could see the humor in life and wasn't afraid to laugh at himself.

The baby was just a month old when they were surprised by a strange visitor. Phebe laid the baby down as she heard the knock on the door. As she opened the door she was amazed at the resemblance. "Is this the George Palmer farm?" The voice even sounded like George's. He took off his hat and walked in the house at Phebe's direction.

"Come in. Yes, this is George Palmer's farm. I am his wife, Phebe. Can I help you with something?" She wanted to ask his name but she waited for his answer.

"I am Elijah Palmer. I believe I am George's half brother. Is he at home?" the young man in his early twenties spoke haltingly.

"Yes, he is out on the farm. You look very much like him. I'll have one of the children go for him." She went to the back door and called out to Eliza, "Run out in the orchard and find Papa. There is a man here to see him. Hurry."

Phebe met George at the back door. His eyes questioned her and she nodded him into the Parlor. George Looked at the young man sitting on the edge of the settee. It was like looking into a mirror fifteen years ago. His long stride took him across the room quickly. He put his hand out to shake the hand extended to him.

"I am Elijah Palmer. I think you are my brother. My Father's name was George and my mother was his second wife, Hannah. I grew up in Quebec and left home when I was about sixteen. My father told me he had another son down here in the Northumberland area. My mother died when I was fourteen. Father and I didn't see eye to eye on many things so when I left I didn't think I would ever go back. I signed on with a ship at Port Cartier. I've been to sea and pretty much around the world these last six years. I went back home to see if I could make it up and found out that Father had died about a year ago. He had left some boxes of things with my name on 'em with a friend, case I did come back. Well, when I was goin' through all the stuff in them boxes I run across this paper about a homestead down here that he sold and some other things with your name on it and a legal lookin' paper with his X on and that of his first wife which I guess was your mother. Someone had written their names above the marks. I brought the boxes with me if you want to see 'em." He took a breath.

Phebe thought the poor boy had never had that much to say in his life. She watched the color rise on his face as he looked to George for a response.

"If what you say is truth you sure could be my brother. My father did draw out on a lot down here but he was no farmer and my ma died tryin' to help him. He married a Hannah but she didn't like me much. Guess I was a little smart mouth. Anyways, they left me here with my aunt and went north. I never heard from 'em again. I joined the Canadian Infantry and fought in the war. My aunt died soon after I got home and I married my dear wife here, Phebe."

"You must be hungry. Let me get you something to eat." Phebe moved to the kitchen to let the men talk alone. They needed time to build a relationship that had been denied to both of them. "George has a brother. How wonderful for him," Phebe thought. She had always felt so sorry for him because he had not known the joy of living in a big family.

Elijah brought the boxes in and he and George unpacked a lifetime of treasures. They tried to establish the age of each of the documents and possessions that had been valued enough by their father to have been saved. Phebe noticed that George had slipped into the family dialect he had used in his language when they first met. He seldom used it any more since Phebe had been so insistent that the children speak properly.

She invited Elijah into the kitchen to have some lunch. She cut a slice of cake for George so he could join his brother at the table. "Elijah, you will be staying with us, I hope." Perhaps she should have discussed the invitation with George first but she was sure he would want to have his brother with them.

"Soon as we eat I'll help ya get settled. We got a room in the back that I built on just fer company. I can sure use some help here on the farm too. My boys are a big help but they need some more growin' ta help with the hard work. Well, listen to me. You're welcome to stay but I guess we need to ask you about your plans. Are you goin' back to sea?" George was glowing with enthusiasm. A brother. A real live brother.

"I hadn't made any plans fer sure until I talked to ya and found if ya were really my brother. I pretty much got everything I own with me 'cause I didn't know what I'd be decidin' ta do. I've had it with sailing. Ya have to deal with some pretty rough types in that business. I guess I'm not cut out fer that kind of life. I was indentured for the first three years and treated pretty bad by the Captain and his men. I don't think I'll want ta be goin' back ta that." Elijah tried to conceal the joy he felt at the idea of making his home here. "I'd like ta try it fer a while if ya'll have me. But I'd be doin' plenty of work ta pay fer ma keep. I don't take no charity."

George helped him pick up the boxes and bring his things in from the little surrey he had driven out to the farm. They put his horse in the barn and then George took him on a tour of the Palmer farm. He wanted to show him everything including the children who were out picking apples.

Phebe prepared supper and put an extra plate at the table. Elijah could tell them about the places he had sailed to. She would get out the geography book and have him tell them about the places as they had read about them in the book.

That night the children got acquainted with their new uncle. He had some difficulty remembering their names. Phebe had each of them introduce themselves to him and tell him three things they liked. Lovina liked singing, reading and Henry, the new boy she had met at school. Asahel liked shoeing horses, plowing and Arithmetic. William George liked reading, writing stories and hunting with George. Eliza liked to say poems, draw pictures, dry the dishes and put them in the cupboard. Lydia liked to play hop scotch with Eliza and sing songs with Lovina.

Phebe opened the Bible, "I hope you will join us. We like to read from the Bible in the evening. 'Blessed are the pure in heart'." She continued to read through the Beatitudes.

Elijah fell into the routines of the family and George had never been happier. He had Elijah's strong muscles to help him with the fall plowing and build some sheds for the sheep he planned to buy. Elijah was full of stories about his sailing days and as Phebe had hoped, his descriptions of places like China and Japan made them come alive for the children. He had seen camels in Egypt and elephants in India. He soon learned that if his language was laced with that of the sea life, Phebe would raise her eyebrows and change the subject. George would smile and look at her with respect for the refinement she maintained in their home.

Asahel was twelve and didn't want to return to school that fall. He had overheard his father say he had left school at that age. His dream in life was to be just like his father. If he stayed home he could help Elijah with all the extra work. Phebe insisted that he go to school and it was the first time she and one of her children had been at cross purposes. "I know you like to be considered one of the men on the farm and you are, Asahel. Your father relies on you more than you realize but everyone needs as much education as they can get. There are always new things to learn and new ways to do them. I read in the paper that they are even considering starting a college to teach farmers better ways of farming down in the States.

"Well, I'm not going and that's, that." He stormed out of the house. Threw the saddle on his horse, cinched up the strap with a yank, put the bit in the horses mouth throwing the reins over the saddle horn and jumped on. He pulled the reins to the left and dug his heal into the horses flank. The horse took off with a start leaving dust clouds in the lane.

Phebe realized this was going to require help from George. They hadn't discussed it but she thought George felt as she did about the children's education. Perhaps the ride would dispel some of the anger Asahel was feeling. She remembered her angry walk to the orchard when she was young and wanted to make her own decisions. She would talk to George and give Asahel a few days before they discussed it again.

"My, where is Asahel off to in such a hurry? I hurried in because I thought there was some emergency in here." George walked to the bucket of fresh water, dipped out a cup and took a long drink while he waited for an answer.

"We had words about him not going back to school this fall. He thinks he has had enough school and should stay home and work with the men. Can you help me change his mind?" Phebe sat down at the table with her chin in her hand and the worry lines creasing her brow.

George hung the water cup back on the hook. "I could use his help and it ought to be his decision. He can read and write and do arithmetic. He's more educated than most of the men in Ontario. Ease up, Phebe. You push too hard sometimes."

Phebe felt the sting of defeat. Asahel would never go back to school unless his Father encouraged him to and he obviously, was not going to do that. She walked from the room and felt an invisible wall start to rise between she and George. It was something she had always known about herself. She did push hard for what she felt was right but she thought George was proud of her for it. This critical remark hurt. She threw her shawl over her shoulders and walked to the orchard.

CHAPTER TEN

"He knelt in the grove of trees. This young boy of fifteen, knelt in the grove of trees and prayed for an answer. *'If any of ye lack wisdom let him ask of God who giveth to all men liberally, and upbraideth not; and it shall be given him.'* He had read the passage in the Epistle of James in the Bible and he believed that God would answer him. God did answer him in a way that he could never have imagined. Two personages appeared to him. He knew the one as God the Father and he heard him say, 'This is my beloved son, Hear him.' They answered the question he had in his heart. 'Which church is true? Help me to know the truth.'" Brother Eleaser Miller clung to the pulpit and tried to control his emotions. The congregation waited. It was as if they too were in the grove asking the question. Phebe felt a transformation within her. A warmth of understanding came to her and she knew that she was ready to accept the answer. She looked over at Charles and Sarah in the pew across from her. They also seemed to be caught up in the spirit of this young man's story.

"They told him none of the churches were true." The young missionary waited for the Spirit to bear witness to this group. He had prayed that he might be able to share this remarkable story in a way that would touch the hearts of those who were ready to accept it. There was a soft rustle that moved through the congregation as they shifted their weight to a new position on the hard benches. It was as if they were adjusting their bodies to meet the change in a lifetime of their religious convictions. Sounds of a nervous cough, a sssh to a child, permeated the silence. Phebe realized she was gripping the Bible on her lap. Then a quiet settled over the group. A quiet of anticipation to hear the rest of the story.

Brother Miller continued, "They told him, 'They draw near

me with their lips but their hearts are far from me. They teach for doctrines, the commandments of men, having a form of godliness, but they deny the power there of.' This boy, Joseph Smith, who had ask which church to join, lay weak, lying on his back looking up to heaven where the light had departed. He had no strength. He recovered enough to go to his home. His mother, seeing his condition, ask him what the matter was. He replied, 'Never mind, all is well—I am well enough off. I have learned for myself that none of the churches are true.' Brothers and sisters, I have more to tell you of this great man and the work the Lord has revealed to him. I will be here tomorrow night at seven O'clock for those of you who would like to hear more, or I can come to your homes."

Lovina stood by the organ and sang, "Amazing Grace, How Sweet Thou Art" Her clear, true voice echoed in their hearts and unexpected tears dampened their cheeks.

Phebe gathered her family together. She wanted to linger and discuss this most unusual message but summer thunder clouds were filling the sky. They needed to get home before the storm hit. Elijah helped her and Lovina into the buggy and handed little Zemira to her. Asahel jumped in the back with William and Lydia. The summer breeze had become a gusty wind and they could see the lightening shooting through the black clouds in the west and hear the bolts of thunder.

George had stayed home today. He wanted to check the crops and determine which ones were ready to harvest. The oat field on the north was headed out and dry. It would probably be first. Eliza was asleep in the house. She had been stung by some bees and her face was so swollen she didn't want anyone see her. Phebe had seen that her little Eliza was not feeling well and agreed to let her stay at home. She ask George to look in on her while the rest of them were at church.

As he walked from the orchard to the grain field he felt some drops of rain. If it turned into a gully washer they would have to delay cutting the oats. It had been so dry with no rain for days he debated in his mind which would be best; a good, drenching, downpour or getting the oats in before a storm came. A flash of light and a crack of thunder, almost simultaneously invaded the quiet of his thoughts. He jumped, startled at the unexpected noise and then realized that the lightning had struck something in the forest. The forest was tinder dry and he feared the worst. He ran to the barn for a shovel and sprinted to the top of the field. By the time he got there the black smoke was billowing out of the dense forest with a wind gusting the smoke and flames toward him. A roaring sound preceded the flames and smoke. He shoveled with all the energy he had to make a fire break between the field and the forest. He watched as the fire burned closer in tongues of flames, skipping some plants and devouring others. Explosions of pine trees were resounding around him and he shoveled harder. It was a hopeless task. The flames jumped the narrow line of fresh turned earth and raced on.

He ran ahead of the flames racing toward him and remembered Eliza. He could feel the heat sear his throat and lungs as he gasped for air. The smoke was so heavy he could hardly see a few feet ahead of him. As he reached the house he looked up and saw the embers blown by the wind had started the roof of the house on fire. Shouting, "Eliza, Eliza," he ran into the house and to her bedroom. She wasn't in her bed. He raced from room to room. The smoke was filling the house and he could hear the small explosions as the fire seared the pine logs of the house. Where could she be? Then he heard, "Papa, Papa," from her room in the other end of the house.

His worst fear had happened. The fire had engulfed the house. He bent low, pulling his shirt tail over his face to ward off the smoke. A beam from the ceiling fell at his side, missing him. The smoke was so thick and the heat so intense that he dropped to his knees to find air to breath. He crawled to her room and found her under her bed. She was unconscious. He picked her up and ran to the window on the south, covering them with a quilt to protect them from the glass, jumped out to escape the flames and heat. Racing to the well, he pulled up a bucket of water, throwing it over his little Eliza. Her body was limp and did not respond. Sobbing, he rocked her in his arms and was overcome with grief. The rains came then in torrents, squelching the fire and covering the blackened fields and house with a deluge of water but it was too late to save Eliza.

Phebe and the children could see the flames leaping in the air across the valley. Elijah whipped at the horse to pick up speed. Phebe was praying that George and Eliza were safe. Fire! that dreaded enemy that seldom came to this moist Canadian land was racing across their farm in a frenzy of destruction. By the time they got to the Palmer Farm the rain was pouring over them and the ashes of their home. The south wall was partially standing and the stone fireplaces that had been lovingly built by the Draper Uncles. The barn and other outbuildings were still intact.

Phebe peered through the rain for a sight of George or Eliza. Elijah drove the buggy to the back of the house and there they found George, huddled over the limp form of Eliza, drenched from the rain and barely conscious himself. Phebe ran to him, pulling her shawl from her shoulders and covering him for protection.

"Eliza, Eliza, I couldn't save her. Phebe, I'm sorry, I tried. I couldn't save her." He was caught up with spasms of coughing and collapsed in Phebe's arms.

Elijah lifted the little lifeless form and carried it to the protection of the buggy. He came back and helped Phebe move George to the barn for shelter. Asahel took care of the horse and threw down fresh hay from the loft. Lovina cradled the baby in her arms and led the others into the barn.

They stared out of the barn door at the rain and the charred scene before them. No one spoke. They were too stunned. Lydia and William George clung to Phebe in desperation. Elijah went to the well for water. As he pulled the bucket up he saw the ashes of the fire had settled on the surface. He skimmed it away and dipped fresh water in the ladle to take to George who was coughing again.

Phebe rolled a horse blanket up to use as a pillow for his head. His skin was clammy and he started to shake. She held him in her arms and sent the children scurrying for more horse blankets. They piled the blankets on and huddled close to him to share their warmth. It had been such a hot dry August and now the rains and wind chilled them.

Phebe knew they needed something warm. Perhaps the tea safe had protected the tea. She picked up the bucket of water and walked in to the charred remains of her house. The big black stove stood like a ghoul in the middle of what had been the kitchen. She found the tea safe and yes, it had been spared. The teapot was black from the smoke but clean inside. She filled it with water from the bucket and poured some dry leaves from the tea can. Half burned chair legs fit into the fire box and a match from the can of matches reignited the smoldering wood. As the tea steeped she looked around to see what the fire had missed in its destructive invasion of her home. The book shelf had burned from the wall and the remains of the books were strewn on the floor with the wind blowing the partially burned pages. The Bible, The Family Bible, oh yes she had taken it with her to church. It was safe in the buggy. A beam lay across the hearth of the west fireplace. She looked up to the mantle and there, blackened by the smoke was the little tea set and Grandma Draper's Cake plate.

It was only then that she allowed herself to give way to tears. Somehow that little tea set had been with her during every crisis in her life, but this crisis was too hard to bear. Her Fairy Child, Eliza, gone. Never to skip across the porch and call her "Mama." George, what of George? She wondered if he would live. She knelt down in the still warm debris and begged the Lord to leave her George. The teapot was hissing. She stood and found some tin cups. Picked up a fold of her skirt to protect her hand from the hot teapot and carried the tea and the cups to the barn.

Charles and Hanah drove their buggy into the yard and saw the remains of the inferno. They had waited the storm out at the church. Then they saw the Palmer family huddled in the barn, staring into space and trying to comprehend what had happened and what to do next. Charles hopped from the buggy and embraced his sister, "Oh Phebe, is everyone alright?"

She cried into his shoulder, "Eliza, Eliza is dead." And then she cried in uncontrollable sobs, "and George is in a bad way. He's having trouble breathing."

Hanah took the baby from Lovina and led the little ones to the buggy where her own children waited. "I'll take this buggy full home and get some food started. Phebe, dear, you and the others bring George over and we'll get him into a good warm bed."

Quiet Hanah, who always relied on Phebe to give directions, rose to the occasion and moved the family into action. Elijah and Charles filled the farm wagon with hay, covered it with horse blankets and carried George to the make shift bed. Asahel led the horses around and threw the harness over their back, hitching them to the double tree. Elijah and Asahel climbed on to the spring seat. Elijah picked up the reins and they followed Hanah out on to the lane. George had fallen into a deep sleep.

Lovina, Phebe and Charles walked to the Palmer buggy and it was then that Phebe realized that Eliza's body was in the buggy. She slipped off one of her petticoats, climbed into the buggy and wrapped the little body in the white ruffles. She sat holding her in her arms in the back, Lovina and Charles rode in front. Phebe looked under the front seat and there was the family Bible, unmarred by the fire or rain. "Why, God? I don't understand." And then she recalled the passage the young brother had quoted this morning from the Epistle of James, *"If any of ye lack wisdom, let him ask of God who giveth to all*

men liberally and upbraideth not; and it shall be given him."
Some day God may help her understand, but for now the sorrow consumed her and she could not be consoled.

PART III

STRENGTH TO BEAR AFFLICTIONS
1832-1834
CHAPTER ELEVEN

The Palmers and the Drapers circled the small grave in the cemetery on Grandpa Draper's farm. Phebe, drawn and pale, looked down at the little cavern waiting for the pine box holding Eliza. Mother Lydia was at her side as she had always been when Phebe needed her. William II was on the other side ready to hold his beloved Miss Phebe if she weakened. The other brothers had carried George, unable to stand, to a chair near the grave. Elijah stood in back of his brother to hold him in the chair and also give him comfort. All of the Palmer children were cared for by one of the aunts or cousins. No one was left without someone to comfort them.

Charles and Carson lowered the box into the grave and Father Draper bowed his head in prayer. "Father; Bless this sacred spot and accept our beloved little Eliza into your arms. Her sweet spirit has brought sunshine to our lives and we thank you for the years you allowed her to be part of our family. Comfort her parents and brothers and sisters. Fill their hearts with solace and understanding of thy hand in all things. This we Pray, Amen."

George wept openly and could not be consoled. Elijah and Carson carried him to Grandpa Draper's home. They put him to bed and Elijah sat by his side. "George, I am so sorry about Eliza. I loved her too, like I do all of your children. I am so glad that I came to find you and that you let me be a part of your family. You must get better and while you are working at that I will take care of the farm. Asahel can help me. The neighbors in the valley and the uncles are going to rebuild the house. You and Phebe and the children can stay with Phebe's folks 'til they get it done." George didn't answer. He turned his head to the wall. Elijah sat quietly at his side.

The Draper clan was gathered again as they so often were to comfort or to cheer. Phebe looked at them and felt the circle of their love supporting her in her weakest hour. How blessed she was to have such a family. She went to Sarah and took Zemira from her. He hugged her neck with his chubby little arms and put his cheek to hers. It was then that she realized she had other children to love and care for.

She slipped away from the group and took Zemira to George. Perhaps the baby could also help ease the pain of this tragedy for him. She nodded for Elijah to leave and she sat at George's bedside. Zemira responded to her silent prayer, "Papa, Papa." and held out his little arms to George. A smile broke the expressionless face and George held out his hand. Phebe laid the baby by his father. She had wondered why this baby had come to them when they thought there would be no more children. Perhaps this was the reason. God knew the pain they would feel when he took Eliza back from them and he sent Zemira to console them. She leaned over and kissed her husband and her youngest son.

George looked at her with love in his eyes but still the guilt he felt for Eliza's death clouded his mind. Could life ever be good for him again? He had worked so hard and built such a good life. Why, if there is a God, did he allow this to happen? He couldn't accept God's will on face value as Phebe did. He turned again to the wall and Phebe lifted Zemira from his side and walked from the room to let him rest.

Lydia and William had made room for Phebe's family and everyone was settled with a place to sleep and a chair at the table. Mother knew how to make people comfortable in any situation. She'd had enough practice since Father always expected her to greet any stranger he brought by with a hot meal and a bed if necessary. Fanny and Lucretia were both married now with little ones of their own. Carson, William II and Zemira had married girls from Loughborough and worked in town. There was plenty of room in the old house for Phebe's family and she needed the comfort her father and mother could give her now.

She walked to the orchard and her father followed her. He quickened his pace and walked stride for stride with her. "Phebe, my dear, I know this is a very trying time for you. I have always felt that the greatest test of our faith would be to lose a child. They are so innocent and it seems so unfair. The Savior loved little ones more than any of us can realize. I am sure he will care for her until that time when we join her in heaven. He said, 'Let the little ones come unto me.' They die without sin. What a gift she was for the time we had her. We have so many happy memories of that little pixie who gave love to everyone she met.

I wanted to share with you something that happened the last time your family was here. Eliza and I were together here in the orchard. She looked up at me and said, 'Grandpa, I love Jesus too. I know you do because mama said she didn't know anyone who loved Jesus more than you. Mama loves him too, and I want to be so good that Jesus will want me to come and live with Him.'

Phebe, you taught her well. Thank you for letting her know how much I love the Lord. I've thought of that conversation often in the last few days.

Now, my dear, you must let that love the Lord has promised, comfort you and take that strength to give your love to George and your other children. They are suffering this terrible loss too, you must be strong and help them. Keep in mind that he said, 'Love one another as I have loved you.' I promise you that as you pour your love out to them your heart will heal."

Phebe rested her head on her father's shoulder. "You give me strength, Father. When my faith wavers I think of you, sitting in your chair with your Bible open and reading the scriptures to us with such conviction. I have tried to be that kind of example to my children also. I sometimes wonder about myself. George thinks I am too intense about things and as he said, 'Push too hard'. I do have an inner drive that seems to propel me to try harder at whatever the task seems to be.

I see so much of you in me and also many of Mothers traits. I love you both with all my heart. Thank you for spending this time with me."

They walked back to the house arm in arm. "Father, have you heard about a Brother Miller that is in the area? He gave the sermon, if you could call it that, in our church last Sunday. There was something so moving about the story he told of a fifteen year old boy having a visit from God and Jesus Christ? I had the strangest feeling come over me. In fact, the whole congregation seemed to be very caught up in the spirit of his story. He said none of the churches are true. What do you think of that?"

William hesitated and then looked down at Phebe, "Yes, I have spent many hours with him. I too feel of his sincerity. He is coming to the house tomorrow night to meet with some of the family. Would you like to join us?"

"Yes I would. Maybe George will feel well enough to be with us too."

Lydia smiled as they entered. She could tell that what ever William had said to Phebe had helped her. That familiar light was back in those steel gray eyes that had always seemed to say, "I'm ready for the challenge, what ever it is."

"Is George awake? I should take some food to him. He has hardly eaten anything these last few days." Phebe went to her mother's cupboard and lifted down a bowl and cup and saucer.

"He was coughing again just a few minutes ago. Maybe some warm tea and a bowl of the chicken soup will taste good to him." Lydia gave her a tray and napkin and cut a slice of bread to go with the soup.

Phebe carried the tray of nourishment to the bedroom. It was as Father had said. She needed to care for her family and get George well again. She put the tray down and lifted his shoulders with one arm as she fluffed the pillows with the other. He coughed again and she held the tea to his lips. He sipped the warm liquid. It seemed to relieve the coughing spasms. "Now lets try some of mother's good chicken soup. I never could make soup taste like hers." She spooned the soup to his mouth and he picked up the bread and took a healthy bite.

"Did Elijah and Asahel leave? There is so much to be done at home. I can't just lay here." He tried to sit up but the coughing spasms started again and he fell back on the pillow.

Phebe picked up the napkin and wiped the perspiration from his forehead. "George, I need you to get well. You must rest and let us take care of you. I know it is very hard for you to stay in bed. I can't remember a day since we were married that you weren't up at daybreak, but please, let me help you get better."

He let her feed him and ate all of the soup and bread, finishing it off with the last of the tea. He grinned at her and said, "Now are you satisfied, Miss Phebe?"

"Oh George, it is so good to see you smile. I love you so much and I don't know what I would do without you." She leaned over and gave him a kiss.

He kissed her back, "Or I, you." he said.

She sat by his side holding his hand until he fell into a restful sleep. She whispered to herself, "How did Father know I could only heal my own wounds by helping others heal theirs?"

She slipped out of the room and went to find the children. They needed to know she loved them just as much as Eliza. They sat on the porch together in the twilight hours of the day, and taking turns, shared the things they would remember most about Eliza. As they talked, they healed, and Phebe repeated the scripture her Father had quoted earlier. 'As I have loved you, love one another.' They hugged each other and kissed their mother goodnight before they went to the bed Lydia had assigned to them. Lovina took little Zemira with her.

Phebe sat on the porch contemplating the future. How could she repay Charles and the neighbors and uncles for rebuilding the house? They would need some money for supplies and she needed to go back and see what little their might be that she could salvage from the ruins. As she had in the past, when faced with hardship, she started to make a mental list of what she would do. She and Lovina could take the buggy and go to the bank in Loughborough. They could then go on to Cramahe and leave the money with Charles. The cellar would still have food in it and the animals had survived so there would be eggs and milk. They could use the big old stove to heat water to wash things that could be used. She would borrow some bedding and dish towels from mother. Maybe Eunice would come over and help Mother with George and the little children while she was gone.

Yes, tomorrow she would get busy and take care of her family. Then she remembered her father's invitation to listen to Brother Miller tomorrow night. Well, she could get ready tomorrow and leave on Saturday, but the bank would be closed. Maybe Monday would be soon enough. She'd pray about it. Come to think of it, she had a lot of things to pray about. Another list began to take form.

It had been another hot August day. The children had taken turns fanning their Papa, trying to keep him cool. There was still ice in the ice house so Father brought some in for Lydia to make Ice tea. The evening was welcomed as it brought a cool breeze that wafted through the open windows.

George seemed to feel better. The children had been good for him. Lovina had told him about a friend who's mother was a milliner and wanted her to model hats for her in Loughborough. "She thinks my dark hair makes her hats look better. She has even offered to teach me how to make hats. Now what do you think of that?"

"Oh, 'Vina, you make everything look beautiful. But I don't know how your mother could spare you now. She'll need all the help she can get. We'll see how things go." George looked at the beauty of his sixteen-year-old daughter. She would make any hat look beautiful. All the women in town would like to look like Lovina. She would make the hats sell like hot cakes at the village breakfast.

Little William George came in to take his turn and started to tell his father about the conversation he had over heard when the Uncles were planning the rebuilding project for the Palmers in Cramahe. In a deep voice he said, "Now you brothers, be here at the crack of six in the morning Thursday next. We want to put in a good day. I've loaded my wagon with tools so you load yours with all the logs you can find. We'll stop in town and pick up nails. And make sure your wives send along plenty of food." He imitated his great Uncle Carson's voice. "Then Uncle Joel said, 'Maybe you older men ought to stay here and let David and William II and I go up to do the heavy work.' Well, that made Uncle Carson pretty upset." His voice dropped again, "I can out work you any day of the week and don't you forget it."

His imitations were so exact that George had to laugh. He laughed so hard he started to cough again and William George had to run for Phebe. "I'm sorry Mama, I didn't mean to make him cough. I was just trying to cheer him up."

Phebe brought him a drink of water and saw he was still chuckling between coughs. He repeated William George's story and they laughed together.

The parlor was filling with guests who had come to hear Brother Miller. Phebe took the younger children to their room and found a book William George could read to them. Lydia Elizabeth promised to mind Zemira and listen to her big brother.

"George, Father has invited that missionary over that I told you about. Would you like to come out to the parlor and listen for a while? If you get tired, I'll help you back to bed." Phebe held up his shirt to help him dress.

"I'm not up to it Phebe. The last thing I want to do right now is listen to religion. As I see it, God hasn't been to kind to me of late. Go on and do your prayin' with 'em. I'm not a mind to." The barrier was there again. Phebe turned and walked from the room.

"The parlor was full and some were sitting on the porch within hearing distance. Father William welcomed them and introduced Brother Eleaser Miller. "Let us pray together first. Brother William Jr. would you start our meeting with a word of Prayer?"

Phebe's brother stood and ask the Lord to bless them with discernment to recognize the truth. It was short and sincere.

The young missionary opened the Bible and turned to the Gospel of Luke where he read of John, Baptizing Jesus. "— 'it came to pass, that Jesus also being baptized, and praying, the heaven was opened, and the Holy ghost descended in a bodily shape like a dove upon him and a voice came from heaven which said, Thou art my beloved son; in thee I am well pleased.' Just as God was there to witness the baptism of His son, so was God the Father there to witness His son introducing the beginning of the last dispensation to Joseph Smith. He said, "This is my beloved Son, hear him." They appeared to Joseph as he prayed to them in the grove in answer to the query as to which church was true.

That happened in 1823 and so much has been revealed and will yet be revealed to the Prophet Joseph until the fullness of the gospel is restored. An ancient Prophet from this continent appeared to him and led him to discover golden plates on which were written another testimony of Jesus Christ. About Him appearing on this continent. The ancient prophet was named, Moroni. He was the son of another great prophet, Mormon, who had compiled this history. It is called the Book of Mormon. He pulled the book from his pack and began to read, "And again, I would exhort you that ye would come unto Christ, and lay hold upon every good gift, and touch not the evil gift, nor the unclean thing.—Yea, come unto Christ and be perfected in him, and deny yourselves of all ungodliness; and if ye shall deny yourselves of all ungodliness, and love God with all your might, mind and strength, then is his grace sufficient for you, that by his grace ye may be perfect in Christ; and if by the grace of God ye are perfect in Christ, ye can in no wise deny the power of God.'

I have come to you as an emissary of our Father-in-Heaven. I have been chosen to come to you and you have been chosen to hear my message. The prophet has been told that the voice of warning shall be unto all people by the mouths of my disciples, whom I have chosen in these last days. And they shall go forth and none shall stay them, for I the Lord have commanded them.

And verily I say unto you, that they who go forth, bearing these tidings unto the inhabitants of the earth, to them is power given to seal both on earth and in heaven, the unbelieving and rebellious. —Prepare ye, prepare ye for that which is to come, for the Lord is nigh. And the arm of the Lord shall be revealed; and the day cometh that they who will not hear the voice of the Lord, neither the voice of his servants, neither give heed to the words of the prophets and apostles, shall be cut off from among the people;—Wherefore, I the Lord, knowing the calamity which should come upon the inhabitants of the earth called upon my servant Joseph Smith Jun. and spake unto him from heaven and gave him commandments and also gave commandments to others, that they should proclaim these things unto the world —that man should not counsel his fellow man, neither trust in the arm of flesh —But that every man might speak in the name of God the Lord, even the Savior of the world —that mine everlasting covenant might be established.'

Brothers and sisters, I come to you as an emissary of the Father to proclaim this gospel to you. I testify of its truthfulness. As the Holy Ghost rested upon the Savior at his baptism, so has the Holy Ghost born witness to me of the truthfulness of this gospel. I pray that you will open your hearts to this message. This I pray in the name of Jesus Christ, our Redeemer, Amen.

Silence filled the room. William Jr. held his wife Bett's hand and was obviously over come with the spirit. Lovina, who was sitting by her mother, put her arm around Phebe and whispered, "It's just like at the church when I sang. I have that same feeling. It's true, I know it's true."

Father William arose and thanked the young missionary for his stirring message and solemnly ask, "Where can I get a Book of Mormon?"

Brother Miller passed his book to him. "It was just published a little over a year ago. Brigham Young is coming to Canada in a few months and I am hopeful he will bring some more copies with him. I have to go to Kingston for a few days. I will stop by when I get back and pick up the book. Thank you for letting me share my message with you tonight. You have a lovely family, Brother Draper." He walked to the door and as he left it was if an invisible thread, tying him to them, was stretched thin and they didn't want him to leave. He had brought them a message that would change the direction of their lives and they had no idea where it would take them.

Gradually, they went to their own homes. Father William was sure Phebe and William Jr. would want to read this new book. Perhaps he and Lydia could read it together.

Phebe looked in on the children. Lydia Elizabeth and

Zemira were asleep on either side of William George. He was also asleep with the story book open on his chest. She pulled the cover over them and kissed each one, trying not to think of Eliza. She closed the book, laid it on the table and blew out the lamp.

George was sleeping quietly so she slipped off her clothes in the dark and stepped into the flannel nightgown her mother had loaned her. She knelt on the braided rug by the bed and conversed with the Lord. There was much she needed to pray for; thanks to be offered, questions to be answered and strength to do the things she must do in the next few days. Phebe prayed with energy and sincerity and opened her mind to inspiration.

Slipping quietly beneath the covers so as not to awaken George, she lay quietly looking into the dark and contemplating Brother Miller's message. She wished George had heard it and felt the spirit as she had. She could never tell it to him the way Brother Miller told it, with such conviction. She had never felt the spirit of the Holy Ghost so she wasn't sure if that is what had happened to her but it was that same strange feeling that she had when she heard him speak at the church.

Then the memories of that dreadful Sunday poured over her and she wept quietly. Tomorrow she would talk to George about her plans to go to the bank for money and go home to see what she could salvage. There were things she needed to check on before the men came to rebuild. She tried to recall the list of things to do again.

CHAPTER TWELVE

Phebe and Lovina bounced along in the buggy on the way to Loughborough. George had agreed that Phebe needed to get some of their savings from the bank to help pay for the rebuilding of the house. He signed a note to the bank president so there would be no question about releasing the money to her.

Lovina was glad to have this time alone with her mother. "I have had an offer that I think I would like to pursue with your permission. I discussed it with Father yesterday and he was concerned because he felt you needed me. Mrs. Kenny has ask me to model hats for her Milliner Shop. She will also teach me how to make hats. I was thinking, if you agree, I might be able to stay with Aunt Lucretia or Uncle William. Uncle William's shoe repair shop is next door to the hat shop. I could help Aunt Bett with her children when she gets called to deliver a baby. Now I am out of school I want to learn something new and earn my own money."

Phebe remembered how she felt at Lovina's age and how proud she was when she bought the material for the red dress. "Perhaps we can stop and discuss it with Mrs. Kenny while we are in town. You have such artistic traits that I'm sure you would be very successful and modeling her hats for her would certainly help them sell. Hats are so popular now and the decorations on them are works of art. I have been thinking of buying a hat from Mrs. Kenny myself."

"Oh, Mother, do you really think I may be able to make hats? I think she has every color of the rainbow in ribbons and she knows how to make them into flowers and birds and-" Lovina was lost in her thoughts of a new adventure.

"What about Henry? You have seen him quite often lately." Phebe had been reluctant to bring up the subject of Henry

Munro but she had noticed how he always met Lovina at church and she had seen the looks they exchanged when together.

"Well, He has ask Uncle William if he can apprentice in his shoe repair shop." It was obvious that the two youngsters had made some plans to be conveniently together. They were quite the industrious pair. "Mama, I really like to be with Henry. We have a lot of fun together and he is a very kind person. He was the smartest boy in our class at school. The only thing I was better at in school was Penmanship."

"If you were to accept this position, I think it would be better for you to stay with Aunt Lucretia. Have you ever heard the phrase, 'Familiarity brings contempt?'

Sometimes being around someone you like for long periods of time cause you to see their faults. You can lose friendships that way." Phebe expected the next question.

"What about when you marry someone and spend all your time with them?" Lovina's brow wrinkled as she ask the question.

"That is different. You have a commitment to love and honor each other and as you build a home and have a family, your love grows stronger. Working together to raise a family bonds you together in a way that you can only understand when you are married. Just yesterday, your Father and I had one of those special times when we laughed together about William George mimicking the Uncles. Have you noticed how Grandpa William and Grandma Lydia seem to think of the same thing at the same time?" Phebe hoped she had explained the difference between relationships before and after marriage. This was a crucial time for her beautiful Lovina.

"How much farther is it to town? Aren't we over half way there?" Lovina smoothed out the skirt of her dress and pulled her bonnet to one side a little at a jaunty tilt. It was a beautiful day and she was so happy. Then she sat quietly wondering if it was alright to be happy after all that had happened to her family.

Phebe was lost in thought also. Her Father had finished reading the Book of Mormon on Saturday and she had spent several hours reading this most unusual book. George had slept most of the time while the rest of the family were at church. It read like the Bible and some of it was exactly like Isaiah. The names were so unusual. She always felt guilty when she skipped to the back of the book but she was so intrigued by Brother Miller talking about it being another witness of Jesus Christ. She had leafed through the book until she found the part about the Savior appearing to, were they called Nephites? There again was the message of His love for little children. She had brought the book with her to give to William Jr. She would be anxious to discuss it with him after he read it.

She reined in the horse at the hitching post of the bank. She walked in and ask for Mr Green, the bank president. "It is most unusual to release money to a woman without the presence of her husband to whom it belongs."

Phebe started to seethe. This wasn't any more George's money than hers. They had both worked for it and it was theirs together. She opened her purse and pulled out the note with George's signature. "Here, my husband is ill so he wrote this note and signed it so you would release the money to me."

Mr. Green adjusted his spectacles and held the note at an angle so he could focus on the scribbled note. He reluctantly counted out the money as if it were a gift from his own supply. Phebe put it safely in her pocket book, walked out and crossed the street to Mrs. Kenny's Milliner Store.

Lovina was walking from table to table trying on hats and primping in the mirror with each new choice. The Ladies shopping in the store would follow her and pick up the hats as she put them back on the table. Phebe smiled to herself. She would like to look like Lovina in the hats too.

"Is Mrs. Kenny in the store, Lovina?"

"Yes, Mother, she just stepped back in the work room to get a customer's hat."

Phebe and Lovina waited until the women in the store finished their purchases and left. "Mrs. Kenny, I am Mrs Palmer, Lovina's mother." She held out her hand to the milliner, a small, pretty woman who appeared to be of French Canadian decent.

Her dark eyes sparkled as she smiled and extended her small soft hand to Phebe. "I am so happy to meet you. You have a lovely daughter and she sells hats for me every time she comes into the store. I would very much like to have her work for me. She has a natural beauty that attracts people and a sense of style. We could set it up as a form of apprenticeship. I would pay her a modest allowance and teach her how to make hats. Most of them I weave my self or make from felt that I shape on a mold. Of course the thing that sells them is the decoration in ribbon, silk and lace. Would you consider such an arrangement?"

"I would have to consult her father. I think it would be an excellent opportunity for Lovina. I have recognized her creative talents since she was a small girl. We recently had the misfortune of loosing our house to a fire. We are on our way to see what we can salvage. It will be several days before I have an opportunity to discuss this with my husband. Will the position still be available in two weeks?" Phebe liked Mrs. Kenny. The store was clean and the clientele that visited the store seemed to be some of the most fashionable ladies in town

"Yes, even longer if it is necessary. I hope to hear from you soon, however." She turned to Lovina, "You put on that pretty smile for your Papa so he will let you come and work for me. I can make and sell twice as many hats with your help."

"Come Lovina, we must get over to the Shoe Shop. Good day, Mrs. Kenny." They walked down the board walkway to the next shop and went into see William Jr.

He was pounding away at the leather with his hammer. He held small nails between his lips which he took one by one to nail the sole on the shoe. Shoe lasts of every size lined the shelf at his side and the shelves in back of him were filled with everything from rough, home made brogues to fancy leather pumps. He looked up and that old familiar smile that he kept for his favorite Miss Phebe crept across his face. "George agreed to the plan, I see. I hoped he would. Hard as it will be, you need to go back to what's left of the house. I have a young man coming in to run the store for me. I'm going with you."

Henry Munro walked in the door whistling. Then he spied Lovina and went right to her side. "Hello, I didn't know you were going to be in town today. My, don't you look pretty." Then he realized Phebe and William were listening to them and the color rose in his face.

Lovina flashed him her coy smile and took his hand. "Henry, have you met my Mother? This is Mrs. Phebe Palmer, my Mother. Mother, this is Henry Munro.."

"I'm happy to meet you, Henry. I have seen you at church with your family. Lovina tells me you are a very good friend." She smiled and shook his hand as she would another adult.

"Glad to meet you Mrs. Palmer. Lovina is my good friend too." He walked over and picked up a leather apron from the counter and tied the strings behind him.

"Henry, I'm glad you came a little early. Try to finish those boots I am working on. Mr. Terry will be in to get them this afternoon. Close up at dark and take the money up to Bett. I'll see you in the morning if you can come in again."

"I'll be here," Henry said with a smile and then winked at Lovina when he thought no one was looking. They pretended not to see.

"Oh, William, it is wonderful of you to go with us. I wasn't sure how I would handle going back to that burned out home and all the terrible memories of that sad Sunday." She took his hand as he helped her into the buggy.

"You going with us too? I thought you might stay here and keep Henry company." William lifted Lovina into the buggy and tweaked her cheek.

"Uncle William, you must stop treating me like a child. I'm sixteen years old."

He smiled at her attempt to act so grown up, loosened the reins from the post, joined Phebe and Lovina on the seat and flipped the reins on the back of the horse. "Did you get a chance to read the book, Phebe? I'm sure Father wouldn't give it up until he had read every page."

"Father read all night and finished the book the next day. I read most of it yesterday and brought it with me for you to read. I really would like to have a copy of my own so I could study it more. There are many similarities to the Bible. It is almost as if it is another chapter or story of the same or related people. I won't say any more because I want to know your impressions first." She pulled the book from her pack and slipped it into William Jr.'s pocket.

"I was so impressed with Brother Miller, Phebe. I haven't been able to get him or his message out of my mind. Something tells me that this message will have a great impact on our lives.

William helped Phebe and Lovina empty the supplies they had brought with them into the granary, unhitched the horse and took him to the barn. They changed into some old work clothes Lydia had found for them and walked to the house. Starting at the newer part of the house on the east end, they saw that Elijah's room was totally burned. Phebe remembered the boxes of papers which were George and Elijah's only tie to the past. She would have to ask Elijah if he found any remains of those boxes. Even a scrap of paper with a note or signature would be something worth having.

They went to what was left of the girl's room. Phebe steeled herself for this part. She went to the partially burned bed that had been Eliza's. The strong stench of the damp burned wool from the quilt batting was stifling. She pushed it away with her foot, revealing the remains of Eliza's rag doll. Her memories took her back to her preparations for Christmas last year. She had made rag dolls for Lydia and Eliza. Funny how you remember little things. Finding black buttons for the eyes had created a real problem. She searched the rag bag for buttons on old clothes, finally settling for blue ones on Lydia's doll and yellow ones on Eliza's. As it had turned out, that was the way they told them apart. She picked up the half burned doll and wiped the black soot from the yellow eyes.

Lovina searched for any of her personal things that might be buried in the black charred debris. "Oh, look Mama, Here is my necklace you and Papa gave me for my sixteenth birthday." She started to polish away the black with the hem of her skirt.

The trunk in the girl's room had protected the clothes in them; winter coats and some extra dresses and underclothes. She would have Asahel and Elijah carry the trunks to the granary. William was out in the fields looking for them. She moved on to the boy's room and the trunk there was intact also. And then to their bedroom, George had made the crib so lovingly when they had realized they were to have this unexpected baby. The crib was almost completely burned as was their bed, the ticks and quilts. Even the new coverlet she had just finished crocheting was a blackened mass of scorched wool. She sat on the trunk in her room. It was the only item that could be saved except the china lamp with the hurricane glass lamp shade that had somehow settled into the ashes and was covered with the black residue from the fire.

The books, the books, were any of them still readable? They lay on the floor, damp from the rain and charred beyond belief. She picked them up one by one trying to decide what to salvage. There, between the Geography and Algebra books was the unburned little book of poems that John had sent. She opened it and found the letter still tucked between the pages. She wondered if they had moved to Ohio. She would probably never hear from them again.

Lovina and Phebe gathered up the unbroken dishes, silverware and pans. They heated water on the stove and tried to wash up the remains of the kitchen utensils. Phebe carefully carried the tea set and Grandma's cake plate to the soapy water and washed them clean. She wrapped them in some of the towels she had brought from home and packed them carefully between the clothes in her trunk.

William Jr. walked in with Elijah and Asahel. They started to laugh as they saw the women. "I hardly recognized you Mama. You and Lovina are all streaked with soot."

Phebe and Lovina had been so busy they hadn't even looked at each other. They laughed too and it made it all easier. Lovina pulled a face at Asahel and chased him out to the yard. "Bring some fresh water in so we can wash up." Phebe called after them. "Elijah, did you find anything left of your father's treasures?"

"No, not a thing. I'm glad George and I went through it all together. I guess all we'll have is what we can remember."

"How are the crops? Was the fruit damaged?" Phebe asked.

"The oat crop is gone, of course, but the peaches and apples look fine. The Tobacco wasn't hurt and I think we can start harvesting that in time to meet the broker when he comes to Loughborough. The animals are all fine and the granary and the barn. The red hen has a new flock of chicks and the spring lambs have grown a foot. I've fed some of the milk to the lambs and took the rest over to Hanah. We've been sleeping and eating over there. I think the neighbors and Uncles plan to start working on the house tomorrow." Elijah gave a complete report and Phebe was impressed with his thorough observations.

William Jr. had calculated the value of the crops and was relieved that this devastating fire wouldn't wipe out all of George and Phebe's assets. "Look at it this way, Phebe. The Lord has blessed you with abundant crops. The Lord Giveth and the Lord taketh away. We will all work together and things will be back to normal soon."

"How would we survive without the family and our friends

here in the valley?" Phebe put her arm around her brother's waist. The shock of being back here was wearing off and the work had been good for her. She directed the men to the trunks to be carried to the granary.

Lovina and Asahel carried the water in. It was soon heated and the girl's washed their hands and faces. The men washed up too and they walked out to a grassy spot and sat down to eat the lunch Lydia had packed for them.

It was a warm late August afternoon. As Phebe looked over the farm she said to her self, "We can rebuild this. George will be well soon and other than loosing our little Eliza, things will be back to normal soon.

When the animals were cared for they all piled into the wagon and buggy. Sarah would be waiting for the boys for supper and Phebe knew they would all be welcome at her table.

"Thank you, Sarah. That was a delicious meal. I do believe the Draper boys marry the best cooks in Northumberland." William Jr. smiled at his sister-in-law.

Lovina and Phebe helped Sarah clear the dishes and carry them to the side board to wash. The men sat at the table discussing the challenges of clearing the burned part of the house and what they could possibly save as they rebuilt it. Phebe remembered the money she had brought from the bank and took it to Charles and William Jr. "We have some savings in the bank. George and I appreciate all the work everyone is contributing but we will buy any supplies that need to be purchased. I'll leave this up to the two of you and if you need more we will make arrangements for it." She went back to help Sarah.

William Jr. was soon giving an animated description of the meeting with Brother Miller. "I wish you could have heard him, Charles. He said another missionary is coming in a few months who will bring us some copies of the Book of Mormon. I haven't read it yet but Father and Phebe have."

"I heard him speak at the church and talked to him after, while we waited for the storm to blow over. The way he describes this Joseph Smith is incredible. Do you think he really had a vision?" Charles was curious about William Jr.s impressions. Even though he was a younger brother, Charles had great respect for him. William Jr. was probably the brightest of the Draper children, except for Phebe, and Charles often ask him for advice.

"Charles, I have been trying to reserve judgement but I have to tell you that I received a strong witness of its truthfulness at that meeting. I would love to meet this Joseph Smith that Mr. Miller calls a prophet. There is so much we don't know about it but I have the feeling that Mr. Miller has more to tell us." William Jr. moved his chair and motioned for Phebe and Sarah to join them. "Phebe, What are your impressions?"

"Like you, I had an unusual feeling that surprised me. It was as if something warm was generating within me. It surprised me because I am so analytical. I have not been impressed by the shouting preachers that have so often visited our area. I agree with what Mr. Miller said was revealed in this so called vision. They shout of the fire and brimstone interpretation of God's will but I have never been caught up in a feeling of their sincerity or even intelligent analysis of the scriptures. I briefly scanned the Book of Mormon yesterday, but certainly reserve judgement until I can read it more thoroughly. I hope we can keep it a little longer so I can read more."

"I plan to read it tonight when I get home. You can pick it up on your way back to Richmond. Charles, can I borrow a horse? I rode out with Phebe and Lovina. I'll bring it back when I come out to help with the house. I'll ride back with the Uncles." William rose to leave.

"Anytime brother, take the bay. He needs a workout.

How's the shoe repair business? Sure you can get away to help with the house?" Charles always chided William for investing in a business that didn't challenge that wonderful mind of his.

"Sure, I have a new apprentice and I know he will work his head off for me because he wants to impress my niece." He grinned at Lovina and she blushed.

Elijah broke into the conversation, "Did I ever tell you how much I enjoy this family? If any body cares, I was impressed with the Miller preacher too. Come on Asahel, we had better get some sleep so we can hit that tobacco field tomorrow."

Phebe found herself alone with Charles and Sarah. "I'm glad to have a few minutes alone with you two. Thank you for all you have done for me. Sarah, you have cared for my children and fed my family. You are a real sister to me. I hope someday to be able to repay you. And Charles, we have always been so close. It was right that you should be the one to come to me when I lost Eliza. I love you both."

Charles walked to his sister, "Remember when you used to fight my battles for me when we were kids down in Rome? I owed you." He gave her a hug.

CHAPTER THIRTEEN

George and Phebe sat in the new rockers on the porch of their rebuilt house looking north over the oat field. Elijah had plowed under the burned stubble. The leaves on the trees that were not destroyed in the fire were turning bright reds and yellows. The haze of autumn hung low over the valley and the days were shorter. Phebe wrapped her shawl around her. "George, are you warm enough? I can get an extra shawl for you."

"Phebe, stop fussin' over me. Ya make me feel like a invalid. I can take care of maself. I'm goin' to help with the apples tomorrow." He stood and walked in the house. She could hear him coughing as he pumped him a drink of water.

Zemira had built her beautiful cupboards and he and William Jr. had installed a pump in the house that pumped water from the well. Not only was the house rebuilt, it was rebuilt with conveniences she had never had. George seemed to resent the fact that he had not been able to help. He said he didn't even feel like it was his house. She hoped that his attitude would change as he became stronger and was able to work again. Men certainly didn't enjoy being sick.

Elijah had been a Godsend to them. He kept the Palmer farm running almost as efficiently as George had with Asahel as his constant companion. Asahel and Phebe had had another discussion about school but it had not gone well. She finally agreed that he could decide for himself. William George and Lydia Elizabeth were going into school each day with Sarah's children.

It seemed strange to have Little Zemira to herself so much now. She spent a lot of time telling him stories and teaching him some of the games she used to teach the children in school. He was a bright little boy and learned them quickly.

Her favorite time was when he snuggled on her lap and said, "Sing to me Mama," She would sing the lullaby's she knew over and over until he fell asleep, his dark hair curling in wisps around his face.

Lovina was living with Lucretia in town and working at the Milliners. They saw her once a week when they went in for supplies and she would came home with them from church on Sundays. Henry came out on Sunday afternoons and took her back to town. It had just been two months and it seemed like she was growing away from them so quickly.

By Christmas they had all settled into a routine. George was able to care for the animals and, other than shoeing the horses, did quite well. Elijah had done all the fall plowing and George went to the orchard with he and Asahel to supervise the pruning.

William Jr. had totally embraced the new religion and had found a place for them to hold meetings on Sundays in Loughborough with the missionaries. It was the hall where the town men's club met during the week. Several families from Loughborough were attending the meetings with them, including the Munros and Mrs. Kenny. If the weather was good, William and Lydia would come from Richmond. The Uncle's families would often come also but Aunt Olive and Uncle Peter had chosen to stay with the Catholic Church and went to Mass in Richmond.

They planned a special Christmas service at the new meeting place. One of the missionaries had left a Book of Mormon for all of them to share. Phebe suggested that they read the first chapter of 3rd Nephi. William Jr. agreed and ask her to do the reading. "But people will be shocked to hear a woman read in church. Do you really think I should?"

"Father and I will give the prayers and Lovina can sing a Christmas song. You, dear sister, will read from the Book of Mormon. It doesn't look like we will have a missionary here. Phebe, I have been thinking about something. You know there are very few people who can read well, and if it hadn't been for you and Mother, there would be even less. I think the Lord blessed you and Mother with the special gift of teaching so we would be ready to learn his word when it came to us. Do you think we can get George to come to our meeting?"

A feeling of sadness engulfed Phebe and she looked away. "I'm afraid not, William. He gets very angry if I even mention this new religion. He used to go his way and let me go mine but he has very strong feelings against this movement. Have you noticed that Asahel seldom comes also? It is as if we are on opposite sides and Asahel has chosen to take that of his father's. He won't even come when Elijah invites him. I am so torn. This issue seems to be cutting a chasm between us that I can't bridge."

"Miss Phebe," William put his arm around her. "I have noticed the change in George. I had hoped it would go away as he started feeling better. Perhaps Satan is working on him to deprive you of the blessings of the true church. We will both pray about it and maybe he will have a change of heart."

Brigham Young came as a missionary in the later part of January 1833 and he did bring more copies of the Book of Mormon. It was better than Christmas to the little group who had embraced the gospel. He was a very likeable man who talked to the men about their trades. Zemira was taken with him when he told him he liked to work with wood also. Zemira and Agnes insisted that he stay with them in order to share his new ideas of ways to shape wood in his workshop. "Zemira Draper, I promise you, you will be a great blessing to this church."

In their own self styled way they had formed their own congregation with William Jr. as their leader. Brother Young recognized the talents of this young energetic, enthusiastic convert and encouraged him to continue as he had. After several meetings with Father William and William Jr., Brigham Young broached the subject of baptism. He was surprised to find that they already believed in baptism by immersion. Now he explained that since the power of the priesthood had been taken from the earth and was only now restored that only those with that priesthood had the authority to baptize.

In a meeting with monumental implications for the Draper family, Brigham Young invited the progeny of Thomas Draper to be baptized members of the Church of Jesus Christ of Latter Day Saints. He explained that this baptism was not to be taken lightly. It would cleanse them of their sins and they would take upon themselves the name of Jesus Christ. They would then be confirmed a member of the Church and receive the Holy Ghost which would be a guide and protection to them

Phebe discussed it with George and he was not willing to even consider it nor did he want her to. She prayed about it and talked to her Father. "I am torn between following the desires of my husband or accepting the invitation to join the church which I have come to know is true. You are so wise. Tell me what to do."

Father William took her hands and looked into her eyes. "Phebe, I have always felt that you were a special gift from God and can be a great influence on others. We are caught up in something greater than we can even imagine. We each have to make this decision for ourselves. I can promise you this, what ever your decision is, it will have a profound effect on your family."

It was February and the only place with water deep enough for baptisms was the nearby river. A warm flow of air came down through Canada and as Phebe stood in the water flowing down from the snow packs of the north she felt at peace. Brigham Young, raising his hand to the square repeated the short baptismal ordnance and immersed her in the water. She was one of the first of her family to become an official member of the church. Lovina and her sisters wrapped her in quilts as she walked from the water. She sat on the chair by the side of the river and Brigham Young laid his hands on her head and confirmed her a member of th Church of Jesus Christ Of Latter Day Saints and said, "receive ye the Holy Ghost." Tears ran unabated and the power of the Holy Ghost bore witness to her that her decision was right.

When she returned home she waited until after supper and they were alone to tell George the news. "George, I was baptized into the Mormon Church today. It was something I felt I had to do and I was hoping you would allow me to share my feelings about it with you." The look in his eyes startled her.

"So, you weren't satisfied until ya got yer backside wet," and he stormed out of the house.

Mending fences with George was not easy. He turned his back to her in the bed and seldom spoke. She searched for ways to please him and tried to ignore the hurtful way he treated her. The children noticed the rift and gave their father a wide birth. Except for Zemira who toddled to his father and reaching up his hands would say, "Papa, Papa." George would swing him in the air and the baby's giggle would bring a smile to his father's face.

The winter storms hit again with a vengeance, piling the snow high in the lane with drifts that could not be penetrated. Elijah and George would bundle up in warm clothing and wade through the deep snow to the barn to feed the animals. One day a ground blizzard raged all day and they could not see the barn and granary from the house. George tied a rope to the back porch and he and Elijah headed to the out buildings, hoping the rope would provide them a way back to the house if visibility remained as it was. They reached the end of the rope before they found the barn. Thinking they were on the right path, George dropped the rope and trudged on. Elijah followed, but they were soon aware that they had traveled beyond the distance of the barn. Trudging through the deep snow was exhausting and the biting wind burned his lungs as George gasp for air. He fell in the snow, unable to go on.

Elijah helped him up and they tried to retrace their tracks

but the wind had destroyed the foot prints as fast as their feet left them. They wandered in the bone chilling wind and snow, peering through the sleet at disappearing images.

"How can we be lost? This is my farm, I know every inch of it." Panic was in his voice. Elijah heard this strong man, who was his brother, start to cry and he stood helpless by his side.

"George, I know you don't give much credence to prayin' but the way I see it, that is about our only hope now." Elijah knelt down in the snow and begged the Lord to help him find the way back to the house or the barn. He put George's arm around his shoulders and moved on in the direction he felt guided to go. As they moved to the edge of their visibility, shadows loomed before them and they could see the outline of grotesque snow covered figures. A few more steps and they recognized the outline of trees in the orchard.

Elijah helped George to the nearest tree and helped him lean against it for support. He brushed away the snow from the limb and recognized the apple wood. They had skirted the barn completely and were at the far end of the orchard. He hoped George had enough strength to get back to the house.

Phebe was pacing the floor. The men had been gone too long and she could hear the milk cow bellowing to be relieved. They were not in the barn or the cow wouldn't be making such a fuss. Were they lost out in this blizzard? She wrapped up in her warm shawl, covering her head, and went out on the porch. The daylight hours were almost gone. The rope tied to the porch pillar lay limp in the snow. She picked up the lantern by the door and carried it into the house to light it. Back on the porch she waved the lantern and called as loud as she could, "George, George, Elijah, Elijah."

Her voice carried through the crisp air and she heard back, "Keep calling, we're coming." It was Elijah and the sound was coming from the direction of the orchard. She shouted their names until her throat was raspy and waved the lantern, hoping they could see the light also.

Finally, the two figures appeared through the haze of the storm and the dusk of oncoming night. She kept waving the lantern and ran to them, not feeling the icy snow packing around her feet and ankles and clinging to the hem of her skirt. She helped Elijah get George back to the house. He was so weak he could hardly lift his feet to walk up the three steps to the porch.

Once in the house, Elijah added wood to the stove and Phebe helped George out of his snow packed clothes and wrapped him in quilts. William George and Lydia stood wanting to help but not knowing what to do. "Here, you each take one of Papa's hands and hold them in your hands until they are warm." Phebe poured some hot coffee from the pot into a cup and brought it to George. She spooned it into his mouth and he accepted it greedily.

He started to shiver and then his whole body was shaking. She took the flat iron from the stove, wrapped it in paper and slipped it between the covers of the bed. "Asahel, hold that quilt from our bed by the stove and get it warm. She opened the oven and put some towels in to heat. "Come on, George, get into this nice warm bed." She took the towels from the oven and put one under him and one over him and then the warm quilt. Finally, the shivering subsided and he fell into a sound sleep.

Elijah had changed his wet clothes for dry ones and the saturated clothes were hanging, draped on chairs around the stove. He held a hot cup of coffee in his hand and it was then that Phebe realized he too was shaking. She had relied on his strength so much the last few months that it almost frightened her to see that he too was vulnerable. "What happened out there?" she asked.

"We just got lost in the blizzard. I've never seen anythin' like it. We couldn't tell where we were headed. It was like swimming in white water. I thought George was goin' to die on me out there. I finally knelt down and prayed that I could find our way back. It was just after that, that we found we were up at the far end of the orchard. We started toward the house and heard ya yellin' and then we saw the light. Phebe, between you and the Lord, we made it back."

They heard the cow bellowing again and Asahel went to the door. "The storm's let up some. I'll go take care of the animals and milk the cow." He pulled on his coat and picked up the milk bucket. Phebe followed him to the porch and held the lantern to light the path to the barn. The blizzard had subsided and the sky was clear with stars so bright the lantern light was small in comparison.

Asahel picked up the rope and pulled it in the direction of the barn. It was long enough to reach to the barn door. They would be safe in another storm. He went into the barn and Phebe soon heard the contented sounds of the animals. She could also hear Asahel whistling.

After a hot supper of chicken stew and freshly baked bread, they were all ready to crawl into their warm beds. Phebe banked the fire for the night, blew out the oil lamp light and crawled in by George. He stirred from his sleep and threw his arm around her. "Phebe, thanks for takin' such good care of me. I didn't deserve it the way I been treatin' ya. Did Elijah tell ya we was lost and he kneeled down right there in the snow and prayed fer us ta find our way out. An then we found the trees an' heard ya callin' and we saw the light. I didn't have an ounce of strength left in me. Phebe, I won't give ya no more trouble about prayin' and religion." He hugged her tight and they fell asleep.

The next few weeks were filled with the men shoveling snow paths and Phebe sewing to replace some of the things lost in the fire. As her nimble fingers stitched at seams or sent the tatting shuttle flying to make lace, she taught the children new stories she had read in her Book of Mormon. She told them of the good king Benjamin and how he worked with the people, never asking them to do anything he would not do himself. She quoted his message, "—that ye may learn wisdom; that ye may learn that when ye are in the service of your fellow beings ye are only in the service of your God." She told them the story of Nephi, the great prophet, who as a young man was sent with his brothers to get the family records from the evil Labon. As she recounted Father Lehi's vision of the tree of life and the iron rod that would lead them to the truth, she thought of the rope that led to the barn and how prayer had led George and Elijah to the orchard and ultimately to safety.

George sat in his rocker and listened to the stories with fascination, as did the children. Phebe wove the accounts of brave warriors and of a people who fought for liberty to defend their land and beliefs. She told of the great leader, Moroni, who tore part of his garment away and made a flag which he called the "Title of Liberty." How he raised it and declared the land a Land of liberty where people could maintain their religion and the Lord God would bless them.

Phebe remembered the stories her Grandfather Lathrop had told again of the Grandfather Rev. John Lathrop and his fight for religious freedom in England. When the sun was shining, she took the children to the porch and turned the rope. As they jumped, she repeated the Lathrop genealogy chant as she and Charles had done so many years ago.

It was a happy family time for the Palmers and George seemed to recover from his sadness and his illness. He watched his children play "Button, button, who has the button." and endless games of hide and seek. He planned the crops he would plant in the spring and he and Elijah talked about the work that would have to be done to prepare the soil.

They missed Lovina who could not come to see them through the drifts of snow. Phebe wondered how she was getting along with Henry Munro and if she had learned to make hats well enough to sell some.

Many evenings they popped popcorn over the fire in the

fireplace, sometimes covering it with molasses or a sprinkle of salt and butter. Lydia Elizabeth helped Phebe make candles and polish the chimneys for the oil lamps. Phebe taught her how to crochet and tat lace and doilies.

George tried his hand at whittling on some apple wood and soon had his boys and Elijah shaping the wood into little animals or wagons. Elijah made a boat to resemble Noah's ark and they were busy for days carving the pairs of animals to fill the boat. Little Zemira played with them as they were finished and William taught him how to imitate the sounds of the animals. He would pretend to be Noah and call the animals to the ark in a deep prophetic voice. Zemira would walk the little figures forward, oinking or bleating or neighing depending on the animal.

Phebe reviewed some geography and algebra with Asahel. He was reluctant but his father encouraged him now to cooperate with his mother.

One night, as they sat around the fire, Elijah started to tell them about his experiences as a sailor. "The storm was heaving the boat to the tip of the waves and crashing it down. The sails were out and the Captain sent me up the mast to help pull 'em in. He said the young 'uns could go cause if they got blowed into the sea he wouldn't be missin' much. I was a good climber but the mast and the ropes was wet and slippery. I'd climb up a step or two and slip down one, all the time looking at that mean sea water and wonderin' if I would be drownin' in it before night come.

I finally reached the top an' released the riggin', letting the sail fall free. I slid and slipped down the mast and had no sooner touched me feet ta' the deck when that mast popped like a twig and came toppling right after me. I scrambled out of the way but it caught ma foot. I could feel the bone snap. Some of me mates pulled the mast off me and carried me down below ta me bunk.

I was in pain that night an ta stop my moaning they filled

me with rum. The next day my head was a hurtin' as bad as ma foot and spendin' all the time down in my bunk while the boat was a rollin' and pitchin' I got sea sick. I wasn't sure which hurt the most, ma head, ma foot or ma stomach. Well, I crawled out o' my bunk and hopped to the ladder so as I could climb up ta the deck and get some air. I fell on the wet deck just as the boat tipped on the wave and I slid across the deck, right ta the feet of the Captain. He was an ornery cuss and I was scared o' what he'd do but he looked at me in ma sorry state and took pity on me. Had 'em wash me and clean me up in some fresh clothes and put me in a nice clean bunk. Then he gave me somethin' he said was fer the pain an' I didn't wake up 'til the sun was a shinin' and we wus on smooth water. He told me I was a brave boy ta climb that mast in the storm and the rest of the time I served on that ship he treated me like a son. I'll tell ya' I was sure someone was a watchin' over me cause young boys don't count fer much with old sailors and many of 'em just disappear.

Phebe was glad Elijah had come to them. In many ways he taught her boys things that neither she nor George could. He was a good man and would always be welcome in her home.

CHAPTER FOURTEEN

April came with the promise of new life. There were several baptisms every week. William Jr. and Bett were baptized in March and Brother Brigham Young was staying in the area where so many God fearing people had been waiting for a religion that they could commit to whole heartedly. They loved him and he loved them as they learned this new gospel together.

The small congregation of saints were meeting on a regular basis and filled the men's club hall once or twice a week. William Jr. would accompany Brother Brigham on short missionary trips to outlying areas when he could get away from his shoe shop. Phebe was often called upon to read from the scriptures, comparing excerpts from the Bible and the Book of Mormon. George would go with her some of the time but put most of his limited energy into the farm.

He planted tobacco where the oats had been and corn in the wheat fields. Neither of them would be as susceptible to fire as the oats or wheat had been. He tried to put the nightmares of the fire behind him but he would wake in the night from a dream where he was running from the flames and calling for Eliza. Phebe would console him and rub his back until he drifted off to sleep.

The warm April sun beckoned George and Phebe to leave the house and take a stroll through the orchard where they checked the progress of the blossoms. They talked about their children and what was ahead for them. Lovina had announced that she and Henry were going to marry in the fall after he had finished his apprenticeship. Elijah was getting serious about Sarah's sister who was living with Charles and Sarah on the adjoining farm. Lanky Asahel was developing muscles and whiskers which he liked to show off to William George who would be twelve in August. Lydia Elizabeth was six and Zemira almost two.

"Phebe, remember the dance we went to when you wore the red dress. I fell in love with you that night but I didn't think you would ever marry me. You came from such a fine family and were so smart and beautiful. When I look at our family now, I can hardly believe it is mine, mine and yours. I couldn't have done it without you and you have been so good to Elijah, treating him like your own family.

Phebe you are a good woman and I love you very much." George took her in his arms and gave her a long kiss.

An April rain was suddenly drenching them and they ran for the house.

April storms soon gave way to May and then June sunshine that bid the newly planted crops to break through the ground. The new lambs were past the wobbly stage and wild flowers bloomed on the edge of the forest.

Phebe and George sat in the rockers on the porch past evening until the chill of the late June night drove them to the warmth of their bed.

That night George woke Phebe. He was throwing the covers and he was burning hot. He was gasping for air and the pallor of his skin frightened her. She pumped cool water on to a cloth and wiped his face and hands trying to cool his burning fever. He called for her in his delirium and try as she might, she could not break the fever. She called for Elijah and sent him hurrying to get Charles and Sarah. Sarah seemed to have a talent for nursing sick people. Perhaps she could help George where Phebe had failed.

Phebe tried to get some cool liquid into George's mouth but he would cough it out and then gasp again for air and his face would turn blue. She bathed him again and again with cool water to no avail. The fever raged on. He threw the covers and she covered him again over and over.

Charles and Sarah came back with Elijah as the morning

light was creeping across the valley. Phebe was exhausted and Sarah took over with the bedside vigil assuring Phebe she had been doing all she would have done. Charles and Elijah propped up the head of the bed, hoping it would help George breath. The heavy mucus in his throat rattled as he tried to force the air to his starving lungs

The delirium subsided and he slipped into a sleep. They could not rouse him. Sarah got the children up and dressed and they gathered around their father's bed. Charles led them in prayer and as he finished, George opened his eyes and smiled at each of them, Phebe last. And then stopped breathing. They could not revive him.

"Oh, no! Not you too George." Phebe embraced him, not comprehending, and then at last accepting the loss. She called her children to her and in a calm and reassuring way explained that Papa had gone to live with God.

Another loss of one so close within the year and Phebe was numb to the reality of it all but she knew she must be strong for the children. Asahel turned and walked from the room and Elijah followed him. She let them go, knowing that her loss was not any greater than theirs. They would have to work through it the best they could and they had each other.

Sarah prepared some food that was hardly touched. Charles pushed his chair back from the table, "Ill go to town and tell Lovina and William Jr. I'll send Lovina back to you and go to tell the rest of the family." He and William Jr. would take care of things from here on.

Again, as before, the family gathered at the small cemetery on Grandpa Draper's farm. Brother Brigham joined them and spoke of the Heaven that would open up to George, where the Savior would love him and bring comfort to his soul. "And one day you will all be together again, you Sister Phebe, and your children here, with George and your Little Eliza, on the morning of the first resurrection. You have a great work to do on this earth and George has a great work to do in Heaven. Have faith in the Lord and he will comfort you."

William Sr. and William Jr. were on either side, as they walked back to the old family home.

Phebe was thirty-seven years old and a widow with five children and a farm to run. Lovina would soon be married and she knew Henry would take good care of her. So that left four, though she would always be on hand for Lovina, as her mother had been for her.

As she had in the past, when facing challenges, she started to make a list of what needed to be done. Somehow the legal papers for the farm and the money in the bank needed to be transferred to her name. The crops needed to be planted and then harvested. How much could she expect Elijah and the children to do? Elijah was courting Sarah's sister, Martha, and he should be free to make his own life.

She would ask Father and Charles and William Jr. to counsel her. They were all good business men. Of course, she wanted them to understand however, that she was in control and would, after their suggestions, make the final decision. George's words came to her then, "Phebe, some times you push too hard." She would think about that and perhaps let the brothers help her as she knew they would.

William Jr. met her at the bank. Mr. Green was again very cool and reluctant to carry out business directly with Phebe. "My sister has a sizable account in your bank and it is necessary that she have control over it. You have a letter on file from her husband giving her permission to draw on that account as it becomes necessary. We will expect you to honor that request."

"Mr Draper, I will be happy to honor the request but as you know it was written while Mr. Palmer was still living. I may have to take this up with the local Barrister." He looked down the sheet showing the assets of said, 'George and Phebe Palmer.'

"Mr. Green, I see by that ledger that the account is listed in the name of both George and Phebe Palmer. I am sure the Barrister will agree that Phebe has as much claim to it as George and so thereby should not be challenged." William Jr. held his ground and it was finally agreed that Phebe could, in fact, have access to the money.

William and Phebe stood and shook hands with the banker, who reluctantly accepted the gesture. "I would like ten Pounds in cash today to set the precedent." Phebe's steel gray eyes met his and he counted out the money to her. "And I will stop by tomorrow for a full accounting of my assets in you bank. My husband kept very accurate accounts so I will bring them with me to compare them with yours."

She looked back, as she walked through the door William Jr. had opened for her, and saw Mr. Green remove his pincer glasses and heard an audible sigh.

Out on the street, William Jr. laughed and looked at his sister with admiration. "Miss Phebe, I think you put him in his place. There should be no more trouble with that account. I have to get back to work. Why don't you go up and talk to Bett." He went into his shop and she walked up the stairs.

She was puffing when she reached the door at the top of the stairs. Perhaps she had been taking it too easy of late and needed to work harder. She was getting soft. Bett answered her knock and invited her in for a cup of tea and a piece of cake. They sat chatting, "I must be getting old. I was out of breath when I got to your door. Perhaps it has been losing George and all that has happened lately, but I really don't feel very well and I have so much to do now."

Phebe liked Bett. It was easy to talk to her and she knew why William Jr. had fallen in love with her. She was a good listener. She smoked a small clay pipe, which was common with many of the women from Loughborough where tobacco was one of the main crops of the area. She was rather plain but her warm brown eyes conveyed a genuine concern for others. She was the local practicing Mid-wife.

Bett pressed Phebe for more information about her health, "Phebe, I think you are expecting another baby. The later births don't always have the same signs as the earlier ones."

To say Phebe was in a state of shock would be an understatement. She was sure

Zemira was her last. She had to admit that Bett was right. She had all the signs but had refused to recognize them.

Bett put her arms around her and held her as the tears flowed down her face. George had given her one last gift and one last challenge. Hadn't their lives been like that from the first? One challenge after another, beginning with the dance when they first met and him challenging her to bake better pie than her sister Lucretia.

She wiped her eyes with her handkerchief, "Thank you Bett, for the tea and cake and for being my friend as well as my sister-in-law."

She walked down the stairs. Her next stop would be to see her sister Lucretia and Lovina and tell them she was expecting a baby. She could put off announcing it but she would need their help. She would have to add more items to her list.

The Men's Hall was filled to capacity and Brother Brigham was addressing the congregation. Most of the Draper's, Woods, Palmers, Boyles, Van Luevens, Brunos and Bradshaws were there with other curious neighbors who had heard the rumor that something special would happen at the meeting.

"Brothers and Sisters, you have been so devoted in your study of the Gospel. The Lord has blessed you with a desire to learn and the Holy Ghost has born witness to you of the truthfulness of the message I bring to you and that of the Book of Mormon. It is time for us to proceed with the Lord's will and organize this group into a branch of the church. As you know, Brother William Draper Jr. has been given the Aaronic

Priesthood and has been ordained to the office of a Priest. In that capacity he has traveled with me and helped me spread the gospel through many areas of Ontario. He bears a strong witness and I am calling him to be your leader in my absence. I can not always be with you. I will be called to other fields to preach the Gospel where others, as you were, are looking for the truth.

All those who feel they can support Brother Draper in this call, please raise your hand." Brigham Young scanned the audience with his eyes and found every person had raised their hand. He had not called for a vote from the baptized members only.

With that official action, the Church of Jesus Christ of Latter-day Saints was organized in Loughborough. Phebe and the children and Elijah had raised their hands. Phebe was so proud of her younger brother and she thought to herself, "I knew you were someone special when I named you, William II."

Brother Brigham continued, "I want you to know that the saints are gathering in Kirtland, Ohio where a city of the Saints is being built. I am not asking, or even suggesting that you sell your places here and move to Ohio, but if you should decide to do so, let Brother William organize the move. The church will be strengthened by your presence there if that is your decision. The Prophet Joseph Smith received the following revelation in 1829.

'This great and marvelous work has come forth unto the children of men. The field is white already to harvest. Whosoever will thrust in his sickle and reap, the same is called of God. Therefore, if you will ask of me you shall receive; if you will knock it shall be opened unto you. Seek to bring forth and establish my Zion. Keep my commandments in all things. And if you keep my commandments and endure to the end you shall have eternal life, which gift is the greatest of all the gifts of God.'

My time with you has been precious and you will always be part of my memories and brothers and sisters to me. I know the message I have brought to you is of God and I say this in the name of His son, Jesus Christ, Amen."

Father Draper gave the closing prayer and they filed out, shaking Brigham's hand as they left. Several were heard to say, "We'll see you in Ohio."

Phebe looked at this sturdy man who had taught them so much and helped them on the path of learning the Gospel. His spirit was as strong as his body and she knew he was a man of God. "Brother Brigham, thank you for all you have done for us this last few months. It is my hope that our paths will cross again."

"Sister Phebe, you are a strong woman and have been tested by the Lord. He has your welfare in mind and will bless you. I promise, our paths will cross many times in this work we have begun. This is just the beginning." He held both her hands and she could feel his strength extend to her as he looked into her eyes. It was as if he had a picture of the future flashing in his mind.

Lovina walked to the buggy with Phebe. "Mother, I am coming home to live with you. Henry and I have discussed it and we feel my place is with you, at least for the next few months. Mrs. Kenny has given me permission to take supplies home with me. I can make a few hats in my spare time."

"Oh my dear, I don't want you to change your plans. I will get along just fine, though I would love to have you near me." She took her beautiful daughter's hand.

"Mother, I have decided and have made all of the arrangements. My things are over here in Aunt Lucretia's buggy. Elijah, can you help me get them?" Lovina took Elijah's arm and pulled him to the Van Leuven buggy. Henry met them there and the two young men carried hat boxes and a trunk to the back of the Palmer buggy.

Henry followed them out to the Palmer farm to spend the

Sunday afternoon with Lovina and her family.

The family sat around the big table after dinner and speculated about which families would decide to leave the valley to go to Ohio. "How important will it be to go there?" Elijah ask. "Martha and I have been talking about our future plans and she still has questions in her mind about the church. Her family is very opposed to her having anything to do with it. They are devout Catholic. She hasn't told them yet that I have been baptized."

"I think Brother Brigham made it clear that the decision was ours. Some of us may feel compelled to go and others could stay here and continue to spread the gospel. I couldn't possible go now, but I may feel differently in the future." Phebe looked around at her responsibilities. Zemira was on her lap and she was reminded of the new life growing within her.

"I will never leave here. This is my home and I will always stay here and work my father's farm. I haven't decided about being baptized either. Father didn't think it was important." Asahel pushed his chair back and left the room.

Phebe changed the subject. She would talk to Asahel later. He was his father's son and she would not dissuade him from his loyalty to George. "Henry, how is the apprenticeship proceeding? You must be carrying a lot of responsibility with William spending so much time proselyting."

" I have been able to keep up with the work while Brother Draper is gone. He is a good teacher and seems to have confidence in my taking care of the business." Henry was not boastful, but proud of his position.

"Lovina, will Mrs Kenny be hiring another girl to take your place in her milliner shop? Are you leaving her without the help you had promised to give her?" Phebe expected her children to live up to their commitments.

"She has a niece coming to live with her who can help her in the store and she will teach her, as she did me. to make hats. I will be able to make hats here at home to keep up her inventory while she is teaching her niece. She may give me some direct orders from some of her clients. Some of them have already requested my work. We have agreed that I will go back for brief periods if she finds that she needs me." Lovina had worked out all the details and Phebe was proud of the new maturity she saw in her. Lucretia had been a good influence on her also. She could see that Lovina had picked up some of the natural refinement of the lovely Lucretia.

Elijah and William George excused themselves to attend to the chores and Henry and Lovina left for a walk to spend some time alone. Lydia Elizabeth had gone home with Charles and Sarah to stay with her cousins. Zemira had fallen asleep on Phebe's lap. She carried him to his bed for his afternoon nap.

She sat in the rocker contemplating the impact of the meeting that morning. What did it mean to her? She recalled the last words of Brother Brigham. How would their paths cross in the future? Why had George died at such a young age and left her with this family? Sometimes she felt angry at him for not fighting harder to live and then guilt feelings filled her heart and she wept because she missed him and wanted him to be in the rocker next to her. Some of him was still alive in her and she must remember that. As long as she carried this baby, he was still a part of her.

She heard the children returning. She wiped her eyes and picked up the Bible from the table but she had trouble concentrating on the printed page before her. She must face the problem of Asahel.

CHAPTER FIFTEEN

"Elijah, I would like to go over a few things with you if you have some time today." Phebe picked up Elijah's breakfast plate that held few traces of the meal he had just finished of side pork, fried eggs and biscuits. She carried the plate to the side board where Lovina was washing the dishes in a soapy pan of water. Phebe rinsed them in a pan of hot water and wiped them with a clean white towel, returning them to the cupboard.

Elijah finished his coffee and carried the cup and saucer to Lovina. "I have a few minutes now. Asahel and William are hoeing the corn field. You can almost watch that corn grow but the weeds are growing just as fast." They walked to the porch and sat in the rockers looking out over the fields.

Phebe searched for a way to begin, "Elijah, George was so proud of you and I am aware that the Palmer farm would be in poor shape had it not been for your hard work. The small wage George agreed to pay you has not compensated for all the work you have done. I have some ideas of what we might consider.

We could operate the farm as if it were a partnership, dividing the profits. You could go ahead with your plans to marry Martha. There is plenty of room on the farm for another homesite with the necessary outbuildings. I feel sure that George would have made this offer to you if he had lived. There is even adjoining land that has not been filed on that you may consider acquiring.

Our agreement would include the profit from the crops that will be harvested this fall. I will continue to pay your wages until the first crops are harvested which will probably be the tobacco, cherries and peaches. After that time we will divide the proceeds evenly. Asahel will be paid a wage from your half and William George from mine. The girls and I will prepare the meals, do the laundry and take care of the chickens. You can make your home here until you and Martha have a house to move to. I will keep the accounts which you may inspect at any time. We will have to agree on the crops we will plant in coming years and each pay our share of the seed or other expenses as they arise." Phebe waited for Elijah's response.

"I, I don't know what to say." Elijah had trouble controlling his emotions. He looked at his feet and shifted his weight, "I came here practically as a beggar to your door. I have done only what I needed to do to repay you for your kindness."

"Elijah, you are family and families share what they have. You brought so much joy to George. You gave him the family he had never had and you have literally helped us to survive this last year. I love you as a brother and I believe this is the best solution to my dilemma at this time. Hopefully, it will give you an opportunity for you to establish some independence on your own." Phebe waited.

"How can I refuse you? It is the best opportunity I have ever been given. I would like to talk it over with Martha, though I can't imagine that she would not agree for me to accept the offer. Let's think it over for a day or two. We may think of other things we need to consider and that will give me time to talk to Martha. Phebe, you are a good and generous woman. I have no reservations about casting my lots with you. I am proud to be called your brother." He stood and put his hand on her shoulder.

"We'll talk again when you are ready. Just let me know." Phebe stood and walked in the house to help Lovina with the housework.

"Lovina, have you talked to Henry about your wedding plans?"

"We talked about it yesterday. I don't see how we can make any plans until you have decided what you are going to do. Do you know when the baby is due?" Lovina hated to bring up the subject but it had to be part of the decisions ahead of them.

"I can't be sure but Bett and I think it will be some time around the end of February or the first of March. You go ahead and make your plans. Lydia Elizabeth helps me and the boys can take care of themselves." Phebe felt so guilty that Lovina was considering her welfare over her own happiness. She and Henry were so right for each other.

"The harvest season is just around the corner and you know how demanding that is with the harvesters to feed and the long hours spent by everyone. I need to help you cook and clean. We also need to get clothes ready for the baby. All of Zemira's things were burned in the fire. Mother, there are many reasons why I need to help you and I won't take 'no' for an answer. We can make plans for my wedding as we prepare for the new baby. I have always thought a spring wedding would be just perfect." Lovina picked up the rag rugs and took them to the porch to shake.

Phebe retrieved the broom and swept the crumbs and dust into a pile which she pushed into the coal shuttle. She lifted the lid from the firebox on the stove and fed the dust balls and crumbs to the smoldering fire. After washing her hands she took the mixing bowl from the cupboard and and put some milk in a pan on the stove to to scald. As she measured out the flour to prepare the day's bread she considered the Israelites who were called to leave Egypt before the bread had a chance to rise. Could she walk away today if the Lord commanded her to do so. When she entered the waters of baptism she had taken upon her the name of Jesus Christ and had promised to obey his commandments. Each day, as she learned more about the Gospel, she tried to contemplate what the ramifications were to her.

When the bread was mixed she made some apple pies. They could bake while the bread was raising. Apple Pie was Asahel's favorite as it had been George's. Somehow, she had to show him she loved him and understood the sorrow he felt at his father's death.

The Chicken was steaming on the stove and Lydia Elizabeth came in with the peas and new potatoes she and Little William had retrieved from the garden. It was one of their favorites as it had been to Phebe when she was a child. She started to prepare them as she had so often watched her mother do. She boiled the new little potatoes and when they were semi soft, added the peas and some thickening, salt and pepper and a bit of sugar to bring out the flavor of the new peas. She sipped a bit of the liquid to taste the flavoring. It was almost as good as her mother's. She never seemed to be able to replicate that wonderful taste memory she carried in her mind. She looked out of the window and saw a horse and buggy coming down the lane.

If they were to have company, she was prepared with a good warm meal for them. As the dust cleared she saw it was her Mother and Father. How she had longed to have some time with them. She always felt comforted by their love and concern for her.

Phebe ran from the house and embraced her parents as they approached the porch. Then to her surprise she started to cry. She had tried to be strong but suddenly realized she needed someone to lean on and who better than her father? He held her until the tears subsided and they found a seat in the shade on the porch.

Lydia sat close to Phebe and held the hand of her daughter who had brought so much joy to her. Her heart ached for Phebe and she searched in her mind for a way to console her. "Phebe, you have been in our prayers and your Father and I both felt you needed us today, so we have come to be with you. I don't really know what we can do to help you, other than to be here and let you know that we love you."

"Oh, I need you so much. Sometimes I feel so overwhelmed with all the people I am responsible for and the work that needs to be done. I am trying to make some decisions that will be good for everyone and hopefully, be what George would have wanted me to do. I have even felt his guidance at times."

Father William looked at his daughter, remembering the once gangly ten-year-old who knew exactly what she needed to do, and who now was struggling with decisions for the future. "Phebe, we will stay with you for a few days. Your mother needs to be assured that you are alright and I can help Elijah with the farm. The boys are taking care of things at home for us. Let's just enjoy being together. Where's the baby? I want to see that little guy." He went in the house knowing Zemira would be close by. Lovina had him in the back yard with her while she was gathering the sun dried clothes from the clothes line. William found them and basked in the hugs from his little grandson.

"Phebe, how are you feeling?" Lydia was glad to have a few minutes alone with her daughter. "Lucretia told me about your condition. She said you had given her permission."

"I am feeling pretty good. I haven't had any morning illness but I do get tired so quickly. Lovina has been a God send to me. She is so mature now and she takes over just like a grown woman. She sees things that need to be done and does them without asking. Lucretia was a positive influence on her. We have fallen into a routine and I rest when I need to. Lovina and Henry have decided to wait until after my baby is born to get married. I feel guilty about them altering their plans but they will not be dissuaded.

Bett feels that I am in good health and should be able to carry this baby to full term. It is due in late February or early March. This little spirit must have an important reason for coming to me. Perhaps it is to help me remember the good things that George and I shared.

I have offered Elijah a partnership in the farm that he is considering. I'm glad Father is here. He can help us work out

the details and advise us as to how to proceed. I have never
needed you more."

"It's a girl, a darling little girl." Bett placed the little bundle
in Phebe's arms and Lydia wiped the moisture from her forehead.

It had been an easy birth and she had the best of care with
Bett and her mother with her. She had felt George's presence
there, encouraging her on and giving her strength. No
Laudanum this time had left her mind clear and she looked
down at her new daughter remembering that George always
wanted her to name the babies. "Her name is Rhoda. I don't
know a Rhoda but I read the name in the Scriptures somewhere and I like it. Yes, we will call her, Rhoda."

Phebe fell asleep with the baby in her arms, Bett took the
baby from her and motioned Lydia to follow her. "This will be
the last baby Phebe will give birth to. She has lost a lot of
blood and will be weak for some time. I am going to recommend that she come and stay in town until she is fully recovered. Do you think Lucretia would let her stay there? Our little
place on top of the shop is filled to capacity with our brood but
I would like her close by."

"I'm sure she will, Lucretia is a very loving sister and John
always makes people welcome in his home. It will be the perfect place and I know just what will help Phebe get better fast.
I'll write a note to Fanny to come for a visit. She could cheer
Phebe if no one else could. Should we have William come in
and give his sister a blessing?" Lydia's concern was evident in
the tone of her voice.

William, the only member of the church in Laughborough
holding the priesthood at that time had been schooled by
Brigham Young in using his priesthood to bless the sick.
Brother Brigham had explained the power of healing, accom-

panied by faith, that came with this marvelous priesthood.

"I'm sure he will want to. He came with me because he was concerned about her. I'll get him." Bett went to the Parlor and announced that a new little girl had come to join the family and that Phebe had named her, Rhoda. Lydia followed with the baby to show her to the family.

Not wanting to alarm the rest of the family, Bett asked her husband to come to the kitchen to help her with some hot water and towels. "William, Phebe has lost a lot of blood and I think she should have a blessing. Can you come with me now to her room? I need to stay close to her. I don't want to show any undue concern at this time. They have all had enough to worry about."

William took the small vial of sacred oil from his pocket. Brigham had helped him bless it before he left. He walked with Bett, laden down with towels, to Phebe's room. He carried the heavy bucket of water and closed the door behind them.

The transparent look of Phebe's skin proved Bett's assessment to be accurate. He opened the little vial and put two small drops of the sacred oil on Phebe's brow. She didn't stir. He put his hands on her head and plead with the Lord, if it be His will, to allow his, Miss Phebe, to live to raise her children and continue to be a strength to the family. The bond between Phebe and William had never been stronger and it was as if he was holding on to her with all the faith he could generate. Tears were streaming down their faces as Bett and William embraced. They both loved her and knew how much they needed her. And there was her family, they needed her too.

"Are you sure you are comfortable?" Lucretia had Phebe in the softest feather tick she could find covered with snow white sheets and bolstered by Pillows galore. "I'm just going to spoil you, big sister."

"I am very comfortable but all I want to do is sleep. Where am I? I can only vaguely remember being put in this bed. Who was it that carried me up here?" Phebe tried to focus her eyes and her mind.

"John helped William bring you in town and up here to our house. Phebe, you have been very ill since the baby came and we are all trying to help you get better. William gave you a blessing and we have all prayed for you. Mother is here with me and Fanny is coming too. Won't that be fun? We will all be together again, just like when we were girls at home." Lucretia fluffed a pillow.

"My baby, where's my baby ?" She voiced the panic that was overtaking her.

"The baby is fine. She is a cute little girl. Remember, you named her, Rhoda?

Mother has her downstairs. Bett has been coming over every day to check on you and the baby. She will be so glad to see you awake. We were afraid we were going to lose you. I'll get some tea for you. Bett gave us some herbs to put in tea as soon as you were able to drink it. I'll be right back. Just lie back and rest." Lucretia hurried off for the tea.

Phebe was trying to remember. The farm, who was taking care of the farm? What about the rest of the children? Lovina and Henry! what about there wedding? Did she sleep through the wedding? How long had she been asleep? She tried to lift herself from the pillow but fell back, exhausted.

Lydia brought the baby in and laid her in Phebe's arms. Phebe opened the blankets to find the tiny hands and look at the round little face. "Oh, Mother, she is beautiful. George would be so proud. I was dreaming about George. He was bringing this little girl to me and smiling at me and he put his arms around me. I can still feel his arms around me." She drifted back to sleep and Lydia took the baby from her and tiptoed out of the room.

Fanny arrived with her smile and chatter that never stopped. She ran up the stairs to see Phebe and rushed into the room. "Oh, Phebe, I am so glad you are alive. I've been worried sick about you since I received the note from Mother. We'll have you up and around in no time. When is Lovina getting married?" She didn't wait for an answer but hurried on. "I haven't even seen the baby yet but I hear she is a doll. Do you think she will look like Lovina? It is going to be so fun to all be together here; you, Mother, Lucretia and I. I brought some things for the baby and for Lovina for her wedding. I'll get them unpacked and show you. My neighbor sent some herbs for you. I can't remember the names but I'll have Bett look at them before you take them." Her voice trailed off as she realized how weak her sister was.

Lucretia came in with the tea and supported Phebe with her arm while she sipped the warm tea from the cup. The cold March wind was blowing outside but this house was filled with love and comfort. Phebe fell asleep again and her sisters quietly left the room.

Lovina was a beautiful bride in the white satin gown with hand tatted lace and little buttons all the way down the back and up the tapered sleeves. The veil was attached to a cluster of ribbon roses laced with pearls. Lovina had designed it herself. It cascaded over her shiny black curly hair. Her tiny waist was circled with a single strand of pearls and the train fanned out from the back of the skirt. She glowed with happiness.

Henry was in a black frock coat and a white pleated shirt with the popular stand up collar and a cravat caught by a single pearl. His blue eyes and blond hair in contrast to Lovina's snapping black eyes and brunette hair was startling. Lydia Elizabeth scattered the apple blossoms in front of the bride as she walked toward her Uncle William Jr. who would perform the ceremony. Her Grandfather walked by her side and relinquished her to the young man who would promise to love her forever.

Phebe stood with her mother. She was thin and pale but the color was coming back to her cheeks. As Lovina and Henry took each other's hand the audience was seated and waited for William Jr. to start the ceremony.

Here in William and Lydias parlor their granddaughter was being married. It was a beautiful wedding. Uncle William left out that part about 'til death do you part and inserted a part that said forever. Lovina and Henry's eyes met in total commitment and eagerly kissed as the words, "you may now kiss the bride." were uttered.

The brothers and their wives, Lucretia and Fanny and their husbands lined up to congratulate the couple. But first her grandfather and grandmother Draper with Phebe between them embraced the young couple. "Welcome to the Draper family," William Sr. took Henry's hand in a strong grip, "Giving you my darling granddaughter doesn't mean you can take her away from us."

Phebe held her daughter's hands, trying to control her emotions; "You look so lovely, my dear. I want you to be happy. Thank you for all you have done for me."

Lovina threw her arms around her mother, "I am so happy and I love you mother. Thank you, for all you have done for me. I wish Papa could have been here but I think he was in spirit."

The celebration after was the traditional Draper gala sharing it with the Munro's and all of the friends of both families. The older cousins were visiting and comparing memories of Grandpa Thomas Draper and the myriads of children were involved in all kind of activities. As always, with the Draper's, there were enough creative people around to keep games and activities going.

The bride and groom slipped out to the buggy to leave only

to find that the cousins had decorated it and tied cans to the spokes of the buggy wheels. They were showered with rice and the Uncles helped them escape as was the family custom.

William Jr. called a family meeting after the newlyweds were safely on their way. "I want to discuss the possibility of some of us going to Kirtland to join the other saints there. It must be an individual family decision that should be made after fasting and prayer. Bett and I have decided we are going to try to be ready to leave by September. The Wood family has also committed to that date.

If we make our plans together in a group it will be less costly and also safer. We have had very little trouble with our neighbors about our new religion but in some places there have been serious threats. Do you have any questions?"

"What shall we do with our property here? Will there be housing for us there? Has the Prophet called us to come? Who will preside over the church here if you leave?" The questions were coming rapidly as the new saints were facing a decision that had been hovering over the congregation since Brigham Young left several months ago.

"Each of you will have to make your own financial arrangement as to the disposal of your business and homes or farms. It may be wise for us to leave in small groups so that we will not be putting all of our land on the market at once. We don't want to devalue our assets. I plan to keep my shoe shop and have Henry operate it on a share basis with first right of refusal if I should decide to sell it. We can rent them the flat upstairs that we have been living in.

There are no promises of housing for us in Kirtland. There again, we will have to make individual arrangements, which will be another argument for us going in groups. We can help build housing for each other as we have here.

If we go in groups of people with different talents we will have the opportunity to make a living and assist each other. I plan to take some farming equipment and some of my shoe making tools. Mr. Wood will also take some blacksmithing equipment. We can take some seedlings from our trees and some planting seeds. Most of us have learned to survive on the frontier from our experience here. Ohio is a new frontier also, though parts of it have been settled for sometime. Some of the basic needs will be to find enough property to have a garden and some animals to provide milk and meat and eggs. We hope to always have someone with us that can teach our children and work with the local government. I would think that it would be wise to try to take enough supplies with us to help us through the first winter.

If you decide to go with this first group, let me know as soon as possible. Again, let me remind you to make it a matter of prayer. I love all of you and that love nor the love of our Savior is predicated on your decision." William Jr. made his way through the group, answering individual questions and reassuring family members that they were not being compelled to move.

"Mother, are we going to Kirtland?" Thirteen-year-old William George voiced the question that they were all thinking about as they traveled back to the Palmer farm from Grandpa Draper's house where the wedding festivities took place.

"I don't know, We will have to follow Uncle William's advice by fasting and praying. There are many things to consider. I'm sure the Lord will guide us in our decision." Phebe thought of her situation now. Elijah was managing the farm well and he and Martha would be married next month. Lovina was married and she and Henry hoped to start a family. He would be operating the shoe shop so their future looked promising. They were both ambitious and quite independent. Lydia Elizabeth was almost eight, Zemira would soon be three and the baby just two months old. Asahel, fifteen, had a mind of his own and had become an integral part of the work on the farm.

"Don't count me in. I told you before that I would not

leave my father's farm. I don't need to fast and pray about anything." Asahel was driving the buggy and he snapped the rein
on the horses rump to keep the animal moving and to show his
control over the situation.

Phebe held the baby close to her and put her arm around
little Zemira. It had been a long day and now was not the time
to discuss the pro's and con's of moving to Kirtland, but she
would pray about it.

PART IV

THE HOLY SPIRIT WILL COMFORT THEE
1834—1838
CHAPTER SIXTEEN

The Trunks were in the middle of the floor in the little house she had rented close to the Peter Whitmer store. William and Zemira had helped her move in the few items of furniture she brought and had set up the beds. She looked at the windows to see what she would need for curtains. She had never lived so close to a store. It would be convenient for her to get the material she needed but she should unpack first.

Bett had taken all of the children for a walk around town to become acquainted with their new surroundings. All but the baby, of course, and little six-month-old Rhoda was sound asleep on the feather tick beside the big bed.

Phebe opened her trunk to get the baby clothes. She would need them first. She laid them on the table and the towels were next. Stacking them in nice even piles, she folded back the next layer of linens, there was the tea set she had so lovingly packed. One of her little girls would have this someday but it was still her childhood treasure. The shelf between the windows would be perfect. It wasn't large enough to hold Grandma Draper's cake plate but the gold rimmed plate would fit on the mantle as it had on the Palmer farm.

The Palmer farm, yes it was still the Palmer farm, but she had signed it over to Elijah. He had promised to watch out for Asahel and send her one third of the profits from the farm for six years. He had given her one thousand dollars in cash. She had taken her savings from the bank to make the trip and get her started in Kirtland. She smiled as she remembered Mr. Green's face when she withdrew her money. He looked like he was in great pain. He had made it clear to the members of the church that he did not condone their new religion or the exodus that was taking place.

It was hard to leave Asahel and Lovina. Asahel was angry about her decision to throw her lot in with the Mormons. She hoped one day he would be touched by the spirit and with Elijah's influence, join the church. Lovina was expecting her first baby in a few months but Mother Lydia had promised to take care of her granddaughter.

The Lord had answered Phebe's prayers and made it known to her that she should move to Kirtland with William and Zemira, their wives and families. Her preparations were never thwarted and as her plans were completed, one by one, she knew she had made the right decision. Somehow, she also knew, when Brother Brigham had said their paths would cross again that her life would play out with the body of the church.

She took her Book of Mormon and the Family Bible from the trunk. The final entry on the birth page had not been recorded. She found the pen and ink packed in her valise so she could write to Lovina and Mother when she arrived. She opened the ink bottle and dipped the pen into the liquid. There was just room at the bottom of the page. She wrote:

> *Rhoda Palmer born*
> *March 15, 1834*

She turned the page and on the back wrote: *Deaths*
> *Eliza Palmer died*
> *August 3, 1832*
> *George Palmer died*
> *June 27, 1833*

She held the page open to let it dry. So many important

things in her life were recorded here? And then she remembered the old adage, "When one door closes another opens."

She hurried on with her unpacking. She wanted to get this done because tonight Brother Brigham was going to introduce them to the Prophet. He and his wife Emma had just arrived in town and were to be at the Whitmer's. Yes, she was ready to walk through this open door to a new life because the Lord had directed her path to it and she would do as the Lord commanded in all things.

She took the new blue hat Lovina had made for her from the hat box and held it by the darker blue cape mother had given her as a going away present. She did want to look her best to meet the Prophet of God.

Brother Brigham ushered them in to the upper room of the Whitmer store. The Prophet was there to meet the new arrivals. "Brother Joseph, this is part of the Draper family I told you about when I returned from Canada. William Jr. and his wife Elizabeth, Zemira and his wife Agnes, and Phebe Palmer, their sister."

They each shook his hand and tried to hide the awe they felt at being in his presence. He soon put them at ease, "Brigham could not stop talking about the Draper's when he came back to Kirtland. He told us about your acceptance of the gospel. Zemira, you must be that finish carpenter he raved about and William, you are the brother with the wonderful mind and leadership ability. Phebe, you have made great sacrifices to help build the Kingdom. Please accept my condolences at the loss of your daughter and husband. Brigham tells us that you have become quite the scholar of the Bible and Book of Mormon. You have been a teacher I understand. Your help with schools will be needed as the saints pour into our city."

Phebe was impressed with his sincere interest in each of them. She looked into his eyes and saw a man of strength and honest concern. "Thank you, Brother Joseph. I am afraid Brother Brigham exaggerated a bit. I do love to read and study the scriptures but I am far from being a scholar. There is so much to learn. I hope I can help with the schools. I have four young children of my own that need to be taught."

The Prophet moved to William, "I hope you will join us in our learning sessions here in this room tomorrow night. The Lord is revealing so much to us so fast that we need to study together to assimilate it. We need your help."

"Zemira, as you can see with all the building going on here, we need your carpentry skills. As soon as you are settled, report to Bishop Partridge. He knows where the most help is needed." He smiled at the group and then introduced them to Emma.

Phebe was impressed with the respect he showed to Emma. She could see the love and pride in the Prophet's eyes as he made them acquainted with his beautiful Emma. She looked fragile but conveyed a strong personality. Phebe had heard of the trials and challenges that Emma had been called upon to endure. She prayed she could be as strong.

New buildings were under construction on every street. William and Zemira were renting temporary housing also but planned to look for something more permanent where they could build homes and plant gardens.

"Phebe, when we find a place, I hope you will put in with us. I know I am going to be called upon to leave on church assignments when we get settled and it would be good for you and Bett to be together. Think about it, Miss Phebe. You know Zemira and I will take care of you and your children. Father gave us firm instructions before we left Loughborough." William was such a dear brother and Phebe appreciated his concern.

"I hope not to be a burden to anyone, but it is good to know I have two brothers to watch out for me. The Prophet gave me something to think about tonight when he mentioned schools. I am sure many children are coming to Kirtland with their parents. When I get settled I will inquire about the schools and see if I can be of help." Phebe was planning ahead.

Kirtland was a bustling city with many new inhabitants, most of them Mormons. The Prophet had been directed by the Lord to build a Temple. They were called upon to contribute money and labor to complete the edifice. William and Zemira were both working on the construction of the temple along with other friends from Canada and new converts that were pouring into Kirtland.

Phebe counted the money she had left. She would make a deposit in the Kirtland Bank tomorrow. She set aside a contribution for the temple. She would give it to Bishop Partridge on Sunday. Her share of the harvest money from Elijah should arrive soon and if she could arrange for a teaching position she would be able to take care of her family. Her faith was strong that the Lord would bless her if she kept her part of the bargain.

She left the baby with Bett and instructed William George and Lydia to take care of Zemira while she went to investigate the local school. She slipped quietly in at the back of the room and sat on one of the benches next to a writing shelf. The school master was only teaching the ten to fourteen-year-olds. Most of the children were still learning very basic skills of reading and arithmetic. It was a typical frontier school. She remembered Master Park and the enthusiasm for learning he generated in students. The teacher noticed her and walked to the back of the room, monitoring the students as he went. "Can I help you? We don't have many visitors in the school. It is quite distracting to the students."

"I am sorry. I was hoping the children would be at recess. It is you I came to see. Actually, I have a son who I need to enroll in your school. Also, I have had some experience with teaching a Primary school. Have you, or would you consider adding a Primary school? Perhaps we could trade some of my teaching services for my son's tuition. I'm sure there are many people moving to Kirtland who have young children that could benefit from a Primary school. I am Phebe Palmer, a widow with four children. I have a two-fold responsibility; one to help earn a living for my family and second to make sure my children are educated." Phebe hoped she had presented herself well and not been too presumptuous.

"Mrs. Palmer, I would have to discuss this with the school committee. It is a new concept to me. I have heard of Primary and Kindergarten schools in the large cities but it is very rare out here. Perhaps we should talk to Brother Cowdery. He was a teacher in the state of New York. I must get back to my students. How can I get in touch with you so we might discuss it further?"

"I am renting the house across the street from the Whitmer store. I hope to hear from you soon." She nodded and walked from the room.

Phebe was encouraged but realized that some of these frontier people may not feel that education is that important. On the other hand, how can they study the scriptures and learn the gospel if they can't read? She hoped she would have an opportunity to talk to Brother Cowdery too.

She stopped at the Bank and deposited her savings and then on to get the baby from Bett. "Thanks for taking care of Rhoda for me, It seems that I am always in your debt. If I can find a teaching position, I have a plan that I hope will allow me to carry my part of the work."

Bett was washing the dishes and Phebe picked up a towel to dry them. Rhoda was on a quilt on the floor; gooing, kicking and playing with her hands. She was such a happy baby. Bett's toddler, Moses, was walking from chair to chair and then crawled over to the quilt and gave Rhoda a big kiss. The mothers laughed at the little cousins. "They should be such great friends, just as we are." Phebe smiled at her sister-in-law and lifted the towel dried plates to the cupboard shelf.

William knocked on Phebe's front door, opened it and walked in before she could answer the knock, "Phebe, I am so excited. I had to tell you before any one else. I have just come from the meeting Brother Joseph invited me to attend. To my surprise, it is called the 'School of the Prophets' and its purpose is to train future leaders of the church in doctrine and church government. Its second purpose is to to give the brethren the opportunity to learn about all things above and below the earth from the best books. It will be like attending a university with the Gospel as the curriculum.

The Prophet introduced the meeting tonight with the theme, 'The Glory of God is Intelligence or in other words; Light and Truth.' Some of the men have had little schooling and others have a vast knowledge of different subjects. It will be a marvelous opportunity to learn. The greatest, of course, is to be taught by the Prophet as he has been taught by the Lord.

The Prophet told us that he has designed a model city plan for Kirtland and the City of Zion in Missouri. The city plot is to be one mile square, divided into blocks containing ten acres each—forty rods square—except the middle range of blocks running north and south; they will be forty by sixty rods, containing fifteen acres, having their greatest extent east and west. The streets will be eight rods wide. the center tier of blocks forty by sixty rods will be reserved for public buildings, temples, tabernacles, and school houses.

As he talked about the design for the city of Zion and Kirtland I was reminded of my experience working with the Civil Engineer in Kingston. Do you remember how he marveled at my ability to calculate land measures. He even offered to send me to Engineering School. Well, I offered to help with the measurement and division of the lots here in Kirtland. I will be paid for the service by receiving a home sight in the new development. We can be in our own home by spring. Phebe, we are just what Kirtland needed. The Lord has truly guided us here. What did you find out about the school today?

I didn't have time to ask Bett about it before I left for the meeting." William pulled up a chair and sat at the table.

Phebe poured two cups of tea and set them on the table, pulling up a chair for herself to join her brother. The children were all asleep, "I was a little disappointed in the school as it is designed for only ten to fourteen-year-olds and just teaches the basic skills of Reading and Arithmetic. The school master seems bright enough and was open to discussing a Primary school He is going to talk to the School Committee and get back to me."

"If the Prophet's design for the city is implemented, there will be many schools. His emphasis on learning will support your philosophy as well as those of higher learning. Phebe, you can help in this great design. I'm sure the Lord needs you here." He looked at his, Miss Phebe, with admiring eyes. She had been the first to open his eyes to the joy of learning and now, here he was, invited to learn in the "School of the Prophets."

"My only concern is taking care of Rhoda and Zemira. I can't be in two places at once. Bett and Agnes and I talked about the possibility of me teaching the children, ages six to ten in the family free of tuition and they would tend my little ones while I was teaching. Agnes, though she hasn't been blessed with any children, seems more than willing to help us. "I am reluctant to leave my babies so much but I do need to supplement my income. What do you think about that arrangement?" William's approval was important to her.

"Phebe, that sounds like a perfect solution. You know Bett and Agnes love your children like their own." He finished the last drop of tea in his cup and left for home

Phebe picked up the paper she had bought at Whitmer's Store today along with a copy of The Book of Commandments and one of the Pearl Of Great Price. She felt very extravagant, but it had been so long since she had had new reading material and there was so much to learn about this new religion.

The headlines of the paper read EVENING AND MORN-
ING STAR changed to MESSENGER AND ADVOCATE.
The accompanying article explained that the EVENING AND
MORNING STAR had been the publication from The City of
Zion in Missouri. The presses there had been destroyed by the
mob action. New presses were purchased for Kirtland where
messages from the Prophet would be printed and distributed in
the future. The Kirtland editors felt the new name was more in
keeping with the purpose of the paper.

Phebe's worry lines appeared on her forehead as she read
of the atrocities visited on the Saints in Jackson County and
the loss of their homes and holdings. Why would people treat
such God-fearing people like that? As she went on she read
some of the complaints registered by the people of Jackson
County: A document was in circulation that was called "THE
OLD SETTLER'S SECRET CONSTITUTION" setting forth
the alleged grievances of the mob and binding all who signed
it to assist in "removing the Mormons." —They were
described as "The very dregs of society; poor, idle, lazy and
vicious." claiming to receive direct revelation from God; to
heal the sick by the laying on of hands; to speak in unknown
tongues by inspiration all of which is derogatory of God and
Religion, and subversive of human reason. They also claim
that God has given them the land of Jackson County and that
they would possess it as an inheritance."

Phebe shook her head and felt outrage at the treatment and
insinuations that were so eschewed in their interpretation. She
was relieved that there was such a peaceful feeling here in
Kirtland. The Drapers had always been known as good neighbors where ever they had lived and she planned to live her life
out that way. Her father had always respected the views of others and made them welcome in his home and had taught his
children to follow his example. How different their lives would
have been if he had turned away the old Indian, Okinihah,
from their door.

She took some paper and the pen and ink from her small desk and started a letter to Lovina,

October 2, 1834
My Dear Lovina,
We have arrived here safely and are getting settled in our rented homes. Your Uncles, William and Zemira hope to start permanent homes for us soon. I will help pay the expenses of building and we will have adjoining homes. That will allow Bett and Agnes and I to help each other when the men are away on church assignments. They will be working on the new Kirtland Temple at least one day a week. It is already under construction. We, the women, are to sew clothes for the workers and ease their burdens wherever possible to compensate them for the time they devote to the work on the temple.

I have already visited a school and hope to help with the teaching of the younger children. Bett and Agnes have agreed to help care for Zemira and Rhoda while I teach. I will teach Bett's older children tuition free in exchange. I am hoping to talk to Brother Cowdery about my teaching ideas.

The exciting news is that we have already been introduced to the Prophet by Brother Brigham. The Prophet greeted us with open arms and made us feel so welcome. His wife, Emma is beautiful and a very refined lady. I wore the new hat you made me and the cape Mother gave me when I left.

It is very exciting to be here in the heart of the church. They have set up a new printing press here in Kirtland where they will publish any messages or revelations from the Prophet. Uncle William has been invited to a very special school called, "The School Of The Prophets." It will be much like a University to learn the Gospel and other subjects. It is designed to train the leaders of the church so it is a great honor to be ask to attend.

There are many saints moving to Kirtland. The Prophet has designed a city plot to accommodate the growth and

schools are a part of the plan. Uncle William is going to help with the survey of the property.

The children enjoyed the trip here. They especially liked sailing on the ships across the lakes. We were fortunate that none of us suffered any illness. It was wise for the men to take the wagons and animals on the barges and the rest of us to sail on the passenger ships. I am sure we were much more comfortable. As you know, we left on September 11th and arrived here on September 24th. The last part of the trip was the hardest after we met the men with the wagons at North Kingsville. The roads were very rough and muddy from recent rains. Needless to say, we were glad to arrive in Kirtland.

William George was up to his usual antics and I often found him conversing with other travelers and entertaining them with his impressions of the Captain or other workers on the ship. Lydia Elizabeth was so much help with Zemira. Some times the water was a little rough and he needed someone to protect him from falling. Rhoda is growing so fast, you would not even recognize her. She can turn over by herself and is such a happy baby that she requires very little attention. She has a good appetite and sleeps through the night.

I hope you are feeling well. Only two more months and I will be a grandmother. It is hard to believe. It seems like just yesterday that you were born. It is my hope that this baby will bring you as much joy as you have brought to me.

Have you heard from Asahel and Elijah? Please give them this address in case they do not receive the letter I sent yesterday. The mail is not too reliable in Cramahe, as you know.

Please give my love to Mother and Father when you see them. I will try to write to them soon. Also, remember me to my dear sisters and friends in Loughborough.

You and Henry are so dear to me and I miss you very much. I hope you will consider joining me here someday.

My love to you,
Mother Phebe

Phebe addressed the envelope to Mrs. Henry Munro with her Loughborough address and added her return address to the upper left hand corner. She folded the letter and put it in the envelope thinking, "I wish my love was tangible enough to visibly enclose it in the envelope."

Her eyelids were heavy and she set aside the letter. Bedtime was a lonely time for her since George's death. She often laid awake to the wee hours of the morning trying to relax. Tonight she hoped to sleep soundly but she had a lot to think about. She found herself making another mental list. Her method of putting things in order. The top of the list was how she could arrange for a meeting with Brother Cowdery.

CHAPTER SEVENTEEN

"William, wash the breakfast from your face and comb your hair. We need to get you started in school today." Phebe was combing Lydia Elizabeth's long blond hair and braiding it into a single braid. She should be in school also but she was only eight. She washed Zemira's face and hands. He tried to wiggle away from the washcloth but his mother was persistent and kissed him on the forehead when he was clean and dry. She wrapped the baby in a small blanket to protect her from the crisp, October air.

Phebe walked down the Kirtland street with her little family. She smiled and nodded to her new neighbors as she encountered them. They had brought food into her family as they were getting settled, which was most appreciated. The Weavers lived on one side and the Terrys on the other. She hoped she could remember their names and those of their children. Having close neighbors was a new experience for her also.

"Good morning, this must be William." Master Baker greeted them as they approached the school and walked with them into the one room school. He assigned William a desk and told him where to put his nap sack with his lunch and writing materials.

"Mrs. Palmer, isn't it? I have thought about your suggestion for a Primary school and have discussed it with the committee. They have some concerns but would be willing to hear your ideas. We will be meeting this afternoon after school. I didn't realize you had such young children. How will you care for them while you teach school?" He looked down at Lydia holding Zemira's hand and baby Rhoda in Phebe's arms.

"I moved here with my brothers and their wives and families. They have agreed to help me. That should not create a problem. With your permission I will attend the meeting this afternoon and describe the Primary school program I have taught before." Phebe smiled and turned back toward home with the children.

"I have a letter to post. I understand you do that here at the store." She pulled the envelope addressed to Lovina and passed it across the counter to Mr. Whitmer.

Mrs. Whitmer came from the back of the store. "Good morning, Phebe. Let me take that baby. I love to hold babies. She held Rhoda in one arm and reached into the large glass container and pulled out some hore-hound candy balls for Lydia and Zemira.

Phebe paid Mr. Whitmer for the postage and looked at the bolts of curtain lace on the shelf behind the counter. She took her window measurements from her pocket book and determined how many yards of material she needed for each room. She chose a small check for the kitchen windows and lace for the parlor and bedrooms. Mr. Whitmer was measuring off the yardage from the bolts and cutting the lengths with large black scissors.

Phebe was distracted as the door to the store opened and a gentleman she had not met entered the store. "Good morning, Peter. Isn't it a lovely fall day. I think fall is my favorite of the seasons."

Mr. Whitmer looked up from the fabric he was cutting. "Good-morning, Oliver. It's good to have you back. You look well considering the affairs in Jackson County. How long have you been back?"

"Just yesterday Brother Phelps and I arrived to consult with Brother Joseph about our next legal approach for redress. We will be here for some time waiting for court dates." A worried expression crossed Oliver Cowdery's face as he looked at his good friend Peter Whitmer.

"Mrs. Palmer, have you met Brother Cowdery? Oliver, this is Phebe Palmer. She and her brothers have just arrived from

Canada. Her brother is William Draper who was the presiding officer there." Mrs. Whitmer passed the baby back to Phebe.

"I am happy to meet you, Sister Palmer. I met your brother last night. He is a good man. He said his widowed sister had accompanied him here and that you were a talented teacher." He shook her hand and smiled at the baby in her arms.

"Brother Cowdery, I believe this is an answer to my prayer, meeting you today. I have been discussing the possibility of a Primary school with Master Baker. We both agreed that we would like your opinion on the roll of a Primary school in the educational plans for the church. I have been invited to meet with the School Committee and Master Baker after school this afternoon." Phebe took her handkerchief and wiped Zemira's sticky face.

"Brother Joseph and I have spent many hours talking about the educational needs of the Saints. We are certainly open to new ideas. I'll come to the meeting this afternoon and we can all discuss it together." Oliver Cowdery walked over to the shelves to consider his purchase needs.

Phebe had the children thank sister Whitmer for the candy and paid for the fabric. She left the Whitmer's to visit with Brother Cowdery. He obviously had something very serious to discuss with Brother Whitmer.

It was not yet ten o'clock in the morning and she could check off four items from her list; William was enrolled in school, she had met Brother Cowdery, mailed the letter to Lovina and purchased the fabric for the curtains. She could work on the curtains while she put her thoughts together for the meeting this afternoon. She hoped she hadn't overstepped the appropriate bounds by discussing the meeting with Brother Cowdery. It may have been too presumptuous. Perhaps she should have waited to see the makeup of the committee. She remembered the politics of the school committee in Richmond but this was a Zion community. She would expect better.

Zemira and Rhoda were having a long afternoon nap.

Lydia was playing with the little Terry girl next door. Phebe took a sheet of paper from the cubby hole in her desk and picked up her pen.

> Primary School: Ages six to nine.
> Curriculum: Basic reading skills
>   Arithmetic, Addition, Subtraction,
>   Multiplication, Division
>   Literature
>   Penmanship
>   Art
>   Music.
>   Manners
> Questions about funding and money for books and
> materials.
> Length of school term and school day.
> Teaching methods
> Discipline philosophy
> Parent's responsibilities
> Reimbursement to teachers.

This would be a full agenda for the meeting and, after all, it wasn't her meeting but she did want to be sure that these things were discussed. Agnes stopped by to see how the curtains were coming and Phebe shared with her the plans she planned to present to the committee. They both threaded a needle and took a curtain panel to hem. As they sat, taking small blind stitches that would not show from the right side, they talked about what they would want the men to build into their new homes.

It was time to leave for the meeting. Agnes agreed to stay there with the children until Phebe returned. Phebe took off her apron, straightened her hair and put on the hat Lovina had made for her and carried her cape. It may be cool before she returned. She picked up the piece of paper containing the school notes and slipped it into her hand bag.

"Mother, where are you going?" William George was walking toward home with a group of new friends from school.

"I'm on my way to a meeting at the school. I shouldn't be long, Aunt Agnes is at the house with the children. Would you help her with them, please? I see you have some new friends." She smiled at the three boys with her son.

"This is Adam, Philip and David. They are all good marble players. I will have to practice if I am going to win my good migs back. They live close to us so we can go to school together." The boys looked shyly at Phebe and she wondered if they had won the marbles fairly but she wasn't overly concerned. William George Palmer could take care of himself.

She walked on down the road passing other small groups of children walking home. They seemed happy and that was a good indication that their day at school had been a productive one. It was her opinion that happy children learned faster and better than those that were afraid of the teacher and disliked school.

The school committee was made up of three gentlemen. Two long time residents of the area and one of the recent converts from Pennsylvania. As Master Baker introduced them to Phebe, he wisely indicated some of their background, giving her the opportunity to couch her words carefully. The long time residents didn't appreciate being called Brother and Sister and did not want to be controlled by the new "Mormons." Phebe graciously nodded to each as they were introduced and waited for Master Baker to proceed with the meeting.

"Mrs. Palmer comes to us with some background in what is called, Primary education. She would like us to consider expanding our school offerings to younger children in order that they can progress faster in the regular program we now have in place." Having said that he nodded for Phebe to begin. As she pulled her sheet of notes from her handbag the door opened and Oliver Cowdery walked in. He congenially shook hands with each of the members, calling them by name.

"May I join your meeting? I met Mrs. Palmer this morning and she told me she would be discussing her Primary School ideas with you this afternoon." Oliver pulled up a student chair and sat in the circle.

No one invited him to stay or ask him to leave. Phebe glanced at the "Old Timers" and tried to read their expressions. They seemed receptive enough so she proceeded with her presentation, explaining that she had taught formally in a classroom as well as teaching her children at home when the weather was too bad for them to attend school.

"If your son, William George, is an example of your teaching ability, I can certainly recommend you. In just one day, it is evident that he can compete with the brightest students in the school." Master Baker was encouraging her to go on.

She continued with the presentation of the curriculum that she thought was important for the Primary age children. They listened attentively waiting for her to continue. She explained her philosophy of discipline and desire to have parents understand the program so the could assist their children at home. Mr. Brown, one of the Old Timers, finally spoke, "It sounds pretty good but ya know, some of the folks around here don't cotton ta too much edjucation. Ya start askin' them ta help an they're just as likely ta keep their kids home."

The group discussed where to hold the school, since there was only one room in the present school and how they would get money for books and a salary for the teacher. Phebe suggested that the parents pay her a tuition fee which she could accept in money or commodities. "I wouldn't want any child denied the opportunity to learn. I could be very flexible but I would need some compensation."

"I am not a voting member of this committee and so have not taken part in the discussion. I will, however, make this offer. If you decide to proceed with the plan I will personally see to it that another room is added on to the school by volunteer labor. Mrs. Palmer certainly gives me the impression that she knows what she is doing. Let me know what you decide and I will keep my promise." He left as quietly as he had entered with a smile for each member of the group. Phebe noticed that he had called her Mrs. Palmer instead of Sister Palmer.

"Do you have any other questions?" Phebe was putting her list away.

"How soon can you start?" Mr. Allen seemed ready to make a decision.

"I can begin as soon as there is a place to hold school. I can teach without books until we can find a source to get them. Thank you for listening to me and I'll await your decision." She stood up, shook hands with each of them and nodded to Master Baker. As she closed the door she heard the animated discussion start in the room she was leaving.

Brother Cowdery caught up with her as she hurried toward home. "Sister Palmer, the Lord has truly guided you to us. If the church is to grow, as the Lord has revealed that it will, we need to provide for an educated group of saints to learn His doctrine. We can't rely on word of mouth to spread the Gospel. We must have missionaries who can read and distribute printed messages to members and converts.

I sensed that you understood the dynamics of the committee and were careful not to present the school concept as church inspired though well it may be. You were wise in your presentation. Some of us get so caught up in the joy of the Gospel that we over step our bounds with our non-member friends. We must always remember that they were here first, and though we will soon out number them, we cannot intimidate them or we will have the same problem as the one I just left in Missouri.

I hope the decision is to proceed with the school, and if it is, we will get some of our members to help put up that school in short order." He smiled, tipped his hat and turned at the corner as she went on toward home.

Phebe slowed her pace even though she was anxious to get home to her family. The men were called to be missionaries and spread the gospel. No one ever said anything about women being missionaries. Of course, someone had to take care of the family while the men were gone and continue to have children to give spirits to those waiting in the pre-existence. But she could not have more children. Perhaps this was her mission; to prepare the children to learn the gospel and take it to the ends of the earth.

"Sister Phebe, you have a letter." Sister Whitmer called to Phebe as she was returning home from school. Phebe walked across the street to get the letter from her new friend.

"Thank you. I am expecting news of my first grandchild but I don't think it has arrived yet." She looked at the envelope and recognized the scrawl of Elijah. "Oh, it is from my Brother-in-law with his report on our farm." She put it in her hand bag and hurried on home to relieve Bett of the children. Those three little ones under the age of three were a hand full.

Lydia and William George had gone on ahead to help Bett while she finished her preparation for the next day. Bett's children of school age had gone with them. This little Draper/Palmer clan made up a good part of the school population. There were eight of them all together with three in Master Baker's class and the other five in Phebe's. She had fifteen other children in her class ranging in age from six to nine. In the two months the school had been open, they had made great progress in their reading and settled into a well behaved group of students with the older children helping the younger ones. It was now almost time for the Christmas Holiday.

"Bett, how did it go today? I hope Zemira didn't get into

too much trouble. He wants to climb onto and get into every-thing." Phebe put her handbag down and picked up the baby. Little Rhoda put her hands on her mothers checks and gave her a big kiss.

"You sweetheart. I missed you so much today." Phebe hugged her baby and looked around for Zemira, William George and Lydia. "Where are the the other children? I sent them on ahead to help you."

"They took Zemira over to Agnes's. William George and the other children had been making up a play about some story they read today and they wanted Zemira to be one of the char-acters. He needed to get out and play with the older children and Moses is still having his afternoon nap." Bett was making a dress for her daughter, Roxanna, and the two friends sat in the rockers. Phebe, holding Rhoda, was resting for a few min-utes before the demands of evening meals and bed time.

"How did you feel about Brother Brigham's report on the Zions camp trip in sacrament meeting Sunday? After all the suffering and trials they endured, he seemed to feel it had a greater purpose. How did he say it? 'I would not exchange the experience I gained in that expedition for all the wealth of Geauga county.' He always seems to see the positive aspects of every encounter." Bett picked up her little pipe, put it in her mouth and went on sewing.

"He is a great leader. I am always so impressed with his undying devotion to the Prophet Joseph. Oh, I forgot, I have a letter from Elijah." She picked up her hand bag from the table beside her and holding the baby in one arm, opened her purse with the other hand and pulled out the letter. It was postmarked November 10, 1834. It had taken over a month to reach her from Cramahe. She read it aloud to share with Bett. They had no secrets from each other.

November 8, 1834
Dear Phebe,
    The crops are in and I have been paid for them that we usually sell. Martha and I sat down and did the figuring and we come up with the following amount as your share, 500 f. We had a good crop of tobacco that brought the bulk of the cash. We lost some of the cherries to a late frost but the peaches and apple crops was big. Any money we get for the potatoes and squash I'll put to buy seed for next year.
    Asahel is working hard and is a big help to me. He's growin' like a weed. We had to buy him some new clothes. He paid for them out of his wages and was mighty proud to do it. I'm sure he misses the family but he don't say much.
    Martha's expectin' a baby in the spring so we will have a family of our own. I hope we can be good parents like you and George. We haven't heard from Lovina but she'll be havin' her baby soon.
    How are things in Kirtland? Sometimes I wish I was there with you but I don't say much to Martha. She can't feel the spirit like I do. I just keep prayin' and go into church in Laughborough as often as I can. Asahel won't go with me so I usually go with Charles and Hanah. Charles is good at presidin' over the branch and the meeting house is full every Sunday. I hear some more saints are plannin' to come to Kirtland.
    Thanks for helpin' me with the farm and I hope this is enough money for you. I bought the bank note from Mr. Green and he said you would be able to cash it there.
    This other letter come for you so I am putin' it in too.
    Elijah and Martha

Phebe looked at the bank draft and it was made out for five hundred pounds. Elijah had done well. She wondered what Mr Green thought when he made out the bank draft. She smiled to herself, knowing how suspect he had been of her.

She looked at the other envelope. It was postmarked, September 27, 1834 and from Ohio. The return address was from Mr. and Mrs. John Park. Ohio University, Athens, Ohio.

> *September 20, 1834*
> *My Dear Phebe,*
> *Mary and our family have moved to Athens Ohio to take the position I wrote about in our last letter. We have a new son. His name is, John Rocky Park. Rocky is Mary's mother's maiden name. His sisters have spoiled him, I fear. They were so delighted to have a brother.*
>
> *One of my associates here is John William Draper. He is very renown and has published some important papers. The name was such that I thought he may be a relative of your family. When I inquired, he said he was indeed a cousin of your father. He told me he had heard through mutual relatives that misfortune had visited you. I hoped it was not true that your little girl was killed in a fire and your husband George died a few months later. The coincidence of names and location convinced us that it was our own dear friend, Phebe, who had suffered such a great loss. We truly grieve for you.*
>
> *Mary's health is much better and the Ohio air seems to agree with all of us. The Philadelphia air was becoming so filled with the smoke from the factories that we were hard pressed to breath on some days. It was especially bad in the winter months.*
>
> *I am teaching some pre-medicine classes and enjoy that much more than practicing.*
>
> *Please write to us and let us know of your welfare.*
> *As ever, your good friends,*
> *John and Mary*

Phebe felt guilty. She should have written to them. So many changes had taken place in her life that she could fill a volume.

"Well, I must get my brood home and fed. That was a lot of news. It is good to hear from home." She put the letters in her pocket and wrapped the baby in the blanket as she went out to collect the other children. She really wanted to read it all again.

She felt a wave of homesickness that she had suppressed for several days. It was almost Christmas. The first Christmas away from home and family. The snow started to fall lightly as she and the children walked home. What could she do to make this a memorable Christmas for her four children? They were certainly making the most of their new surroundings. She could hardly do less.

"Let's sing a song while we walk." William George and Lydia led out with one they had learned at school about a three cornered hat. They sang it in a round, each starting on a different phrase, and then all together. Phebe started at the wrong time and they all laughed and started over.

The snow was heavy when they reached the house. They brushed the white crystals from their coats and stomped their feet. Inside, Phebe lighted the lamp and added wood to the fire she had banked as she left that morning. It was soon warm in the little kitchen and the aroma of supper warming, encircled the family. They sat at the table and bowed their heads, holding hands. "Father, we thank thee for this day and for the food that we have before us. Bless it that it will give us strength to do thy will. Bless our loved ones in Canada. Watch over the leaders of our church and bless the saints in Missouri who have suffered so. Help us to love one another and keep thy commandments. We say this in the name of Jesus Christ, Amen." Phebe filled the children's plates and poured them each a glass of milk. She fed Rhoda bits from her plate.

"Mother, William George made up the most exciting play and we practiced it. Zemira is in it too. Do you think we could have a big family party for Christmas like we used to have at Grandmother Lydias? We could put on the play for the family." Lydia Elizabeth had the Christmas spirit and Phebe wouldn't dampen it.

"Of course you can. Maybe I could help you with some costumes."

With the children put to bed, Phebe opened the letters and read them again. Her homesickness took over and she cried. William and Zemira and their families were so good to her but it wasn't like being home. Suddenly, the empty feeling of being a widow in a strange city with four children to care for was overwhelming. She picked up her Bible and it fell open to the beatitudes. "Blessed are they who mourn for they shall be comforted." She was reminded of the Savior's love and she allowed it to encircle her. It was not easy to forget the confirmation she had received of her decision to come to Kirtland nor was it easy to live with the decision.

As she closed the Bible she was drawn to the new Book of Commandments. She turned to the page where she had left a marker and her eyes found that message meant for her, *"Wherefore, I now send upon you another Comforter, even upon you my friends, that it may abide in your hearts, even the Holy Spirit of promise, which other Comforter is the same that I promised unto my disciples, as is recorded in the testimony of John.*

This Comforter is the promise which I give unto you of eternal life, even the glory of the celestial kingdom."

She read of the Kingdoms of Heaven and then another verse that seemed directed to her *"Draw near me and I will draw near unto you; seek me diligently and ye shall find me; ask and ye shall receive; knock and it shall be opened unto you."*

"Teach ye diligently and my grace shall attend you, that you may be instructed more perfectly in theory, in principle, in doctrine, in the law of the gospel, in all things that pertain unto the Kingdom of God that are expedient for you to understand.—

"Organize yourselves; prepare every needful thing; and establish a house, even a house of prayer, a house of fasting, a house of faith, a house of learning, a house of glory, a house of order, a house of God."

Then the passage came to her again; *"I will go and do as the Lord has commanded. Blessed be the name of the Lord."*

CHAPTER EIGHTEEN

"William, please take this bank draft to pay for the house you are building for us. I am getting along just fine on the money I earn from teaching and I still have savings in the bank. It is important for me to be as independent as possible." Phebe gave her brother the note.

"Phebe, you are a dear. I have invested everything I have in the shoe repair shop and I have hired two apprentices to run it for me while I work on the house and do the rest of the surveying. All that and a day a week on the Temple doesn't leave me much extra time. As you know, I spend several evenings a week in the Prophet's school. With the growth in the church and in Kirtland we should all be quite comfortable financially. I have borrowed money from the bank for my part of the house so your money will help out." He put the note in his pocket and looked at his sister. She was so strong and always carried her load, though it was a heavy one.

"Last night we learned about the Word of Wisdom that was revealed to the Prophet last year. Have you read that revelation?"

"No, not yet, Bett and I have talked a little about what we have heard of it. What did the Prophet say? Is it a commandment or just a suggestion for good health? There seems to be some confusion about its importance." There was so much to learn. Phebe couldn't get to it all as fast as she would like.

"I think it is a commandment for the leaders of the church. It is for the temporal salvation of the Saints given for a principal with promise, adapted to the capacity of the weak and the weakest of all saints, who or can be called saints. There were a lot of questions and I didn't get all the answers. If everyone is commanded to live by it to be a member of the church it will be a great hardship on them. I don't know how Bett could give up her little pipe and we all drink a lot of tea and coffee and have all of our lives. We could eat less meat and we usually have fruits and vegetables in season. None of us have imbibed in the spirits, thanks to Father. He was pretty firm about that. I guess we need some more direction on it. Many of the brethren used to smoke and chew tobacco in the "School" but after the prophet had the revelation there is no more of that."

Phebe made a mental note that she would read that revelation and see what the Lord had told Brother Joseph on the subject.

"How soon do you think the house will be ready for us? I need to give Mr. Wright notice as to when I will be moving."

"It has been a mild winter and we have been able to get a lot done. If the weather holds we should be in it by the end of March. It is saving a lot of money to have our houses connected with a common wall. If we can be in it by then we will have time to plant a garden and have plenty of vegetables for summer. This is a great time to be in Kirtland. I just hope I can start spending more time on the Temple." William walked toward the bank and Phebe went on to school.

They had made Christmas special for the children with gifts from Father Christmas and the original play by the children. While Phebe was putting costumes together for the play she also filled a bag of scarfs and robes and made a star from some shiny material. They dressed up like the nativity characters and Uncle William read the story of the birth of Jesus from the book of Luke just like his father had on every Christmas he could remember.

Agnes and Bett made all the goodies that had been traditions for their families and Phebe made fruit cake and Christmas pudding like her mother had made every year since she was a child. They roasted two of the chickens and stuffed them with sage dressing. The potatoes and gravy and vegetables were just perfect. It was a wonderful Christmas dinner and then they all went to hear Brother Joseph give a special

Christmas Message.

As Phebe walked to school she thought, "The Children will remember this Christmas. Maybe we have depended on Mother and Father to make Christmas for us when we could have done it ourselves. They showed us how, but the spirit of Christmas is within each of us. It is service to others and trying to spread the message of "JOY".

Master Baker was ringing the bell and she hurried on. The children had gone on ahead while she talked to William. She was puffing as she got to the school but soon caught her breath and moved to the front of the room.

A new little girl was sitting on the back row, still wearing a hat and coat, which she was clutching to her as if for protection. She looked frightened and she dropped her eyes as Phebe looked at her. Phebe walked back to her, "Good morning. I'm Mrs. Palmer. What is your name?" She put her hand on her shoulder and smiled, waiting for an answer.

"My name is Julia, Julia Spencer." She looked up briefly but dropped her head again. Phebe had caught a glimpse of her dark brown eyes.

"Julia, we are happy to have you in our class. You may hang your coat and hat on this hook over here and I will get you some things to use today." Phebe picked up a small student slate, chalk and a piece of cloth and passed them to Julia as she returned to her seat.

After the children had said the pledge and prayer, Phebe ask Julia to come to the front of the room and tell the class something about herself. Julia reluctantly walked forward, and Phebe put her arm around her sensing that she would need a lot of encouragement to talk to the class. "Have you just moved to Kirtland?" Julia nodded. "Where did you live before you came here?"

"In Georgia, ma'am." She was polite.

"My, that is far from here. How did you get here?" There were not good roads to travel on in Ohio let alone any kind of public transportation to Kirtland.

"We come in a wagon." She was warming to the questions and the children were sitting eagerly awaiting her answers. They sincerely wanted to know more about her.

Phebe looked at her curly black hair and the dark tone of her skin. She had a beautiful face with fine features. She wondered if she had left the slave state of Georgia with parents who were fleeing for freedom. It would be best if she didn't press the introduction any further at this time. The children would make friends with her at recess and she would feel more at home. "We are very happy to meet you, Julia. This is Lydia Elizabeth. She will be your special friend for today and help you get to know the other children." She could rely on Lydia to make Julia feel at home.

Julia was smiling by the time the school day ended. Julia's mother came to pick her up. She was obviously of the negro race. Holding Julia's hand, she walked into the school and to the front of the class where Phebe was writing the next day's assignment on the board. "Are you Julia's teacher?"

"Yes I am. I'm Mrs. Palmer. You must be Mrs. Spencer." Phebe shook hands with her. "Won't you sit down. I would like to know a little more about Julia. Has she been to school before?"

"I was taught by my owner in Georgia but he died and the new owner wanted us to be field workers, so my man and I up and left and brought our Julia to freedom. I been teaching her some letters and she's a smart girl. I want her to be able to read like I can. We just come on this town last night and it seemed like a good place to stop. People seemed real friendly. When I seen the school I just sent her in. We was kind of cold in the wagon and I knew she would be warm here. Can she come to your school?"

"Of course she can. We are happy to have her. Do you need help finding a place to live?" Phebe wondered how she could help this family.

"We don't have much money but we're good hard workers and we can earn our way." Mrs. Spencer, if that was her real name, seemed sincere and Phebe, who had always been a good judge of character, took her at her word.

"You come on home with me and I'll get my brother to help you." They walked to the door and saw Mr. Spencer waiting in the wagon filled with what little the family owned. "It is near by. We can walk and your husband can follow us in the wagon." Lydia took Julia's hand and they skipped down the walk.

"William George, will you go to Aunt Bett's and get Zemira and Rhoda? Tell Uncle William I need him to come over when he has a little time." She invited the family in and started to prepare some supper. She wondered how long it had been since they had eaten a warm meal.

Lydia was showing Julia her doll and the doll clothes she had received for Christmas. The two little girls were already good friends.

Phebe invited the Spencers to wash up and she set the table with a plate for everyone, just as her mother would have done. She said a prayer of thanksgiving on the food and invited them to eat. Mr. Spencer broke the silence, "We're Christians too. We've been baptized and accepted Christ in our lives. He was watchin' over us and brought us here."

William came by as soon as he finished his evening chores. Phebe introduced him to the Spencers and the four of them evaluated the situation and tried to come up with a good solution. It was still too early in the spring for this family to live out in a wagon. William invited Mr. and Mrs. Spencer to go home with him and Julia stayed with Lydia. Phebe made a bed for them on the floor. She could hear them giggling after the other children were asleep.

Tomorrow she would see what reading skills Julia had and then she would know where to start helping her. She wondered what their legal responsibility was. They had admitted to her

that they were run away slaves and she didn't know what the
law was in Ohio. William would have to look into that tomorrow. As for now, they were all warm and well fed, just as they
would have been if they had come to Father's house. Again
she remembered their old friend, Okinihah.

William gave Jason Spencer a job in his shoe shop. Bett
and Phebe made an arrangement with his wife, Serena, to help
with the children and the house work in exchange for Julia's
school tuition. That would free Bett up for her growing Mid-
wife practice. William suggested that Jason help him add a
room to the back of the house for the Spencers. The house
would then have a main house for William and Bett, a smaller
home attached for Phebe and her children and another room
added on for the Spencers. Each of them would have their privacy. They could help them with a summer garden and share
the harvest. Zemira and Agnes, who were building on the next
lot agreed, and so the Drapers once again followed the admonition taught them by their father.

Phebe walked out of the family meeting, hoping William
would follow her. He saw that his sister had something on her
mind. "You work out the details with them, Bett, and I'll check
on what supplies we need to work on the house tomorrow."

"Phebe, you are concerned about something? Do you think
we have gone too far to help the Spencers?" He looked seriously at his sister.

"No, my only concern is our legal position regarding runaway slaves. Do you know what the law is in Ohio regarding
slavery? I personally don't think any person should be a slave
to another. The whole concept of slavery is abhorrent to me but
I am not willing to break the law. Who can we talk to without
initiating problems for the Spencers? One of the complaints of
the Missouri Mobsters reported in the paper was that the
Mormons were anti slavery and protected runaway slaves.
Missouri seems to be in sympathy with slavery but I don't
know about Ohio."

"I'll ask around at the "School" tonight. In the meantime we will keep quiet about what we know about the Spencers. They seem like good, hardworking people and that is all I need to know about them." They started back to the house.

"There is a conference to be held this weekend for all the brethren that accompanied the Prophet to Missouri. It is rumored that the twelve apostles, will be chosen. I wonder if our good friend, Brigham, will be one of them." William was totally engrossed in the workings of the church.

William held the door open for Phebe. "Well, do you think our plan will work?" He ask Jason.

"Yes Sir, Mr. Draper. No one has ever been so good to us except our old owner who died. We'll work as hard as we can and we won't be no bother to you." Jason put his arm around Serena and they smiled at their new benefactors.

It was agreed that the families would continue as they had until the new building was finished. Julia would stay with Phebe and go to school with she and the children. Jason and Serena would stay with William and Bett. Serena would help with the little children while the older ones were in school.

The following morning after the students were busy with their assignments, Phebe had Julia read some simple sentences and compute some very simple arithmetic problems. Obviously, Serena had indeed helped her learn to read and Phebe recognized Julia's ability to learn quickly.

The first few days went smoothly and all the children played together congenially. Julia and Lydia Elizabeth were both good leaders with ideas for games to play and giving clear directions.

William had reported to Phebe that as far as he knew, there was no law that governed runaway slaves in Ohio at that time. Some of the people in the Southern part of Ohio would capture them and take them back to slave owners for a reward. It was his opinion that they were within the law to befriend them.

Master Baker and Phebe met after school and discussed the

possibility of having the children from their classes prepare a program for each other. William George had been pushing the idea until Master Baker accepted it. William George was always trying to put programs together. Phebe had to smile. She knew her son. He was a natural actor and she wondered where it would take him. "I think it would be good for the children. The winter gets long and dreary. It will give them something new to think about."

They planned the program for the following Friday. Master Baker would let his class put on the original play by William George Palmer and Phebe's class would sing some songs and recite poems. "Phebe, it makes teaching school so much more enjoyable, having another adult to work with. How are things going with your new student?"

"She is a bright little girl and the children in my class have accepted her very well. Do you see any problems?" Phebe had been very sensitive to the social interaction of the children since Julia came.

"Every thing seems good from my perspective. If we have any trouble, it won't be from the children. Prejudice is an adult trait. Working together we may be able to teach these children the folly of being prejudice." Master Baker picked up his notebook and went back to his classroom.

The children were delighted with the program idea and started to make suggestions as to how they could participate. Phebe allowed them to decide what they wanted to do. Some of them agreed to memorize poems and others wanted to sing songs. Lydia and Julia chose to sing a song together. Phebe helped them find a song that the class had not sung before. As they practiced, the blend of their voices was beautiful. Lydia was a clear soprano, like her sister Lovina, and Julia was a true alto.

When Friday came the children were prepared and the program started in the large classroom of Master Baker. The Primary class sang, "America", then they each recited a nursery rhyme and Lydia and Julia sang "Little Maggie May". The older children started the play and to Phebe's surprise it was the story of an Indian helping a family travel across the ice and snow to grandmother's bed side. William George was the Indian and Bett's Henry played the part of his grandfather.

All of the children sang, "Wait For The Wagon" and the program was over. All of the children clapped and left humming "Wait for the wagon and we'll all take a ride." It had been a great success and they were all proud of themselves.

That night, as the children were finishing their prayers, a rock crashed through Phebe's window, with a note wrapped around it. Phebe kept the children back from the broken glass and picked up the missile that had invaded her room. On the paper was written in bold letters "SLAVE LOVER." She crumpled it and put it in her pocket. "Someone must have thrown a rock harder than they intended and it went right through our window." I'll put some paper over it for tonight and Uncle Zemira will repair it for us.

After the other children were asleep, William George got up and came to his mother's side, "What did the note say?"

"Don't be concerned. Some citizen in town doesn't like us befriending the Spencers, but we will ignore it. They are good people and we will do as the Savior had commanded. 'Love one another.' Your play was excellent today, William George. I am so proud of you for writing that play about our family history." Phebe kissed her growing son and sent him back to bed.

She hoped the rock incident would be forgotten and not repeated if it was ignored. She reflected back on the little girls singing and decided that maybe someone was jealous because it was so well done. Her scriptures were close by and, as she did so often, Phebe picked them up to find solace from the concern she felt at the disturbing incident with the rock.

Monday morning Mr. Brown knocked on Phebe's door. It was early and the children were still eating their breakfast. "Mrs. Palmer, I've had some people comin' ta me pretty up set about that little black girl in yer class. They've a mind ta keep their kids home if they're goin ta be goin' ta school with blacks. Some are sayin' ya spend all yer time with her cause she's sa slow an can't catch on like the other kids."

Phebe stepped outside to avoid the children hearing the accusations by Mr. Brown from the School Committee. "I'm sorry you have heard such unkind and untrue rumors, Mr. Brown. Julia Spencer is a very bright little girl and she requires no extra help. In fact, she has helped other children in the class. She was helping your little girl one day last week with a subtraction problem. The only individual help I have given her was the second day she came when I had her read for me to see what level of material I should assign her. Her parents have been educated in the South and will certainly be an asset to Kirtland. They are hard workers and good honest people. Would you have me deny a child of this ability the opportunity to come to school because of the color of her skin?"

Mr. Brown looked down at his feet and dug a hole in the dirt with the toe of his shoe. "That may be so but folks are still a talkin' an' I thought I best come over an' warn ya that some of the kids might not come ta school today. Course it don't matter to me. I'm a God fearing man an I don't judge nobody. By the way, did they come here ta join up with the Mormons?"

Phebe tried to hold back the anger she felt at his insincerity and pious excuse. Her future as a teacher in Kirtland may hinge on how she handled this. "Mr. Brown, I appreciate you coming by. I know you want what is best for the children and so do I. Why don't you come over this morning while the children are reading and listen to them. They are all doing well and would love to read for you. That way, you can hear your daughter read with the class and see how well Julia fits in with the other children."

"Well I'm pretty busy this morning. You know I have my farmin' ta do and that don't wait around for nobody. By the way, why didn't ya let my little girl sing with your girl and the black girl Friday. She felt pretty bad about that." He was on the attack again.

"I'm sorry, I didn't know Jenny wanted to sing with them. We'll work something out so that can happen. The children chose what they wanted to do on the program and Jenny said she wanted to say a poem. I'm sure those three little girls can sing together and I'll find a new song for them to learn. Now, any time you can get away from your farm, you just come right over to the school and I'll have the children read for you, even if we are in the middle of something else." Phebe was not going to let him out of the hole he had dug for himself.

"I'll try, but I got ta do some spring plowin' today. Just thought I'd let ya know how things was." He turned and walked back down the path.

Phebe hurried to get the children ready and all of them off for the day. She had better be to school early if their was going to be trouble. Somehow, she felt that most of the trouble was centered right in the Brown family over a little jealousy. She could work on that with the girls at school.

CHAPTER NINETEEN

William and Zemira had finished building the house with the help of Jason and the older boys. William George was fourteen now and could carry his share of the load. It was just the end of March. This Saturday was the designated day to move in. Phebe had organized the move, giving everyone assignments. Lydia Elizabeth, Julia, and Juliana were to tend Little Zemira, Moses and Rhoda while the older children helped pack the clothes, dishes, pots and pans and bedding into the wagon. The men would move the large furniture and the women would be at the new house to direct the unpacking and placement of furniture.

It was a wonderful big house for three families. After a full day of exhausting work, the families fell into their beds in their new house. All was well with the Draper/Palmer/Spencer clan.

This was truly a golden time for Kirtland. New businesses were opening and new homes were being built as fast as the lumber could be hauled into town. The bank was advertising loans to new comers to build and William was surveying more lots the bank had purchased from the farmers. The twelve apostles had been chosen and all but three ordained as special witnesses to Christ. They were to spread the gospel over the land. The other three, William Smith, Thomas B. Marsh, and Parley P. Pratt were away on missions and would be ordained when they returned. As William had heard rumored, Brigham Young was chosen as an apostle along with his good friend, Heber C. Kimball.

The following Sunday afternoon, William assembled the family for a special announcement. "I was called to a special meeting today. I have been assigned to go on a Mission."

Bett looked up at him in amazement. "I thought you were on a mission here. You work on the Temple more than any of the other brethren and spend night after night at the "School".

"The Prophet has told us that the Lord expects great sacrifice from us and we know the Prophet has sacrificed more than any of us. I am to leave in two weeks for Canada." He knew they would be excited about him going home to Canada so he had saved the best of the news for last.

"Oh, William, how exciting for you. You can see the family and even hold my new little grandson." Phebe had finally had a letter from Lovina announcing the arrival of another William. He was to be named William Munro and was born on Dec. 2, 1834. They were trying to find someone to run the shoe store because they wanted to come to Kirtland.

William grinned and they all rushed to congratulate him and give him messages to take home. All except Bett. She would like to have been told first but she knew that was the way it was in the Draper family. She hadn't told William that a new baby was on the way. Maybe it was just as well. At least she would have Phebe. Zemira and Jason could take care of the heavy work and the older children could help them. She put her pipe in her mouth and walked out to contemplate just what sacrifices were expected of them in this new religion. William hadn't said how long he would be gone. Perhaps he didn't know.

Phebe watched Bett leave and joined her good friend on the porch, "At least the house is finished so we don't have to pay rent any more. We'll get the family working on a garden. School will be out in a few weeks and we can spend some good time together. Maybe we can make some new quilts for the beds. Serena showed me a new pattern I would like to try. I have been cutting out pieces and sewing them together. I think the pattern is called, "China Plate".

The next two weeks flew by and William was on his way before the trees were in bud. He had letters for everyone and presents for the new baby. He had just been called to the mission for the summer. He should be home before Bett's baby was born. He left with other missionaries who were traveling to the East. He would go to Rome, New York, see their relatives there and introduce the Gospel to them on his way to Canada.

School was out two weeks later and the summer lay before Phebe, Bett, Agnes and Serena to decorate their new houses and enjoy the Kirtland society. They helped each other with curtains, towels, quilts and chair covers. They refilled the down comforters and ticks. They were invited to sewing bees with neighbors and invited neighbors in to help them quilt. The children worked in the garden and played in the fields, going barefoot most of the time. Lydia, Juliana and Julia delighted the little ones with hollyhock dolls they made from the flowers growing on the ditch bank.

Phebe missed the apple orchards of home. One day she took Bett for a ride in the buggy to the outskirts of town to find an apple orchard. They followed lane after winding lane but finally came upon an orchard full of trees covered with little green apples. Phebe's mouth watered and her lips puckered as she remembered childhood days when she would break a green apple from the stem and bite into the crisp, sour, unripened fruit. "Bett, I would love to have one of those green apples but I think the farmer would suspect our sanity if we ask for one. At least we know where an apple orchard is now so we can come back in the fall for our winter's supply." She flipped the reins on the horses back and they headed back home.

On their way they passed the partially finished temple. It was almost up to the top of the second floor. Men on ladders were hammering away and lifting boards up to each other. Zemira spied them and waved. He was working on the window frames. Tomorrow would be their turn to help with the noon meal for the temple workers. Phebe had baked some cakes this morning before the day got too warm to have a fire in the stove. Tomorrow morning she would bake bread. It was decidedly warmer than it had been in Canada in the summer. They planned activities around the cool of the morning and evening with quiet things to do during the hot afternoons.

"Phebe, Phebe," Bett rapped on the common wall.

Phebe jumped from her bed. slipped into some clothes and hurried to Bett's side of the house. "Bett, what's the matter?" She found Bett writhing in pain on her bed.

"Phebe, get some towels and my bag of herbs. I'm loosing the baby." She moaned as another contraction enveloped her body.

Phebe brought the towels and the herb bag. Bett chose the bag of herbs that she prescribed for herself to stop the bleeding and another to ease the pain from the contractions. She directed Phebe as to what she needed her to do. "I may lose consciousness so follow the directions I have given you." Phebe held a cup of tea to Bett's mouth. She had measured the herbs into the warm liquid.

Bett's strength was waning and with a long moan the baby came and Bett slipped into unconsciousness. Phebe followed the directions that had been given to her. After she cared for Bett's needs she snipped the cord and wrapped the little premature body in a towel. It was a girl and had been born alive but died in Phebe's arms. William was not there as his fifth child was born and died. When Bett awoke, Phebe was by her side and told her about the little girl. "I will name her, Harriet. The other baby that I lost was a girl also. I named her Roxanna."

Phebe remembered those days in Loughborough when Bett lost the other baby. It seemed so long ago but was in fact only four years. Henry, her oldest was nine years old, Juliana was six and Moses had just had his third birthday.

William arrived home in late September. He brought letters and gifts from home. All was well there but many of them were planning to come to Kirtland and join the main body of the church. Lovina and Henry were most anxious. They had tried to find a solution to the shoe shop dilemma. William needed the income from it to help make the payments on the loans he had from the Kirtland Bank.

"Bett, I'm so sorry about the baby. When I got Phebe's letter there wasn't time to write back. I just started back home as my mission was filled. I'm glad Phebe was here with you." William put his arms around Bett and comforted her as the tears rolled down her cheeks. Bett, who was a strong woman and seldom reduced to tears, wept at the joy of having her husband home and at the loss of their baby girl.

Sunday, as the saints poured in to the meeting, William was greeted by the many friends he had made since coming to Kirtland. Bishop Partridge ask him to report his mission and he told of wonderful conversions. Following his report he was called to be the president of the priest's quorum in Kirtland. Bishop Partridge and Brother Whitmer laid their hands on his head to set him apart for this assignment.

He was appointed to attend the "School" again and started to work with a renewed zeal on the temple. "Brother Draper, welcome back. We have missed you but from the Bishop's reports, your mission was very successful. With the completion of the temple so close, we have some very sacred information to learn in our school sessions." The Prophet shook his hand and smiled at this faithful brother.

The temple would soon be completed and the saints were passing it daily to see the progress. The men working on the temple were ask to wear white shirts and the sisters made the shirts for them. As the construction neared the end it was determined that the temple should receive a coat of protective stucco. The workmen assigned to the stucco work experimented with various formulas. Adding broken glass to the mixture gave off a special glow as the light caught it when dried. The problem was that most glass came from Germany and was very expensive by the time it reached Kirtland.

"Sisters, we have a special request for our new temple." Bishop Partridge looked over the congregation making eye contact with the Sisters. "I know that some of your most prized possessions are your china and glass wear. I've packed enough of it myself as we have moved from place to place to know it is valued above husbands themselves." He laughed and the sisters laughed with him. "If you could find it in your heart to spare a plate here or a glass there it will add a glow to our new temple that will be a tribute to our Father in Heaven."

It was obvious that each sister in the congregation was making a mental inventory of her china and crystal at home. Phebe thought of her tea set. She had been saving it for a special occasion. What could be more special than the Temple of the Lord. "Those of you who can find it in your hearts to share some china or glass, bring it to the temple site tomorrow. We will have workers there to accept them."

Phebe took the tea set from the shelf, holding each little cup and saucer in her hand, looking at the luster of the china. Then she held the teapot and removed the lid. She remembered the day she heard John was going to marry Mary and wanted to know what tea leaves would tell about her future. She looked deep into the tiny vessel and again wondered at her future. She walked to the the temple site and placed her tea set, a piece at a time, carefully in the barrel. Someone else would have to break them. She couldn't bring herself to do that.

The dedication of the Kirtland Temple was set for March 28, 1836, just two weeks away. The finish on the outside was almost complete and Zemira and the other finish carpenters were completing the carved wood trim on the inside. Painters were following them as soon as the nails were set. Special lettering was being attached to the raised pulpits on either end where the priesthood leaders would sit. The lettering was to be painted gold. The best painters were assigned the task of carefully painting the the letters so that the lines were crisp and straight.

When the painting was finished the cleaning began.
"Phebe, can you reach the top of this door molding?" Phebe
was teetering on the top of a ladder trying to reach the top of
the tall doors. She took the soapy cloth from Sister Pratt and
wiped the sawdust from the top of the door molding Women
were cleaning everywhere with wet cloths, dry cloths, scrubbing brushes, mops and brooms. The lye from the soap and the
new wood blended into a smell of cleanliness unequaled in all
of Kirtland. The windows shone and the brass handles glistened. The Temple was ready as the ladders were taken down
and the cleaning tools carried out. Tomorrow was to be the
day.

"William George, did you scrub your neck? I don't want to
be embarrassed by grime rubbing off on the new white shirt I
made for you." Phebe was braiding Lydia Elizabeth's hair. She
had taken the rags from her bangs so they curled around her
face, emphasizing her blue eyes she had inherited from her
grandmother. Lydia Elizabeth dressed Zemira in the new suit
Phebe had made for him and Phebe put the white, smocked
dress on Rhoda. The tucks on the bottom held the hem just
above the little black shiny shoes. When they were ready,
Phebe put on the hat and cape that she wore on special occasions and a new pale blue dress that she had made for this
momentous time. Lydia's white pinafore ruffles were starched
and ironed, standing out from the ten-year-old's shoulders. Her
long blond braid tied with a blue ribbon fell down her back.

Phebe inspected her children for every detail. They must be
at their very best. "This may be a long meeting but it is very
important for you to listen carefully because things will be said
that you may never hear again." She put some small pieces of
hardtack in her hand bag to appease Zemira and Rhoda if they
became fidgety. Extra handkerchiefs would make little cradles.

As they entered the large doors of the temple she could see
that the Priesthood holders were already in their places.
William sat with the Aaronic Priesthood as the president of the

Priest quorum. The Prophet Joseph and his counselors were at the other end with the Melchizedek Priesthood. His Father, who was the Patriarch of the church, appointed by divine revelation, sat a few seats away from his son.

The benches were filling up fast and each family group sat as closely as possible, allowing room for others to come in. Phebe held Rhoda and William George held Zemira. Lydia Elizabeth sat between them. It was a cool spring March day. the windows were opened slightly to let a light breeze flow through the building filled to capacity.

Phebe looked up at her brother, William. His face glowed with happiness and as the meeting proceeded the glow increased. He would later write in his journal, "My pen is inadequate to write or my tongue to express what happened there. Many present spoke in tongues and had visions and saw angels and prophesied."

They sang praises to the Lord in a new song; "The spirit of god like a fire is burning, the latter day glory begins to come forth. We'll sing and we'll shout with the Angels of Heaven, Hosanna, Hosanna, to God and the Lamb."

Shouts of Hosanna filled the air.

Phebe witnessed all of this with her four little children pressed on the bench between Bett, her children, Zemira and Agnes. When the meeting was over they were astounded at the length of time they had sat there. Even the children were in awe. The hardtack had not been removed from the handbag and the handkerchiefs had been used to wipe away tears of joy and unbelievable spiritual enlightenment. The spirit of the Lord reigned over the meeting. It was His house.

That evening, Phebe and the children returned to the temple site. It was as if they wanted to stay in the aura they had experienced that day. As they neared the temple the lights in the sky radiated in the glistening white temple. Phebe thought she could identify one glimmer that had been a part of her tea set.

They walked slowly home and into the part of the house Uncle William had built for them. Phebe knelt by the chair at the table and each child followed her lead. "Dear Father-in-Heaven, We thank thee for the blessings we have received by being allowed to attend the dedication of thy Temple today. We have experienced the strength of thy power and we come before you in gratitude for the things we have witnessed this day. As the mother of these children, help me to be an example to them and never do anything that would distract from the miracles they have seen this day. Help us to live worthy of thy love. We ask in thy Son's name, Amen"

Phebe could not fall asleep that night. The scenes of the day played over and over in her mind. The feelings she felt burned within her, testifying to her of the Savior's love for each of them and the importance of the work that had been revealed to the Prophet. Everyone in the dedication meeting had witnessed a revelation. She would have sacrificed everything on earth to have been there. She rededicated her very being to His will.

As the morning light started to appear she fell asleep and dreamed of George and Eliza walking toward her, smiling. George was holding his arms out to her and then she awoke. It was Monday morning and the children had to be fed and cared for and she had to get to school. She moved through the day with the usual activities but held on to the feelings and memories within her, not wanting to let the daily routines rob her of the spirit.

As she was preparing supper that night, she heard a knock on her door. She opened it to none other that the Prophet's Father, Patriarch Smith and his scribe, Sylvesta Smith. "May we come in, Sister Palmer?"

Phebe opened the door wide and ushered them to chairs in her sitting room. "How kind of you to come by." But she wondered at the purpose.

"Sister Palmer, Bishop Partridge has told us that you are a

widow with four children. He has explained some of the trials you have had and the sacrifices you have made to follow the Lord's direction in your life. I watched you yesterday in that glorious meeting and felt impressed to come to you to give you a Patriarchal Blessing, if you feel inclined to receive one at this time."

Phebe was overcome. She had never felt more in tune with the Lord than she had the last two days. "Father Smith, I would be honored and it is the desire of my heart to receive a blessing, that I might know of His will for me." She had heard of the blessing meetings but had been reluctant to go and ask for a blessing. The Lord had sent it to her.

The kindly Patriarch placed his hands on her head, *"Sister, the Lord hath favoured thee from thy cradle, I lay my hands upon thy head in the name of Jesus according to the order of God desiring in my heart to bless thee if thou wilt ask for blessings thou shall have blessings. according to thy desires in righteousness so shall it be, thou hast been afflicted and left a widow with children to care for but the Lord hath been merciful unto thee and given thee power to bear up under thy afflictions, and shall give thee the fullness of his holy spirit to comfort thee. I seal the blessing of a father upon thee because thou hast no father to bless thee nor companion to impart thee, but if thou will be wise, thou shalt have a companion who shall be a man of God and thou shalt be able to bring up thy children so that none of them shall be lost, keep the commandments and thy life shall be long and thou shalt see good days, and happy days, and the destroyer shall have no power to harm thee. keep the word of wisdom and all the commandments and be a pattern for thy sex. be wise, trust in God, he will deliver thee and provide for thee in all things which thou shalt need for thy comfort in this life and an inheritance in the life which is to come. I seal all the blessings which thou shalt need and I seal thee up unto eternal life in the name of Jesus. AMEN.*

Sylvesta wrote as the Patriarch's rich humble voice

mouthed the message to Phebe from the Lord. Then she wrote Phebe's name, birth date and place of birth on the blessing with the following heading. *A PATRIARCHAL BLESSING BY JOSEPH SMITH IN KIRTLAND OHIO MARCH 28, 1836. Sylvesta Smith, Scribe.*

Phebe sat motionless, filled with the spirit of understanding that her life would hold many challenges but that the Lord would bless her in all things. She folded the parchment paper and put it in her Family Bible.

CHAPTER TWENTY

The following weeks and months were filled with unbelievable revelations and spiritual meetings. Small groups of people assembled on the roads and in the places of business. The main topic of discussion was the Kirtland Temple and the things that took place in that holy edifice. They were of such magnitude that it was impossible to keep secret, though they were very sacred.

"Phebe, this is the golden time of the Church. I have been called to fill another mission in Canada and this time the apostles are going with me. I leave in June and will be back in the fall. I have discussed it with Bett and she is willing for me to go. We both know the Gospel must be spread as quickly as possible and I have been blessed with some talent in touching the hearts of people with my testimony. I will travel a different route this time by way of Toronto and across the Lake to Lewiston and along the Erie Canal. We have some Draper relatives up that way that I hope to contact."

"Thank you for all the help and friendship you have given Bett. I will need to rely on you again while I am gone. Do you have any concerns?"William and Phebe were analyzing the family needs and their responsibilities to the church.

Phebe looked at her brother, "Things seem to be in good order. I have banked the checks that Elijah has sent so I feel I have some security there. I won't be teaching while you are gone so I will be free to spend time with Bett as we did last summer. Other than her loosing the baby, things went quite well."

"I do have some concerns that I think we should deal with. There has been some overt acts of prejudice against the Spencers and some directed at me and the children. I thought we had it under control but with some of the action of the non-mormons and the bitter feelings of those who are leaving the church, I am becoming more concerned for their welfare. People seem to direct their anger at the weak who are unable to defend themselves. They may see me in that position, though I do not. The combination of me being a widow, you out of town and the Spencers living with us may set us up as a prime target for them to play out their anger."

William shifted his weight and leaned against the porch railing, "I have some of the same concerns. Jason and Serena have accepted the gospel and want full fellowship in the church. They have been reluctant to be open about it because they were afraid they would bring condemnation to the church. I have a suggestion for what may be the best solution but it would put more responsibility on your shoulders.

My plan is to take the Spencers with me to Canada. Our family up there could help them get established and there is much less concern up there about slavery. In fact, there is a colony of escaped slaves up there now, out of the reach of slave owners in the South. Jason knows the shoe repair business and I have in mind that he could take over for Henry Munro. That would allow Lovina and Henry the freedom to come and join us here."

Phebe was ecstatic at the thought of having her lovely Lovina in Kirtland and seeing her new grandson. "That is a perfect solution. We know that the good folks of Loughborough would accept the Spencers with the sponsorship of our family there. I will write to the school and report Julia's academic progress. Have you discussed this with Jason?"

"No, I have just been praying about a solution to the Spencer's problems and future in the church. When things settle down here, they will always be welcome to come back. We have all become very fond of them and they are so helpful. I feel this is an answer to my prayer. Let's talk to them together." Phebe and William walked to the back of the house to talk to Jason and Serena.

"We'll help you pack your wagon and I will be able to go most of the way with you. I can assure you I will get you over the border into Toronto and help arrange the rest of the trip for you. I will write ahead for Henry to meet you and help you get settled. I should be there a few weeks after you arrive so if there are any problems I can help you." William was reassuring in his presentation of the plan.

Phebe put her arm around Serena, "It will be so hard to have you leave us. Someday, when the world accepts the concept of Zion, we can all be together again."

"The good Lord sent us to your school room and he is watching over us now. Your kindness to us has brought us more happiness than we have ever known. We will do what you suggest but it will be hard for us to go away." Jason looked at Serena with mixed feelings.

Phebe then shared with them some of the things that had led her to believe they were in some danger if they stayed. She had been reluctant to tell them before. A group of older boys had attacked Henry and William George on their way home from school one day, roughing them up pretty bad. They threw out a lot of bad accusations and threats. She didn't tell them about the rock incident.

The Drapers and Palmers were quiet about their plans for the Spencers and tried to help them pack and make preparations with out drawing any attention. William suggested that they leave in the night. They knew the road well for the next twenty miles and there was a full moon. He had shared the plan with the apostles he was to travel with and it was determined that he would meet them in Toronto.

It was a warm June night and time had come to implement the plan. William mounted his horse early in the evening and headed for town as if he were on his way to the "School". His traveling supplies were hidden in the Spencer's wagon. He passed the Whitmer store and the Temple and then circled town picking up the main road where it entered the heavily wooded hills.

He waited in a rock quarry that was off the road. The spring rains had left surface water and small streams were creeping over the rocks into a clear pool. His horse drank from the pool as the shadows lengthened.

He heard the sounds of approaching horses but it was not the plod of horses pulling wagons. They were coming fast and as they neared the quarry, William moved back into the shadows and held his horses head to his chest. He did not want to be discovered there.

"We'll help those blackies get out of town. They shoulda been gone long ago. This ain't no place fer runaways." They drank from their bottles and raced by. William led his horse quietly back into the woods. He needed to intercept the Spencers. The horse picked his way through the shale and between the trees. William came back to the side of the road and could see the Spencer wagon approaching. He beckoned them off the road and found a clearing that was wide enough to accommodate the wagon. They were able to wind their way back into the protection of the woods.

Jason and Serena were practiced at avoiding trouble. Julia and Serena hid under the blankets in the wagon while Jason and William worked with the horses to keep them quiet. An hour passed. "They must have gone home. It should be safe to leave now." William started to mount his horse.

"No, stay quiet. I hear em." Jason held William's arm.

The rowdies' boisterous voices were carrying into the density of the forest. The moonlight was fading and Jason hoped they would not see the wagon tracks where they had left the road. He and William should have taken time to cover the tracks. Their only hope was that the men had been drinking enough to not notice them. He held his breath, listening.

The sounds faded as the men rode back to town, somehow convinced that that they had missed them. Racing through the night, drinking and planning evil deeds had filled their need for a good time.

The travelers found their way back to the road and continued on. William was convinced that taking the Spencers to Canada was an answer to prayer. He could only imagine what would have happened to Bett and Phebe if he had left the Spencers there.

As Kirtland had grown, so had the need for more schools. The closest university was in Athens Ohio and few trained teachers moved to the frontier towns like Kirtland. There were, however, many well educated people who were joining the Mormon church.

Eliza R. Snow had opened a school for young ladies. Phebe and others who had taught Primary schools met together to share ideas, as they planned for the opening of another school year. It was evident that they were all converts to the new religion. "We must be careful not to show partiality to the children of the Saints. Some of the "Old Timers" and the non-believers could take offense if they see any favoured treatment." Phebe warned.

Master Baker had joined them in the meeting, "I am hearing more and more resentment from towns people about the Mormons running everything. Many of them are very concerned about the new Kirtland Safety Society. We must try to stay neutral at the schools and not be drawn into the conflict."

When school started Phebe found her self resolving disagreements between children. There was much more name calling and seldom a recess period that didn't end with out some of the boys fighting. The peace that had existed in the little country school had vanished. Try as she would, Phebe could not seem to change the tone of the atmosphere in the school. Master Baker was encountering the same problems.

William returned home to find many of his old friends disenchanted with the Prophet and with each other. He sought out his old friend, Brother Brigham, who himself had just returned. "What is happening to Kirtland? Our beautiful city seems to have turned into a den of selfish, greedy, jealous people. They seem to be more concerned about what they have than who they are."

Brigham Young put his hand on William's shoulder and shook his head. "The Prophet is very disturbed. It seems that we are having trouble being a Zion people. The financial demands of so many flocking here in need of housing and business opportunities are overwhelming. Many are bringing their life savings with them but the money is to no avail if they don't have a roof over their head. We can't seem to build fast enough."

"Do you think we should all transfer our money to the new bank? Phebe and I have a fairly substantial amount and have discussed the possibility." William didn't see himself as a financier though he was good with figures.

"The Prophet is very clear that he is not urging the saints to use the Bank. He has made it very clear that, though he is the treasurer, it is not instituted by the will of God. Some still insist on supporting it as an arm of the church. We each have to follow our own feelings as far as business is concerned. Some would like the Prophet to make all their decisions for them which would then clear them from any responsibility for their own actions. We all have a lot to learn about being members of this church but what we must always remember is that it is the church of Christ and we must treat each other as he has admonished us, with love and compassion."

Brother Brigham changed the subject, "How were our friends in Canada? did you see your parents and Charles? How is the Branch doing there? I think I left a piece of my heart there. Remember how strong the spirit was in our meetings? You Draper's all have a special way that endear you to others.

I think it is the closeness and love within your family."

William reported to him about their mutual friends and the general growth of the church in Canada and they both went their way.

Hostility was so evident between members and non-members that Phebe found herself arbitrating fights and arguments with even the little ones at school. The children of the apostates seemed to show the most anger.

Phebe met with William in one of their usual strategy meetings. "I have decided to transfer my money to the Kirtland Safety Society. I have been reading in some of the out-of-town papers about the economy in the states since VanBuren was elected. It sounds like none of the banks are all that safe. My last check from Elijah was half of what it was last year because of the tariffs in the south on tobacco. It seems that everyone is greedy."

"Brother Brigham said we should follow our own feelings on the matter. I have a loan on the place in the other bank but I may borrow from the Safety Society to pay it off. I think the Interest is lower. My shoe shops are doing well and I should have it paid off in a year or two at the most." William often followed his older sister's lead as she did his.

There were discrepancies in the banking laws concerning the technicality of the Kirtland Safety Society acting as a bank. In January of 1837, Samuel D. Rounds found an opportunity to make some extra money and harass the Mormons. He brought accusations against the Kirtland Safety Society for issuing notes written as bank notes when it was not chartered as a bank. By becoming an informer he received a portion of the penalty of one thousand dollars. It was later reported as a malicious prosecution but the Prophet and Sidney Rigdon were arrested upon a charge of violating banking laws. They were later released.

The business panic of 1837 began shortly after Van Buren took office as President. An order had been issued for public lands to be paid for in gold rather than bank notes issued by wild cat banks. Mills and factories in the east were closing and many were thrown out of employment. Gold and silver vanished from sight. Kirtland was visited by the same panic and the Kirtland Safety Society ended in disaster.

Phebe, William and Zemira with their wives met for a family council. "The bank has closed. Our property will revert back to William Branch. He is gloating over the fact saying, 'it is better for me to have it than for old Joe Smith'. Where do we go now? The leaders of the church are making plans to move the headquarters of the church further west." William looked defeated. They had come to Kirtland with such high hopes and they had all worked so hard.

Zemira, who left the decision making to his brother and sister, squared his shoulders, "The Lord brought us here and now he has something else for us to do. We have a few weeks before they can evict us. We have our health, each other and spring is coming on. Spring always brings good feelings and new life. Remember when the Apple orchard would blossom. We would all feel like celebrating. Let's take stock of what we have and see what tomorrow brings."

Phebe looked at her youngest brother who had quietly worked away at helping with every project, receiving no special church assignments, but following the council in all things. Her admiration and love for him burned within her, "You're right, Zemira. Our faith hasn't been tested one whit yet. We'll do all we can and the Lord will provide. We have expected it to be too easy."

On April 16, 1838 the caravan of The Draper's and Palmers left Kirtland with all their worldly possessions packed in wagons and headed west. William had been ordained a High Priest and set apart to preside over a branch of the Church in Morgan County, Illinois.

As they passed the temple block, Zemira pulled his team to a stop. The others followed. Zemira pulled the wagon brake on, jumped down from the spring seat of the wagon and walked over to the temple door. He ran his hand down the painted wood of the door jam, feeling the polish that had come from planing and sanding. Tears rolled down his weather worn cheeks. He walked back to the wagon, released the brake and flapped the reins on the horses.

Phebe looked up at the white glistening walls catching the morning sun and said a silent goodbye to her tea set and remembered the words they sang at the dedication; *The Spirit Of God Like A Fire Is Burning.*

She turned to her children in the wagon, "We may not always remember what was said there but we will never forget how we felt." She too gave her team of horses their cue and they followed the wagon in front of them.

PART V
THE LORD WILL PROVIDE
1838—1842
CHAPTER TWENTY-ONE

The Draper/Palmer Caravan consisted of three wagons filled to capacity. They were accompanied by cows, extra horses, pigs, some crates of chickens, and a few sheep. Many of their possessions had been sold at auction to provide cash for the trip.

William Draper and his wife Elizabeth (Bett) and their four children; Henry H. (12), Juliana (10), Moses (6), Wm. Lathrop (5 weeks) were in the first wagon with trunks filed with clothing, bedding. cooking and eating utensils. Furniture and other items to help them sustain life in a wilderness environment were packed as well. William was on his way to fill the assignment by the leaders of the Mormon Church to preside over a branch of the church in Morgan County Illinois. He carried with him books and pamphlets, published by the church and printed in Kirtland. Bett had her medical supplies and herbs in pouches, labeled for their designated use.

The next wagon was that of Phebe Draper Palmer and her four children; William George (17), Lydia Elizabeth (12), Zemira (7), and Rhoda (4). They also carried trunks of personal belongings, furniture and household necessities. Phebe had brought books and supplies to conduct a primary school for the younger children in Morgan County. She had left some of her things behind to be sold at auction also but she had carefully packed Grandma Draper's cake plate with the gold trim between quilts for protection. The Family Bible with her blessing carefully folded and placed between the leaves of the book was tucked in beside it.

The third wagon was that of Zemira Draper and his wife, Ellen Agnes. They had no children. Zemira, William's younger brother had traveled with him from Canada to Kirtland, as had Phebe and her children. Their wagon was filled with carpentry tools and their household belongings. Agnes kept her spinning wheel so they could make woolen yarn and thread from the sheep's wool.

As Zemira had suggested at their first planning meeting, they had taken stock of what each had that all could use. Their family training to help each other and work together had served them well in their preparation.

After weeks of travel on muddy roads they finally had to stop for a few days as the roads were not passable and the spring storms were relentless.

Another company of evacuees from Kirtland and converts from Illinois found refuge in the same camp. They joined together for a testimony meeting and were encouraged to forge ahead and found strength in numbers. One of the families was that of Ebenezer Brown and his wife Ann Weaver Brown with their four children. They had sold their farm in Pennsylvania in 1836 to join the saints in the West.

They had stopped for a time in Illinois where their youngest son, John, was born and now were joining the saints in their move to Zion.

Phebe, Bett, Agnes and their new friend, Ann, sat huddled under a makeshift canopy, protected by the steady cold drizzle of the rain. Ann and Bett were rocking their babies as they sat on the tarp they were using to protect them from the muddy ground. "Let me hold little Billy, Bett." Agnes took the baby and held him with his head on her shoulder so she could feel the soft fuzz of the newborn's head on her cheek. Agnes longed for one of her own but tried to fill the void with loving the little nieces and nephews.

Ann told the women about their conversion in Pennsylvania. "I was so impressed with the missionaries that introduced the Gospel to us. Ebenezer and I both received a testimony at almost the same time. It was made know to us by the spirit that we should follow the saints. We were going to join them in Kirtland when we heard of the movement west. Now we have everything we own and the profit from the sale of our farm in Pennsylvania, to put in with the church. Ebenezer is a strong man, and even though he has not had the opportunity to learn to read, he seems to remember every word he has heard about the church. He likes me to read to him from the Book of Mormon and when he retells the stories to the children it is almost word for word the way I read it." Ann's pride in, and love for, her husband was evident in her voice.

Phebe recalled how she had felt at George's attitude to her conversion and baptism and the feeling of that loss of oneness in that important event left an emptiness even now. She envied Ann's joy in sharing the gospel so completely with her husband. The sadness she felt was almost overwhelming, but she turned her thoughts to other things. "I saw a loom in your wagon. Do you weave cloth?

"Yes, I do. I have for many years, and I thought it may be wise to bring the loom with me having four children to clothe as well as Ebenezer and myself. I am concerned about getting thread, however. That was always available in the East but here on the frontier it may be hard to find."

"Now we know the Lord led you to us. I have a spinning wheel and we have sheep with us. I wasn't looking forward to knitting, tatting or crocheting everything." Agnes smiled at Ann as she contemplated them working together with loom and spinner. "Phebe fashions clothes and teaches children and Bett is a Midwife and takes care of us when we are sick. We will make a great team."

"William is a shoe maker and land plotter and Zemira is a fine carpenter. We are all farmers. We could start our own town and fare quite well." Bett added. She could see the group working together in peace and harmony.

The men were also swapping stories of past experiences as they cared for the animals and surveyed the camp site for dry wood and forage for the stock. The other wagons from Kirtland had moved on this morning. The rains had suddenly stopped, as spring rains do and the sun was shining brightly, bringing warmth to the camp and optimism to the travelers. "We should be able to go on tomorrow if the weather holds. If we give the other wagons a day's start ahead of us the road should be better. We may have to graze the stock farther away from camp though as their animals will have taken care of the nearby grass." William checked the wagon wheels for loose spokes and to see if the metal bands were tight on them.

The other men followed his lead and and they rounded up the horses to check their hoofs and shoes to prepare for the next day's journey. Zemira picked up his hoof hammer and tightened some nails that were loosened by the travel in the wet mud. Ebenezer worked with the hoof pick to clean away the rocks embedded in the hoofs. "When did you men join the church? If you were in Kirtland it must have been some time ago."

"We were converted in Canada in 1833 by Eleaser Miller and Brigham Young. Most of our families were baptized by Brother Brigham but only three of the families came to Kirtland. Once things have settled down, we expect more of the Drapers to join us. I have been back to Canada on two missions. The church has many strong converts there."

"I was so disappointed to hear about Kirtland and the hard feelings of some of the members. I can't understand people turning their backs on the Prophet like that." Ebenezer wiped the sweat from his brow .

"It was a shameful thing in many ways. Satan is there to tempt us on every turn and it seems he usually uses material ways to do it." William put his hand on his new friend's shoulder. "We are happy to have you join with us as we travel to Morgan County. I have a church assignment there. Will that fit in with your plans?"

"Ann and I talked about it last night and was hoping you'd ask us. It seems like the Lord has led us to you and that is what we should be doing."

Zemira walked over and shook Ebenezer's hand. "Glad to have you with us, brother."

Wet tarps and clothes dried in the sun as the women prepared meals and repacked the things they had used the last few days. The children were playing and helping with the preparation to move on. After their confinement in makeshift tents and wagons they were glad to move about and explore the area. Phebe organized them into a water detail, carrying pails of water to camp from the stream nearby. Rhoda insisted on following the group and took a little pail with her. Not realizing the swiftness of the water, she dipped her pail in the stream and the pressure of the stream pulled her down the bank and into the stream. Seventeen year-old William George, supervising the water carriers, sprinted down the edge of the stream, watching the little body bobbing in the water. "Get help! Rhoda's in the water." He called back as he ran quickly enough to jump into the water ahead of her and pulled her limp body to him. He threw her over his shoulder as he waded out of the stream.

Phebe was ahead of the crowd running to the stream. "Not Rhoda, not Rhoda!" she sobbed as she ran. Then she saw her strong young son carrying his little sister to her. Rhoda was coughing and shivering. Phebe grabbed her and held her tight as if she could will her to live by doing so. Bett flipped her shawl from her shoulders and wrapped it around mother and daughter. As she did so she clapped her cupped hand hard on Rhoda's back. Rhoda gasp in air and spewed out water from her mouth and started to cry.

Before the evening meal, the four families knelt in a prayer of thanksgiving for the survival of Rhoda and the sunshine that would allow them to proceed to their destination.

William George was the center of attention for being so brave. He tried to distract the attention and the seriousness of the experience by going into his imitations of everyone, including Rhoda coughing. Rhoda, sitting on her mother's lap laughed at her big brother and Phebe hugged her. William got out his Jew's harp and started to play some lively music. Soon they were all dancing and singing around the camp fire.

The fire was dying down and the children were all asleep. Phebe sat poking the charred wood with a stick and let her mind wander. "Could she have been able to let another little one die? If the Lord had expected her to do that, would she have accepted His hand in all things? What challenges lay ahead? How would her faith be tested in the future? Would she remain firm in her convictions?" She thought of Ann and Ebenezer and the story of their conversion. Had the Lord guided them to the Draper/Palmer caravan? She pulled her shawl tightly around her to protect her from the cool April evening.

Her brothers came and sat by her on either side. Zemira put his arm around his sister. "Are you all right?"

"I'm fine. I was just sitting here wondering about the future and if I will be strong enough to pass the test."

William took her hand, "Miss Phebe, you are one of the strongest women I know. You will help all of us pass the test. Zemira and I came out alone to give you a blessing." They stood and laid their hands on her head and invoked the Lord to give her strength to meet the challenges ahead.

She hugged them both, "Thank you. What would we do with out the blessings of the Priesthood? What would I do without my brothers?"

They walked her to her wagon where she climbed into the makeshift bed and put her arm around her little Rhoda who was sleeping the peaceful sleep of a child.

William walked into the country store, "Sir, I'm looking for a Mr. Isaac Weeks. Do you know any one by that name in this area? My name is William Draper. I was told I might find him in this vicinity.

The proprietor of the store looked up at William, "He lives on the west end of town. He and his Mrs. settled here a couple of years ago. He's already built himself a nice house and barn. You'll recognize the house, it has a big front porch and the house is built of logs."

William looked at the jars of candy on the counter and decided it was time the children had a treat. He reached in and took a handful and paid for them with change in his pocket. "I'll be back for supplies when we get settled. Thanks for the information."

The trip to Morgan County, Illinois had taken seven weeks. It was the end of May and the weather was warm. The four wagons approached the village of Prattsville and circled to make camp on the outskirts of the small settlement. William, Ebenezer and Zemira had saddled their riding horses and went in to town to look for accommodations and find the members of the church.

After the stop at the store the three riders headed west looking for the house described by the store keeper. The church authorities had given William Brother Weeks' name to contact on their arrival. He had been forced out of Clay County, Missouri during the problems and was with a group that had moved back into Illinois for protection from the mobs in Missouri.

The three men dismounted as they reined their horse in at the gate of a nice log house with a large front porch. A sign over the door said, "WEEKS." "This must be it. Shall we go in together or do you want us to wait here?" Zemira looked at his brother for direction.

"Lets all go in. I'm sure the Weeks family will be glad to have some members of the church stop in." William walked up to the door and knocked. The men removed their hats and brushed the road dust from their trousers.

A middle aged woman answered the door. Her smile and demeanor put the men at ease. "Hello, may I help you?"

"We have been sent from Kirtland. I am Brother William Draper and this is my brother, Zemira and my friend, Ebenezer Brown. Is Brother Weeks at home?"

"He's out working in the barn. I can call him in or you can go out to the barn. Why don't you come in and have a cool drink? I'll call him." She opened the door wide for them to enter and motioned them to chairs in the sitting room as she walked to the back of the house to call her husband.

Brother Weeks walked into the room and shook hands with the men as William introduced them again. "I have been sent by the church authorities to preside over this branch of the church. I was to contact you when I arrived. How many saints are in the branch?"

"We have about fifty families here in the area. Most of them came from Jackson, County when the persecution started. The people here have been very good neighbors and it has given us an opportunity to get started again after having lost everything we had in Missouri. We had to literally run for our lives and it feels good to be in a safe place." Brother Weeks took a glass of cool liquid from his wife after she had served the other gentlemen.

"There is a little problem as I see it. Since we didn't have anyone here for several weeks to preside over the Branch, the members voted last Sunday to sustain me as the presiding elder. I don't know what we should do about it. Do you? I would gladly step aside." Brother Weeks impressed William with his sincerity and humility.

"Since there are no church authorities here I would say that it is up to us to decide. What Priesthood do you hold?" William tried to recall the lessons they had in the School of the Prophets about succession of authority.

"I was ordained a High Priest in Missouri before we came here. I am the only High Priest here so I guess that's why the members voted to sustain me in the position."

William stood and shook his hand, "Brother Weeks, it sounds like things are in good order here. We will stay on through Sunday and attend meeting and then move on to Far West to see what the Brethren want me to do." He looked to his companions for approval. They nodded.

"Thank you, sister Weeks, for the refreshing drink. We must get back to our families and let them know of the plans." William walked to the door.

Brother and Sister Weeks said in chorus, "Your families? Where are they?"

"We are camped on the other side of town. They are waiting for us to find accommodations for them to set up house-keeping here. It seems we will have a few more miles to go before we put down roots."

"Bring your families here. You can use our well and we have plenty of pasture for livestock." Brother Weeks walked out with them to the hitching post. "You can pull your wagons in here West of the house and graze your stock in that west pasture there. The grass is tall from the spring rains so there should be plenty to sustain your animals for several days."

"Thank you Brother, that is very generous of you. We will be happy to pay you. We will collect our families and be back in a few hours." William shook his hand again and mounted his horse.

As the three men rode into camp they were greeted by all of the traveling flock. William took the candy from his pocket and distributed it to the children. "Let's assemble over here in the shade." They followed him to a nearby grassy spot under a tree.

"It seems that our travels are not over, at least not mine. Brother Weeks, the man I was to contact here, was sustained by the members here because they had been without leadership for so long. He is also a High Priest and since there are no church authorities here to give us direction we have decided that he should remain in that position and I will continue on to Far West to meet with the brethren there. We have been invited to camp at the Weeks farm until Sunday. I will not ask the rest of you to go on with my family if you choose to stay here. There seems to be a good size group of saints here." William waited for a response from the others.

"I don't think it would be wise for one family to travel alone through Missouri with the feelings of unrest there. Some of those mobsters could be dangerous to a wagon traveling alone. We have come this far together. Agnes and I will go on with you." Zemira looked at Agnes for agreement and she nodded her approval.

"I need to stay with my brothers. William George is seventeen now and can drive our wagon as well as I can. If we won't slow you down, I think we should stay with you. As Ruth said to Naomi, 'Whither thou goest, I will go.'" Phebe motioned her children to her. "Do you feel as I do?"

Her strong, young son put his arm around her shoulders, "We're part of the family. I say we stay together."

Ebenezer had been quietly discussing the matter with Ann. Gurnsey (14), Harriet (12), Norman (8), their three older children huddled close to hear the decision of their parents. They had been traveling for several weeks and the novelty of the trip was no longer exciting to them. They had made friends with the Draper and Palmer children and enjoyed being part of the group. Ebenezer stepped forward, "Ann and I feel that we should stay with the group. The Lord directed us to you and we will go on with you."

"We told the Weeks we would be back in a few hours so we should get packed up and on our way so we can be settled by dark. They have a well we can use so we don't have to get more water and they have also offered us pasture land for the animals. Let me just say that I appreciate your decision and commitment. If at any time, in the next few days, you should decide to stay here, I will understand and there will be no hard feelings. I suggest you make it a matter of personal and family prayer to receive confirmation of your decision." William and the other men started rounding up the animals.

The women repacked the cooking pans and straightened up the bedding and clothes in the wagons. They met between the wagons when they had finished. "I was so looking forward to stopping here. The baby is so young and even with the extra herbs I still don't seem to have the strength I had by this time after my other babies were born." Bett, realizing that William had made the decision for their family without discussing it with her first, had those feelings again that she felt when he announced his first mission.

Phebe knew her sister-in-law well and loved her. She also understood her brother William's enthusiasm and dedication to the church. "Bett, we must make your load easier. You always take care of us and it is time we took better care of you. I suggest that we free you up from all cooking by Ann, Agnes and I cooking for all four families. We can also keep the washing up with the help of the older children. Harriet, Juliana and Lydia can take care of the little ones. They are old enough to accept that responsibility. A few days rest in good weather with plenty of water available from a well can give us the boost we need to go on."

Bett looked at Phebe, "Thanks, I'm glad you decided to go on with us. I don't know what I would do without you."

The caravan was soon on its way through town. They stopped at the Country Store and purchased supplies they would need for another trip of over a hundred miles.

At the Weeks farm they were surprised by a group of people who had prepared a welcome dinner for them. A beef roast was cooking on a spit over a bonfire and tables on the big porch were laden with fresh bread, pies, cakes, pickled beets and all the goodies they could only have imagined. Sally

Weeks had activated the saints in the area by sending her son on his pony with a message of the new arrivals and an invitation to come and help greet them. Buggy's of saints were still arriving after the travelers were camped at the west of the house and the animals secure in the pasture.

Samuel Weeks was introducing the men around and Sally was getting acquainted with the women and introducing them to the other women, letting them know which sister brought which specialty dish. As they visited they found that they had common friends in the church and were soon catching up on the recent events in Kirtland and news from the Saints in Missouri.

William was ask to speak at the Sunday service and his testimony was inspiring to the saints there. He admonished them to follow the prophet and not be influenced by those who would malign him and undermine the church. He thanked them for their generous welcome, "Your Christ-like actions the last few days have brought new hope to us and we are one in the spirit of the gospel with you. Some day we will meet again and on that occasion we will welcome you, whether it be on this earth or in heaven."

Monday the travelers were on their way again, rested and spiritually renewed. The future looked brighter to them and they looked forward to meeting old friends from Kirtland at Far West.

CHAPTER TWENTY-TWO

The caravan was half way to Far West as they approached the settlement of Huntsville. The trail for the last two days had been rough with several bogs requiring the wagons to be double teamed to pull them through the quagmire. Intermittent storms drenched the camps and strong winds preceding them sent the campers scurrying to tie down wagon tops and keep the cattle from scattering.

As the women had promised, they doubled up on the cooking and washing to relieve Bett of some of the pressures of the trip. Henry called softly at the Palmer's wagon in the night. "Ma needs you, Aunt Phebe. Pa's sick."

Phebe slipped into her clothes and climbed down from the wagon bed. She walked quietly to William and Bett's wagon, finding her way around rocks and logs in the star light. "Bett, how can I help you?"

"William's running a high fever. I can't seem to break it with cold water or any of the herbs I've tried." Bett held the canvas back for Phebe to join her at William's bed side. He was delirious.

"I think we had better get the men to give him a blessing." Phebe hurried to Zemira's tent, calling to him, and then to the Brown wagon. Both men came quickly.

"William is very ill. He is running a high fever and talking out of his head. Do either of you have any consecrated oil to give him a blessing?"

Zemira ducked back in his tent and came out with the little vial in his hand. The men ask the Lord for William's recovery using the priesthood power bestowed upon them. William settled down almost immediately, but Phebe and Bett stayed by his side through the night.

The following day he was lucid but very week, unable to

raise his head from the pillow. They set up a permanent camp under an old oak tree in a grassy area near by. A rider came into camp, "You folks Mormons?"

Zemira and Ebenezer were reluctant to answer, not knowing the reason for the question.

"I had a dream last night that there was someone out here who needed me so I jumped on my horse and rode out. I'm Edward Weaver. I live up the road in Huntsville. I'm a convert to the Mormon church and I've been trying to help the saints when they come through on the way to Far West." He got off the horse and shook hands with Zemira and Ebenezer.

"We are Mormons and we have a very sick brother with us. We gave him a blessing last night and he rallied but he is still very weak." Ebenezer led Brother Weaver to William's Wagon. "This is Brother Weaver. He lives in Huntsville and has come to help us."

Phebe got down from the wagon bed and greeted their benefactor. "I don't think he can survive another night out and it looks like we are in for more storm." A streak of lightening shot across the black cloud overhead and the thunder following it vibrated the wagons and spooked the animals.

"I'll go and get a buggy and come back for him and his wife. They can stay with us until he recovers." Edward mounted his horse and was off without a response to his offer.

Phebe helped Bett get her things together. She would need to take the baby who was still nursing with her. They cleaned William up as best they could while Agnes and Ann prepared breakfast for the families. None of them had been able to sleep much and it was a camp of weary people.

Brother Weaver was soon back and the men carried William to the buggy filled with quilts and pillows. They helped Bett in and Phebe handed her the baby, bathed and dressed in clean clothes. Zemira put the valise Phebe had packed in the back of the buggy. Brother Weaver told them how to find his house and invited them to come and see

William at any time. "Now don't you worry, We'll take good care of him." Bett held William against her and the baby on her lap. She looked so forlorn.

"All will be well, Bett, I promise you. We will come and see you as soon as we get a permanent camp set up." Phebe tried to reassure her sister-in-law as the buggy pulled away from the camp site.

The storm clouds blew over and the sun came out again. The discouraged travelers did what needed to be done and rested while they assessed how they could set up a permanent camp to stay in until William was well enough to go on. The men hitched a team to the wagons one at a time and pulled them into a little meadow beyond the big oak tree and closer to a stream of fresh water. They set up some temporary barriers to keep the cattle confined to a grassy area where they could graze and sent the children scouring to find rocks to form a fire pit for cooking. They had learned many survival skills on the trail in the last few weeks of travel. The comforts of home were almost forgotten.

Phebe sat alone under the oak tree, watching as the children played games at the bottom of the grassy knoll. It was time to get some of the books out and spend some time reviewing their reading and math skills. It may take several days for William to recover enough for them to move on. Keeping busy with scheduled activities would help the time go faster and give the children a greater sense of security living in this temporary environment. As she had in the past, she started to make a mental list of how she could organize the day for the campers. When she had it firm in mind she would present it to Zemira, Ebenezer and their wives.

Phebe's mind wandered and she thought of her two older children, Lovina and Asahel. Just before she left Kirtland a letter had arrived from Lovina. She and Henry had moved to Sagamon, Illinois and they had a little girl, Ester Ann, who had been born there. Mother and Father Draper, William and

Lydia, with others from Canada had settled their for a time, waiting for direction as to where the center of the church would be. Lovina had no news from Asahel. The last Phebe had heard from Elijah and Asahel was a short note from Elijah with a final payment on the Palmer farm. The depression in the States had affected the economy in Canada making the check smaller than Phebe had expected. It did come after the Kirtland Bank failed so she had this small payment to help sustain her in this trip.

Phebe presented her proposed daily schedule and it was agreed that they should proceed with it until William recovered and returned to camp. After breakfast each morning the camp was put in order and the children met with Phebe under the oak tree. She read stories and poems to them and listened to them read from the primers she had packed into her wagon. They memorized poems and practiced calculating sums. William George wrote a play about funny things that happened while they were traveling. He assigned the parts out to the children and taught them how to perform them. Lydia and Juliana made up a song to sing in the play. Their goal was to have it ready to present when Uncle William recovered and came back to camp.

Each day, two or three of the travelers would go to the Weaver Farm to visit William and Bett. They would report to him on the activities of the camp and assess his progress to tell the family as they returned. Bett was improving also in the comfort of the Weaver home. Two weeks after the illness struck, William was better and Brother Weaver returned he and Bett and the baby to camp. There was a great celebration with William's favorite food and culminating with the play presented by the children. Hearty laughs and clapping interspersed the performance. William George was lauded for his direction of the play and the cast gave him a bouquet of wild flowers gathered from the surrounding area.

William stood and thanked everyone for their support

during his illness and asked them to kneel in prayer as he thanked the Lord for the blessings they had received. The camp was soon quiet as the performers and campers snuggled in their makeshift beds.

Midmorning the following day, a new group of travelers joined the camp under the big oak tree. It was another group from Kirtland. Among the new arrivals was the Prophet's mother and father and their sons Hyrum and William and their families. It was a joyous time in camp to have the kind Patriarch and his sweet, little wife in camp. They were soon swapping stories of the last few weeks and catching up on the news of friends and families who had been separated since leaving Kirtland.

The members in Huntsville heard of their arrival and soon they were joining with the travelers in testimony meetings. Father Smith was invited to give the members blessings. At the culmination of one of the meetings, William was inspired to speak to the members, sharing his testimony and warning of trials that would come to them to test them. He was inspired to warn of trouble ahead for the Smith family. Father Smith bowed his head to hide the tears. He too had premonitions of problems ahead. He had lived the past several years with concerns for his son's safety. Now that concern was for the whole family and their beloved friends who had embraced the gospel with them.

Father Smith rose and dedicated the "Camp Under the Oak Tree" as a resting place for those who were worn out in their travels from the east. William Draper was called to preside over the camp and the Smiths resumed their journey.

The Draper/Palmer/Brown group stayed with William until he was released from this call in August when he was sent a message to move to Caldwell County, Missouri because of strong indications of Mob violence.

After a few days of preparation, the camp was transformed into a moving caravan again. They proceeded along the trail but soon came upon evidence that travelers who had preceded them had been harassed and some of their belongings burned, the remains marking the trail. Some slaughtered animals were left bloated and rotting by the road.

William called a conference. It was determined that they would proceed on an alternate route, approaching Far West by the Haun's Mill area. They pushed forward and found a place to settle on Log creak a few miles short of Far West. The men began to cut logs and clear land for cottages, barns and sheds. Extra rooms were added to William and Bett's cabin for Phebe and her children. Log Creek was soon organized as a branch of the church with William presiding. William took up his shoe making. Each family had about seven acres of fertile ground to farm and they started preparing the fields to plant in the spring.

Phebe organized the school for the children of the settlement. Several families had joined them at Log Creek and the early days of September was a good time to start school again. She met another young teacher, Miss Mary Ann Duty, who had started a school in an abandoned log cabin. Together they were able to continue to educate the children as families came and settled in Log Creek.

The Prophet visited the small branch and encouraged them on. There were still rumors of mob violence in the surrounding country but things were going well in Log Creek. The men never left the settlement, however, without protection and the children were instructed to watch for strangers and not go out into the woods alone. The men taught the women how to load and fire the muzzle loading guns and an escape route was plotted in case they had to evacuate.

The few long time residents of the area were friendly to them and had willingly sold the farm land to them at a reasonable price. The comfort and safety of the Log Creek community was not to last. In October of 1838 hostilities were so rampant that the Prophet ordered his followers to move into Far West for their mutual protection. Once again Phebe, her brothers and the Browns filled their wagons, rounded up the cattle and joined the droves of saints pouring into Far West.

The wagons were lined up along the streets, their drivers waiting for direction. The Prophet, seeing the great need of the multitudes moving into Far West, had assigned some of the residents to direct the new arrivals to various locations where everyone could find some kind of shelter. Hyrum Smith, recognizing the drivers of the Draper Caravan, motioned them to the east of town.

"Brother William Carey will help you over at that old log house, Tell him I sent you." He waved them on and walked on to the next wagon in line.

Several families were sharing the facilities of each homestead. The Careys already had a family named Fowler with them but they greeted the Drapers and Browns graciously. The well near by offered fresh water and there was still pasture land for the cattle to graze. After seven months of living in wagons and makeshift cabins, the new arrivals were somewhat self sufficient. The days were still warm as Indian summer tarried and gave the saints time to prepare for winter.

Phebe knocked on the door of the old farm house. She smiled at Sister Carey when she opened the door. "I'm Phebe Palmer. I hope we wont be too much trouble to you. We are all hard workers and have adequate supplies for our needs. I am a widow but I have a son who is seventeen and carries his load like a man. My brother, William Draper, is the leader of our group. We also have another brother with us, Zemira Draper, and the Ebenezer Brown Family. How can I help you?"

Sister Carey put her arm around Phebe, "How can I help you? You are the one who has been traveling. Sit down and tell me more about your family. If we are going to live together we had better get acquainted."

Phebe sat in the welcome rocking chair. It had been a long time since she had felt the comfort of a rocker. She looked into the warm brown eyes of Sister Carey and knew at once they would be friends. She was short and round, probably in her early fifties. Her smile was sincere. "I'm afraid there are a lot of us. We left Kirtland in April and have been on the road most of the time until we settled at Log Creek about a month ago. We had cabins built there but, after the Haun's MIll raid and the atrocities that happened there, the Prophet advised us to move into Far West. So, at his direction, we are here."

Sister Carey handed her a cup of warm herb tea. Phebe held the saucer in one hand as she lifted the cup to her lips with the other. It felt so good to be in a real house again drinking tea from a china cup. "We can make beds in and under our wagons. We have tents and tarps to protect us if the weather holds out until we can get some cabins built" She was going to explain the strengths of each of the family when Sister Fowler burst into the room.

"Who are all these people in our yards and fields? It looks like we have been invaded by a caravan of Gypsies." She walked straight to Sister Carey and pointed her finger at her. "My husband and I made it very clear we weren't sharing this house with any more than one family. There isn't room for all of us as it is."

"Brother Hyrum sent the Draper wagons to us. They have just come in from Log Creek. They have their own supplies and can care for themselves. We just need to share our well with them. This is Phebe Palmer. She is William Draper's sister. We were just getting to know each other. As you well know, we have been directed by the Prophet to share what ever we have." Sister Carey tried to ease the tension.

"Well, we'll just see about that. I am going to talk to Brother Fowler about this. Hyrum Smith can't dump a big family on us, even if he is the Prophet's brother." She turned without speaking to Phebe and left the room.

"I'm sorry. It must seem like a terrible imposition to her but we really have no alternative. The brethren seem to have their hands full trying to find a little space for everyone. I'll help get our group organized so we will be as little trouble as possible." Phebe thanked Sister Carey for the tea and started to leave.

"This house was all mine before it was part hers. The properties were allotted to us when we came to settle here. You are welcome for as long as you need to stay. As soon as you get settled come back in and finish telling me about your family." She walked with Phebe to the door and smiled at the children playing in the yard. "Come here children. I have some cookies just waiting for some hungry cookie eaters." She took the plate of cookies from the table and met the children on the porch.

The men had met Brother Carey and were moving the wagons and animals at his direction. The four wagons and a buggy were soon located in the South pasture with the well between them and the house. An adjacent field of corn stubble left from the fall harvest was a good location for the animals. The team of oxen William had purchased in Log Creek along with the horses, cows, and sheep were herded into the corn field. Brother Fowler rode up on his stallion and surveyed the activities. He dismounted and called to Brother Carey, "What is going on here?"

"These are the Draper and Brown families. Brother Hyrum has sent them here to share our homestead. The Prophet has called them in from Log Creek for their safety. Brother Draper was the Presiding Elder there." He motioned to William who stepped forward to shake Brother Fowler's hand.

"This sharing has gone far enough. My wife and I are leaving. If they want to stay they can buy out my part of the homestead. If they can't, then I expect you to buy me out. We'll be leaving in the morning and I expect my money by then." He turned and stocked into the house.

The men conferred with Brother Carey. The Saints had been directed not to sell the land they had been allotted but to share what they had until further allotments could be determined. To keep peace and avoid further conflict with Brother

Fowler, they determined a fair price for the pasture, corn field and the adjoining few acres to the south. It was obvious that they would have to build another two or three cabins before winter. Brother Carey assured them there were plenty of logs available to use for more building and to burn for heat in the winter. He pointed to a large pile of logs that were stacked in back of the house. "With your help, we can bring more timber in from the back acreage and start on the new buildings. I was hoping to get another house built before winter my self. Now I will have lots of help. Brother Fowler wasn't one to lend a hand to much work. By insisting on payment for the land he will lose his good standing in the Church."

As promised, the Fowlers left the next morning with bag and baggage, signing a quick claim deed to the property over to William, Zemira and Ebenezer. They indicated they were not only leaving Far West, but also the Church. Phebe had offered to pay her share also but the men refused to accept it. Now, with the Careys, they sat down for a planning meeting. Zemira, William and William George would start the cabins while Ebenezer and Brother Carey took a wagon pulled by the oxen to bring down more timber.

Phebe expressed her concern for William's health and arranged with the Careys for he and Bett and the baby to stay in the room the Fowlers had used. The rest of them could camp out until the cabins were built.

Brother Hyrum came by and they reviewed their plans with him. "The twenty souls in our household will be just fine. Don't you worry about us and tell the Prophet and Bishop Partridge we are here to help if he needs us." Brother Carey smiled as he surveyed the group. He and his wife had not been able to have children and he felt like he had just been blessed with a big family.

Sister Carey insisted that they do the cooking in the house and they set up planks on saw horses for tables on the porch to eat their meals. The women were soon making quilts and sharing recipes as they cooked and cleaned and sewed together. Ann Brown, with her daughter Harriet at her side learning the weaving skills, was busy at her loom. Agnes was spinning thread at a record rate on her spinning wheel. Supplies of bedding and clothes for the coming winter had become a necessity because of the limited space they had for extra supplies as they left Kirtland in April.

Phebe had the children spend some time each morning reviewing their reading and arithmetic but the rest of the day they were busy helping the men with the building. The fourteen-year-olds, Henry Draper and Gurnsey Brown, could pound nails as fast as the men. Lydia, Juliana and even little Rhoda picked up nails and ran errands for the builders. The little boys, Norman Brown, Moses Draper and Zemira Palmer had the responsibility of straightening nails and picking up wood scraps for the wood pile. It reminded Phebe of her happy childhood days when the Uncles were building the house for them when they moved from New York to Canada.

Ann's and Bett's babies were napping on a quilt on the floor. Sister Carey looked down at the little ones, "It is so wonderful to have babies in the house. Brother Carey and I have longed for a time when we would have a family to care for and here we are with a house full. The Lord seems to answer our prayers in very unexpected ways." Baby John wakened and before he could cry for attention she had picked him up and was rocking him back to sleep.

Phebe was at the stove stirring the stew for supper. "Are there any apple orchards around here? I'd love to get some apples for some fresh apple pie. We could make some applesauce and even dry some for winter. We had acres of apple orchards in Canada. The autumn weather always seems to make me homesick for apples."

Sister Carey looked up at Phebe, "I think there are some apple trees up at Di-Ahman. Did you see any out by Haun's Mill when you came in?"

"I didn't notice any but I think I'll walk up by the store and ask around. Surely someone will know where to get some apples." She pulled the stew pot to the back of the stove and slipped off her apron. "Harriet, do you want to come with me? You have been at that loom all afternoon."

"I would love to, Sister Palmer. May I go, mother?"

Ann shooed her away from the loom taking her place on the stool and picking up the threads and shuttles so as not to lose the pattern. "You may go. You have picked up the art of weaving so quickly. You are a true weaver. It runs in our blood you know. That is why my maiden name is 'Weaver'. My ancestors for several generations back have been weavers." The shuttle flew under her adept fingers.

Phebe and Harriet put their bonnets on and walked out into the yard. The noise from the saws and hammers was ringing through the air. Brother Carey and Ebenezer were just pulling in with a load of timber. The team of Oxen were plodding along as if the load of heavy logs they pulled were as light as a load of straw.

"William was so fortunate to find those oxen. It was as if he knew how much we would need them when we got here." Phebe waved at the men and kept pace with Harriet as they walked toward town.

There was still a stream of wagons pulling into town. The population was now more than 5000 people. The city had been laid out by the prophet as he had the other cities, including a temple site. Phebe was glad they had arrived when they did and been assigned to live with the Careys. Ahead of them, at the side of the road, they could hear a small band playing. A handsome young man with dark hair and a mustache was playing the violin. He looked at the ladies and winked at Harriet. She looked away as the color rose in her cheeks. She was twelve-years-old and had never been winked at before. Not like that.

Oliver Straton grinned and continued playing with his

brothers and father. He sang the chorus of "Nellie Brown", not knowing that the pretty young lady he had just winked at was Harriet Brown. As she turned the corner she heard the rich baritone voice sing, "She's a young thing and cannot leave her mother."

Harriet took Phebe's arm as they walked into the General Store. Phebe bought some buttons for the sewing projects and inquired about the apples. The only apples available were in the south end of the county. She would have to ask Brother Carey if it was safe to go that far south. The Missourians had made it clear that the Mormons were to stay together in the northern part of the state. Phebe wasn't sure where the boundaries were. If she was still in Canada she would not be concerned about going alone even in to Indian territory, but the unreasonable hatred for the Mormons in Missouri was something she hadn't yet come to understand.

CHAPTER TWENTY-THREE

The three cabins had been built in record time. The families were settled in and William had set up a shoe shop in town. Phebe's cabin was built with a large room for school. She soon had several students. They paid a small tuition, giving her some income. She limited the school day to three hours because the children were needed at home. On Fridays they would bring their lunch and spend an extra hour with music or drama. William George helped her with the drama and Oliver Straton, the winking violinist, came to give music lessons.

Ebenezer was scouting the county for more livestock. He and Brother Carey would leave early in the morning and usually come home later in the day with another milk cow or bull calf. Sometimes they would take some to sell. There was plenty of meat and milk for the four families and the Careys shared the crops they had harvested with their new extended family.

Zemira and the older boys became a building crew helping to build cabins for new saints. They were still arriving in the late fall months. As hard as they worked they could not keep ahead of the demand. Families were still doubling up in cabins as the weather turned cold and they needed shelter.

The sun was shining bright one October afternoon and Phebe decided she would take her children for a ride south of Far West to find some apples. William George was working on the building crew so she harnessed her favorite horse to the buggy and took Lydia, Zemira and little Rhoda with her. She called to Ann and Bett as she left, "We are going for a little ride to find some apples."

The children were sitting on a quilt they had brought in case the afternoon turned cool and Phebe had packed a lunch for them. Soon they were singing and the horse was trotting along at an even gate. They followed a road south for a few miles and then it turned East. Phebe could see what she thought was an orchard across the valley. She flipped the reins on the horse and it trotted faster. Her mouth was already watering, just thinking about apples.

As they neared the clump of trees she could see they were just that, a clump of trees. She stopped the horse and decided this would be a good stop for the picnic. The children jumped down from the wagon and spread the quilt under a tree in the shade. Phebe led the horse into the clump of trees and tethered it to an old oak. They sat on the quilt and ate the sandwiches and cookies from the lunch box.

The spot they had chosen was back, away from the road. They were folding up the quilt and putting the lunch box in the buggy when they heard riders coming from the east. The heavy pounding of the horses hoofs on the dry dirt road sent warning signals to Phebe and the children that there were several riders and they were moving fast in their direction. Almost daily reports had circulated of small bands of marauding mobocrats, harassing and even torturing Mormons.

Phebe was terrified. How foolish she had been to come out here alone and bring her children. "Lets get farther back into the woods. Maybe they will go on by and won't see us." She put the quilt and lunch box in the buggy, untied the horse and led it into the dark recesses of the clump of trees. The children clung to her as she put her finger to her lips to warn them to stay quiet.

The men reined their horses in and dismounted on the grass next to the trees. "We'll give our horses a rest here and watch for some of them Damn Mormons to come by. They seem to be comin' from every direction. That Doniphan must be a Mormon lover to tell 'em they could have all of Caldwell County." A dark, surly looking man took a drink from his canteen and wiped the moisture from his shaggy moustache.

"Ain't none of 'em goin' to settle in Missouri if we can help it. If we kill off 'nouf of 'em they won't be able ta keep having more. They's just an ignorant lot. Bet most of 'em can't even make their mark let alone read."

Phebe put her hands over Lydias ears to keep her from hearing the vulgar bragging of the men about what they had done and would do to the Mormon women. They were crouching in back of the buggy. Phebe leaned her head on the buggy wheel and prayed that the men would go on and not find them in the woods. A feeling of peace came over her and she knew the Lord would protect her and her children. That faith that had directed her to Kirtland and on to Far West burned within her and she knew the He had important things for her to do. This was not her time. She whispered to the children, "Just stay quiet, we will be fine. The Lord will protect us." It was as if an invisible aura surrounded them that could not be penetrated by the evil of men on the road. They could no longer hear the wicked things they were saying.

The men soon mounted their horses, turned back to the East and rode away.

Phebe waited until she was sure they were out of sight. "Get in the buggy children." She untied the horse and led him through the trees to the west end of the protective foliage and on to the road. She climbed up on to the buggy seat and flipped the reins on the horses back. He responded with a quick trot. She did not look back. She thought of Lot's wife and wondered what she would look like as a pillar of salt.

The children were quiet all the way home. The realization of the danger she had exposed her children to haunted Phebe. As they neared the cabin, little Zemira broke the silence. "When you prayed I knew we would be safe. He gave his mother a hug and a big kiss on her cheek. You are such a good mother."

William George was waiting for them by the gate. "I have been so worried about you. Brother Carey said it is not safe for women to be out alone." He helped them out of the buggy and took the reins to lead the horse back to unharness and curry it.

Phebe walked with the children to her cabin and there on the porch were two large boxes full of apples. Ebenezer walked over from the Brown's cabin, "Brother Carey and I ran on to a farmer who had some apples for sale so we traded a calf for apples for the lot of us. We even have some extras to put in the cellar so we can have apples for the winter."

"Ebenezer, you are a dear. The Lord seems to keep guiding you to help us. How did you know I needed an apple so much I would risk my life and that of my children for it? The Lord has blessed me in so many ways, but I need Him to bless me with patience." And then she told him of the harrowing experience she had endured that afternoon and of the answer to her prayer.

"You are a fine woman, Phebe. You bring great strength to this family. I'm glad we found the apples. We weren't looking for them though. It just happened. It's a good thing you came home safe to us. We will all thank the Lord for that in our prayers tonight." He smiled and turned back to his cabin.

Phebe looked after him thinking what a kind man he was. She was sure the Lord had guided he and Ann to them.

A few days later word reached Far West from some of the surrounding areas of house burnings, property destruction and murders. The Prophet formed a company of seventy-five men to scout the situation. Brother Carey volunteered to go from their group because he had lived there longer and knew the area. At Crooked River they encountered a mob and a conflict ensued. Apostle David Patten, Simeon Carter, and Patterson O'Banion were killed and several others were wounded. A war of extermination had been declared again against the Mormons and gloom settled over Far West. They placed men on twenty-four hour watch and plans were set in motion to defend the town.

The last of October, a group large enough to be an army was seen approaching from the south. All the men, young and old, were assembled and marched to the south boundary of the town. The army from the south reached a scattering of timber where they halted and had scouts climb the trees to assess the strength of the Mormon force. Seeing the numbers of the Mormon force, they sent out a detachment with a flag of truce. Col. George M. Hinkle and three other men rode out to meet them as the people of Far West watched with concern. Col. Hinkle returned to Far West Reporting that Governor Boggs had sent out the army to investigate and settle any difficulties with the Mormons and non-Mormons. They requested that Joseph Smith and other leaders of the church consult with them to try to settle the problems.

The Prophet, his brother, Hyrum, and other leaders saw this as a reasonable request and marched out to the enemy camp. As they innocently walked into the encampment, they were declared to be prisoners of war. A contingency was sent back to report that the Church leaders would be kept in camp overnight for further discussions but would be sent home at eight-o-clock the next morning. They were encouraged to keep a night watch for there were ungovernable characters at large who might stir up trouble.

The following morning it was reported that a treaty had been signed by Joseph Smith and the Army officers. The terms of the treaty directed the Saints to lay down their arms, and deed their property to the State to pay for the expenses of the Army. The Army was directed to carry out the terms of the treaty immediately.

William, Ebenezer and Zemira were on the south line as the Army approached the city. They watched as the Army formed a square. Col. Hinkle led them into the Square and it was then that the men realized he had betrayed them.

"Lay down your arms, including guns, knives, whips or any other weapon." the general of the Army barked out to them. Some of the soldiers roughly searched the men taking even their pocket knives, while the other soldiers formed another square into which the unarmed men were marched, leaving their weapons behind.

They were allowed to relax for a time and men sat in small groups by friends but were not allowed to talk. Zemira caught William's eye and the Brother's communicated to each other that they were in this together and would protect each other to the end. They nodded to Ebenezer and he moved next to them.

General Clark strutted into the square, "Arise to your feet for further orders." He was letting them know that he was in command. "You may return to your families but must remain in town. At night you are to stay in your houses or be shot." The soldiers aimed their guns at the men as they dispersed to their homes.

Phebe was with Sister Carey trying to comfort her. The early detachment of men that Brother Carey had gone with had not returned. It was evident that they were in a state of war and that first group was already imprisoned, or worse.

When the men returned to the cabins, William directed them to get their families and meet at the Carey House. "There is safety in numbers so I recommend that we all stay together here with Sister Carey. We men will take turns at the windows and you women make the children as comfortable as possible. If need be, hide them in the cellar. We will use the firewood for clubs and the kitchen knives for protection if it comes to that. Each of you take a kitchen knife with you. These men are savages and have no value for human life."

The women hurried to their cabins for extra bedding and night clothes. Phebe picked up her family Bible and it fell open, revealing the blessing paper. Her eyes fell to the line that said, "The destroyer shall have no power to harm thee." She remembered the dear voice of Father Smith as he gave her this promise. This blessing was a format of her life and she had faith that it would be fulfilled.

Her heart ached for the Smith family. The Prophet's parents, Emma and the families of the other leaders who had gone willingly to settle affairs, only to be betrayed. She wondered how one could live with that kind of betrayal on their conscience. She put the Bible, with the blessing still folded inside, under her arm and carried as much bedding as she could. William George was helping the children with their nightclothes and getting the knives from the kitchen as Uncle William had directed.

The younger children finally slept but no one else in the cabin could rest. They could hear guns firing, dogs yelping, hogs squealing and men howling like demons and cursing. When the light of morning came they could see hogs, dogs and sheep lying dead in the streets. They had been shot by ruffians who amused themselves by pretending they were Mormons running away on all fours. Zemira's cabin was ransacked with clothes and bedding strewn about. The spinning wheel was broken beyond repair.

Agnes picked up a piece of the wheel that had been thrown out in the yard. She stared at it in unbelief and fainted. Zemira carried her into the log house and put her on a bed. Bett was at her side with some smelling salts and Phebe ran to the well for some fresh water. As she looked into the well she was appalled to see the head of a calf floating on the blood red water. "How could they?" she cried to herself and went back to the house with an empty bucket.

Agnes was soon revived and lay white and motionless on the bed. Bett motioned for Phebe and Zemira to follow her outside. "Agnes is pregnant. She didn't want to tell you, Zemira, until she was sure but we decided yesterday it was quite certain. Stay by her and let her tell you. She has wanted a baby for so long." Zemira returned to the house and Phebe and Bett surveyed the mess outside.

"Lets get everyone busy cleaning up. If we have work to do it will take our minds off the terrible night we have had. Don't let any of the children go to the well. One of the men will have to clean that up." As usual, Phebe was organizing the family to move on with life.

A soldier came to each door with quick claim deeds to be

signed to all the properties so the Prophet could be released. All the deeds were signed but the Prophet and Hyrum were not released. Four of the prisoners were released to bring back Brother Carey whose head had been bashed in by a mobster.

The men helped him to the log cabin and knocked on the door. William answered and caught Brother Carey as he fell to the floor. His head, an ugly mass from the bludgeoning was wrapped with a makeshift bandage to stop the flow of blood. They took him to his bed and Phebe called for Bett. Ann and Ebenezer tried to comfort Sister Carey as she saw her husband so mutilated.

Bett and Phebe nursed him through the night and the men gave him a blessing. William could not promise he would live, as it was revealed to him that the Lord was calling him home. He dedicated him to the Lord and he passed away that night. The "family" rallied to Sister Carey, giving her love and support. During this short time they had become so close. The men dug a grave in the back yard that morning and after a short service buried Brother Carey and disguised the grave so it would not be disturbed by ruffians who may do despicable things.

Later that day, Joseph and Hyrum were returned to Far West in a roughly constructed cart with a ceiling and bars on the sides resembling a cage that might hold a strange animal for a side show. They had been sentenced by court marshal to be shot the next morning at eight o'clock. It was said they were brought to say good- by to their families, but it was also to warn the saints to fear and obey the demands of the Missouri Army.

The saints lined the streets and sobbed as they saw this man of God treated with such indignity. Phebe heard him say to his mother as she clung to his hand, "All will be well. God will protect us."

Emma stared at him in disbelief as he bravely gave her directions, "Take care of the children. I will be fine. I love you."

A gloom settled over the Saints in Far West and they slowly returned to their homes. Some to ponder the reason for this turn of events and some to reject the church and deny the testimony of its truthfulness. Others, strengthened by the trial they had endured and atrocities they had suffered.

Again, William called the family together. "We must be strong and give strength to our neighbors. The Prophet has taught us well and we have much more to learn. He will be in our midst again. In the meantime, we will try to live in our usual manner. We will care for each other and use our individual talents to keep our family together." They all knelt in prayer. They would all stay in the log cabin until it was safe to leave.

William jumped from the horse, ran to the log house and threw open the door, "General Doniphan has saved the Prophet. He resisted the order for the execution."

An audible sigh of relief spread through the room and they were soon hugging each other.

"The bad news is that they are still held in the Liberty jail in Clay County." The celebrating stopped as they realized the danger Mormons would be in in Clay County where there was so much hatred for the saints. "General Clark has called all the men in town to a meeting. I have to go back, but I wanted to give you the good news." He turned and left.

The men were gathered in front of the general store by the large public square. There was much speculation about what the General would have to say. He rode up on a large stallion and dismounted handing the reins to an aide who accompanied him. Standing on the porch of the store he looked down over the group of Mormon men with obvious disdain. "You have been dealt with leniently, in view of the extermination order previously made, but final provisions of the treaty has still to be carried out. You are to leave the State of Missouri by planting time next spring. You are advised, as I discharge you, to go back and provide for your families and make speedy preparations to leave the state and scatter yourselves like other people, and never gather again in companies under presidents, prophets, bishops, or apostles to govern you. If you do, you will bring down the wrath of a just people upon you as you have already done. You are now dismissed to carry out these measures." He strutted off the porch and mounted his horse, kicking the horse in the flanks and leaving the group of saints in a cloud of dust.

They had little recourse and they each turned away from the group and walked toward home. Zemira and Ebenezer were with William. They now felt free to survey the damage and losses from the siege of the city by the mobsters. The cattle and livestock was scattered and it was unclear as to how much of it had been slaughtered. William walked out toward the deserted Army camp. There he found the heads of his oxen on the road. He had only his riding horse and a cow to leave the state. Mrs. Carey still had a team of horses, Phebe's team was gone but Ebenezer and Zemira still had their teams of horses. Some of the sheep and cattle had been slaughtered or disappeared but there was some left and the men rounded them up and returned them to the Carey farm.

The three men returned to the house to report on the General's directive and the assessment of the livestock and their condition. Phebe's heart sank as she realized they had to move again and that her horses were gone, giving her no way of retreat without relying on her brothers again. Was there no end to this harassment?

Ebenezer stood and moved to the back of his chair for support. "The Lord will direct our ways until the Prophet can return to us. The apostates have left the area and we still have Brigham Young and the other apostles to help us. If we combine the resources we have, we can prepare and leave this hateful state by spring. I am willing to share what ever I have as I am sure each of you are. We will need four teams of horses which we have and we also have until spring to leave. Sister Carey and Phebe, this includes you and we will help you get ready to leave."

William responded, "Thank you, Ebenezer. Most of the cattle and livestock belongs to you and if we use them, we will find a way to repay you."

"Thanks to both of you. Sister Carey and I appreciate your help. We will help with the preparation every way we can." Phebe looked at Sister Carey for confirmation and then to her children. They nodded in agreement.

Little Rhoda clung to her mother's skirt, "Can we leave soon so those mean men won't come back and hurt us?" Her mother gathered her into her arms to comfort and reassure her.

"We can't leave until spring, dear. The men won't come back now because they know we are going to leave. We'll move back into our cabins and try to get our lives back to normal. We have to prepare for winter and Christmas." The reference to Christmas seemed to cheer all of the younger children and give them something fun to look forward to.

William George was amazed at how his mother had the ability to put people at ease and give them something good to work for. He stood and put his arm around his mother's shoulders. "We Palmers will pull our weight."

A knock on the door diverted their attention. Ann Brown opened the door to a very anxious Oliver Straton, "Is everyone here alright?" His eyes scanned the room, resting on Harriet. He breathed a sigh of relief. "Rumors are flying all over town about how the young girls have been treated by the mobsters. I have been going to some of my friend's homes to see if they need help." It was obvious that he was trying to cover up his special concern for Harriet.

William George saved the awkward situation, "What a good friend. We are all fine. We lost some live stock and Uncle

Zemira's house was trashed but we came through the siege without any personal injury. Of course, we lost Brother Carey. How is your family?"

"We are all fine. They broke some of our instruments but my father is good at repairing them. We'll be playing together soon." Oliver smiled at the family, "I'm glad you are all well. I heard about Brother Carey. I'm sorry Sister Carey, I loved that man. He was always so kind to me."

Sister Carey dabbed at her eyes, "Thank you Oliver. He loved to hear you play and sing. I hope you will come over often and play for us. It will help me remember the good times with him."

"I'll do that as soon as Father gets my fiddle repaired. I'll see you all soon. He glanced at Harriet and left."

Ann looked at her daughter and then at Ebenezer. They realized their daughter was growing up. In spite of the horrors of the last forty-eight hours they found joy in looking at their children and feeling their love for them. "Family; this is what it's all about." thought Ann. She moved to Ebenezer's side and he put his arm around her.

Zemira was glad the tension had cleared, "Agnes and I have good news. We are going to have a baby in the summer. Finally, we are going to have a family too." He looked at Agnes and she beamed back at him. She was still a bit pale but Bett's remedies were helping and having things back to normal would help considerably.

The family meeting ended and each family went to assess the condition of their cabins. Bett and William had stayed with Sister Carey and they continued to do so. Baby Lathrop spent most of his time on Sister Carey's lap and filled the empty arms of the sweet lady who had lost the love of her life.

Phebe and her children found that the mobsters had gone through their cabin but had only scattered some of the books and personal belongings. They soon had it straightened up when Phebe remembered Grandma Draper's cake plate. She opened up the trunk and there it was. Still protected by the quilt she had wrapped it in. She sat down and held it in both hands. As the sun caught the crystal it was like a kaleidoscope changing patterns and reminding her of scenes from the past: The old Indian, Okinihah, that took them to Canada; Grandpa and Grandma Draper; Father William walking with her in the orchard when Eliza died; Mother Lydia helping the girls make quilts; George, dancing with her in her red dress; Master John at the Christmas party, Lovina, her beautiful Lovina in her wedding dress; Eliza, her fairy child, wrapped in her white petty coat in the buggy; The Palmer farm with the orchards in blossom; Brother Brigham baptizing and confirming her; the day she met the Prophet and Emma; Sitting in the Kirtland Temple and witnessing angels; Saying good-by to the tea set as it shone on the Kirtland Temple; Driving the wagon through bogs of mud as the rain poured down on them.

"Mother, are you alright?" Lydia Elizabeth brought Phebe back to the present.

"I'm fine, darling. Just thinking about all the special things that this plate of Grandma Draper reminds me of. I must tell you all about them sometime." She packed the plate back in the trunk and closed the lid. It was time to get on with the future. With her cabin in order she went next door to help Agnes.

William went back to his shoemaking and Phebe started to hold school again. Zemira and his carpenter crew were busy with repairs and helping the saints repair wagons as they prepared to leave in the Spring. Ebenezer took his son, Gurnsey, with him to buy and sell livestock. The women spent their spare time making clothes and quilts for the baby Agnes was expecting.

By the end of March the exodus had begun. Brigham Young had helped facilitate the moves. Families were leaving daily to often unknown destinations. Most of them were going to Illinois because the political climate there was more conducive to peaceful living. The Prophet and Hyrum were still in the Liberty jail, surviving under deplorable conditions. In their absence, the organization of the Church continued under the Quorum and the Bishopric.

Letters to Emma and the saints from the Prophet occasionally found their way to Far West and on those occasions new hope came to the beleaguered members. Joseph continued to receive revelations for the church while he was imprisoned. So in spite of the extermination order the faithful saints knew the Lord was still guiding the church. As they dispersed to unknown locations they did so knowing that in the future they would be together again as they had in the past.

William was able to purchase another team of oxen. Sister Carey's team of horses and a team he bought on time from Ebenezer for Phebe provided he and the two widows with animals to pull their wagons to Illinois. Zemira and Ebenezer had teams to pull their wagons and their caravan, once again with wagons packed and livestock herded along with them, headed to Illinois.

It was the later part of March of 1839 when they crossed the Mississippi and stopped at the little town of Atlas. Bett Draper's brother, Nathan Staker, lived in Atlas and encouraged William and Bett to stay with them for awhile. Phebe and Zemira stayed with them also but Sister Carey followed a group of saints going north, hoping to find some of her relatives. Ebenezer and Ann headed south to find a place to settle. The Drapers and Palmers promised to follow after they had rested for a few weeks.

Agnes was not well. The traveling had been wearing on her. Bett thought it best that she be given an opportunity to rest from the travel. The Stakers welcomed them and the group was happy to be out of Missouri and with peaceful people. There were stores in Atlas where they could shop for food and supplies that had not been available to them in Missouri.

Though they were still camping in their wagons, they were

resting. The past year, spent mostly on the move, had prepared the adults and children alike to make the best of living in wagons and tents. The women could cook good meals over campfires and wash their clothes in river or well water available to them. Local fruit and vegetables were purchased from farmers and campsites were chosen where there was plenty of grass for the livestock to eat.

Phebe shook the quilts in the fresh air and refolded them to put them in her wagon. The extra quilts they had made at Sister Carey's had replaced some that had worn thin on the trip from Kirtland. She hoped Sister Carey would find her relatives to the north. It was hard to say good-by to the dear woman who had taken them into her home and her heart. Bett's baby, Lathrop, still cried for her. She missed Ann and Ebenezer also. They had gone through so much together and they were like family.

"Lydia, get Zemira and Rhoda. We are going to walk to the store and buy you a treat." William George was off with the older boys getting acquainted with the town. The children ran to her in anticipation. A new chapter in their life had begun.

CHAPTER TWENTY-FOUR

The stay at Atlas extended beyond a few weeks. The men found work and the women were satisfied to live in the camp. Agnes was having trouble with her pregnancy. Bett was concerned about her and encouraged the family to stay in Atlas until the baby was born.

The Straton family came to Atlas looking for other saints from Far West. William George saw Oliver on the street, "Hello, friend. Did you get your violin repaired?"

"Yes, and we are going to play for a dance tonight. Are the Brown's here too?"

"No, they went south. Uncle William is leaving tomorrow to find them. We haven't decided just where we are going to settle yet. I've been picking up odd jobs here and there, mostly when the boats dock and need to be unloaded. It would be fun to travel that river. I've been thinking about signing on a boat but I haven't been brave enough to talk to my mother about it." William George waited for a response from Oliver.

"I've been thinking about the same thing. How about if we get some kind of act together and travel the river as performers. We can both sing and with your natural acting ability and my violin we could wow 'em." Oliver took William by the arm and they walked down the street making plans as they went. By the time they arrived at the Draper camp they had both committed themselves to the idea and had all the arguments in place for any objections Phebe might present.

Phebe was hesitant but listened to the young men with their enthusiastic plans almost convincing her. She knew that William George was old enough to start making plans of his own. He had been so good to help support her through this last year. How could she deny him the freedom to find some adventure away from the responsibilities of the family. Maybe after one trip down the river and back they would both be satisfied to stay with their families. It wasn't really like going to sea. She remembered the stories Elijah had told them and he had been much younger, traveling the open seas to foreign countries.

"Well, lets work on a plan and see if it is feasible. Do you know a ship's captain that will let you travel as performers? How long will it take to get something prepared to present to a ship owner? You have to be prepared to end up as deck hands and indentured crew men if it doesn't pay off." Phebe tried to present some of the problems that would arise without being negative about the whole idea.

"Lets ask around, Oliver, and see what we can find out. In the meantime we can get an act together and present it to some of the locals. Maybe a ship's Captain will see it and ask us to take it on the river." William George was already putting ideas together and the boys turned to walk back to town.

"Thanks for the help, Mother." He looked back and then took an extra skip to catch up with Oliver.

Phebe wondered what William would think of the idea. She would wait until he returned from his trip to find the Browns and discuss it with him then. She knew he was anxious to pay Ebenezer back for the team he had loaned them to pull her wagon. The boys may find themselves in pretty bad company on a river boat. They both had expressed strong convictions about the church. Maybe they could be missionaries or at least help some of the converts that were coming from England to New Orleans and up the Mississippi. Now there was not a center of the Church to come to, new converts would need all the help they could get from any source.

"Mother, Aunt Bett said to come to the Stakers as fast as you can. Aunt Agnes is very sick." Lydia Elizabeth was out of breath. She had run all the way.

Phebe grabbed her bonnet and hurried back with Lydia. Bett met her at the door. "It doesn't look good for her. The

baby is almost full term but she has started to swell and that is
a bad sign. She is very hot and I can't seem to cool her down.
Zemira is with her now, but she is barely conscious." The two
women walked to the room the Stakers had turned over to
Agnes and Zemira.

Zemira looked at his older sister with eyes pleading for her
to help his dear, Agnes. A moan came from the bed as Agnes's
body tried to extricate itself from the invader that was challenging her very life. The contractions followed rapidly and
Bett sent Phebe scurrying for towels and hot water. Zemira
reluctantly let go of his wife's hand and walked out side. He
was just in the way.

A baby boy was born later that day. Zemira named him
Edward Joseph Draper and he died that evening followed by
his mother, Agnes.

Sorrow followed. Agnes had endeared herself to all the
family including all of the children that she often cared for as
she would her own. William postponed his trip south.

Phebe seemed to be the only one that could comfort her
brother Zemira. Perhaps because he realized she had lost a
child and a husband. They sat together on a log in the back
yard. Phebe held his hand and chose not to speak but just comfort him with her presence. The tears rolled down his cheeks.
The despair he felt was all consuming. William joined them on
the log. Once again the sister and brothers were facing the trials of life together with compassion for each other.

After the funeral and burial of Agnes and her baby son,
William headed south to find his friend, Ebenezer, and pay him
for the team of horses he had loaned to them.

A few miles south he found the Browns settled in the small
town of Pleasantville. It was in a beautiful valley carved out by
the Mississippi River. The ground was fertile and it was easy
for Ebenezer to convince William to join him there. William
found a log cabin and three acres of land that he was able to
rent. He also found a small house for Phebe to rent close to the

Brown's. Zemira would be welcome in either home.

The Browns were shocked at the news of the death of Agnes and her baby. Ann remembered the hours they had spent together spinning and weaving. Agnes always had expressed her desire to have a child and Ann had to feel that the Lord had answered her prayers and they would be together in Heaven. One had to wonder if things would have been different if Agnes had not had to suffer the siege of Far West and the difficult trip to Illinois.

William hurried back to Atlas to share his plans for the family to move to Pleasantville and get settled while the weather was still good. His description was so glowing that the family caught his enthusiasm for the move and were, in fact, anxious to get settled.

Once again they packed their wagons and headed south for what they hoped would be a permanent home. William George helped his mother pack the wagon and assured her he would help her get settled before considering going on the River. He and Oliver had come up with a show about traveling on the river with some original songs and William George's impersonations of various kinds of travelers. Oliver offered his assistance in helping the Palmers move to Pleasantville. He endured the teasing that he had ulterior motives having to do with a little Brown girl. It was all in good fun and they were glad to have all the help they could get.

By the end of August the families were settled and William George and Oliver were off to the river to find their fortune, with promises that they would return in the fall.

Phebe was so happy in Pleasantville. It was just what the name implied. The neighbors were kind and welcomed them to the village. A small village school was in need of a teacher and she was soon employed as the primary teacher. Rhoda was now old enough to go to the primary school and Lydia and Zemira could once again attend a regular school. The house she was renting had a garden planted in the back and, to her delight, an apple tree.

William had soon established himself as a shoemaker and quickly had a large cliental. Zemira's talents as a carpenter were also recognized and once again the Drapers and Palmers were productive members of the village, as they had been where ever they had lived.

There were enough members for them to hold meetings in each other's homes. They were able to study the Bible, Book of Mormon, and the revelations that had been received by the Prophet Joseph. The men were still able to exercise their priesthood. They were very careful, however, not to encourage neighbors to join them. The experiences in Missouri still lay heavy on their minds.

Ann, Bett and Phebe worked together on sewing projects and maintained the "family" as a unit. Ebenezer was industrious, enlarging his herd of cattle and was fairly well off, compared to the other residents of the village.

Oliver and William George, as promised, returned in the fall with graphic stories of their experiences on the river. The Ship's Captain had negotiated with them to return to his ship when the season started again in the spring. In the meantime they would spend their time entertaining in the local communities up and down the Illinois side of the river.

Phebe took her blessing from the family Bible and reread it. The Lord had filled the promises except for the part about a man of God who would marry her and help her care for her children. Perhaps he had decided she didn't need a husband when she had such good brothers and their friend, Ebenezer.

News reached Pleasantville that Joseph and Hyrum Smith had escaped from Liberty Jail. They had started immediately to look for a location where they could once again establish headquarters for the Church. By the Fall of 1839 they had settled on a swampy area about fifty miles up river from Quincy, Illinois called Commerce. Word went out to the saints to come to a conference.

William was packing his bag and Bett was packing him a lunch. Henry had his father's horse curried and saddled waiting for him. Phebe ran in to say good-bye. She gave William a big hug, "I wish I could go with you. It will be wonderful to see the Smiths again and so many of our other friends. Give them all our love. Maybe at the next conference we can make it a trip for the whole family."

William kissed Bett good-bye and waved to the family as he mounted his horse and headed north. As he traveled he encountered old friends heading for the same destination. Many of them were ill from camping on the river for the whole summer and were still trying to recover from the trials they had encountered in Missouri. He noted in his journal that night, "they looked more like ghosts that had neither flesh nor blood." Many of them had suffered from Malaria as they camped at Commerce on the Mississippi and many had been miraculously healed. William realized how blessed they had been to have the Stakers to go to and the help they had received at their hands.

Commerce was organized as a Stake of Zion and its name changed to Nauvoo. William was chosen as a high councillor in the stake but he soon resigned so he could continue his work in Pleasantville. Newel Knight organized Pleasantville into a branch of the Church and directed William to preach in the vicinity whenever invited by respectable citizens to do so. The Prophet Joseph promised him that when the branch reached one hundred people, he would come himself and organize it into a stake of Zion.

Shortly after William's arrival for the conference as he approached a gathering he saw a familiar figure going into the meeting. "Father, Father; is that you?" He shouldered his way through the crowd.

William Draper Sr. turned and saw his namesake just a few feet away.

"William, my boy." They embraced with tears of joy. They hadn't seen each other since William had left Canada after his last mission. Nor had they had any news from each other during the trying times in Missouri. There was so much to to catch up on but it would have to wait until after the meeting. For now it was enough to know that they were both alive.

Phebe looked up from her desk and thought she was seeing a vision. "Look who I found in Commerce." William grinned as his father rushed forward to his daughter and folded her in his arms.

"Father, is it really you?" The years that had separated them dropped away and it was as if she was again a young girl in her father's arms. "Where is Mother?"

"She and Lovina are in Sagamon. I came here directly from the conference to see you and Zemira and look into the possibility of moving the rest of the family here. We have been separated far too long. William has given me such glowing reports of Pleasantville, I think it is almost certain that they will want to come here.

Lovina and Henry have dear little children. I know you want to see your grandchildren. Little Billy and Ester Ann are the joy of our lives. Helping Lovina care for them has helped your mother through these last years of worry. We have some other good news for you. Asahel is married to a nice girl. Her name is Evaline Carter. They are living in Sagamon by Lovina and they are expecting a baby in a few months."

Phebe caught her breath. "What about the farm and Elijah? Has Asahel joined the church?"

Her father put his arm around her. "No, and he really doesn't want anything to do with the church. When he found that Lovina was leaving Canada with us it was evident that he couldn't let go of the last tie he had with the family. He and Lovina have a special bond. Elijah payed him half the value of the farm. Asahel has bought a fertile piece of land in Sagamon and is building a house for them there. He is happy, Phebe, and we just have to leave his feelings about the church up to him and the Lord."

Rhoda came into the class room and looked quizzically at the older man who looked so much like Uncle William. "Rhoda, this is your Grandpa Draper. He hasn't seen you since you were a baby." Phebe took her hand and introduced her to her grandfather. She let him hug her but reluctantly. Then she looked into his eyes, smiled her little wistful smile and gave him a big kiss. "Mamma said you were wonderful."

William and Zemira went with their father to help with the move to Pleasantville. It was only a matter of weeks until the family was reunited. Phebe's joy in having her parents and her daughter and family with her was immeasurable. She was disappointed that Asahel and his new wife had not come with them but they were not too far away.

Along with the happiness of the Draper family was the optimism of the saints in Pleasantville. They were once again able to have church gatherings and share the gospel with neighbors who wanted to know more about the Church. William became a prominent speaker in the area. Doors were opened to him by many prominent and respectable citizens. Many believed and were baptized.

The church grew rapidly in Pleasantville and soon exceeded the one-hundred members the Prophet had determined would qualify them to become a stake of Zion. True to his word, the Prophet sent his brother, Hyrum and Bishop George Miller, to establish a stake at Pleasantville. William Draper Jr. was called to be the Stake President and William Allred the bishop. They were instructed to obtain a piece of land and lay it off in town lots and build a meeting house. They were to provide comfort to the saints as they gathered in Pleasantville.

Phebe was anxious that her Parents and daughter meet the Browns who had become like family to them. Soon after their arrival a celebration was held. William George and Oliver provided the entertainment. Ebenezer contributed the beef to be roasted and the women cooked their favorite dishes. Ann Brown endeared herself to the family by making enough pies to feed them all. The crusts were so flaky that all the women were asking for her recipe.

When Oliver was taking a short break from his fiddle playing he called Ebenezer aside, "Brother Brown, I have a question to ask you. May I have your permission to court Harriet? I know she is considerably younger than I am but since the day I saw her in Far West I have known she would one day be my wife." having said all that with one breath he exhaled and waited for an answer.

Ebenezer hesitated, not wanting to accept the inevitable. His Harriet was so young but it had been obvious to he and Ann that her future would be with Oliver. "She will not be fourteen for another year. Until she is fourteen you may just see her in the company of others. When she is fourteen then we will discuss it again. You are a fine young man and I appreciate your honesty and candor. She could not make a better choice, but lets give her some time to grow up. It will be her decision at that time. I hope you can be patient."

"Thanks, Brother Brown. I can wait. One more season on the river and then I can think about settling down." He went back to his fiddle playing and grinned the rest of the evening. Trying not to look at Harriet too often.

Phebe sat with Lovina and Henry and watched as the children danced to the fiddle along with the grownups. William and Bett had formed a square with Ebenezer and Ann. William George was calling the dance and everyone was clapping them on. Phebe held her four-year-old granddaughter on her lap. Little Ester would clap to the music and soon wiggled off her grandmother's lap to dance to the music herself.

Phebe noticed that Zemira was sitting by himself and she would have encouraged him to dance with her but it was too soon. His grief for Agnes was still too painful. Father and Mother Draper walked over and sat by him, noticing his loneliness. He was their shy, sensitive son, always ready to help and never expecting any special privileges in return.

William George held his hand up for attention and as the group quieted he looked to his older sister, Lovina, "We are missing the best entertainment in town. We haven't heard my sister sing since her arrival."

Lovina blushed and shook her head in denial but William George would not be silenced, "She has the most beautiful voice I have ever heard and I insist that she come up here and sing for you." Phebe encouraged her with a little push and her husband beamed as she walked toward the entertainers. She was still beautiful with her dark curly hair and slim figure. She looked too young to be the mother of two children.

After conferring with Oliver about which songs he knew and what key they would use, her soprano voice, starting softly, was soon exceeding the volume of the accompaniment as she sang several songs and then invited the audience to join her. The music brought them together as one and Phebe beamed with pride at her two children performing for their friends and family.

The party was a great success. Phebe's prayers were lengthy that night. She had so much to be thankful for. The Lord had blessed her on every turn through the trials of the last few years and now to have her family together again was more than she had ever hoped for. She had just turned forty-two but she felt like a young girl. Could she really be a grandmother? Little Billy and Ester Ann were proof of that.

Mother Lydia came for a visit the next day, "Phebe, there has been so much going on since we arrived that we have not had time to catch up." She saw Grandmother Draper's plate on the mantel and smiled. "Looks like you are still taking care of the plate for Olive. Where is the tea set?"

"I donated it to the Kirtland Temple. They broke up fine china and added to the plaster to make it glisten. Oh, Mother, I wish you could have been there for the dedication. We saw angels and heard people speak in tongues. The spirit was so intense that we sat for hours not realizing the time. And the following day the Prophet's father, Patriarch Smith, gave me the most beautiful blessing." She picked up the family Bible and took the folded sheet from between the pages. "I want you to read it. It has sustained me through some of the most difficult times." She passed it to her mother who opened it up and read the blessing quietly to herself.

"What wonderful promises. I would say that you have a lot to look forward to."

Lydia scanned the sheet of paper again noting the date and the scribe as well as the name of the Patriarch. She carefully folded it and passed it back to Phebe who put it back in the Bible. "Who is this 'Man of God' promised to you? Is there something else you have to tell me?"

"Mother, that is a dilemma to me. I am not interested in anyone nor is anyone interested in me. I have decided that the Lord knows I have such a good family to care for me that I don't need a husband. The brothers and their wives have helped me every step of the way. Agnes and Bett tended my babies so I could teach and Bett is like a true sister to me. We have endured a lot together and are very close. I would give my life for her and she for me. We have you and father to thank for it all. You taught us how to be a family." Phebe walked to the mantle and replaced the Bible.

"You have been a binding influence on them as well, dear. Perhaps our love for one another was why we were so ready to accept the gospel. It is a gospel of love. As for the blessing, I have not known the Lord to change his mind before. You should prepare yourself for all of the promises." Lydia looked at her oldest daughter and remembered the concerns she had always felt for the challenges Phebe would have in her life. The blessing was another confirmation.

CHAPTER TWENTY-FIVE

Harriet and Oliver stood before William Draper Jr. to be married. Harriet wore the dress Phebe had helped Ann design. Ann had woven the fabric from beautiful silk thread from China, imported to Quincy Illinois. They had sewn tiny pearls into the material to form beautiful designs. The scalloped train was caught up with clusters of pearls.

Oliver was handsome in his cutaway coat and ruffled shirt. He looked at Harriet and still could not believe that since her fourteenth birthday in February she had declared her love for him and was not interested in anyone else. It was the twenty-second day of August and it was their wedding day. After lengthy advice from President Draper, William George handed Oliver the ring and Ebenezer put Harriet's hand in that of her adoring fiance.

Phebe sat by Ann and they dabbed their eyes as the young couple took their vows and were declared man and wife. Lydia Elizabeth and Juliana were the bridesmaids. Rhoda and Ester Ann scattered rose petals as the newlyweds walked back down the aisle to be congratulated by their guests. The little boys carried the train until Oliver picked up his new bride, placing her in the fringed surrey. They were soon on their way followed by shouts of advice from the crowd.

They made a brief appearance at the party that followed, dressed in their traveling clothes. They were going on their honeymoon down the river on a river boat.

The new church building was filled to capacity. "You Mormons sure know how to throw a wedding party. What a beautiful bride your daughter is. By the way, where is the hard punch?" Emanual Green, from the town council winked at Ebenezer.

"I'm afraid you won't find any here. We have a special

code of health we call the Word Of Wisdom. We don't drink any alcoholic drinks. There is some tasty fresh grape juice over here. Come have some of that." He led him to a table laden with fancy cakes and cookies. A large bowl of grape juice graced the center of the table. Emanual accepted a cup of the juice and picked up a fancy cake.

"You Mormons have made Pleasantville more pleasant than it was before. You are an ambitious lot and the town is thriving. I can't figure out why those people in Missouri would treat you so poorly. I think I can speak for the whole town council when I say how happy we are to have you here."

"We are happy to be here. You are good neighbors. I, for one, would like to put my roots down and stay here the rest of my life. I just bought another thirty acres and I'm looking for more cattle. My buyers want more beef to send up the river." Ebenezer was always putting feelers out to expand his herd.

"I'll let you know if I hear of any. Thanks for the juice. It was almost as good as the hard stuff." Mr. Green moved around the crowd shaking hands. It didn't hurt a politician to get to know new people. His assessment of their value to the town had been sincere. Most of the local businesses were about to close when Ebenezer Brown came to town and now they were a booming community with new businesses starting every day. They would have more than their share of taxes to send in on that new bond to improve the roads.

Phebe walked home with Lydia Elizabeth and Zemira. Rhoda had gone to stay at Lovina's with Ester Ann. Lydia Elizabeth was also fourteen but Phebe hoped she wouldn't be interested in marrying soon. She would like to send her east to school. She had a good mind and Phebe would like to see her have more education. She wondered if her old friends in Ohio, the Parks, would know of a school there. It would be much closer. Perhaps she would write to them. In the meantime, Lovina could teach her how to make hats.

Bett had given birth to a new baby boy in December with

no complications. It made for a Merry Christmas for everyone. They named him Albert Edward. The whole family enjoyed him to his delight. His grandparents spent every spare minute with him and by the time he was nine months old he seemed more like theirs than his own parents. They had missed being with the families when the last few babies were born.

Illinois passed a new law having to do with state sponsored schools. Since Phebe did not have a teaching certificate she was not able to continue teaching that September. As she pondered over her possibilities of ways to provide for her family she went to her father for advice.

"My girl, your mother told me about the promises you were given in your blessing. I think it is time for you to put your independent ways aside and have faith that the Lord will provide. You have some money saved and you know how to live frugally. We will not let you or your children starve or go without. Harvest your garden, preserving what you can for winter, and take good care of your milk cow. Just enjoy taking care of your family and spending time with your mother and daughters. I promise you, the Lord will provide." Father William put his arm around her, reassuring her that she didn't always need to do everything for herself.

"But I don't want to be dependent on others. I should be helping you, not you helping me." Once again she started to make her proverbial mental list of what she would need to make it through the winter.

"Don't deny us our blessings, Phebe. Put your trust in the Lord." He left her deep in thought.

School started and it was strange to send Zemira and Rhoda off without her. She kept herself busy working in the garden and cleaning house. She tried Ann's pie recipe and took one over to have her test it. Ann was at the loom weaving. "Will you teach me how to do that? I should be able to learn if Harriet could. Of course I don't have Weaver blood." Phebe sat by Ann and watched her work the shuttle.

Ann laughed, I am sure you could learn anything you set your mind to. I want to make a quilt for Harriet and Oliver. Can you come over tomorrow and help me put it on the frames?"

"I can. You and I will get all kinds of things done this winter, just to keep me busy." Phebe appreciated Ann's concern for her and she would enjoy spending more time with her. Ann was always smiling and finding things to laugh about. She could repeat something her little John had said in such a way that it sounded like the funniest thing a child had ever said. Ebenezer was gone a lot and often took little John with him leaving Ann alone when the children were in school.

Lydia Elizabeth and Lovina had set up a hat shop in Lovina's new house. They spent every free minute weaving straw, fashioning decorations from ribbon and taking orders from the ladies in town. Father and Mother Draper had convinced Zemira to live with them. They were always making the rounds to the families with something Mother Lydia had baked or to repair something Father had seen that needed fixing.

The winter snows came early that fall of 1841. By November the garden was frozen and covered with vines to protect it for the winter. Phebe had picked and stored the apples from her tree in sand pits in the back yard. She sat down and tried to write to her old friends in Ohio to inquire as to the possibilities of Lydia Elizabeth getting more education there. She walked to the store to post the letter. Hopefully they would still have the same address after all these years. Lydia knew nothing of her mother's plans for her and Phebe wanted it that way. If she heard from the Parks she could discuss it with her then.

Phebe walked to the Brown's. Ann hadn't been her old self lately. Phebe was not surprised to see Bett knocking at Ann's door. The two friends were greeted by Ebenezer and ushered into Ann's bedroom. She lay languid on the bed and tried to force a smile for Phebe and Bett. Bett gave Phebe some herbs and sent her to the kitchen to make Ann some tea. She added some wood to the stove and filled the teakettle with fresh water, putting the measured herbs to steep in the water as it heated.

"Phebe, I need your help." Ebenezer sat down in the chair by the table. "I have to be gone a lot with my cattle business and I can't leave Ann alone. She can't take care of herself, let alone the rest of the family. With Harriet married, I don't have anyone to cook the meals and take care of the house. I've been trying to keep it up myself but I'm no cook or housekeeper. You are Ann's best friend. Would you consider coming to live here and take care of us until Ann is better. I would be happy to pay you as much as you earned teaching. Maybe you could let your house go back to your landlord. That way you would-n't have to pay rent and would have a salary too. We have plenty of room here for you and your children."

"How can I refuse you when you have done so much for us? Let me talk to Ann and see how she would feel about it. It is hard for anyone to give up their kitchen to someone else, even if they are sick." Phebe poured some steaming tea into a cup and put it on a saucer. "I'll do all I can to help you Ebenezer." She carried the tea to the bedroom.

Bett gave her a knowing look as she turned away from Ann. Phebe held the tea to Ann's lips and she took a sip of the liquid pulling a face from the bitter taste of the herbs. "I know it doesn't taste very good but if you want to carry this baby you will need to have some of it every day." Bett encouraged her to take a few more sips.

Phebe fluffed her pillow and brought some warm, soapy water and washed her face and hands. "Ann, do you mind if I take your laundry home with me? I'm going to do my washing in the morning so I can do yours along with it. If the sun shines like it did today it will dry and I'll have it back by tomorrow afternoon."

"Oh, thank you, Phebe. I have been laying here worrying about it. Are you sure it won't be too much?" Ann looked at her with such gratitude that Phebe decided she might consider Ebenezer's solution to the problem. She gathered up the dirty clothes and stuffed them in a pillow case.

Bett took Ann's Little John home with her and told Ebenezer she would bring some supper back for them.

Phebe looked in on Ann. She was asleep so she walked out quietly and picked up the bulging case of dirty clothes. "Ebenezer, let me think about your offer. I'm not sure how I feel about being paid for taking care of a friend. I'll talk to Ann tomorrow. Maybe she will feel a little stronger then. Can you get by for a day or two?"

"Yes, we can get by. Gurnsey and Norman are good help. They just don't know how to do women's work. Then there's Little John. He needs tending and mothering. I'm glad Bett took him home with her. He likes to play with her Lathrop. They practically grew up together when we were on the road so long.

You think it over, Phebe. It would be a great help to me but I know you don't want to hurt anybody's feelings, let alone Ann's. I'll talk to her about it when she wakes up and the two of you can decide tomorrow." Ebenezer held the door open for her and offered to carry the laundry to her house.

"I'll make it just fine. You stay here with Ann. I think you should talk to her about your plan. From what Bett says, she will have to stay down until after the baby comes so it will be for several months. Maybe by then, I will find another way to provide for my family." She walked home in the late fall afternoon sunshine, contemplating the ramifications of moving in with the Browns.

She discussed the possibilities of the move with the children that night. "It would give us some income and the Browns are fine people. We won't do it if you don't think we should."

Lydia Elizabeth was the first to reply, "Could I stay with

Lovina? She needs some help too, with the new baby coming, and I could help her keep the hat business going. Besides, I don't think I could take Gurnsey's teasing on a daily basis."

"I think it would be great. Norman and I could do all sorts of fun stuff together." Zemira was already making plans.

"I don't care where we live, just so I can be with you." Rhoda put her arm around her mother and Phebe realized that of all her children, Rhoda needed the security of family.

Phebe was up early the next morning and had Zemira helping her carry water in to heat for the washing before he went to school. The washing was on the clothes line before the sun came up, almost drying from the frosty morning air and by noon she was folding the towels and ironing the sheets and pillowcases, taking turns with the flat irons heating on the stove. She dampened the shirts and dresses she had starched and sat at the table to have a bite to eat.

As she sat there she realized how much she disliked eating alone. Meal time was family time and she was very lonely, sitting there by herself. Looking back on her life she realized that she had hardly ever been alone. There had always been family with her except when she was expecting Lovina and George was working on the farm. Even then he would come in to eat meals with her.

Moving in with Ebenezer and Ann may be the answer. She had prayed about it and she wondered if she should discuss it with Mother and Father. She knew she would ultimately make up her own mind. That was her way as it had been since she decided to teach school with Master John.

Lydia Elizabeth had definitely decided to stay with Lovina, rather than go to live at the Brown's. She and Gurnsey were good friends but that might not last if they were living under the same roof. She could be of help to Lovina. William George was working up in Quincy now and only came home for visits. The plan just might work for the next few months. The baby was due in June.

Phebe finished the ironing, filled a basket with the clean clothes and started over to the Brown's. Ebenezer saw her coming and came out to take the heavy basket from her. "Ann and I have been talking about you helping us out. Come in and let's talk about it together."

Ann looked better than she did the day before. She had some color in her cheeks and she smiled at Phebe and patted the bed for her to come and sit beside her.

"Ebenezer tells me he needs some help. Phebe, you would be such a dear to help us out. I do want to have this baby and the only way is to stay down. We have shared so much in the past and I would rather have you in my kitchen than anyone else I know. The children love you and we love your children. Please say you will do it." Ann was so enthusiastic about it, Phebe couldn't refuse her.

"I will on one condition, as soon as you are able to take your kitchen back I move on. This is not a permanent arrangement. Now let me help you into a chair while I make your bed up fresh. How soon do I start, Ebenezer?" Phebe looked up at her good friend and saw the relief on his face.

"It looks like you have already started. We'll start moving you over tomorrow. You and Rhoda can have Harriet's room and we can fix a bed up for Zemira in the big room upstairs that the boys share. We can make room for Lydia Elizabeth too. I was thinking of fixing that room up that we added on in the back. I always like to have some extra room in case someone needs a place to stay. William George is welcome here too, any time he comes home." Ebenezer had, obviously, already planned how he could make Phebe and her family comfortable while she cared for Ann and the family.

William and Zemira helped Ebenezer and the children move Phebe's things while Phebe put the Brown's house in order and set up the routines for taking care of Ann and preparing the meals. She enjoyed being busy. It seemed like she was always happiest if she had more work to do than she had time for. As she fell asleep that night she started her list of things she would do tomorrow.

———————————————

Bett walked from Ann's room carrying a new little baby girl. Phebe took it from her to wash and dress. She was so little. As she wiped her off with damp cloths and dried her, Ebenezer looked over her shoulder. "We will name her, Ann, after her mother."

Phebe could tell that the baby's breathing was shallow. She wrapped her in clean towels and passed her to Ebenezer. "Take her to Ann." Ebenezer held his tiny second daughter in the crook of his arm and took her to her mother.

"Zemira, go and get Uncle William. Tell him to come as quickly as he can." Phebe almost pushed her son out the door.

Bett opened the door, "Get more towels for me. I need as many as you can find."

Phebe went to the shelves, filled her arms with towels and returned to the bedroom. Bett looked at her and shook her head as she took the towels and moved back to care for Ann. Phebe took the baby from Ebenezer, "I have sent for William."

Ebenezer looked down at his wife of nearly twenty years and watched her life slip away. He took her in his arms as if he could will her to live but her breathing waned. Finally, she took her last breath and Ebenezer realized she was gone. "Oh, no, not my Ann. What will I do without my Ann." He rocked the lifeless body and wept.

Phebe was stunned. She looked down at the baby in her arms and realized that she too had stopped breathing. "Bett, can you help the baby?"

Bett took the baby and breathed into her mouth, then tipped her over her hand and tapped her back but the baby did not respond. Again she tried, but to no avail. She held the lifeless little body to her face to feel any air that might escape from lungs trying to expand but there was nothing. She could not save her.

"Ebenezer, I am afraid we have lost the baby too." Bett looked at this loving father and husband, realizing the dual loss he had just suffered.

William rushed in and, after seeing the look on Phebe's face, he knew that he had come too late. If it was the Lord's will for them to go he could not have intervened but he maybe could have eased the pain. He walked to his friend and put his hand on his shoulder. Ebenezer looked up, revealing the anguish he felt. He reluctantly laid Ann back on the pillow and gently kissed her. William waited until Ebenezer was ready. Finally, he left his beloved Ann and walked from the room with this friend who had come to be with him in his hour of need.

Phebe laid the baby in her mother's arms and only then let her tears of sorrow flow for the loss of her friend. Bett put her arm around Phebe, "We did all we could. You have taken good care of her these last months. She couldn't have had better care. She just did not have the strength to survive the birth. Once she started to hemorrhage I knew it was over."

Phebe picked up the soiled towels and clothes and carried them to the wash room. She rinsed them through rinse after rinse of cold water, gradually washing away the tragedy of the last few hours. She carried the wet clothes to hang them in the sunshine. The hot summer sun would bleach the final stains away. It also warmed her hands from the cold water but her heart was heavy. She had lost this friend who was like a sister to her. She remembered the sweet voice that had thanked her for every little act of kindness. She would not hear that voice again.

How would they tell the children that their mother was gone? William would help Ebenezer with that.

Mother and Father Draper were soon there to help and Lovina went for Harriet, who lived a few miles away.

By evening the family was assembled to mourn the death of their wife, mother and friend, comfort each other and plan the service.

Ebenezer wanted she and the baby buried in a beautiful spot on Honey Creek, near Quincy, Illinois. It was June of 1842. Baby Ann was buried in her mother's arms.

Old wounds were opened for Zemira Draper as they stood at the grave site. His mother and father stood at his side. He tried to find solace by thinking of Agnes and Ann together with their babies. He remembered them spinning and weaving together. He would try to remember them that way.

Harriet walked through her parents house as if in a daze. What would she do without her mother? Oliver found her and comforted her. The boys clung to their father as if their staying by him could will him not leave them too.

Phebe was at a loss as what to do now. She went to her room and started to organize her belongings. The waves of grief for Ann washed over her again. She had known she would have to make other plans soon but she had been reluctant to forge ahead with it.

Ebenezer knocked on her door. "Phebe, the boys and I would like to talk to you." She walked from the room and little John ran to her, clinging to her skirts. "Phebe, we would like you to stay on and help us."

"Please, Aunt Phebe." Norman looked up to his friend's mother who had filled in for his own mother these last few months.

"I will for a few weeks. You have been good to me and my family and I won't desert you now." Phebe put her arm around Norman and looked at Gurnsey. "How about you, do you feel comfortable with us staying on?"

"Sure, I hope you can. We'd starve if we had to live on Father's cooking." he grinned at her. He was always teasing her about not cooking enough to fill him up. At eighteen his appetite could not be satisfied. "Lydia Elizabeth can come live with us too. I know I tease her too much. But she is so fun to tease. I'll try to be good."

"Lydia Elizabeth is really needed at Lovina's and she is quite happy there, but it is nice to know she is welcome. If you all feel that I should stay, we will try it for a while and see how things go. We will all miss your mother. Maybe we can work together to accept the Lord's will in taking her from us." Phebe smiled at Ebenezer and his three boys.

"Thank you, Phebe. That really takes a load off my mind. Harriet thought she and Oliver should move in with us but I would rather that they go on living as they have been, in Quincy." Ebenezer's sincere gratitude registered in the tone of his voice. "Call your children in. Lets have family Prayer."

Phebe called to Zemira and Rhoda. "It looks like we are going to stay on here a while. I know you two will be happy about that." They all kneeled at their chairs and Ebenezer led them in Prayer.

Phebe was overcome with his sincerity. She had always been impressed with the way he talked to the Lord in prayer, but today it was as if the veil were lifted and the Lord answered his request for comfort in their grief by giving them each a personal witness and peace of mind.

The weeks that followed were uneventful. Everyone was busy with summer work, hoeing and cultivating the fields of corn, feeding the animals and house cleaning. The soot from the wood burning stoves needed to be washed down from the walls and the curtains washed, starched and stretched to hang over the freshly washed windows. Phebe filled the days with hard work, all the while preparing food for the hungry family. She pulled the freshly baked bread from the oven and dropped the ears of corn in the hot water. The meat was cooking in the heavy pot on the back of the stove. It was a warm August day and the heat from the stove had heated the kitchen to the point that Phebe had to open the windows and let the breeze blow through the room. It also carried the smells of the food into the nearby field where Ebenezer and the boys were working. It was as a magnet, drawing them to the house.

Rhoda was setting the table for her mother when the hungry gardeners came in. They washed at the washstand and dried their hands while Phebe put the steaming dishes of food on the table. The meal was soon devoured and the boys pushed their chairs back to return to the fields. "Thanks, Aunt Phebe. That was delicious." Norman picked up an extra roll to eat on the way out.

"Yeah, thanks Mother." Zemira followed Norman with an extra roll in his hand.

Gurnsey looked at his father, "Have you asked her yet?"

Ebenezer looked at his oldest son and grinned. "The corn field's waiting for you. Rhoda, will you take John over to Aunt Bett's? She wants you to help her with Lathrop."

Rhoda took John's hand and they set off to play with their friend.

Phebe started to clear the table and Ebenezer caught her hand. "Phebe, let them wait. We need to talk. Sit here by me."

Phebe wondered what Ebenezer wanted. He had obviously discussed it with Gurnsey. She sat down and pushed the soiled plate aside from her. "What is it?"

"I want you to marry me. I think it is what Ann would have wanted and it is what I want. I can provide for you and your family and I think the Lord doesn't want us to be alone any longer. You are a good woman and we can be good parents to your children and to mine. I talked to William about it and he agreed with me. He let me know right off that no one else makes a decision for you. He said something like, 'don't tell her I said she should or she'll tell you 'no' right off." Ebenezer chuckled as he recalled William's response. "I know you are a strong willed woman and that is what I admire about you. I wouldn't want you to go against your own feelings."

"Ebenezer, I don't know what to say. After living alone for the last ten years I had come to believe that I would live out the rest of my life as a widow. You are such a fine man and I respect you as a Man of God." The words rolled from her tongue as if it was a sign that this was the fulfillment of her blessing. She sat in silence, not knowing how to go on.

"Phebe, I am well aware of the promises you were given by the prophet's father in your blessing. I'm not sure I would be worthy of being called a Man of God but I have committed my life to the tenets of the Gospel since my conversion to the church. I also know of your dedication to the Church and the strong testimony you have to its truthfulness and that Joseph Smith is a true prophet. Together, we can put ourselves in the hands of the Lord and do his will. I would not consider marriage to anyone who was less dedicated." He was holding both of her hands.

"Will you let me think about it? This is such a surprise to me. I know I could never take Ann's place in your heart nor would I expect to. George and I were never one in spirit like you and Ann but I did love him. It was hard to go on without him but I was blessed to have the Church in my life to give me strength."

She hesitated, "I guess I don't really need to consider it longer. If you are sure you want me and can put up with a stiff-necked woman, I will be proud to marry you, Ebenezer." They stood and Ebenezer embraced her as tears rolled down her cheeks.

She was forty-five and he was forty-one. The difference in their age was not important to either of them. Their concerns were for the welfare of their children, the growth of the church and their commitment to it. A companionship relationship would facilitate those goals.

They sent word to Harriet and Oliver, Lovina and Henry, and William George to come home for a meeting. As they met with all of their children and presented their plans for marriage, to their relief, there was no opposition. Phebe could see that it was difficult for Harriet and she took her aside for a private talk. "My dear, I can never take your mother's place either in your heart or your father's. She was one of my dearest friends and by helping your father raise their children I will be doing something I think she would want me to do. I love you, and I hope we will always be good friends. You have so many of your mother's qualities."

"Thank you, Sister Palmer." Harriet wiped the tears from her eyes.

"Call me, Aunt Phebe. That will make it easier. Your father and I have discussed something else. We want you to have your Mother's loom. She taught you to weave and I think that it is part of your heritage that you should keep." Phebe and Harriet embraced and in that act accepted their new relationship.

Phebe and Ebenezer were married by President William Draper Jr. the following week. They took a trip to Nauvoo to see old friends and have some time to get to know each other in their new roles as husband and wife. They were surprised, however, at the growth of the city and were unprepared for the subtle changes they would find that would have far reaching effects on their future and that of their loved ones.

PART VI

A MAN OF GOD
1842—1849
CHAPTER TWENTY-SIX

Nauvoo, once the small swampy community of Commerce, was now a city of several thousand. Sturdy brick houses and business buildings lined the streets of a well planned community. The noise of the busy people driving their wagons down the street and shouting greetings to each other greeted Phebe and Ebenezer as they entered the city. It was nothing like what they had seen upon their arrival in Far West of hastily built cabins and other types of temporary shelter.

"Paper, Paper." Ebenezer bought a paper from the news boy and passed it to Phebe. The headlines read; "Governor Ford Decries Credit, State In Danger of Loosing Solvency" She folded it and tucked it under her arm. She would read it to Ebenezer later.

They saw the impressive Mansion House which was close to completion on the corner and up on the hill, the walls of the Nauvoo Temple. Men were scurrying up and down ladders with rock and mortar. They looked like ants from this view point. Phebe and Ebenezer went into the completed front rooms of the Mansion House to inquire about lodging. They were met by Emma, "Phebe, Phebe Palmer. How good to see you again. And this is Brother Brown as I remember."

"How are you, Sister Emma? I am Phebe Brown now. Brother Brown and I were just married. We came into Nauvoo on a little trip to catch up on the news of our old friends." Phebe looked smart in the new hat Lovina had designed for her and the pale blue dress she had made for the occasion from a light weight fabric Ann had woven for her the year before. Ebenezer cut a striking figure also, in his black, cutaway traveling coat.

He removed his hat and took Emma's hand, "It is so nice to see you again, Sister Smith, and under better circumstances than when we last met, leaving Far West. We must find accommodations for the night. What would you suggest?"

"You must stay here with us. The house is not finished but we have plenty of room for you and I know Joseph will want to see you. How are your brothers, Phebe? I heard William was here for the last conference. You are all in Pleasantville now I understand. It is one of the growing stakes of the church." Emma invited them to sit in the parlor with her.

"Zemira lost his wife, Agnes, over a year ago. He is living with my parents but is still busy in the building business. William is always engaged in the Lord's work as he has been since he was baptized in Canada. He has a very successful shoe making business that my son-in-law, Henry Munro helps him operate. Bett is busy as ever delivering babies. But that is enough about us, how is Mother Smith? We mourned the loss of Father Smith. She must miss him terribly."

Emma looked back toward the kitchen, indicating that Mother Smith was back there. "She is so sad. I try to help her think of other things but Joseph is the only one that can really cheer her."

The Prophet Joseph walked in from the back of the house and they stood to greet him. He shook their hands while Emma told him of their recent marriage. "We'll have to get Brother Brigham over here. He will be anxious to see you too. Emma, send one of the children to the Young's and invite them over for dinner. His converts from Canada will always hold a special spot in his heart."

Emma showed them to a room upstairs and excused herself to supervise the preparation of dinner.

"What a greeting. It was more than I expected. Emma is so beautiful in spite of all she has been through. Isn't it wonderful to see Nauvoo growing so fast. The converts from England and Canada are coming in by the hundreds. It will be wonderful to see Brother Brigham again." Phebe untied the ribbon and removed her hat while Ebenezer put the small cases by the amour. She primped in the dresser mirror, fluffed her hair a little and pinched her cheeks.

Ebenezer looked at her with pride. "You're a fine looking woman, Phebe, and smart too. You'll have to read the paper to me later. From the look on your face, there must be some bad news, but let's not think about it now. We are going to have dinner in the Mansion house with Sister Emma, Brother Joseph, Brother Brigham and his wife. I'd say that is a good start to our marriage." He gave Phebe a big hug and kiss. They walked down stairs hand in hand.

Brigham Young took Phebe's hands in his and looked into her eyes, "Phebe, my dear. They tell me you have married Ebenezer. I am so happy for you. It has been a long time since our days in Canada. Remember that cold day in February when the warm wind came up and I baptized you in the river? You had just lost your little daughter in that horrible fire and then George died soon after. The thing I remember most was the spirit we always felt in your parent's home when we had our meetings. How are your parents?"

"They're just fine. They are living in Pleasantville with the rest of us and are so happy to be there. They hover over us like mother hens and we pretend not to enjoy it. My daughter, Lovina, and her husband, Henry, are there too. I also have two beautiful grandchildren." Phebe glowed as she reported on her family to this good man who had converted the family to the church and taken her into the waters of baptism.

After dinner the conversation turned somber, "I hope you aren't too settled in Pleasantville. It will be necessary in the next few months for the saints in the outer stakes to move in or around Nauvoo. Many of our members have become disenchanted with the Church and it seems that they want to turn the hearts of the other members and their non-member friends away from us. They are stirring up all kinds of trouble. While you are here you may hear many rumors of the most vile nature. These rumors are spreading throughout the state and we are being blamed for all kinds of unreasonable things, even the financial debacle the state of Illinois faces. I anticipate that we will soon have mob action against some of our members, similar to what we experienced in Missouri. The Governor, himself, has accused us of larcenies and robberies of persons unknown but suspected to be Mormons, though he admits they are exaggerated. We may soon need to call the saints to Nauvoo for their own protection and for the protection of the Church as a whole."

The serious countenance of the Prophet brought concern to Ebenezer and Phebe. "It seems that just when we start to take some steps to recoup our losses at Kirtland and Missouri, Satan finds a way to try to discredit us. As you know from first hand experience, most of us have had our life savings stolen or stripped from us in an illegal way. It has been necessary for some of the saints in Iowa to use the Bankruptcy law to place them beyond the power of their unjust creditors. They are being criticized along with the Church even though their actions are legal. They will pay back the money that they owe, but it will take time.

I have been accused as an accessary to the attempt on the life of Governor Boggs in Missouri. It is necessary, as I speak, to watch those around me so that I will not be illegally incarcerated in Missouri again. It is good to be with folks such as you who I can trust completely."

Brigham looked at Ebenezer, "Last December, we had to abandon and dissolve the stake in Ramus and Warren because that section had become a rendezvous for thiefs and the saints were blamed for many of their crimes." Brigham Young shook his head as he recalled the sorrow he felt in having to ask the saints to again give up their homes and move.

The prophet went on, "If we are to have a strong city with a temple, university and other edifices that are necessary for the great work of the last days, we must concentrate our energies and enterprise."

"What are your plans for the Pleasantville Stake?" Ebenezer looked at these men to whom he had committed his life and devotion.

"We have been in the process of drafting a letter to President William Draper, outlining our direction as to the abandonment of your stake. We realized that there have been no overt actions against the saints there but it is spreading up and down the river with farms and cattle herds being raided. I'm sorry, but we need your strengths and talents here. Please keep this information confidential until William is notified. Perhaps you can help soften the blow when it comes." Brigham looked at Ebenezer with the assurance that this confidence would not be broken.

"Tell me about your plans for the university. Will you have any facilities for women to receive additional education? I have a daughter that, in my estimation, is qualified to be accepted at a university. She has finished Normal School with additional tutoring at home." Phebe looked at the prophet for an answer to her question.

"The curriculum for the University has not been fully developed. We have not, at this time, planned classes for women but we know there are many, such as you, Sister Phebe, who would be interested in such a program. As you know, the thirteenth article of faith states that if there is any thing praiseworthy or of good report we seek after these things. The Glory of God is intelligence and I'm sure that applies to women as well as men."

The Prophet changed the subject, "I feel I should indicate to the two of you at this time that you will be part of a movement of the saints to the Rocky Mountains where the saints will assemble. You will assist in making settlements there and building cities and see the saints become a mighty people in the Rocky Mountains. There is much ahead for both of you. The Lord needs you, as he does many other devoted saints, to accomplish His work on earth."

It was difficult for Phebe and Ebenezer to assimilate all they had been taught that evening by the Prophet and the President of the Twelve Apostles. It was as if they had been given a glimpse into the future through the eyes of prophets.

The following day, Ebenezer rented a rig at the closest livery stable and he and Phebe rode around the streets of Nauvoo and then along the road to Carthage, looking at the farm land and homes that were for sale. The more information they had when the time came to move, the better it would be for them and for the rest of the family.

Ebenezer noted that the livestock looked healthy and was relieved that he saw plenty of grazing land which could accommodate his growing herd in Pleasantville. If the time was right he could, with the help of the boys, drive his cattle up to Nauvoo. After what they had heard last night, they wondered how deep they should plan to send down roots here. They had made a commitment not to share what they had been privy to last night and they would not jeopardize that confidence.

On a Sunday in mid September the members of the church filed into a special conference called for the Pleasantville Stake. President William Draper Jr. was presiding. Standing at the pulpit, he took a letter from his pocket, paused for a moment to regain his composure, and began to read:

> *"The letter is dated, September 6, 1842 and signed by the First Presidency.*
> *It reads as follows:*

Dear Brethren,

We regretfully call upon you to sell your homes and acreage as soon as possible and move to the Nauvoo area. The Pleasantville Stake is hereby dissolved and all members who can answer this call are requested to do so as soon as possible.

The Lord appreciates your dedication to the church as do we. Though we know of no mob action in your immediate vicinity it is spreading over the state and we feel the safety of all the members is best served by living together in the Nauvoo vicinity. Your talents and energy is needed here to help with the building of the Temple, university and other edifices that are necessary for this great work in the last days.

Please advise us of your implementation of the proposed plan.

William raised his head and faced his friends and neighbors, many of whom were lifetime residents of Pleasantville. "It will be your decision to comply with this request as you deem appropriate for you and your family. As an emissary for the Church, I have no choice but to sell my properties and relocate in the Nauvoo area. Let me know of your decision and I will report to the brethren. The rest of the meeting was devoted to testimony bearing and the spirit was strong. Some spoke in tongues and many bore testimony of miracles in their lives.

The Draper/Brown families met later in the day to discuss their plans to comply with the request from Nauvoo.

"Your Mother and I can move easily, but the rest of you have homes and properties to sell and children to care for. I recommend that we men go to the area immediately and find homes and property before it becomes more of a premium. Then we can return and organize an orderly sale of our holdings here and the subsequent move.

Mother and I have some extra money left from the sale of our properties in Canada and Sagamon. We can advance down payments on property for any of you who need it until you sell your places here. If we move wisely, we should not have to take a loss on our investments in Pleasantville. We have helped this town grow and are respected by our neighbors. Our farms and houses are well cared for and we should be able to sell for a fair price. We are fortunate that the financial problems facing the rest of the state have not spread to Pleasantville." Father Draper, the patriarch of the family sat down.

"Henry, if you can take care of the shoe shop for a few days, I will go with Father and look for a place for you also." William looked to Henry who nodded his approval.

"I'll go with you also. Phebe and I saw some nice farms when we were up there a few weeks ago. There is good soil and grazing land south of Nauvoo and over toward Carthage. You know, I'm always looking for good land and cattle. I couldn't let an opportunity like that go by, even if we were on our wedding trip." Ebenezer winked at Phebe and no one guessed that they had been given any advance information.

Bett held Albert close to her and wondered if the moving would ever end. No one knew that she was three months pregnant again. In a way she envied Phebe. At least she didn't have to have babies while they were moving from pillar to post. As usual, William hadn't given her any warning. You would think that he could have read the letter to her so it wouldn't have come as a complete shock. At least Nauvoo wasn't like moving to the frontier country of Missouri. 15, 000 people couldn't all be wrong. Phebe said it was a large, exciting city now with schools and newspapers and they had the temple almost ready for the roof. Her testimony was strong too, but sometimes it just seemed like the Lord was asking a lot of them. Just once, she would like to hear news from William without hearing it over the pulpit.

Phebe walked over to her, "Well, here we go again. Some women spend their whole life in one place and one house. They would be jealous of us having so many houses and traveling to different places. You'll like Nauvoo. We can shop in the stores and watch the temple being built." Her effort to cheer Bett was falling on deaf ears but she gave her a hug and went on to visit with other members of the family, giving them reasons to be excited about moving to Nauvoo.

"Zemira, they need your help on the temple. They are just about ready for the finish work and that is your specialty." She smiled at her brother and gave him a hug. She must start trying to find him a wife. He was still so sad and he should be as happy as she and Ebenezer.

That night, after prayers, she and Ebenezer talked to the wee hours about the events of the day. "I don't think anyone guessed that we knew what was coming. Which place would you like me to secure for us? I've been selling off some of the cattle so I have a nice amount for a down payment. Would you like to live out in the country or closer to town? Maybe we could have a house in town and I could graze the cattle on property out a few miles. That is one advantage of beef stock. They don't have to be milked twice a day."

"It would be nice to live in town for a change and it might be safer if things turn ugly as the Prophet warned us it might." Phebe raised up on her elbow and looked at Ebenezer. "What ever we do, let's enjoy what time we have there."

The men left the next morning for Nauvoo and the women took stock of their households. Planning what to move and how to move it. Bett and Phebe were aware that this was going to be easier than the last move when they had to live in wagons for months at a time.

Phebe called the children together and had them try on clothes to see what they had grown out of that could be passed down to the younger children. If no one in their family could wear them they could easily find a cousin that could use them. Norman and Zemira were so close to the same size and growing so fast that it kept her busy making clothes for them. William George kept Gurnsey in some of the latest fashions that he bought when he worked on the river boats. It was fun to sew for Rhoda and John. She had already made two new dresses for Rhoda; one for school and one for Sunday. Lydia Elizabeth and Lovina sewed their own clothes and always looked like the pictures in the stores, except they were more modest. Lovina certainly had a way with style.

Mother Draper came in to help her and brought her a letter she had picked up at the store where it had been delivered. She handed it to Phebe and raised her eyes. "I didn't know you had kept in touch with Master John all these years."

Phebe looked at it. It was addressed to Phebe Palmer so she was quite sure it was an answer to the letter she had written months ago about school for Lydia Elizabeth. "I hadn't heard from them for years. The last I heard, they were in Ohio where he was teaching at a university. I wrote to them some time ago to see if there was a program in their school that would be right for Lydia Elizabeth." She tore open the letter and read:

> *Tiffen, Ohio*
> *August 25, 1842*
> *My Dear Phebe,*
> *Our dear, Mary, died a few months ago and I was so grieved that I put your letter aside until I could write to you in a happier vein. She had been so much better here in Ohio than she was in Pennsylvania that I had high hopes for her complete recovery, but it was not to be.*
> *I am still teaching and it is the one thing that keeps me going. My son, John Rocky, has gone east to Medical School and the girls are all married so I find myself in rather a lonely state except for the companionship of my colleagues.*
> *I have followed, by news accounts, the trials of the Mormon people you have joined. From the little you said of it in your letter, you must have been in some of the worst of it.*
> *In answer to your inquiry about school for your daughter, we have very few programs designed for girls but there*

is a rather progressive girls school near by here. I could give her a letter of introduction to that school and it may carry some weight. Since you are only a few hundred miles from here and there is easy access by river and stage or rail car, would you consider bringing her down here to Tiffen and we could look at the facility together and renew our old friendship. I would love to hear more of your new religion and catch up on news of your experiences on the frontier with those heathenish Missourians.

I will be looking forward to your reply. I do hope you will accept my invitation and forgive me for being so slow in answering you letter.

Sincerely,
Your old friend,
John Park.

"I didn't know you were considering sending Lydia Elizabeth off to school." Mother Lydia looked at Phebe to see her reaction to the letter. She remembered her daughter's feelings for Master John and she wondered what this letter would mean to her.

"I didn't tell anyone, not even Lydia Elizabeth, because I wanted to know what the options were first. Please, don't say anything to her about it. I think there will be just as many opportunities for her in Nauvoo and I couldn't bear to have her away from me. I'll drop John a note of sympathy and thank him for the invitation but decline accepting it. I just wrote that letter on a whim when I was at loose ends. I wouldn't consider leaving Ebenezer and the family to take Lydia Elizabeth on a wild goose chase. I have too many other things to do to even consider it and besides that, I don't want to go. Mother, have I told you how happy I am with Ebenezer. He is such a kind man. He is truly a Man of God and the answer to my blessing. Don't tell anyone about this letter. I am embarrassed that I even wrote to him." Phebe lifted the lid over the fire box on the stove and dropped in the letter. It blazed up and was gone in a puff of smoke. She replaced the lid and in doing so ended a secret desire that was now filled by another source. Once again, mother and daughter shared an experience that only mothers and daughters understand.

Lydia stood and pulled her shawl around her shoulders. The September air was a little cool in the late afternoon. "I wasn't much help to you. I'll come over tomorrow and give you a hand with some of your sewing." She put her arm around her daughter, "I am so proud of you and I am also very happy for you. Remember when I told you how happy your father and I have always been because we have been one in purpose. I think you are finding that kind of happiness now." She walked to the door, "See you tomorrow."

Phebe watched her mother leave and then looked at the lid on the stove. She had direction in her life for the first time. She didn't know exactly where it would take her but she would do it with Ebenezer and it would be the Lord's will. She would give it all the energy she could muster. Isn't that what the Prophet said they needed, their energy? A renewed sense of determination welled up inside her and she remembered the words, "I will go and do as the Lord has commanded."

Chapter Twenty-seven

Phebe walked up the stairs to the children's bedrooms. She measured the windows and jotted down the measurements. As she looked at the wood plank, oiled, floors, she visualized braided rugs by the beds and dressers to protect cold feet in the winter. She walked back to the window and looked out over the city. Other red brick houses resembling this one were on the block across the street. Like this one, there were summer kitchens and wash rooms on the back of the houses, room for small vegetable gardens and small barns for the family horses and/or family cow.

Ebenezer had, as planned, found twenty acres of pasture just outside of town. He and the boys were out there now preparing sheds and mangers for winter feeding. They had brought the cattle up river on a barge and then driven them to the outskirts of town. They did not lose one animal, thanks to the help of Gurnsey, Norman and Zemira. When Ebenezer thanked the boys, Zemira glowed with pride. Phebe could see that he felt like one of the family and was coming to look at Ebenezer as the father he had never really known.

Downstairs she panned out the bread dough that she had set earlier and put it in the sun on the wide window sill in the kitchen. She stoked up the fire under the bonnet oven and picked up a duster to wipe the dust from the furniture in the parlor and their bedroom. Phebe found it hard to believe that she had such a lovely home to care for. She ran her hand over the new velvet love seat in the parlor and looked at the dark carved wood of the small table at the side. The cut glass, oil lamp needed cleaning and she took it back to the kitchen and pumped some water into a pan. She put a little vinegar in the water, and with a soft cloth wiped away the soot.

She had been invited to meet with some ladies in an

organization the Prophet had encouraged. It was to help the poor, help women develop their talents and help with other needs the Church might have. She heard they had been asked to make shirts for the temple workers. The bread would be out of the oven soon. Rhoda and John would be in school for a few more hours so she would have time to go to the meeting.

She took the freshly baked loaves of bread from the oven and put them on the sideboard to cool, covered them with a clean cloth and slipped off her apron. She went to the bedroom and opened the bonnet closet on the dresser. Lovina had made her three new hats and she stood, contemplating which one to wear to the meeting. She chose the dark purple one and looked in the mirror as she put it on and tied the lavender ribbons under her chin. She walked out the door and went to her first Relief Society meeting.

"Phebe, what is all this? Have you gone into some business I haven't heard about?" Ebenezer put his arm around her shoulders and surveyed all the stacks of white fabric cut in pieces.

"I went to the Relief Society meeting today and volunteered to cut out shirts for the men working on the temple. I decided to do several at once to save time. Sister Kimball is going to come over tomorrow and help me sew them together. Oh, Ebenezer, I met Sister Eliza Snow at the meeting. She read some of her poetry to us. It was so inspiring. She writes glowing poems about the Gospel. Emma told us about some new hymns she is adding to the book of hymns. I hope Lovina can go to the next meeting with me. I know they would love to hear her sing." Ebenezer smiled at Phebe's enthusiasm. This move had been good for all of them. They had left their sorrows behind them and had joined in the busy Nauvoo activities.

Ebenezer tried on his new Legion uniform. He was meeting with the Nauvoo Legion tonight. He and some of the other men would take Brother Joseph with them. They could pick him up at the back door of the house where he was hiding and help him slip into the meeting quietly. It was unfortunate that he still had to be in hiding. The last time he was arrested he was released almost immediately because they had no reason to hold him.

The meeting was over and the men were discussing the schedule for drill practice. Men, claiming to be Hancock County constables, grabbed Joseph and Ebenezer, tied their hands and pulled guns against the men who turned and lunged forward to free their friends. Holding the group at bay with drawn pistols, they forced the prisoners to mount horses. "You will learn to plan the overthrow of the State Militia with your legion," the leader shouted as he motioned other riders, partially disguised with blackened faces, from the shadows of the building. They were soon encircled by mounted horsemen and spirited away. Warning shots cut the crisp, October air as the riders galloped away.

Some of the legionnaires mounted their horses trying to intercept the self styled posse by taking a short-cut through the fields. They came upon the group by Green Plain, near William Draper's farm, and followed them as they circled around and head into Carthage. Knowing William was Ebenezer's brother-in-law, one of the men roused him and he joined the group. The prisoner's were taken to the jail, being verbally abused all the way. "We've got Joe Smith now and one of his new legion members." The leader pushed Joseph and Ebenezer into the jail, where the jailer, sleepy eyed, took them up stairs and put them in the upper room of the jail and locked the door.

"Go on home and bring your complaints in tomorrow. It's late, and I want some sleep." The jailer waved the accusers away. "I wish they would let that poor man rest, seems like they're trumpin' up new charges against him every time he turns around. Hope that Marshal from Missouri don't find out he's here or I'll have real trouble on my hands. Some of them ought to be jailed for disturbing the peace, let alone my sleep." He went back to his bed mumbling to himself, hoping his wife hadn't been disturbed.

"I'm sorry to get you into this, Ebenezer. I should have stayed in hiding out on the island like Porter told me to. If the charges brought on us have to do with the legality of the Nauvoo Legion, we have only to produce a copy of our charter. It is my opinion that the men who arrested us were acting out of bigotry and ignorance. If that is the case, we will be released in the morning."

Joseph took this opportunity to talk to Ebenezer about his vision of the Saints in the Rocky Mountains. "I have sent a group of men to survey the possibilities of a move west. When they return we will have more information to help us make our plans. Will you be ready to go?"

Ebenezer looked at the Prophet with love and admiration. "I would go to the ends of the earth for you and this Church. When my first wife, Ann, and I heard the gospel, we knew it was the word of God and we pledged ourselves to go and do what ever the Lord required of us. I have been blessed with a second wife who feels the same. She is a dedicated and faithful servant. We have agreed that anything we are called upon to do, we will do. In the meantime, we are just enjoying our time in Nauvoo with our family and friends."

"Your wife, Phebe, is an unusual woman. I remember the day I met her in Kirtland. I was impressed with her strong testimony and her intelligence. She was a great help getting the school started in Kirtland. She comes from a fine family also. The Drapers are dedicated and loyal. You have made a good marriage, Ebenezer." He put his hand on Ebenezer's shoulder, "Lets have prayer and try to get some rest."

The two men knelt in prayer together and then laid on the

bare mattress on the floor and fell asleep.

News of the arrest reached the Smith and Brown homes shortly after it happened. Each wife called their family together and prayed for the fathers that had been taken away. Phebe sent the children to bed and sat reading some of the latest revelations having to do with baptism for the dead and other ceremonies that would take place in the temple when it was finished. She read until the wee hours of the morning, keeping the lamp filled with oil in case Ebenezer was released in the night.

A knock on the door awakened her in the early morning from where she slept in the rocker. "Phebe, open up. It's William." She threw the door open and he came in, obviously tired from a night without sleep. "Ebenezer and Joseph will be home soon but the Prophet will have to go back into hiding. The trumped up charge the constable tried to pin on them was just that, trumped up. It had no legal grounds or truth to it. The trouble is that if the Missouri Marshall finds out Joseph was in the jail he'll come looking for him here again. Ebenezer is fine. I came on ahead to tell you so you wouldn't be worrying. He should be home by noon."

"I think some of my neighbors were in the group last night. They came and ask me to go with them to get Joseph but I refused. I have tried to be a good neighbor and have made friends out their but I will not join in their harassment of the Prophet."

"I'd best be getting home." William kissed his sister on the check. "You get some rest now."

Phebe went to their bedroom and knelt by the bed. Her prayers of thanksgiving were long and sincere. She had been concerned about Ebenezer but she knew he would survive. They had a greater mission and a few rowdy constables from Carthage were not going to thwart it.

Just as she was about to call the children and start the day, Lydia Elizabeth came running up the path. "Mother, Lovina has another baby girl. Aunt Bett just sent me to tell you they are all fine. Have you heard any thing about Brother Brown and the Prophet?"

"They are fine too. Uncle William just came to tell me about an hour ago. They should be home soon. Lydia Elizabeth, will you stay here and get breakfast for the children and get them off to school? I'd like to go to Lovina. I haven't been with her for her last three babies. Oh, if Ebenezer gets back before I get home, tell him to come over and see our new grandchild." Phebe put her shawl and bonnet on and hurried down the street. She would have to talk to Ebenezer about what he wanted Lydia Elizabeth to call him. It didn't seem proper for her to call her step father, "Brother Brown." Rhoda and Zemira used the same endearing terms as Ebenezer's children; pa, papa or father. All in good time, now she was going to see her new little grand-daughter and if she was anything like Ester Ann she would be a beauty. She prayed that this baby would be strong enough to survive. Her baby born last year lived only a short time. They had named her Phebe Malissa.

Henry Munro answered the door, "Come in, mother. Lovina and the baby are just fine. Aunt Bett said she is a strong baby and from the sound of her crying, I agree with her. Lovina wants to see you." He led her to the bedroom of the small cottage they were renting.

"Mother, I am so glad you are here. I wanted you to be the first to wash and dress her since you missed that before. We have named her Fanny Lucinda for Aunt Fanny. Don't you think she would be thrilled? She already has everyone's attention, just like Aunt Fanny." Lovina passed the bundled baby to her mother who took her to the wash stand to clean and dress her. She was a healthy little girl with dark black hair, much like Lovina's when she was born. She loved her new little granddaughter immediately.

Ester Ann came from her bed with sleepy eyes, "Do we have a new baby, Grandma?"

"We do. Come and see her. She is going to be your best friend. Look at her little tiny hands and feet. You may give her a kiss on the forehead." Phebe held her down for Ester Ann to see her.

"Is she going to die, grandma?" Ester Ann was old beyond her years.

"No, she is going to grow up to be your little sister and you can help take care of her." Phebe finished dressing the baby and took her to her mother. Mother Lydia would be so pleased to hear they had named her after Fanny.

Now life had settled down for her she must write to her sisters and brothers who were still in Canada. She wondered if Asahel would come to see them. He had written to Lovina, telling her they had a new baby girl whom they had named, Phebe. Her heart ached for her oldest son who had chosen to separate himself from the family. Maybe having a family of his own would soften his heart. She would love to see her new little namesake. He had told Lovina that he did not intend to come to the Mormon hotbed of Nauvoo. Perhaps it would be best if they went to him.

Ebenezer came to find her as soon as he arrived home. "Oh, Ebenezer, I am so glad you were not harmed." She held him away from her and looked him over. "Is Brother Joseph safe?"

"He's fine. He has gone back into hiding. I just can't understand the hostility of some of these people. I'm glad you didn't have to hear some of the abusive language they spewed out last night. It was horrible. The Prophet just ignored them. When we finally got to the jail the jailer sent them on their way and treated us fairly. His wife prepared us a nice breakfast this morning and we were released because they had no reason to hold us."

"Now, where is this new baby? Lydia said there was a new baby girl here." Ebenezer pretended to be looking in the corners and around the door until Ester Ann could not be put off.

"She is with Mamma, Grandpa."

The new grandparents went in to see the first baby born to their combined family. Phebe mused over the possibility of a trip to Sangamon to see Asahel. She would have to pray about it before she mentioned it to Ebenezer.

Ebenezer and Phebe stood with their children in the long line waiting to view the bodies of the Prophet Joseph Smith and his brother, Hyrum Smith, the Patriarch. Harriet and Oliver stood by them with their new little son, James Albert. Mother and Father Draper were in line also with Zemira, William Jr., Bett, Lovina and Henry Munro. Thousands of people were standing in lines that stretched for blocks. Shocked at the death of their beloved, Joseph, it was a solemn group. It was a warm June day in 1844 in Nauvoo, the city beautiful, that had been designed by the Prophet himself.

The future of the Church laid heavy on their minds. What would happen without their prophet, Joseph. Phebe mused at the marvelous concepts he had taught them about life after death. She remembered the funeral address when he promised mothers who had lost their babies, that they would be able to raise them in the hereafter. Eliza, her fairy child, would be hers to love and raise. She thought of the School of the Prophets, and how important education was to the prophet. In her mind she could hear that rich, impelling voice reminding them that, "The Glory of God is Intelligence." What of the revealed temple ordinances? Would they still be able to baptize for the dead?

The line moved along and they were soon standing, looking at these beloved men who had made such a profound difference in their lives. Their bodies were void of their spirits and Phebe understood what the Prophet had meant when he talked about mortality and immortality. She could almost feel his spirit there reminding them, "I have a greater work to do." She must move on but it was hard to let them go. Her testimony of the truthfulness of the gospel and Joseph as a true prophet burned within her. Ebenezer's hand on her back reminded her that others were waiting and she stepped ahead to let them have their last moment with the Prophet as she had. Emma stood by the casket in complete control, the demeanor Joseph would have expected. Phebe touched her hand in comfort and moved on, feeling that loss again that she had felt at George's passing. She sensed the feelings of Ebenezer also and took his hand in a tight grip, as if to say, "We know how it feels."

Brother Sydney Rigdon stood before the congregation on the fourth day of August, 1844 . He had arrived from Pittsburgh the day before but had refused to meet with the apostles the following morning. Rather than meet with them he chose to meet with the saints at ten o'clock. He spoke at great length about a vision he had received in Pittsburgh after hearing of the death of the Prophet. "It is my desire, and it has been made known to me that I am to be the guardian of the church." He had recently moved from Nauvoo and been discredited by the Prophet. It seemed strange that someone who had chosen to leave the presence of the Church would be chosen as its guardian. He was the only counselor left in the First Presidency since William Law had left the Church and become one of its most avid opponents.

"Where is Brother Brigham. He would know what to do." Phebe whispered to Ebenezer. "Remember how he took over for the Prophet at Far West?"

The week was filled with meetings, some of which were only attended by High Priests, Stake Presidencies and Apostles. The general membership of the Church was invited to others and they were well attended.

Brigham Young returned from his missionary labors in New Hampshire on the 6th of August. Members thought it providential in light of the claims of Sidney Rigdon. To the priesthood leadership of the Church, he replied to Elder Rigdon's claim, "I do not care who leads this church, —-but one thing I must know and that is what God says about it. — Joseph conferred upon our heads all the keys and powers belonging to the apostleship which he himself held before he was taken away."

August 8th, Phebe and Ebenezer sat toward the back of the crowd. Elder Rigdon had addressed them at great length that morning. In the afternoon session, Brigham Young called the group to attention. He explained the role of the Apostles in the leadership of the church and ask if they wanted a guardian or a prophet. As he went on to explain the leadership of the apostles and the meaning of holding the Keys of the Kingdom his voice sounded like that of the Prophet Joseph Smith and those who witnessed it saw that he also took on the persona of the Prophet.

"Those who want a guardian appointed to lead the church raise your hand." Very few hands were raised. "Those who feel the church should be led by the Apostles raise your hand." Almost every hand raised to endorse the quorum of the twelve, with Brigham Young at its head, to lead the church.

Phebe took Ebenezer's arm as they left the meeting surrounded by those who had crowded in to attend the meeting and had witnessed what Phebe felt was a miracle. She had known Brigham Young since he had come to Canada to bring the gospel to them. She knew him well and never had she seen any resemblance to the prophet until today, but she saw it with her own eyes and heard the voice of the prophet from his lips. At this tumultuous time for the church she knew the Lord was guiding them as she had known when she was at the dedication of the Kirtland Temple.

They walked in silence for a city block or more, not wanting to lose the spirit they had felt in the meeting. Ebenezer finally spoke in a quiet solemn voice, "We have chosen to follow the Lord's way. It won't be easy but it will ultimately bring us great joy. My heart aches for those who are not close enough to the spirit to be led in the right direction."

"Ebenezer, have you wondered why so many fall away from the church while thousands of others are joining? Just last week another large group came from Canada."

"It appears to me that the Lord gives us opportunities to know the truth and tests us to see if we are strong enough to deserve it. Those who cling to the church will have to have the metal to persevere." Ebenezer put his arm around Phebe's shoulders. "Most of those who fall away don't have companions with strong testimonies and determination to help them. I am so thankful for you, Phebe. I know that together, we can endure to the end." He kissed her on the forehead and they walked on home.

Sleep did not come quickly to Phebe, though it had been a long day. She listened to the steady breathing of Ebenezer and knew he was sleeping peacefully. Memories of the past crowded her mind. She was again in the little chapel in Canada hearing Brother Miller telling them the story of the boy prophet, his vision in the grove of trees. All because he believed what he read in the Bible. *"If any of ye lack wisdom, let him ask of God."* Those same feeling she had felt then came back to her again, but now she had a greater understanding of the Gospel of Jesus Christ. It was a Gospel of love. How fortunate she was to have a Man of God, Ebenezer, to share her life, help her with her family and, as he said, endure to the end.

CHAPTER TWENTY-EIGHT

Ebenezer and his brother-in-law, William, were assigned to work on the temple so Bett rode in with William from Green Plain to spend the day with Phebe. She brought little Albert and Parley with her as the older children were in school. The old friends greeted each other with a hug. Phebe found some toys for the boys to play with. For so long they had shared each other's children but now they lived apart and Phebe missed having her nieces and nephews to love and fuss over.

Bett sat in the velvet rocker and Phebe sat on the love seat. The morning sun was shining through the window as they each took up their knitting. Phebe was working on a sweater for her growing son, Zemira, and Bett was knitting a shawl for the new baby she was expecting. As the needles flew, Phebe noticed that Bett had not pulled out her little pipe which had always been her habit. "Where's your pipe?"

Bett shifted in her chair, "I am trying to give it up. William is determined to abide by the wishes of the brethren to live by the Word of Wisdom revealed to the Prophet. If he can do without his coffee I guess I can do without my pipe. The women in my family have smoked pipes for generations. I guess it is time I broke the chain. With this new baby on the way it will be best for me." She picked up the speed of her knitting.

"How do you like your new neighbors in Green Plain? William said they had been very friendly until the night he refused to go with them to Carthage when the Prophet was shot. He said they actually told him he would have to leave town if he didn't go with them." The worry lines appeared on Phebe's brown as she recalled that dreadful time.

"They hardly speak to us now and some of them that paid regularly to use the grist mill have taken their grains to other mills this fall. Sometimes, when I go to the store I notice they stop talking when I come in. The children are being teased at school for being Mormons. To be right honest with you, Phebe, I am very concerned about it. We have always been good to our neighbors and you know how friendly William is to everyone." Bett shook her head.

There was a knock on the door but before Phebe could answer it the door opened and Lovina and Lydia Elizabeth came in. "Mother, we have news from Elijah. Well not directly from him but about him. Some of the new converts from Canada came to see us and some of them had been in Crahame. They had seen Elijah and his new wife. They said he looked fine and the farm was doing very well. Lovina took a breath and went on with other news about friends and relatives in Crahame and Loughborough. "Uncle Charles and Hanah have two more children and Aunt Fanny is planning to come and join us here. Aunt Lucretia and Uncle John are still in their big house in Loughborough."

Lydia Elizabeth was glowing, "Mother, you remember the Bruno's? They have a son Anthony who came here with them. He has invited me to go to the barn dance with him tonight. He is really good looking."

Phebe smiled. Lydia Elizabeth had not shown any interest in any of the young men around, preferring to read books and help Lovina make hats. "What wonderful news. We should have a big party for all of the Canadian saints. Wouldn't that be fun to see our old friends and hear first hand news of our loved ones still in Canada? Bett, what do you think about it?"

Bett was soon in the spirit of the party idea. "Lets talk to William. He is always so good at making plans for this sort of event. Maybe we could have it out at our place. Our barn is almost empty now because we haven't started the last harvest. We could make some of our old favorite dishes we used to make in Canada. It could be a festive welcome for the new-comers. I've felt sorry for those who have joined us at such a sad time. The Prophet would want us to do something just like this."

"Lovina, see if you can find William George. He could get a band together to entertain us. Mother and Father will want to be in on the party too. Lydia Elizabeth, you go and tell your grandparents and get the Bruno's to invite all the new saints from Canada. Lets plan it for next Saturday night." Phebe was glad to have something pleasant to plan on and distract them from their worries about the mobocrats and trouble makers in and out of the church.

William and Ebenezer were infected with the enthusiasm when they came back from working on the temple. Ebenezer was anxious to meet Phebe's friends from Canada and, as expected, William started making plans for the party as Bett was sure he would.

Phebe was anxious to hear from Asahel. After dinner was over and the children all settled in for the night she sat down and wrote him a long letter. Not being able to resolve their differences was a nagging heartbreak to her. She remembered him and his impishness when he was a little boy. The happy child that enjoyed tricking people and making jokes did not resemble the belligerent son who had refused to leave with her for Kirtland. He hadn't answered any of her letters but did write to Lovina. She would keep writing whenever she could. She folded the letter, put it in an envelope and addressed it. Then she wrote letters to her sisters. It would be wonderful to have Fanny with them. She was always so spirited and lively. Phebe smiled as she thought about how Fanny always knew the news and shared it with everyone.

Ebenezer came home from a meeting to find Phebe reading from the Book of Mormon. He sat down next to her and ask her to read to him as she often did. She was reading the message of King Benjamin to his people. "He never ask anyone to do anything that he was not will to do himself. What a humble man he was." Ebenezer loved to have Phebe read to him. He turned to her and ask, "Do you think I am too old to learn to read and write?"

"Of course not. You are a very bright man and if you want me to, I will teach you to read. We can work on it as we study the scriptures together. I think you will be very surprised at how quickly you can learn to read." Phebe had hoped Ebenezer would make this request but she hadn't mentioned it because she knew at his age it must be voluntary. They could work on it in the privacy of their own room and even the children wouldn't know of the project unless he wanted to tell them.

"Phebe, you bring so much happiness to my life and I love you for it." He doused the oil lamp she had been reading by and led her to their room.

The next few days were filled with plans for the Saturday night party. The women were baking and the men cleaned out the barn and set up temporary tables for the food and a platform for the band. William George and Oliver Straton rounded up their musical friends. Ebenezer chose one of his best beef to supply the meat for the party. Norman, Gurnsey and Zemira helped him butcher it and William designed a turning spit to cook the meat on an open fire. The men would take turns turning it for hours to cook it evenly on all sides.

Phebe insisted that they find apples for bobbing, and pies and some to press into fresh apple cider. She sent Zemira with the buckboard to the far side of Green Plain where she knew of an apple orchard. Norman went with him as they had been instructed not to leave Nauvoo alone, even in the daytime. The orchard owner was reluctant to sell the apples to Mormon boys but after they showed him the cash they brought to pay for them and told him it was for a big party at their Uncle William's farm in Green Plain, he consented. "So, you're having a big party at the Draper Farm are ya? I bet you'll have a lot of Mormons there." He lifted the apples into the buckboard for them.

"Yes, we have a lot of new converts from Canada and we're giving a welcome party for them." The boys responded to his friendly exchange. "Our mother wants to make apple cider and apple pies."

"When did ya say the party was? Will the cider have time to turn? It takes several days ta be real good." The farmer licked his lips as if tasting the fermented cider.

"The party is Saturday and we don't need time for the cider to turn. We like sweet cider, freshly pressed." The boys gave the farmer the money for the apples and got back on the seat of the buckboard. Zemira had driven out so it was Norman's turn to drive back home. They would unload the apples for the cider and bobbing at Uncle William's farm on the way and take the rest on home to Phebe for pies.

"He sure was interested in the party. Maybe we should have invited him to come. If Uncle William had been with us he would have, for sure. The Drapers have this tradition of inviting any stranger they meet to eat with them." Zemira turned and picked up one of the apples to eat and passed one to Norman.

"It's a good tradition. If he hadn't invited our family to join you on the trail to Far West we wouldn't have been brothers now." Norman smiled at Zemira and flipped the rein on the horse to hurry it along. "It's strange how things happen to bring people together." The two friends munched on their apples and fed the cores to the horse when they stopped at Uncle William's farm. They unloaded the apples in the barn and went to find their uncle in the grist mill.

He walked out to them, dusting the grain residue from his clothes. "Hello boys. What brings you out here? Who is watching the cattle?"

"Father and Gurnsey let us have the day off. Aunt Phebe sent us to get apples south of town for the party. We got them over at a farm there and dropped the ones off here for the apple bobbing and cider. Do you want us to come out early on

Saturday and run them through the press?" Norman hoped he would. That way they could come out and be a apart of the festivities longer. It would be a lot better than herding the cows. He and Zemira had heard that among the new converts from Canada were some girls about their age. This was going to be some party.

"I can use you to help get the cider and other things ready for the party if your father can spare you. Let him decide how soon he can let you come out." William picked up one of the the apples and took a juicy bite. "They taste almost as good as Canadian apples." He waved to the boys as they drove away from his farm and turned north on the road to Nauvoo.

Two riders from Warsaw were approaching the buckboard from the East. The boys turned at the sound of the hoof beats. Norman slapped the rein on the horse in effort to out run the riders closing the gap between them. They would be no match for the men on the horses nor could their buggy horse outrun them. The riders tried to force them off the dirt road but Norman held the reins tight, keeping the horse under control. The men shouted obscenities at them and then rode off, laughing to themselves for the scare they had given the two Mormon boys.

Zemira and Norman looked at each other, realizing they had narrowly missed having the wagon tipped over and being thrown out into the gully at the side of the road. Norman pulled back on the reins and slowed the horse to a walk.

Zemira shook his head, "I'm glad you came with me. I wouldn't have wanted to be out here alone with those roughnecks. No telling what they would have done to me."

Several of the apples had bounced out of the basket onto the floor of the buckboard and Zemira crawled back to replace them. His mother wouldn't want bruised apples to make into pies. If there was one thing she was fussy about it was apples. He and Norman decided they wouldn't tell her about the men. She would just worry and maybe not let them come out early on Saturday.

The band was tuning up their instruments, the women were putting checkered clothes on the makeshift plank tables and the boys were working at the apple press making fresh cider. The aroma of the beef cooking over the open fire outside wafted into the barn and through the yard. The men had been taking turns all night an through the day turning the spit and feeding the fire to have the meat cooked just right for the party. The fire would pop and crackle as the fat from the roasting meat dropped on to the hot coals.

Wagons started to arrive and people poured into the yard greeting each other and exchanging news about common friends and relatives. The women carried covered dishes to the barn and Phebe was bringing hot, steaming pies from the house. She had come over early with the boys to bake the pies in Bett's oven so they would be hot out of the oven when the guests arrived.

The fiddler in the band started up the music and the other instruments joined in: a bass fiddle, banjo and another violin. As the musicians picked up the tempo, the guests moved into the barn forming squares and following the caller's directions.

Ebenezer met Phebe as he was carrying a large tray of meat into the serving table. "This was such a good idea. Everyone is having a good time and there sure is a lot of food for them to eat. I think we cooked this meat just right. It is so tender it fell off the bones."

Phebe took a sample from the edge of the platter and put it in her mouth "Mmm, It is delicious. I didn't know you were such a good cook. I should have had you helping me in the kitchen. Bring it over here and put it on the end of the table. I want you to meet some of our friends from Canada." Ebenezer followed her to the table and then on to meet so many new people he was sure he would never remember all of their names. The last was a Brother Bruno, a tall stocky man, who took Ebenezer's hand in his large hand with a firm grip of welcome.

Brother Bruno wanted to know how the farming was and if Ebenezer knew of any good farms he could buy. He had sold a large farm in Canada and wanted to get established as soon as possible so he could get the winter wheat in and prepare for spring planting. "I know of a few places out in the country. I'll come by tomorrow and take you around to see some of them. I get out in the country often to buy cattle so I see a lot of farmers. I guess you already know my brother-in-law, William Draper. He may know of some places. This is his farm." Ebenezer motioned for Brother Bruno to follow him over to the cutting table where William was carving away the last of the beef.

"Yes, I know William. We went to school together. We used to call him William Two because there was another William in our class. Phebe was my teacher. Those Drapers are a fine bunch of people. A lot of them are still up in our country."

Brother Bruno walked over to his old friend with a grin a mile wide and put his hand out to William. William wiped the meat drippings from his hands and embraced his old school mate who was at least a full head taller than he was. You haven't changed a bit Old Bruno. You always could whip the lot of us. Have you seen, Miss Phebe, yet?"

"Yes, and she was a sight for sore eyes. I was in love with her when she was our teacher. Did I ever tell you that? And now here she is in Nauvoo, married to a new husband and pretty as ever. I heard about your trials at Kirtland and Far West but she has held up well under it all. You two must have taken good care of her." He included Ebenezer in his comment.

"It always seemed that she was taking care of us. She took care of my first wife until she passed away. She is a good woman." Ebenezer looked across the yard at Phebe with pride and gratitude in his eyes.

Looks like she's found herself a good man too. She has some mighty pretty daughters. My son is really taken up with that Lydia Elizabeth. Does Lovina still sing like she used to? I used to go to church just to hear her sing." Brother Bruno looked around as he spoke, trying to spot the girls.

"I think William George will have her up there with the band before you know it. They sing together sometimes and Lovina sings alone too." As they spoke, Phebe was taking the baby from Lovina and holding Ester Ann's hand. Lovina went up to the band stand and stood by her younger brother. They sang several old ballads together and then Lovina sang alone. Phebe was bursting with pride at her children performing for their old friends from Canada. Little Ester Ann broke away from her grandmother and joined her mother by the band. She tapped her toes and bowed to the audience when her mother finished the song. The barn rocked with clapping and music, drowning out the thunder of approaching riders.

William was at the door by Bett who had just brought out some more hot rolls she had baked. They heard the noise of the riders simultaneously and looked out to the horror of men riding in through the open gate with lighted torches, blackened faces, and shouts of "No more Mormons. No more Mormons." "Go back where you came from. We don't want more Mormons here."

They were riding their horses around the house and barn and then threw a lighted torch into the Grist Mill. It ignited at once in an explosion. Even the arsonists closest to the Mill were thrown from their horses.

William called to the women to take the children and run out of the back door of the barn to the corn fields. Bett refused to go. Her two boys were asleep in the house and she defied the boisterous mobsters by running to her house. As she ran past one of the riders, she recognized him as one of her neighbors who professed to be a Pastor of his church. His blackened face did not conceal his identity. She had delivered his last child without reimbursement. She stared at him in disbelief and he looked away from her, seeing that she knew who he was.

Other riders rode their horses in through the barn doors, forcing the men to the walls. One dropped a torch, but as it touched the floor, Norman Brown grabbed the tub of water where the children had been bobbing for apples and doused the fire that was quickly spreading. Another rider threw a rope around Brother Bruno but did not anticipate the strength of the man who quickly jerked the rope, pulling the intruder from his horse before he could dally the rope around the saddle horn.

The horses in the barn spooked at the sight of the torch fire and bolted out, kicking some of the men crowded to the walls. Zemira dodged to miss the flying hoof and saw that the rider was the farmer who had sold them the apples. He realized that he and Norman had told the farmer about the party and even when and where it was going to be. This was all his fault. He jumped to his feet and pulled at the farmer's leg to try to unseat him from his saddle, but the man whirled on his horse, knocking Zemira to the floor, and then flipped his back with his cat-tail whip drawing blood across the young man's shoulders. "Tell your friends to go back where they come from. We don't want any more Mormons here. We don't even want you here. He flipped the whip again, catching Zemira's hands as he tried to protect his face, the tip of it slicing his cheek.

Norman, seeing his friends plight, went to his rescue with a pitchfork that he threw at the attacker. It missed the man but caught the rump of the horse. The animal bucked as the blood spurted from the punctures. The farmer was thrown from the horse and he ran from the two boys who had innocently bought some apples from him and gave him the information he needed to get a mob together to attack the welcome party.

Some of the riders rode through the yards trying to find the women and girls but they had all found hiding places, safely away from the black faced demons who would have harmed them. Phebe held Rhoda to her as the little girl shook in fear, listening to the riders shouting and riding close to the hideaways. Other mothers held their hands over their babies mouths to smother cries that might reveal their location.

The riders finally closed ranks and started to ride out. The last one throwing his torch through the front window of the house, igniting the curtains and spreading rapidly. Bett picked up the baby and ran from the house while the men fought the fire with water and gunny sacks, confining it to the front part of the house.

Gradually, the women and children came from their hiding places and tried to establish some resemblance of order. William called them together and they knelt in prayer. "We thank thee, Lord, that our lives were saved. Help us to bind up our wounds and care for our families. Bring peace and understanding to our neighbors, that the hate they feel will diminish. Give us the strength we need to stay true to the faith. We beseech thee in the name of our Saviour, Jesus Christ. Amen."

"Now, lets clean up this mess and remember that what we have is so much greater than the hate of our enemies." William found some shovels and brooms, passing them to the men and boys. Phebe and Bett dressed the wounds of the injured and the women who didn't have little ones to care for went to the house to help clean up after the fire and make it as livable as possible.

Some of the horses that had been driven away were rounded up and hitched to the buggies and wagons. One by one the families drove away, leaving William and Bett, Ebenezer and Phebe, and the boys to evaluate the damage. "It would be foolish to ask if there is any chance of legal recourse. Some of the same men who were in the mob that killed the Prophet were with this group tonight. I recognized at least two of my neighbors." William shook his head.

"The Pastor who lives on the next farm was one of them. maybe I should send him a bill for delivering his last baby and taking care of the family until his wife was up and around." Bitterness crept into Bett's voice as she looked at the shambles of her house.

Norman and Zemira looking at each other in unison said, "It's our fault. We told the farmer we bought the apples from about the party. He was one of the mobsters."

Zemira added, "He was the one that whipped me and Norman saved me by throwing a pitchfork at him. It missed him, but it hit his horse."

Ebenezer went to the boys and put his arms around them, being careful not to touch Zemira's wounds. "Don't blame yourselves. We don't. They could have found out in many different ways. The party was no secret. We live in a free country and should be able to have a party any time we want to without having such actions as tonight. We must help our Canadian friends understand that there are people who break the law here just as there are in Canada. I think we should swear out a complaint. We may not receive any satisfaction for doing it but it may stop the men from attacking another time."

"I'm going to see Brother Taylor tomorrow. You know he is from Canada and some of these folks were his friends too. Lets see what he has to say about pressing charges." William was a long time friend of John Taylor's and had great confidence in his judgement. He was the only man William allowed to address him as "Billy Draper."

Phebe and Ebenezer had the boys ride back to town with them and Rhoda. They could come out tomorrow and pick up the other rig. Phebe wanted to come and help Bett with the house anyway. They wrapped some blankets around them to protect them from the cool fall air and drove into the safety of Nauvoo.

CHAPTER TWENTY-NINE

William knocked on the Taylor's door. Sister Taylor opened it and greeted him with a smile. "How nice to see you, Brother Draper. We don't see enough of you. Won't you come in? John is upstairs. I'll go and get him." She motioned for William to sit in the parlor and went up to let her husband know he had company.

Brother Taylor walked slowly down the stairs. He was still pale and weak from the attack on him by the mobsters when they killed Joseph and Hyrum. He had stayed to himself with little outside contact, except for Brigham and the rest of the twelve. They had been trying to protect him from the dissidents who were trying to pull members away from the church.

William stood to greet him and walked over to shake his hand. Brother Taylor was a very dignified and genteel man. William had admired him since they first met in the mission field in Canada. "Well, if it isn't my friend, Billy Draper. How are you? I'm sorry we couldn't come out to the party for the Canadians last night, but as you can see, I'm not up to much partying yet. Tell me all about it." Brother Taylor sat down in the parlor chair next to William.

"We had a grand time for the most part, until some mobsters visited the party. They pretty well ruined the end of it but no one was seriously hurt. They destroyed my Grist Mill and tried to burn the house and barn down but we were able to save them. Zemira Palmer got some bad whiplashes. Remember Sam Bruno from Loughborough? One of the heathens tried to lasso him, but he pulled the brute right off his horse." William laughed as he remembered how shocked the black faced villain looked when he landed right on his backside on the barn floor.

"I wish I could have seen it. I'm sorry your property was damaged to that extent, however. How did the new comers from Canada take it?" The worry lines appeared on his brow as he waited for an answer.

"Many of them were pretty scared, as you can imagine. I called the group together for prayer after and we all worked to clean things up. I came to ask you if we should try to take any legal action. I have been threatened by my neighbors and even ask to leave Green Plain since I refused to go with them the night of the martyrdom. I don't see how we could get any action to help us. They all seem to be pretty set on running us out." William shifted in his chair, waiting for his friend's advice.

"I don't see any recourse for you. We have all agreed not to retaliate from the murders at Carthage and even though it is well known who the perpetrators of that heinous crime were, they have not been arrested. Perhaps you should sell your farm and move into Nauvoo. You still have your shoe shop here that Henry Munro is running. It seems to be doing well. Your parents and the Browns would help you get settled." Brother Taylor's face registered the concern he felt.

"I just needed someone to push me a little. I've been thinking the same thing. Bett is expecting another baby and our little boys were sick all night from the commotion and smoke. I don't think it would be wise for us to stay there. It's a darn shame. I love that farm out there and I was doing pretty well with the gristmill business. I have good crops to harvest this year. I'll do what I have to do, however." William stood and took Brother Taylor's hand in his. "Thank you, I wish they would let us be." He turned and walked out, not wanting to let the apostle see the tears in his eyes.

He rode his horse along the road to Green Plain and as he turned in his gate he saw about sixty-five armed men approaching the house. He knew they were after him so he rode to the woods to hide. A crowd gathered at the house. They forced their way in and tore the straw from the bed ticks, spread in the corners of the room and set fire to it. Bett tried to quench the flames but the roughians forced her out of the house. Some neighbors came to her aid and helped carry the sick boys to a shelter made by putting a bedstead upside down and draping it with quilts. Others were trying to get the furniture out of the house before it burned to the ground. A heavy thunder shower was approaching. When the storm broke, William ventured out to find his family. They were uninjured but in a precarious condition. He helped them into the shelter of what was left of the grist mill. A partial wall, some charred planks and sheets of metal provided some protection to them.

"William, you must go and hide. They are after you to kill you. They told me that and they were still looking for you when the storm hit. I'm sure they will be back. I'll be alright here with the children. Albert and Parley seem better. I think their fever's gone. Thank goodness for the good neighbors that helped me out with them." She pulled the quilts around them for warmth and moved the boys to the shelter of the wooden planks where the floor of what remained of the grist mill was still dry.

"I can't leave you like this. I never should have hidden in the first place." William took Bett in his arms and held her until she stopped shivering.

She looked up at him, "Go. We need you to live and you will be killed if they find you. They won't hurt me or the children. They've shown that much restraint." She pushed him away as the sun broke through the clouds. She knew the sunshine would bring out the posse again.

William dodged in and out of corn shucks. He could see the house had burned to the ground along with the barn and granary. His crops, ready for harvest were destroyed by the hogs, sheep and cattle that were roaming in the fields and paths the marauders had taken, beating down the ripe grain and corn stalks. He hid in a stalk of corn until dark. He went back to the mill and did all he could to keep his family dry and warm. He dared not make a fire.

At daylight, William ventured out and found his way through the fields to the home of George Walker, a Baptist minister. He told him of his plight and the kind old gentleman said. "I know, I saw it all but I could do nothing for you or they would destroy me. How can I help you now?"

"Just let me borrow a wagon to take my family to safety. I'll return it as soon as it is safe to do so." William looked at his neighbor, hoping he would not bring the wrath of the angry mob to his door.

"There it is. Take it and if you return it, all well. If not, all is well." As the good neighbor turned back to his house he called out, "God go with you."

William drove the team and wagon to the mill and started to load up what possessions had been saved when he saw ten armed men approaching. They were clearly looking for him. He dropped to his knees and crept through the brush on his hands and knees. He prayed that the Lord would protect his family and direct his path. He was a mile or so away from his farm when he saw the familiar Brown buggy coming along the road. "Oh, I can't let Phebe walk into this." He rose to his feet and ran to stop the buggy.

"Phebe, Phebe, stop!" He waved his arms and Phebe pulled back on the reins. Zemira was with her in the buggy.

"I'm sorry we didn't get back out yesterday. You look terrible, William. What is happening?" Zemira jumped out and helped his uncle on to the seat by Phebe.

William poured out the nightmarish story of the last twenty-four hours. "Bett and the children are in what's left of the Grist Mill. I've borrowed a wagon and team and I've got to find someone to go and get my family. Ten armed men are out there now looking to kill me. I have been running and hiding and crawling though the brush to avoid them.'

"Oh, my dear William. We will just have to get Bett and the children out of there some way." Phebe put her arm around her brother who had always been so strong for her.

"I'll go and get them." Zemira touched the wound on his cheek and took on a resolve to make up for telling the farmer about the party. "I'll sneak through the fields and get to Aunt Bett and the kids. Is there a team to pull the wagon?"

"I had it all hitched up when I left. You can get to them through the fields. Just get them in the wagon and meet us by that clump of trees you passed a little way back. If you don't get here in about thirty minutes, I'll go and get help" William put his hand on his nephews shoulder. "Thank you son."

"I've an idea that might make it a little safer. Take my bonnet with you. Put one of Bett's shawls and my bonnet on when you drive them out. If they think they have run Bett out alone they will let her go." Phebe was proud of Zemira but she realized he was going into a very dangerous situation.

Zemira hid the bonnet in his shirt and started out through the fields, hiding in the bushes and watching to see it it was clear to make it through the next clearing. He saw the mill ahead of him and looked to see if any of the men were in sight. He saw some going through the shocks of corn. They had their backs to him so he sprinted to the mill. "Aunt Bett, give me a shawl and you and the children get in the wagon. Try to hide so you can't be seen. Uncle William and Mother are waiting for us down the road."

Bett roused Albert and Parley and hurried them into the wagon. She threw in the quilts she had covered them with and climbed in herself. "I'm ready, Zemira."

Zemira bolted to the wagon with the shawl around him and his mother's bonnet tied at a strange angle, but still concealing his face enough to not be recognized. He slapped the reins on the horses and they took off running. As they drove past the corn field, one of the men raised his gun to shoot. Another pulled the barrel down.

"We don't have to kill the women." He shouted. And then hollering after the wagon, "Tell your man we'll find him. He can't get away from us."

Zemira flipped the reins again urging the team into a gallop. The wagon tipped on two wheels as they turned out on to the road but then righted itself. Bett clung to her boys and wondered if this wild ride would cause her to lose the baby.

As they approached the clump of trees where the buggy was waiting, Phebe pulled out onto the road. William lifted Bett into the buggy by Phebe and climbed into the wagon with Zemira. He looked back to see what was left of his farm and shook his head.

Phebe met William George at the door. She had seen him tie his horse at the hitching post and walk up the path. "How are William and Bett? Did you get them safely to the Staker's in Pike County?"

The threats of the mob on William's life had necessitated their exile. They had gone on the sixty miles from Nauvoo to Bett's Brother-in-law, Nathan Staker, who had helped them when they came from Far West. William George accompanied them because he traveled back and forth from Nauvoo to Pleasantville often and had friends along the way that could be trusted.

William George stepped in and took his hat off. "Yes, they are all fine. Aunt Bett had a baby boy the day after we arrived. They named him Isaac Grant. Uncle William said he would come back into Nauvoo after things have settled down and confer with President Young to see what he should do next. Have there been any more attacks on our People?"

"Yes, I'm afraid so. Over one hundred and fifty families have been burned out in Green Plain and other nearby towns. Brother Brigham has told us to prepare to leave Nauvoo and go west in the Spring. He wants all the men to help finish the Temple to complete the work the Prophet started. We have a lot to do. Ebenezer thinks that we should prepare at least two

wagons, if not more. We want you to go with us. Can you stay
and help get things ready?" Phebe had always relied on
William George and she felt comfortable in making this
request of him.

"I'll help all I can. I had already decided to work on the
temple every day. Uncle Zemira will share his finish tools with
me. He has taught me to be a pretty good carpenter. I can
always pick up a little extra work at night playing in a band.
What do we have to do to get ready to go west? Will it be any
different than when we left Kirtland?" He well remembered
the long wagon trip from Kirtland to Far West when he was
just a young boy.

"We used the big Conestoga wagons then but they are
telling us to build smaller wagons, called Prairie Schooners,
for this move. Ebenezer is trying to find all the oxen he can for
the saints to use to pull the wagons. The oxen seem to have
more stamina than horses." Phebe and Ebenezer had gone over
the recommendations from the Brethren and had already started making preparations.

"William George, there is something else I want to discuss
with you. I have already conferred with Lovina. I would like
you to be baptized for your father in the temple. They have
started to do the baptismal ordinances for the dead in the temple font even though the building isn't completely finished.
Somehow, I feel that your father realizes now the importance
of being baptized into the church. The Prophet told us, there
must be a welding link of some kind or other between the
fathers and the children. It is baptism for the dead. For we
without them, cannot be made perfect, neither can they without
us be made perfect. I think your father wants to be part of that
family link that will bind our family together."

"Mother, If that is what you want, I would be happy to do
it. It will be a great honor for me. How does Ebenezer feel
about it?" He picked up a biscuit from the side board and
spread some apple butter on it.

"We have discussed it and we both want to complete as many of the ordinances as we can before we head West. We are both going to receive our sacred temple endowments. Then I will act as Proxy for Ann for her to be sealed to Ebenezer for eternity." She and Ebenezer had not yet decided to whom she would be sealed. William George was so like his father in appearance that sometimes, when she saw him, the memories flooded back of her years of marriage to George. But Ebenezer was a 'Man of God' and she loved him. Phebe poured William George a glass of milk and cut a healthy wedge of pie for him.

Nauvoo was a beehive of activity. Every house had a wagon or two under construction in the back yard. Blacksmiths were working at their forges long hours every day but Sunday and mill workers were milling out wagon boxes and double trees as quickly as possible.

It was October of 1845 and the Spring of 1846 was not far away. That was the deadline the governor had given them to abandon Nauvoo. He claimed he was trying to appease the citizens of Illinois and avoid a major rebellion by giving them this option instead of allowing the Mormons to demand redress or retaliate with the Nauvoo Legion for the murders of their leaders and the raids and beatings of members of the church. The unfairness of the situation was taken to the highest levels of the country by the leaders of the church, only to be told, "Your cause is just, but we can do nothing for you."

Christmas gifts were meager and in every case, items needed for the exodus. The Drapers had their usual Christmas party at the home of Phebe and Ebenezer. The gloom of the situation and the memory of the last party at William's farm hung over the family members. William and Bett came back for the holiday and baby Isaac took the part of the infant Jesus when they reenacted the Nativity, as was their family custom.

Father and Mother Draper glowed with happiness as the children performed and the spirit bore witness of Christ and His mission as Ebenezer, to the surprise of his children, read the words of Luke from the New Testament describing the birth of the Saviour.

Phebe could not control the tears that welled up in her eyes. Ebenezer had been so dedicated and determined that he would learn to read and write. He had been a good student and even, after long days of work and preparation for the exodus, they would practice reading for long hours into the night. He memorized so fast that she would have to remind him to read each word.

"Ebenezer, you read that passage so beautifully. It was as if you were there in the town of Bethlehem, witnessing it yourself." Mother Draper held her son-in-law's hand and looked up to him with love and respect. He had brought so much happiness to her daughter and was also a strength to the family.

Phebe looked over at her father and mother and realized they were aging. It was hard for her to accept the fact that they were in their seventies. Nothing slowed them down and they were preparing for the trip West as vigorously as any other members of the family. She resolved that she would help her mother with the preparation in spite of her independence. They would need all the strength they had to make the journey.

Lydia Elizabeth and Anthony Bruno announced their engagement. They planned to marry before the exodus and so were preparing their own wagon and supplies. Lydia discouraged her mother from making a lot of wedding plans. "We will have Brother Brigham marry us in a quiet ceremony with just the family. I would really like to have Uncle William and Aunt Bett here, and Asahel too if he will come. We have decided to get married right after the new year." Lydia Elizabeth saw the disappointment on her mother's face but she smiled and hugged her. "Lovina will make me a special veil and I will wear the white lawn dress I made last summer."

"I'm sorry you can't have a big wedding. I have tried so hard to keep our family together and make a good life for all of you. Sometimes I wonder why we are called to sacrifice so.

I want you to be happy. I know I must let you go. You have made a wise choice in Anthony. He is a good man." Phebe put her arms around her beautiful daughter Lydia Elizabeth and tried to conceal her tears. She thought to herself, "I must be getting old. I am so emotional about everything."

"There is something I want you to have." She took Grandma Draper's cake plate from the shelf and gave it to Lydia Elizabeth. "Mother gave this to me when I was married and I have taken care of it through all these years. It belonged to my Grandmother Draper. It survived the fire, the trip to Kirtland, Far West, the raids at Far West and the moves to Springfield and Nauvoo. I can't tell you how often I have looked at this plate and remembered my dear grandmother and the blessing she gave me on her death bed. Pack it carefully and take good care of it. Someday, you will have a daughter to give it to and when you do, tell her the story of the Drapers. We are a strong family and the Lord expects a lot from us. I wish I could look into the future to see all that is expected, but if we knew we may not be strong enough to face it."

"Thank you, mother. I know how much it means to you and I will cherish it always. It is a lovely gift." Lydia Elizabeth wrapped it carefully to protect it for the trip and the home she and Anthony would someday have. "You have been a perfect mother. When I look back at all we have done and been through together, I have memories of how you always made me feel safe and loved, even during the siege at Far West. Your faith and prayers gave me a feeling of security that I cannot describe. It was as if I was encircled with a protective shield of your love that defied the forces of evil. I hope I can be that kind of mother to the children that are sent to us."

CHAPTER THIRTY

With the holidays and Lydia Elizabeth's wedding over the Browns were trying to find a buyer for their house. Phebe remembered the disappointment she felt when the short note came from Asahel in answer to the invitation to the wedding. He was not about to bring his family into the city if Nauvoo. It was too dangerous. He did not want them to come and see him because his neighbors may think he was one of the Mormons and burn his house or harm his family. He ended the letter with, "Sorry, but you have chosen your way and I have chosen mine. Please respect my wishes."

Phebe wiped away the tears as she packed clothes, bedding and food and tried to decide what furniture they could possibly take with them. She and Ebenezer had been happy here in Nauvoo, in spite of the problems the church had experienced. They had known it would be for a limited time because the Prophet told them they would someday go to the Rocky Mountains to help establish the church there. Somehow, she had hoped it would be longer, but the situation here was similar to that in Far West. Only those who had seen the venom of the mobs in Far West could realize what happens to people when they become a part of mob violence. Perhaps it was best for Asahel to keep his family away from it.

William had met with Brother Brigham while he was here for the holidays and had been given another challenge that Phebe knew would tax Bett's faith and courage. They had all known that the principle of Polygamy had been revealed to the Prophet before he was murdered but they also knew that only a select few were ask to practice the "Principle". The brethren were concerned for the welfare of the many widows and single women living in Nauvoo who were also eager to go west with the body of the church. William was one of several Church leaders who were asked to marry one or more of the women and help them in the trek west.

William had always responded to any assignment with all the enthusiasm he could muster and seldom did he wait to consult Bett before making a commitment but this time it was different. He was given firm direction by Brother Brigham that he must have Bett's permission to take a second wife. Not only did he want to consult her but he wondered how he would be able to provide for another family after the devastating loss of their home and farm in Green Plain. As had been his custom, he had come to Phebe to help him sort out the ramifications of this call to live the "Principle."

Phebe was in the back of the house taking inventory of the supplies packed and ready to take to the wagons. She heard the door open and recognized William's call to her, "Miss Phebe, are You home?"

When she heard him call her, "Miss Phebe." she knew something serious was to be discussed. He always did that when he wanted her advice or help. She looked up to see this younger brother, who had been her champion and protector through the last few years, pale and exuding the deepest feeling of concern and helplessness. Not even the terrible mob action in Green Plain had left him in such a state.

"What is it, William?" She went to him and took his hand and led him to the kitchen table. "Sit down and tell me. Are you all right?"

He put his elbows on the table and his face in his hands. After several moments of silence, he looked up into those beautiful steel grey eyes of his sister. "I have been called to live the principle of polygamy. I must get Bett's permission and I don't know how to tell her. I don't feel worthy of this assignment nor do I see how I can care for another family. Phebe, what am I to do?" He dropped his face to his hands and they sat again in silence.

"What do you think the Lord wants you to do? Have you

gone to Him for an answer?" Phebe knew the Lord would direct William. He was a good and dedicated servant. "Bett and the children are over at Lovina"s for the afternoon. Go up to the back bedroom. You won't be disturbed. Ponder and pray about it. When Bett and the children come back I'll send her up to you. My advice to you, brother dear, is to ask Bett, not tell her if you decide to accept the call. She has a strong testimony and has sacrificed so much already for the church. Give her the opportunity to make this choice for the both of you."

It was a cold January day and as the darkness crept across the sky in the late afternoon hours the house took on a chill. Phebe added a log to the fireplace and watched as the fire from the embers caught the dry bark on the rim of the log. As the fire engulfed the log she stared into the flames, wondering how she felt about this new challenge given to William. What if it had been Ebenezer who was asked to live the Principle? The warmth of the fire reached out to her and she felt as she had so many times before. The burning of the spirit which testified to her that the Lord was guiding his church and they could do whatever was asked to carry on the work. She remembered that feeling she had felt in the Kirtland temple when it was dedicated by the Prophet and the song they sang: "The Spirit of God Like a Fire is Burning." A feeling of peace came to her and she knew that Bett would be touched by the spirit also. Brother Brigham now held the keys given to him by the Prophet Joseph. He would not lead them astray.

She walked to the bedroom and took her Family Bible from the shelf and opened it to the Family page where she had recorded the births and deaths. The page was full so she turned it over and wrote, *"Married Ebenezer Brown, August, 1842."* She blew the ink dry. She and Ebenezer had been married for three and a half years. It was high time for her to record it in the Bible.

Phebe was stirring the warm soup on the stove when Bett and the children returned. They had walked the few blocks through the new fallen snow and their cheeks and noses were glowing. Rhoda and John had met them there after school and walked home with them. Rhoda pulled her warm gloves off and started to help Bett with the others. "Mother, Lovina made the best cookies for us and we all had hot chocolate before we left. It is so much fun at her house Ester Ann and Fanny were so cute with the baby. You should have been there. Why didn't you go with Aunt Bett?"

"I seem to have a lot to do these days. I should have gone." Phebe wondered why she had decided to stay at home but she really knew it was because William needed her. So often she felt that forces beyond her control guided her actions. "Rhoda, tell the children to come back here by the kitchen stove to get warm and dry. I'll make up for not going by reading a story to you. Bett, William is up stairs. Why don't you go up and tell him we will have supper as soon as Ebenezer and the boys get in from feeding the stock.

She watched with love and compassion as Bett innocently walked up the stairs to face a dilemma that would affect the rest of her life. "Please, Lord, give her strength to pass one more test of faith." She pulled a book of children's stories and poems from the bookcase and walked to the kitchen to keep the children occupied while William and Bett had their talk.

She heard Ebenezer and the boys stomping the snow from their feet as they came in the back door an hour or so later. Ebenezer walked over to Phebe and pecked her on the cheek. His nose was cold and she pulled her face back and then she kissed him. "I'm so glad you are in out of that cold. I have some hot soup ready for you as soon as you and the boys wash up."

"Hear that boys? We have to wash up again. Seems like we have to do that every time we come home. The soup smells good. I guess it's worth the effort." He winked at Phebe and lined up at the wash stand with the boys.

William and Bett joined them at the table. Bett's eyes were

red and swollen and they were both very quiet. Ebenezer looked at Phebe, questioning with raised eyebrows. Phebe nodded to him in their way of saying, "We'll talk about it later."

Ebenezer picked up the cue and kept the children busy in conversation about the visit to Lovina's and quizzed John and Rhoda on their progress in school that day. After dinner he called them to the parlor and proudly opened the Book of Mormon and read to them about the Prophet, Nephi. Bett excused herself to go and feed the baby and put him down to sleep. William followed her upstairs to the room they were sharing.

Phebe watched as the children started to dose and one by one scooted them off to bed. It was fun to have the cousins staying with them and her children didn't mind sharing their beds. Gurnsey, Norman and Zemira had gone off to see friends so Phebe and Ebenezer sat alone by the fire. Ebenezer turned to his wife. "Is there something I missed or is it something I shouldn't know about? Whatever it is, it is having a profound effect on two people who are very important to us."

"I'm sure William will discuss it with you as soon as he can. I don't feel at liberty to break his confidence, though he didn't ask me not to tell you. Ebenezer, have I told you lately how much I love and appreciate you? You are always pleasant and bring happiness into our home." Phebe smiled at this good man who filled her life with so much love.

"You have sparked my curiosity but I will be patient. I knew there was something unusual happening when I walked in the door and got that warm welcome." He grinned at her and her cheeks reddened. "Come on, lets go to bed. I have a lead on some more oxen I hope to get tomorrow. I may have to trade some of our furniture for them or even the house." He took her hand and led her to their room.

William was gone and Bett was downstairs rocking the baby when Phebe finished cooking the breakfast mush. She called upstairs for the children to get ready for school and come down for breakfast. She turned to Bett. "Did William leave without breakfast?"

"Yes. He is fasting today. I would be also if I didn't have a nursing baby." She moved the baby to the other breast and covered him with the soft knitted shawl. "We have decided to accept the call to live the "Principle" William has gone to tell Brother Brigham that he will marry Martha Weaver. She and her husband were so kind to us when William was sick on the road to Far West. Now she has lost her dear husband it is only right for us to care for her in her time of need. We will take her and her children back to Pleasantville with us and prepare for all of us to join the movement west in the spring."

Phebe could tell that the spirit had born witness to Bett as it had to her. There was no more discussion of the matter. If William didn't tell Ebenezer himself before they left, she would share it with him because she wanted him to know of the testimony she had received of the Lord's hand in this difficult "Principle."

The saints were hoping for an open winter so they could continue their preparations to go west but January was unusually cold and stormy. Some barges had taken the lead wagons through the river laced with chunks of ice. When the January thaw was anticipated it just got colder. By the first part of February the freezing weather had caused a phenomena that the old timers in the area had never seen. The Mississippi River was frozen over. It was then that the message came, for the Saints that were prepared, to move across the river.

Governor Ford had sent a letter to Brigham Young apprising him of accusations that had been forwarded to the federal government of the Mormons printing counterfeit money. The accusations were false but the federal troops were said to be heading to Nauvoo as soon as the weather cleared to stop the

Mormons from moving west. It was Governor Ford's admonition for them to go as quickly as possible. Brigham Young was
faced with his people being caught between the mobs on the
East and the Federal troops on the West. His only alternative
was to start the movement west immediately. The frozen
Mississippi offered that option.

Wagons by the hundred were driven along by husbands and
sons. Some horses hitched to buggies followed and many rode
their horses. As the masses crossed the ice it became slushy
and the horses would sometimes lose their footing as did the
people who were walking. As night came on, five hundred
families had crossed the ice and were setting up tents or any
kind of shelter they cold find. Phebe and Ebenezer were in the
first group with their combined families. The Brown entourage
included the two wagons Ebenezer had outfitted; one to
accommodate He and Phebe and their two young children,
Rhoda (eleven) and John (nine). The other wagon was for the
Brown and Palmer boys, Guernsey, Norman, Zemira and
William George. Harriet and Oliver Straton and their two children also had their wagon ready and joined the Brown wagons
as did Phebe's father and mother and her brother Zemira.
Lovina and Henry Munro and their little children would follow
with William and Bett when they arrived from Pike County.
Lydia Elizabeth and her new husband, Anthony Bruno were
also preparing to follow the rest of the family.

Phebe piled the quilts on Rhoda and John as they huddled
in the wagon. She had heated some rocks in the fire to warm
their beds in the wagon box. The cold north wind was biting
and a bonfire in the snow gave off little or no heat. She walked
back to her parents wagon and found them huddled together
shivering. Mother Lydia was grey and her chills were uncontrollable. Zemira was trying to get a fire going to warm some
water for tea but the whipping snow kept blowing it out.

"Ebenezer, come and help me. Mother and father are freezing." The panic in Phebe's voice pierced the coldness of the

night. Ebenezer responded to the call as did the boys from the other wagon. Together the men were able to pitch a tent on the frozen ground between the wagons and after spreading straw and quilts to make a warmer bed they carried Mother Draper from her wagon. Her dear William joined her and tried to warm her with what little heat his frail body could generate.

Phebe carried more rocks from the fire to warm the bed and held some lukewarm tea to her mother's lips. "Mother, sip a little more. We will get you a warm and well. Think about the warm days in Canada when we walked in the apple orchard. Remember the hot summer days when we shelled the peas on the porch." Phebe kept talking, as if she could will her mother to live by keeping these memories alive. "Mother, remember, we made it across the frozen Lake Ontario with the Indian Okinihah?" She rubbed the fragile hands that had comforted her and served her in so many ways. Try as she might, she could not stimulate enough circulation in them to warm them so she held them close in hers. The translucent skin revealed the blue veins beneath and the once long slender fingers now twisted and gnarled by the years of frontier life.

"Phebe, it is enough, she is gone." William held his Lydia to him and wept on the grey bobbed hair that once shone like the sun and blew in the wind. "My Little Lydia, how can I live without you?"

Lydia Lathrop Draper, this pioneer mother and wife who had brought education and gentility to her family on the frontiers of Canada and the United States, died on the west bank of the Mississippi river from exposure to the cold February weather. Would the citizens of the United States of America, and specifically Governor Ford of the state of Illinois, feel justified in the suffering and sorrow they had brought to innocent citizens? Many saints were called home to their creator that night and the camp, though sorrowful and mourning, felt the love and presence of the Savior who had died for them on the cross.

Ebenezer held Phebe to him as she sobbed out her grief. The sorrow she felt was greater than when she lost Eliza or George. It was as if a part of her was gone. Her mother had been her champion, teacher, advisor and protector for all of her forty-nine years. She recalled the quiet, composed Lydia defending her to the charlatan preacher/teacher and the calming effect she always visited upon her when life seemed too hard to bear. "It is funny the little things you remember. Mother always made sure there was a place for everyone at her dinner table and everyone was welcomed with open arms to her home. Oh, Ebenezer, I'll miss her so but I have such wonderful memories."

"You have many of her qualities, Phebe. She taught you well. That is why I love you. We will always revere her memory." Ebenezer kissed her and wiped the tears from her cheeks. He led her to their wagon and she finally fell into a deep sleep dreaming of her mother holding her.

Phebe awoke to the stark reality of her mother's death and the sound of shovels and picks hitting against the frozen ground, trying to pierce the icy crust to find softer earth for the needed graves. Some wagon boxes were being dismantled to use their wood for coffins. Other wagons were headed back across the river for more supplies and some because their owners could not face the reality of the hardships that lay ahead.

Brother Brigham called them to prayer. He talked to God so all could hear. "Please, dear Father, comfort those that mourn this day and help them to know, as I know, that their loved ones are in thy arms and are sanctified this day for their sacrifice. Comfort the parents who have lost children and the children who have lost parents. Help them to see and understand thy plan. This life is but a glimpse of the eternal joy that awaits us all. Give us strength to carry on until it is our time to come to thee." He looked over those hundreds of saints who had survived the freezing night. With overwhelming compassion he wept with them and then stood tall, extending his love to each and every one.

The saints established what they would call, "Winter Quarters", there on the wind whipped plains of Iowa. They built cabins and dug caves into the small hills for any shelter they could find against the winter weather. Phebe observed that those who had made the treks to Far West and Nauvoo, living off the land and camping in wagons and tents were better equipped to survive this relentless deprivation of comfort and rest. It was as if they had been tested before and, having passed the test, could endure any challenge the land or weather would inflict upon them. It was, however, their faith in God and his plan of salvation that helped them endure.

The snow that came in the night or the winds that whipped the snow in blizzards did not deter them from their goal. They would cross this prairie and someday get to the Rocky mountains where they could live and worship in peace.

PART VII

GOD WILL DELIVER THEE
FEBRUARY 1846—OCTOBER 1846
CHAPTER THIRTY-ONE

The Saints pushed on from Winter Quarters, leaving behind them some shelter for those who followed. Many days they traveled only a few miles through the snow and often left graves on the rolling knolls of the Iowa landscape. Some died from exposure and others from hunger or illness brought on by either of the above. Each day, as they marched on to the Missouri River, the road became more difficult. When the thawing winds came, the trail oozed with mud and sucked the wagon wheels into mires. When the freezing rains and snow descended upon them, the cold pierced their shoes and mittens with painful frost bite that left permanent scars.

Ebenezer could see that the cattle needed more nourishment than they could glean from the land. Barks of the trees were gnawed at or browsed off. That is, the few that were left from the autumn fires that had stripped much of the forest from the hills. He sent the four sons south with other young men to find settlers that would let them work for supplies or sell them meal, flour, wheat and corn, or other needed commodities. When the leading body of the saints reached Sac and Fox country, only half way to the Missouri River, spring came at last.

"The water is rising so fast we need to get out of this stream bed. I'll double yoke the oxen to pull out of this mud." Ebenezer jumped from the wagon and motioned to the other men to help him. The women stayed with their wagons and prayed that the water would not rise too high before their wagon was pulled to higher ground. Many days their progress was only to ford a stream bed of rising water from the spring rains.

The young men that had gone south rejoined the caravan at Mount Pisgah with needed commodities. The saints planted fields of grain saved from their meager supplies and from some of the seed replenished by the ingenuity and self sacrifice of these fine young men who had given up their places in wagons and tents to the ill or aged and gone south for help. The fields of grain would furnish food for the saints that would follow.

Phebe was so relieved to see the boys. When they had left the camp in the dead of winter she feared for their lives and had prayed in earnest for their safe return. The four rode into camp together; Gurnsey, William George, Norman and Zemira. Gurnsey was driving the wagon filled with grain sacks and the other boys were riding the horses. "Hello, Hello. Over here. We're over here." She called to them

They brought molasses candy for John and Rhoda. The fresh supply of flour soon furnished the family and their traveling neighbors with hot bread cooked in the big pots over the fires. Phebe pulled out a jar of preserves from a barrel of rice. She had been saving it for a special occasion and passed it around to sweeten the sourdough bread.

That night they sang and danced around the campfire to the Jew's Harp music provided by William George. William George was showing off for a girl in camp that he liked. Her last name was Agnes Draper but they were not closely related. They ended the evening with some hymns and a prayer of thanksgiving for the safe arrival of the boys. William George walked Agnes to her family wagon and Phebe thought. "Well, maybe this will be the girl for him."

Phebe looked at Norman and Zemira. They had grown into men, though they were just fifteen. Their faces, now covered with thin beards, revealed the winter's ferocity and she mourned for the youth they had lost. They had survived and that was the important thing. She was sure Gurnsey and William George had looked out for them but as it had been with the main company, survival was a personal pursuit. It took its toll on the weak and the strong. Their only sacrifice had been mother Lydia. The sight of that frozen hill with the shallow graves on the cold February day on the west bank of the Mississippi was indelibly printed on her mind. And though she had seen it repeated almost daily since that day, the routine of suffering, deaths and burials could not erase that single episode when her mother was buried in the rough hewn casket in the half frozen earth. That night she dreamed that she saw the Savior motioning Lydia to come to him from the grave. She wakened with a start, remembering the dream in detail. A peaceful sleep came to her and the pain of the loss of her mother did not return. She no longer visualized her in the frozen earth, but with the Savior, surrounded by his love.

Ebenezer and Phebe, along with the other family wagons, were preparing to leave Mount Pisgah and head on west. Brigham Young and Heber C. Kimball had left a few days earlier to return, in disguise, to dedicate the Nauvoo Temple and supervise the exodus of the rest of the body of the saints. Camps of weary travelers were now spread over half of the Iowa territory, clustered in groups to assist each other when necessary.

William Draper, with his wives, Bett and Martha and their families, had started west about the first of May. Lovina and Henry with their three little children and the newly weds, Lydia and Anthony, had joined their Uncle William in Pleasantville and started west with his caravan. They came upon the church leaders heading to Nauvoo. It was a great reunion. News from those in the first exodus had not reached them and they were eager for information.

Brigham Young rode his horse up to William's wagon,

"Brother William, I'm glad to see you are on your way. We need fresh travelers to buoy up the group and we especially need your leadership ability. Things are a bit disorganized now but when we get back we will organize the saints into groups of one hundred and we need you to be a leader." He turned and rode his horse along with the wagon as he visited with his old friend.

"How are the rest of the family? We haven't heard a word from them since they left in February." William pulled the jerk line, slowing the oxen to an easy pace for the conversation.

"Pull up for a few minutes and call the family together. I'll tell you all at the same time." A shadow of sadness crossed Brigham's face. The sorrow of the deaths and suffering lay heavy on his shoulders.

William motioned for the others to circle their wagons and called them together to hear Brother Brigham's news. "Tell us. How is every one and how far west are they? I hope they have had better weather than we have had in Illinois."

William watched as Brigham stepped forward. "I'm afraid the news is not all good. The weather has been terrible and the progress very slow. Many of our brothers and sisters have died and been buried along the way."

There was an audible gasp from the group. No one dared to ask who of their loved ones were gone. Brigham continued, "Many families have lost several, but your family has been more fortunate than most. I must tell you however, that dear Sister Lydia did not survive the first night. She is buried at Winter Quarters on the west bank of the Mississippi.

"The rest of the Draper/Brown caravan are well enough. I saw them just before leaving camp. The boys had just returned with several other young men who had gone south for supplies. They brought a wagon load of much needed grain with them."

"I'm sorry to be the bearer of such sad news. I know how much Sister Lydia was loved by all of you. Father William has accepted the loss and carries his share of the burden. He is often found in the tents of grieving families, giving them comfort and leaving his testimony with them. Phebe and Ebenezer are the stalwarts of the group. Phebe teaches the sisters how to cook over the campfire and Ebenezer helps the others care for their stock. They have both been an example of cheerfulness and optimism during the most difficult of times." Brigham Young put his arm around his old friend, William Draper. He remembered those early days of the church in Canada and the light of the gospel in young William. He recalled also the hours they had spent together with the Prophet in the "School of the Prophets" in Kirtland, all eager to learn as much and as quickly as possible. Together they had left Kirtland, Far West and now Nauvoo. Each time under duress from evil men and circumstances beyond their control.

"The rest of your family is at Mount Pisgah. You can probably catch them there. The trails are dry now so you should make good time. You have fresh stock and are not worn out from traveling. I'll be returning soon and meet you at Council Point on the Missouri River. The government has one more request of us but I'll tell you about that when I return." He mounted his horse and joined the small group of riders waiting for him. One of which was another friend of William's, Heber C. Kimball.

Lovina went to her uncle and sobbed on his shoulder. She was Lydia's oldest grandchild and had always felt a special bond with her grandmother. At the Christmas party she remembered looking at the four generations of Draper women, Lydia, Phebe, herself and little Ester Ann. What a legacy. Each one made to feel special and loved because of who and what they were. She must carry on the tradition.

They climbed back into the wagons and continued the endless journey, picking up the pace so as to over take the rest of the family.

Speculation that the Mormons would join forces with the British or the Mexican Government if they left the United States Territory concerned the U.S. government. Some members of the cabinet urged that the government should prevent them from leaving based on the plea that it was contrary to law for an armed force from the United States to invade the dominion of another government, charging that the Nauvoo Legion was an armed force. Letters were sent to members of congress apprising them of the peaceful intentions of the Mormons and asking for Government patronage while journeying westward. It was their hope that they could secure some protection and perhaps earn some subsistence by helping to build forts along the Oregon Trail.

A statement was issued by the high Council of the Church and circulated among the members at Nauvoo in January of 1846 before the trek west began. It read as follows: "Should hostilities arise between the Government of the United States and any other power, in relation to the right of possessing the territory of Oregon, we are on hand to sustain the United States government to that country. It is geographically ours: and of right no foreign power should hold dominion there; and if our services are required to prevent it, those services will be cheerfully rendered according to our ability."

Elder J. C. Little, who was presiding over the Saints in the New England States, was directed by President Young as follows; "If our government should offer facilities for emigrating to the western coast, embrace those facilities if possible. As a wise and faithful man, take every honorable advantage of the times you can. Be thou a savior and a deliverer of the people, and let virtue, integrity and truth be your motto-salvation and glory the prize for which you contend."

Elder Little was successful in finally getting an audience with President Polk and was informed that it was the President's intention that the Mormons give aid in taking possession of California and would receive orders to push through, take the country and fortify it in the name of the United States. Elder Little was to raise an army of one thousand and the people would be protected as good citizens.

The plan was later modified to five hundred men and put under the direction of the Secretary of War. Colonel Kearney, Commander of the Army of the West, received orders to recruit the Mormon Battalion, appointing a Captain from the army to carry out the orders. Other officers of the Battalion were to come from the members of the battalion and elected by their fellow enlistees.

Thus was the situation when Ebenezer and Phebe neared Council Point. Rumors had spread through the camps that war had broken out between the United States and Mexico and a Captain Allen was sent to recruit five hundred young and efficient men from among the Saints traveling west.

Zemira brought the circular, distributed by Captain Allen, to his mother, Phebe, who read the following to Ebenezer and the others in their camp.

> *I have come among you, instructed by Colonel S.F. Kearney, of the U.S. Army of the west, to visit the Mormon camps, and to accept the service, for twelve months, of four or five companies of Mormon men who may be willing to serve their country for that period in our present war with Mexico; this force to unite with the Army of the West at Santa Fe, and be marched thence to California, where they will be discharged.*
>
> *They will receive pay and rations, and other allowances, such as volunteers or regular soldiers receive, from the day they shall be mustered into the service, and will be entitled to all comforts and benefits of regular soldiers of the army, and when discharged, as contemplated, at California, they will be given, gratis, their arms and accoutrements. with which they will be fully equipped at Fort Leavenworth. This is offered to the Mormon people now.*
>
> *This gives an opportunity of sending a portion of their*

young and intelligent men to the ultimate destination of their whole people, and entirely at the expense of the United States, and this advanced party can thus pave the way and look out the land for their brethren to come after them. Those of the Mormons who are desirous of serving their country, on the conditions here enumerated, are requested to meet me without delay at their principal camp at Council Bluffs, whither I am now going to consult with their principal men, and to receive and organize the force contemplated to be raised.

I will receive all healthy, able bodied men of from eighteen to forty-five years of age.

J. Allen, Captain 1st Dragoons

Note—I hope to complete the organization of this battalion in six days after my reaching Council Bluffs, or within nine days from this time. June 26, 1846

Phebe put the paper down. There was silence as the hungry, poorly clad, exhausted travelers looked from one to another. What did they owe the United States Government? Ebenezer was the first to break the silence. "Well, lets read it again and see if there is any thing good about it. President Young will counsel us as to what we should do. We'll be in Council Bluffs tomorrow. Let's pray about it and think it over."

The wagons moved on at a faster pace, hoping to reach their destination early to get direction from President Young.

Phebe read the circular again as she was jostled on the seat of the wagon. Their food was almost gone and it was evident that they would have to spend another growing season here on the plains before they could move on to the Rocky Mountains. Brigham Young would not take them on to another winter of traveling. She was sure of that. What could the government do for them and could they be trusted? She remembered her patriotic stand during the War of 1812. She had always been loyal to her country but the past few years had tried that feeling of trust and devotion. The chant of the Grandfather Lathrops came to mind and she wondered what the good Reverend John Lathrop would have done.

The wagon wheels caught a rut left in the road by the travelers ahead of them and Ebenezer pulled the jerk line to the right to urge the oxen to pull them onto level ground. As the wagon wheels met the edge of the rut the wagon tipped and then righted itself throwing Phebe against Ebenezer. "Sorry, I wasn't holding on. I was letting my mind wander instead of paying attention. What do you think about this request from the government?"

"I think I'll wait and see what Brother Brigham says. We have all had a hard few months and he has suffered through it with us. He knows the Lord needs him to get the Saints to the Rocky Mountains and I believe he will be guided to give us the proper direction. Our group seemed a little down after you read the circular to them. Lets get them to sing and dance around the campfire tonight. We need to cheer them up."

Phebe slipped her arm into the crook of his elbow. "You always make things easier. Don't you ever get discouraged? I have to confess that some days I would have turned back if you had given me the slightest opportunity to go."

"Shame on you. We are more blessed than most. We know we are going to the Rocky Mountains. We just don't know how hard it will be to get there or how long it will take." Ebenezer started to hum his favorite hymn and Phebe joined in. The miles went faster if they sang along the way.

As the darkness crept across the prairie from the east and the sun set in the west, sending glorious rays into the cumulus clouds, the clusters of wagons stopped to make camp for the night. They circled the wagons and tethered the livestock. A fire was built from any brush that could be gathered in the vicinity and the women set up cooking pots and started to prepare the evening meal. The boys found some wild turkeys a few hundred feet from the trail. The birds were drawn and cleaned, ready for the steaming pot of water. Phebe added some herbs and spices and some of the rice. It would be a feast compared to some of the meals they had eaten the last few months. She cooked some bread from the sourdough starter she kept working in the wagon. Sometimes they would wrap the dough around a stick and cook it over the coals of the fire but tonight she baked it in a heavy pot with a lid.

As she adjusted the pots over the fire she heard a rider coming into camp. It was her brother, William. He dismounted and she turned from the fire, brushed her hair back, wiped the soot from her hands and ran to her brother. "William, I am so glad to see you. We have wondered what had become of you and the rest of the family. Are Lovina and Henry with you? Ebenezer! Father! come and see who just came into camp."

The men were hobbling the oxen away from the wagons where they could graze in the grass. They walked into the light of the fire to see a welcome sight. William looked well under the layer of trail dust. He was thirty-nine years old and moved with the vigor of a twenty-year-old. The men embraced and the questions started to fly. "Where is your family? Who came with you?"

William threw up his hands, "One at a time, but first let me look at you. You don't look too bad considering what I have been told about your plight the last few months. Brother Brigham met us on the trail." His voice broke but finally he was able to utter the words. "He told us about Mother." He put his arm around his father's shoulders as the family patriarch allowed some tears to trickle down his weathered cheeks. William's tears fell on his father's shoulders. After an awkward silence he straightened and started to answer the questions.

"The rest of the family is back a few miles. We had hoped to overtake you before dark but when we realized that was not going to happen they agreed that I should come on and find you. They will join us in the morning if you can wait up for a few hours. Yes, Lovina and Henry are with us. We didn't start until the middle of May so we have had an easy journey compared to yours. We have passed groups of Saints all across the Iowa prairie, asking if any of them had seen you. The Brunos are back a few miles and told us we were close. They had seen you a few days back." William walked around the group hugging his brother Zemira and his nieces and nephews.

Phebe finished preparing the evening meal and called the group to supper. Father Draper invited them all to join in a family prayer before the meal. It was a prayer of thanksgiving for William's arrival and the food that had been provided for them in the wilderness.

Phebe could hardly sleep that night. She was so anxious to see Bett and she must get to know more about William's second wife, Martha. Most of all, she wanted to see Lovina and Henry and her grandchildren. Little Billy Munro was twelve and Ester Ann was almost eleven. Fanny would be four in October. Tomorrow would be a great family reunion, one long to be remembered.

CHAPTER THIRTY-TWO

It was the morning of June 27, 1846. The second anniversary of the martyrdom of the Prophet Joseph Smith Jr. The sun rose over the camp of the Browns and Drapers somewhere east of the Missouri river. The lowing of the cows near the campsite wakened the boys and they dutifully crawled out of their bed rolls and slipped into their britches and shoes. Each taking a bucket to milk the cows, they moved quietly to avoid waking the camp. They would have a few hours rest today while they waited for Uncle William's family to arrive.

Ebenezer was already up and out with the livestock. A new calf was born that morning joining some of the other young offspring; lambs, shoats and a colt. The colt was born to Ebenezer's favorite white mare and was promised to John if he would care for it during the journey. Ebenezer thought to himself, "New life goes on, even under the worst of circumstances. Our herd of livestock has grown since we left Nauvoo, in spite of the wretched winter weather." They had lost some lambs who were born too early to survive in the spring snow storms but for the most part they had been blessed. They could help provide meat for the camp as well as milk and wool to spin and weave for clothes. His daughter, Harriet, had found room in her wagon for the loom. She and Phebe would be busy when they finally arrived at Council Bluffs and the sheep were sheared. He went back to the circle of wagons, started the morning fire and put the water on to heat.

Phebe slipped out of their wagon bed, trying not to disturb Rhoda and John. She joined Ebenezer at the camp fire. "The prairie is alive this morning with new grass. It is going to be a beautiful day. I think I will make Johnny cakes for breakfast. I can make them fresh for William's camp as they arrive. Ebenezer, this is really an adventure isn't it? Now the bad weather is past we can enjoy this beautiful land. Sometimes, out here, it seems you can see for ever. It is very different than the wooded covered hills of the East." She took some warm water from the pot and poured it into the wash basin. She washed her face and hands and brushed her hair, braiding it into a plait and pinning it up for the day. Her muslin dress was worn and faded but she had some calico to make her a summer dress when they arrived at Council Bluffs.

The rest of the camp stirred and they were soon up washing faces and smelling the coffee perking over the fire. Brigham Young had listed coffee on the supplies to take with them and advised them to use it wisely for warmth and energy. Phebe mixed the Johnny cake batter and was soon frying them in the hot grease. They disappeared as soon as she cooked them and she had to mix up another bowl of batter. As William had predicted, the rest of his company arrived before ten o'clock and they too enjoyed the Johnny cakes. Phebe was so busy over the fire she hardly had time to give the new arrivals an adequate welcome, but the rest of the camp was taking care of that. She would have her time with Bett and Lovina and the grandchildren soon enough.

Some important visitors arrived that were totally unexpected. President Brigham Young, Heber C. Kimball and Willard Richards were riding back to Mount Pisgah, visiting all the intermediate camps on the way as recruiting sergeants. Ebenezer was right. The President would give them direction and they all circled the campfire to hear his message.

"It's good to be with you again. I always feel like I am coming home when I am with the Drapers and Browns. As you know, the United States Government has requested five hundred of our healthy, able-bodied men to join the Army of the West in protecting the States in the war with Mexico. We want to conform to the requisition made upon us, and we will do nothing else 'til we have accomplished this thing. If we want the privilege of going where we can worship God according to the dictates of our consciences, we must raise the Battalion. I request that you make a distinction between this action of the general government, in calling upon us for volunteers, and our former oppressors in Missouri and Illinois."

Brigham Young looked over this family group he had known since his early days of membership in the church and remembered the fertile Canadian farms they had left to follow him and the other leaders of the church. They had been dedicated to fulfill every request made of them. He knew he would have recruits from this family. "Discuss this among your family and make it a matter of prayer. If you find it within your hearts for some of you to answer this call, you may enlist when you reach Council Bluffs."

Phebe filled plates with Johnny cakes and side pork and passed to the visitors. They chatted about mutual friends as they ate and then took their leave to visit other camps with their recruitment message.

As they rode away, Brigham's heart was heavy and he tried to hide his discouragement from the other men riding with him. He had received word that the President of the United States had made a commitment to Thomas H. Benton, Senator from Missouri, that "If the Mormons did not respond to his request for volunteers he would have the privilege of raising volunteers in the upper counties of Missouri, to fall upon them and use them up." He had not shared this with the others because he did not want to intimidate anyone. He would keep this to himself until the saints had an opportunity to respond without being coerced.

Father Draper called the family to prayer. "Dear Father, help us to know thy will in this matter. Let us each search our souls for an answer to this request. This we ask in the name of our Lord and Savior, Amen. Now go to your wagons and make your decisions. We will decide what is to be done before our evening prayer.

The dear old patriarch walked back to his wagon alone.

If he were only younger, he thought, he could go and represent the family. He wondered who would respond to the call.

Phebe and Ebenezer climbed into their wagon. They each had a son old enough to enlist; William George and Gurnsey, and each another son almost old enough; Zemira and Norman. William George had just married Agnes and she was not well. Gurnsey, Norman and Zemira had taken over the care of the live stock that would be so crucial to sustain them on the trip and after they arrived in the Rockies. Lovina's husband, Henry, had been ill since they left Nauvoo.

They listed the conditions and needs of each member of the family. Ebenezer took Phebe's hand and looked in to those steel grey eyes, "I think we should go. I have had experience with the Nauvoo Legion and even though I am forty-four, I'm in pretty good shape for my age. You could go with me as a laundress and cook. We could both earn money to help our families make it to the Rocky Mountains. We have a promise that we will someday be helping to build the kingdom in the Rocky Mountains and the special blessing that we will run and not be weary and walk and not faint. We have been blessed in the past to bear the burdens put upon us and I have a strong feeling that we should volunteer to represent our family."

The possibility was spinning in Phebe's mind. She too had faith that they would arrive in the Rocky Mountains, but what of their other responsibilities? "What about John and Rhoda? Who will take care of them?" They had tried to give these two youngest children the security of a family with a mother and father who would care for them. Could they leave them now to the mercy of other members of the family?

"Harriet and Oliver can watch out for them and the other boys. William and your father and brother Zemira will be with them also as well as Lovina and Henry. Perhaps they will stay in Council Bluffs until we have filled our assignment. Then we can come back for them." Ebenezer's practical organization took over. "The boys can take care of the animals and herd them along with the caravan as they have been doing if they decide to go on West before we return. If we send money back to them, they may be able to buy more stock along the way. I have taught them how to buy and sell. Let's present the plan to the rest of the family and see how they respond."

Phebe smiled, "They may not let me go because I am too old. Remember, I am older than you. I'm forty-eight years old. Come to think of it, I'm an old lady."

Ebenezer put his arm around her. "You are the youngest and healthiest of the lot. You can out work, out cook and out clean any woman I know and still be good natured about it. Besides, I wouldn't go without you."

Young Zemira came to the wagon, "May I speak to you? I don't want to intrude." He could see that they were having a very private conversation.

"Come on up in the wagon with us." Ebenezer reached out his hand to his stepson, giving him a lift onto the wagon seat beside them. "We are just following your grandfather's admonition to consider our responsibility to Brother Brigham's request. What do you have in mind?"

"I want to enlist and go with the Battalion. I am sure I could be a good soldier and I am big enough to pass for eighteen. Most people say I look older than fifteen." It was obvious that Zemira was caught up in the excitement of marching off to do battle for his country.

Phebe put her arm around this fine young zealot and remembered his bravery in saving Bett and the children from the marauders at William's farm in Green Plain. "We wouldn't want you to lie about your age. Nothing works out well based on dishonesty. Wait until you hear our recommendation and you may see where you are needed. Let's see what happens when we get to Council Bluffs."

That night Ebenezer and Phebe presented their plan to the rest of the family. To their surprise, William was not enthusiastic about any of them going. "We have suffered so much at the hands of the government. It seems very unfair for them to ask further sacrifices of us. I get the feeling it is not a request for volunteers but more of a conscription."

"We feel the Lord wants us to accept this. We both feel that He will protect us and that we can be the greatest help to the family and the church in this capacity. How else could any of us earn money to help finish the journey? We will have to impose on you to help with John and Rhoda." Ebenezer looked at Harriet who nodded an acceptance.

Oliver walked over to his father-in-law and took his hand. "We will do our best. We love John and Rhoda and we will see that nothing happens to them while you are gone, if that is your decision."

Bett had been standing at the back of the group but now she stepped forward and put her arm around Rhoda, who seemed a little bewildered by the announcement. "I'll make sure Rhoda is loved and cared for too. She has always been like my own daughter. I helped bring her into the world and I have helped Phebe raise her. She is a very special young lady and I will help her while her mother is making this sacrifice for the family. I hope all of you realize why these two generous people are suggesting this. It is so none of the rest of us will have to go." She looked briefly at her husband and hoped he would take the cue to express his appreciation.

William walked over to Phebe and Ebenezer, "We are indebted to you. I should have known it would be the two of you. How will the rest of us survive without your strength to support us?"

Each member of the family now contemplated the changes and added responsibility they may be called to accept. Phebe started making a list in her mind of what she needed to do for each one before she left them and what she would be able to take with her. She would leave the family Bible with Lovina because she knew she would guard it with her life. She walked away from the family group to sort out her thoughts and Bett followed her.

"I have missed you so much. I could hardly wait for us to catch up with you and now we will be separated again. Phebe, let me help you with your preparation. One thing you will need are several cans of different herbs to help with sickness. I hear that the army doesn't take very good care of the sick." Bett stood by her sister-in-law and friend. Together they watched the large orange sun sink over the western horizon. They were both lost in thought. How long would they travel into the west and when and where would they meet again?

Come, Come Ye Saints, no toil nor labor fear, but with joy wend your way
Though hard to you, this journey may appear, grace shall be as your day.
"Tis better far, for us to strive, our useless cares from us to drive,
Do this and joy, your hearts will swell—All is well!! All is well!!

They sang the song in unison to build their spirits and unite them in their determination to go on.

The large assembly of the saints was gathered at Council Bluffs for the grand farewell party to wish the Battalion on there way. Five hundred volunteers had been recruited and several were taking their wives, and some their families with them. Long tables laden with food prepared by the sisters from their meager supplies were under the shade of the trees. A temporary stage had been constructed for President Young and Col. James Allen to stand on to address the group as they crowded forward to hear the messages.

Brigham looked over these devoted followers and his message rang loud and clear on that sixteenth day of July, 1846. "My dear, brave saints, the Lord looks on you today with gratitude for your faith and devotion. This was not an easy decision for you nor is it easy for us to see you leave our presence, but I make you these promises: Your families will be cared for and will fare as well as I do. They will be helped along the way. Not one of you who have enlisted will fall by the hands of the nation's foe. Your only fight will be that of warding off wild beasts. There will not be as many bullets whistle around your ears as did around Dr. Willard Richards' at Carthage jail. Let us dance and sing and celebrate together. We are a blessed people and any hardship we are called upon to make is a small price for the blessing of the gospel of Jesus Christ in our lives. Now take your turns at the feast and Brother Richards, start the music." He stepped down off the stage and taking his wife by the hand, led them in a lively reel.

Ebenezer and Phebe joined the dancers and smiled as they do-se-doed with each other and friends down the line. Phebe had finished her new calico dress and Ebenezer's new white shirt. They wore new shoes that William and Henry had made for them. They seemed to glisten in the sun as they danced and sang. Phebe's face was aglow with the spirit of the occasion. She didn't feel forty-eight, but as young as she had when she danced with George in Loughborough those many years ago. She danced with her sons and step sons, her brothers and neighbors. Finally, out of breath, she went to a grassy knoll and sat to rest.

Rhoda came to sit by her and she put her arm around her young daughter who could not quite comprehend the need for her mother to leave. "Rhoda, I love you. I will pray for you every day and I promise you, we will be in the Rocky Mountains together. There are so many people who love you and will take care of you. Will you pray for me every day?" Phebe brushed her daughters hair back and kissed her forehead. She could not control the tears. She had tried to be strong and accept what was to be but she had never been separated from her mother.

Phebe held her tight and turned her own face away to hide the tears that wet her cheeks. "Rhoda, you are my special present from God. You came to me after your father died to give me comfort and love. You will always be precious to me. Please know that am going so I can help you as well as the rest of the family. Someday you will understand. Please help Harriet and Lovina with their little ones since I won't be here with them. You will have to take on some of the work I have done but I know you can. You are very responsible and my lovely, almost grown up daughter. Now, lets wipe our eyes. We don't want anyone to see us crying." She brushed her cheeks with the back of her hand and wiped Rhoda's tears away also. They smiled at each other and held hands as they walked back to the dancers.

Col. Allen stood at the podium and called the group to attention. "I have had several young men approach me with a desire to accompany the Battalion even though they are not old enough to be regular enlistees. I have interviewed them and consulted with their parents as to their permission for them to join the march. I have chosen the following seven young men. As I call their names, I would like them to join me here. First, Zemira Palmer to be my personal aide."

Phebe caught her breath, happy for Zemira but not knowing what it would mean to him. At least she and Ebenezer would be there to watch over him.

Col. Allen continued; Second, William Byron Pace assigned to Lieut. James Pace; Wilson D. Pace, assigned to Lieut. Andrew Lytle; N.D. Higgins, to Captain Nelson Higgins, Charles Edwin Colton to adjutant P.C. Merrill; James Mowrey, to Lieuts. George Rosecrans, Samuel Thompson and Robert Clift, and Elisha Smith to Capt. Daniel C. Davis."

The seven young boys took their place on the stage by Col. Allen. He shook hands with each of them and they beamed with pride. Zemira was first in line to accept the handshake and he was elated that he was chosen to be the Colonel's aide.

In the two weeks since Col. Allen had been amid the saints, he had earned their respect and Zemira deemed it a great honor to be chosen for this singular assignment. He looked down and saw his mother in the sea of faces. She hid her feelings of apprehension and smiled at him. Zemira could go with them. At least she would have one of her children by her side.

Ebenezer gave her a squeeze, "Isn't that great. He wanted to go and now he can."

Somehow, Phebe knew Ebenezer had had a hand in this but he wasn't taking any credit for it. Col. Allen said he had conferred with parents but he hadn't ask her. If Ebenezer had done this as a surprise to her and Zemira he had certainly succeeded. She looked up at this man who seemed to know her needs better than she did herself, and gave him a peck on the cheek. He smiled back at her and feigned innocence.

Ebenezer had been elected second sergeant of Company A to serve under Captain Jefferson Hunt. Phebe was happy to be with that group. Celia Hunt was one of her friends and she knew she would want to have some women to associate with while the men were filling their army assignments She wondered just what her work as laundress and cook would entail. How many would she cook for and how often would she be doing laundry? She had so many questions about the future.

The extra wagon Ebenezer had outfitted for them would provide her transportation. Some of the women accompanying their husbands were planning on walking along with the troops. Ebenezer inspected all the oxen and chose two he felt were the strongest and healthiest. One was a mottled brown and the other was white. He would take his favorite horse and one of the mules. The rest of the stock would be cared for by the family and allowed to rest and regain their strength to move on, should they leave before the Battalion returned.

Brigham Young called the twelve elected officers from each of the five companies, to a special meeting. He admonished them to keep the commandments, exercise their

priesthood, help one another and hold religious services whenever possible. He repeated his promises to them concerning
their protection from their enemies and advised them to be
wise in their use of medicines offered to them by army doctors.
He offered a special blessing in their behalf and sent them
back to their families to prepare for their departure.

Ebenezer gave each of his sons and Rhoda a special blessing before they made the rounds of the rest of their family and
friends to wish them goodbye. Phebe's brothers, William and
Zemira met with them alone. William embraced them both and
looked away, trying to control his emotions. They had come so
far together and had relied on each other for strength through it
all. He looked at Ebenezer, "I still think it is too much to ask of
us from a government who has given us no protection or support. I will watch out for your families to the best of my ability. Please be careful and remember how much I love you
both." He kissed his sister, "Oh, Miss Phebe, take care of yourself."

Phebe's brother, Zemira, kissed her goodbye and shook
hands with Ebenezer. "I'll watch out for your families too and
don't worry about Father. He will be fine until we meet again,
either here or in the Rockies."

Company A was the first to be mustered in and the first to
leave on the long, hot march to Fort Levanworth. Ebenezer
marched with his men. Phebe and her son, Zemira, rode in the
wagon following along with the other families accompanying
the soldiers. The white horse and mule were tethered to the
back of the wagon. The stream of humanity, strung out along
the banks of the Missouri river, seemed endless and as they
looked back across the Iowa planes. There were camps of
Saints as far as the eye could see.

The Battalion trek had begun. Where would it take them?
When would it end? Phebe put her trust in the Lord and a
smile on her face. "Here we go on a great adventure, Zemira."
She slapped the rump of the oxen with the jerk line to encourage a pace at least equal to the rest of the travelers.

CHAPTER THIRTY-THREE

The hot, unrelenting, July sun bore down on the marching soldiers. Officers, caught up by their new found authority, pushed them on with infrequent stops for water. The heat, combined with the humidity from the Missouri river, took its toll on several of the marchers and in spite of requests from the noncommissioned officers to slow the pace, the mounted officers pushed them on.

Phebe's wagon was one of the few pulled by oxen rather than horses, causing her to travel more slowly than the rest. She soon fell behind company "A" and found herself with the wagons from company "B". She and some of the other women with wagons were picking up the stragglers who had been overcome with the heat. The wagon tops provided some shade from the sun and most of them were carrying an extra supply of water, which they used to relieve the suffering.

Finally, the first day of the march ended. Samuel Boley from Company "B" was over come by the heat and was dangerously ill from the effects of the march. Phebe nursed him with cold clothes, trying to stabilize the temperature of his body. Ebenezer and Captain Hunt gave him a blessing and he fell into a deep sleep.

They had reached Sharpy's point, a French trading post on the Missouri River. Capt. Allen issued camp kettles, knives, forks, spoons, plates, coffee, sugar and blankets. The Captain could see that the new enlistees were in need of some time to adjust to the rigors of Army direction, so he held them over at this post for four days.

On the fifth day they left for Fort Leavenwerth.

On July 21, 1846 they awoke to the sound of the bugle and drenching rain. Most of them had slept in bed rolls on the ground. They would not be issued tents, guns and uniforms until they arrived at Fort Leavenwerth. After a breakfast from their own packs they rolled up their soggy bedrolls, now heavier than ever and trudged four miles through wet sand and mud.

The fifth company was finally filled and had marched on, following the trail of the other companies and overtook the main body of the Battalion at Mosquito Creek. The name of the creek lived up to its reputation and the soldiers and their families were besieged by the pesky bites of the hordes of mosquitoes.

Samuel Boley was dangerously ill. Phebe looked through the many containers of herbs Bett had packed for her with instructions for their use but nothing seemed to help Brother Boley. As she drove the wagon on, her heart ached for him as he moaned in agony, seeming to come in and out of consciousness with the bumps of the trail. He slept fitfully through the night and then fell into a coma. Phebe dozed as she held vigil through the night.

"How is he?" Ebenezer looked in to the back of the wagon as the morning light crept up over the horizon.

"I'm afraid he won't make it through the day. Nothing I do seems to help. Dr. McIntyre spent some time with him last night also but he could do nothing for him." Phebe climbed down from the wagon and leaned her head on Ebenezer's shoulder. He could see that she was weary from a night with little rest.

The bugle sounded and he turned to go back to his men. "I'll try to check with you later. I'll see if one of the other women who doesn't have to drive a wagon can ride with you." He blew her a kiss from his two fore fingers and the tired lines by her eyes wrinkled as she smiled back at him.

The men marched on in the heat and humidity. Some with damp clothes covering their heads and others with felt hats that seemed to attract the heat more than protect them. They carried extra clothes so they could send their clothing allowances back to their families. The pace was still unrelenting for men who were already weak from the hard winter months of travel and deprivation across the Iowa prairie.

Capt. Hunt and some of his subordinates, one of which was Ebenezer, approached Captain Allen. "The pace is too fast. Our men can not go on at this pace. Many are ill after just a few days. Is there some way you can intercede for us." Capt. Hunt kept eye contact with Captain Allen and saw a flicker of compassion.

"I'll confer with my men. We are under orders to reach Fort Leavenwerth as soon as possible." Capt. Allen rode back to council with his cadre of regular army. All of them, to a man, insisted that the pace remain the same. The color left Captain Allen's face as he returned to report the decision. He was not feeling well himself and he had a horse to ride.

That night, Brother Samuel Boley died from heat exhaustion. Sister Hunter, wife of Capt. Hunter of Company "B", had spent the night with Phebe. The following morning the death of Brother Boley was announced to the enlistees. His closest friends dug his grave and he was buried on the banks of the Missouri River on July 23, 1846. He was the first casualty of the Mormon Battalion.

Phebe straightened up her wagon, putting Brother Boley's few possessions in a small knapsack to send back to his family at Council Bluffs. They had been in the Army for a week now and she had laundry to do for the officers of Company "A". She heated water in the big pots while she cooked breakfast for Captain Allen and his men. Zemira helped her as he was Capt. Allen's aide. It was also her turn to do the laundry for them. The women from each of the companies would take turns. Since she was the laundress for Company "A" she was first to have the assignment.

The lye soap made the skin on her hands tingle as she scrubbed the clothes on the wash board. The mud from the day before was so embedded on the legs of the pants she had to soak and scrub several times. She hung them on lines in the back of the wagon to dry and was ready to leave when the main body moved out for Fort Leavenwerth. She rubbed her hands with tallow and put some cotton gloves on to drive the wagon. She remembered Bett warning her to always use the tallow so her hands would not crack and bleed from the harsh lye soap.

As the oxen moved along the trail, Phebe let her mind wander back to the main body of the church where most of her loved ones were. She thought of each of her little grandchildren and wondered if she had given them enough attention. Ester Ann was reading already and she was sure Lovina would help them all keep up with their reading and ciphering. And then she thought of Rhoda, the sadness she felt as they parted and the look of abandonment in Rhoda's eyes. She hoped she had found the letter she had left for her by now. She had hidden it in a little carved wooden box they had let Rhoda bring with her from Nauvoo for her special treasures. Perhaps she could write to them when they reached the fort. The men would be sending their uniform allowances back so someone would be taking mail back to the families.

The dust from the trail seemed to filter back to her as her oxen slowly plodded along. Ebenezer had promised her he would trade them to the army for some horses when they got to the fort. That way she could keep up with Company "A" and be closer to Ebenezer and Zemira who were always at the head of the marching soldiers. The dust may not be as dense either. She wiped the perspiration from her forehead and the cotton gloves were streaked with dirt. "I must look a sight and I can't stop and wash my face until we halt for the night. I'm glad I have that extra water in my wagon for emergencies." She finished wiping her face and took the dirty gloves off. She would wash them out when they made camp for the night.

Ebenezer, filling his assignment as Second Sergeant, slept in his bed roll with the men in Company "A". Phebe was lonely in the wagon alone at night. She spent many hours in prayer and meditation, reading the small copy of the Book of Mormon she had packed with her personal possessions. Her kerosene lamp was often still giving off its yellow glow within the tent long after the troops were asleep.

Captain Allen noticed the hours she kept and chided her, "Don't you like to sleep or do you sleep with the light on? Are you afraid of the dark? Since you are a volunteer laundress I can't command you to keep the same hours as the soldiers but I do hope you are getting enough sleep." He had been concerned about accepting her as a laundress because she was older than any of the other women, but he observed that her energy seemed endless and she looked much younger than some of the others.

"I like to read at night when it is quiet. I am better able to concentrate on what I read. I seem to sleep more soundly then and arise better rested." Phebe appreciated his concern for her.

"What is it you are reading?" he asked. He liked to read also and had read everything available to him.

"I'm reading the Book of Mormon. Are you familiar with it? It is a history of the natives of the American continents." Phebe picked up her book and passed it to the Captain.

"Oh, yes. I've heard it is the Bible for your church, but I haven't read it. Is it this book that teaches your people to be so dedicated, honest and loyal?" He turned the book over in his hand but acted reluctant to open the cover.

"The message in this book will change one's life forever. There is much to learn from its contents. Would you like to borrow it?"

The Captain passed it back to her. "I'm not ready for such a drastic change at this time of my life but I may take you up on your offer at a later date." He knew if some of his fellow soldiers from Missouri saw him reading the book he would have serious problems, but he was curious about the book that had such far reaching effects on people. He tipped his hat to

her as he rode away thinking about the graciousness of this
woman and wondered at her reasoning for joining the
Battalion.

They crossed the Nishnabotany River at Hunsaker's Ferry
and camped near Lindon, Missouri. It had been another hot
day and several more men had succumbed to the heat, finding
shelter in the wagons. Some of them even purchased ponies to
ride from local farmers. They tried to sing as they marched to
make the time go faster. Many Missourians were surprised to
hear the joyful mood of the people who had been driven from
their homes and persecuted. It was amazing that they were
now volunteering to serve their country in the Battalion.

There were, however, still some Missourians who refused
to do business with a Mormon. The troops ran out of flour and
after traveling almost forty miles, with little or no food, they
found a man had been ordered to deliver flour to them but had
refused to let a Mormon sign for it. When he was threatened
with arrest, he soon delivered the flour.

Day after day they traveled toward the fort, crossing rivers
and traveling on rocky, dusty roads. Phebe listened to the men
singing, "The Girl I Left Behind Me" as they marched through
St. Joseph and on out of town to camp. The tenacity of the men
never ceased to amaze her. One day seemed to be threading
into the next. It was much further to Fort Leavenwerth than she
had imagined. Ebenezer estimated that they had traveled about
two hundred miles down the Missouri River in fifteen days.

After they made camp they went in groups to bathe in the
river. The women and children first. Phebe basked in the cool-
ness of the water and was refreshed as the trail dust drifted
away into the river. She watched as mothers bathed their little
ones. It made her homesick for Lovina and the children. She
took one last dip in the water and then moved closer to Lydia
Hunt. "Here, let me help you with the twins." She took one
and rolled it in a blanket while she dried and dressed herself
and then dressed the baby.

That night, when the troops were quiet, Ebenezer came and spent the night with her in the wagon. It was so comforting to have him close to her. They talked in hushed voices way into the night and then she fell asleep and slept soundly. She awoke at dawn. Ebenezer was already awake. "Will you be in trouble for leaving your men?" Phebe's worry lines were showing as Ebenezer slipped into his clothes.

"No, Capt. Hunt gave me permission. He put Sergeant Wright in charge for the night." He pulled on his boots that William and Henry had made for him before he left Council Bluffs. They were well made and he, unlike many of the men, was not having trouble with blisters from the long marches.

They sat on the back of the wagon watching the sun come up and just enjoying some quiet time together. Phebe looked up at him, "We have only started and it seems like it has been forever. Some aspects of this army life make me feel like I have lost my free agency. Does that bother you?"

Ebenezer grinned at her, "You never did like people telling you what to do, did you? Just be patient. The Lord will protect us. Perhaps it is our test of obedience. We must remember those promises we made in the Nauvoo Temple and we will be blessed to survive the test." He left her there in the wagon and returned to his men.

Phebe tried to recreate in her mind those sacred promises. She couldn't remember them word for word but she knew the essence of her commitment. She put a smile on her face, shook the dust from the dresses and petticoats she would wear for the day. If this was the work of the Lord, she would give it her best. When she was washed and dressed she started the fire for the morning meal and mixed up a batter of sour dough bread for breakfast. Now the Lord had sent them the flour, the least she could do was to make it as tasty as possible for the men.

That night they camped on a small creek a little past the town of Bloomington. It was a late July night and the air was heavy and sultry until well after eight-o-clock. When the cool, evening breezes drifted over the camp, the men fell into a deep sleep, exhausted from the long day's march. Phebe sat reading when a strong gust of wind rocked her wagon. She put her lantern out and jumped from the wagon just as it tipped over from a second onslaught of wind. She saw the smoldering fires of the camp rekindled from the gale force of the wind and trees were falling all around the camp. The animals were tethered in a field of dead wood near by but miraculously survived the hurricane like winds that pelted everything in their wake with sand and limbs. Lightening streaks lighted the sky and the roar of thunder seemed to shake the earth. Then the rains came but were brief, evaporating before they settled the dust. Soon the men who had been routed out of their slumber by the storm were putting the camp back in order and settling back down for the night.

Ebenezer and Sergeants Allred and McCord came to Phebe's aid. They righted the wagon and tied the canvas top back in place where the winds had ripped it free. The other men agreed that Ebenezer should stay with his wife since the weather was so erratic. The wind had been a blessing in disguise. She had Ebenezer beside her for one more night.

On August first they reached the ferry on the Missouri River where they would cross the river to the fort. It took five long hours in the sun and heat to ferry the battalion members and the rest of the entourage across the river. They were issued tents on their arrival and were directed to make camp in the public square of the fort. The tents gave them shade from the sun but as the sun bore down on the tents it made them very warm inside. They pitched the tents in army fashion and again broke into song conveying a positive image to the other troops housed at the fort, most of whom were companies of Missouri volunteers.

"Phebe, I have traded the oxen for a nice team of horses. Come and see them." Ebenezer took Phebe's arm as she climbed down from the wagon. They walked to the holding pens for the stock and Ebenezer pointed out two matching blacks with stocking feet and blaze faces. He pulled some oats from his pocket, encouraging them to come to the rail fence.

Phebe rubbed her hand down the blaze face of the horse nearest her and looked into the big brown eyes. She had always insisted she could tell the temperament of a horse by looking into its eyes. "They will be fine, Ebenezer." She crawled between the rails of the fence and was patting the neck of the horse when the matching horse came over and nuzzled in to be petted also. "What shall we call them? Did the other owner give them names?"

"Name them them anything that suits you. I'm glad you like them."

"To be honest, I was always a little afraid of the oxen. They were so big and clumsy. I never did get around to giving them a name. I'll have to spend some time and come up with some very good names for this beautiful matched pair." Phebe put a hand under the chin of each horse and looked from one to the other. After considerable inspection and contemplation she said, "I think I'll call them Joe and Hy for our beloved prophet and his brother. Do you think that would be alright? They always worked together as a team, pulling saints along with them. Not only that, but they both loved their beautiful horses. Do you think that would be disrespectful?"

"I think they would both be pleased and consider it a complement. That is what you mean it to be." They walked arm in arm back to the center of the fort.

"I have to get in line to get my paycheck. They will give us $42.00 for a years uniform allowance and as a sergeant I will be paid $13.00 a month. I think the laundresses are on the same pay as the Privates, $7.00 a month. We will be able to send $65.00 back with Brother Pratt to help with the trip to the Rockies. I think we both have clothes to last us a year. Thanks to Bett, William, and the girls for helping us make new clothes and shoes for the trek. My boots are much better than those issued by the army, and the shoes they made for you look quite sturdy."

Ebenezer got in line and signed his name on the pay sheet. After the men were paid the women got in line to sign for their pay. Phebe heard the pay master turn to his aid and say, "Did you see that every one of those Mormon men and women could sign their name. Someone told me they were a bunch of ignorant people but I don't believe it. A lot of the Missourians just make their X."

Phebe found Ebenezer in the crowd and gave her pay to him. "Will you get this to Brother Pratt? I'm going to try to get some letters written to the family before he leaves with the mail pouch." She turned and hurried to her wagon.

She tried to fill the letters with descriptions of the land and some of the humorous things she had seen. It would be soon enough to tell them about the hardships when they were all safely back together. She was just sealing the letter when Ebenezer came to the tent. He was wearing a wide white belt and shoulder straps over both shoulders to carry a scabbard and bayonet. He held his new flint lock musket in one hand and more camp equipment in the other with a large cartridge box under his arm. An Army issue caplock pistol was stuck in his pocket. With a twinkle in his eye he looked at Phebe, "Do you think I can carry all of this to California without some help?" They both started to laugh. He looked so funny loaded down with all the newly issued equipment. "I hope they don't ask me to salute. I would surely have to drop something." Hanging from other shoulder straps was a knapsack to carry clothing and other necessities. He also had a haversack and a half-quart canteen with shoulder straps. "I think I need more shoulders." He dropped the equipment to the ground and started to assemble it in better order.

The August heat was more intense than that of July and the Fort was miserably hot. Even without the forced marches the men were getting sick and many of them were in need of medical help. There never seemed to be enough drinking water. A Doctor George B. Sanderson, of Platte County, Missouri was appointed as surgeon in the United States Army to serve with the Mormon Battalion of volunteers. Many more of the men had become ill while at the Fort from the extreme heat. Some of them working long hours as blacksmiths or other trades in the heat of the sun. Col. Allen was seriously ill and lay in his quarters for days with no improvement.

Zemira would report on the health of Col. Allen to his mother each day. On August eleventh he came to her wagon and told her they were going to be moving out the next day for Sante Fe. Captain Jefferson Hunt had been directed by Col. Allen to direct the march and advance with the command while he remained at the fort to complete the business of out-fitting the Battalion.

Phebe readied her wagon for the move and went to help Celia Hunt with her wagon and the twins. Finally, they would be on their way. She hoped her new horses would be as easy to handle as she had anticipated. That night she prayed for Col. Allen. He had been so kind to them and after being in camp for almost two weeks with many soldiers from Missouri, she felt the Battalion may need a sympathetic ear as the march proceeded. She wondered if she should leave her Book of Mormon with him, he said he may want to read it later but she didn't want to go on without it.

Light was just breaking in the East when Ebenezer and Zemira hitched the team up to the wagon for Phebe. She petted each of her new horses. She hadn't decided which would be Joe and which would be Hy. In fact it was hard to tell them apart. As she climbed into the wagon, Zemira handed her the reins. In time she would get to know the personalities of the horses. The one with the most leadership ability would be Joe. She slapped the reins lightly on the rump of each horse and they moved out to join the other wagons in line.

CHAPTER THIRTY-FOUR

Most of the wagons carried some of the soldiers who were running high fevers and Phebe's was one of them. The lack of water at the Fort and the requirement that they only drink from their canteen ration had caused a considerable amount of illness. They were still commanded to go on with the Battalion and promised care from the new Dr. Sanderson. Three privates from Company "A" lay in the back of Phebe's wagon. She encouraged them to drink from her water supply. A mixture of Catnip and Yarrow was added to a cup of water twice that day from the herbs Bett had given her. They traveled five miles and found little or no water to replenish the canteens.

That evening, Dr. Sanderson came to Phebe's wagon, "I am told that you have some sick men here. Come on men, on your feet. Let me take a look at you." By this time their fevers were down considerably but they needed more water to quench their thirst. The men helped each other up and out of the wagon. The Doctor inspected the mouth and throat of each of the men by holding their tongue down with a rusty spoon. Using the same spoon he had used for each inspection, he filled it with Camomile and poured it down each man's throat. "They are not to ride tomorrow. There seems to be a lot of lazy Mormons in this Battalion and I will see that they each fill their assignments."

"Doctor Sanderson, they have all been running fevers. I have treated them with Catnip and Yarrow and it has seemed to help but they are far from well enough to march with the men." Phebe assumed that any doctor would appreciate the observation of someone who had been with the patient all day, but she didn't know Dr. Sanderson.

"You are telling me that you are more capable to prescribe for these men than I am, Mrs. Brown? You are not to administer any of your herbs without my authorization. Do you understand me?"

Phebe stood and looked him in the eye with a resolution that she would not back down from what she knew to be right. "Dr. Sanderson, I am not a Doctor but I have nursed many sick people back to health. If I have something that will improve the health of a soldier or anyone else in the trek, you may be assured I will give it to them." The color rose in her cheeks but she did not drop her eyes from his.

The veins on his neck pulsated as the red crept up from his collar until his face was totally flushed with anger. "I have warned you, Mrs. Brown." He turned and stomped off to the next wagon. She was sure she had not heard the last from him. He reminded her of the charlatan teacher that had come to Laughborough those many years ago and challenged her ability to teach the little children. A smile crossed her face as she remembered her mother's firm denunciation of the man. "I guess Ebenezer is right. I am more like my mother than I thought."

The men crawled back into the wagon, falling asleep almost immediately from the sedative effects of the Camomile. Phebe kept rousing them enough to take more moisture. She knew the fevers would not break completely without it. She prepared the evening meal for the officers and went back to her wagon to care for the men. The cool clothes she bathed their faces with seemed to relieve the fever as the evening air cooled the camp. She went from one to the other in an attempt to keep them as cool as possible.

"I understand there is a pretty haughty woman in this wagon that needs to be reprimanded." Ebenezer looked in on her as she dipped the cloth in the water. "The good Doctor came to see me about putting you in your place. I told him I had no authority to do that since you weren't one of the soldiers under my command. He then went to Capt. Hunt and complained. Capt. Hunt said you probably knew more about taking care of sick people than he did. It did not sit well. You know the Doctor and Lieutenant Smith are not of a mind to take orders from Capt. Hunt. In fact, they seem to feel that they have more military authority here than the Captain and that Col. Allen should have put them in charge. Phebe, you may have stirred up a hornet's nest this time. I wish I could have been here to see it." He climbed into the back of the wagon with her and looked at the poor sick men. "They will never be ready to march tomorrow. What can we do?"

Phebe smiled at him. "I have an idea. After dark we will move them to Celia's wagon and I will take the twins with me. Then, if the good doctor comes to inspect the wagon he will just find two darling little babies here. I'm sure he doesn't know all the men well enough by now to know if they are marching in the ranks or not. I don't recall him asking their names. If he does ask for them tomorrow you can have some of your men answer for them. There are several soldiers with the same last name. I am sure they can confuse him."

"Sounds good to me. Just try to take care of these poor sick men until we can get them on their feet. In the meantime, I'll tell Capt. Hunt that I put you in your place. He'll know from the grin on my face that your place is just where it has always been. Right here in my heart. Good luck!" He gave her a peck on the check. "I'll come back after dark and help with the move."

Phebe returned to her vigil assured that Ebenezer would take care of letting Celia and Capt. Hunt know the plan. He was such a good man. He was, as the Prophet's father had promised her, a man of God. His men were lucky to have him for a sergeant. He held no malice for any one and she had never seen him abuse any power or authority he had over man or beast.

When all was quiet in the camp the sick men were moved to the Hunt wagon and the babies to Phebe's. She slipped Celia some of the herbs she had been using with directions as to how to administer them and then in turn, was given directions for the needs of the babies. If they needed to be nursed, she would take them, one at a time, back to their mother. Doctor Sanderson could use his old rusty spoon to take care of some of his Missouri friends.

The following day the scheme worked as planned. When one of the babies needed their mother, Phebe would take her bonnet off and wave it at Celia who would pull her wagon up close to Phebe's. Her thirteen-year-old son John would take the baby that needed to be fed to his mother's wagon. As Phebe had predicted, Dr. Sanderson came to inspect her wagon and found only the babies asleep in the wagon bed. He did not bother to speak to Phebe, thinking he was slighting her, when in reality she was relieved because she didn't have to answer any questions.

After two days of this routine the men were able to march part of the time with their troops and when they needed rest they would drive the wagons for the women. Giving the impression that the women needed their help.

They came to the Kansas river and were ferried across on flat boats by some Delaware and Shawnee Indians who were cultivating the land near-by. After a few more miles travel they came to Spring Creek, a beautiful little place with natural springs about every twenty yards. The water was clear and had a refreshing taste that finally quenched the thirst of the travelers. Many of the sick men started to recover after receiving plenty of water and some rest. They bathed in the springs and the stock grazed in the green meadows.

Phebe used the soft spring water to wash the laundry of the officers and her own clothes as well as the bedding from the wagon. The women strung ropes from wagon to wagon to hang the wet clothes to dry. As they waved in the fresh breeze, it was like a renewal. They would like to have stayed longer but the stock started to graze into the fields of the Indians who had befriended them so they moved on a few miles to Stone Coal Creek.

One of the men Phebe had nursed back to health brought her a surprise. "Sister Brown, I brought you a present." He handed her a handful of honey comb he was hiding behind his back. "I figure you saved my life and when I found that Honey Tree I made up my mind that you would be the first to have some of the honey."

She took it from him and put it on a tin in the wagon. "I'm so glad you're better, Brother Bliss, but you didn't owe me anything. I'll render the honey down and we'll have some on some Johnny cakes in the morning. I hope the bees didn't sting you."

"No, ma'am. I've been taking honey from bee trees all my life and never been stung once. I got chased by a bear once out in Pennsylvania but I out run him. Actually, I kept circling around until the honey tree was between us and so he kinda got distracted and gave up chasing me." He walked over to the spring and rinsed the residue of the honey from his hands.

Phebe followed him and stooped down to rinse her hands also. "Thanks for the honey Brother Bliss. Make sure you stop by my camp fire in the morning for a Johnny cake."

Phebe stopped at Celia Hunt's wagon and found her and both of the babies running high fevers and taking chills. She picked up the babies and went to find Capt. Hunt. He took the little ones into his tent while Phebe went back to help Celia. She was making some catnip tea for her when the sky suddenly became black and a wind, stronger than the one that had tipped Phebe's wagon, blew through the camp. It over turned some of the other wagons and Sister Coray jumped from the carriage she was in just as it was tipped and driven before the wind. The hale and rain pelted everything in its wake, dousing the fires and soaking the tents and bedding.

Capt. Hunt protected his babies with his body while the tent blew down around them. They were soaked to the skin as was everyone else in camp. It seemed to last only a few minutes but was a cleansing storm to the camp. All those who were still suffering from the chills and fever were miraculously cured. Even Celia and the babies ceased to suffer another symptom of the dread disease that had plagued the camp.

Companies "D" and "E" straggled in after the storm. They were always a day or two behind the front companies, having to wait for the ferries and sometimes waiting for the dust to clear from the companies in front of them.

Colonel Price's command of Cavalry was also camped at Stone Coal Creek. His animals scattered in the storm. Many of the Battalion men helped with the search to round them up. The rest of the camp dried out their tents and clothes and by afternoon was called together for a meeting with Capt. Hunt who had witnessed the miraculous healing of his wife and babies. He spoke with the men about the blessings and miracles they had witnessed so far on the trip. The spirit was strong and others stood and bore testimony of the blessings of the gospel and the answer to prayer.

Phebe stood by Ebenezer during the meeting. "We have been blessed, haven't we? The Lord has been with us. Look at those sweet little Hunt babies. I had given up on them. I must exercise more faith in the future. The Lord has sent us a sign that he will protect us and we must keep the faith."

Brother Bliss walked into the meeting with another bucket filled with honey comb. "Look what the Lord sent us. Some more honey."

Dr. Sanderson stood at the back of the group with a look of disgust on his face. He took on a dark countenance that belied his sincerity in caring for the sick. He was obviously not moved by the spirit of the meeting and gave no credence to the miracles that had occurred. He turned away with a smirk and walked into his tent.

Word came by a courier that Col. Allen was not recovering from his illness and may not be able to join the Battalion. The news flew through the camp and many prayers were offered in his behalf. The Captains of each company determined it would be best for Lieutenant James Pace to return to Fort Leavenworth to see for himself, the condition of his good friend. He left the camp, which they had named Hurricane Point, and headed East. He was unaware that Lieutenant Smith and Dr. Sanderson had already left camp to return to Fort Leavenwerth. When he arrived he learned that Col. Allen was not expected to last more than a few hours. He died at six o'clock a.m. on August 23, 1846. Lieutenants Gully and Pace were at his side.

Lieutenant Gully had stayed behind with Col. Allen acting as quartermaster to complete the orders for the Battalion. At the announcement of the Colonel's death Lieutenant Smith and Dr. Sanderson ordered Lieutenant Gully to leave and join the main group of the Battalion.

Lieutenant Gully looked at the two Missourians, "You have no authority to order me to do anything. I am not under your command. I will finish filling the requisitions for the Battalion just as Col. Allen instructed me."

He turned to walk from their presence without saluting them when an aide to Major Horton entered the tent. "Major Horton would like you and Lieutenant Pace to come to his quarters immediately."

The two Battalion Lieutenants followed the aide to Major Horton's tent. Sanderson and Smith followed them and paused by the entrance into the tent, just close enough to hear Major Horton ask, "Lieutenant Gully, are the requisitions for the Battalion completed?"

"I have completed the requisitions and was just in the process of supervising the loading of the wagons in preparation to send them to the Battalion. Lieutenant Smith and Dr. Sanderson have ordered me to leave immediately and join the

Battalion. I told them I would not leave until I had completed my assignment and it was my understanding that they had no jurisdiction over me or Lieutenant Pace." Lt. Gully knew Smith and Sanderson were lurking by the tent and raised his voice in this report to Major Horton so the eavesdroppers could hear.

The Major sensed the situation and very pointedly, so that he could be heard, said, "No one has any right to assume command over the Battalion. You are a separate corp from the rest of the army and as per the agreement with your President Young, you are to elect your own Colonel. I have written a letter to this effect to Captain Hunt and requested that he send an express on to General Kearney to this effect. I would also suggest that one of you return to Council Bluffs and apprise President Young of the death of Col. Allen and the need for the Battalion to organize itself to move on to Sante Fe. I would suggest that Lieutenant Pace make the journey to Council Bluffs while Lieutenant Gully completes the supervision of loading the supplies."

As Lt. Pace left the Major's tent, Lt. Smith and Dr. Sanderson asked him in a very congenial way if he would please take a letter from each of them to President Young. He agreed to this request and by noon, August 23rd he was on his way back to Council Bluffs on a fresh horse with enough food and supplies to last the trip and letters from Major Horton, Lt. Smith and Dr. Sanderson. He carried few other letters because the main body of the Battalion was over forty miles south and unaware of his assignment to make the trip back to Council Bluffs. The weather was cooling down and he enjoyed his ride, contemplating seeing his family and friends again, he made the trip in three days and found the main body of the Saints at Cutler's Creek on the west side of the Missouri River.

He went immediately to Brigham Young's tent and delivered the letters and the news of Col. Allen. "Col. Allen's death is going to be a great blow to the Battalion. There are other's who would like to take command of the camp but do not have the best interest of the men at heart."

President Young put his arm around the young Lieutenant, "You have had a hard ride. Find your family and have something to eat. I see you have a few more letters to deliver. I am going to call a council together. Come back and meet with us about three o'clock this afternoon. We need to hear more about the Battalion and the welfare of the men and their families that are traveling with them."

"Thank you, President Young. I would like to see my family. I'll be here at three o'clock."

They assembled and Lieutenant Pace was questioned and instructed at great length. He was given messages to take back to the Captains of the Battalion one of which was a reminder of a direction President Young had sent to them at Fort Leavenwerth which read as follows, "If you are sick, live by faith, and let the surgeon's medicine alone if you want to live, using only such herbs and mild food as are at your disposal. If you give heed to this counsel, you will prosper; but if not, we cannot be responsible for the consequences. A hint to the wise is sufficient."

Howard Egan and John D. Lee were asked by the president to accompany Lt. Pace. The three men traveled in a carriage and upon reaching Fort Leavenwerth were greeted warmly by Major Horton. He gave them all the supplies the carriage would hold, letters for different commands and a fresh horse.

They found the Battalion camp on September 11th. The soldiers, being free of the oppression of Lt. Smith and Dr. Sanderson, had nursed their sick and moved on toward their destination of Sante Fe. Large tracks of fertile soil spread for miles but were intersected with streams and small rivers. Phebe was following Company "A" in her wagon filled with several recuperating soldiers. She turned and saw that they needed help. "I'll pull over and ask Sister Hunt if she can help us. Maybe the Boscos can ride with us."

She pulled the wagon over and waved her bonnet to Celia Hunt.

"Can the Boscos ride with us for a while. The sick men need help and I can't drive and help them at the same time."

Celia Hunt motioned to the Boscos who were riding in the back of her wagon tending the twins. "Brother Bosco can drive your wagon so you and Sister Bosco can help the men. I'll get one of the girls from the next wagon to help with the twins."

The women reigned in the teams and the elderly Boscos climbed down from the Hunt wagon and up into the Brown wagon. They were a happy couple who could have been the mother and father of any of the soldiers. They fussed over the soldiers and the children in the camp as if they were family. They had never been blessed with children so when the Hunts had asked them to go with them to help with the twins, the Boscos could not resist the opportunity.

After Benny Bosco helped his little rotund wife, Betsy, into the back of the wagon with Phebe, he took his place on the wagon seat. Phebe smiled at the scarlet suspenders he wore to hold his trousers up over his round belly. Benny was easily spotted in the crowd by his bright red suspenders.

"Giddy-up, Hy and Joe. We got miles to go" Benny jiggled the reins on the rumps of the horse and they moved on behind the marching soldiers.

Behind them were other wagons, carts of supplies pulled by oxen and more companies of soldiers. As Phebe looked out of the back of the wagon the stream of humanity stretched as far as she could see, a cloud of dust hovering over the serpentine trail.

She and Betsy poured the men cups of water, wiped their faces with cool clothes and chatted with each other and the sick, weary men. Betsy found a seat in the corner of the

crowded wagon. She looked up at Benny, "How you doin'
Benny? Do you need a drink of water?"

"No. I'm doin' just fine dearie. You just tend to them sick
men. I'll be fine. You better hold on tight. Looks like we're
comin' up on a little stream here. You may get jostled some."

Phebe and Betsy braced themselves for the bumps and jos-
tles that would follow and felt the wagon ease into the stream
bed. Suddenly it dropped several feet and the horses jerked at
the harnesses to pull the wagon from the unsuspected
whirlpool it had fallen into. The wagon tipped, the water
rushed in and within minutes the passengers of the wagon were
in the swirling stream, trying to keep their heads above the
water.

The men in front of them and behind them were trying to
get to their drowning friends to pull them to safety. Phebe held
her breath as she sank to the bottom and then gave a push with
all her might to reach the surface. She gasp for a breath of air
to fill her lungs. Her shoes were like dead weights on her feet
and her dress and petticoats floated up around her face and
then pulled at her. She was going down again, she needed
more air. She lifted her chin for one more gasp as the back-
wash wiped over her and filled her mouth with water. Just as it
seemed that she would surely drown, strong arms encircled her
body and pulled her to the surface. Ebenezer held her tight and
kicked with all his might to propel them through the water to
safety.

He picked her up over his shoulder and waded through the
shallow water to the shore. She vomited out the water she had
swallowed and breathed the fresh air into her lungs. This survival scene was duplicated all along the bank as other rescuers
helped the men and the Boscos from the water onto the sandy
shoal. The whirlpool had almost claimed some of the rescuers
as well and they lay on the banks with the passengers of the
wagon, trying to recover some semblance of strength to move.

"Oh, Phebe, I thought I had lost you." Ebenezer held her

tight in his arms and they both laid back on the sand and let the sun dry them as their lungs gradually adjusted to the normalcy of breathing and their muscles relaxed from the strenuous ordeal.

As Phebe turned her head she saw Captain Hunt and his aide placing two bodies on the sand. The red suspenders caught her eye. "It's the Boscos. Ebenezer, the Boscos were in the wagon with me. He was driving and she was helping me with the men."

Ebenezer helped her to her feet and they joined the circle around Benny and Betsy. Their faces were blue. Captain Hunt was leaning over them, listening for a heart beat. Finally the suspenders started to rise and fall slowly but Benny did not respond to Capt. Hunt. His eyes were closed and his breathing shallow. Betsy was blue and barely breathing also. Capt. Hunt motioned to some of his men, "Help me get them to our wagon." The bodies hung lifeless as they were gently lifted and carried to the Hunt wagon. They did not survive the hour.

Ebenezer and Phebe went to the waters edge to try to retrieve items from Phebe's wagon that were floating by the banks. The team of horses had been freed from their burden and the wagon righted and pulled from the water by the men from Company "A". Ebenezer bent over and picked up the water soaked copy of the Book of Mormon from the reeds. "I hope you can dry and save this." It was their only copy and one of the most precious of the rare possessions they had brought with them.

Air tight cans of Herbs were floating around and Phebe waded out to retrieve them. They took stock of the wagon and found the small trunk of clothes was still inside. Phebe opened it to let the extra dress, shoes, stockings, underwear and petticoats dry. The cooking pots were put back on their hooks.

They looked up as Sergeant Shelton, the messenger from Fort Leavenwerth, rode into camp with the news of Col. Allen's death and the letter from Major Horton advising

Capt. Hunt to take temporary command. The news of Col. Allen's death was a blow to the men. They saw him as their advocate and protector. An aura of sadness and grief was felt through the camp, enhanced by the news that both of the Boscos had passed away.

It had been the Bosco's wish that they would not be parted, even in death. Some of the men prepared a grave sight. Benny and Betsy were buried together and a stone wall was built over and around the grave sight. A funeral service for the Boscos and Col. James Allen was conducted by Captain Hunt. Adjutant Dykes preached a funeral sermon.

The following day, August 30th, the officers met to determine who should assume command of the Battalion. All of the officers agreed that Captain Hunt, the senior captain, should take command. The unanimous decision was noted in a letter to the President of the United States, informing him of the death of Colonel Allen and asking him to honor the agreement that the Battallion would choose their own leader. It requested that Gen. Kearney be directed to appoint Captain Hunt to the command. Captain Hunt knew it was necessary to get the request to the President as soon as possible. "Ebenezer, I think you have the fastest and strongest horse in the company. Will you take this letter to Independence and post it to the President?"

Ebenezer saddled his big white horse while Phebe packed some food and put a bed roll together for him. He winked at his wife and kissed her, "No more swimming while I'm away." He waved good-bye and was off on his mission within the hour.

Everything seemed easy and pleasant to Ebenezer. Phebe wondered at her good fortune to have a husband that never complained and accepted acts of fate or assignments with a positive attitude. She went to the solitude of her wagon and prayed for his safe return to her.

Captain Hunt led the march on to Council Grove the

following day and was advised by an advance aide that Lieutenant Smith was on his way to take command of the Battalion. The officers met again and appointed Jesse D. Hunter, Captain of company "B" and George P. Dykes, 1st Lieutenant of Company "D" to study the matter of who had the right of command and report back to the council.

The voices of the two could be heard outside their tent in heated argument and they finally emerged and reported to the council, Captain Hunter spoke first. "It is my recommendation that Captain Hunt, the senior captain has the right of command."

Lt. Dykes interrupted, "It is my opinion that since we are enlisted by the United States government that an officer of the regular army of said government should command us. It is my concern that the U. S. Government will not keep their promises to us if we are not aligned with the regular army."

The officers were discussing it when Lt. Smith and Dr. Sanderson came in with some additional army personnel and handed a letter to Captain Hunt from Major Horton informing him that the Government property in the possession of the Battalion was not receipted for. Since Lt. Smith was regular Army he had the authority to sign for the government property. It was not clear from the letter that Major Horton was advising that Smith be given the command of the Battalion but the men in the council assumed that was the intent.

Captain Hunt stood and cleared his throat, "I have been directed to lead the Battalion and am very capable to carry out this assignment. I am a Captain and Smith is but a Lieutenant. I was elected to this position under the direction of Col. Allen and just because the official papers have not been forwarded to us does not prove that I should not maintain that command. We would be well advised to wait until we have official instructions from Washington or General Kearney before we change horses in the middle of the stream. You are wise men. I leave it in your hands."

Lt. Dykes repeated his concerns and called for a vote. It was moved by Captain Higgins of Company "D" and Seconded by Captain Davis of Company "E" that Lt. Smith be given the command.

Samuel Gully stood, "I was with Col. Allen when he died. I heard Major Horton say that Captain Hunt should take command. I can not, in clear conscience vote for this man. It is my understanding that all the enlisted men should have a vote. It should not be at the discretion of the officers only. They were all given an opportunity to vote when we were elected to our positions in Council Bluffs."

Dykes called for the vote and all but three of the officers voted for Lieutenant Smith. The pompous Smith glared at Lts. Clark, Gully and Willis, the three dissenters. They stood without saluting and walked from the council tent.

As the word spread through the ranks, a gloom prevailed that was more intense than when the news of Col. Allen's death was reported. The men felt they should have been given a vote and there was great concern about the character of Lt. Smith. They also knew him to favor the advise of Dr. Sanderson.

August 31st. they broke camp at 7:00 a.m. under the command of Lt. Smith and traveled to Diamond Springs where they stood for inspection by the new commander.

Phebe and the other cooks were advised to cook for two days because there would be no fuel at the next camp. Zemira came to her campfire while she was preparing the food. "I am concerned about being an aide to Lt. Smith. I have been trying very hard but I can't seem to please him. What should I do? I wish Captain Hunt was in command or that Col. Allen hadn't died. They both appreciated everything I did for them and treated me with respect. Lt. Smith treats me worse than he does his black slaves. He even accused me of drinking his brandy and you know I would never do that."

The frown lines on Phebe's brow deepened, "Just do as he

asks and ignore his poor manners. When Ebenezer gets back we will discuss it with him. You are only here under our permission and we can send you back to Council Bluffs if you are treated badly. Part of learning to get along in this life is to put up with some people who disagree with us. Do your best and we will see what happens." She gave him a slice of bread and some of the stew which he ate rapidly and then returned to his assignment.

The next camp was at Lost Springs which was deserving of its name. Water was heated over small fires made from burning weeds in trenches and the following day they moved on the Cottonwood Creek in Comanche Indian country. The Comanches were known to be hostile so guards were alerted to twenty-four hour duty.

Phebe prayed and watched for Ebenezer's return. A rider alone in Comanche country could be easy prey for the Indians. He rode into camp that night after dark. Some braves had spotted him earlier in the day but he had been able to out run them on his horse and found a dugout to hide in until dark when he slipped into camp. He stayed with Phebe that night and reported to Capt. Hunt the following morning. Phebe had told him of the change of command so he chose to report to Capt. Hunt over Lt. Smith for obvious reasons. If Smith knew why he had been away from camp his vindictive nature could make life miserable for Ebenezer and he didn't need that.

Phebe was concerned about the food supply. Somehow the orders had been altered after Lt. Gully left Fort Leavenwerth and only three-fourths of the rations ordered were sent. Lt. Smith ordered a forced march and cut the rations to three-fourths per man. It was early September and still very hot on those southern plains. The men started to get sick again and many were soon in need of wagons to carry them.

The men were routinely called out each morning for sick call. The fifes and drums would play a diddy called, "Jim along Joe", reminding anyone who was ill to go to the

Doctor's quarters for treatment. His treatment always consisted of a vile tongue lashing and the order to take either Camomile and/or arsenic. At first he gave them in little paper packets which the men discarded on their way back to the wagons. When the Doctor discovered the packets thrown in the weeds he became furious and forced the men to take the medicine from his old rusty spoon. The same one he had used to examine and treat the men in Phebe's wagon.

The mail was delivered by Lt. Pace and the two men who had accompanied him. When the message from President Young was circulated pertaining to the use of herbs rather than the Doctor's medicine the men became even more emphatic that they would not take the prescribed medicine from Sanderson. They were threatened by Smith that if they refused the medicine they would be pulled from the wagons, tied by a rope and dragged behind the wagon.

Dr. McIntyre, a botanic physician, had been appointed assistant surgeon by Colonel Allen on the day of enlistment but he was warned by Sanderson that he would cut the throat of any man who administered any medicine without his orders. The women tried to do what they could but the harassment of the sick continued. Some of the men appealed to Smith on the grounds of religious scruples against taking mineral medicine but Lt. Dykes repudiated this claim by insisting that the "Brethren" back at Council Bluffs used mineral medicines.

They were camped on the banks of the Arkansas River on September 11th when Lt. Pace delivered the packets of letters from Council Bluffs. He stopped by Phebe's wagon with an envelope containing several sheaths of paper. Phebe looked at the writing and recognized Lovina's handwriting. "Thank you Brother Pace. Did you see any of our family?"

"I saw William on the street but didn't have time to talk much. He said everyone seemed to be fine in the family. He looked well enough." Lt. Pace rode on to deliver the rest of the mail.

Phebe ripped open the letter. It was the first word from family since they left Council Bluffs in mid July. Tears filled her eyes and blurred her sight as she tried to read the even lines of handwriting, written small to fill the paper with as much news as possible. The letters were formed perfectly, as she had taught Lovina when she was a child. She wiped the tears from her eyes and sat in the shade of the wagon to read the letter.

CHAPTER THIRTY-FIVE

August 26, 1846
Dear Mother, Ebenezer and Zemira,
We miss you terribly and pray for your safety every day. Some general news has filtered back to us about your whereabouts but nothing personal until Brother Pace arrived in camp and told Uncle William you were all well. I hope you are getting enough to eat. It has been very hot here this summer and we have worried about the effect of the heat on those of you in the Battalion.

Now, for news of the family here. Grandpa Draper is as well as ever and always helping someone and cheering them up. We know he misses Grandma but he doesn't dwell on it. Uncle William and Aunt Bett are busy also. Aunt Bett delivers a baby almost every day and Uncle William is in charge of one hundred families so he has his hands full. He has also been asked to take another widow as a polygamist wife, Sister Bigsby. Both she and Sister Weaver are expecting babies in the next few months. Zion is growing.

The exciting news is that Aunt Fannie and Uncle Ben have joined the Saints here. She is just as lively as I had remembered and keeps us all laughing at her descriptions of the people and the activities here in camp. It has been very good for Grandpa to have her with us.

Rhoda is a great help to both Harriet and myself with all our little ones. She misses you very much and I often find her alone reading the letter you left her. It seems to be a great comfort to her. I think she has grown three inches this summer. Harriet and I were just talking about the need to make her a new dress, as she has grown out of the last one you made.

William George keeps busy, as usual, with his music. He and Oliver have put a good group together that play for the camp dances. He also spends a lot of time with his wife, Agnes. She is still quite ill and doesn't seem to improve. She has such a sweet disposition and we have all learned to love her.

All of the Bruno's have decided to go to southern Iowa to find farm land. It was hard to see Lydia Elizabeth leave. They promise that they will join us when the Saints are settled in the West. She thought she was expecting a baby when they left. I am happy for her. She is very much in love and promises she will come to us when we are all together again.

Harriet and Oliver and their children are well. She has been weaving cloth for shirts for the men and boys from the spring shearing wool. Norman and Gurnsey are taking good care of the stock and take after their father in finding good animals to increase the herd.

William, Ester Ann and Fanny are growing so fast. William takes over for his father in a lot of ways. He helps with the stock and carries water for me. Henry has had several bouts with chills and fever and each time it seems to take a little longer for him to recover. He and Uncle William are very busy making shoes. Brother Brigham wants us all to have sturdy shoes before we start west.

We may wait for another season to start the trek west as Uncle William has been assigned to stay here and help the converts as they come in. Grandfather feels that we should stay together as a family and we all agree.

Uncle Zemira leads a group of men who help families build cabins or other sorts of shelter. They will be used for other migrating saints when we leave. Our Winter Quarters are on the West bank of the Missouri river, a little north of Council Bluffs. As more converts join us we have to find places to live where there is enough food and water for the stock. The crops we planted in the spring are starting to ripen so we should not want for food this winter. I have tried to preserve the berries and currants that we have found growing wild, just as you taught me. The men go out hunting and have found enough deer and some buffalo to dry for jerky and supply fresh meat.

Please give my love to our friends traveling with you. It

is my prayer that God will bless and protect you.
    Your loving daughter and sister,
    Lovina Palmer Munro

Phebe read the letter again, savoring every word and trying to picture each member of the family as Lovina had described them. Then she went to find Ebenezer and Zemira to share the letter with them.

The buffalo meat was tough. Phebe was trying to keep the fire going to boil the meat as long as she could. If she could bank the fire enough it would keep the pot boiling while she did the laundry for the officers.

They had traveled along the Arkansas river for four days, stopping just long enough to eat meals and sleep. It was the fifteenth day of September and they had made a permanent camp to cook, wash and draw provisions. As usual, it had taken several hours to cross the river where the Cimmeron cutoff intersected the main trail to Bent's Fort.

Colonel Price and five of his Regiments were there. They had word from General Kearney that he had taken possession of Santa Fe. The Battalion was to change course from Bent's Fort and come directly to meet the General at Santa Fe. Colonel Price met with the Battalion officers. "You will need to take provisions for several days. You have a forty mile march ahead of you and there is no food or water. It will be a difficult stretch. I doubt that the women and children with you can make the trip without putting undo burden on the rest of the men. Perhaps you should consider sending them up to Pueblo to winter."

The five captains met to decide what they thought would be best for everyone concerned. They had been advised before they left Council Bluffs that they should all stay together but they had no idea at that time how much sickness they would experience or how many problems they would encounter. Captain Higgins of Company "D" volunteered to lead the detachment. Two sergeants, a corporal and eight privates were chosen to help Captain Higgins escort the group of twenty-seven women and children.

"Celia, I can hardly bear to see you go. I have become so attached to the twins and you have been a good friend." Phebe held a baby in her arms as Celia secured the last pot to the side of her wagon for the journey.

"Jefferson feels that it is best for me and the children and I think he is right. He has chosen our son Gilbert to the escort detail, so I will not be without family to help me. You have been a dear friend to me also, Phebe. Lets hope we both make it to the Rockies so we can be together again." Celia took the baby from Phebe and passed it up to her son before climbing into the wagon.

All the women with small children had been commanded to go for the welfare of them and the rest of the Battalion. Phebe watched as many of her friends and their little ones clung to husbands and fathers, not knowing when they would see each other again. Finally, the small band of travelers headed north while those remaining prepared for tomorrow's journey.

Ebenezer and Zemira came to Phebe's wagon and ate with her after the officers were fed. Ebenezer finished the stew on his plate and licked his lips. "Phebe, you are the best cook in camp. I am glad they didn't send you to Pueblo. It sounds like we have some rough traveling ahead of us, however.

Zemira, how are you getting along with Colonel Smith? Is he unkind to you?"

Zemira swallowed his food and took a drink from his cup, "Oh, no more than usual. I can handle it. He isn't very good to anyone but I think I need to be around to help you with my mother. She may get herself in trouble yet with Dr. Sanderson if she doesn't stop sneaking those sick soldiers the herbs. I think he is getting wise to her. I wouldn't have been surprised if he had insisted on her going to Pueblo."

Ebenezer grinned, "I was afraid he would too but I had some good arguments ready and Captain Hunt and I had a plan if we had to use it." He wouldn't tell what the plan was even when Zemira and Phebe begged him to. "We may still have to use it and I don't want you to be co-conspirators."

Zemira went back to his tent and Ebenezer stayed with Phebe, knowing that the days ahead may give them little time to be together.

The camp was strangely quiet that night without the sound of children's voices or babies crying. Phebe wondered how long it would be until she heard another baby cry or held one in her arms. Ebenezer was soon in a deep sleep and she lay watching him. The wagon had been their only home for seven months and they had many more miles to go. What lay ahead for them in this wilderness of sand and weeds? Could she endure it? And then she reminded herself of the promises she had been given of a long and happy life. She snuggled close to Ebenezer for warmth from the chill of the night air and the comfort of it brought to her to be by him. She drifted off to sleep wondering what Ebenezer and Captain Hunt had plotted.

The blowing sand and sun burned her cheeks as Phebe guided and urged her team along. Her bonnet was no match for the wind that kept whipping at the wide brim made to shade her face. She tied it on as tight as she could but the buffeting of the wind loosened the knot, allowing the protective bonnet to blow off her head and rest on her back. Finally, she gave up, and concentrated on Joe and Hy. They were receiving the full effect of the blasts of sharp sand, often turning their heads to avoid the piercing pain to their eyes.

The wagon was full of men, exhausted from marching into the wind. They were taking turns riding and receiving their meager ration of water during their time in the wagon.

The officers were mounted on their horses and preceded the wagons to help pack the sandy trail. The foot soldiers marched behind with kerchiefs tied over their faces to protect them from the dust. Some of them dropped behind, unable to keep up the pace.

As the day wore on the wind subsided only to be replaced by the excessive afternoon heat. Many canteens were dry but there was no hope of stopping, as their would be no relief from the thirst. Phebe looked ahead and thought she saw, in the distance, a lake or pond. "I can hold on until we get there," she thought to herself, and rolled the pebble around in her mouth to keep the saliva flowing. The marching men and animals needed the water more than she did. She could see some scrub trees by the pool but when they got to the trees they discovered the pool was just a mirage, a trick played by nature, to lure on the desert traveler.

Captain Hunt and Ebenezer saw a large black lagoon off to the north and rode off to investigate its contents. They found a large pond filled with insects and hundreds of buffalo. It was water, though brackish and riled by the buffalo. They shot their muskets into the buffalo herd to drive them from the life preserving water, returned to the thirsty travelers and sent them to quench their thirst..

Phebe could see the familiar white horse as it came over the sandy bluff. Ebenezer was waving his hat for them to come his way. She pulled the rein on the right and eased Hy and Joe into the softer sand. As thirsty animals do, they sensed the closeness of the water and bolted toward the muddy pond. Phebe hung onto the reins and tried to hold them to a steady pace but finally gave them their head and held onto the wagon seat. One of the men in the wagon came to her aid and reigned in the team as they neared the water.

The pond was circled with men and animals parched from the long hot day on the dessert floor. Ebenezer brought some water to Phebe in his cup but she sipped from her canteen of tepid water. She was glad she had some of the clean water left. The troops were soon on their way again and when the darkness of night crept on them from the east, they made camp and it was noted in the log that they had traveled twenty-five miles that day. The officers were convinced that sending the women with children north had been a wise decision. They could, in fact, travel faster without them. Perhaps the other women should be sent to join them. This was harsh country, worse than any of them had ever dreamed it would be.

The following day was much the same as the last and the soldiers and animals were spent from the forced march. The following day they started at four o'clock in the morning to avoid the treacherous heat of the mid-day sun. In the cooler environment they were able to travel ten miles before breakfast. But there was still no rest for them. After ten days of similar travel with only occasional water holes and buffalo chips for fuel, both men and teams were failing fast.

The night of September twenty-first Zemira came to Phebe's wagon. They had traveled eighteen miles that day and had to dig in the Cimmeron river bed for water. Zemira whispered to his mother, "How can we get some important information to Captain Hunt? I overheard something I think he should know."

"Go and get Ebenezer. Tell him you stopped by the wagon. That I was ill and needed him." Phebe pulled the army blanket around her and laid down in the wagon box.

When Ebenezer returned with Zemira the three of them huddled in the wagon and spoke in whispers. "What did you hear, Zemira? It must have caused you grave concern to come to us this way."

Ebenezer put his hand on the boys shoulder to reassure him that his confidence would be protected. "Tell us, boy. Is there something we can do?"

Zemira looked from one to the other. "I was clearing the area around the Colonel's tent when I heard he and

Dr. Sanderson talking. They were laughing about how they were going to kill us all off with the forced marches and the medicine. They are reducing rations to two-thirds tomorrow and no more water will be issued. Only the water from the sink holes we find will be available. Dr. Sanderson admitted to Colonel Smith that the medicine he gives the men just makes them thirsty."

"Go back to your camp, Zemira. You were wise to warn us. We can help the men make allowances for what is to come. Conserve what food you can, Phebe. I'll meet with Captain Hunt and see what we can do."

The Captains called a special prayer meeting invoking the blessings of God in protecting them from the elements and providing them with the needed food and water to survive. Nothing was said in a public way of the Colonel's plans but all the men were forewarned to conserve food and water. They were also reminded to avoid reporting to sick call. Again the women made their wagons available in any way they could for the sick and the ailing men took guard duty at night in the cold rather than take the medicine. They were often relieved by a friend who knew of their condition. In spite of the treatment of the unsympathetic, conniving Colonel and his medical assistant, the men survived through compassion for one another.

It was the twenty-fourth of September, almost two weeks since leaving the Arkansas River, when they saw two high mountain peaks resembling rabbit's ears ahead of them. Fur traders coming past stopped at their camp and told them the peaks had served as guides for travelers. The traders spent the night with them and related stories of severe storms in the area and the loss of a hundred of their mules to a winter storm. The following day they came across the bones of the dead mules and also a human skull.

Phebe wondered where they would be when the winter months came. As she dressed the next morning she noticed that her dress was much looser on her than it had been when she had made it last July in Council Bluffs. Gradually, she had become thinner with the deprivation of food and water. She dropped to her knees for morning prayer and thanked her Father-in-Heaven for preserving her to help the many that needed care. She had not had a sick day so far. Some of the other women were not faring as well. She took some tallow from the jar and rubbed on her hands. They were brown but the skin was not broken even though she had worn calluses on them from holding the reins.

That day they marched another twenty miles over rough terrain and came to a spring of water. It was the first good water they had found in several days. They could even see some timber on the horizon. The following days they found deer, elk and antelope as well as timber for fuel but little food for the animals so they pushed on until dark and started again at daybreak, hoping to find some grazing land.

A council of officers was held on October third. Word had been received from General Kearney that if the Battalion had not arrived by October tenth they would be discharged. Colonel Smith suggested that they select fifty of the healthiest men from each company and the best teams to go on a forced march to Sante Fe. The sick and weak teams would follow as best they could.

Ebenezer mounted his strong white horse and Phebe with her matched team of horses was also in the advanced guard. Zemira rode an Army horse as did the black slaves Colonel Smith kept with him at all times. There was now plenty of water and feed. The caravan moved out quickly, arriving on the night of October ninth.

It was Phebe's forty-ninth birthday but it passed by, unobserved.

They were greeted by an old friend of the Mormons, General Doniphan, who was in charge of the post. It was he who had saved the Prophet Joseph from the lynch mobs in Missouri. He declared a holiday and ordered a salute of a hundred guns to be fired from the roofs of houses in honor of the Battalion. In spite of all he had done, the prophet had been killed by so called patriots at Carthage, Illinois. Here were Joseph's people, sacrificing all they had for their country. Tears came to his eyes as he saw their deplorable condition.

The second wave of the Battalion was not far behind them, arriving on the twelfth of October. They had been better off without the Doctor and Col. Smith. They had come upon some small Mexican towns where the friendly people offered to sell them bread and cakes.

The Battalion was called to the square for an announcement. Colonel P. St. George Cooke addressed the group. He had been appointed by General Kearney to take over the command of the Battalion. "I commend you for your dedication to duty. Your march so far has not been easy nor will it be in the future. Because many of you are ill and the road ahead will challenge the best of us, I will have further instructions tomorrow as to how we will proceed from here. All officers are to meet with me in my tent to discuss the details." He saluted the men and turned to go to his tent.

There was an audible sigh of relief as the men and the twenty women who were still with them, realized that Colonel Smith was no longer in command. It was as if they had received a reprieve from a death sentence.

Lieut. Col Cooke read the following order dated October 15, 1846, Santa Fe.

Agreeable to instructions from the Colonel commanding, Capt. Jas. Brown will take the command of the men reported by the assistant Surgeon as incapable, from sickness and debility, of undertaking the present march to California. The Lieutenant Colonel, commanding, deems that the laundresses on this march will be accompanied by much suffering and would be a great encumbrance to the expedition;and as nearly all are desirous of accompanying the detachment of invalids which will winter near the source of the Arkansas river, it is ordered that all be attached to Captain Brown's party. The detachment will consist of Captain James Brown, three Sergeants, two Corporals, and sixteen privates of Company C; First lieutenant E. Luddington and ten privates of company B; one Sergeant and corporal and twenty-eight privates of company D; and one Sergeant and ten privates of company E and four laundresses from each company. Captain Brown will without delay require the necessary transportation and draw rations for twenty-one days. Captain Brown will march on the 17th inst. He will be furnished with a descriptive list of the detachment. He will take with him and give receipts for a full proportion of camp equipments.

The commanding officer calls the particular attention of company commanders to the necessity of reducing the baggage as much as possible; transportation is deficient. The road most practicable is of deep sand and how soon we shall have to abandon the wagons it is impossible now to ascertain. Skillets and ovens cannot be taken, and but one camp kettle to a mess of not less than ten men.

Company commanders will make their requisitions on the Assistant Quarter Master, Captain W. m. D. McKissock, for mules and wagons, provision bags, pack saddles complete, and such other articles as are necessary for the outfit.

By the order of
Lieut. Col Cooke

The council of officers was dismissed to enact the orders. Ebenezer went directly to Phebe's wagon. "The Colonel is sending all the laundresses back to the Arkansas River to winter with the last detachment as well as the men who are too sick to go on. He thinks we may have to abandon the wagons before we reach California.

Phebe's chin came up, "I have not come this far to turn back when the trail gets hard. I have not been sick one day or delayed the progress of the Battalion in any way. You tell that

Col. Cooke that I am going on if I have to follow behind in the dust."

Ebenezer laughed, "I knew you wouldn't take the news lying down. Remember that I told you about a plan Capt. Hunt and I had back when the last detachment was sent to Pueblo? Well, the time has come to implement the plan with some deviations. What other women would you think are strong enough to stay with the Battalion?"

Phebe put her hand to her chin, running over the names of the other women. Some, she was sure, would want to go back, but others would want to go on. Most of the women were wives of officers. "Susan Davis, the wife of Captain Davis of Company E seems to be a very strong person. Captain Hunter's wife, Lydia is also strong and a born leader. And then that little Melissa Coray. She would not leave her husband for any thing. She is the youngest of the women but she has a lot of courage. She has walked many days when she could have ridden in a wagon because her husband had to walk. She is also a good cook. She has a close friend who they may allow to go. Her name is Sophia Tubbs. Her husband is William Tubbs in Company D."

"Let me see what I can do. I have a lot of people to contact and help get ready for the move. I'll get back to you as soon as I know for sure if you have to leave." Ebenezer rubbed the nose of his horse and patted the neck of this white horse he had purchased in Nauvoo at a pretty price. He always felt a little stronger and a little taller when he rode his white horse. He put his left foot in the stirrup and threw his right leg over the saddle. He picked up the reins from the horses neck and looked down at Phebe. "I'll do every thing in my power to keep you with me. I think that is where the Lord wants you to be."

Ebenezer conferred with his good friend, Capt. Hunt and then went to converse with three of their friends; Jesse hunter, Dan Davis, Bill Coray and William Tubbs. The six men walked to the Colonel's tent and ask for an audience. The details of the conversation were never revealed but modified orders were forthcoming. Five women would be allowed to continue on in the roll of laundresses. They must furnish their own transportation and go at their own risk.

Lieut. Col Cooke made the announcement the following morning sitting astride a beautiful white horse. "The following women will be allowed to continue on with the Battalion; Susan Davis, Lydia Hunter, Melissa Coray, Sophia Tubbs and Phebe Brown. They are to be commended for their courage as we will not be in any position to make any special allowance for their welfare."

Phebe looked at the familiar horse and then at Ebenezer. He grinned at her and she loved him more than ever.

PART VIII

THE DESTROYER WILL HAVE NO POWER TO HARM THEE
OCT. 1846—JULY 16, 1847
CHAPTER THIRTY-SIX

The five women sat in the shade of Phebe's wagon. Phebe broke the silence, "If we are to survive we will have to make some plans and work together. Our husbands will help us every way they can but they have their Battalion duties and Col. Cooke made it clear that we would have to take care of ourselves and not be a burden to anyone."

Lydia Hunter looked up from her tatting. "Let's make a list of what we have and how we can use our facilities together. If we cook and do the laundry together it should help our energy to last the trip."

"I don't have much to offer but I will work hard. I am so glad I can stay with William." Melissa had walked almost all of the way with her husband, helping to carry the meager necessities to keep them alive. "I am so happy that Sophia can go too. She is such a good friend and a hard worker."

"Perhaps we can get by sharing two wagons and put what we have together. Melissa, you and Sophia can ride with me." Phebe put her arm around this young wife who had risked her life to stay with her husband and smiled at Sophia. They could be her own daughters and in some ways, they reminded Phebe of her daughters, Lovina and Lydia Elizabeth.

Susan and Lydia looked at each other and Susan smiled, "Looks like that puts us together and that's fine with me. We will have an extra wagon we can loan to the army but have it in reserve if we need it."

"Lets present our plan to our husbands. They may have something to add or see some problem with it. I'll see if Capt. Hunter can get them together to meet with us." Lydia Hunter stood to leave. "I can see we are going to be a good group. We are sisters in the gospel and together, we will survive."

Phebe was aware of the women and the special strength they could individually contribute to the group. She remembered how the combined efforts of the women in the move from Kirtland to Far West had eased the burden on all of them. She thought of Bett and Ann, Ebenezer's wife and Zemira's wife, Agnes. How she missed them. Their love and respect for each other had helped them survive those terrible days. She remembered Brother and Sister Carey and their kindness to the Draper/Brown caravan when the Prophet's brother Hyrum directed them to their door.

Her thoughts turned to Ebenezer's Ann and her sweet countenance as she lay on her death bed. Sometimes she felt Ann's spirit with her, thanking her for helping Ebenezer and she felt a love for her that transcended death. She thought it interesting that she had never had a jealous feeling concerning Ann.

"You seem to be a million miles away in thought, Phebe." Susan Davis looked at her friend.

"Actually, I was remembering Ebenezer's first wife, Ann, and what dear friends we were. I miss her very much." Phebe smiled at Susan.

"Did you know that I am Daniel's second wife? Sophronia, his first wife, also died while I was taking care of her and then he asked me to marry him and help him raise his family. We have something in common, Phebe."

The husbands returned with Lydia and the plans were drawn up for the merger of the wagons and the duties of the women. When possible, the men would take turns staying with their wives and privates would be assigned to care for the teams pulling the wagons and help with the heavy chores of carrying water and firewood or buffalo chips.

A payroll call was issued and they were paid in a small amount of cash but the bulk of it in checks, redeemable back in the states. John D. Lee was still with the battalion and was going to accompany Lieut. Pace back to the main body of the church. He volunteered to take the money back to be distributed as each person desired. For this service, he charged them fifty cents. Most contributions were divided between money for families, missionary funds and immigration funds. All of the checks were sent back as there was no where to cash them out here in the wilderness.

Ebenezer, Zemira and Phebe combined their checks, sending $26.00 in checks with Elder Lee. They each kept $3.00 which had been paid them in cash after paying Elder Lee $1.50 for the delivery. They anticipated passing some villages that may provide food or needed clothing if they had some cash. Phebe sewed a money pocket to the inside of underwear for each of them to carry the cash.

Captain Hunt called a meeting for all of the Battalion. Testimonies were shared and the women and men who were leaving the group were honored and blessed in their return trip. After the meeting, the musicians played and the dancing began. Col. Cooke stood at the outer circle of the large group of tired, poorly clad people, many of whom were ill. He wondered at these people who could pray, laugh, sing and dance under such conditions. Most of all he observed their love and respect for one another. He had heard of the treatment meted out to the Mormons in Ohio, Missouri and Illinois and he wondered at their continued commitment to a country that had treated them so badly. Obviously, they had been pushed beyond the point of reason by the self appointed Col. Smith who he was now happy to demote to his rightful rank of Lieutenant. As for Dr. Sanderson, he would have to keep him under his command, but he would certainly control his unkind behavior toward the men he was suppose to care for.

The returning contingency of sick soldiers, women and the men under Capt. Higgins command left the following morning. Brigham Young had told them not to be divided but again, the circumstances warranted it. Capt. Hunt observed that each of the two groups who had been sent back had strong priesthood leadership who had been among those given special instructions from President Young before leaving Council Bluffs.

Phebe and Ebenezer found some of the discarded paper used to wrap army supplies and started letters to their daughters. Ebenezer hadn't finished his letter to his daughter, Harriet, when he was called to help assemble the returning wagon train. Phebe finished her letter and rushed over to Brother Gully, "Please give my love to my family along with this letter and God bless you on your trip back to your family. Thank you, we are proud of you for your strong stand against the tyranny of Col. Smith. You are wise to go back."

"Thank you, Sister Brown. May the Lord attend you and Brother Brown to California." A cloud of concern covered his face as he looked over the remaining soldiers. "They need you, Sister Brown."

Samuel Gully, John D. Lee, Howard Egan, Roswell Stevens and Lieut. Pace bade their friends good-bye and rode from the camp. It was October 19th, 1846.

Ebenezer hurried to the wagon to finish his letter but it was too late, the men had gone. "I'll finish this anyway and put it in my knapsack. You never know when someone may come by that will take it to Harriet." He sat on the tongue of the wagon and took the stub of a pencil and the paper from his pocket. He could not write as fast as Phebe, but thanks to her, he could read and write now. His brow wrinkled as he laboriously wrote the words and chained them together in thoughts.

Meanwhile, Col. Cooke wrote in his diary:

"Everything conspired to discourage the extraordinary undertaking of marching this Battalion eleven hundred

miles, for the much greater part through an unknown wilderness, without road or trail, and with a wagon train.

"It was enlisted too much by families; some were too old, some feeble and some too young; it was embarrassed by many women; it was undisciplined; it was much worn by traveling on foot and marching from Nauvoo, Illinois; their clothing was very scant; there was no money to pay them, or clothing to issue; their mules were utterly broken down; the quartermaster department was without funds and its credit bad; and animals were scarce. A small party with families was sent—to winter at a small settlement close to the mountains, called Pueblo. The Battalion was now inspected, and eighty-six men, found inefficient, were ordered, under two officers, with nearly all the women, to go to the same point; five wives of officers were reluctantly allowed to accompany the march, but furnish their own transportation.

"With every effort, the quartermaster could only undertake to furnish rations for sixty days; and, in fact, full rations of only flour, sugar, coffee and salt; salt pork only for thirty days and soap for twenty. To venture without packsaddles would be grossly imprudent and so that burden was added."

Following his entry in his diary, Col Cooke informed the troops they would move out the following morning, October 20, 1846, on their way to California.

Ten days rest had done wonders for the troops and they started out with high hopes of meeting the challenges ahead and traveled six miles to Aqua Frio, a good grazing spot for the animals.

Phebe was glad to have Melissa and Sophia with her in the wagon. There were no sick men to transport since they had all been sent back to Pueblo. The oldest and the youngest of the women sang songs as they rode along together and talked about their families and their conversions to the church. Phebe was surprised to learn that Melissa was also from Canada, though not from the Loughborough area. The miles rolled by much faster with someone to talk to and Joe and Hy were spry after the rest, good water and adequate grazing. Melissa and Sophia laughed when Phebe told her how she had decided to name the horses, Joe and Hy, after Ebenezer procured them for her at Fort Leavenwerth. She still hadn't decided which one was the better leader, after all these miles, so they both responded to Joe and Hy collectively.

Melissa looked over at Phebe, "I have a confession. I really should have told you before we left but I was afraid they would send me to Pueblo and I did want to stay with William. I'm expecting a baby. I have tried to keep it a secret but sometimes I get very sick in the mornings."

Phebe looked over at her and smiled. "That is exciting news and I won't share it with anyone until I have your permission. It will make it easier for you to spend more time riding in the wagon. See, the Lord has ways of working things out for us if we have faith and try to do the best we can. I'll look through the herbs my sister-in-law, Bett, gave me and see if there is something that will help you. She is a midwife and I have helped her with many births, so you put your mind at ease. You will have all the help you need when the time comes. Who knows? We may be back with the saints in the Rockies by the time the baby comes. It will be a wonderful summer baby. They are always the strongest."

Phebe's encouragement eased Melissa's concern. "Sister Brown, you make me feel so much better. Tell me how you felt when you were expecting your first baby."

Phebe's mind went back to those early days with George when they were building the Palmer Farm. She told her about helping with the plowing and the planting. Then she told her about Lovina, her beautiful baby girl who had brought so much joy to her. They both became silent but Phebe's mind kept helping her relive those days, and she thought of recording the names of the children in the Family Bible given to her by Grandfather Draper. She did hope Lovina was taking good care of that precious book.

Phebe looked up in time to see Colonel Cooke raise his hand to halt the advance guard of Company A. Three riders were coming toward them from the southwest and she recognized them as Antoine Leroux, Pauline Weaver and Jean Baptiste Charbonneau, three of the guides Colonel Cooke had chosen to help him reach California. All three were familiar with the southwest territory and Colonel Cooke had told the officers of the Battalion that their very survival was dependent on the information these guides would share with them.

The Battalion slowly came to a stop and the Colonel dismounted his white horse as did the guides, giving their mounts a rest while they discussed the hazards of the trail ahead.

Phebe finished serving the officers and the guides their dinner. They had traveled fifteen miles that day on a road that had been traversed enough to make it more passable than much of the previous trail. The three buckskin clad guides with their unkept appearance ate most of the food from their tin plates with their hands, ignoring the silverware she had provided for them. Their long beards, hair, and weathered skin testified of the rustic and sometimes treacherous lives they led.

Charbonneau sopped the gravy from his plate with the last of his sourdough biscuit, "Colonel, there's water about fifteen miles up that-a-way from the river. I'd suggest ya take that route come mornin'. You'll have to be leaving the Rio Grande sooner or later and them water holes are mighty important to survival in this country."

Charbonneau was born to be a guide. He was the son of the Indian woman, Sacajawea, who led the Lewis and Clark expedition to the Northwest Territory. His father was a frenchman. He had spent his life in the wilderness areas of the country and knew them well. Phebe could see that his features carried traces of both of his parents. He was a Lamanite, a descendent of Father Lehi in the Book of Mormon. His people had been given great promises. She may have an opportunity to tell him what she knew of his ancestors, but now was not the time. She gathered up the plates and took them to the dish pan of hot water to wash them.

Before leaving Sante Fe the rations had been cut to three-fourths pound of flour, three-fourths rations of sugar and coffee, one and one-half pounds of beef for one day. Col. Cooke had established some procedures that brought more of an army atmosphere of discipline to the Battalion. The commander of each of the companies was directed to select a non-commissioned officer to report on daily duty, whose duty it was to issue rations and superintend the loading of the wagons and the care of the mules. They were to have immediate command of the teamsters and assistants. The commanders were held responsible for the careful issue of rations. The Colonel made it clear that the welfare and safety of the Battalion may depend on it.

The officers were expected to live the letter of the law as well as the soldiers under their command. The morale of the men was much better than when Lieut. Smith was in command, ignoring the officer's infractions while punishing the privates for every little imagined offense.

Col. Cooke issued this additional order:

> *"Hereafter, no muskets or knapsacks will be carried in a public wagon or on a public mule without orders or express permission of the commanding officer. After roll call the ranks will be opened and an officer will pass down each rank and see that all are fully armed and equipped. Immediately after roll call, breakfast will be disposed of and everything packed in the wagons by a sufficient number of each mess under the acting Quartermaster Sergeants of the*

company, as provided for in the order. All this will be done
without waiting for signals or the loss of a moment. — I call
all the officers and the Quarter master Sergeants of compa-
nies and the teamsters and the assistants to do the best for
them possible."

"By order of Lieut. Col. Cooke. Signed by G.P. Dykes,
Adjutant."

So it was the following morning, and when all was readied
the Battalion made up primarily of foot soldiers traveled about
sixteen miles up hill to a rocky chasm. The water was there as
the guides had attested to but it was about one hundred feet
down through a narrow gorge in a well about thirty feet in
diameter. Col. Cooke sat on the edge of the ravine directing the
watering of the animals. It took over two hours for the men to
lead the animals down single file to water and return with
water for the camp.

While the soldiers were working the water detail, the
women were catching up on some cooking. Extra bread on
hand allowed for speedy breakfast toast. Phebe, Sophia and
Melissa were always on the alert for ways to save time and
stretch the short rations.

Ebenezer was on duty to care for the animals that day so he
came for Hy and Joe to lead them down the narrow path to the
well for water. The matched team followed Ebenezer down the
rocky trail and around to an open space by the water where
they drank their fill and munched on some grass by the edge of
the water. Ebenezer took a bucket with him to carry water back
to camp as did the others. He cupped some water into his
hands and drank from the well. It was good water and he took
another drink in the same manner remembering the bible story
of the soldiers who were chosen because they drank from
cupped hands rather than lapping at the water like a dog. He
grinned as he thought about it. "I guess I qualify as a good soldier. At least I could be one of Gideon's men." He took hold of

Joe's halter rope with one hand and carried the bucket of water in the other. Hy followed as they climbed back up the steep trail to the camp. Joe gave Ebenezer a gentle push when the grade was hard and finally, they made it to the top.

Ebenezer took the water to Phebe, "With the help of your team we made it back with a little water in the bucket. When I get through with the mules and oxen I'll go down and get some more." He gave her a peck on the cheek and whistled as he moved on to the next animal in line.

That night the musicians from each company, organized by Brother Levi Hancock, came together and played and sang to the delight of everyone. Phebe and Ebenezer danced as did the other couples. Most of the men danced together since their wives were not with them. They laughed and changed partners as one of the men called some squares. Brother Smith played some stomping music on his fiddle and some of the men from his part of the country danced their own original dances to the fiddle music.

Col. Cooke smiled as he watched from the sidelines. He had never seen a happier people. They accepted their assignments without complaint, worked harder than any soldiers he had commanded and still had energy to dance and sing. He looked up at the wide expanse of the Autumn sky and saw the harvest moon in full array, hanging in the sky. This was a good land. He was determined that he, with this unusual group of people, would make it to California.

The following morning he ordered his guide, Leroux, to take six men with him to scout the area. He was to send one back to camp after each days travel. It was November 14th and they traveled about twelve miles in a southwestern direction. One of the old white oxen Ebenezer had traded to the army for the matched team gave out that day. It was recorded as one that had been procured at Fort Leavenworth, which it was, but before that it had pulled the Brown wagon across the Mississippi on that cold February day and trudged through blizzards across the Iowa plains.

Phebe was glad she had not named the old white ox. It made it easier when it was butchered the following day and the little meat left on the emaciated animal was divided among the soldiers. She cooked some for the officers, helped salt and preserve the hide, but that day she chose not to eat the meat.

Melissa and Sophia helped her strip what little fat was on the hide and salt it down. They stretched the hide out in the sun to dry. Phebe wished she had her brother, William, with her to help her tan the hide. He had used some kind of acid that smelled very bad but he performed some sort of miracle that turned the stiff hides into soft leather. The men's shoes were worn and some were wrapping the soles on with ropes or rags to protect their feet from the hot sand. Perhaps they could use this hide to make shoes for some of the men.

She decided she would ask Charbonneau about softening the hides. He and his mountain men friends must know some methods of making leather. She would ask Ebenezer also. Maybe he could tell her.

Some of the men found some wild grape vines when they were rounding up some stray cattle. They picked all the grapes they could carry and brought them back to camp and then returned with buckets to pick more. The grapes provided a delicious diversion to the bland diet of bread, meat and coffee. They made sure the four women had a share of the find and Phebe relished the sweet taste of the grapes. She remembered the fall apples in Canada and wished they had a wagon load to feed the men. This country was so barren it was doubtful they would be finding much wild fruit to supplement their supplies. Perhaps the Lord had provided the grapes for them as he did the manna for the Israelites in the wilderness.

They had traveled over twelve hundred miles since July. It was now mid November so they had averaged about ten miles a day. Many days they had pushed ahead for twenty-five or thirty miles, some days they had rested and other days made only a few miles. She guessed it would be much the same. There was ice on the water bucket this morning. Even in this desert country the nights were cold.

The army started across the valley and soon found themselves in deep sand. Col. Cooke had the foot soldiers walk two abreast in two rows across the sand in front of the wagons to pack the trail for the wagon wheels.

Phebe kept her team in line to avoid the soft sand. Melissa and Sophia insisted on walking with their husbands and Phebe did not object. They were plucky young girls and Phebe had come to admire there determination. Neither Melissa nor Sophia liked to drive the team so Phebe had maintained that role from the time they started to share the wagon. The horses were so used to her anyway that they needed little attention when following the troops.

She felt the soothing stone in her pocket. It was comforting to know it was there in case they ran out of water. She had taught the girls to carry one in there pockets also. As she told them, "It is nice to just feel the smooth stone in your pocket but if you get thirsty and there is little or no water, you can put it in your mouth and you don't feel so thirsty."

Phebe could see Melissa up ahead. Her red and yellow sunbonnet with auburn curls falling down her back was easy to spot among the drab hats of the soldiers. She saw Col. Cooke ride up beside Melissa on his white horse. He seemed to be offering her a ride but she saw the bonnet move from side to side so she knew that Melissa had not accepted the offer. Perhaps she and Sophia would come back to the wagon after the next rest stop. They could talk about what they could make for the new baby. Material and yarn was in very short supply but they would think of something. Phebe decided one of her petticoats would be just the thing to use for some little baby gowns. After so much washing it was very thin and soft. She could pick the hems out and save the thread to sew the gowns together. She smiled as she thought of the new baby. Her bonnet had slipped back on her shoulders and she pulled it up to protect her from the midday sun that had crept overhead. They would be stopping soon now and she would encourage Melissa and Sophia to join her in the wagon.

Col. Cooke rode past and tipped his hat to her. She smiled back. He was a gentleman and treated all the women with respect. In fact, Dr. Sanderson and Lieut. Smith were even more congenial under his command. The Lord had blessed them by sending someone as wise and good as he to take them to California.

The columns of marchers stopped in front of her and she pulled on the reins. "Whoa, whoa."

CHAPTER THIRTY-SEVEN

The level plains brought them to the Mimbres River lined with welcome green grass and water. Another sick detachment of soldiers had been sent to join their comrades in Pueblo. One of the sick men was Sophia's husband, William Tubbs. Sophia had left with him. Phebe and Melissa wondered what the trail ahead held for them.

The mules and horses were freed after being in harness for over eleven hours. The women gathered up the laundry from the officers and started the water heating and the meat boiling for the evening meal. The river water provided extra water that had been so scarce. They would work into the night to get the laundry done.

Melissa tied a rope to the top of the wagon cover and Phebe stretched it to one of the few trees growing by the river. She circled the tree with the rope and took it on to the clump of bushes a few feet away. They washed the clothes in the hot soapy water and then carried them to the river to rinse out the soap. The bank to the river was steep and the heavy wet clothes made the trip down to the river and back up to the wagon taxing. Phebe's back ached from the burden but she took more than her share to free Melissa from carrying more than her small frame could handle. After a few trips, Phebe saw Melissa's strength waning so she sent her on to monitor the cooking food while she finished the laundry her self. Her hands were cold as she draped the wet clothes over the ropes. If it was as cold tonight as it had been the last few nights, the clothes would freeze and they would have to finish drying them on the trail.

Phebe climbed into the wagon and found the can of mutton tallow, rubbing it into her cold, red hands and pulled the cotton gloves on to cover them. The gloves were no longer white as they had been when she started the trip, but they still protected her hands from the cold and kept the tallow from smearing on everything she touched. Her supply of tallow was running low. She would have to save some more when they butchered more of the sheep.

Ebenezer came to her wagon. He had walked the trail all day, packing the sand for the wagons. He was tired but not complaining. She rubbed his shoulders and pulled the boots from his feet. "Ebenezer, leave those stockings with me so I can darn the holes. Do you have some others in your pack?"

"I have another pair but they aren't in much better condition. Do you have any yarn to knit me some more?" He had seen some of the other men trying to mend their clothes and darn their stockings. He was mighty lucky to have Phebe.

"I have one ball of yarn left. I hope it will make a pair for you and one for Zemira. It was all I could get before we left Sante fe. I've been working on them the last two days." Her eyes wandered to the ox hide she had draped over the top of the wagon to dry. "Ebenezer, I saved the white ox hide but I don't know how to soften it. Melissa and I scrapped the inside and salted it. What else should we do. It seems to me that a lot of the men are going to need some leather to repair their shoes."

"I've heard that the Indians use brains or urine to soften the hide. I'll ask the men that are on butcher duty to save the brains for you next time they slaughter some animals. I think you could soak it in the river while we are here and that would soften it up. I hear Col. Cooke is going to hold up tomorrow to see if the guides come back to give him suggestions for the direction we should go, so it may have time for a good soaking."

"I don't have watch tonight so I can stay here with you if you can put up with a tired old soldier. I'll help you take the hide down to the water and secure it so it won't float away."

They pulled the salted hide from the wagon top and

Ebenezer carried it to the water. He tied a rope around one end of the hide that had once covered the foreleg of the oxen and the other end of the rope to a bush at the side of the water. He put some rocks on the hide to hold it down and he and Phebe sat by the river, watching the old white hide gradually absorb the water and sink out of sight. Ebenezer put his arm around Phebe's shoulder and pulled her to him. "That white ox got us across the frozen Mississippi and the snow covered plains of Iowa, and even down to Fort Leavenwerth. It may help us make it to California by protecting our feet. I never dreamed when I bought it in Carthage that it would be so useful."

The moon was not quite full now but its light shimmered across the river. The weary travelers crawled under the blankets to protect them from the cold and slept soundly. Phebe was comforted by the nearness of Ebenezer.

Phebe awoke to the trumpeter's reveille. Ebenezer was already gone. The air was cool and it was tempting to stay under the warm covers but she had work to do. The laundry needed to be retrieved from the makeshift rope lines and she mustn't forget the ox hide down in the river.

Dressing quickly, she threw her shawl around her shoulders and walked down to the river to check for the hide and also wash her face and hands. The cold river water was stimulating and the residue of sleep soon vanished as the cold air hit her wet skin. She wiped her hands on her apron and started to untie the rope that held the hide in the water. It was almost more than she could handle to pull the wet hide up out of the water with the rocks holding it down. The river bank was lined with soldiers washing their hands and faces in the cold water.

"Let me help you, Sister Brown." It was William, Melissa's husband. "I just walked Melissa back to the wagon and came down to wash up. You must have a buried treasure down there." He helped Phebe pull on the tie rope and soon the ox hide surfaced and they pulled it up on the river bank.

"Thank you, William. If you will help me lay it over the

top of the wagon it can dry as we travel." She turned at the sound of hoof beats and saw Col. Cooke and the guides riding out of camp toward the top of the hill southwest of camp.

Charbonneau pointed to the west. "If ya stay on that trail ya won't have water for most a hundred miles."

Weaver and Leroux, the other guides agreed. Old Weaver looked south, "Now there's some Mexican villages down that way and they might be sellin' ya some of their crops or other things ya might be needin'."

The men returned to camp and the Colonel called the officers together for a strategy meeting. After explaining the possible peril of crossing the arid country with no water for a hundred miles he announced his decision. "I have decided that we should take the advice of the guides and travel south to Mexico. This will delay our arrival in California but at least we will live to see it."

There was an audible sigh of disappointment among the officers. It had been the intent of all of the Battalion that the sooner they reached California, the sooner they would be reunited with their families. Long days of marching with limited food and water was worth the sacrifice if it brought them closer to their goal. The officers left the meeting with heavy hearts, knowing they must break the news to the men under their command.

It was Sunday and the Colonel announced that they would lay over a day to make their plans. It was determined that two of the large wagons would be left behind and the oxen used as pack animals. The men were also directed to leave their tent poles in a pile, using their musket barrels to support the tents. They had purchased some Mexican sheep and would heard them along the trail, butchering them as they went for meat.

Brother Pettigrew and Brother Levi Hancock went quietly from tent to tent counseling the men to, "Pray to the Lord to change the Colonel's mind."

The women met together in the Hunter wagon. Lydia was

in tears, "I cant go to Mexico. I haven't told you I am pregnant and I don't want my child born in Mexico." She covered her face with her hands and sobbed.

Phebe tried to assess the situation and find some words of encouragement but for once, she too was devastated. Only four women and two of them pregnant with the hardest part of the journey ahead. Going into Mexico they could face a people already angry with the Americans. "Our only solution is to pray with all our hearts that the Colonel will choose the right path. We must also have faith and remember the promise of Brigham Young that there would be no bloodshed." The women knelt in the wagon, holding hands, as Phebe petitioned the Lord for help.

The women joined their husbands as they met together for a Sunday service. Their voices raised in the new song that Brother Clayton had written on the Iowa plains. "Come, come, ye saints, no toil nor labor fear but with joy wend your way." As they came to the last verse, voices broke as they sang, "And should we die before our journey's through, Happy day, All is well.—-If our lives are spared again to see the saints their rest obtain. Oh, how we'll make this chorus swell. All is well, All is well."

Colonel Cooke heard the singing as he wrote in his journal. The faith of these people was more than he could understand. In light of what may lay ahead of them in Mexico, they were still singing, "all is well."

The whole camp slept fitfully that night and were ready to go early. They moved in a southerly direction for a few miles and then the trail veered sharply to the East. The Colonel raised his arm to halt the troops and called the officers forward. "Since the word came that the Mexican war was over and that we should proceed quickly to California, that has been our goal. I was ordered to California. I will go there or die in the attempt. Bugler, blow to the right." The Colonel heard a murmur from the troops, "God bless the Colonel" He smiled to himself. If this was the way the men felt, they would survive.

The long line of marchers and wagons gradually wound its way in a westerly direction. The word moving back through the ranks that the decision had been made to take the trail to California they traveled another eighteen miles to a dry camp.

Zemira came to Phebe's wagon after camp chores were finished. "Mother, have you ever felt that your own personal prayers were answered?"

"Many times, Zemira. Why do you ask?" Phebe took his hand and looked at this tall son. He must have grown a foot since they left Council Bluffs four months ago. They sat together on the tongue of the wagon.

"When Col. Allen announced that I was to be his aide I was pretty sure it was an answer to prayer. Then, when Lt. Smith took over I wondered what I had done to deserve his anger and I prayed that I would please him or be assigned to someone else. Colonel Cooke took over and he has been so good to me. He even gave me these old army pants because mine were too small. I am sure that his decision today was an answer to our prayers." He looked into his mother's beautiful steel gray eyes, "Do you think we will live to see California?"

"I'm very sure we will. And someday, we will be with our loved ones again in the Rocky Mountains." She told him then, how the Prophet had told she and Ebenezer that they would one day help settle the "New Zion" in the Rocky Mountains. "We decided we would never tell anyone about that promise but I think you should know. It will help you in the hard times ahead. Please help us keep this secret as I am sure it was given to us as a personal blessing. Yes, Zemira, we will see California."

Zemira went back to his tent and Ebenezer stopped by to say "Good night." She told him she had shared the promise with Zemira. He smiled, "This was the time to tell it. He needs all the encouragement we can give him. I have often wondered if I had done him a favor by agreeing to let Col. Allen bring

him along but I feel now that it was a good decision for him
and for us." He kissed her good night and went back to his
assigned tent, supported by the musket barrels.

As Phebe undressed for the night she heard her soothing
stone drop from her apron. She picked it up, held it for a
moment, then slipped it back into her pocket.

The officers, mounted on horses, rode ahead and the men
were marched again in two lines to pack the trail for the wagons that followed. They were now down to two wagons for the
women and three wagons for supplies. The four oxen were
weighed down with supplies tied on them as were the twenty
or so pack mules. The women's wagons led the wagon train
and today, Phebe's was in front. They had started early to take
advantage of the sun being at their backs. After about eleven or
twelve miles they came to a small moraine jutting out from a
higher mountain. At its point was a rocky crevice that
appeared to be a source for water.

"There isn't much water here. I think the horses need it
more than the men." The Colonel directed the men on horses
to the water and motioned for the horse drawn wagons to pull
around to the water hole. When it was time for the men to file
up to the water for a drink they had to wait for drops of moisture to leak from the rocks. Some of them had only a table-
spoon or less.

Seeing their plight, Phebe put the pebble in her mouth to
stimulate the flow of saliva. She hoped Ebenezer and Zemira
had been able to get a drink. Over three hundred people trying
to get a drink from a dripping rock was close to ridiculous.
When the Colonel ordered them to move on, those who had
not been able to get to the rock waited for the last minute to
fall in at the back of the line. With no moisture to quench and
unending thirst, they trudged on, trying to keep up with the
troops.

Six miles over the ridge they were met by the guides
telling them that there was water nine miles further on.

Mirages of water continued to plague them as they pushed on. It was dark when the first contingency arrived at the western shore of a dry lake bed and found water in some swamp holes. The men continued walking into camp until morning light. Some of them had been without water for almost forty-eight hours.

When the last of the men came in they fell into the water and some of them drank in excess after the long thirst. They became ill and were treated with the usual dosage of Calomel which they held in their mouths until they could spit it out into the fire. Phebe watched with fury in her eyes as she saw the men subjected to the treatment. She took note of those who were ill, hoping she would be able to find them and give them some herbal tea to relieve their suffering.

The colonel recognized the need for another days rest to recuperate from the arduous trip. Some of the brethren went quietly to the ailing soldiers to give them a priesthood blessing.

Phebe spent the resting time to do some knitting on the stockings for Zemira and Ebenezer. Melissa was sewing some baby gowns from the soft muslin petticoat. The wagon was a far cry from the comfort of the house in Nauvoo and the rocking chair Phebe loved to sit in when she was knitting. She found herself rocking back and forth to the rhythm of the knitting needles and repeating the stories she had told Melissa about her childhood, her family and the apple orchards.

Several of the men were sent ahead to open a trail over the ridge of the Rocky Mountains. Phebe could see mountain peaks far to the north and she wondered where they would finally settle. With plenty of water and fresh meat from the mountain animals she threw herself into finding a variety of ways to cook the wild meat, trying to stretch the supplies as far as she could and adding a few herbs to the pots of steaming stew. The men were always on the lookout for wild berries.

Charboneaux came into camp with a grizzly bear he had

shot on the mountain. He had eluded two others he frightened off with his well timed shot. The bear meat became part of the evening meal and Charboneaux told his tale over and over at the camp fires as the men chewed on the bear meat.

Phebe wiped her brow. It had been difficult to drive the team up this steep mountain. Ebenezer finally asked permission to help and it was granted. The men had made a trail but it was far from a wagon road. Phebe climbed out of the wagon and started to trudge up the steep hills. She was soon out of breath and her legs felt weak. "I have become soft, riding in that wagon. I should have walked more like Melissa, but then, who would have driven the wagon?" She stopped to rest and then found new strength to go on further. If the men could do it, she could. The weeds and thistles clung to her skirts and she was glad for the protection of the high shoes William had made for her to protect her ankles.

It was the twenty-eighth of November and they were camped on a south summit of the Continental Divide. Phebe looked over the vista. It seemed she could see forever. Everything west was down hill and she knew everything East was down hill also. Especially the last few miles she had climbed on foot. When she looked down the steep descent that would be the next challenge her hands were cold and clammy. She had never liked heights. She walked back from the brink of the hill to the camp. Ebenezer had unharnessed the team and the wagon was in place, ready for her to start her chores for the evening meal.

Col. Cooke called the men together and outlined the plan for moving the wagons and supplies down the steep grade. The pack animals, including the oxen, would transport all the supplies down, tied to their backs.

It took all of the daylight hours to tie the packs to the

animals and lead them down the steep hill, then return to tie another load, and another. Some of the mules bucked and the Oxen, not accustomed to being used as pack animals, made quite a game out of it. The men would laugh at their antics. The wagons were next on the list for the following day. The wagons would be emptied of everything, including any heavy parts that could easily be removed. Ropes would be tied to the wagons which the men would hold from the top as they eased the wagons down the incline. When they ran out of rope they would dally them around the trees, repeating the process until they had the wagons to the valley floor.

Phebe's wagon had been emptied and she kept only her blanket to wrap up in to keep her warm on this mountain ridge in late November. She was glad when Ebenezer came to her aid and slept by her to help keep her warm through the night. They had all filled their knapsacks with some bread or jerky for the morning meal. At daylight the wagons were pulled to the precipice and eased over the edge. The weight was more than expected and the men held to the ropes until their muscles rippled under threadbare shirts. It was slow, tedious work and took all the strength the men could muster as several hung to each rope. It was a tug of war with a heavy wagon and the pull of gravity against dozens of men holding fast to ropes. Two ropes broke while they were lowering the third wagon and it crashed, end over end, breaking into pieces with wheels rolling, unattached to crevices below. The men finally won and a cheer went up as the last wagon safely reached the valley floor.

The women were trying to pick their way down, taking a gradual descent by following the switch back trail the animals had made the day before. As they reached the camp sight they looked back to see the sun shining on the rocks and trees all aglow in tints of red, orange, purple and yellow. Phebe felt immersed in the beautiful autumn hues and the warmth of the glowing sun. It was as if she were engulfed in a fire, feeling the protection of God. Aside from the loss of the wagon their had been no injuries. Surely they had received help from on high. Before she knew it she was singing, "The Spirit of God like a fire is burning the latter day glory begins to come forth—" and the others joined her until there was a chorus of the sacred song bouncing off the vermillion rocks and precipices. Many fell to their knees in a silent prayer of thanksgiving.

It was now early December and the troops had worked their way down more canyons that allowed easier passage. The varied types of trees dressed in autumn colors contributed to the landscape. A wild vegetable called Mezcal was added to their meals. Charboneaux taught them how to roast it Indian style. It became a welcome diversion to what had been a long journey of sand, weeds, a limited diet of mutton, beef, some wild meat, wild berries, and little water.

Phebe and Melissa were finishing the evening chores and watching another glorious sunset. Phebe looked up at the beautiful scene as she scrubbed on the brown, crusty residue in the pot. "Oh, Melissa. I wish I could paint that picture so I could always remember it. Look, the clouds are even reflecting the color." The water soaked the pot clean while Melissa and Phebe enjoyed the ecstasy of the moment.

"Sister Brown, I love the way you make little things important and more meaningful. The Lord has blessed you with a special spirit to serve and teach others. Thank you for being my friend." Melissa wiped the dishwater from her hands and gave Phebe a hug.

Tears came to Phebe's eyes and she tried to hide them. Melissa could never understand how much her presence had eased the loneliness Phebe felt for her own daughters. Lovina, her beautiful raven haired daughter, now a grown woman with a family, Lydia Elizabeth expecting her first baby and Rhoda, left to the care of others while growing into those tender years.

"Melissa, you have brought me more happiness that you know. You are young and vibrant. You glow with that special beauty that happens when you are giving life to a new spirit. Thank you for being my friend."

They hung the pots on the side of the wagon and walked into the maze of tents to find Ebenezer and William. Many of the men spoke to them as they walked by with the usual respect, referring to them as Sister Brown and Sister Coray. Phebe felt very safe in the company of these good men who respected women and lived moral lives.

They found their husbands among a group of sergeants from Companies A and B. Captain Hunter and Captain Hunt were giving directions for the move to what the guides called, Rancho San Bernardino. The Mexicans and Indians had lived their together but the Apache Indians had finally drivin out the last Mexican rancher. It would not be a long march. They would arrive sometime the following day.

The women waited until the meeting was over and their husbands walked them back to the wagon. "Get a good night's sleep. We'll be in Rancho San Bernardino tomorrow." With that, the men left their wives to the comfort of the wagon and went back to their bedrolls in their tents.

Sleep did not come quickly for Phebe, "Hmm, Rancho San Bernardino. What would it be like? Did Apache Indians still live there? Would they welcome this army of three hundred and fifty or more Americans coming into their rancho? Would there be little Indian children there? She hoped so." Gradually sleep came and she dreamed of teaching a little group of Apache children to read.

CHAPTER THIRTY-EIGHT

It was a nightmare. The wild bulls were charging the men who were shooting and reloading muskets in a life saving frenzy. A dozen men were under Phebe's wagon, using it as a protection while they shot volley after volley of balls at the raging animals. It took a half dozen or more to bring down one animal. Some men were laying on the ground, protecting their faces from the onslaught and hoping the bulls would jump over them as they stampeded across the compound.

Phebe and Melissa huddled in the wagon bed as they heard men screaming and guns firing. Phebe looked up to see Amos Cox's body fly through the air after being gored by a bull and tossed away like a rag doll. Mounted officers were firing into the wild herd, trying to chase them away from the unprotected men who could not find cover under the wagons, behind mesquite bushes or by the remnants of the old adobe walls of what was once the San Bernadino rancho.

They had arrived at the rancho and made camp by a small stream of water. Some of the men were sent to hunt for meat. To their surprise, they came upon a large herd of wild bulls. After several shots they were able to bring one down. One man, exhausted from the conflict, stayed with the carcass while the others returned to camp to get help. Little did they know that they would drive the herd right into their camp of unprotected comrades.

The battle raged on until the stampeding herd moved on, leaving a ravaged camp. The Colonel assessed the damage and found that the wagons were all in one piece and only a few of the mules had been injured by the bulls. The horses that were loose in the adjoining field had scattered to avoid the goring bulls. Tents and personal belongings of the soldiers were strewn across the camp.

Ebenezer limped over to Phebe's wagon arriving just as Zemira did to check on Phebe's safety. Phebe assured them she was just fine. Ebenezer had been kicked in the leg and Zemira's face was covered with dirt from laying flat on his stomach during the melee. The three of them, after being assured they had survived the stampede, started to make the rounds of the camp to help where they were needed.

Phebe heated water and started washing wounds, binding them with what ever she could find. The most serious casualty was Amos who was gored and thrown into the air. He suffered a nasty slash in his thigh and broken ribs. Phebe got to him before Dr. Sanderson. She held the gash closed, hoping to stop the excessive bleeding. The Doctor pushed her out of the way and took over the care of the wounded man, sewing up the gash in a crude manner. To her surprise, he later had Amos carried to her wagon and ask her to care for him through the night. He brought her whiskey to give him for pain. She found some herbs in her collection to use instead. When the wound started to bleed she packed it with comfrey and replaced the soiled dressing, using the whiskey to clean the strip of cotton. She steeped a mixture of ginger and spearmint which he sipped to ease the pain.

Captain Hunt and Ebenezer came to the wagon and gave him a blessing. "He should sleep now." Ebenezer looked up at Captain Hunt who was replacing the lid to the bottle of consecrated oil he kept with him at all times. The men left the wagon with Phebe sitting at the side of the wounded soldier who was dosing off. She was astonished when she was awakened by the morning light and realized that both she and her patient had slept through the night. When he asked for water and food, she knew he was on his way to recovery. She made him comfortable and started her morning chores. The officers would be hungry too.

The slaughtered cattle were skinned and the hides soon claimed by the soldiers to be used to repair shoes that were so ragged they gave little protection to the soldier's feet. The flesh was cut into strips and dried into jerky. This windfall of meat could help them survive until they reached California. The supply wagons were filled with drying meat. The pots were full of boiling beef. Many of the soldiers were putting their own private supply into their knapsacks. After five days of intensive work the Colonel announced they would be moving on the following day. There was still meat that had not been preserved. Phebe worried at the waste. As the wagons rolled out of Rancho San Bernadino, she looked back at the unused carcasses lying on the ground waiting for the hovering vultures to consume the carrion.

A group of Apaches approached the camp at midday. As they rode up on their Indian ponies they held their backs straight with pride and addressed the Colonel in limited English. Phebe noticed that they seemed to be more dignified and intelligent that those that visited her cabin on the Palmer ranch in Canada. She could see they were conferring with the Colonel on some serious manner but it wasn't until later she discovered the purpose of the meeting. They were angry about the wasted meat left at the rancho. When the Colonel ask them if they had food to trade or sell they refused. They rode away from the marchers after delivering their message.

Phebe was disappointed. She had not seen one Apache woman or child. She imagined families of them not too far away and wondered how they lived.

They traveled on through mesquite brush, often having to cut a trail. A black cloud appeared in the West and a cold rain started to fall soon turning to snow. They moved ahead to a grove of ash trees by a stream and set up camp to wait out the storm.

Darkness fell on the camp early and the men huddled in their tents, using the heat generated by the warmth of their bodies and their army blankets to protect them from the cold night air. Campfires were built as close as possible to the opening of the tents, allowing some heat from the coals to warm the low shelters.

Phebe and Melissa made a common bed in the wagon. They put the old white ox hide under them and both of their blankets as covers. They wrapped their shawls around their heads and shoulders and huddled close to each other to stay warm. The cold night air was pierced by the howling of wolves. It seemed as though they would never stop and an eerie quiet settled over the camp. The howl of a wolf seemed somehow, foreboding.

Phebe worried about her horses. She remembered the cold night she spent with her family near Lake Ontario when the Indian, Okinihah, spoke in a quiet voice to the horses to keep them from bolting when the wolves howled. That was forty years ago and here she was, clear across the continent, almost to the Pacific Ocean. In her mind she retraced her steps from this place somewhere near Mexico and close to California back to Rome, New York. Mind pictures came back to her of Grandma Draper giving her a blessing, teaching school with Master John, dancing with George in his red British uniform, walking through the apple orchard on her father's farm, the little tea set, the fire, looking at the graves in Grandpa Draper's cemetery, smelling the apple blossoms at the Palmer farm, Brother Brigham baptizing her in the river, the glorious Kirtland Temple, Far West and the ravages of the mob. There was so much to remember in forty-nine years of living. Then she thought of the Prophet and his promise to Ebenezer and her about the Rocky Mountains. She had done a lot of living but there was a lot of living yet to do. She drifted off to sleep as the howling wind joined the howls of the wolves.

Morning came and the camp was slow in moving. A dusting of snow covered the ground and the damp wood was slow to take the flame. One of the teamsters had died in the night and a sadness permeated the air. It was the first death since this band had separated from their comrades at Sante Fe. The men dug a deep grave and Elisha Smith, one of Capt. Davis' hired teamsters was laid to rest by the grove of Ash trees. The grave was covered by wood and brush that was subsequently burned and raked over to protect the remains from the wolves.

When Reveille blew the next morning the men responded as they had been trained by Col. Cooke. The camp was soon fed and baggage packed. They moved on, leaving the lonely grave and the howling wolves.

Phebe had spent some time with Elisha's wife before she left with the group to go to Pueblo. Someday she would see her again and tell her about her husband and his passing.
She hoped, however, that she could forget the wolves. The wild animals seemed more of a threat to them than the Indians or Mexicans. She wondered if Brother Brigham had seen a vision of the wild bulls and the howling wolves. It would not surprise her if he had.

The following days they averaged close to twenty miles a day. There was plenty of grass for the animals along the way. Hy and Joe pastured on the grasses and their thick coats they had grown as the weather cooled became more glossy and they pulled the wagon with more energy. Phebe took the curry comb and brushed them down, combing the burrs from their manes. They were a good looking team. She patted the blaze faces and gave them each a biscuit she had saved from breakfast.

A variety of animals seemed to be following the Battalion at a distance. They sighted antelope, deer and more bulls.

The guides brought word that the best route was now to Tucson, a garrison town for protection against the Indians. The alternate was a hundred miles out of the way over mountains, rivers and hills. The men had been ordered to carry their muskets unloaded. Colonel Cooke did not elaborate on the purpose.

Colonel Cooke's order read—

We will march then to Tucson. We came not to make war on Sonora, and less still to destroy an important outpost of defense against Indians; but we will take the straight road before us and overcome all resistance. But shall I remind you that the American soldier ever shows justice and kindness to the unarmed and unresisting? The property of individuals you will hold sacred. The people of Sonora are not our enemies.

By Order of Lieut. Col. Cooke

Small bands of Indians and some groups of Mexicans observed the Battalion and took an exaggerated account of the size of the force of American soldiers. A Mexican sergeant came into camp, "I talk with commander. He order to not let army force pass through town."

Colonel Cooke sent word back to the commander that they need not be concerned. The approaching army was friendly and would do them no harm but would simply purchase some supplies and pass on. He ordered the men to load their muskets and had them march ahead of the wagons to protect the supplies and women.

The army messenger, Foster, had been taken into custody at the garrison and in retaliation some of the Mexicans were arrested and held as hostages. The negotiations proceeded as the Battalion moved on toward Tucson. Ebenezer was in an advanced guard of fifty to enter the city. When they reached the gates they were greeted by a small band of Mexican soldiers who escorted them through town. Only a few women, children and old men were visible. The town had been evacuated.

As the main body moved through town with loaded muskets, they greeted the Mexican women, children and old men with smiles. The townspeople brought them water and sold them Quinces and other semi-tropical fruit which were unfamiliar to the Easterners. They were also able to buy flour, corn and beans as well as much needed salt. Phebe looked on the new supplies as manna from heaven. The diet for the last few days had been limited to almost straight beef with no salt to flavor it.

The Colonel took a large quantity of wheat from the public storehouse to use for feed for the animals but many of the men used small quantities of it to supplement their daily rations.

They made camp a few miles out of town and observed a church on a nearby hill. It was Sunday and as the day wore on they could see the Mexican men coming back into town from the church. They had obeyed the commanders orders to not allow American soldiers to pass through by going to church and ignoring them.

Again, a few men were called from Company A to return and watch for any suspicious movement of large groups of men. When a group was observed of a larger number than the Col. had identified as being safe, the signal was given and a circle of guards were posted around the camp. The women were together in Phebe's wagon and a small group of soldiers were assigned to protect them. About an hour passed and it was determined there was no threat of attack so the troops were ordered to bed but the women stayed together in one wagon with the guards still posted in case of a surprise attack.

The march began again through sand and mesquite with no sign of water. The guides would promise water ahead to encourage them on but there was no water to be found. Strange gnarled cactus bushes were prevalent and the sharp, spinney segments would stick to the animals and pierce the threadbare clothing of the soldiers. Tall cacti grew like trees. It seemed that there were forests of them. They had no leaves but were barrel like with curved arms growing out and reaching upward. They left Tucson on December seventeenth and did not find any appreciable amount of water until the twentieth. By then the first to come upon water filled their canteens and carried them back to the thirsty troopers. Some were almost crawling to find water to stay alive and others had given up and were lying by the side of the trail, and would have died without the compassion of their comrades.

Phebe and Melissa kept their pebbles in their mouths and tried to stay in the shade of the wagon cover. They shared one canteen of water in the three days of deprivation. The Colonel ordered the Captains to march at night and rest for only a few hours at a time, knowing that they must keep moving on or they would never find water. Phebe wondered how many more trials the weary men could withstand. She watched as they filtered into camp for hours and hours. Many, hardly able to walk.

The day's march ended after ten laborious miles, at the Gila river. Phebe and Melissa started to wash the officer's clothes. The men lined the river washing their clothes and some went down river for a long awaited bath in water deep enough to float in. The camp was in disarray as the men had dropped their belongings and rushed to the water. Phebe looked up from her scrubbing to see hundreds of Pima Indians walking through camp. She felt some alarm but Weaver, the guide, was nearby and assured her all was well, "They are just curious. They are known for their honesty and would never take anything that didn't belong to them."

Phebe observed them looking at various items that must have seemed strange to them but they didn't touch anything. Before long, they walked away as quietly as they had arrived. Phebe wondered at their heritage. She knew they were Lamanites as described in the Book of Mormon. Had their ancestors handed down those values taught by the Savior when he visited this continent?

The following day they marched on to the Pima village. She saw the Indian children she had longed for. Many of the children and women met the travelers long before they reached the village. Phebe saw the happiness and love in their eyes. When she smiled at them they smiled back at her and she longed to hold some of the little ones in her arms. The women were beautiful, moving gracefully. They followed them back to the large village of several thousand inhabitants.

Many of the Battalion men traded buttons and even clothing, ragged as it was, for bread, stewed pumpkin, corn, beans, molasses and squash. The Colonel gave the chief three ewe sheep and congratulated him on his prosperous and happy people. He also took his silk handkerchief from his pocket and tied it around the head of one of the little girls.

Phebe spent her time with the women and children. She wrote letters in the sand and voiced their sound. She drew simple pictures and named them. The children drew pictures for her in the sand. She played a singing game with them and they held hands and sang the chant of the game. The women looked at the print of her faded calico dress with envy. She would have given it to them if she had another to take its place. Then she had an idea. They seemed to have an abundance of leather so she took a piece of charcoal and wrote her name on a small piece of leather in clear letters. Soon they brought many pieces of leather for her to write on. Each time she wrote it she would pronounce "Phebe" and point to herself.

Zemira and some of the other young aides were playing stick ball with the children using a bundle of leather tied with a string. It was like a holiday. A diversion from the routine of travel, chores and hardship.

They camped in the village that night and, as was their custom, they sang songs, played their fiddles and danced. The Indians were delighted. They rocked to the music and some of them tried to imitate the dancers. When the Battalion dancers rested the Indians danced their tribal dances. The women brought out more cakes and fruit for their guests to enjoy.

"This was like visiting a little spot of heaven after all the hard days we have seen." Phebe's arm was linked in Ebenezer's as he walked her back to her wagon.

"Have you noticed that just when we think we can not go

on or live through another day without water or food, something happens to help us survive. The Lord is watching over us. Our prayers are being answered but I have to admit I sometimes wonder why we are being tested so." Ebenezer looked down at his worn shoes and ragged trousers. He wondered if they would last the trip.

That night they climbed into the privacy of the wagon and knelt in prayer. Taking turns, they thanked the Lord for his protection and prayed for their loved ones back with the saints. They pled for strength to survive the road ahead and thanked the Lord for these kind Pima Indians who had given them a day of rest and happiness.

Ebenezer kissed Phebe goodnight and went to his assigned tent and lonely bed roll. He would be glad when this was over and they could at least share a bed each night.

Phebe rolled up in her blanket in the wagon and thought about the children she had played with that day. They had such beautiful brown eyes and amber skin. Their dark hair shown as the sunlight reflected on their long braids. She had helped some of them do a reverse braid which she called a "French Braid" by folding the locks under instead of over. The first little girl sat still as a post while Phebe braided her hair and the mothers watched. Soon they had more little girls in line waiting for their hair to be braided by the white lady. Yes, it had been a wonderful day and she dozed off to sleep smiling.

The reveille blew much too early and the army routine started as if there had never been an interruption. The men were instructed to take only those things they had bartered for if they could carry them on their backs. They were not to be carried in the supply wagons. The disappointed men assessed the purchases against their strength to carry them and many of them were left on the ground.

Breakfast chores were finished and the horses hitched to the wagon. Phebe took the reins and pulled her wagon into line. The children and mothers stood at the side and waved at her as the wagon moved on through the village. She waved back and looked into their innocent faces. "Each one is a child of God and is blessed with the spirit of Christ. And if so, why do people experience life in so many different ways?" She was lost in thought for many miles.

They were traveling through rich, cultivated grounds and the fertile land seemed to reach for miles in every direction. While they stopped at midday some riders came into camp who had been in San Diego with General Kearny. "The General will be surprised. You are closer than he expected. It took him twelve days from here with pack mules and he expected it would take from forty-to-sixty days with wagons. The Mexicans have revolted again and the General's got his hands full."

Colonel Cooke shook his head. "We are making a trail by foot and traveling as fast as we can. I'm afraid the General will have to rely on his own troops to control the Mexicans."

They camped that night and the following day, December twenty-third and twenty-fourth, at a village of the Maricopa Indians who were estimated to number in the thousands. They lived in dome shaped houses, thatched with corn-stalks and straw, varying from about twenty-to-fifty feet in diameter, with arbors in front, on which lay piled up cotton stalks, with unopened bolls to dry. They had horses, dogs, mules and even some tame Spanish chickens. They were not afraid of the soldiers. They were much the same temperament as the Pimas.

As the officers sat around eating their evening meal, Colonel Cooke commented to the Mormon officers, "This might be a good place for your exiled saints to settle." The head chief of the Tribe, Don Jose Messio, thought that would be a good plan. He smiled at the officers, "General Kearny left sick mules here. We feed and they healthy now. You take with you."

Again the honesty of this tribe as with the Pima's belied the rule so often heard by regular army that "The only good Indian is a dead one".

Phebe again sought out the children and played with them as she had those in the Pima village. She wrote in the sand and played games with them. She was trying to finish knitting the stockings for Zemira and Ebenezer so she let them watch her knit. They were fascinated by the speed of the knitting needles and the rhythm of the clicking. They seemed confused at the use of the stockings. Phebe showed them how they would wear them on their feet. The children looked down at their little brown feet and shook their heads as if to say, "We don't want anything like that on our feet."

Phebe was able to get some fresh corn from the Indians and boiled some on the cobs for the officer's dinner. She kept a cob for herself and relished every bite. Their diet had been limited to beef for so many days that the taste of fresh fruits and vegetables at the Indian villages was a welcome treat.

She worked late into the night on the stockings. Seldom did she keep a lantern lit after dark but she wanted to have the stockings for a surprise. Tomorrow would be Christmas. The shank of yarn was getting small so she unraveled the last row of her shawl to finish off the top ribbing of the stockings. She cut four pieces of the white ox hide into a shape she had designed for a leather moccasin. It wasn't much of a Christmas present but it was the best she could do.

She blew out the lamp and curled up in her blanket and recalled the last Christmas in the Nauvoo house. They had all been together then and Lydia Elizabeth had announced her engagement. So much had happened since then. Nauvoo was thousands of miles away and she would likely never return. A wave of homesickness engulfed her and, for the first time on the trek, she allowed herself to cry until she fell asleep.

CHAPTER THIRTY-NINE

The five hundred, foot sore and heart weary, Mormon Battalion soldiers were following a dry sand river bed that was the beginning of a forty mile stretch of dessert. Phebe urged her team on, trying to keep then in the path the men had made by walking two abreast in parallel line to pack the sand for the heavy army wagons. some of the men pulled ropes tied to the oxen and horse teams to help them through the sand. The last two of the wagons on the trail were those of the four women who were the laundresses and cooks for the officers.

Phebe put the soothing stone in her mouth to assuage the ever present thirst. She would save what little water she had for later. She tried to ignore the drops of blood on the sandy trail. Some of the men had abandoned their shoes completely while others had rags holding parts of shoes on their feet. Many had open bleeding wounds from blisters and festered cuts from the cacti and rocks.

It was the first Christmas Phebe could remember without a Christmas tree. Only five months ago she, Ebenezer and Zemira had said their farewells to family and friends on the Iowa prairie. It was almost impossible to believe that only last Christmas they were in the big house in Nauvoo having a Christmas party with all the Drapers and Browns. She remembered the smell of the pine tree and the spicy aroma of the holiday food. The pangs of hunger reminded her of the meager breakfast she had eaten and she rolled the stone in her mouth once more to stimulate some moisture. Her lips were dry and cracked from the sun and wind of the southwest dessert and her hands were calloused from pulling on the reins to guide the horses that pulled her wagon. Her gloves had worn out long ago and the tallow, once used to soften the skin was now used for nourishment, not comfort.

They traveled eighteen miles that day and camped at yet another dry camp. the melancholy of the men permeated the air, each one lost in his own memory of other, happier Christmas days. Phebe had saved the hard brown crusts from the toast she had made for the officers. It may have been wrong of her to let it toast longer than she should have so she would have an excuse to trim the edges.

She had saved them for Ebenezer and Zemira. Their rations had been cut so drastically that even burned toast scraps would seem like manna from heaven. Her tin of herbs was almost empty but there would be enough for some herbal tea to go with the toast.

Phebe sat on the wagon tongue and started to sing in a quiet voice, 'Silent Night, Holy Night, All is calm, all is bright.' She looked up at the starlit sky and wondered at the brightness of the stars. "Which one is the brightest? Just how bright was that star on that first Christmas night that guided the wise men? Which one will guide us back to our loved ones?" And then a tear drop wet her cheek and she wiped it away with the sleeve of her faded gingham dress. The desert could get very cold at night. She climbed into the wagon and put on her shawl. Seeing there was a loose wisp of yarn on the bottom of the shawl, she quickly wove it into the adjacent stitch, tied it in a knot and lit her lantern.

Ebenezer and Zemira came to her wagon. Ebenezer grinned as he handed her a little basket woven from reeds by the Pima Indians. He had kept it in his knapsack until now. It was the only gift he had for her. She took it in her hands and her eyes shone with tears as she carefully examined her treasure. "Oh! Thank you, thank you. What a wonderful surprise. I will always remember those beautiful, brown, children and their mothers. Remember how we sang together and I braided their hair?" She carefully lifted the small woven lid from the basket and inside was a miniature doll woven from black hair.

Now it is my turn. I have a surprise for you." She poured

the warm tea into two tin cups and handed them to her husband
and son. Then she took the blackened, bread crusts from her
apron pocket. "Here is some toast to go with your tea. When I
was a little girl I always had tea and toast parties for special
occasions.

The men sipped the tea and savored the toast as though it
were the finest of Christmas cake. "Mother, I was so hungry.
This tastes better than my favorite chocolate pudding." Zemira
looked at her and tears came to his eyes.

Phebe opened her trunk and took out two small bundles
wrapped in ox hide, handing one to Ebenezer and one to
Zemira. Quickly, they unlaced the bundles to find a new pair
of knitted stockings and the makings of moccasins. They
untied the rags that were holding their boots together and
pulled them off revealing stockings that were so worn they
looked like fish netting. Phebe gasp as she saw the condition of
their feet.

Zemira pulled on his new stockings and felt the comfort of
the soft knitted wool on his tender feet. "Thank you, mother
You always seem to find something for us when we need it
most." He picked up the moccasin pieces and fit them around
his feet. "A soft moccasin may be better in this deep sand than
those old boots. It seems to work for the Indians."

Ebenezer dunked the last of his toast scraps into his tea,
relishing it to the end. He looked at Phebe with a twinkle in his
eye. "I see the tops of these stockings are the same color as
your shawl. How did that come about?"

Color came to Phebe's cheeks, "I have lost a lot of weight
and my shawl was too long so I unraveled the bottom of it and
there was just enough yarn to finish the stockings. I hope you
wont mind the green tops."

Col. Cooke rode his white horse up to the wagon. "I was
wondering where my trusted aide was. Here he is with his family. Mrs. Brown, you have a very fine son and I would like to
let him know how much I appreciate him. I would like to give

him one of my shirts. I have noticed that he has grown right out of that shirt he has been wearing." He picked up the shirt from where it lay across the saddle and tossed it over to Zemira.

"Wow! new socks, moccasins and a new shirt in one day. I don't know if I can handle all this. What a Christmas!" He jumped from the wagon with his new treasures to go to his tent to try them on.

"Mrs. Brown, Zemira is the kind of son I would hope to have someday. I couldn't have a better aide. Let me tell you something about your son. Every morning when I awake, there are my boots by my bed, polished and ready for another day. I have tried to catch him at it but I haven't yet. I don't think he sleeps. I wish I could make this trek easier for him but I have to admit that I need him." He patted the neck of the white horse. "I'll try to make it as easy on him as I can. From now on he will eat with the officers."

He seemed embarrassed by his confession. He always had to be harder than the hardest and tougher than the toughest. He didn't want to ever seem soft to anyone. His leadership could not be challenged nor could he appear to be vulnerable. "Oh, and Mrs. Brown, thank you for all you do for the officers and so many of the other men. You too Sergeant Brown. I know I can depend on both of you. Merry Christmas." He tipped his hat and rode the white off to the officers tents.

"I guess he was feeling the Christmas spirit. I'm glad he realizes what a good boy he has as an aide." Ebenezer put his arm around Phebe. Melissa is spending the night with William and I am going to stay here with you."

Reveille came at 4:30 a.m. and the next challenge was the Pima pass in the Maricopa Mountains. They were on again through brush, gullies and sand. The Colonel lightened the load of the wagons by abandoning hundreds of mule shoes and nails. Eight miles on the following day brought them to the Painted Rock Mountains where they faced a bluff that needed a wagon trail cut to facilitate the ascent over the pass.

Phebe looked with awe at the ancient writings on the large rocks. She would like to stop and study them. They were like picture writing. What did they mean? Arrows, stick horses and what seemed to be stick figures of people. Some appeared to be running. Others seemed to depict some kind of royalty with people bowing or kneeling to them. She wished there was paper available so she could make a copy of it to look at later. Regretfully, they were on their way again before she could study them longer.

They had taken the short way to avoid crossing the river several times but it had been a difficult trail. Now they came back to the river bed and as they moved along, the grass became more scarce and the animals suffered. The Colonel made a makeshift pontoon boat out of two of the wagons to float the supplies down the river in an effort to ease the burdens of the animals. The currant of the river was stronger than expected and twenty-five hundred pounds of their precious supplies were out of sight after the first day. Several days later, a troop of men sent to save what they could of the floating supplies, found them grounded on sand bars. They were only able to retrieve a small part.

When the salvagers came back to camp almost empty handed, Phebe turned to Melissa, "If they reduce rations anymore the men won't have anything to eat at all. We hardly have enough to make the meals for the officers."

The men had been cutting down the cottonwood trees and chopping them up for the horses to browse on. It was January 1, 1847 and a number of mules and sheep died with symptoms of poison making them unwise to use for food.

By January seventh, even with men fainting from hunger and exhaustion another reduction was made in the rations. The remaining provisions were weighed and it was announced that only four days of rations were left. After seven more miles of rough terrain they camped again by the river. The animals swam to the far side to browse what they could from the flag grass and willows.

They came upon a variety of mesquite that provided them with fruit and seed pods which they resorted to grinding into meal and cooking into small cakes. Phebe had one of the few Coffee grinders in her wagon so she and Melissa spent much of their time grinding the pods that were gathered by the men as they marched along the trail.

January ninth they came to the Colorado River and made camp. It looked much like the Missouri but not as deep. The officers met to plan the crossing. As they sat in the Colonel's tent they missed the arrival of the last of the men who had tried to retrieve the lost supplies. They brought with them about four hundred pounds of flour but were in a pitiful condition, having to travel and crawl through thorny brush until their clothes were mostly torn from their bodies and they were covered with scratches.

Phebe's supplies of herbs were getting low but she managed to find some that she mixed with the mud and applied to the scratches to relive the itching and help the healing begin. Her heart ached as she saw their condition and she wondered at how much more would be required. Now they had to cross the Colorado and she had been told to have her wagon ready by morning, as it would be used as a pontoon to ferry what supplies were left across the river.

"Put those wagon planks on top of the wagon boxes. You men, put the supplies on top. Some of you lead the mules across. I hope you can all swim because that is the only way you will get to the other side." Colonel Cooke barked out the orders as the other officers lined up the men to take their turns loading and guiding the mules, horses, sheep and cattle into the water.

Phebe felt a moment of panic. She remembered her near drowning in the small creek and she wondered if she could make it across the river without help. She had driven her horses across streams sitting on the wagon seat but never had she crossed an expanse of water this wide. The crossing was well over a mile wide and she could see that the men who were piloting the wagons across could not reach the bottom in some places with their poles.

The ferrying took all night and into the morning of the following day. Phebe had kept her blanket with her and her few personal belongings. She rolled up in her blanket and slept part of the night but the worry of how she would get across was ever with her, even in her dreams.

The other women slept by her as they had given up their wagon to the ferrying also. To her relief, the Colonel ordered them all on the last wagon crossing the river. As they floated into the murky water, riled by the animals and men wading back and forth, it seemed much farther than a mile to reach the other side. They held onto the planks, hoping they would not slide from the wagon bed. The murky water splashed over them as the mules pulled the wagon against the current of the river.

The four women in long faded calico dresses and sunbonnets, clung to the few belongings they had with one hand and held on to a plank with the other. Animals were all around them in the water along with soldiers, trying to keep their footing in the sand of the river bed. As they came to the first channel a soldier lost his footing and reached out to the wagon for help. It tipped, but then righted itself by the buoyancy of the water. One mule had drowned in an earlier crossing and Phebe held her breath as the mules tried to swim the deep channels while pulling the wagon.

The shallow water of the far side was finally in view and the women started to relax. At last, they were across. They waded the few feet up to the sandy bank and sat exhausted on a ledge cut away by the water. Lydia Hunter and Melissa Coray were feeling the extra weight of the babies they were carrying. Susan Davis and Phebe picked up the blankets and sacks of the pregnant women and carried them with their own, a hundred yards or so up the hill to the encampment.

The wagons were reassembled and the supplies either tied to the mules or replaced in the wagon they were assigned to. Phebe's box of clothes and herbs which also contained her Book of Mormon was placed back in her wagon along with what was left of the old white ox hide. She thought they would camp here to rest from the crossing but it was not to be. The men were hitching up Hy and Joe to the wagon as the signal came for the men to assemble and fall into line to march. They traveled on another fifteen miles to a well that had been dug by General Kearny's men.

Phebe looked back to see Lydia's wagon only to hear that it had been bogged down on the river bank and the men of Company C had stayed back to retrieve it. She hoped Lydia was safe. She noticed an unhealthy puffiness of her hands and face when they stopped at the river crossing. They were warning signs of troubled pregnancies. Her load would need to be lightened whenever possible.

"The well is dry and we need a wash tub to hold the dirt back while we dig deeper. Col. Cooke sent me over to get your tub from you, Sister Brown." The private started to lift the tub from the hook on the side of the wagon.

"Just a minute. The Colonel has no right to take my tub from me. It does not belong to the army. I let them use my wagon on the river without complaint but I need my tub to wash clothes. I've supplied my own transportation and my own equipment to wash their clothes and cook their food. Tell the colonel he will have to devise another plan to dig the well." Phebe left the private in complete astonishment. He dared not take the tub and wondered at his fate or hers when he reported her response to the Colonel.

The Colonel was soon at Phebe's wagon. "Mrs. Brown, we are in desperate need of your tub. The well was dry when we arrived and we have gone down two or three more feet without success. We have already commandeered a tub from Mrs. Davis and we need yours also. It is not safe to send the men down deeper without some protection from the walls caving in. You have the only tub left and I need it. We may be sixty miles or more from the hope of more water."

Phebe was convinced of the Colonel's concern. "I can see the emergency of the situation It is just that I seem to have everything stripped from me. But I am better off than the men. Many of them are in ragged clothes and barefoot with only beef jerky to sustain them. At least I still have my wagon and horses. Take the tub, Colonel, but you will only have clothes washed in streams of water from here on."

"Thank you, I knew you would help if you understood the urgency of the request. I have great concern for the plight of the men, Mrs. Brown. That is why I have sent up a prayer to heaven that we can find water. I would appreciate your prayers for our success as well." He lifted the tub from the hook where the private had left it and carried it to the well diggers.

An hour later he carried a camp kettle back to Phebe's wagon, "Here, you deserve the first water from the well. Our prayers have been answered. There seems to be enough flow to water the animals and enough for the men to quench their thirst. As with you, my faith had not failed, thanks to the tubs." he did not wait for a response. Phebe started a fire and put the kettle to boiling for what little she might find to make a meal.

The colonel sent the guides ahead with a detail of men to burn a trail through the brush and dig wells ahead of the main body of the Battalion. Phebe smiled as she saw them leave with some pack mules following them. Tools and supplies were tied to the mule's backs. On top of one was perched one of the tubs they had retrieved from the well. The bottom had been cut from it to let the water surface. The tin, tub ring bounced on the mule and she wondered if it would help provide water for them again.

The trail burned by the guides was hot on their feet. The blistering sand and cacti needles took their toll and blood droplets dotted the trail. All hides had been used up to provide some covering for their feet. Ebenezer wore his moccasins until he saw a barefoot comrade with bleeding feet. He gave him his moccasins and dropped back to the wagon to cut some more leather from the old white ox hide.

Their only food that night was the last of the starved sheep. They were divided equally between the men with each tent having a small portion to share with each other. Even the hides and entrails were divided and cooked in pots. They ate what they could to abate their hunger and saved any hide they could not chew to cover their feet.

Twenty-five miles more after a night at a dry camp they came to Pozo Hondo wells where, though the water was limited, they could quench their thirst. The most encouraging event was the arrival of a group of men who had been sent ahead to find some food. They rode into camp with thirty-five mules and ten fat beef. One was killed for a quick meal and by late afternoon they were on the trail again.

The nights were very cold and the days very hot on the desert. The men suffered from being so poorly clad to protect them from the extreme temperatures. Phebe encouraged Ebenezer to stay with her in the wagon but he was determined to stay with his men and not take advantage of having his wife with him. So many of the men mourned for their wives and families.

Thirty more miles bought them to the first running water they had seen for five days. It was called the Cariza Creek but the Battalion called it "First Running Water", the first they had seen since leaving the Colorado. The wagons arrived about noon but the last of the troops were still straggling in the following morning, weak and thirsty. Some comrades had gone back with mules for those who had given up before reaching the creek.

January eighteenth the Colonel wrote: *"I went through the Companies this morning; they were eating their last four ounces of flour; there has been no sugar or coffee now for some weeks."*

A messenger from the Governor of San Diego arrived and announced that the men who had been sent ahead for supplies had arrived. The message also promised prompt assistance. Colonel Cooke let the men rest for a day after receiving the news that help was on the way. They were to clean their guns as the messenger had also reported several battles that were still taking place in California. Some of the Mexican troops may confront them as they retreated to Sonora.

One day ran into another for Phebe but she tried to remain pleasant. She was weary and when she saw the haggard looks on the faces of the men she wanted to cry. She was glad she didn't have a mirror with her to reflect her dry, sunburned face. They were approaching another range of mountains and her heart sank as she heard Charbonaux report, "We are penned up. There is no way over those mountains for the wagons. There was a rugged ridge about two hundred feet high to surmount.

The Colonel looked at him and exclaimed, "Either you find a passage through these rocks and gorges or I'll find someone who can. I am not about to abandon the wagons after all we have gone through to keep them with us. Charbonaux followed on his horse and they rode to the hills.

Messengers came back to tell the men to follow them but they soon found themselves in a narrow gorge. It became at least a foot narrower than a wagon. Most of the axes, picks, shovels and other tools had been lost on the river. The few that were left were commandeered by the Colonel and when the wagons arrived the men were chopping away at the pass. The mountain appeared to be a huge pile of rocks. There was no soil beneath the rocks. As they moved one layer there was another layer of rock to dislodge. The Colonel, himself was wielding a pick and his stern look of determination gave hope to the men that they would succeed.

By the time Phebe arrived with her wagon, the first wagon had been taken apart and carried through the pass. The men were still chopping away at the stone walls with their picks and the gorge was now wide enough for her to drive through. Another steep sandy ridge was ahead of them and it took twenty men with ropes to pull each wagon over but as they descended they came upon an Indian village called San Phillippi. It was the twentieth of January and the animals were turned out to graze.

As the officers approached the village they could see that it had been abandoned. Probably out of fright of the oncoming troops. The only food left was the beef so the last two were slaughtered and divided among the men. After a brief rest they moved on to a low mountain pass and it was there that a messenger found them with orders for them to proceed to San Diego instead of Los Angeles. The Warner's Ranchero was just ten miles away.

Phebe felt she was spending her last ounce of energy as she cleaned up after the evening meal. She went to her wagon and knelt in prayer. "Please Lord, help us to come to the end of our journey soon. Give me strength to finish." She laid down in her wagon bed once more, rolled the army blanket over her and let sleep overcome her exhaustion.

CHAPTER FORTY

The live oaks, tall green grass, plenty of water and a real house greeted the weary travelers and a feeling of joy permeated the air. The guides who had been sent on ahead for more supplies and instructed to meet the Battalion at the Warner Rancho arrived on the same day, January 21, 1847. It was the first full meal since Rio Del Norte but they still had no salt. The rations were raised to four pounds of beef per day per man. Their only bread was a few flourcakes purchased from the Indians.

A warm spring of water was near where the troops camped and the women were allowed the privacy of bathing first. Phebe sat in the warm water, letting it sooth and refresh her. The other three women were with her. They washed their hair and let the long locks float away from them in the water and then dried themselves with their blankets.

With the trail dust washed away they felt renewed energy to take up their duties. "I'll tell the officers to get their clothes to us to launder. This warm water will clean them and our hands won't be cold. We'll have to do it here in the spring because, as you know, we no longer have a tub to wash in." Phebe dressed quickly, wishing she had clean clothes to wear but she would try to find time for that with the officers laundry. She braided her hair and let the long plait fall down her back. She saw it was streaked with grey. Her age and the trip were taking their toll on her.

The weather the next morning was like a spring day. The sun shone through fluffy clouds and then the clouds darkened and the wind blew and the rains followed. They moved on the next day on a muddy trail with only wet blankets to shield them from the weather. A detail of men who had been sent back to the Gila River to retrieve some of the supplies left there arrived with four hundred pounds of flour, allowing the rations to be increased to about a fourth of a cup a day per man.

As the wet, bedraggled army approached the Temecula Valley they saw a line of mounted horsemen. "Halt, Take up arms." The Colonel directed. Even though the war was officially over their were continual reports of skirmishes between the Mexicans and the Californians as well as Kearney's troops. "We may have unfriendly Mexicans ahead."

The men were in battle formation when the riders came closer and it was discovered they were friendly Indians. The leader of the Indian band rode up to Col. Cooke and shook hands. A sigh of relief went through the troops. The men had commented to each other earlier that a small army of twenty men could wipe out the whole Battalion because of their condition.

As they approached the San Luis Valley the steep sandy ravine was more than the horses could handle. Phebe urged and cajoled her team but to no avail. The men came to her rescue with ropes and what little strength they could muster to help the horses pull her wagon and the others over the crest of the hill.

The valley was full of grasses and once again the men were encouraged to move on through a land more promising to survival. They found wild mustard which they added to their limited diet of beef. There were large herds of horses, donkeys and cattle, as well as many varieties of fowl. Phebe looked out over the valley to see gulls by what she calculated to be in the hundreds or thousands. "We will not starve in this land, Melissa. I think the worst of it is over."

Melissa smiled at her with the enthusiasm of a child, "I am so excited about seeing the ocean. I wonder how much farther it will be."

"It can't be too much farther with pelicans and gulls so prevalent." Phebe flipped the reins on Hy and Joe to urge them on.

A large white building appeared ahead and as they neared they could see it was a church of some sort with a bell steeple. It was white stucco and had many adjoining rooms and pillars. It was the San Luis Rey mission. Looking in the windows they could see that it was furnished with dark carved furniture and pieces of beautiful art. There were planted gardens outside and a sundial. It was a far cry from what they had seen so far on the trail. Trees bearing strange orange fruit lined the courtyard.

"I hope we camp here. This looks like a palace." Melissa was getting ready to climb down from the wagon when the Colonel signaled for them to move on. It was January 27, 1847 at about 1:00 p.m. when they caught sight of the ocean. The blue expanse seemed to curl over the edge of the earth to the West and South but they were miles away from it.

A great shout of "Hooray! hooray!" went up as they realized the goal was finally in sight. They could actually see the great pacific ocean they had dreamed of for almost two thousand miles.

That night they camped in the San Diequito Valley. After traveling a winding hilly road that was little more than a path for another sixteen miles the following day, they arrived at the old San Diego Mission. The Colonel directed them to make camp and allowed those who wanted, to go on down to the edge of the ocean. Zemira and Ebenezer got into the wagon with Phebe and they followed a trail down to the water. Phebe sat between them gazing at the unusual foliage and could hear the strange sound of the waves crashing against the rocks. "We are really by the Pacific Ocean. I want to wade in the water." Phebe started to pull off her shoes and Ebenezer pulled on the reins to stop the team.

They walked bare foot across the sand for several hundred feet. The sea shells and star fish dotted the sand and cut into their feet but that was nothing compared to what they had been through. As they walked into the water the salty brine tingled the skin on their feet and they watched as the small waves crept up over their ankles. The ocean lured them out farther and before they knew it they were all sitting in the sand with the waves washing over their shoulders. Ebenezer and Zemira helped Phebe to her feet and they walked back to the sandy beach and let the warm air dry their clothes before they started back.

"Now the war is over, do you think they will let us leave before our enlistment time is up?" Zemira was anxious to get on with life. He was tired of the army routine as were most of the Battalion.

Ebenezer picked up a sea shell and studied it, "I don't think so. I think General Kearney has given Col. Cooke enough assignments to keep us all busy until July. I hear that some of the other army men are leaving and have refused to reenlist. Col. Cooke plans to train us in regular army drills. No, I think we will be here for a few more months at least. Thank goodness we are in such a beautiful place where the weather is so nice."

Phebe held her face up to the warm sun and felt the sea breeze. "I wonder if they will still keep me on as a laundress and cook. For that matter, I wonder if we will ever be paid for the time from Sante Fe. That was the last pay we received."

"I would be satisfied if they just found us some uniforms to wear. The ragged clothes are a disgrace to the army. One of the privates in Company A had to make himself some pants out of an old abandoned wagon cover or expose himself to the world." Ebenezer looked down at his own pant legs and saw they were in rags from the knees down.

Zemira fared a little better, thanks to the extra pair of pants and the shirt the Colonel had given him.

The warm California air had dried their clothes and it was time to get back to camp. They climbed into the wagon and Hy and Joe headed for camp.

Phebe found the other women and they prepared another meal of beef for the officers with some biscuits. It seemed that the officers always made sure their rations were a little more generous. The women each put a biscuit in their apron pocket. They had already decided they would spend the night with their husbands and they knew they would appreciate an extra biscuit.

The following morning the soldiers were called to attention to hear the order of the day. It was January 30, 1847. It read as follows:

Order Number 1
Headquarters Mormon Battalion,
Mission of San Diego, January 30, 1847
The Lieutenant-Colonel commanding congratulates the Battalion on their safe arrival on the shore of the Pacific ocean and the conclusion of their march of over two thousand miles. History may be searched in vain for an equal march of infantry. half of it has been through a wilderness where nothing but savages and wild beasts are found, or deserts where, for want of water, there is no living creature. There, with almost hopeless labor we have dug deep wells, which the future traveler will enjoy. Without a guide who had traversed them, we have ventured into trackless tablelands where water was not found for several marches. With crowbar and pick and axe in hand, we have worked our way over mountain, which seemed to defy aught save the wild goat, and hewed a passage through a chasm of living rock more narrow than our wagons. To bring these first wagons to the Pacific, we have preserved the strength of our mules by herding them over large tracts, which you have laboriously guarded without loss. The garrison of four presidios of Sonora concentrated within the walls of Tucson, gave us no pause. We drove them out, with their artillery, but our intercourse with the citizens was unmarked by a single act of injustice. Thus, marching half naked and half fed, and living upon wild animals, we have discovered and made a road of great value to our country. Arrived at the first settlement of California, after a single day's rest, you cheerfully turned off

from the route to this point of promised repose, to enter upon a campaign; and meet, as we supposed, the approach of an enemy; and this too, without even salt to season your sole subsistence of fresh meat. Lieutenants A. J. Smith and George Stoneman, of the First Dragoons, have shared and given valuable aid in all these labors. Thus, volunteers, you have exhibited some high and essential qualities of veterans. But much remains undone. Soon you will turn your attention to the drill, to system and order, to forms also, which are all necessary to the soldier.

By order
Lieut. Colonel P. St. George Cooke.
P.C. Merrill, Adjutant.

The following day the drills began and the only thing that resembled those of an army were the guns and the straight lines of men turning on command. The ragged attire belied the role of a soldier of the United States government.

A few days later General Kearny addressed the Battalion. Praising them for their patriotism and service to the country He promised to report on their great contribution to the president and congress when he returned to Washington. "Napoleon crossed the Alps, but you have crossed a continent."

The future of the Battalion was still unclear but there was no indication that there would be an early mustering out. Ebenezer was called to report to the Colonel with Lieutenant Oman and Sergeant Hunsaker of Company D. "You are to choose thirty privates to stay here with you at San Luis Rey, nine from company A, eight from Company C, five from Company D and eight from Company E. This will comprise the detachment to remain to garrison this post." Colonel Cooke signed the order and dated it March 14, 1847.

"Sir? What about Mrs. Brown? May we have permission for her to stay with us?" Lieutenant Oman waited for the Colonel's decision.

"I will send captain Hunter's wife with him, since she is

not well and leave Mrs. Brown with you. The other two women can maintain their assignments as cooks and laundresses with the rest of the Battalion."

Ebenezer breathed a sigh of relief. He did not want to be separated from Phebe now but he was sure Zemira would be going with the Colonel. They saluted the Colonel and proceeded to notify the men who would be staying. Ebenezer went directly to Phebe's wagon and told her the news.

Phebe had been with Lydia Hunter who was suffering the last stages of a complaint that often accompanied pregnancies. Her legs and hands were very swollen and she periodically lost consciousness. Phebe hoped the baby would soon come to relieve her friend of her misery.

Captain Hunter was ordered to march to San Diego the following day with his Company as garrison for the protection and defense of that location. His wife was allowed to go with him. Phebe hated to see her friend, Lydia, leave before the baby came but she was glad for her that the baby would be born in United States territory. "Captain Hunter, Lydia's time is very close. Find one of the local women in San Diego to help her as soon as you get there. I wish I could go with you."

Phebe put a smile on her face to cover her concern and said good bye to her friend.

Four days later the rest of the Battalion were to leave for Pueblo de Los Angeles to maintain a military hold on what had been the Mexican capital in the California territory. Melissa was concerned about leaving but Susan assured her she would take good care of her. Her baby was not due for a few months and now she was over the first months of nausea she was able to carry her load of the work.

On March nineteenth the rest of the Battalion not assigned to San Diego or San Luis Rey moved out for Los Angeles. Phebe waved at Melissa until she was out of sight and then turned to see what she could do to help the men. She walked into some of the quarters where the men were to stay and saw that they were infested with fleas and other types of vermin. The dirt floors were soft sand that seemed to be crawling with various kinds of insects, She was glad she had her wagon. She had been directed to provide her own transportation from Sante Fe and she would keep it for her housing here. Living in a wagon had become second nature to her. Now if she could convince Ebenezer that he should share her wagon they could get by just fine.

She took stock of the supplies that were left and decided she would recommend to Lieutenant Oman that she be allowed to prepare meals for the whole garrison. If two privates were assigned to help her each day she could manage and the food would go farther.

She started making a list in her mind of what she could prepare for the evening meal. Supplies had arrived from the Sandwich Islands before the main body left for Los Angeles so rations were increased. Bolted flour, soap, sugar, coffee, candles and the much needed salt. Beef was plentiful at less than one cent a pound.

With the greens and vegetables available in the mission gardens, Phebe had several options to choose from for a much deserved full meal for the men.

The men worked hard to clean up the mission and Phebe helped where she could. Occasionally some small groups of Mexicans or Indians from nearby villages would come by to sell some of their breads or vegetables. But most of the time it was because they were curious about the new inhabitants of the old mission.

None of the men or Phebe were allowed to try to enter the main building of the mission. It was locked so they respected the ownership of the Catholic Church. They only used the out buildings for housing, pastures of grass for the horses and mules and the garden spots that provided much needed nourishment. They found the orange fruit on the trees to be tart but tasty and the dates from the palms trees like a Christmas treat.

Lieutenant Oman with the help of the sergeants held a short practice drill each day. Ebenezer and Brother Abraham Hunsaker conducted meetings on Sundays. Most of the meetings were testimony meetings and Phebe was invited to participate. she often led them in songs as they realized none of the musicians had been ask to accompany them.

A week into March a rider came to the mission with the word that Lydia Hunter was suffering and asking for Phebe. Lieutenant Oman and the sergeants encouraged her to go. It would be faster by horseback so they saddled a horse for her and she rode to San Diego with the messenger.

Captain Hunter had found a Mexican lady, Juanita Machado Wrightington, to help and Phebe found her in the captain's quarters attending to Lydia. The baby was already on its way and Lydia's body writhed in pain as the contractions came and went. She was almost unconscious and Phebe was shocked at the yellow color of her skin. "Lydia, Lydia, it's Phebe. I'm here." She put her cool hand on Lydias hot forehead.

"Let's get some cool clothes and we need towels, lots of towels." She motioned to the Juanita to help her but she just received a puzzled look and a response in a language she did not understand. She looked around the barren room and saw that a pot of water was heating over the fire. A dingy cloth hung by the wash basin on a small table. She grabbed the cloth and poured the hot water over it in the basin. Then she pulled off her petticoat, put it in the hot water and hung it to dry. Juanita wiped the perspiration from Lydias forehead with her skirt.

A healthy little boy was born but Lydia did not regain consciousness. Phebe wiped the baby dry with the cloth and wrapped him in the petticoat that had dried by the fire. She gave the Senorita the water bucket and pointed for her to fill it. "Agua, agua." she said as she took the pail.

Phebe stepped to the door and called Captain Hunter. She

laid the baby in Lydia's lifeless arms and left while the Captain spent the last moments of his wife's life at her side. Phebe stood out in the California sun facing the ocean and tears streamed down her cheeks. Her thoughts went back to the other times she had seen mothers give their lives to bring a new life into the world. It seemed to be the Lord's plan but so much was expected of women. They paid a great price to be co-creators with God. She wondered what more she could have done to help her friend. She had seen the signs and been helpless. She went to find the pack she had brought with her. Her only other petticoat, the one with out the ruffle, was in her pack. She slipped it on and went back to meet Captain Hunter as he came out of his quarters.

Lydia was buried not far from the camp the following day and the Mexican Lady promised to take care of the baby. Phebe wanted to take the baby with her but she knew that was not possible. The messenger rode back to San Luis Rey with her and she broke the news to Ebenezer and the other men.

April and May came and went with the weather getting warmer. They had received their pay by messenger about the middle of May but there was no way of spending it to buy clothes or other necessities they had been without for many months. Some of the men were sent to San Diego to buy some pants or shirts and Phebe sent money for some calico. The ships coming into harbor in San Diego were bringing more supplies now they saw a market for them with the additional three hundred or more people in the Battalion. Somehow they also seemed to know when the army pay was coming and scheduled their arrival to coincide with it.

When the men arrived back at San Luis Rey with the commodities they had purchased there was little left of the money. The inflated prices for shipped in supplies had depleted the money before the requests were filled. By the end of June they were relieved from their duty at San Luis Rey by a regular army detachment and ordered to Los Angeles. They arrived on the third and were there to celebrate the country's birth on the fourth of July.

At sunrise the flag was raised and the musicians formed in a band played the Star Spangled Banner. Phebe stood between Ebenezer and Zemira in the new calico dress she had made. Zemira was now taller than Ebenezer and dressed in an Army uniform. With his dark curly hair and mustache he looked very much like his father, George, when Phebe first met him in Loughborough. Ebenezer, slim and brawny from the trail and the army routine, at least now had some respectable looking clothes but they were far from army issue. He had purchased them with his army pay.

The Declaration Of Independence was read and the band played, "Hail Columbia, and Yankee Doodle. Levi Hancock sang The Star Spangled Banner as the flag was raised on the flag pole and the men stood at attention. Phebe was again filled with the pride of a patriot in spite of the trials she had experienced at the hand of the government. The soldiers were each treated to a glass of weak wine and dismissed to their quarters.

Discharge time was near and the dilemma of reenlistment or setting out to find the main body of the church was the continual topic of conversation. Most of them had spent what little money they had and they knew from their past experiences how demanding a trip across country could be with out supplies, pack animals, wagons and sturdy horses.

Phebe took up her usual duties with the rest of the women. It was good to see Melissa and Susan again. Melissa was large now in the last few weeks of her pregnancy. Susan and Phebe did the lifting and left the lighter chores for Melissa. They missed Lydia and had spent time grieving for her. Phebe reassured Melissa that she did not show the same signs of problems that she had seen in Lydia. They made some more baby gowns and a shawl for Melissa and Phebe gave her a tiny pair of moccasins she had made from the last of the old white ox hide. She had pounded the tough old leather with a rock, as she had watched the Indian women do, until it was soft and pliable. She cut narrow strips of the leather to lace the little booties together.

July 16, 1847 the troops were lined up with Company A at the front and the other Companies behind them in order. It was three o'clock in the afternoon. The unpopular Lieutenant A. J. Smith marched down one way between the ranks and back the other and in a low tone of voice said: "You are discharged." That was all, after the sacrifices and suffering of a patriotic, religious group that had made a two thousand mile trek in answer to their country's request. Just a "You are discharged." The band of volunteers, as they were referred to, who chose to defend their country if need be and represent their church in the noblest way had submitted to the army regulations and to the tyranny of Lt. Smith and Dr. Sanderson without revolt and now they were free to go their way. It was ironic that it was Lieutenant Smith who discharged them. Col. Cooke had been reassigned before the Browns returned to Los Angeles.

Captain Davis was making the rounds of the troops, urging them to reenlist. He came to Phebe's wagon where she and Ebenezer were discussing their future plans with Zemira. "I promise you a new wash tub if you will consider staying with us." He grinned at Phebe. "I was hoping you three would stay for another six months. I think our assignment will be to stay in San Diego and help the settlement there. You will have regular hours and can work for extra pay in your free time. The settlers there are anxious to build up their town and hope some of the Battalion will stay and help them. Captain Hunter's detail has already dug several wells and started a kiln to make bricks. Let me know what you decide." He rode away to the next group of men.

Phebe climbed down from the wagon, stretched her back and turned her face to the blue pacific ocean. She was forty-nine years old, thin and browned from the months of travail with the Mormon Battalion. She was the oldest of the four women who had finished the trek, but she may have been the strongest. With them she had cooked, washed clothes, delivered babies, cared for the sick and encouraged the others with her fervent desire to move on. She had felt the pangs of hunger, the thirst for water and the fear of wild bulls. The heat of the sun had weathered her skin and the cold desert nights had chilled her bones. She was still a thousand miles from her destination but today she could rest and enjoy the warm comforting sea air. As the waves crashed against the rocks and receded back into the calm waters they were as a mirror of the happiness and hardships she had and would endure.

Ebenezer came to her side, his arm encircled her waist and she leaned on his shoulder. Most of the money they had received had been sent back to the main body of the church. The joy of their freedom was dimmed by the stark realization that hard decisions lay ahead of them. They had few options. They could reenlist as Captain Davis had urged them to do, or they could travel northward to the Rocky Mountains with some of the other Battalion members who had been mustered out which would require them to live off the land and enter the new Zion in the Rockies with nothing to start a new life. They quietly climbed into the back of the wagon where they knelt and ask the Lord to guide them in their decision. As they left the wagon, Zemira came to question his mother about their future. Phebe put her hand on his shoulder and said, "We will know tomorrow. The Lord will let us know." He accepted the answer to his unvoiced question. He could wait until tomorrow. Mother always seemed to know what was best. Hadn't her faith saved them 'til now?

PART IX

A PATTERN FOR THY SEX
JULY 1847 -1849
CHAPTER FORTY-ONE

Zemira came to the wagon. "Captain Hunt has called a meeting for all the Battalion. He has some special instructions for us before any of the men leave."

Phebe and Ebenezer walked toward the large assembly tent, went in and sat by Susan Davis, William Cory and his wife, Melissa. Zemira joined them after he had completed his assignment to notify the men of the meeting. Captain Hunter, Captain Hunt and Captain Davis were at the front with Colonel Stevenson, now in command. Colonel Stevenson had met with the men before and urged them to reenlist, promising that they could elect their own officers.

Captain Hunt urged those who could to reenlist. "We must not lose the ground we have gained. The officer elected from our ranks would be third in command in California. We must each consider our own situation. If it will take all of your resources to get you to the main body of the Church and then have nothing to offer, you should consider staying. A committee has drafted conditions under which the re-enlistment would take place. These conditions, after first being rejected, have been modified and after mutual agreement, Colonel Stevenson has agreed to accept them. As you know, my wife and family left us at Pueblo and I feel compelled to make every effort to find them. Many of you have loved ones who left for Pueblo with the sick detachment and may wish to accompany me. Captains Hunter and Davis have chosen to stay on. Captain

Davis will be the Captain of the reenlisted Company.

Some of you have strong feelings about staying or leaving and we have heard these arguments in a previous meeting. I am of the opinion that the Lord will direct each of you in the path you should take. There is no question about the great sacrifice you have made for your country and the Church. If you go, go with my blessing, if you stay, stay with my blessing. We will one day be united together with the body of the Church.

Those who plan to leave should organize in to groups of fifty and elect leadership. I would like to meet with each group after your decision is made. President Young gave me an assignment before leaving on this journey and I do not think that assignment would be filled if I did not see that you were safely on your way. May God go with you as He has been with us all the last year."

The band played a lively "Yankee doodle". Levi Hancock and Zemira Palmer, sang "Come, come, ye saints. No toil nor labor fear, but with joy, wend your way." Slowly small groups started to join in the song and finally they were all standing and singing together ending the last refrain with resolution in their voices, "All is well, All is well."

The meeting adjourned and groups started to cluster to discuss their future. William Coray looked at his wife, heavy with child, and saw the dedication in her face to make the best of his decision. "We will head out with the Captain Hunt. I just hope I can find a wagon and a good team to make the journey as easy as possible for Melissa. I hope she never has to walk another step."

Ebenezer turned and winked at Phebe, "William, we won't be needing our wagon and team. You and Melissa take it. Melissa is well acquainted with Hy and Joe. She knows she can trust them. I am going to reenlist. We will have quarters provided for us. Go, and take it with our blessing."

Phebe was surprised to say the least, but she shouldn't have been. Ebenezer had provided a wagon and team for her to leave Far West. He was truly a "Man of God", always willing to share with others. As she looked back over the time she had known him, it occurred to her that the Lord had always blessed him with more in return than he had given away.

"That will be best for you, Melissa. I won't worry about you if you have the wagon. Just try to get word to me when the baby comes. I wish I could be with you but it looks like we will be going in opposite directions." Phebe looked at Ebenezer and smiled. She wondered if he had consulted Zemira. She had felt in the meeting that it would be best if they stayed and earned some money to take with them. In the last news she had from the family, William was staying in Winter Quarters to help the saints there before they started West. She was confident the rest of the Drapers would stay with him.

They started for the wagon and Zemira joined them, "Captain Davis ask me if I would stay on as his aide. I told him I would if you agree."

"We are all staying. I told you we would know today. Go and tell Captain Davis to plan on you before he asks someone else." Phebe gave him a reassuring smile. "By the way, How long have you been singing with Brother Hancock?"

"Most of the time you have been in San Diego. We just started harmonizing one night and found our voices blended. As you say, I better get over to tell Captain Davis I will stay and help him." He walked away whistling a tune to himself.

Phebe and Ebenezer returned to the wagon to sort out what they would keep, what they would leave for the Coray's and what they would give to others. There wasn't all that much. The few clothes they had, the water stained Book of Mormon and the little reed basket that had been her Christmas present, was about all they kept. Melissa would need the cooking pots and the bedding.

"Ebenezer, I am so glad you gave the wagon and team to William and Melissa. I have been so worried about her. There are plenty of mules and horses around here to buy for one or two dollars but the wagons are scarce and bring a high price."

Ebenezer looked at this plucky wife of his, realizing she had come a long way in adapting to what life dealt her. "I'm glad you feel as I do about staying. I wanted to talk to you about it first but I was afraid William would rush off and use all the money he had to buy a wagon."

"That's fine. There was a time in my life that I would have been hopping mad about not being consulted, but not this time. I think we both had the feeling we should stay. Captain Davis will be glad to hear the news and so will Susan. Let's go and tell them together. Oh, and lets tell Captain Hunter too. Now I can see his little son and maybe help take care of him. Did you know they named him Diego Hunter?" The two pioneers locked arms and walked across the compound with heads high, ready to start their next adventure.

San Diego was warm but the evening breezes off the ocean gave relief to the tropical heat. Phebe and Ebenezer had a room to share in the compound Company B had built in the Spring. It had a door and window on the Ocean side and a window on the far side. The windows were open most of the time, letting the air flow through. Ebenezer had purchased four mules in Los Angeles and Phebe had ridden one, packed their belongings on the other three while Ebenezer marched with the men back to San Diego.

The people in San Diego were so happy to see the Mormon Battalion soldiers return they lined the street and clapped and shouted. The men were offered work when they weren't on duty and the town continued to flourish as it had while Company B had been quartered there. More wells were dug, bricks baked, and buildings built. Supply ships continued to come to harbor there, bringing commodities from the Sandwich Islands.

The Army continued to pay Phebe and Susan to launder the officer's clothes and cook for them. With only fourteen officers to cook and wash for, they found extra time to knit and sew. Phebe would spend some of her afternoons with small groups of Spanish children, teaching them how to speak English. It started with just one or two, but before long the mothers were bringing their little ones to her. They would sit in the back and listen, learning along with their children. By November she had a few who were learning to read. She was learning many Spanish words also and before she knew it, she could converse with the mothers in a limited way.

Juanita, who cared for Diego Hunter, brought the baby to Phebe often to cuddle and love. She made him dresses and knitted booties for him. While she was here she was determined to give him all the love she could as a gift to her friend who had suffered with them on the trail and given her life to have her child born in the United States. He was a happy baby and Captain Hunter beamed when Phebe held him up to the men to show him off.

The time seemed to fly by and Phebe realized that her fiftieth birthday had come and gone in October without her even thinking about it. She had lived half a century and it had been filled to the brim. Now the ships were bringing in paper, pencils and ink, she would start to write down her history. Some of the men managed to keep a journal on the trek but her time was so limited. After traveling all day, she would have to prepare meals and launder clothes. This was a good time to start. There were so many things to remember and she wanted her children to know all about it.

She opened the notebook to the first page and wrote, "History of Phebe Draper Palmer Brown" Born, October 9, 1797 in Rome, New York.

It was still warm in San Diego in December. Signs of the Christmas season seemed to be appearing everywhere. Simple nativity scenes appeared in the windows of the small adobe houses and sometimes in the courtyard among the cacti and rocks.

"Felis Navidad, Felis Navidad, Miss Phebe." The children and their mothers greeted her often with their Christmas greeting. Phebe helped them make paper chains to decorate and told them about the Christmas tree traditions in other countries as well as some of the other traditions from the east.

There was soon a mixture of Mexican traditions as well as those of the Eastern Battalion members appearing in town. The men remembered the last Christmas on the trail and how much they had missed their families and the special activities of the Christmas season at home. Most of them had no idea where their families were now, if they were alive of dead, but they were sure they weren't back in the warm homes in Nauvoo where they had celebrated the 1845 Christmas season.

Phebe was determined to make this a happy holiday if it was at all possible. She and Susan Davis put their heads together to plan a Christmas party. With the help of Captain Davis they were able to get some special requisitions of extra stockings and shirts from the army supplies, for surprise gifts for the men. They planned a special dinner, making Christmas cakes with the abundant fruit in the area. Some of it was dried and they used it to decorate the cakes.

Phebe taught the children some Christmas Carols in English and they taught her some in Spanish. The townspeople came together with the Battalion and they had a religious service depicting the Nativity with Diego Hunter being the Baby Jesus. Phebe read the account of the birth from the Bible and then read from the Book of Mormon about the Savior's visit to the American Continent. Zemira sang, "Silent Night" in his clear bass voice.

Captain Davis and Captain Hunter spoke to the people about the blessings they had all received from their time together including all they had learned from each other.

The Catholics went to Midnight Mass and the following

day, Christmas 1847, they had a big feast together with the
Battalion. Each group showed respect for the others beliefs and
traditions. The Battalion members danced and sang and some
of the townspeople joined in.

Ebenezer and Phebe were exhausted from the day's activities when they returned to their room for the night. "You and
Susan really know how to plan a party, Phebe. I think it almost
made up for that sad Christmas we had last year. I wonder
what our families are doing tonight. Our best gift could have
been some word from them about where and how they are."
Ebenezer pulled off his boots. He and Phebe knelt by the bed
together to thank the Lord for their blessings and to ask for His
special blessings on their loved ones.

In spite of the busy day, Phebe could not dose off to sleep.
Her thoughts were with Rhoda. She would be fourteen next
March. Tears dampened her pillow as she thought of missing
those special years that had changed her little girl into a young
lady. She hoped Bett or Lovina had made her a new dress for
Christmas and perhaps William might have made her some
new shoes. Where ever they were they would have a Christmas
party and there would be dancing and singing. Lovina would
be singing and the boys would be playing their instruments.
She imagined Rhoda dancing with a tall blond young man and
wearing a new blue dress with a bonnet to match that Lovina
would have designed. Father Draper would be sitting on the
side lines, watching with a wide smile and clapping his hands
to the music. Yes, where ever they were they would be together and showing their love for each other as they always had.
She wanted desperately to be with them. Finally, sleep came
and she dreamed of being fourteen again on the Draper farm in
Canada and walking along the path with Charles and Joel in
the apple orchard. It was spring and the blossoms were full on
the trees. And then it seemed that she saw Rhoda ahead of
them hiding behind a tree and when she got to her she had
made a wreath of apple blossoms and put on her head. She ran

ahead of them and then the dream ended.

Phebe wakened, still smelling the wonderful aroma of the apple blossoms, only to realize she was still in the dingy army room in San Diego with the smells and sounds of the ocean invading her senses and crowding out the memories of the apple blossoms and Rhoda.

Their six month reenlistment was up in December but they had been urged to stay until Spring. They knew the weather would be harsh in the Mountains in the winter, making travel difficult and dangerous. The townspeople still had projects they wanted help with and the men agreed to help finish the work they had started. There was very little need for army protection because of the good will that prevailed. Capt. Davis cut the drills short and encouraged the men to work in town and earn as much money as they could to take back to the Rockies.

Ebenezer and Zemira worked together in the brick kiln making adobe bricks. It was hard work but they enjoyed it. The men would often make a game of it to see how many bricks they could make in a day and the production soared. New adobe structures were covered with a stucco plaster. Stuccoed adobe walls surrounded the courtyards. The Spanish influence on the architecture was prevalent. Almost every house or building had a well, lined with bricks and capped with a decorative row of tile to add design to the structure.

The blacksmiths made heavy ornamental iron gates, heating the metal and bending it in artistic forms. The carpenters carved designs in the large timbers they used in the door and window casings. These Mormon men had come from a variety of backgrounds and had many specialized skills. One was a glass blower and he made beautiful stained glass panes to add to a carved door or window to reflect a kaleidoscope of colors into the house.

Zemira was carrying the cooled bricks from the rack by the kiln to the wagon when he looked up and saw two men riding into town. They had obviously been on the trail for a long time as their long, unkempt hair hung around their shoulders and bushy beards concealed their faces. Their horses were in a lather and the pack animals that followed them were covered with dust. They carried rifles and side arms.

Zemira put the bricks down and walked quickly to Ebenezer to point out the new arrivals. Ebenezer put his hand above his eyes to shade them from the sun and help him focus on the riders. He saw the initials on the apron of the saddle as the first rider lifted his canteen to take a drink. The familiar "OPR" was almost more than he could comprehend. He had seen it plenty of times in Nauvoo and on the Iowa plains. Yes, it was Orin Porter Rockwell behind all that dust and beard and hair. Ebenezer gave a hoot and went running forward to greet the riders.

Other men heard the commotion and soon there was a group surrounding the men, barking out questions about where the saints were and if they had seen their families. Porter and James Shaw, who was with him, looked at the men who were so eager to hear from and about loved ones. "One of you get Captain Davis and we'll all get together so I can report the news to everyone at once." Porter threw his leg over the saddle and dismounted as did James.

Zemira rushed into the cooking room. "Where's Captain Davis? Porter Rockwell's here and he has news to tell us." Susan and Phebe threw cloths over the food they were preparing and followed him from the room.

Susan found Captain Davis in his quarters and soon all the men were assembled in the bowery waiting for Porter to tell them anything he could. Phebe and Susan joined them.

Porter took his old felt hat off and hit it against his leg to knock the dust off. He wiped the dirt and perspiration from his forehead and gulped down a cup of cold spring water one of the men had brought him. "I was assigned by Brother Brigham to come with Captain Hunt to get cattle, horses and mules to take back to the Rockies. I was also given special instructions to round up twenty-five of you soldiers to go back with me to the Great Salt Lake Valley. Brother Brigham figured your enlistment was up in December and that some of you would be anxious to get back to the saints. He needs your help in building cabins for the pioneers that are coming into the valley by the hundreds.

Captain Hunt started back with his men and the cattle they had rounded up, but James here and me, we came on to find you and finish doin' what Brother Brigham asked us to do. Looks like you're really settled in here. Maybe none of you want to leave."

A loud murmur went through the group. "Can you tell us where our families are?" someone shouted from the back.

"Well, I'm not right sure where every family is cause they're pretty much scattered from Council Bluffs to the Great Salt lake Valley. Last Spring, a little later than this, Brother Brigham and some of the Saints started west to the Rockies. They got to the Great Salt Lake Valley on July 24. About a week after that here comes the Battalion soldiers and families from Pueblo and the Mississippi Saints." Porter took another drink of the cool water.

"There's high mountain peaks all around the valley and this big salty lake to the west. That lake's so salty you can float on it but you sure don't want to get any of it in your eyes. Brigham says that the water flowin' down from the mountains is goin' to make that valley blossom like a rose if we get to plantin' and making the water go where we need it to raise our crops.

Last August, Brigham, and over a hundred men left to go back to Winter Quarters to help more saints get ready to move west. Lots of them that went were some of the Battalion boys who wanted to find their families.

Well, that's about it. Captain Davis, if you can decided which twenty-five are goin' back with me we'll start making our plans. The rest of you are supposed to go up the route the men took from Los Angeles. A man by the name of Sutter has got a mill up there and he needs workers in the worst way. There's a rumor that they have even found gold up by the mill. Brother Brigham needs as many of you that can to earn money to bring back to the valley so we'll have cash to buy the things we can't raise.

I'd like to get myself a good bath and somethin' to eat and then I can try to tell each of ya where your families are, if I know."

Some of the men took the travelers to their quarters and to the warm springs for a relaxing bath. Susan and Phebe went back to the cook house and continued to prepare the evening meal. They cut up some of the fruit they had picked from the trees and made biscuits to go with the meat they had been stewing all day. This was a day to celebrate. Finally, there was news from home.

Ebenezer came in and tested the meat. He often did that to get a little taste of what was coming for supper. "Well, Phebe, here we are at decision time again. Do I volunteer to be one of the twenty-five or do we go up and work at the mill?"

Phebe wiped her hands on her apron, "Lets see if he knows anything about where our family is. If they are in the valley I'll walk every step of the way to get there as soon as I can. We may not have a choice. I guess its kind of like a story. You just have to wait and see how it turns out."

CHAPTER FORTY-TWO

Eager as they were, the men let Porter and James finish their meal before asking more questions. Porter pushed his plate back. "Thank you, ladies. That was a fine meal. Now let me tell you some things of interest to all of you. When Capt. Hunt got to the valley his wife was there and he learned that one of the twin babies had died in Pueblo. That was a hard blow to him, as he took great stock in those twins and had great faith the Lord would look out for them. Some of the other men died on the way to Pueblo or while they was there. Most of 'em made it to the Valley.

Brother Brigham's organizin' the Saints in groups of tens and hundreds to move west from Winter Quarters. It's hard to explain to you how that place is. People are all up and down the river on both sides of the Missouri. Every kind of shelter you can imagine has been thrown up to house them and there has been a lot of sickness. It seems like the same river fever that struck the saints when we first went to Nauvoo. Converts are comin' faster than you can imagine. They's comin' from England, some by way of the Eastern states and some by way of New Orleans and up the Mississippi. It's all the Brethren can do ta keep ahead of getting 'em organized fed and ready to move west. Some of the good leaders have been ask to stay at Winter Quarters to help keep things under control.

Sister Brown, the last I was there I seen your brother, William. I think he'll be stayin' on at least another year. He's good at organizin' people and gettin' 'em to work together. His brother, Zemira, had a crew helpin' ta build the cabins and they couldn't keep ahead of the Saints movin' in.

I heard your Lovina lost her husband, Brother Munro. But they all seemed to be rallyin' 'round her and she is as beautiful as ever. She sang in the last meetin' I was to."

Phebe turned away and tried to compose herself. How would Lovina survive without Henry. They had always been so much in love. She remembered the day she met him in the hat shop and how, even then, she knew they were right for each other. She didn't wait for any other reports from Porter. She picked up one of the serving kettles and carried it to the cook house. She needed to be alone.

Ebenezer followed her. He put his arms around her and let her weep on his shoulder. "There, there, my dear. It is a great loss but Lovina will be taken care of."

"I know, but I should be with her to help her with the children. I wonder if I write a letter to her if Porter could get it to her some way?"

"Ebenezer, you go back and see if you can find out about the rest of the family. I'll get the kettles washed up and write a letter to Lovina."

Ebenezer left her and she put her work apron on and attacked the black kettles with determination. She had thought they were making the ultimate sacrifices. She hadn't let herself think of the trials the family might be enduring. She indulged herself in self pity and then she remembered the wonderful promises Father Smith had given her in her blessing: "You shall have a long and happy life." She wiped the pan dry, hung it on the wall and went to her room to write to Lovina.

Ebenezer returned with news that the rest of their families were well, as far as Porter or James knew, and would not be coming west until the summer of '49. William's call from Brother Brigham was to stay there at winter quarters for three years to help with the charter of the town and help supervise the planting of the crops and harvesting so that no one would go hungry.

"Does that mean we will go to Sutter's mill to work? How will they choose the men to go back with Porter?" Phebe was full of questions.

"Captain Davis will go for sure and then the first twenty-five to volunteer. They need to round up beef cattle, mules and horses to drive back with them. It will not be an easy trip. They are going to take a southern route that Porter is familiar with but it has not been traveled by wagon. I guess they will take the Davis wagon and one of the Army wagons with them. Captain Hunter is going to stay here and work with the government to keep peace with the Mexicans and Indians."

It was well into March before Porter's group headed out and the rest of the mustered out soldiers headed toward Los Angeles and then up to Monterey.

Ebenezer had six mules, one for each of them to ride, and three pack mules. They had learned to travel light and by now they knew the area well enough to know they could pretty much live off the land. Between the three of them they had about two hundred dollars and they hoped to earn more at the mill to take back to the Rockies.

They stopped at the the little village of Monterey before heading inland. A few scattered cabins and a trading post dotted the hills by the ocean front. The waves beat against rock cliffs with eddies whirling around large boulders out in the water. The smooth sandy beaches of San Diego were contrasted here by sharp, jagged rock formations eroded by the unrelenting waves. As they looked out to sea they could see the waves cresting and rolling in. The sun was shining on the rocks and some of the weathered rocks away from shore were covered with sea animals, sunning themselves and barking at each other.

They rode up to the trading post, dismounted and tied their mules to the hitching post. The proprietor was a crusty old man who looked at them with a suspicious stare. When he noticed they weren't carrying sidearms he seemed to relax and ask, "What can I do fer ya?"

"We need some flour and beans. We're headed to Sutter's place and we may not have a chance to get supplies there." Ebenezer started to pull his money pouch out to let the storekeeper know he could pay.

"On your way ta get some of that gold, are ye? I don't know if ya can believe them stories goin' around. I have seen some pretty good sized nuggets and a fair amount of dust. You a part of that soldier group? I see you're wearin' army pants." He pulled the lid off the flour barrel and picked up the scoop and a cloth sack.

"We heard that Sutter was looking for workmen. We are on our way to the Great Salt lake Valley and just want to earn some money on the way." Ebenezer watched as the old man filled the sack with the course ground flour.

"Some of your company come by here a few months ago and headed up that way. I here tell it was some of them that found the gold."

Phebe had been standing back with Zemira taking stock of the supplies on the shelves. Now she stepped forward. "Was a pretty young woman with them? She may have had a new baby with her and they had a team of black, matched horses."

"Yes, I think I know who you're asking for. They was here for a few weeks last summer but her baby died. It's buried out here in back in the buryin' plot." He motioned to the back of the trading post. "After they buried the baby they was pretty shook up. I felt sorry for 'em out here in this country, just the two of 'em and so young. One mornin' they just packed up, stopped by the babies grave and left. They made a little marker for it. You can go out back and see it if ya want."

Phebe hurried ahead of Ebenezer and Zemira. She was sure it was Melissa's baby and when she caught sight of the little marker she was positive. "Baby William Coray" was carved into the wooden marker and hanging from a nail below it was a little pair of white leather booties. New spring grass covered the small mound of dirt.

Phebe tried to hold back the tears but when she looked at Ebenezer and Zemira and saw the tears rolling down their cheeks she let the tears flow. They held each other there, the three of them, remembering William and Melissa and their sacrifices to be together and have their baby.

"I hope they will still be at Sutter's when we get there. I just want to put my arms around her and comfort her. I know how hard it is to lose a child." Phebe walked back and stood by the mules while Ebenezer and Zemira finished their business with the trader and tied the supplies on one of the pack mules. She didn't want him to know she had been crying.

It was hard riding the mule and she hated to get on it again. She was getting used to it, however, and Ebenezer had given her the tamest of the six. She had named her "Jenny". Jenny seemed to sense Phebe's sorrow, accepting her burden without complaint which she usually registered with a buck or two.

They rode in silence for a while, taking the trail marked out for them by the trader. He had drawn a crude map for them on a piece of brown paper, directing them to the easiest route to Coloma on the American River where Sutter had built his Mill.

The trail was rough but the mules picked their way through it. Their Battalion friends that had preceded them by several months had left evidence of their trail and it was not hard to follow. Some of the passes were narrow and they wondered how they had been able to get wagons through. Looking back on their experiences on the Sante Fe trail, they knew that if any group of men could traverse a hard trail it would be the Battalion boys.

Upon reaching the Sutter's mill area at Coloma they found the saw mill was completed but they continued to find old friends from the Battalion who told them of gold finds in many of the nearby canyons and streams. Ebenezer and Zemira purchased some picks and panning equipment at Sam Brannon's store and the three of them set out to find their own rich gold deposit. The Prophet had told them to earn money to bring back to Zion and here it was for the taking. They found a stream south of Hangman's Gulch and set up their tent.

Phebe rode around to the camps and found old friends from the Battalion. She heard stories of great gold finds and some of robbers and cheaters. There was a great stir among the men because Sam Brannon, who had brought saints from Brooklyn to San Francisco, was claiming he had the right to collect tithing from the miners. He wasn't satisfied with a tenth. He was insisting on thirty percent. As she rode from camp to camp she looked for William and Melissa. She also observed the various methods the miners were using to retrieve the gold. There were very few women in the camps and Phebe became an object of curiosity in her independent ways. There were enough of the Battalion men around to provide protection for her if she needed it.

After a day of searching, someone told her the Corays were with a group on up the river at a place they called "Mormon station". She found her way back to camp to report on her findings.

"Phebe, Phebe, come and see." Ebenezer held out the shallow pan with about three ounces of gold dust shining up at her. It represented about fifty dollars worth and Zemira had panned out an equal amount.

"I guess I had better start helping you. I've heard stories about the miners being robbed. Maybe you should keep your guns loaded and ready in case we need to use them. I'll make some leather pouches to put the gold dust in. Then we will have to find some way to keep it in a safe place. Oh, I have good news, I heard that the Corays are up stream to a place they call Mormon Station." Phebe started the pots heating to get them something to eat.

While they were heating she went to the stream with the men and tried her hand at panning gold. She watched as the gold settled in the bottom of the pan as she slushed the water over the glittering sand. She couldn't believe her eyes. Who would have thought that Miss Phebe from Canada would be in California panning for gold. She would have a long page to write in her journal tonight.

There were small camps of people in almost every stream

or creek and more people were coming in every day. On Sunday they met with a group for church services and then a planning meeting followed. It was April 1848 and many of them decided they would mine as much gold as they could and prepare to leave for the Great Salt lake Valley the first of June. Most of them were from the first volunteers mustered out of the Battalion the summer before. Many of them had helped Sutter build his saw mill and worked on the grist mill but had not received any payment for their labor. Gold fever had taken over and though Sutter was an honest man he was without help to manage his financial affairs. Ebenezer shared the message he had been given by Porter Rockwell that they should earn as much as they could to take back to the valley.

The Corays came to the meeting and the Browns had a wonderful reunion with them. They were like family to them now and Melissa poured her heart out to Phebe about the loss of their baby. Phebe and Ebenezer told them about their visit to the little grave and somehow it seemed to help.

"We are not going in June with the first group. I want to mine enough to send for my family in the East." William put his arm around Melissa, "But we are anxious to get to the valley, get settled in our own place and raise a family. We may leave a little later in the summer. Some of the members up on Mormon Island are making plans to leave about then."

Ebenezer looked at Phebe, "From what Porter said, our families won't be coming west until '49 so we have decided to stay here and earn or mine as much as we can until then. Maybe we will pull up stakes and move up to the island. Are the streams as rich up there?"

"Some say they are even richer. We'd be glad to share our camp with you. I still owe you for the wagon and horses. They were a life saver for us. Without them I think I would have lost Melissa as well as the baby."

Ebenezer put his hand on William's arm, "You don't owe me anything. The Lord has blessed us with plenty for our needs and it looks like he filled these hills and streams full of gold so the Saints can survive in the Rockies." He turned to Phebe and Zemira, "How about it, shall we move on up the river with our friends here?"

"I'd like that. I have missed Melissa and it is much more pleasant to have another woman around." Phebe smiled. She had tried to be a good sport but it was hard being the only woman around and she knew Melissa felt the same way. Here in the gold camps there were a few more women who had come from San Francisco but they weren't like Melissa. In fact she had only seen one of them and she reminded her of the unsavory women in Los Angeles that the men were warned to avoid.

Early the next morning they broke camp and went on up river to be with the Corays and many other friends from the Battalion. They counted from 100 to 150 Mormons there. There was safety in numbers. These men and women had been through so many trials together there was a bond of loyalty between them. Sam Brannon was not well received there when he tried to collect money from them in the name of the church. They agreed that they would send their money back to Brigham Young by a reliable messenger and not one who was trying to divide the church. It was well known that he had disagreed with the Prophet's decision to stay in the Rockies instead of moving on to California. He was already exploiting the members by setting up the only stores and charging exorbitant prices for even the most basic commodities and mining supplies.

William and Melissa were able to retrieve enough gold by the end of May to join the Mormon group that was leaving for the Valley. They assembled in a place called Pleasant Valley, East of Hangtown. Three of the men went as an advance party to find a better route than the Donner party had used the year before coming West. When they did not return after several days the party set out on their journey to the Great Salt Lake

Valley. William took with him Ebenezer's tithing, six ounces of gold dust and six dollars in Spanish coin. This was valued at $100.00 and represented $1000.00 in earnings.

The travelers also bought some army surplus canons from Sutter, wagons and mules, outfitting themselves to safely get to the Rockies. News came back to camp that they had found their friends in the advance group killed by poison Indian arrows and buried in shallow graves. Phebe and Ebenezer were glad the group had taken the Canons with them.

Ebenezer and Zemira were always trying new methods of extracting the gold as were the other men. Some of them used shallow pans and others used tightly woven baskets. To hasten the work they experimented with larger tub like vessels they called rockers. A variety of methods were used to move the dirt to be washed.

The cooperative efforts of the Battalion members made the process even more efficient. They organized into groups of five or six, helping each other move the dirt. Sometimes they would move it on large sheets of canvas and wash it away to leave the gold flakes in the bottom of the rocker.

Phebe worked along side the men helping to remove the overburden until they found the start of a vein. She panned gold in small flat tins and made small leather pouches to hold the gold dust. It was pleasant there at Mormon Island. The weather was mild even though it was in the mountains. There was plenty of wild animals, foul and fish to provide meat and berry bushes lined the streams.

Phebe was dusting the fresh trout with flour as she prepared to fry it for supper. She used the flour sparingly as it was a dollar a pound. Even though the Saints were amassing what seemed like fortunes compared to the meager wages they had earned in the army and at day labor, they still were very careful with their money. They saved it for the valley while many of the Non-Mormon miners wasted it away gambling and drinking as fast as they mined it. Sam Brannon again was taking advantage of the circumstances. He quickly erected a hotel to house the transient miners and advertised in his paper, *The California Star*, about the rich gold fields along the American River. The saints at Mormon Island chose to sleep in their army bed rolls and tents to save their money.

Ebenezer, Phebe and Zemira, along with about 100 other former members of the Battalion, held their regular Sunday meetings. They encouraged each other in their work to provide a sizable nest-egg to take with them to start their new lives in the rockies. Phebe was often the only woman in the meetings after Melissa left and it was a lonely time for her. She wrote in her journal and read her Book of Mormon while the men were working on the mill races or scouting out new sources.

She looked up from her reading as Zemira poked his head in the tent. "I went north a ways and found what looks like a rich vein. Lets all three go there tomorrow and see what we can find."

They were up before dawn and on their way with some jerky and hard tack in in their pockets to chew on and a pick or shovel over their shoulder. Ebenezer had a sack stuffed in his back pocket in case they found some nuggets or dust to bring back to camp.

It was even better than Zemira had imagined and the three of them worked feverishly. The bag was gradually filling with the precious dust. Phebe took a break while the men dug in another direction. She walked up stream. The early afternoon sun was warm on her shoulders. Looking around, she realized she had walked up stream farther than she had anticipated. She knelt by the water, scooped her cupped hands into the cool liquid and lifted them to her lips for a refreshing drink. She splashed some of the water on her face and dried it with the edge of her skirt. As she looked down into the crystal clear water she caught a glimpse of a sparkle as the sun rays shone through the ripples of the water.

Her long sleeves absorbed the water as she kneeled and

reached down toward the stream bed. It was deeper than she anticipated and the refraction of the light through the water caused her to direct her hand away from the glistening rock. She adjusted her weight, pressing her foot against a rock to give her more leverage and reached again for the precious stone. Just as she clasp the nugget in her hand the pressure of her foot on the rock dislodged it and she fell face first in the stream.

Still clasping the nugget in her right hand she pushed with her left hand and her right fist to get her face out of the water. Pulling her knees toward her she was able to get her feet under her and push herself up out of the water. She stood finally and looked at the nugget in her hand. It was almost as large as a walnut. Pushing it deep into her pocket she turned her attention to the wet, oozing mud that covered her hightop shoes. She was soaked from head to foot. Unlacing her shoes, she pulled them off and rinsed the mud from the scuffed leather shoes. Putting them in the sun to dry along with her stockings she tried to wring as much water as she could from the heavy folds of her dress.

Sitting on a rock, facing the sun, she laughed to herself. It was a good thing she was alone. She would have been embarrassed if anyone had seen her fall in the water. Pushing her hand deep into her pocket, she pulled out the nugget to evaluate its size and lustre, and wondered at what it might buy for them in the Great Salt Lake Valley. She put it safely back in her pocket.

As she pulled her wet clinging clothes away from her she looked up stream and saw a good sized bear crossing the stream. Hopefully, the breeze had not carried her scent in that direction. Cautiously, she reached for her shoes and stockings. They were still damp but she pulled them on and was lacing the shoes up as quickly and she could when she heard a rustle in the bushes behind her. Thinking it was another bear, she looked for something she could use to defend herself.

Ebenezer and Zemira walked out of the bushes laughing, "Swimming with your clothes on again I see." Ebenezer grinned from ear to ear. Then they confessed that they had followed her trail after she had not returned in a few minutes, only to find her falling into the water as they arrived.

Phebe took the nugget from her pocket and they took turns holding it and judging its weight. It may have as much value as all the dust the two of them had mined that day.

In the late Summer of 1849 another group met to plan an exodus to the Valley. This time the Browns were ready to go with them. They estimated that they had about $5000.00 between them and determined they would use their six mules for travel rather than to invest in the inflated prices of wagons and horses. Phebe had sewn small packets into the clothing of Ebenezer and Zemira. She made her a belt resembling a corset which held little packets for the gold and the rest of the precious metal was distributed among the packs on the mules.

Ebenezer chided her for her industrious effort to protect their earnings. Her retort was, "My Mother always warned us not to put all of our eggs in one basket. One way or another we will get this gold to the valley. We have done what the Prophet has asked us to do and the Lord will provide if we use good judgement."

Zemira winked at Ebenezer, "You can't argue with mother's faith. If she is willing to ride that mule, Jenny, all the way to the valley, I guess we will have to let her have her way as to how we carry the gold."

CHAPTER FORTY-THREE

The line of travelers wound through the tree covered hills, climbing out of the Sacramento valley heading East. They followed the trail their friends had opened the year before and on which many gold seekers had and would use to travel west to the gold fields. The trail took them North of Trukee Pass and the dangerous route the Donner party had traveled. They would circle the high mountain peaks, the barren desert of salty sand and the Great Salt lake approaching the valley from the north. It was the last of August and they estimated it would take them about six weeks to two months to reach the Saints in the Salt Lake Valley. A trip judged to be between seven or eight hundred miles. They had poured over the rough maps and tried to plot how far they could travel in a day, where the water sources were and where they would most likely be vulnerable to Indian or robber attacks.

Ebenezer, Phebe and Zemira were with the group of fifty people, most of them Mormons and former Battalion members. Phebe was the only woman. To appear less conspicuous she wore men's clothing. It was much less cumbersome than the long skirts and petticoats when riding the mule but she was very self conscious about it and longed for the time that she could be a lady again in pretty clothes. She looked at her hands, now rough and calloused from the past three years of driving teams, cooking and washing on the trail, and last of all, digging in the bedrock and panning gold. She was thankful for her good health and most of all the promise she was waiting for of a long and happy life.

All of the company were carrying gold dust or nuggets East. Traveling close together, the men took turns riding in the front or rear of the group with their guns loaded to protect them from Indian attacks or marauding bands of robbers.

Stories had circulated through the mining camps of the dangerous trail to Great Salt Lake.

These seasoned pioneers knew the rigors of travel and paced themselves in order to average fifteen or twenty miles a day. Phebe prepared for the challenges of the trip and was eager to get on with it. Finally, she was headed for her family. It had been three years since they had parted in Iowa. She wondered if she had known what was in store for her if she would have been so willing to go.

Her mule, Jenny, followed Ebenezer's mule, Buck, and Zemira followed behind their three pack mules. The six mules had served them well the past year since they bought them in San Diego and they knew what to expect from each other. Buck knew if he was peaceful, unlike his name, Ebenezer would have a sugar cube or extra hand of oats for him. Jenny was protective of Phebe and seldom shied, side stepped or balked as she had when first acquired. Phebe talked to her in a gentle tone and respected her needs for food, water and rest. What more could a mule want. Ebenezer and Zemira tended the feet of the mules carefully, picking out rocks and trimming their hoofs. They were well aware of their dependency on these mules to get them to their destination. Phebe was grateful that Ebenezer was so good with animals. She had seen so many mistreated on the Battalion Trek but never by Ebenezer.

They were a few days out and it was a beautiful early September day. The air cool and refreshing. The tenderness Phebe had experienced the first day or so from the long rides was subsiding and she decided that just as she had become used to the long days on the hard wagon seat, she would also become used to riding Jenny. She kept a bandana handy to pull up over her face if the trail became dusty and she pulled the brim of the old felt hat down to shield her face from the sun. At Ebenezer's insistence, she had a side arm in a holster strapped to her waist. Her hair was braided and twisted in a bun under her hat. Because she was tall and slim, she could easily pass as any one of the men traveling in the group.

They were unaware of a group of men following them. It was a swarthy group of what was commonly called mountain men. Jed and his son, James led the group. The beaver trapping had been poor so they had followed the tales of gold in California and found themselves at a saloon called Murderer's Bar. There they met the three Carson brothers and after several rounds of drinks, started to make plans for what they hoped would be a lucrative adventure. Mr. Brown, the tavern owner heard the boisterous brags of the men and their plans for the Gold Train of naive Mormons heading East with their gold. As the night wore on, Brown, which was an alias, formed his own plan and by morning was enlisting some of the best sharp shooters in the area to carry it out.

The five trappers were staying about three miles back of what they termed, "The Gold Train." When the train moved, they moved and when the train camped they camped with a cold camp so as not to arouse suspicion with smoke from a fire. They were nearing the summit and as the morning sun broke through the density of the trees they could see the train of travelers descending into the valley below. There would be less foliage to cover their surveillance so they separated to scout the outreaches of the trail, agreeing to meet at dark when the Gold Train had reached the other side of the valley.

The men took off on either side of the trail and distanced themselves from each other as well as the train. They were nearing Indian country so their scouting instincts made them alert for nearby bands of braves that might thwart their plans.

Meanwhile the Mormon train was moving through the valley. As the day wore on the late summer heat became more intense since they had dropped several hundred feet in elevation and no longer had the protection of pine and aspen trees for shade. The map showed a water hole ahead and they moved on to take a midday break where they could fill their canteens. It was nothing more than a small stream that had survived the thirsty desert sands but it was enough and they could see hills ahead where they would camp for the night.

Phebe filled her canteen from the stream as did Ebenezer and Zemira and the other men. They each ate from their own rations in their packs, mostly jerky, let their stock graze and drink by the stream knowing that the short break would help them with renewed energy to go on.

They were a jovial group, laughing at and with each other. Some of them teased Phebe about her manly appearance but she took it well and reminded them that she had seen most of them in less than appropriate attire on the Battalion trek. Though they were headed to a new destination, foreign to all of them, it was as if they were going home. Home to friends and family and to the leadership of the Church. Brother Brigham would take care of them and they would help build the new Zion.

Soon they were on their way again across the valley to the hills ahead. They had already exceeded their twenty miles for the day but they had not been hard miles. Tomorrow was Sunday and they would have their day of rest.

Their small campfires dotted the small ravine where they camped for the night. It was a beacon for two other groups of travelers. The tents were pitched and the animals tethered nearby. Charlie, the fiddler, tuned up his fiddle and began to play. Soon they were all singing the old tunes and before long several were dancing to the jigs he played.

A rider came into camp, his horse in a lather, and he jumped from his saddle. The music stopped and they all turned to see the intruder. Ebenezer and some of the other men reached for their guns realizing they had neglected to assign some of the men to stand guard. Mr. Brown, the tavern owner, dismounted and was immediately recognized. "Brother Rockwell, come and join us. We're just resting from the trail with a little music and dancing."

"The names Brown. Please call me Mr. Brown. I have

some friends meeting me here and no one is to know my real name." He took a sip from his canteen which was a signal for his men to come in to the camp.

Three sharpshooters who the men recognized from the shooting contests at Mormon Island rode in. "O.K. Brown, now what do we do?"

"Smith, you take the south point up there, Jones up the north slope and Henry, you take cover down stream a ways until they pass you. I judge they'll be ridin' in shortly. I'll meet 'em head on." The men left for their destinations, *Mr. Brown*, led his horse to the brush nearby and then joined the group.

"Start up the music and dancing. Everybody relax. We've got it under control. Ebenezer, round up about five of your best marksmen and take cover close by in case we need a back up. Oh, you better make sure you have some guards on your mules and horses. Sister Brown, you get to the back of the group. It'll be safer there."

Phebe moved to a spot behind the fiddler and sat down on a rock. She felt her gun at her side but it gave her little comfort. She tried to decide if she should load it but she knew she would never be able to shoot anyone. Her best option was to pray for protection for all of them. She closed her eyes and said a silent prayer. The fear that had made her legs shake as she sat down subsided.

As had been predicted, the five ruffians rode into camp, and Jed called out, "Stop the music. I have a message for you Mormons. Bring out your gold and give it up and no one will get hurt. If ya give us any trouble, I can't guarantee nothin'."

The fiddler stopped but no one moved. As Jed pulled his gun from his holster *Mr. Brown*, shot the gun from his hand. As the other four drew their guns, shots rang through the blackness of the night and all five were disarmed. Ebenezer and his men pulled their guns and the would be robbers found themselves surrounded as the marksmen rode in from their assigned posts.

"Get off your horses. It doesn't pay to mess with the Lord's people. We'll follow you back to the gold fields where you can get your own gold. Hope you won't mind walking. Smith, get their horses and put 'em with the Mormons' stock. They may need some extras 'fore they get to the Rockies. You boys escort 'em back. I'm goin' to stay with the train for a day or two." Port holstered his gun.

The sharpshooters pushed the ruffians out of camp and on their way. They had been paid well by Mr. Brown for a few days trail ride and they would enjoy the trip back. Not only had he paid them but he had agreed not to enter the next shooting contest which would mean more money in their pockets.

With the crisis over, old friends clamored around Porter Rockwell and thanked him for being there when they needed him. He chided them for being so trusting and not taking better precautions. He added, "Somehow, the Lord seems to let me know when I'm needed. Brother Brigham sent me out here with Brother Lyman to see about a postal route and help straighten out Brother Brannon. He didn't say nothin' about helpin' you but he did say I was ta' help collect the tithing so as soon as ya' get to the valley ya' better be payin' up the Lord's share."

They enjoyed their Sunday together. It was a day of rest and rejoicing. Many testimonies were offered that day and they knew they were a blessed people.

Porter rode along with them for the next day, showing them how to watch for trouble on the trail and sharing stories of the past few months since he had been with them in San Diego. He had been back to Iowa with Brother Brigham and helped put down an Indian uprising south of The Great Salt Lake Valley after he got back, before coming to California. He'd seen some of their family members again and told Phebe he had delivered her letter to Lovina. He sat by Phebe as they gathered around the campfire. "I know you folks are anxious to settle down after all your travelin' and I can't blame ya.

It's goin' to be good in the valley for ya and I hope to be your neighbor someday." He looked into the fire, 'Yes, I hope the Lord will see fit for me settle down. I'd like to have a wife and family agin'. I'm hopin' to find my oldest daughter out here somewhere. She up and disappeared and I don't know if she was kidnapped or if she went of her own will. I'll find her though."

Phebe looked at this good man who had put his life on the line so many times for the brethren that she was aware of, and probably many more that she didn't know about. She remembered the love Brother Joseph had for him. She had seen him embrace Porter in Nauvoo and say, "I love this man and the Lord loves him."

Porter left the group the next morning to return to his California assignment. The rest mounted and moved on East. Phebe put her heal into Jenny's flank, "Come on, Jenny, lets get to the valley."

What seemed like endless days of rolling, sagebrush, covered hills and scrub oak, finally, was nearing its end. The train of travelers had turned in a southeasterly direction. They could see the majestic Rocky Mountains to the East and the streams flowing down from them were reaching out into the flat lands nourishing a lush growth of grasses. They came to a river flowing south and from their maps they determined it was flowing into the Great Salt Lake. They followed the river south until they came to some narrows where the river was not too swift and divided to circle a natural island. The first riders tested the depth, finding it fairly shallow, motioned the rest of the riders to follow them into the waters.

Phebe hesitated, remembering the fear from her near drowning before, but she put her confidence in Jenny's ability to carry her across. She had forgotten that she had wedged her journal beneath her bedroll and the saddle. Jenny moved into the deep water at Phebe's urging and before she knew it the water was up to the saddle and and washing over the rump of the mule. She looked back and saw her journal floating away from her but there was no way to retrieve it. All of the other riders had their hands full fording the stream. As she saw the pages flip in the water and then the whole sheaf of papers submerge her heart sank. She decided, "If I wrote it once I can write it again. I have a good memory. I'll start it all over when we get settled."

She hung on to the saddle horn and clamped her legs to the mule's sides. She didn't want to be washed away as the journal was. Everything else seemed secure. One more to cross on the other side of the island and they could dry out. The late October sun would dry out the bedrolls and clothes in a hurry. Perhaps she could even take some time to go up stream for a bath and wash her hair. It would feel so good to be clean again. She was also determined that she would ride into the valley wearing a dress and bonnet, not looking like a man.

"I hate to ask again, but how many more days until we reach the Saints?" She looked at Ebenezer, feeling guilty because she had ask so many times before in the last few weeks.

"I think we have one more good days ride and the next day we should be in the Salt lake Valley if the map is right. It's hard to judge. The mountains look so close but as we get closer to them we can see that the foot hills extend way out into the valleys. We will be able to see the lake long before we get to the valley where the saints are." Ebenezer pulled her close to him as they sat on the bank of the river drying in the sun. "Have I told you lately how proud of you I am. No man could have a better wife. You have been a real trooper and some day I will make it up to you for all you have been through."

"Thanks, I love you for saying that. The Lord has guided our steps and that promise the Prophet made us so long ago is coming true. Here we are at the foot of the Rocky Mountains. We both have good health and I'm sure He has a lot more in store for us in the future. I'll just be glad to see our families and settle down for awhile. I hope He doesn't ask us to travel back to Iowa." She sighed and leaned her head on his shoulder enjoying the comfort she felt from being near him. The sun was warm on their faces and an evening breeze was just starting down from the high mountains at their backs. They looked across the wide vista of miles they had traveled the last few days, watched the horizon curve away from them and the sun creep down to join it.

"I want to go up river for a bath. Do you think I need a chaperone? We haven't seen any Indians for miles." Phebe stood up and stretched. Pulled her hair out of the bob and unbraided it, letting the grey streaked locks fall over her shoulders.

"I'll go with you and keep a look out. Port said there were Indians all around the area so we can't be too careful." Ebenezer picked up his rifle and followed her upstream away from the other travelers until they were out of sight. There were some tall bushes that provided some privacy so he sat there with his gun loaded incase an intruder came by.

Phebe slipped her clothes off and got in the cold, clear water. It felt like it had just melted from the snowy glaciers tucked into the northern crevices of the mountains towering in the East. She shook off the chill and as her body adjusted to the temperature of the water it was as if it was feeding her soul with new vitality. She let her head fall back in the water and her long hair float away from her. She scrubbed at her scalp, loosening the caked dust that had gathered there beneath the sweaty rim of the old leather hat. It felt so good to be clean again. If there was one thing that had been the hardest of these last three years, it had been the days she had to spend feeling dirty. It was not her way and she hoped when they were settled she would be able to resume her old habits of cleanliness.

She heard Ebenezer stir in the bushes and looked up to see two Indian boys looking down his gun barrel. Frightened, they turned and ran away through the tall reeds and bushes that lined the river, their bare feet sending wafts of river sand behind them. She wondered how long they had watched her bathing before they were discovered. She dried herself off with her shirt and quickly slipped into her clothes. They were just innocent children and had probably never seen a white woman before.

Joining Ebenezer, they hurried back toward the safety of the group. Ebenezer warned the men as he and Phebe entered the camp. "There are some Indians not too far from here. We had better keep our guard up."

Guard duties were assigned and the whole camp was on alert. Some of the men shot their guns out into the sagebrush, hoping it would be a deterrent. The animals were tethered within the camp and the group opted not to pitch tents that night, making it easier to fend off an attack. They huddled in their bed rolls listening to the night noises, wondering if they were Indian signals. The October chill was in the air but no fires were started.

Needless to say, sleep did not come quickly to Phebe even though the men around her were alert and ready for an attack if it came. She had so much to think about. She probably wouldn't have slept anyway. Just two days away from friends, and she hoped, family. Had William brought the family to the Valley yet as Porter said he had planned to do this summer? How tall would Rhoda be now and Ebenezer's John? He was such a handsome young boy. What about Lovina and her children? Would they remember her? She was sure Ester Ann would. They had always had something special between them. And Bett, how good it would be to see her again. Her good friend, Bett. Then, there was the rest of Ebenezer's children, Harriet, Gurnsey and Norman, and her dear father. Let's see, there would be brother Zemira and William George? Oh my, and old friends from the Battalion too. It was like counting sheep, and before she thought it would have been possible, she was sound asleep and Ebenezer was listening to her patterned breathing, glad that she was resting.

Morning came and the camp stirred, getting ready to be on their way again. there was frost in the air and the dew was icy on the grass. They built quick fires for a warm drink. As they looked to the bluff on the north they saw four or five braves sitting on their ponies, watching them. They turned their pintos and rode away. How close they had been to camp during the night no one knew. They would soon be safely on their way south. By noon they should be in sight of the Great Salt Lake.

Phebe had unpacked one of the bundles on the pack mule that carried her clothes. She had found the lavender dress and the pink bonnet with the lavender ties as well as her petticoats. She tried to shake out the wrinkles and refolded them. She put them carefully back in the bundle and tied them to the back of her saddle. They would be ready for her when it was time to enter the valley.

The miles seemed to pass so slowly. Jenny felt the antici-pation of her rider and stubbornly slowed her pace. Phebe scanned the scene before her seeing the sandy moraines jutting out from the foot hills. Higher up on the mountains there were spots of bright red and yellow where the frost had touched the oak and aspen. And finally, to the southwest, she saw what she thought was a glimmer of water. Parched white beds of dried sand seem to stretch for miles to the west. By afternoon they could see the beautiful lake in the distance but realized it would be another day before they would reach the Saints. They could see a lone rocky peak cutting the blue sky in the south-east. A glacier of snow clung to a north slope. Lower peaks were closer but Porter had told them to watch for that lone rocky peak. When they could see it they would be within a day of their destination.

CHAPTER FORTY-FOUR

The Brass Band was playing in the bowery and people lined Temple street watching as the "Gold Train" rode into town. It was a motley group of weary travelers on mules and horseback with an entourage of pack animals loaded down with their gear. One lonely woman in a lavender dress and pink bonnet broke the monotony of the drably clad band. Some in the remnants of old army uniforms and others in worn pants and shirts from the work in the gold fields. The beaming smiles on their faces belied their appearance as they saw friends and family waiting to greet them.

They were the last of the Battalion to return and many of their comrades were there to welcome them home. Families that had been parted for three long years were reunited, husbands and wives and children who had lived with the dread of never seeing their loved ones again. Shouts to loved ones filled the air as they tried to be heard over the sounds of the band. A few of the men were still searching the crowd for a familiar face when the Browns and Drapers encircled Phebe, Ebenezer and Zemira. They held their own celebration right there in the street, oblivious to the others. Tears of joy streaked their dusty faces as they let the reality of the long awaited reunion permeate their senses.

Brother Brigham was there to participate in the celebration and moved among the crowd shaking hands and welcoming them to Zion. He came to the group encircling Phebe and Ebenezer. He remembered the day he had stopped at the Draper camp on the Iowa prairie and ask for support in forming the Battalion. He felt a sigh of relief to see them all here safely together. He held Phebe's hands, "My dear, you have come a long way and how we appreciate your sacrifice. Many of the Battalion members that preceded you have reported on

your kindness to them. Welcome to Zion. The Lord loves you."
He moved on to greet the others.

William had led the family group in with Judge Appleby
and Judge Clark just one week before. His brother Zemira had
come to the valley the previous summer so it was at his home
the Browns and Drapers were gathering. It was hard to take it
all in. Everyone was talking at once, asking questions and
reporting on their trip across the prairies. They had been
caught in a bad storm east of the Rockies and lost some of
their cattle but they had come through it without losing a single life.

Zemira had married Amy Terry and they had two little
girls. Amy seemed to feel a little overwhelmed with all the
family arriving within a few days. The yard was full of animals
and wagons and the little three room cabin had bed rolls in
stacks against the walls. She had tried to bake and cook in
preparation for the arrival but as she looked over the group she
was afraid the food would not go far enough.

Phebe was in a daze. She couldn't get to everyone fast
enough. First she sought out Rhoda, holding her fast. She was
almost as tall as her mother and Phebe was shocked at her
beauty and maturity. Her auburn shock of hair circled a pretty
face and her eyes seemed a darker blue than when she was a
child. Phebe held her hand, not letting go as she went from one
to another.

"Miss Phebe, I've missed you so much and have so much
to tell you." William held his sister close. "I have a new wife
and three more children. Mary Ann, this is my sister, Phebe.
Bett is here somewhere." Mary ann, the new wife, held a new
born baby and a little two year old girl clung to her skirt.

"I'm glad to meet you Mary Ann. As soon as I get to see
everyone I want to hold that baby. Oh, it is so good to be with
family again." She searched the sea of faces for Lovina.

"Rhoda, where is Lovina?" still craning her neck to see
over the group.

"They are still in Iowa. Did you know about Henry's death?" She said it almost reverently, registering the personal loss she felt. Henry had been like a father to her and she missed him terribly.

"Yes, yes, Brother Rockwell told us, but I thought she would be with the family. Is she alright?"

"Lovina has remarried and is expecting her second baby by her new husband this winter. They decided it would be better to wait until next year to come west but I am sure she will be coming. You will like her new husband Mother, his name is Thomas Brandon."

Phebe tried not to show her disappointment. She had missed Lovina but there were so many other family members to see. "What about William George?"

"He will probably be coming out with Lovina. He has remarried also and has two little boys. They are so cute. They look just like their father." Rhoda felt very important to be the one to tell Phebe about the family.

Father Draper came to her side, put his feeble arms around her and suppressed his sobs of joy. He could only say, "My girl, my girl, my dear Phebe. It has been a long hard journey but I kept the faith that I would see you again. The Lord has blessed us all."

Phebe felt the stubble of his beard on her cheek, remembering the many times that his faith and wisdom had carried them all through hard times. She realized that so much of her determination in life had come from her father's strength and testimony. She was suddenly so weary and wished she could curl up on her father's lap as she had when she was a child and listen to him read to her from the Bible in the old log house in Rome, New York. She had tried to be strong for so long and now, for just a fleeting moment, she wanted to lean on her father's love. "Father, it is so good to be with you again. It has been a long hard journey for all of us."

Then she saw Ebenezer with his children and quickly

moved to be a part of their reunion. Zemira had Norman and Gurnsey in deep conversation swapping trail stories and young John stood by his father listening to Harriet tell about the letter.

"Father, you can't imagine what comfort your letter brought to us. It was the one you wrote in Santa Fe. We were in western Nebraska and so tired from the journey and worried about you, Aunt Phebe and Zemira. I was riding on the seat by Oliver when a man rode up on a horse and handed me the letter. We called to the children from the back of the wagon and read the letter to them. It was only then that we turned to thank the rider that had brought it to us. He was no where to be found. Our wagon train stopped and the men searched everywhere for the rider without finding him. They came back to me and ask exactly where we were when he rode up. I told them it was back about a mile by the only two trees in the area. They went back there but could find no sign of the man or even any hoof prints.

There were so many saints in our company who had loved ones in the Battalion and they had not heard a word of there whereabouts or welfare. We shared the letter with everyone. Realizing it had been written almost three years earlier we still took heart that it had come to us at one of our most discouraging points on the trail. We were all of one accord that it was one of the three Nephites who had been promised, like the Apostle John, to never taste of death, but to stay on the earth to serve God's promised people." Harriet pulled the brown worn paper from her handbag. "See, Here it is. I have kept it with me all the way."

Ebenezer looked at the letter, looked at Phebe and then at Harriet, "I wrote this letter in Santa Fe but I didn't get it finished in time to send it on with Brother Lee. I have kept it in my pack all this time." Handing it back to her he went to his pack but the letter was not there. "It has truly come to you by some miraculous means. I'm glad it brought comfort to you. Let me see it again."

Harriet handed the letter to her father. He looked at it more carefully and then held it for Phebe to see. "Remember, I wrote it on the tongue of the wagon. Look, you can see the grain of the wood where the pencil lead skipped the ridges. I don't write all that well so I am sure this is the letter I wrote."

Phebe looked at the letter and recognized the careful printing. She remembered his effort to learn the letters and form them correctly. He was consistent in substituting a capital "R" for a small "r" and had trouble with when to use "ee" or "ea" in a word. The letter started, "DeeR HaRRiet," Yes, this was definitely Ebenezer's writing and she had seen it in his pack long after they had left Santa Fe. In fact, she remembered it being there when they packed to leave San Diego.

She handed the letter back to Ebenezer, "Yes, it is your letter. I put it in your pack myself in San Diego over a year ago after Porter had left with my letter to Lovina. I remember thinking at the time that we should have sent it with him. Obviously the Lord wanted Harriet to have it and found a way to have it delivered. It is one more miracle we have witnessed.

Ebenezer and the boys rode their horses through the deep grasses and marshes. They were in the southeast corner of the valley and they looked up to see the towering peaks to the east and the traverse mountains forming a barricade to the south. On the north was a sandy moraine bordered on the east by a hidden valley still covered with green undergrowth and scrub oak.

"It looks like at least four good streams carry water down from the mountains. Even this late in the fall the water is still running from the snow capped peaks. After all the places I have traveled I have come to appreciate the importance of water. This looks like an ideal spot to settle." Ebenezer urged his horse to higher ground where he could get better footing out of the marshes.

Norman rode his horse up beside his father, "I thought you would like this. We drove the cattle herd we brought across the plains out here to pasture. When it is hot in the summer the cool breezes come down from that corner canyon and in the evening as the sun still shines up on the mountains the cool evening air settles here in the valley. Gurnsey and I came out last week and rounded up some of the cattle. They are nice and fat. We found almost every one of them. Some of them may be in the foot hills or the Indians may have helped themselves to one or two."

Gurnsey picked up where Norman left off, "There's plenty of deer in these mountains too. We've seen cougar and bear tracks when we were lookin' for the cattle. I'm glad we came ahead last year so we could find this spot before someone else settled on it."

As they rode on a big pheasant hen flew out of the marsh and two or three more followed her. The horses balked a little at the unexpected disturbance of the quiet solitude. The men reined them in and surveyed the surroundings again. Ebenezer stood high in his stirrups and looked around him. "It seems that the water all runs down to this one area that is so marshy. One of the first things we will have to do is to decide how to control it so we can build our houses on dry ground. One thing for sure. We should never go hungry here. Lets get back to the city. I can hardly wait to bring Phebe out to show her. We knew the Lord had a special place in mind for us and I think this is it."

Norman and Zemira offered to follow the others and watch for Indians. They were so glad to be back together. The last three years experiences had brought an obvious maturity to them and they were comrades once again. John and Gurnsey rode on either side of their father as they picked their way through the undergrowth and then followed the barren trail for several miles back to Salt Lake City. They could see several other canyon coves in the east at the foot of the mountains but none intrigued them like the one they had already claimed with the clear mountain water flowing down in a creek through the willows.

"There seems to be plenty of timber in the mountains to build our cabins. Zemira and I learned a lot about making bricks in San Diego but it takes a lot longer to build with bricks than with wood." The wheels were already spinning in Ebenezer's head. He had a town to build, fine sons and a wife to help him, a good herd of cattle, some gold in his pocket, a lot of friends and no Missouri Mobsters to run them out. Yes, this is what the Prophet meant when he promised he and Phebe that they would help build Zion in the Rockies. He nudged his horse with the heel of his boot until he broke into a gallup. The trail was more open now and he could hardly wait to report what he had found to Phebe.

The boys saw their father's move as an invitation to race the horses and they were only too happy to join in. Zemira and Norman were sure they would out do the rest, but they had underestimated or forgotten their father's ability to ride. After a few miles Ebenezer pulled his horse to a slow walk and the four boys caught up to him. They walked the lathered, dusty horses into the city, daring Ebenezer to give them another chance.

"We'll have lots of races and parties and dances. When we get some cabins built we'll build a bowery for parties. Maybe William George will be here by then. He and Oliver can start up the band and we'll have a great time."

The October sun seemed larger than a pumpkin, setting in the west over the lake as the men dismounted, loosened the cinches and pulled the saddles and halters from the horses. They carried some water from the well to the trough and turned the horses into the corral. They dusted off their pants, took off their hats, and wiped their faces with their kerchiefs they had soaked in the trough. "Looks as if we are ready to go and break the news to the ladies." They all remembered that

Phebe expected them to clean up a bit before coming in the house. It didn't take long to get back into the swing of things.

Phebe was setting tin plates on the table while Bett was stirring the stew in the large pot hanging on the Iron arm that could be moved over the fire and then out over the hearth. Amy and Mary Ann were tending their babies. William and his brother, Zemira had just returned from a scouting trip to the Millcreek cove. Father Draper sat in the only rocker that had made its way across the plains in the Draper wagons, rocking Mary Ann's little girl. Rhoda was rounding up all the little ones to eat at the first sitting. The adults would eat later.

Ebenezer burst in the door and went right to Phebe, lifting her off her feet and swinging her around. "I have the best surprise for you but you will have to wait until tomorrow." He winked at the boys, as if to request their silence and support in the intrigue. "First, I have to go to the tithing mint and try to see Brother Brigham. If all goes well, you will know the surprise by tomorrow afternoon."

Phebe looked at the boys for a clue but they looked away, avoiding those steel grey eyes that usually melted their determination to keep any secret from her. She could see that Ebenezer had the upper hand and he was grinning from ear to ear. he started to hum a tune and took her arm and started to dance. Everyone began clapping and singing the words, "She's a young thing but cannot leave her mother."

Phebe caught her breath as they came to the end of the stanza and her cheeks were bright from blushing with all the attention. "That must be some surprise. You weren't this happy when we found water after almost dying of thirst or when we found gold in California. Ebenezer, how good can it be?"

"Mighty good, mighty good, and that's all I'm goin' to say about it 'til tomorrow." He picked up Harriets baby and held her as he continued dancing around the room.

Phebe shook her head and accepted the fact that she would have to wait until tomorrow. She had news to share with

Ebenezer also but it wasn't good news. She would tell him later. He was so happy now, as was everyone else in the family. She was just starting to get a glimpse of what the Prophet meant when he talked about eternal families.

She helped dish up the stew for the children as they found a place on the benches by the table. Amy had put a cloth on the table and Phebe realized it had been over three years since she had sat at a table covered with a cloth. Her brother Zemira ask his father to say a blessing on the food. Father Draper stood at the end of the table and bowed his head, asking the Lord to bless the food and thanking Him for the abundance of nourishment to spirit and body.

After the children were settled down for the night, William was conversing with Bett and Mary Ann about their future plans. Phebe and Ebenezer walked out to have some time to themselves and watch the harvest moon climb up over the ridges of the mountains. They had seen the country from the East to West and North to South but never anything more spectacular than these Rocky Mountains. It felt so safe here, like the home they had been dreaming of.

Ebenezer put his arm around Phebe's shoulders. It was chilly out and she had put on her green shawl, still with her to warm her on cold nights. "I hope you can find some yarn to make you a new shawl. Every time I see this shawl it reminds me of the green stripes on the stockings you knit for Zemira and me. How about a blue shawl next time? You look pretty in blue."

Phebe smiled, "I'll try to fit it in. Bett and Harriet brought the spinning wheel and the loom with them so our winter will be filled with work to clothe this family. Did the boys bring some sheep with the cattle?"

"Yes and I think they still have the wool from the spring sheering waiting for use. They are good boys and have been careful guardians of the herd. I saw the cattle today and they are healthy. We should have a good crop of calves and lambs in the spring." He was getting close to revealing his secret so he changed the subject. "Did you see any of our old friends today?"

It was time for Phebe to tell him her news. "Yes, I saw Melissa Coray. She has a new baby boy. The sad news is that William died last month. He got very sick on the trail coming back last year and never recovered. It was heartbreaking to hear her story. They loved each other so much. Oh! she gave me this to give to you. She said William made her promise to tell you that it was the first tithing paid into the Mormon Mint."

Ebenezer took the small piece of paper from Phebe. "Read it to me Phebe, I guess my eyes are getting bad and I haven't been practicin' my reading for some time."

Phebe took the receipt from him and held it to the light seeping out of the cabin door. She read, "Ebenezer Brown, a Battalion veteran paid in tithing, six ounces of gold dust and six dollars to total $100.00 in tithing." It was dated November 23, 1848. That was the day the Corays had arrived in the valley from the gold fields last year. The first business William took care of was to deliver the tithing Ebenezer had entrusted to him. It was the first receipted gold dust paid into the mint. The dust was valued at $15.67 an ounce.

Ebenezer took the receipt and held it in his hands and then folded it and put it in his pocket. "I knew I could trust William. He was like a son to me. I had hoped he and Melissa would settle near to us." He swallowed hard to rid himself of the lump in his throat. "I'll take the rest of our tithing into the mint tomorrow."

They walked into the cabin and found a spot on the floor to put their bed rolls. The army blanket covered them as they lay amid the sounds of the family members sleeping in every available spot. Phebe wondered at Ebenezer's surprise. She had looked at some of the cabins that were for rent. They would be taken up quickly by the other new arrivals. The family needed more room and they could afford to spend some of their money to rent a cabin until they got settled. Brother Brigham had been wise to have the cabins built and reserved for new arrivals. He seemed to think of everything. She put her arm around Ebenezer and smiled to herself about his enthusiasm for the surprise. He always gave her something to look forward to.

Chapter Forty-five

Ebenezer stood in the tithing office with some of his friends waiting to have his gold dust weighed and receipted. They were full of stories and plans for settling in the valley. Some of them had already received their assignments from the Brethren.

"Good morning, Brothers. I knew I could count on you to come in with your tithing. I don't know of a more dedicated group of men." Brigham Young took his hat off and made the rounds, shaking hands and giving words of encouragement. When he came to Ebenezer he invited him into his office and closed the door.

"Have a seat Brother Brown. Let me tell you how pleased I was to see so many of the Browns and Drapers reunited here in the valley. It's people like you who are the backbone of the church, accepting assignments willingly and carrying them out cheerfully.   One of the returning Battalion soldiers told me that you were one of the most amazing of all the men because you never seemed to get discouraged. He said you and Sister Phebe often helped others or shared with them, leaving little for yourself."

Ebenezer was embarrassed, "I only did what I thought the Lord expected of me and it wasn't that much. They all suffered a lot. If we hadn't helped each other we would not have survived. I was blessed to have Phebe with me. She encouraged me to help others and had ways of seeing to their needs. Did anyone tell you about how she stood up to that Dr. Sanderson and tricked him so she could help the sick men? I'll have to tell you about it sometime. She is quite a woman."

"Yes she is. I've known her since my early days in the church. I baptized her in Canada, but I'm sure she has told you about that." Brigham shifted in his chair and pulled a sheath of papers in front of him.

"Brother Brown, I'm trying to get everyone settled before winter comes on. With your group coming in from California and the other company just arriving from Iowa we are a little hard pressed to find housing for all of you. Do you think your family could share a cabin with another family for the winter until we can get more built?"

"If we can get one of the larger cabins, with Zemira Draper's help, I'm sure we can make do for all the Drapers and Browns. We have a few more wives and children to take care of now but we have worked together in the past. Phebe and Bett always seem to make things work and the older children are good sports. We can still use the covered wagons they brought with them and our army tent. If we need more we will build it." Ebenezer felt confident in speaking for the family.

"Brother Brigham, when the boys and I were out checking the cattle, I found a spot I'd like to have for our family. It's in the far southeast corner of the valley and there seems to be plenty of water running down from the mountains. I believe it would support many families once we get the water directed where we need it. It's beautiful out there. How would you feel about us settling there?" Ebenezer almost held his breath. He hoped no one else had asked for the spot.

President Young grinned, "I know the spot. It's yours if you want it. I know you are a cattle man and you need grassland. I may have to send others out to join you. It seems to me that it would support a good sized community and I think you and Sister Brown are just the two to make it work. If I know her, she'll have a school organized for the children and you'll have the men making ditches and building homes. Before long there will be a branch of the church there. You've made a good choice. You have my blessing." He stood and shook hands with Ebenezer and moved to the door, ready to get on with his next appointment.

Ebenezer put his tithing receipt in his pocket, thanked Brother Brigham again and was out the door like a shot, not even waiting to say good-by to his friends. He could fulfill his promise of the surprise for Phebe and if they were going to get out there today they would have to hurry. It must be a good twenty miles. It was already almost nine o'clock. The morning was slipping away fast.

"Zemira, could I borrow your wagon and horses? I'll have them back by tomorrow night. I need to take Phebe on a little trip." He knew his brother-in-law would share anything he had.

"Take them with my blessing. Does this have anything to do with the surprise for Phebe?" Zemira grinned at his good friend.

"It does and I'll tell you all about it when we get back. Thank you for being so generous. I'll make it right with you when I get my feet on the ground again. I need to find a wagon to buy and many other things. It seems we came back with money in our pocket but few of the necessities." Ebenezer shook Zemira's hand and hurried into the cabin to find Phebe.

"Phebe, we are going to take a little trip. We will need some food and our bed rolls. Maybe Amy could loan us an extra blanket. It may be a little cold tonight. I'll have the horses hitched to the wagon in just a few minutes and be ready to go. As soon as you have the things together let me know." Before Phebe could respond, he was out the door and she was quite sure this had something to do with the surprise he had promised her.

They rode out of town in Zemira's wagon heading south. "Are you going to tell me where we are going?" Phebe looked at Ebenezer and saw that he was trying to hide his excitement. His eyes twinkled and he let a smile cross his face.

"Just you wait and see my dear. We have quite a ride ahead of us. I will tell you this, I talked to Brother Brigham about it and we have his blessing. Let's enjoy the ride. Have you ever seen such beautiful mountains covered with the brightest colors of autumn leaves? There is everything from dark green to dark red and the brightest of yellows." He flipped the reins on the rumps of the horses and they moved ahead at a faster pace.

Phebe decided she would give up and just enjoy the ride. She had never had much patience waiting for surprises. It was usually she who planned the them. They drove along a rough trail lined with sage brush and dry grasses. There was an occasional cluster of bushes or oak brush where small streams reached down from the foot hills. She pulled her shawl around her. The October sun was not strong enough to warm the cool fall air but it felt good on her face.

The mountains that lined the valley on the west were much lower than the high rocky peaks on the east and there seemed to be much less foliage on them. The western part of the valley looked barren.

About the time the sun started down its arc to the west they came to an area covered with more foliage and Ebenezer turned in an Easterly direction. The grasses were deep and there were large clusters of willows growing on the banks of the streams of water. The horses pulled the wagon through some marshes and finally to higher ground. Phebe looked up at the mountains. "This has to be the most beautiful view of those rocky peaks. What a pretty part of the valley."

"Happy Birthday, my dear. This is going to be your new home. I'll build you a house here and we'll invite our relatives and friends to come and live by us. Before long we will have cabins all over this little corner of heaven. I'll build a bowery for us to have parties in and a school where you can teach the children. Of course, we will build us a church for meetings and plant gardens." Ebenezer gave her a big kiss.

Phebe had forgotten about her birthday. She was fifty-two years old but she felt like a new bride. What a wonderful surprise. Yes, here she was going to have a long and happy life, just like Father Smith had promised her. Tears of joy were running down her cheeks. It was all too good to be true. She turned to Ebenezer and asked, "Can we please have an apple orchard too?"

They rode around on the high ground looking for possible places to build the house. They finally settled on a spot about a mile and a half west of the foothills and not too far from the sandy banks on the north. Some larger cottonwood trees lined the stream there providing shade and shelter. They chose a spot to spend the night and set up camp. Ebenezer guided the horses around so they could watch the moon come over the tops of the mountains from the back of the wagon. He unharnessed the team and let them graze in the tall grass and drink from the stream. Phebe unwrapped the lunch she had folded in a napkin and they sat on the tail gate of the wagon and ate their meal.

The light was fading and they went for a walk, picking their way through the brush. They found wild berry bushes and some late fall wild flowers. Circling back to the wagon under the tree Ebenezer stopped and took Phebe's hand, "We have something to do that is very important." He knelt down and she knelt beside him. They took turns praying and thanking God for all the blessings they had received. For his protection in their long travels, protecting their families, and finally, for bringing them to this special place.

The birds nesting in the tree above them sang their evening song. Phebe and Ebenezer made their bed in the wagon and watched the stars shimmering in the dark sky while they waited for the moon to rise over the mountains. Listening to the chirping of the crickets, they fell into a peaceful sleep. They were home.

Bett and Phebe sat knitting in the matching rockers Ebenezer had taken in trade for one of the gold nuggets. The wagon trains of people rushing to the gold fields were coming through almost every day in spite of the oncoming winter weather. Most of them were anxious to trade anything they had for food or bedding. They were encouraged to take the

Northern trail to avoid the high Sierras and become victims of the weather as the Donner party had. Some of them took the advice and others were determined to take the straightest trail to what they hoped would be their fortune.

The large cabin Ebenezer and William had rented in the city was almost full of furniture and even sported a big cast iron stove with a large oven and a water reservoir on the side. Great sacrifices had been made by the previous owner to get it across the plains and over the rocky mountains to Salt Lake City. When he heard the High Sierras were even steeper than the Rocky Mountain passes he was more than willing to trade it for some meat and flour to feed his family.

The cabin had four rooms and the full loft above was divided by the steep stairs that led to it from the great room below. The girls slept on one side of the loft and the boys on the other. Phebe and Ebenezer had a room as did William and Bett. Harriet and Oliver shared the other. A trundle bed pulled out for the little ones to sleep on. William had also purchased a cabin and rented a small farm about six miles south of the city in the Millcreek area where he could plant spring crops and set up a grist mill. Mary Ann and her little ones were living there. William shared his time between Bett and Mary Ann. Bett now had eight living children ages two to twenty-four and Mary Ann, the two-year-old and a new baby. He planned to plant crops on the lot in the city and other rented property in addition to the Mill Creek farm. Flour had risen to the price of seventy-five cents to a dollar a pound. He was sure they would have enough to be well fed through the first winter, but with this large family to support, his first concern was raising crops the following year to feed all of them.

Father Draper lived with Zemira and his family in a cabin close by. They shared the barns and corrals in the back and the well that produced a good supply of water. As happy as they were to be living in houses again, they knew it was temporary. Ebenezer had convinced them that once the water was controlled and diverted in the Willow Creek area they would all want to move south to what he and Phebe described as a little bit of heaven. The rented houses they lived in would be needed by those migrating to the valley the next summer.

The women spent their time spinning thread, weaving cloth and knitting. In addition to that they had to cook and wash for the big family and help with the animals while the men went south to work on the Willow Creek project.

Phebe also found time to get the children together for an hour or so each day to teach them. Some of them had been without any schooling for almost three years. The older boys were a little resentful as they struggled to remember the letters and put words together in sentences. They liked the arithmetic best so Phebe emphasized that and wrote problems in stories they would have to read to determine the answer. Rhoda helped her with the younger children just starting to learn letters and words. She was patient with them and Phebe realized Rhoda was about the same age as she had been when she first taught the little ones with Master John in Canada.

On this cold afternoon, Phebe and Bett had stoked the stove with wood, and had a nice warm fire crackling in the fireplace. They were alone in the great room and the knitting needles were flying fast as the two friends matched the rocking of the chairs to the cadence of the needles.

Phebe held out her knitting to examine it. Her mind had been wandering and she wondered if she might have dropped a stitch. Satisfied that she hadn't made a mistake she resumed her knitting. "Bett, this reminds me of the days in Nauvoo when we would knit together and share our thoughts. I've been wondering about something but haven't had time alone with you to discuss it. How have things gone with you and William practicing the Principle? What happened to Sister Weaver? And wasn't there another wife named Mary Ann Crosby?"

Bett put her knitting in her lap and stared into the fire for a time before responding. It was as if she was thinking back and reliving some of the last years. "Sister Weaver died in the fall of '46 after you left us. I loved her, she had been a good friend to us since we were back on the trail to Far West. William was put in charge of so many things at Council Bluff and Council Point. New converts were joining us almost daily and many of them were single women with no one to care for them. Mary Ann Crosby was a widow with small children so William was asked to marry her and take care of her and her family. We all seemed to work well together and I thought everything was just fine. She and William had a son, a strong little baby and William was very proud of him. One day she asked to meet with William and I. She told us she no longer could follow the Saints West and had decided to go back East to her relatives. We both urged her to reconsider but she would not be dissuaded. She insisted that she had not been treated fairly and that she would not let the new baby carry his father's name. They had named him Nephi and his mother now insisted he be known as Nephi Crosby. It almost broke William's heart. You know how hard he tries to do what is best for everyone. Some women aren't the sort to live the Principle and Sister Mary Ann seemed to be one of them.

Mary Ann Manhardt is another story. She came with a large group of converts, many of them being single women without any idea how they would survive on the prairies. The brethren explained the principle of polygamy to them and most of the leadership in the Priesthood offered to marry them and help them cross the plains to meet with the rest of the church. Mary Ann is a sweet girl and has helped me with my family as well as her own. I think William loves her very much and I am not jealous of that. He deserves every happiness and our love is strong enough to share. You remember the time we were called to practice the principle and my conversion to it. I have not wavered from that conviction. It is not always easy, but I think it is more challenging to the men than the women. William carries the burden of this large family and I know he will do everything in his power to provide for us. Your brother is a good man."

Phebe looked over at her sister-in-law with respect and new understanding. She had thought that the trials she and Ebenezer had endured were almost unsurmountable and she knew the degree of faith they had exercised to stay close to the Lord and carry out their commitment. Now she better understood how her brother and Bett had also been challenged to have the faith to follow the direction of the Prophet. "Bett, you are a good woman. Have I told you how happy I am to be close to you again. You have been a very stable influence in my life and I will always love you for that."

Ebenezer and the rest of the men were returning from Willow Creek. Dark clouds had filled the western sky and the cold wind that preceded them gave the men warning to head for the safety of home. They had chopped trees down on the foot hills and pulled them on drags behind the horses to the location of the cabin. Some of the swampy area had to be crisscrossed with willows for the horses to to cross without sinking into the mire. They had a good pile of logs, enough to get started on the cabin when the weather improved. Ebenezer was anxious to tell Phebe about their progress. He was grateful for the help of the men from the family. He was not surprised however. As long as he had known the Drapers he had seen them work together, shouldering each other's burdens. Phebe had told him the stories of the Uncles building the houses and cabins in Canada. This is what he hoped would happen in Willow Creek, everyone working together to build a town for all of them to enjoy.

Snow was falling by the time the men reached the edge of town. They hurried the horses along and by the time they had them in the barns and free of their saddles and bridles the snow was four or five inches deep. It was a quiet snow falling in large flakes landing on their hats and shoulders. Ebenezer looked up and large flakes caught his eyelashes. He opened his mouth and let the snow flakes float in. What he wouldn't have given for this snow to quench his thirst when they were in the barren dessert on the Mexican border.

They stomped the beautiful white snow from their boots and entered the warmth of the great room. The aroma of hot bread baking and a spicy stew greeted them. The wives were setting the table for the first group. This time it would be the men. The children could wait. They were in the loft listening to Rhoda read stories to them from a book of fables Phebe had found at the store.

Ebenezer gave Phebe a hug. "We cut enough wood today to start the cabin as soon as the weather cooperates. The way it's coming down now we may have to wait for spring. Have you looked out at that beautiful snow? I swear, even the snow falls reverently in Zion."

PART X

GOOD AND HAPPY DAYS
1850—1879
FORTY CHAPTER-SIX

Bedsteads, chairs, tables, pie safes and cupboards filled the wagon box. Another wagon was burdened down with the big black stove and sacks of flour, grain and sugar. Phebe and Rhoda were following in the buggy pulled by a small black mare Ebenezer had bought for Phebe. The back of the buggy was piled high with bedding and clothing. They were on their way to their new home in South Willow Creek.

Zemira and Norman were herding the cattle, sheep and extra horses along in back of the buggy. Gurnsey and John were already at the new cabin. They had spent most of the last few weeks there while the calves were being born and the sheep lambing.

There was an air of excitement with the family. They wanted to get the cabin furnished and the crops in before Lovina and William George came to the valley. Harriet and Oliver were staying in the city for a while. He was playing with the brass band and working in a new mercantile store.

Rhoda smoothed her skirt out and held to her bonnet as the buggy moved along at a steady pace, "Mother, it is so far out here. I wonder if any of my friends will come clear out here to see me. I may never have anyone to marry me if only our family lives out here in Willow Creek."

Phebe hadn't realized that her optimism in the move may not be that of all the family members. "You can always go in to the city and stay with Harriet but you may be surprised to find that your friends will love to come out to Willow Creek once they have been there. Are you a little worried about one special friend? I noticed you gave that Joseph Allred most of the dances at the last party even when the other young men were asking."

"Oh, Mother, he is quite special. I really don't know a lot about him and I may never learn any more. I may never see him again. Brother Brigham will probably send him on a mission to some far away island." A tear was forming in the corner of her eye and the expression on her face was one of complete sorrow and foreboding.

Phebe was amused at the sincerity and depth of sadness Rhoda felt but she did not allow herself to show her feelings. The few months she and Rhoda had been back together had been wonderful and she was well aware of the tender feelings of young women when they are feeling quite grown up but still not in full control of their lives. "Rhoda, my dear, be brave and try to look on the bright side. There will be so many new converts coming to the valley this summer and Brother Brigham will be sending other families to South Willow Creek. We may have many new neighbors in just a few months. Also, I noticed that young Mr. Allred had a fine looking riding horse that he rode away on after the dance. I'll just bet he will test the speed of his horse by riding him out here very soon. In the meantime, we will stay so busy getting the cabin ready the time will fly. Just you wait and see. Brother Knight has given Zemira permission to visit his daughter, Sally and Guernsey has Brother Lorenzo Young's permission to court his daughter, Harriet. I'm sure Norman has his eye on some pretty girl too so you will have plenty of social life."

With the help of all the family members the wagons were unloaded and the necessary furniture in place by night fall. Ebenezer had braced the wooden slab floor where the heavy iron stove would sit. The fireplace still needed some additional stones or brick and Phebe was hoping her brother Zemira would make a mantle for them similar to those he was carving and staining for some of the houses in the city. The logs had been caulked on the outside but there was still the inside to finish. She felt certain, that with Rhoda's help, they could finish the inside while the men were busy getting the farm started.

It was a fairly good sized cabin with two bedrooms, a great room downstairs and a full loft above that could be divided off. Phebe was glad that Ebenezer had built it large enough to accommodate more than the family. She was sure they would have many house guests as the Saints continued to move into the valley. Just the extra family members would fill it in no time. The men had talked about building another cabin and, perhaps, a bowery on the East of the house after the planting was finished, but realistically there was a lot to be done before building another cabin. A barn and other out buildings may have higher priority.

They had plotted out about one-hundred and seventy-five acres and though much of that would be grazing ground, it would take a lot of work to get the corn and wheat planted, let alone the garden. They brought dried peas and seed potatoes with them and Phebe had left word with Harriet and Oliver to keep an eye out for apple tree cuttings. She was determined to be diligent in getting an orchard started. Brother Brigham was continually sending word back to the wagon trains to bring greater varieties of plants and seeds to help this valley blossom as the rose. They needed to grow all the food possible to feed the thousands of immigrants that were joining the church and coming to Zion.

Amy and Bett had made them a basket of food for their first meal and the family sat around the table in their new cabin enjoying the fresh bread, sliced meats and the new milk Gurnsey had put in the creek to cool. To Phebe's delight, Bett had included a small sack of dried apples, a delicacy she had brought from Iowa. Phebe covered them with fresh spring water from the creek and heated them on the stove until they resembled fresh, sliced, cooked apples from the apple orchard in Canada. She added a little sugar and some cinnamon from her spice safe.

Ebenezer ask them each to kneel at their chair for family prayer. His voice broke as he thanked the Lord for all their blessings and asked for the food to be blessed so they might receive nourishment to complete the tasks ahead as they helped build their part of Zion.

While the family ate the last of the supper the discussion turned to their next assignments. Norman volunteered to start the plowing on the acres to the south. He brought out a sack he had secreted away during the move. "I brought this corn seed with me from Iowa and I can hardly wait to get it in the ground and see if it will sprout. The old wooden plow should turn this damp soil without too much trouble. I'll use Old Molly to pull the plow."

Pride showed in Ebenezer's eyes as he saw the ambition in his young son's face. "The rest of us will need to get that water directed in ditches over to where he plants the corn. I think I have enough shovels to go around. How about it boys?"

Gurnsey, John and Zemira nodded in agreement. Zemira spoke first, "Maybe we can make ditches like we saw those Indians use. What did Col. Cooke call it? 'Irrigation?'"

"Yes, I think your right. Remember how they had water running all over that hard parched earth in little troughs dug between the plants. With all the water we have here, I'm sure we can raise acres of crops. Maybe we can get some spring wheat in also. We'll need plenty of flour to feed this family and the rest of them that will be comin'." Ebenezer pushed his chair away from the table which was the signal that the meal was over and they were free to leave the table also.

Rhoda and Phebe had made beds in the loft earlier and now they gathered the tin plates from the table and the rest of the dishes and washed them in the hot water steaming on the stove. When they were put away in the cupboard Phebe lit the coal oil lamp on the table and sat down in one of the rockers. Ebenezer sat in the other. She opened the Book of Mormon she had carried with her from Nauvoo. Some of the pages were water stained and a little brittle. She started to read to the family from the beginning. 'I Nephi, being born of goodly parents.' I thought perhaps we should start from the beginning again. It is our desire that you wonderful young people will also feel that you have been born of goodly parents. We are so proud of all you have done while we were serving with the Battalion and since our arrival in the valley." She continued on reading from her favorite scripture, and concluded with the passage, "I, Nephi, will show unto you that the tender mercies of the Lord are over all those whom he hath chosen, because of their faith, to make them mighty even unto the power of deliverance." She closed the book.

"The Lord has delivered us from many who would have destroyed us without his protection. We are now safe and free to do his will, keep his commandments and build his Zion. Lets get a good nights rest so we can get an early start tomorrow." She stood up and placed the book on the lamp table.

"Amen." Ebenezer said solemnly.

The family went to the city for the 1850 October Conference. President Brigham Young and his counselors greeted them. They found seats on the benches and listened to the Brethren's talks of encouragement and reports of progress. They were encouraged to continue to live the principles of the gospel and continue to donate all they could in time or money to the immigration fund. Men were needed to go to Iowa to help with the migration and many saints in foreign countries were in need of help for passage money to come to Zion.

Those saints who had arrived since the last conference in April were welcomed and given information about new settlements and how to best use their talents to help establish Zion. President Young announced a new mission that was to be under the direction of Apostle George A. Smith. It was to be called the Iron Mission about three hundred miles south of the Salt lake Valley. "We have chosen men for their specific talents such as farmers, blacksmiths, shoemakers, stone masons, bricklayers, teachers, smelters, doctors, midwives and others to establish a community there and find a source of iron for the Mormon Colonies. The following men are called to go. Some, but not all of them, will be ask to take their wives and children to make it their permanent home."

Phebe and Ebenezer listened to the list of names. Some of them were friends from the Battalion and others they had known in Nauvoo. When Ebenezer's name was read it was a great surprise. They had just begun to get settled in South Willow Creek and winter was coming on. The crops had been harvested but there was still much to do.

Ebenezer looked at Phebe and saw that silent determination to do what she had to do. "I'll meet with Apostle Smith after the meeting to find out what is expected. We both agree that we do what we are ask to do. Brother Brigham promised us South Willow Creek and I have never known him to go back on his word."

Phebe relaxed, knowing Ebenezer would do what was best, but in the corner of her mind hoping that she would not have to move again.

When the meeting was over, those being called to new missions were directed to meet with their leaders for instruction. Ebenezer gave Phebe a peck on the cheek and a wink. "I'll meet you at Zemira's as soon as I can. Go on with the family but be sure to save me some of that cake you made for dinner."

The Drapers and Browns were all gathered at Zemira Draper's cabin. The October weather was warm enough for extra tables to be set outside with planks on saw horses. Church conferences were times for family reunions and parties. The boys and Rhoda brought their friends to dinner. Rhoda introduced Joseph Allred to the family. The color rose in her cheeks as Joseph boldly announced, "It is nice to meet my new family. Rhoda has agreed to marry me in January."

Phebe was surprised. Rhoda hadn't told her they had decided on a date. She began to click off a mental list of what needed to be done so Rhoda would have the necessities to set up housekeeping. There would be quilts to make and new dresses to be designed and made. She had dried and preserved enough of the fall crops to share with them. They would be slaughtering some beef and pork in a week or two and making soap.

Having been caught up in Rhoda's announcement she had forgotten about Ebenezer's new assignment. If she was to go with Ebenezer to the Iron mission she would have to leave Rhoda again at a time when she needed her. Remembering Ebenezer's request, she walked to the table laden with pies, cakes and cookies. She cut a healthy slice and wrapped it in a napkin. Slipping away she started to walk back to the bowery where the meeting was being held.

Ebenezer met her on the way. Another time he might have teased her and withheld the information he knew she was waiting for but the serious expression on her face let him know it was not the time to make fun. "My assignment appears to be of a temporary nature. I am not required to take my family. I am to travel with a group of men on horseback. We are to help determine a location for the community and help them cut timber and build cabins. There is always concern about Indians so we are also expected to take our rifles with us to help protect the settlers. Some of our friends from the Battalion have been telling exaggerated stories of my sharpshooting abilities. I guess that is one reason they called me. John D. Lee is going also and is appointed to be the recorder for the group. It was good to see him again. I hadn't seen him since we were in Santa Fe.

I wish you were going with me but you have done enough

pioneering. I need you to stay on here and keep the work going at South Willow Creek. They are talking of appointing postmasters at each of the small settlements. If they do that I will need you to take care of the mail. My reading and writing skills aren't good enough for that. As soon as the other families get settled out there you'll be wanting to start up a school for the children.

If I can keep the men moving on the logging and building I may be back in just a few months. I hope it won't be long. There is so much I want to do on our own place."

Phebe felt a wave of relief. Since her long ride back from California on Jenny she had not looked forward to another trip on a mule or in a wagon. In fact, she always took a pillow with her to sit on in meetings or when they rode in the buggy or wagon to town. "I guess I'm getting old but I am quite relieved that I am not called to go. Rhoda and Joseph just announced to the family that they are getting married in January so I have a lot to do to help her get ready.

Ebenezer, I hope you won't be gone too long. I'll miss you and I hate to think of the first winter in the cabin without you. The boys will take care of me but it just isn't the same." She put her hand in her pocket and pulled out the cake wrapped in the napkin and passed it to him.

"I guess it won't ruin my appetite for dinner if I eat cake first." He put one arm around Phebe and ate the cake with his other hand as they walked back to Zemira's cabin.

The family, eager to hear about the new assignment, stopped in the middle of their dinner and looked to Ebenezer for news of the mission. "It looks like I'll be heading south on horseback in early December to help them get settled on the Iron Mission. They needed a good rifleman to protect them from the Indians and a strong back to help cut timber and build cabins. If I work hard and help make friends with the Indians I may be home in a few months. Now, this doesn't mean that we stop our plans for South Willow Creek. I hope you are all still planning on making your homes out there. There is plenty of land and water for all of us. Phebe will be staying here to keep an eye on things. If you have any questions while I am gone, just ask her. She may need a little help from time to time so I'd appreciate you watching out for her." He sat at the table and Phebe brought him a plate filled with hot food and fresh bread.

She poured him a large glass of milk. "You'd better eat hearty and keep your strength up if you are going to get all that done." She stood with her hand on his shoulder as he ate his meal. It was a sign to the family that she supported him in his call and would make the best of things while he was gone.

Father Draper raised his glass, "A toast to Ebenezer and Phebe. They show us the way and we follow. You can be assured that we will all come to live by you at South Willow Creek. The Browns and Drapers stick together and care for one another. Ebenezer, by the time you get back, you won't know the place."

The rest of the family joined in the toast, "Here, Here!!" they shouted together.

December came all too soon. The meat was salted and/or dried and stored in the cellar. The lye soap had been made, some with tallow from the mutton for hand soap and some with suit from the beef for laundry. It had been cut in bars and stored in tins. Phebe and Rhoda had a quilt on the frames Ebenezer had fashioned for her. When they weren't busy with the quilt or household chores they were knitting or crocheting collars and cuffs for dresses and the edging on table clothes and towels.

Phebe had been so busy she had not had time to dread Ebenezer's departure but as the first of December rolled around and the days got shorter and colder her spirits dropped. She had to talk to herself and pray for courage to keep her spirits up. If this was to be a part of her long and happy life, she would have to work harder at being happy. She baked Ebenezer's favorite pound cake and cooked some pork chops with some sage dressing. She skimmed some cream from the top of the pans of milk, and poured it over the fluffy mashed potatoes and made a white pork gravy. Rhoda put a jar of wild choke cherry jelly on the table with the fresh hot biscuits.

Ebenezer and the boys stacked the wood they had chopped for the stove by the door and came in to enjoy the meal. They washed up at the wash stand and dried their hands. The four boys were as big as their father and they all had healthy appetites. Phebe and Rhoda served the meal and then joined them at the table. Ebenezer called on Zemira to bless the food.

"I'm going to miss your good cooking, Phebe. But while I'm out there pioneering I'll think of you back here in this comfortable cabin with a warm fire and plenty to eat. That will warm my heart." He smiled at each of them. "Before I go I want to give each of you a blessing. Lets do it after supper. They may come for me tomorrow."

Once again, Phebe listened to Ebenezer talk to the Lord. She was always impressed that this man who fretted because he couldn't read or write well could communicate so beautifully with his Father in Heaven. His prayers brought peace of mind to each family member. The boys were visibly touched by their father's concern for them and Rhoda wept openly. She realized that Ebenezer, who was the only father she had ever known, would not be here for her wedding.

Brother Isaac Goodale came by on his horse early the next morning. The other men on horseback were waiting on the main trail south for Ebenezer to join them. His bedroll and pack had been ready for days. Phebe quickly packed the perishables in the lunch sack. He kissed her good-by and mounted his best horse, saddled and laden down with the few possessions he was taking. Norman passed him his riffle and he put it in the scabbard at the side of the saddle. He touched his lips as if to throw them all a kiss and rode away to meet the rest of the missionaries.

Black clouds were forming in the west and starting to cluster in the corner canyon to the south east. A winter storm would set in before night fall. Phebe hoped the travelers would get ahead of it. That night she had a hard time sleeping in their bed alone. The wind was whistling around the cabin and even the canvas covers over the isinglass windows didn't keep the chill from creeping in. It was going to be a long hard winter.

CHAPTER FORTY-SEVEN

Phebe sat in the shade of the bowery, enjoying the view of the beautiful mountains to the east and resting for a few minutes before starting the evening meal. It had been over a year since they moved into the cabin in South Willow Creek and she checked off in her mind, all the things that had been accomplished.

Ebenezer had filled his mission and returned home in the early spring. The boys had kept the wood box full and carried water in for her all winter. They had taken care of the cattle and even added to the herd. Her brothers had come out often to make sure she had what she needed. Her brother, Zemira, had finished the fireplace with a carved wood mantle and rocks of river stones polished by the mountain stream water. They had kept their word to Ebenezer. He was amazed at all that had been done.

The cabin was finished on the inside and whitewashed. She had made curtains for the windows and the isinglass would soon be replaced with real glass that was being brought in from the east. The farm had given them a good yield last fall and promised an even better harvest this year. Tender new leaves were developing on the apple, peach and apricot cuttings in the new orchard. Seed saved from last year had provided them with plenty to plant extra acres of wheat and corn. She had a nice garden in the back with potato plants already two inches high. The rows of carrots and onions were showing strong, green growth and the sweet corn was breaking through the ground.

Rhoda had married Joseph Anderson Allred in January and they were starting to build a cabin close by. Rhoda was a pretty bride. Locks of her auburn hair circled her face in a natural curl. Though her skin was fair she did not freckle. She was slim and lithe, almost as tall as her mother.

Lovina and William George and their families had arrived late in the fall of 1850 so most of the family was here for the wedding festivities except for Ebenezer who was sorely missed. Lovina brought a special gift to the wedding party but it was not for the bride, it was for her mother. Phebe opened the package to find her Bible Grandfather Draper had given her for her wedding. Lovina had protected it from the elements in all the travel. Phebe held it in both of her hands. Tears came to her eyes as she opened it to the family page listing births and deaths in her own handwriting and the folded sheet of paper on which was written the blessing given to her by the Prophet's father in Kirtland.

Lovina's arrival had been bitter sweet. Her new husband, Thomas Jefferson Brandon, was not as attentive as Henry had been and Phebe struggled with her concern for Lovina. Soon after they arrived she and Thomas had announced that they would be settling in Provo. Lovina's oldest son, William, was a strong sixteen-year-old and his stepfather relied on him to help with the family. Ester Ann was twelve-years-old, Fannie Lucinda, nine and Henry Brigham was five. After Lovina had married Thomas Brandon in Iowa, they had Thomas Jefferson Jr. who was now three, and George Washington who was two. She had lost two of her children from her first family at birth so they had made the trek from Iowa to the Salt Lake Valley with six children. This past April, Lovina had given birth to a little girl in Provo and they had named her Phebe Lovina. It was her ninth child.

Phebe and Bett had gone to Provo to care for Lovina and Bett had grave concerns for this niece that had been like her own daughter. Each pregnancy seemed to take a greater toll on Lovina's strength. Phebe convinced Thomas that they should take Lovina and the children home with them until she was stronger. He finally conceded if they would leave her son, William Munro to help him.

Phebe was delighted to have Lovina and her family with her. A new baby to care for and little ones to teach and play with. Ester Ann was a big help to her grandmother. The children blossomed as they ate the good farm food, had plenty of milk to drink and basked in the love of the extended family.

"A penny for your thoughts," Lovina came out of the house and sat by her mother in the bowery. "The baby is asleep and I must have dosed off too. It will be time to get supper ready soon. Where are the children?"

"Ester Ann took them to see the baby lambs. They will be back soon. Did you have enough milk to satisfy the baby?" Phebe's concern showed though she tried to conceal it.

"I must have because she went to sleep. Oh, Mother, I think she will look just like you. We chose the right name for her." Lovina changed the subject to avoid causing her mother any more concern. She too worried about giving the baby enough nourishment. She was glad Aunt Bett and Uncle William had moved out to South Willow Creek. Maybe Aunt Bett would have something to help her. She would ask her tomorrow after church. They would all be getting together for Sunday dinner here in the Bowery.

"How does Aunt Bett get along with Uncle William's other wife? Mary Ann seems like a very nice person but she is so young." Lovina had missed the chats with her mother and it was good to sit here in the shade and visit.

"Aunt Bett gets along with everyone and she likes Mary Ann very much. She is totally committed to living the Principle. Only unselfish and dedicated women can make a success of it. I think they are all happier now they are out here with their family together and I am so glad to have William and Bett close by. Zemira and Amy are starting their cabin next week so they will move out with their children and bring father with them. It will almost be like it was when we were all together in Nauvoo." Phebe smiled as she remembered the sales talk Ebenezer had given her brothers to move out and share this part of the valley with them.

"Gurnsey and Zemira are hauling logs for cabins also. They haven't made official announcements but they both have permission to marry the girls they have been courting. Don't let on you know until they tell but I think it will be in the winter some time. Harriet and Oliver want to come out also. It should be a great Christmas this year." Phebe, like most mothers, was happiest when all her family was together.

"William George is trying to persuade Mary Ellen to stay here in the west with him but she seems quite determined to go back East to her parents and take their baby daughter with her. He ask Ebenezer and I if he could bring the boys with him and come out to live with us. Ebenezer assured him he was welcome but encouraged him to try to convince Mary Ellen to stay." A cloud crossed her face as she recalled that sad conversation. William George, her happiest child, had lost the lilt to his voice and the mischievous twinkle in his eye. His first love had died shortly after they married in Iowa. Now his second marriage seemed to be headed for disaster. It was hard to see him so down hearted.

"Life isn't always easy, Mother. We all have to face the hard times and learn from them in our own way. You know that as well as anyone. You have tried so hard to make our lives happy but we each have to face our own problems." Lovina stood and moved to her mother, putting her arm around her shoulders. "It is so good to know you are here to help us and it looks like we will keep you plenty busy."

Little Phebe Lovina cried out to them and they both stood to go to her. Her colic cry was familiar to them. They had taken turns sleeping since she was born. She seemed to be in so much pain and they tried all the remedies they knew to soothe her. Phebe put a pinch of soda in a spoon of water and let it drip in the baby's mouth. She rubbed the little stomach with warm castor oil until the spasms seemed to stop. Bett had suggested that Lovina chew some ginseng root hoping that would help but it just appeared that baby Phebe had a persistent problem. Phebe held her namesake over her shoulder and patted her back. The baby let out a loud burp which seemed to relieve the pain. She snuggled into her grandmother and was soon asleep.

Phebe put her back in the cradle and started supper. The children's voices could be heard as they neared the cabin. They were shouting, laughing and imitating the antics of the baby lambs. Lovina jumped up and stepped outside to remind them to be quiet so the baby could sleep. "Why don't you wash up out here. Looks like you have been playing mud pies. What dirty faces!" She dipped some water out of the water barrel and put it on the washstand for them. "I'll get a towel for you. Ester Ann, help them get clean."

Ester Ann lined them up in order; youngest to oldest, and supervised the face and hand washing. Fanny was at the end of the row and she informed her older sister that she could take care of washing her own face and not only that but she was going to get clean water. Lovina chuckled to herself, recognizing that her Fanny had some of the same traits as her Aunt Fanny. Ester Ann and Fanny were inseparable but Fanny was firm in her independent spirit. Ester Ann was mature for her age and more "easy going". She washed up after Fanny and they kept the children on the bowery until they were called to supper.

"Grandfather, something bothered me today. When we were watching the lambs one of the mother sheep went to the pond to drink and walked into the water. She seemed to sink right into the pond and she didn't come out. It wasn't like she was trying to swim out. I wanted to go in after her but I didn't dare leave the children." Ester Ann's brow was furrowed with concern.

"You were wise, my girl, not to go after her. I think there is quick sand in one end of that pond. It was best to stay with the children. I'm glad it was one of the sheep and not one of you children. We need to get that fenced off before we have a tragedy. Boys, lets get it done before we go to bed. Tomorrow is the sabbath and we can rest. We'll have to use some of the logs we were saving for cabins but it is worth it if we save a life." Ebenezer pulled one of Lovina's little ones on his knee. "These blessed children are too valuable to be lost to the devil, quick sand."

The men finished their supper and headed for the pond with saws and shovels.

"Mother, what about that sheep's lamb? Won't it be hungry?" Little Henry looked at Lovina, his eyebrows knit together in concern.

"I'm sure that lamb will need someone to feed it. If the girls will help their grandmother with the supper dishes, you and I will go and find the lamb. We will bring it back to the house and find a way to give it some milk. Maybe Grandfather will let it be your special lamb, because you cared enough to worry about it." Lovina threw her shawl around her shoulders and put a sweater on Henry. The early summer evening was cool as the breezes drifted down from the foot hills.

Phebe was reminded of the story in the Bible having to do with the lost lamb.

Lovina and Henry would find the hungry lamb wandering out there somewhere crying for its mother. The joy of having her grandchildren with her again was almost overwhelming. They were such precious spirits and the Lord had blessed them to survive the hard trek across the prairies. He must have something important in mind for them. She put her arms around the girls, "Come on, my dears. Lets get the dishes done up before they get back. I'll braid your hair for you like I did the little Indian girls on the desert. But I haven't told you that story yet. I'll tell you while we wash the dishes. I'll also show you the little reed basket they wove for me. I have so many stories to tell you."

Phebe opened the mail pouch and distributed the few let-ters into the small boxes hanging on the wall. Ebenezer had been given the postmaster position and she handled the mail as it arrived. There were now 20 families consisting of 222 peo-ple living in the organized precinct of Little Willow Creek on the official records.

She read off the names she had written and attached to the boxes in alphabetical order: Andrew Jackson Allen, George Bankhead, Ebenezer Brown, Joseph Gurnsey Brown, Andrew Burnham, Henry Day, James Downs, William Draper, Zemira Draper, John Enniss with brother-in-laws (John Boulter and William Boulter), Perry Fitzgerald, Harvey M. Rawlins, Joseph Sharp Rawlins, Robert Shipley, Absolom Smith, John S. Smith, Jacob Terry, Joel E. Terry, William R. Terry and John P. Wright. She knew each member and the story they had to tell of their conversion to the church and the sacrifices they had made to come to Zion.

She and Ebenezer had welcomed each family and helped them get settled. Ebenezer was known for his charity. It was not unusual for him to give a milk cow, a pig or horse to a new family to help them get settled. His herds had grown and he willingly shared his blessings. Phebe was on hand to help Bett when new babies arrived and had started teaching school in her cabin as soon as there were five or six children to teach.

William Terry had been a teacher in the East so he and Phebe organized a school. He had brought seeds of apples and peaches from Rhode Island, so like Phebe, he also planted orchards as well as ideas and learning. He taught the older children and she the younger ones as she had in Canada. The men built a small adobe school for them. Brother Terry had brought some books with him and some of the other settlers contributed books to the school.

They also used the building for church meetings. It wasn't finished. For now it had only willows for a roof and cloth at the windows, but they could hold meetings in it. Phebe hurried with the mail so she could get over to the church to help the women sweep and clean. They had received word that some of the church leaders would be at the meeting tomorrow to organize them into a branch of the church. It was September of 1852 and already the frost had nipped the trees on the mountains. As she walked from her house to the new adobe building, she looked up at the beautiful sight of the yellow Quaking Aspen trees nestled between the dark green pines. "They will have to hurry with the roof and windows of the school to get it closed in before winter," she thought.

The rough pine benches were filled by 10:00 a.m. the following morning as Brother Smith rose to call the meeting to order. William and Ebenezer had taken turns conducting the flock because of the priesthood they held and their past experiences but today a delegated authority from the church had been sent to organize the Branch. He called on Father Draper to open the meeting and Sister Fitzgerald to lead them in a Hymn. The Sacrament was blessed and passed by priesthood holders and then Brother Smith proceeded with the organization. "We have called Brother William Draper to be the Presiding Elder of the Branch, Ebenezer Brown to be his First Counselor and Zemira Draper to be his Second Counselor. Brother Draper has held the office of Bishop for many years and has acted in that capacity in several locations. He studied with the Prophet in Kirtland Ohio and has been a stalwart in the church. His counselors also have had years of experience in the church and are found worthy to hold the offices for which they have been recommended. All those in favor raise your right hand. Thank you. If there are any opposed raise your hand." All attending had voted in favor of the three brethren.

Phebe smiled. The three friends were officially working together again. She remembered the day the Browns had met them on the trail to Far West. It had been a long friendship. They complimented each other in various ways. William was the born leader with a special charisma to charm all he met.

Ebenezer was an organizer of work, always willing to carry his load and a little bit more. Somehow, he always seemed to have extra resources to help facilitate the task. His good nature carried over into the work. People enjoyed putting their shoulder to the wheel with Ebenezer. Zemira was more quite but was always on hand to help finish the task. His adoration for his older brother and brother-in-law was evident. They were a good team with the skills to pull together for a common goal.

Within the week the community had met to make another decision. South Willow Creek was a long, awkward name and they wanted to choose a name for their new town, post office, school and church. They wanted identity and a committee was organized to make some recommendations. Brother Day and Brother Terry met with the newly appointed civil officers to officially name the town. A few days later they called another meeting to present their findings. Brother Terry addressed the group. "Our first recommendation was to name our town Brownville after Ebenezer but the authorities said they had already received an application for that name. We talked it over and came up with our second choice. We propose that we name the town Draperville after our first Bishop, William Draper."

Everyone agreed with the choice and complimented the committee on the good work they had done. Now they had an identity. Phebe went home and made a sign to put over the bank of mail boxes. It read, "DRAPERVILLE POST OFFICE"

Ebenezer came in a little later. He had stayed to a meeting with the Branch Presidency. Some of the brethren from the city had come out to meet with them on some church business. Phebe didn't ask about it knowing it was not proper for her to pry into the business of the Branch. "You seem a little quiet. Are you disappointed about them not naming the town Brownville?"

"No, no, that is the least of my worries." He sat down in one of the rocking chairs. "I have something very serious to discuss with you."

All kinds of possibilities ran through her mind but Phebe was not at all prepared for what came next.

"We have been called to live the Principle. Here I am in my fifties and I am ask to start a new family." Tears rolled down his cheeks and he put his face in his hands. "The only way out for me is for you to not give your permission. I just want us to have our long and happy life here together building our new town. I understand the Principle and believe in it but I have always felt that only the most worthy would be called to practice it. My reluctance is evidence enough that I am not worthy."

Phebe's face was ashen and she felt her strength slip away. She dropped into the other rocker. "It is Ann's permission that you need. You are sealed to her for eternity, not to me. I can accept any call you have and support you. I too believe in the doctrine of Polygamy as it has been revealed to the brethren. As for your worthiness, there is no question in my mind that you are worthy. You are a man who is compassionate, fair and moral. You are the kind of man the Lord needs to help fill His kingdom on earth." She hesitated organizing her thoughts. "I won't deny it is a shock to me but we have been so blessed, the Lord must need a little more in return." She stood and went to him putting her hand on his shoulder. "Why don't we pray about it and discuss it again in the morning."

"Oh, Phebe. What would I do without your strength?" They walked together to their bed and knelt on either side in private supplication to the Lord.

Phebe slipped out of bed early the next morning, made a fire in the stove and put some water on to heat. The cracked wheat cereal was soon cooking and she walked out to the cooler on the north of the house to get a pan of milk from last nights milking. The fresh cream that had risen to the surface rippled as she put the pan on the table. The cream was soon skimmed into a small jar and the milk poured into a pitcher. She put the sugar bowl and spoon holder on the table and turned to the pie safe for a loaf of bread to slice for toast.

Ebenezer walked out of their room into the great room. His eyes were swollen and he obviously had not slept well. He sat at the table, took Phebe's hand and pulled her into the chair beside him. "Ann came to me in a dream last night. I haven't dreamed of her for so long, but she came to me last night. She was beautiful and she smiled at me. I felt that great love I had for her and all she said was, 'Yes, and Phebe too.' I reached out for her but she was gone. All night I kept going over in my mind what she had said. 'Yes, and Phebe too.'"

Ebenezer took both of Phebe's hand in his, "We haven't talked about this since our days in Nauvoo when we received our sacred endowment and I was sealed to Ann. Phebe, would you consider being sealed to me as my second wife in the endowment house? If I take additional wives, as I have been called to do, I would have to have them sealed to me. You have never said if you want to be sealed to your first husband, George. It is your decision but I would like you to be my wife for eternity and I know that is what Ann wants also." They both stood and he took her in his arms and kissed her. "No one has ever had a better wife. I love you, Phebe Brown."

Chapter Forty-eight

It had been a warm spring and the streams feeding into Draperville were teaming with water. All the men and boys had worked to control the water as it rushed down the stream beds from Corner Canyon, Bear Canyon, Rocky Mouth and Dry Creek. The water falls in Cherry Canyon were spewing over the rocks and sending rivulets of water down the sloping hills between Corner Canyon and Bear Canyon.

It was the second week of April and the 1853 General Conference had adjourned for six months. Phebe and Ebenezer rode home in the buggy pulled by Phebe's black mare. The rest of the family had stayed on for some of the parties that followed the conference. Ebenezer wanted to get back and make sure the dams and ditches were holding the water from flooding out the crops planted on the lower fields.

"Phebe, we haven't talked again about me taking a second wife. The brethren were very firm in the Priesthood session of Conference that those who had been called to live the Principle should accept that call and do all they could to fulfill it. I just don't know what to do. We don't have any single women in Draperville or even any young girls that the boys haven't spoken for. Anyway, what young woman would want me when she could have one of the handsome young men in town?" He seemed a little relieved that he hadn't found someone available to marry.

"I guess, if the Lord needs you to marry someone, He will make sure to make her available. Don't worry about it, Ebenezer. If it is to happen, it will happen." She moved over closer to him on the buggy seat. "I've been thinking about our discussion about the sealing question. With your permission, I would like to discuss it with my children. At least those who are here. Perhaps we could go to Provo and visit Lovina and

Thomas. I haven't seen her since Lydia Alice was born last spring and little Phebe Lovina is already two years old."

"As soon as the spring run off is over we will take a trip to Provo. It is quite a large settlement now. I saw some of the boys from the Battalion who live there now at Conference. They invited us down to have a party with them. Seems like a group of them are getting together in a couple of weeks. We are all invited to bring our families." The twinkle was back in Ebenezer's eye as he thought about being with his old friends again. "Oh, I also heard that Port Rockwell is going to settle out by the point of the mountain. Down close to the 'Hot Pots'. He's still looking for mail contracts with the government." Conference was definitely the time to get caught up with the news.

The traverse mountains on the south of Draperville formed a gradual slope down to the Jordan River. Close by were some natural springs of warm water where some of the young men went to swim. Tales of near drowning had surfaced as the boys bragged about the outings there. Some declared that no one had touched bottom and only good swimmers could survive there. Phebe's fear of drowning made her shudder when she heard their tales and she encouraged their boys not to go swimming there.

"That would be nice to have Porter close by. He certainly came to our aid on the trail from California. The boys tell stories of all kinds of dangerous things he has done to protect Brother Brigham. I guess we are not completely safe from those who would harm the church and our leaders, even here in the valley."

The dams and ditches held. In a few days the streams had subsided and the Browns made plans to spend a few days in Provo. Phebe had been making new dresses for her granddaughters. Ester Ann and Fanny were almost young ladies now. She fashioned theirs out of bright yellow and lavender cotton with a bodice, full skirt and bonnet to match. For the little girls she made white lawn dresses with lots of tucks and bloomers to match. She edged the bottom with some tatted lace and put a blue ribbon on one and a pink ribbon of the other. Now that Sister Fitzgerald had opened her store it was much easier to get fabric, buttons and ribbon.

Phebe packed the new dresses along with her own things in a small valise she had purchased in the city. She packed a lunch for them and carefully folded the high collared white shirt she had starched and ironed for Ebenezer. His best suit was neatly packed in a suit bag she had made to protect it from the dust on the trail south.

William George and his boys were going with them as were Zemira and his new wife Sally. They would take two buggies. Rhoda and Joseph had moved north to Davis county, Norman and John had agreed to stay and take care of the animals and Guensey was busy finishing his cabin. His wife, Harriet was expecting a baby and didn't want to travel.

It was a beautiful spring day as the little caravan traveled the hard packed dirt road south. The road followed the foothills of the east mountains and as they looked west they could see the large expanse of the Great Utah Lake. The water from that lake flowed north to the Great Salt Lake in the Jordan River named after the river in the New Testament. To the East a high sharp ridge cut the skyline. The Indians called it Timpanogos, meaning sleeping maiden, as it appeared to be the shape of a young woman lying on a bed. It was still covered with snow as if white sheets blanketed the bed.

Phebe sat on her pillow and held her bonnet with her left hand to shield her face from the morning sun. They stopped for lunch in a grove of trees by a stream of fresh mountain water, let the animals rest, drink and graze for an hour or so and then continued their journey. It was almost dark when they crossed the Provo River. The settlers had fashioned a bridge over the river that flowed into the Utah Lake. Finally they saw the first cabins of the Provo Settlement and soon were at Lovina's door.

The children were so excited to see their grandparents and aunts and uncles. Phebe opened her valise and gave the girls their dresses. Ebenezer took four baby lambs from the crate in the back of the buggy and gave to the boys. Lovina looked tired and the grey streaks in her hair belied her age of thirty-seven. The delicate contour of her face and large brown eyes conveyed a fading beauty that was once the talk of the town in Loughborough, Canada. She had prepared a fine supper for the travelers and after the meal William George picked up the banjo he had with him and started to strum some of the old favorite songs. Lovina's clear soprano voice was soon filling the room with the lyrics and melody. A light came back into her eyes and soon the family was singing together. Ebenezer took Phebe by the hand and they surprised the children by dancing a Polka.

The Battalion party was well attended. Whole families came with there lunch boxes and quilts to picnic on the grassy slope by the river. The little children ran and played while the men clustered in groups reciting again the stories of there experiences in the Battalion. The women sat on quilts in a group. They ask Phebe to tell them her side of the story, intimating that the men may exaggerate a bit.

Phebe described her fright when the wild bulls attacked, her near drowning and the days of thirst when only a pebble in her mouth helped defray the thirst. She then looked around at the women knowing all of them had sacrificed and suffered in similar ways to reach the valley. "I would like to know about you and your experiences. I didn't mean to take up all the time. Lets take turns. How did you get to the valley and who were your loved ones in the Battalion?"

One by one they talked about husbands, fathers or brothers who had left them on the prairie to go with the soldiers. One pretty young girl explained that her brother and brother-in-law had been with the company. "My brother is David Pulsipher and my sister's husband is Sgt. Daniel Tyler. It was hard for us to have them leave us as we had no transportation to cross the plains. My father died in Far West. Our home was burned before our eyes in Nauvoo. Mother made an agreement with one of the men as we left Council Bluffs to hitch our cow with another animal to pull his wagon so our belongings could be carried. When mother became ill and couldn't walk he was vexed. He loosened the cow from the team and left mother and I, the cow and our belongings by the side of the trail. We waited there until a kind soul came along, tied the cow to the back of his wagon and let mother ride until she was well enough to walk. I walked all the way ."

Phebe was impressed with this young woman who had also been a survivor of Far West, Nauvoo and the trail west. She judged her to be about eighteen. It was hard to tell. The hardships of the trail often took a toll on the traveler. Some of the young children seemed old for their age. She remembered the sorrow she had seen in the eyes of children when they were driven out of Far West after seeing the carnage wrought upon them and their loved ones there.

Phebe turned as she felt a hand on her shoulder. Ebenezer was standing behind her and had obviously been listening to Samantha Pulsipher's story. He motioned to Phebe, "Will you come with me. I need to discuss something with you." She stood and followed him away from the party and up stream until they were in a secluded spot.

He took her hand, "I think I have my answer. I have a very strong impression that the young lady we were listening to is to be my wife. I had this premonition to leave the men and walk over to you. Standing there, listening to her story, I felt a strong desire to take care of her. How do you feel Phebe? You are the one who is the most sensitive and discerning of people."

"I felt great compassion for her also and a depth of her commitment and willingness to do what needed to be done for the building up of Zion. Perhaps we should pray for a confirmation of our feelings." They knelt together there by the river and prayed, knowing that this was a decision not to be entered into lightly.

As they finished their prayer they looked into each others eyes and simultaneously nodded the affirmation they both felt.

"Samantha is a sister to David Pulsipher and her brother-in-law is Sgt. Daniel Tyler. You remember him. He was the one who kept the journal of our trek so religiously. Why don't you discuss it with them and see how they feel before you approach her. If it is the proper thing to do, they will have the same feeling also." Phebe felt the gravity of the situation and she walked back to the group of women in a somber mood.

That evening after supper, Ebenezer excused himself to meet with some of his Battalion friends. When the children were in bed, Phebe asked Lovina, William George and Zemira to take a little walk with her. They walked away from the house and down a lane to the river. Phebe watched the water flowing briskly down the river and thought how much it was like life; always moving on and changing. She turned to her children who were now adults with their own families and responsibilities. She cleared her throat and hoped she could frame the question in her mind so that it would be received as she meant it to be. "I have something I need to discuss with you. Ebenezer has been called to live the Principle and before he takes another wife he wants me to be sealed to him for eternity in the new Endowment House in Salt Lake City." She paused for a minute to give them time to ponder the conse-quences. "What do you think I should do?"

Lovina was the first to answer, "What ever you think is best, I can accept. Ebenezer has always been very good to you and all of us. I remember how adamant Father was against the church even when he had the same opportunities to learn the beautiful principles of the gospel. Your faith is so strong and you are so willing to do the Lord's will I feel impressed to leave the decision to you."

William George put his arm around his mother, "We want for you what you want. As Lovina said, Ebenezer has always been good to us and treated us like his own."

Zemira nodded in agreement. "He has been a good father to me. He stood up for me in the Battalion. You were promised a 'man of God' to help you raise your children. Even though we are all adults now I am sure the Lord still wants Ebenezer to take care of you. If that is for eternity, so be it. We all love you and want your happiness." He threw a stick in the dark river and they watched as it floated away from them.

Phebe looked at her children, "Thank you. I hoped you would feel that way. I'll tell Ebenezer when he gets back." They walked back to the house together.

Phebe was in bed when Ebenezer returned. She wasn't asleep. He sat on the side of the bed and pulled off his boots. "Samantha is only sixteen-years-old. I thought she was older than that. She seemed much older when she was talking about their trials on the plains. I asked David and Daniel about me asking her to be my polygamist wife and they gave me their permission. I stopped by her mother's cabin to get her permission and Samantha was there. We talked about it together and from what I could tell, she and her mother knew that she would be asked to be a polygamist wife. They had been praying that she would be asked by a good man who would be kind to her. I told them to pray about it and I would stop by in the morning for an answer."

He slipped off his clothes and climbed into the makeshift bed by Phebe. "If they say yes, I guess that will be the answer. I hope I'm up to this. Starting all over with a young wife and family won't by easy."

Phebe rubbed the tight muscles on the back of his neck . "I'll help you all I can. I have news for you also. My children have encouraged me to be sealed to you for eternity. If the offer is still open, I accept. We can still help build Zion together."

Ebenezer turned and kissed her, "Thank you Phebe. I can't do it without you." They lay quietly trying to sleep, but both lost in thought of what the future held for them.

A spring rain had just washed the valley clean and the sun shining from the west reflected through remaining moisture on the mountains to the east creating a double rainbow that reached from Little Cottonwood Canyon to Corner Canyon. It seemed to be an omen to Ebenezer as he drove the buggy south toward Draper. The day, May 19, 1853, had been one of mixed emotions. Phebe and Samantha had been sealed to him in the Endowment House. The promises and covenants he had made in that Holy edifice lay heavy on his mind. He missed Phebe and wished she was with them.

Phebe had insisted on staying in the city with Harriet allowing Ebenezer and Samantha to have time alone. She had prepared the other bedroom in the cabin for them. New curtains were at the window and a fresh straw tick on the bed with new sheets she had made. A quilt made from the double wedding ring pattern covered the bed and a bolster pillow was adorned with a white muslin case decorated with twelve inches of tatted lace. Samantha would bring her own things but Phebe wanted her to know they had made preparation for her entrance into the family. The pie safe was full of bread and pastries and Bett had agreed to have a hot dinner in the oven for them when they returned from the city.

Phebe had waved goodbye as they pulled away in the buggy. If her smile seemed a little forced it was the best she could do. She had just been sealed to a man she loved with all her heart and she had sent him off with a new, young wife. She had committed to give all that she had for the good of the church but this was very hard. Working hard or giving money or food or clothes was easy compared to this. She remembered her mother's statement, "People are more important than things." Now she understood the meaning of that in the deepest sense possible.

Time was wasting and she would not allow herself to wallow in self pity one more minute. She quickly checked off a mental list of the numerous blessings she had received and pulled her shopping list from her handbag. She had only about two hours to shop before the Mercantile closed and then Harriet and Oliver would be expecting her for supper.

She bought some hore-hound candy for the children at the candy counter and then went to look at the shoes. Some black high button shoes would look nice with the new black skirt and cape she had made. She seldom dressed in all black and after it was made she thought it quite dreary. Lovina had helped her fashion a hat decorated with lavender ribbon. Lavender ruffles on the collar of the cape reflected the soft tones of her skin. She remembered the times when a red dress was just the thing and the argument she had with Fanny over the red ribbon. Now she liked softer colors.

The streets were filled with wagons, horses, buggies and ox carts. Wagon trains from the east carrying goods for sale lined the sides of the streets. Boards were laid along the roads next to the stores for people to walk on. Phebe kept to the board walks as long as they were available. She walked past the temple site where there seemed to be hundreds of men and horses digging a very deep hole. Others were guiding horses pulling drags loaded with rock. She was glad they had moved out of the city where it was quiet. She hurried on the few more blocks to the house the Stratons were renting.

The children were delighted to see her and it was no time until she was reading them stories and treating them to candy. Harriet had been working at the loom most of the day and had woven a beautiful piece of fabric. "Aunt Phebe, will you help me make this into a dress for Malissa? We can spend the day tomorrow making it."

"Oliver and I have been discussing the possibility of us accepting Father's offer to come to Draper. Oliver isn't much of a farmer but Father and the brothers could teach him what he needs to know."

"I would like that very much, Harriet. I've missed you and I know your father has. I keep wishing Lovina would come to Draper also but Thomas is quite set on them staying in Provo. I'll be glad to help you make Malissa a dress. She can wear it to her baptism." Phebe started to set the table while Harriet worked at the stove.

"Harriet, do you think you could teach your father's new wife to weave? If we keep a new little family clothed it would be very helpful to have a weaver handy. We will have to find a loom or have one made. I wonder if Zemira could make one by copying yours. Your father would be so happy if he had another wife who could weave like your mother."

"You amaze me, Aunt Phebe. You always find something to plan ahead for and it is usually something that will make life better for someone else." Harriet left the dinner preparation and came to Phebe, putting her arms around her, she gave her a big hug. "You are special, and I love you. Of course I will teach Samantha to weave. It's an old family custom." She had sensed Phebe's need to feel loved and appreciated.

Ebenezer came for her after a few days. She and Harriet showed him the sewing they had done and he spent some time with his little grandchildren. James Albert told him about catching fish in City Creek and Malissa proudly read a story from a little book for him.

On the way back to Draper Phebe was reluctant to ask Ebenezer about his first days alone with his new wife. She decided that she would just wait for him to tell her what he wanted her to know. It didn't take long. "Phebe, Samantha is really quite a remarkable young lady. She makes good bread and she likes to milk the cows."

Phebe laughed, "I'm so glad. I dislike milking cows. I have

never offered because I was afraid I would have to assume that responsibility if I once started. If she makes the bread and milks the cows, I can probably handle the rest of it."

Ebenezer looked at her and grinned, "There have always been enough boys around to milk the cows but I didn't know you were so opposed to doing it? Maybe I should teach you how, just in case you need to sometime."

"I'll teach myself if the time comes, thank you. I can't stand the thought of a cow switching her tail in my face. I've done a lot of things for you, Ebenezer Brown, but I don't intend to milk cows. Now a goat I might try. They aren't so big."

Ebenezer kept up the banter, "I wonder where I could get a herd of goats. I'm sure they would thrive on that pasture grass in Draper. Now I have found a goatmaid, I'll have to work on that." He chuckled, knowing the ridiculous conversation was only a cover for the deep feelings and concerns they both felt but knew it was not the time to discuss them.

Samantha had a nice supper ready for them when they got home. She had set the table with a new table cloth she had embroidered and edged with fine lace. Phebe let her invite them to the table and accepted the role of guest. This was Samantha's opportunity to be the hostess.

"What a pretty table cloth and napkins to match. Did you do the crocheted trim?" Phebe admired the fine handwork.

"Yes, my mother taught me how to crochet when I was a small girl. I enjoy doing handwork." She served Phebe and Ebenezer their supper and sat down at the left of Ebenezer.

That seemed to start a pattern that would continue. Where ever they went, Phebe sat at Ebenezer's right and Samantha at his left. They soon fell into other routines, dividing up the household chores and the meals. Phebe taught Samantha the art of pie making and how to tat lace. She also read from the scriptures each night after supper and introduced Samantha to some new books of poetry she had bought in the city.

After the routines had been established the boys moved back into the house. There was just Ebenezer's son John and William George's sons, David Moroni and George Alma who were only five and six. They had stayed with Bett for a week or so while the Brown house adjusted to a new wife. Bett helped them know what to expect in a family living the Principle.

William George had left his boys with Phebe while he went back to Council Bluff to help with the migration of the saints. His wife's decision to leave him and take their daughter with her had hurt him deeply. He seemed to handle it better if he was on the move and they always needed teamsters to help the saints move west.

Phebe filled her days with teaching the little ones in the village to read and do simple arithmetic. She left the house to Samantha for a good part of the day knowing that too much togetherness can ruin a friendship. Samantha was like a daughter to her but they were also friends. Ebenezer divided his time with them and because of his good nature and their pleasant dispositions, the arrangement worked well.

By September, Harriet and Oliver had decided to move to Draper. The men helped them build a cabin and Ebenezer designated some property for them to farm. Harriet put her loom in her father's house and taught Samantha to weave. Samantha was a quick learner and a hard worker. She seldom sat idle and was glad to learn this new skill. As she and Harriet sat at the loom working on an intricate design Samantha became ill and ran from the room. When she returned she was still pale. Harriet had her sit down away from the loom. "Sometimes weaving makes you feel a little dizzy if you don't look away."

"Oh, It wasn't the weaving. I think I am expecting a baby but I have been afraid to tell any one. If you were me would you tell Ebenezer first or Phebe? I wish my mother was here so I could ask her. This is all so new to me. Phebe has been an angel to me and I hope she won't resent me having this baby."

She looked to Harriet for an answer.

"If I were you, I would tell them together. They will both be happy for you and excited about having a new baby in the house. I have never known two people who love little children like my father and Aunt Phebe. I can't wait for you to tell them. They will be so excited. I'm going on home so you will be alone when they come in." Harriet rolled up the unused yarn and put it in the sewing basket by the loom.

Phebe came back from a visit with Bett. She had also stopped by at Sister Fitzgerald to see if she could help her. Her baby was due any day now. Ebenezer came in from the field and washed up at the wash stand. "Well, how are my two favorite girls?" He kissed them each on the cheek and sat down in his rocker.

Samantha sat on the floor in front of him and Phebe sat in the other rocker. Bravely, Samantha cleared her throat, "Harriet said I should tell you both together so I have decided I will. I think I am going to have a baby." Then she broke into tears. Once the flood gate was open she started to sob and they both went to her, trying to comfort her.

Phebe lifted Samantha's chin and wiped the tears away. "This is wonderful news but I know it is frightening. Don't be afraid. We will take care of you."

Ebenezer lifted her to her feet and put his arm around her and walked her to her room. He looked at Phebe and she nodded for him to go with Samantha.

Phebe sat back down in her rocker and pulled some yarn and a crochet hook from the sewing basket. She chained one hundred and fifty stitches, held one end to her nose, held her arm out and stretched the other end to the tip of her finger. Yes, that would make a good size shawl for the new baby. She visualized the new pattern Sister Fitzgerald had used on the baby shawl she had just finished. After a few attempts and some variations Phebe determined a series of stitches that would make a nice pattern for the new baby shawl. The crochet hook was flying and her mind was completely absorbed in her work. It had been her philosophy of life to keep busy doing something constructive to take your mind off things you would worry about but could not change. Samantha would need her help and Phebe silently committed herself to be as helpful as possible. The words to a tune often sung in church came to mind, *"You can make the pathway bright, fill the soul with heaven's light, if there's sunshine in your heart. You can turn the night to day as the shadows fly away, if there's sunshine in your heart today."*

CHAPTER FORTY-NINE

Small bands of Indians often walked around the foothills to the south and east of Draper. They had burial grounds on the sand hills to the north. They were known as the Timpanogos Utes and made their more permanent homes around the Timpanogos lake to the south. The Mormons had named it Utah Lake.

Many of the settlers in Draper were afraid of the Indians. Mothers would call their children into the house if they saw the Indians close by. If they were within shouting distance, the older youngsters would call them names and then run for shelter. Phebe assured them that she had met many different kinds of Indians from New York, Canada and Mexico and had found them to be easy to please. When she was teaching the little ones she would tell them stories of, Okinihah, taking them across the icy Ontario and about the little Indian children with beautiful bronze skin and large brown eyes that greeted the Mormon Battalion.

One afternoon as the neighbor women were having a "quilting bee" Phebe thought it a good time to discuss the Indians. "Brother Brigham has encouraged us to feed the Indians, not fight them," she explained to the women around the quilt.

"We have to protect our children from them. We encountered Indians on the plains that would have killed us all. They set fire to our wagons and I'm sure they would have stolen our children. I'd just as soon stay away from them." Sister Fitzgerald gave Phebe a defiant look and then concentrated on pushing her needle to make tiny stitches on the quilt. The other women nodded in agreement.

Phebe could see that the possibility of her changing their minds was slim. Hostile Indians were a constant threat to them as they crossed the plains and she couldn't alleviate that fear with her personal stories. She had seen more hostility from white men at Far West and Nauvoo than she had from Indians but she knew her defense of them fell on deaf ears.

The fear of the Indians mounted as stories were told, retold and embellished. One night some Indians did raid a herd of horses in the south end of town. They stole several of them and the news flew through the village. A town meeting was called and it was determined that a fort should be built to protect them from marauding Indians. Ebenezer volunteered the property to encompass his home, the Fitzgerald store and the school house. The dimensions were 35 rods by 23 rods. Most of the summer of 1854 the men spent their spare time building a wall, one foot wide and eight feet high.

Ebenezer had became a man of substance. His herds increased and his ground yielded good crops. He supplied wagon trains with meat and other commodities. His generosity was always returned with more than he could imagine. He was a man of vigor and optimism. He was viewed with respect by his neighbors and the leaders of the church. The brethren encouraged the church leaders who had been called to practice the Principal, to take additional wives if they had the means to care for them. It was in this capacity that Ebenezer was encouraged to take another wife.

Many Immigrants came to the valley with little or nothing except what they carried with them. They had spent all they had for passage on boats from England and on wagons and teams to get them to Zion. Another crisis was facing the church leaders. There were many young women alone or with relatives that needed someone to provide a home for them. Many went to work for some of the wealthier families but that solution was not adequate to meet the demands.

John Wright, his Wife Mary and daughter Mary Elizabeth were assigned to Draper when they arrived from England. Ebenezer helped them get settled in the cabin Zemira had built for Sally before they went to live in Provo. The Wrights were dedicated members of the church and hard workers. John had been a carpenter in England so Ebenezer introduced him to Zemira Draper who hired him to help with the many building projects in town.

Mary Elizabeth became good friends with Samantha. Phebe watched their friendship grow as did Ebenezer. The two girls would take long walks together as Samantha's pregnancy progressed. It was during this time that Mary Elizabeth learned about living the Principle. When Ebenezer ask her to be his fourth wife she was ready to accept the challenge.

Ebenezer hired Zemira and John Wright to build another room on the east of the house and Phebe enlisted the aid of Samantha to help make the curtains and rugs. Samantha wove fabric for new sheets and pillow cases and Phebe tatted the lace for the edging. It was during this preparation that Samantha had her baby, a little boy they named Ebenezer Brown Jr.

Bett and Phebe were with her during the birth. She was a strong girl and the birth was normal for a first baby. After the baby was washed and wrapped in clean soft homespun he was put in Samantha's arms and Ebenezer was invited in to see his new namesake. The last time he had come to the bedside of a wife after childbirth had been that tragic day when he lost Ann. It was with mixed feelings that he went to Samantha's.

Bett walked from the room with Phebe, picked up her clay pipe from the stove, put it in her mouth and took a deep puff. She sat in the rocker to rest, "Samantha will be able to have many children. The baby was a little slow in breathing but he will be fine. How will it be to have a new baby in the house?"

Phebe didn't comment on the pipe. If Bett had returned to her old habit, it was her business. She was still her best friend. She sat in the rocker next to Bett sipping a cup of Camomile tea, "I am looking forward to it. My arms often ache for a new baby to hold. I hope I can be wise enough to let Samantha do the mothering."

Bett nodded, "That is one of the fine lines we walk in living the Principle. Who disciplines the children and who comes to their aid when they are sick? But I've had my own to care for so it hasn't been much of a temptation for me to take over for Mary Ann, except when she was sick and needed me."

"Ebenezer's taking another wife. He and Mary Elizabeth Wright will be married this fall." Phebe made the announcement without fanfare. She and Bett knew each other well enough to share their thoughts openly.

"I thought as much when I saw him adding the room to the house. Mary seems like a nice girl. She and Samantha appear to be quite congenial. That always makes it easier." Bett smiled at Phebe, "Who would have thought, when we were living in Canada, that one day we would be out here in the rocky mountains sharing our husbands with other women. The gospel has brought unbelievable changes into our lives."

"Yes, it has. The important part is that we understand the concept of eternal progression and the plan of salvation. The Savior has guided our footsteps and protected us to be a strength to these spirits that come to our families. It takes strong, faithful women to live the Principle. The responsibility of it weighs heavy on the men and I feel sorry for those who have to live with jealous and selfish women." Phebe looked over at Bett who was more like a sister than sister-in-law. "You have set a good example for me. I hope I can follow your lead."

Their conversation was interrupted by the pounding of nails on the addition to the house. The dishes rattled in the cupboard. The roofing would soon be finished and that should stop the noise and vibration. Ebenezer came from the bedroom with a smile on his face, "That is a fine boy isn't it." It was a statement, not a question. "Thanks for taking good care of her. You two make quite the pair."

He went out to supervise the work on the house and the fort wall. There was always so much to be done and he was not one to waist his time. The sheep needed shearing and he and the boys had an order for ten head of beef to be delivered to the city tomorrow.

Bett left Phebe to care for Samantha. She walked quietly into the room and saw that the new mother was resting peacefully. The baby started to fuss so Phebe picked him up and carried him out so Samantha would not be disturbed. She sat in her rocker and hummed her favorite lullaby. There was something about a new baby in the house that brought happiness and hope for tomorrow. A sense of well-being filled her soul as she sat there holding this new little spirit from heaven and she thought to herself, "This is part of my promise of a long and happy life."

She took the sleeping baby back to Samantha's room and laid him in the cradle. Tiptoeing out, she heard a rap on the door and opened it to find the mail currier with a good sized bag of mail. "Come in, I have a bag for you," and she handed him the burlap bag she had filled that morning with mail from the village. After he left she opened the bag to distribute the mail to the family boxes on the wall. There were two letters addressed to her. One was from Lydia Elizabeth in Iowa and the other from Lovina. She put them aside and finished sorting the mail.

Lydia Elizabeth must have received the letter she sent to her months ago. She hadn't been sure of the address, knowing only the town she lived in. It had been over five years since she had heard from her. With her mail duties finished she sat to read the letters from her daughters.

April 1854
Hamburg, Iowa

Dear Mother and Ebenezer,
I was so happy to hear from you. After so many years of not having word we were afraid something had happened to

you when you were with the Mormon Battalion. It sounds as if you are comfortably settled now. We were surprised to hear that both Rhoda and Zemira are married. We did know that Lovina had remarried but did not meet her new husband before we came south to to live in Hamburg.

Several of Anthony's friends from Canada came here to settle and we have a large flourishing farm. I wish the saints had stayed here to establish Zion but with the political upheaval at the time, I understand their decision.

You have four grandchildren you have not seen. We have two sons and two daughters; Anthony Jr. is seven years old and looks just like his father, Isaac is five and resembles the Lathrop side of our family, Clara is three and looks like Lovina with dark curly hair and our baby, Josette, is one and it appears that she has my features and coloring. They are all healthy children and I am teaching the boys to read as we do not have a school nearby. I am also expecting another baby in the winter. It seems that even though I was an old twenty-two when I married I still am to have a good sized family.

In answer to your question about coming west, I doubt that we will ever do that. We have such a thriving farm here and Anthony is very happy with his friends that settled here with us. We hold church at our home on occasions and the missionaries stop by on their assignments to the east. Neither of us seem to have the commitment to the church that the rest of you enjoy. Life is much easier for us this way. I hope you understand.

If any of the family come east, tell them to come and see us. We are about sixty miles south of Council Point on the Nishnabotna River which flows into the Missouri just a little south of here. Give them all my love and do write to me often. I miss you very much.

> *Your loving daughter,*
> *Lydia E. Bruno*

Phebe read the letter again. She was relieved to know that

Lydia Elizabeth and Anthony were doing well but she was sorry they didn't plan to come to Zion. She appreciated the description of the children.

Lovina's letter was just a short note;

> *Dear Mother,*
>
> *With our large family and small house we are very cramped and I worry about the girls, Ester Ann and Fanny. They have no privacy here and Thomas does not have a lot of patience with them. Would it be possible for them to come and stay with you for a while? I'll send them up with friends when the opportunity arises. It will be on a trial basis and if it doesn't work out let me know.*
>
> *Thank you for helping me. I don't know what I would do without your help. I will miss them terribly. I am not sure exactly when they will arrive.*
>
> *Give my love to all,*
> *Lovina*

Phebe read it twice and then tried to read between the lines. It would seem that Lovina would need them to help her with all her little ones but if she thought they were better off in Draper they were certainly welcome.

Phebe decided to rearrange the loft so the girls could have some privacy up there. Her grandson, David Moroni, was still with them and Ebenezer's son, John. They could have their room in the east of the loft and the girls could share the west end. When the carpenters were through with Mary's room she would have them erect some walls and make some doorways. They would have to cut some windows in also to make it lighter.

She told Ebenezer about the girls coming and he was delighted. There was always room for one more in his home and it would always be so. With the new baby and the girls there would be eight of them and there was plenty of room at the table.

Phebe was glad she would have the girls and Moroni to look after. As Bett had told her, it would be easier not to interfere with Samantha raising her baby if she had other children to care for. Tomorrow she would go to the store and find some calico to make Ester Ann and Fanny new dresses.

The girls arrived in time for the Fourth of July celebration. They had planned a sunrise service where the Mormon Battalion and Nauvoo Legion soldiers would wear their uniforms and raise the American flag. William gave a patriotic talk about their allegiance to the United States Government. There were races for the children and a horse race around the outside of the fort. Ladders were leaning against the fort to enable people to climb up and watch the horse race. There would be a big picnic on the grass in the middle of the fort and a platform of planks was built so they could have a dance in the evening. The Boulter brothers had put together a band. John Boulter played the fiddle, Sam Frost the Bass Fiddle, and William Boulter was the prompter.

When John and Elizabeth Enniss came to Draper they brought with them Elizabeth's two brothers, John and William Boulter. Their parents had died at Council Point and so, as with other families, they came with their sister. They were both grown young men. The oldest, William, had hired on as a teamster for migrating wagon trains and came to Draper when he was in the area. John stayed in Draper and worked making adobe bricks, farming and playing his fiddle for every occasion that needed some music. He wrote many of his own songs and could pick up the melody of most anything without written music.

The Munro girls were excited to be with the big Draper/Brown family. They loved their cousins and their grandmother. They put on their new calico dresses for the festivities. Phebe braided their hair and pinned them in a twist that made them feel very grown up.

Grandpa Draper sat in a rocker in the shade of one of the

trees, adoring his grandchildren and great grandchildren. His son Zemira and his daughter-in-law, Ann, sat beside him. They relayed the names of the winners of the races and games. With each announcement, Grandpa was the first to cheer for the winner. Phebe came and stood in back of her father and put her hand on his thin shoulder. Now in his eighties, his frail body seemed almost transparent. The twinkle was still there in his eyes. As he felt Phebe's hand he turned, "There you are my dear girl. I hoped you wouldn't miss all the fun. I'll bet you have been taking care of that new baby at your house."

Phebe smiled. Even in his advanced years he kept track of everything and everybody. "I was braiding the girls hair. Have you seen Ester Ann and Fanny. They are growing up so fast. It seems like just yesterday they were toddlers in Nauvoo."

"Yes, they came by and gave me a hug before they went on to see their friends. How well I remember that party in William's barn when Ester Ann had to hold her mother's hand while she sang. That was the happy part before the mobsters came." A shadow crossed his face as he remembered the brutality they suffered at the hands of William's neighbors.

The horse race was next. John had agreed to race Ebenezer's fastest filly. Bishop Draper had reminded them there would be no wagering on the race but their would be a prize for the winner. Six boys had entered the race; Albert Draper, Joe Day, Bob Shipley, Bill Terry, Jack Smith and John Brown. They were to make three laps around the fort. Henry Day shot the starter gun and they were off. The crowd around the fort were cheering them on. Each family pulling for their son to win. The lead changed at almost every lap. John was in the lead at the last lap but Bob Shipley's black moved up from fourth to over take the Brown filly. Bob won the race. The other boys dismounted and walked over to congratulate him. Bishop Draper announced the winner and gave him a ten dollar gold piece. It was the biggest prize of the day.

The father's of the boys moved in to congratulate the

winner and tried to cover the disappointment of their losses. Brother Shipley was bragging about the speed of the black. Ebenezer shook his hand, "Perhaps you and I should race our horses and see which horse is the fastest." Brother Shipley was a large man, about twice as big as Ebenezer. They both knew if they raced the horses Ebenezer would win. They both laughed as did their friends who overheard the conversation.

Phebe introduced her granddaughters to the Boulter boys and the next thing she knew they were sitting by them at the picnic. There was a large group of young people joking and laughing as the boys who ran the horse race joined them. Phebe took some extra fried chicken and rolls to the group. It was devoured before she was back to sit by Ebenezer and Samantha.

Everyone joined in the dance from little children to Grandpa Draper. He took one short turn with Phebe and then begged off. "I'm just not as young as I used to be. I'll just sit here and tap my toe. I think that is the best I can do."

Phebe walked him to a chair by the side of the plank floor and brought him a cool drink of Draper spring water. Ebenezer touched her arm and they were off into a reel line with a swing and a doe-se-doe. Ebenezer amazed her. He never seemed to run out of energy.

Phebe was surprised when Ester Ann joined John Boulter to sing with him for some of the songs. Her voice was not as true as her mother's but it was beautiful and the dancers clapped and wanted more.

The girls were happy in Draper and Phebe was glad they were with her. They could go to school there in the winter and she could help them with the schooling they had missed the last few years. Ester Ann and Fanny gathered reeds along the ditchbanks and made hats from them. Lovina had taught her girls the millinery art and they both enjoyed fashioning hats. Ester Ann had a little more patience with it than Fanny and within a month or so was making hats for some of the ladies in the village.

Phebe's Sister, Fanny and her husband John Van Leuven finally reached the valley but were sent almost immediately to a Dixie Mission where they supported Zemira Palmer and his wife Salley in the implementation of the United Order in Orderville, Utah. After a brief visit with her family, Fanny wished them goodbye and was on her way. Phebe often had short notes from her or Zemira's wife Sally, telling about the progress of the Saints in living the United Order. Phebe was always glad to get the little extra tidbits of information that only Fanny would provide. Zemira Draper had joined his sister, Fanny, and nephew, Zemira Palmer, in Orderville also.

Ebenezer married Mary Elizabeth Wright in October. They spent a few days in Salt Lake City after the sealing. When they returned home, Phebe and Samantha had their room prepared, and the family settled into a routine with three wives sharing the work and the love of Ebenezer. They taught Mary how to cord the wool and spin it on the spinning wheel. Samantha still did the weaving and Phebe the cutting and sewing. They prepared and ate their meals together. By December, Mary was expecting a baby. Phebe and Samantha assumed extra work to allow her to rest when she didn't feel well. She held Samantha's baby and looked forward to the time she would have her own.

Grandfather Draper took ill in December of '54 and died on Christmas Eve. It was a sad Christmas for the family and the whole community. He had endeared himself to everyone. Phebe felt a great void in her life but also knew that her mother was close by. As her father took his last breath he opened his eyes, looked beyond those around his bed, smiled and whispered, "Little Lydia, my Lydia," and he was gone.

John Boulter had been a frequent visitor at the Brown home and had ask permission to court Ester Ann. Lovina had given her permission by letter and the two were married by Ester Ann's uncle and Bishop, William Draper, in January. They built a small cabin by the foothills below Cherry Canyon.

They had several acres of farm land with a gradual slope that could be easily irrigated. One of the ditches the men had dug was just west of the home site. John was twenty-one and Ester Ann was fifteen. They were a happy couple and were always in demand to sing together at church and town parties. John would often compose an original song for the occasions.

Phebe was delighted to see Ester Ann so happy and decided that Lovina's decision to send the girls to her had been a wise one. As grandmother's do, she made her quilts, bed linens, table linens and filled her cupboards with fresh baked goods and staples for cooking. Lovina and Thomas came for the wedding party. Lovina had made Ester Ann a beautiful dress and designed a special hat of white ribbon to attach to the veil.

Mary's baby was born the next September and at October Conference Ebenezer's name was called again to fill a mission. This time he was to take his family and help establish the town of Carson, Nevada. His son John was called to the Hawaiian mission and was to accompany his father as far as Nevada.

Ebenezer was again surprised at a call of this magnitude at his age. When they arrived home from conference he took Phebe by the hand and they walked outside. "What are we to do? With two young wives to support, as well as you my dear, I wonder how I can leave everything here. My head has been spinning since I heard my name called."

Phebe took his hand as they walked out of the fort and down their favorite path to the orchard. The new trees were heavy with apples and Phebe thought of the many times she had made grave decisions in an apple orchard. "I will be fifty-eight next week and I am responsible for two grandchildren. People depend on me to help teach the children in the village school and we also have the mail contract. Perhaps I should stay here and you take Samantha and Mary with you. They are young and will enjoy the challenges of the mission. We can hire men to help Gurnsey run the farm and the cattle. I can help with the book keeping. It won't be easy for any of us but William and Bett will help me. You have no choice but to accept the call."

"I never questioned that but my concern was mostly for you. It is too much to ask you to give up everything and start over. I did consider our holdings here and what we would do about them. They want us to leave and get established there before winter sets in." Ebenezer looked out over his farm and back at the fort. "We have accomplished so much here in five years. I love this place and I don't want to ever leave it. Nor do I want to leave you."

"I don't want to live here without you, Ebenezer. This is our promised land but the Lord has been so good to us. It is out of our hands." Her voice broke and she turned her head to hide the tears welling up in her eyes.

"Let's go over and discuss it with William and Bett. After all, he is our Bishop and should certainly have some direction for us." Ebenezer knew what his old friend,

William, would tell them but it would somehow make it easier if the advice came from him.

As expected, Bishop William Draper suggested the same solution Phebe and Ebenezer had discussed. He offered his help as a brother and their Bishop. They both knew they could count on him. He stood between them and put an arm around each of them. "Miss Phebe, I promise you, you will want for nothing and will be protected in Ebenezer's absence. Ebenezer, I have the feeling that this will be a temporary separation and that you will be called home sooner that you think. Now, go and get your affairs in order. We will have a big farewell party next Saturday and you can be on your way the following Monday.

On the appointed day for departure, two wagons loaded to capacity and pulled by strong teams of draft horses were driven out of the fort by Ebenezer and John. Each of the young wives in their homespun dresses and sun bonnets held their babies in their arms as they sat on the wagon seats. Mary's baby was just three weeks old and Samantha's, a little over a year. A riding horse was tethered to the back of each wagon as was a milk cow.

It had been a busy week. Phebe was exhausted, both physically and emotionally. Ebenezer and William had given her a blessing the night before. Ebenezer had spent his last night home with her and she cherished the brief time alone with him.

Phebe walked to the gate of the fort and watched until she could no longer see the wagons. A deep sense of loneliness engulfed her. She turned and walked back toward the house.

CHAPTER FIFTY

Winter set in early. Not only did it snow but the temperature dropped so rapidly that frost covered the windows of the houses in early December. The winds out of Corner Canyon were relentless, pilling up the snow into high drifts. If it continued the families in the outlying areas from the fort would be stranded for many days. The Indians were suffering from the severe weather also and there were more and more incidents of thefts from the farms on the perimeter of the town.

William called a town meeting to discuss the problem. He was not only concerned about the safety of his flock from the Indians but also from the weather. He stood before the group in the school house and offered a solution. "We can all move into the fort for the winter. There are about twenty buildings within the fort, counting the school, store and homes. We can double up in some of the homes and use the school and store for families. There is at least three more months of winter to survive. I'll leave it up to you to decide who you invite to share your house. If there is anyone without an invitation by the time we finish refreshments, come to see me."

The women in town had been asked to make cakes and pies and hot cider was steeping in a large black pot on the stove. Phebe invited the Enniss family and John and Ester Ann to share her house. With Ebenezer and the young wives gone there was plenty of room. They would each have a bedroom and the Enniss children could sleep in the loft rooms with Fanny and David Moroni. Her cellar was full of potatoes, apples, squash, parsnips and preserves. Ebenezer had filled her storeroom with flour, sugar and beans. The ice house was lined with smoked pork and cured beef. She was sure there was plenty for the three families to share.

Ester Ann was expecting her first baby in late December

and Phebe wanted her close by so she and Bett could be with her. Perhaps the storms had been a blessing in disguise for her. She wouldn't be lonely with Ebenezer gone. There would be plenty of people around.

Long before the refreshments were consumed every family had a place to stay for the winter and plans were under way for the move. Little clusters of women were discussing what supplies of food they would need. The men decided to bring all the stock into the nearest corrals and sheds along with what feed they could move from the snowbound barns. Wood for the stoves was also addressed and groups of men were assigned to furnish wood piles. There were three wells in the fort, the Browns being one of them. The water level had always been high so drinking water was not a concern.

William adjourned the meeting and encouraged the saints to move into the fort as soon as possible. There was every indication that more storms were on their way. He felt inspired to urge the families to move at once.

They had met on a Wednesday and by Sunday the move had been made and they were all in attendance for their Church meeting. Bishop Draper announced that the meeting would be devoted to personal testimonies. The spirit was very strong, as the members of this humble group, stood one by one to thank the Lord for his blessings and protection.

Lauritz Smith, the first Scandinavian convert to move to Draper, was a blacksmith. He had built a small blacksmith shop in the fort in the summer of '55. He and his wife had now set up housekeeping in the back of the shop to ride out the winter storms. It was difficult for him to speak in English and he often became very frustrated as he tried to communicate. Today he rose and bore his testimony in Danish and to their surprise, all understood him. He told of his conversion to the gospel in Denmark and his journey by boat across the ocean to the mouth of the Mississippi River. He had married his young wife, Mary, on the ship. He expressed his unwavering testimony of Joseph Smith being a prophet of God and his commitment to do the Lord's work.

Others stood and spoke in tongues unfamiliar to most but understood by all. Phebe had never felt the spirit in a meeting to this degree since the dedication of the Kirtland Temple. Her worries over Ebenezer left her and she felt at peace as her faith returned to sustain her.

The winter was long and it seemed that spring would never come. The families fared quite well living in such close proximity. Occasionally William would have to intercede in a dispute but they were minor. The men took turns guarding and feeding the cattle. The Indian problems anticipated did not materialize but this group of people learned to live together in harmony. Phebe was sorry Ebenezer was not there to see it. He had set the stage for neighborliness with every family that moved in and he would be proud to see how they had functioned in a time of crisis.

Spring did come and the families moved back to there homes, planted their crops and life returned to normal. More Scandinavian families moved to Draper and they were graciously welcomed, in a large part because of the blacksmith who had lifted their spirits in that testimony meeting.

Phebe was reluctant to let Ester Ann and her new baby daughter, Lovina Cumfort Boulter, move back to the cabin but John assured her that he would take good care of them. The baby was three months old and Phebe was sure that her first great grandchild was the prettiest baby the Lord had ever created. She held the baby and rocked her to sleep while Ester Ann was packing up their clothes. Phebe looked at the baby and wondered what challenges she would meet in life. She came from a long line of strong women.

Phebe recounted the women in her past; Grandmother Draper who had given her a blessing when she was just a small girl, Grandmother Lathrop who's refinement had trained her own mother Lydia to be so serene and beautiful in all situations. She looked inward and wondered if some of her qualities might be emulated by this little girl when she grew to womanhood. Lovina, with her loving disposition would be one to be revered and certainly her sweet happy little mother, Ester Ann.

William Boulter returned to Draper that spring and ask for permission to marry Fanny. Lovina again gave her consent so the Munro sisters were married to the Boulter Brothers. William staked out a farm and joined his brother in making adobes and building houses.

The following year passed by with out major problems or events. An occasional letter from Samantha or Mary kept them up to date on the progress of the Carson Settlement. Gurnsey was called to go to the aid of the Willey company stranded on the plains near Fort Bridger. He brought back two of the young girls who had witnessed their parents freezing to death on the plains. The community took them into their hearts. That winter was not nearly so severe as the preceding one but some of the families chose to move to the fort during the worst of January and February.

In the summer of 1857, President Young had declared a holiday for all the saints to celebrate the tenth anniversary of the arrival in the valley. Saints from all over the valley went up Big Cottonwood canyon to celebrate the momentous occasion. It was during this celebration that Porter Rockwell rode in to tell Brigham Young that a United States army was advancing toward Great Salt Lake because of a so-called insurrection in Utah by the Mormons.

Brigham Young sent riders to the outlying missions to have the saints return to the valley. He also enlisted the aid of Lot Smith and Porter Rockwell to organize legions of men to delay the arrival of the army headed by Col. Johnson. They were to use any means available to them except blood shed. In the meantime President Young sent negotiators to Washington to plead for a peaceful settlement with the government.

Ebenezer and his young wives returned to Draper. As William had predicted, their call had not lasted long. His son Norman, who had gone to find his fortune in California, returned with him. Phebe was delighted to have them all home. They once again moved into the routines they had established before the mission call.

Lot Smith and Porter Rockwell came to Draper and enlisted the help of many of the younger men. Norman, known for his shooting ability, was one of the first to volunteer. He went with Lot Smith as did some of his friends. Others joined forces with Porter Rockwell and they were on their way by September after harvesting their crops and providing for their families. They were to hamper the progress of the army without bloodshed. They were successful in that the army was delayed and had to spend the winter in the Fort Bridger area

Brigham Young directed all the saints in the valley to prepare to move south when spring broke. In his determination not to give into unfounded accusations and submit to unfair treatment again from the United States Government, he sent directions to all the communities to abandon their homes and farms. They were to leave only enough men to burn it all to the ground, should the Army advance on the valley.

It was a somber group that met at the meeting house and heard the letter from the First Presidency read by Bishop Isaac M. Stewert, who had replaced William in this position the year before. They were directed to leave the territory at once if they were not willing to destroy everything.

Phebe and Ebenezer walked back to their house, the other wives following with the children. They walked to the well to get a drink of the fresh water. Ebenezer looked at his wives. His jaw was set, and in a tone unlike his nature, he lashed out, "I'll leave as I am directed but I will be back. This is our promised, Zion, and it will be ours." He left to help organize the wagons.

The town was evacuated as requested and the long line of

wagons and cattle wound up through Corner Canyon to the alpine valley over the Traverse ridge. It was a secluded valley, lush with grasses and fed by the streams on the south slope of Lone Peak. They pitched tents and covered the wagons with tarps. Some made dugouts to protect them from the storms that would surely come.

Phebe found herself, once again, cooking over campfires and sleeping in a wagon box. Samantha and Mary slept in the tent with their children. As the evening breezes brought down the cold air from the glacier covered mountain, the campers built their fires high to keep warm.

Phebe poked at the embers with a long stick. She was sitting on a rock close to the fire circle. "I wonder how many times we will be driven from our homes."

William and Bett were enjoying the warmth of the fire with her. William looked at this sister and wondered at her tenacity. "Miss Phebe, keep the faith."

Ebenezer came to her and put his arm around her shoulders. "At least we are camped in a beautiful place. We are with the saints in the Rocky Mountains as the Prophet promised us. What more can we want?"

Ebenezer's wives were housecleaning. The walls were getting another coat of white wash and the wooden floors scrubbed. Every nook and cranny was washed down with lye soap. The bed ticks were refilled with straw and the bed linens washed and hanging in the sun to dry. The children were beating the dust from the rugs hanging on the rail fence. It took at least three days to accomplish a thorough housecleaning of this magnitude and the children loved it. They slept out under the stars and Moroni, now in his early teens, told them scary stories and pointed out the star constellations starting with the first evening star.

This was the second housecleaning since their return from the high Alpine valley. President Young had negotiated a settlement with the United States Government and Johnson's Army was stationed in the remote Cedar Valley with the scrub oak, sage brush and wild rabbits. The soldiers were not allowed in the city and the Saints were encouraged not to mingle with them.

Phebe was putting the last polish on the lamp chimneys while Samantha and Mary put the freshly washed dishes back in the cupboard. The house sparkled as the sunshine danced through the clean windows with newly starched curtains hung and pulled back in evenly measured folds. Clean towels hung by the washstand and a bowl of yellow and purple pansies sitting on a crocheted doily graced the center of the table. They felt the satisfaction that comes from hard work as they looked around at their accomplishment.

Phebe was proud of the nice home they had provided for Ebenezer and the children. It was always open to visitors and had several each day as they stopped by to check for mail. When Phebe answered the knock on the door she was surprised to see that it was not one of the neighbors, but a soldier and one she recognized immediately. "Col. Cooke, come in. How nice to see you again after all these years. Someone told us you were with Johnson's Army. Let me send one of the children to the field for Ebenezer. He will be delighted to see you."

Col. Philip St. George Cooke took his hat off and walked into the room. Phebe motioned him to a chair and called out the door to Moroni, "Go and find your grandfather. Tell him we have a very important visitor."

"Samantha and Mary, let me introduce you to Col. Cooke. He was our commanding officer when we were in the Mormon Battalion. Col. Cooke, these are Ebenezer's other wives, Samantha and Mary Brown." The women nodded to him and left the room realizing he was Phebe's guest.

"Mrs. Brown, you are looking well. I was delighted to hear

that you and Sgt. Brown made it here safely. How is Zemira? He was such a good aide for me and a fine young lad." He started to light his pipe but thought better of it and held it in his hand, unlit.

"He is married now and living about three hundred miles south of here in a Mormon community called Orderville. He and his wife have a special assignment there for the church. They have had five children but just have three living. They had twin girls in '55 but they did not survive. Zemira has followed the trade of his uncle, Zemira Draper, that of carpentry, and he is very good at it." Phebe enjoyed praising her children and she was proud of Zemira.

Ebenezer came in and his familiar grin creased his face, "Well, as I live and breath, if it isn't Col. Cooke. Welcome to our home. We are glad you came to visit us. Phebe, would you get this fine gentleman a drink of our famous Draper spring water? It's the best you'll taste in the valley." Phebe brought the two men a drink of fresh cool water from the well.

Col. Cooke savored the refreshing drink. "Thank you. That is a lot better than the brackish water we get from our well at Cedar Fort. Sgt. Brown, I came on business. I hear you have some of the finest beef for sale in the valley. Our supply is getting low and we are expecting to be called back east any time now. I would appreciate you selling the U.S. Army some of your stock. We would pay you well. After the problems our army has caused your people, I would understand if you chose not to sell them to us.

I have another request. I need a strong horse to get me back east. Knowing you to be a good judge of horse flesh, I was hoping you would have something similar to that white you sold me in Sante Fe."

Ebenezer smiled, remembering the negotiations over the white horse and the women being allowed to stay with the Battalion. "I will be happy to do business with you. I have plenty of beef cattle on hand and several horses. You can look them over and take your pick. It looks like you will be going east to fight another war. I hope it ends as peaceably as your war with us."

Col. Cooke shook his head. "I told them they wouldn't find anything but a peace loving people out here but I was never able to get the ear of the men making the decisions so I just had to come along. Your boys did give us plenty of trouble up there in the Wyoming country. I'm glad it's settled. I'll never forget that ride into the Great Salt Lake City with your Brigham Young standing there defying us to get out of line before we reached the redwood fence. I had bragged you boys up so much I just grinned all the way and took my hat off in respect to the men I rode with into California."

"I'll pay you well for the horse and cattle but I also have a gift for the two of you. It may not be much of a gift but I brought you a new Army issue rifle. It is touted to be one of the best. It shoots a fifty-six caliber slug and has a good sight. We have been directed to destroy all of our fire arms and equipment to make our trip east easier. If some of your people can use some of the wagons or other equipment, have them come out and ask for me. I'll see that they get what they need. Maybe we can make it right by you for all the trouble we put you through. If the men drive the cattle out for us I'll see that they are well paid in army issue as well as money."

Ebenezer looked at Phebe and they both smiled. The little Danish blacksmith, Brother Smith, had just last night told them he was in need of iron to make nails for the new meeting house and school they were building. He must have prayed for some to come his way because here it was. "Thank you, Colonel. I know it will come in mighty handy for some of our needs. Let's go out and look at the horses. Phebe, set another place for supper. Our friend here isn't leaving until he has had a meal with us."

The children sat at the supper table, enthralled at the retelling of the events on the Battalion trail. Phebe enjoyed the retelling of them much more than she had the living of them. Before long Colonel Cooke was on his way and Samantha insisted on clearing the table and doing the dishes. Mary was busy with her new baby.

Phebe and Ebenezer decided to take a walk up to Brother Smith's to tell him about the source of scrap iron they had just been offered. They held hands on the walk and reminisced about the first night they stayed here in Willow Creek before it was named Draper. "What a high time we had. The two of us all alone here looking up at the mountains and listening to the crickets chirping. I hope we never have to leave again. Phebe, we've done and seen a lot of things. The Lord has made a beautiful world for us to live in but I think he saved the best spot for us." He put his arm around her waist.

"I have no complaints. I couldn't be happier." Phebe leaned against his shoulder and they stopped for a few minutes looking up at the grandeur of the mountains. The setting sun reflected a brilliant hue on the colorful rocks and ledges. The glaciers of snow took on a pink cast. As they walked toward the foothills some deer jumped from the oakbrush and loped away.

The new school was almost finished and there were already enough students to fill it every day. Phebe taught only the youngest ones and held school for them in her home, leaving room for the older classes in the school. Mr. Frampton had taught there until the evacuation of the town. He went on south to teach after that and did not return. The last few years Andrew Jackson Allen's son-in-law Thomas V. Williams, had been the teacher. He was a mathematician and Phebe respected him for the way he taught and treated the children. He also helped the community devise a way to schedule watering turns out of the ditches so they would all have a fair share. It was

1861 and Master Williams had better offers from larger schools. The trustees of the school were anxious to find a replacement.

Absolom Smith, a convert from Virginia, lived in the western part of town by the main thoroughfare to Salt Lake City. A traveler stopped by to acquire temporary work on the farm. After visiting with him for a short while, Absalom realized that he was a well educated man and invited him to ride up to the center of the village to meet some of his neighbors. He stopped to show him the new school house that had just been completed. Ebenezer and Brother Day were there in the center of the fort when they arrived.

Phebe was on her way back from Sister Ann Fitzgerald's. She had taken her some hot biscuits and preserves. She also had to go over the Relief Society accounts with her. Phebe had been called to be the treasurer of the women's organization and Ann was the president.

As she walked past the men, Phebe, looked at the stranger talking to them and her heart skipped a beat. She stopped in her tracks. She felt fifteen again. He looked exactly like her old friend from Canada, Master John Park. But it couldn't be. This was a young man about the same age as Master John was the last time she saw him. He would be in his sixties by now, even older than she. Ebenezer called her over to meet the man. "Phebe, this is Dr. John R. Park from Ohio. He is passing through and needs work. We would like you to talk to him about our school. You know more about it than the rest of us."

"I would be happy to. Welcome to Draper, Dr. Park. I apologize if I seem a little startled. You look very much like a teacher I taught with in Canada years ago. His name was John Park also. He went to Pennsylvania, became a doctor and was living in Ohio the last I heard of him. It's a big country though. They say we all have a look alike somewhere." She stopped, embarrassed that she had made such an issue of his resemblance to her old friend.

"And what was your name when you lived in Canada? It wouldn't have been Phebe Draper?" His warm smile was familiar to her.

"Why yes, but how would you know that?"

"My father and mother often talked about you and Canada and the little village school. Weren't you my mother's girl-friend?" He was as delighted to meet her as she was him.

"Your name then is, John Rocky Park? They wrote me let-ters about you. The last I heard from your father must have been almost twenty years ago. Your mother had just passed away." She could not believe that Master John's son was standing here in front of her in the Rocky Mountains. His hair line and the set of his jaw was identical to that of his father's.

Ebenezer cleared his throat. "Well, it is a small world isn't it. Phebe, why don't you take Dr. Park over to the house and see what he knows about teaching school?"

"I think he would like to see the school. I can show him the books we have acquired for our library." She took Dr. Park's arm and they walked into the new school that had been built with a vestry in the east end.

"Tell me, Dr. Park, what brings you out west?"

"When I finished Medical School in New York, I went back to Ohio to live with my father. I started my medical prac-tice there but I guess my father's love for teaching was an over riding influence. I didn't enjoy practicing medicine any more than he had. He passed away last year and I decided it was time to see the country and find out what I want to do with my life. I am on my way to the Northwest but I ran out of money so I needed to work for a while to earn enough to go on. I think I would rather teach than be a farm hand. Is there somewhere I can find lodging if I decide to stay?" He walked over to the book case and looked at the small collection of books on vari-ous subjects. It was more than he would have expected for such a small remote village in the west. This school had possi-bilities. He decided to stay and try it.

Phebe was delighted to introduce him to the townspeople. The more she came to know him the more he reminded her of his father. He was very professional, treating children with respect, but requiring their best. He let them know that it was his opinion, if a subject was introduced in the proper manner with the proper teaching techniques, any child could learn.

He was often called on to use his medical skills also. His pay for teaching was $60.00 a year with a third of it in cash, a third lodging and the other third in produce. When he did any doctoring he was usually paid in produce.

Bett was relieved to have him in town. She had been the only medical help available for eleven years and she had often found herself in situations that were far beyond her training.

Dr. Park endeared himself to the villagers. He joined the church that first year he taught in town and was soon an important part of the community.

When he decided to go on to the Northwest the following year, the students and their parents were disappointed. They were happy, however, to convince a Dr. Ruel M. Rogers to take his place on a temporary basis. They had a half promise that Dr. Park would return if he wasn't happy in the Northwest country.

Phebe hoped Dr. Park would come back someday, but for now the Lord had sent Dr. Rogers at a time when they needed his skills.

CHAPTER FIFTY-ONE

The town was agog with excitement. Brigham Young had sent word that he would visit Draper and its famous village school at 10:00 a.m. on July 27, 1867. Dr. Park had been training a group of boys into a military marching band. Uniforms were made by the mothers from homespun cloth and a tailor had helped cut the pattern. The trousers had white stripes down the sides. This group was the pride of the community as they marched in precision order holding wooden guns made by Brother Pearson and Brother Smith. This marching group was to meet the President of the Church at the station and escort him to the school house which also served as the town meeting house.

Dr. Park, having returned from the Northwest, had established a school of renown reputation during the last four years since his return. The saints had been admonished by the church to bring west all educational materials they could fit into there wagons and carts. To that collection, Dr. Park had added several books. His school averaged about one hundred students. In addition to these he taught English to the adults who had migrated to Draper from foreign countries. He taught from McGuffey's Readers, Willson Readers, Spencerian Speller, Ray's Arithmetic, and Spencerian Penmanship. In addition to that he taught Geography, History, Botany, Zoology, Orinthology and Philosophy. On Saturdays he took the students on field trips to collect insects, leaves and rocks. He was now paid $1500.00 in gold for each school year.

Phebe was proud of the school. It lived up to her lifetime dream of what a school should be. Several hundred children and parents had visited the school at one time to hear Dr. Park explain the curriculum of the school. The town had welcomed them and made a celebration of the occasion. It was with the same enthusiasm that they looked forward to this day and the arrival of President Brigham Young, the most revered man in the territory.

Phebe helped Samantha and Mary get the children ready for the prophet's arrival in Draper. Samantha had seven children and Mary four so the three women had worked diligently to wash and starch the clothes and were now braiding the girls hair and combing down the unruly locks of the boys. The Brown children were to set an example of well dressed and well behaved children. Clarissa, Eunice and Mary Elizabeth had colorful new ribbons for their hair.

While Phebe braided the girl's hair and tied the ribbons on she told them about Brigham Young baptizing her many years ago. She told them about the cold February day when they walked to the river and about the warm wind that came just as she was to go into the water to be baptized. "And Brigham Young would come to my father's home in Canada and teach our whole family about the church. He was a very young man then but he had a special spirit about him that helped us all to realize that the church was true."

Ebenezer wore his good suit, a freshly starched white shirt and a dark cravat with a pearl stud in the center of it. He walked with his wives who were in their very best dresses to the meeting house. The children followed them with the older children holding the hands of the little ones. They stood at the entrance of the church with the other towns people and peered down the road to see the Boys Marching Band preceding the carriage of the President.

The Bishopric were first in line to greet him as his aides helped him from his carriage. The children were in such awe that it seemed as if they were not even breathing. There was definitely not the usual chatter that accompanied a gathering such as this. Brigham Young nodded to the crowd and proceeded into the building. The families followed, each taking the bench they were accustomed to occupying.

The Browns took their usual seats on the first bench. Phebe carried her cushion and placed it down at the end of the bench at the right of Ebenezer. Samantha sat on his left followed by her children. Then Mary and her children filed in and sat on the bench in back of them.

Phebe looked up at Brother Brigham sitting on the riser at the front of the vestry. He smiled at her and nodded his head. She wondered if he still remembered her. He had become so famous now. He was much heavier than when she first knew him and he was starting to look older. She smiled to herself as she realized she too was much older.

She was lost in thought about the many times they had met in the past. When she had arrived in Kirtland and he introduced her to the Prophet Joseph Smith and his wife Emma, in Far West during the terrible days of mob violence when he was trying to hold the saints together, in Nauvoo after the martyrdom of the Prophet when she sat in the audience and witnessed his appearance change to that of the prophet, on the west bank of the Mississippi when her mother died, his request for volunteers for the Battalion, his welcome when they arrived back at Great Salt Lake. She remembered that day well. She was wearing that lavender dress and bonnet and riding her mule, Jenny. That was almost twenty years ago.

The meeting started and she tried to attend to the speakers but her mind kept wandering back in time. She was caught up short, when Brother Brigham was speaking and referred to those days in Canada when so many Drapers joined the church. He talked about dedication and sacrifice required by the Lord from those who would be numbered in his fold. Then he looked at Phebe. "Sister Brown is one of those the Lord has chosen to lead the way. Her sacrifices have been many, as have many of yours. The Lord loves you for your dedication to his work."

She smiled back at him and then dropped her eyes in embarrassment. She was not one to be singled out for keeping the Lord's commandments. Somehow, that took away the blessing of it all.

After the meeting was over he walked from the stand and shook her hand. "Sister Phebe, It is wonderful to see you again. I wonder at the events that have happened since that day I left Loughborough, Canada. How many times our paths have crossed in our service to the Lord. May it continue to do so." He walked on to shake Ebenezer's hand and marvel at the lovely family. He walked down the aisle greeting each family and shaking hands with all of the children. Most of them he had met when they arrived in the valley and he had an uncanny memory for names.

When the day was over Phebe said goodnight to the family and went to her room alone. It was not her turn to have Ebenezer spend the night. She didn't mind being alone. There was so much to think about, so many memories to cherish. She took her Patriarchal blessing from the old family Bible and unfolded it. It had been years since she had read it. She looked at it written in beautiful script and remembered the evening Father Smith had come to her home in Kirtland. It was the day after the temple was dedicated. They had witnessed miracles and seen angels. This blessing was a miracle to her. She read, *"Sister, the Lord has favored thee from thy cradle. I lay my hands upon thy head in the name of Jesus according to the order of God desiring in my heart to bless thee. If thou wilt ask for blessings thou shalt have blessings according to thy desires in righteousness, so shall it be. Thou hast been afflicted and left a widow with children to care for, but the Lord has been merciful unto thee and given thee power to bear up under thy afflictions, and shall give thee the fullness of his holy spirit to comfort thee. I seal the blessing of a father upon thee because thou hast no father to bless thee nor companion to support thee, but if thou wilt be wise thou shalt have a companion who shall be a man of God, and thou shalt be able to bring up thy children so that none will be lost. Keep the commandments and thy life shall be long and thy shall see good days, and happy days, and the destroyer shall have no power to harm thee. Keep the word of wisdom and all the commandments and be a pattern for thy sex. Be wise, trust in God. He will deliver thee and provide for thee in all things which thou shalt need for thy comfort in this life and an inheritance in the life which is to come."*

She knelt by her bed and poured out her heart in thanksgiving to the Lord for all of his blessings. There was one unfulfilled spot that still worried her. She never heard from Asahel, her oldest son. She wrote him a letter every year, expressing her love for him and telling him the family news but he never answered her letters. Lovina had received a few letters from him so they knew he was still in Illinois and he and Evaline had ten children. She had letters from Lydia Elizabeth and Rhoda. William George was married now and Zemira was still in charge of the United Order for the church in Orderville. Lovina came to see her more often now that Ester Ann and Fanny were living in Draper. She would like to resolve her situation with Asahel but perhaps it was not to be. Other than that, her blessing had been fulfilled.

As she stood up and turned the covers back she heard a light tap at her door. It was Ebenezer. "Phebe, can I spend the night with you? Samantha said she didn't mind and I would like to be with you."

"Come in. I need some comforting." She turned down the other side of the bed.

Ebenezer and Phebe stood at the grave side of Elsie Samantha Pulsipher Brown, third wife of Ebenezer Brown. It was April of 1877. Samantha had been pacing the floor, grasping for breath. Suddenly she said, "Good bye all, I'm going to die." and fell to the bed. Her seven living children stood by the grave with their father and Phebe. Three small graves beside Samantha's, were those of two sons and a daughter who had died from epidemics that routinely plagued the children of the town.

The marker on the other side read, "Mary Elizabeth Wright Brown, fourth wife of Ebenezer Brown, 1837-1870." There were four of Mary's children's graves. She had died of a sudden illness after her last baby was born in 1869. Ebenezer had just built a new house for the large families of his two younger wives. It was really two houses divided by a common wall. Phebe stayed in the old house as it was home to her but when Mary died Phebe had moved in to the new house to care for Mary's children. Brother and Sister Wright, Mary's parents, had moved into the old home and took Mary's Baby, Edward, to raise.

Phebe looked around the cemetery at the many grave sites. John and Ester Ann had lost five little children. Fanny and William had lost two. Most of the deaths were from Diphtheria or Pneumonia. Very few families had been spared the sorrow of a child's death.

She and Ebenezer tried to comfort Samantha's children. Little Elisha would not go to his father, but clung to his sister, Eunice. Mary's oldest daughter, Mary Elizabeth, nineteen, had volunteered to care for Samantha's family. She encouraged the children to go with her to the house. The children from both of the families had been raised as brothers and sisters, taught to love and respect all three wives and be loyal to each other. They went with her willingly.

Ebenezer faltered as they walked away from the cemetery. Phebe held his arm. She noticed that he no longer used his left arm and seemed to limp, favoring his left leg. He leaned on her now, "I guess I'll have to have a little help getting home." Norman came to his father's side and helped him to a nearby buggy. The cemetery was only a block from home but it was evident that Ebenezer could not walk that far.

Phebe rode with him in the buggy. She was eighty years old and Ebenezer was seventy-six. She sat straight in the buggy. As her shoulders rounded with age she was determined she would not lose that posture that had been so important to her. "I could probably still balance a book on my head," she thought, and then chastised herself for such a vain thought at a time like this.

Ebenezer allowed some tears to streak his cheeks. "She was a good woman, Phebe. I tried to be a good husband to her. It is hard when you want to please three women." He fumbled in his pocket for a handkerchief.

Phebe pulled one from her handbag and handed it to him. "You have been a fine husband and father to all of your family. The Lord giveth and the Lord taketh away for His own purpose that we will understand one day."

Ebenezer took the extra handkerchief and blew his nose. "I will stay with Samantha's children if you will stay on with Mary's. Most of them are able to care for themselves except for little Elisha. I wish I could get close to that little boy."

"We will both be in the same house with just the common wall between us. We should be able to manage. I'll cook the meals with the girl's help. The boys are good to bring me wood for the stove. It may be best for us to eat in Mary's house until things get into a routine." Once again Phebe was making a mental list of what she would need to do to help fill the vacancy of the stalwart, Samantha. The children were cooperative and helpful. Between the two of them, they could handle one more challenge.

By January, Ebenezer had lost the use of his left side completely. Phebe had organized the older boys into a routine of helping him dress and getting him into and out of bed. The neighbors were good to come by to visit with him. Sister Fitzgerald was the Relief Society president and she came to check on him every day. They had always drawn water from the Brown well so she used that as an excuse. Phebe started preparing the meals in Samantha's side of the house so she could be closer to him.

One evening, as the dark settled over the village, Bishop Stewart came by to cheer his old friend. Ebenezer was in a melancholy mood. "I have always tried to do what the Lord has required of me and do it to the best of my ability, but now I am afraid I will have to leave all these children without a father to care for them." The Bishop invited the children and Phebe to join him at Ebenezer's bedside. He gave him a blessing, asking the Lord to accept the great sacrifices he had made in his life and to give him peace of mind.

Ebenezer drifted off to a quiet sleep while Phebe held his hand. It was not long until he was gone. After the family had been notified and the children comforted and put to bed, Phebe went to her room and prayed that she could endure to the end.

Lovina and Ester Ann stood at Phebe's side as Ebenezer's grave was dedicated to the Lord. She had been his wife for thirty-six years. She was so happy that she was sealed to him for eternity. They had made a good team, pulling together to fill the assignments and challenge that came their way. Just like the matched team Ebenezer bought for her at Fort Leavenworth.

Samantha's daughter, Clarissa, was married to Joshua Terry's son. Ebenezer had left his vast holdings in Joshua's hands. The Terry's took over the care of Samantha's younger children and a tight control of the proceeds from the farm. Mary's boys were in there twenties now and no longer needed, Aunt Phebe, as they called her, to care for them. Mary Elizabeth, realizing that Aunt Phebe could no longer take care of her, went to work for a family in Bingham Canyon.

Phebe continued to live in Mary's home. Lovina, now sixty years old and having lost her third husband, Newman Bulkley, came to live with her mother. Lovina suffered from diabetes so mother and daughter cared for each other with Ester Ann's help. Ester Ann would bring her little son, Roy, with her to her grandmother's house. Phebe loved to have the little ones around, even at her advanced age. Roy was a bright child and started to learn to read with his great grandmother's help. He was probably the last child she taught to unlock the magic of written words.

Sometimes John would come with Ester Ann in the evening and they would sing the good old songs that Phebe loved. Lovina would join them, still singing in her clear soprano voice. Little Roy learned the songs too and the three generation trio sang about children playing in the sand,

> *"Two little children, a boy and a girl,*
> *were playing one day in the sand.*
> *They built them a house of pretty sea shells,*
> *with only their little brown hands.*
> *When the boy, just for fun,*
> *gave a kick and then run*
> *and down came the house on the sand."*

Phebe's last days were happy ones with her family nearby. As she heard them sing she wondered how soon her life would come down into the sand. At eighty-two years old, she knew her days were numbered.

Lovina came to her mother's side, fluffed the pillow at her back and tucked the blanket around her shoulder. She then took an envelope from her pocket. "Mother, I have a letter from Asahel. I wrote to him weeks ago and ask that he get in touch with us." She opened the letter and read the brief note.

> *"Dear Lovina,*
> *I am sorry you and mother are both in ill health. I am getting older also. I thought I would never see my sixtieth birthday but here it is. Our ten children are all well with families of their own. Evaline and I are alone here on the farm but our children and grandchildren come to visit us often. I have appreciated your letters from time to time.*

Give Mother my love. I regret that I could never bring myself to answer her letters. I know she always wanted the best for me but I seemed to have more of our father in me than the kind characteristics of our Mother. I still cannot understand why all of you have made such great sacrifices for the Mormon church.

Mother would be happy to know that all of our children went to school and did quite well. Phebe, our oldest, even taught school until she was married. She is very much like her grandmother.

I send my love to all the family. Thanks to you, I know something of them after all these years.

Your loving brother,
Asahel

Phebe held the letter in her hand as if feeling it would connect her, somehow, to Asahel. "Well, he writes with adequate penmanship and spelling, even if he wouldn't stay in school. It was always important to me that my children be educated. Oh, my dear Lovina, thank you for staying in touch with him over the years. You are the peacemaker in the family. There is one more thing I need you to do for me."

"What is it, Mother?" Lovina leaned close to hear her mother's voice.

"There is a wooden box under my bed that Zemira made for me years ago. I have kept important papers in it and the little woven basket the Indians made. Please give it to Ester Ann and tell her she must keep it until she needs to pass it on to one of her children. You may look in it. There may be something you want to add. It is a legacy of our family." She smiled at this daughter who had brought so much happiness to her since the day she was born in Canada. Suddenly, she felt very tired. The lids closed over those steel grey eyes that had witnessed more than most.

A path of light opened up to her and she could see Ebenezer, Ann, Samantha and Mary walking to greet her with

Beverly B. Thompson

arms outstretched. She was running to them when she saw in
the distance, George, holding Eliza's hand.

Epilogue

I had many experiences while I was writing this book that I would like to share with the reader. I often felt that Phebe was guiding my writing as I tried to put myself into her life. On many occasions I would be writing the "Novel" as a story and then discover from subsequent research that I had written it as it had happened. It was my intent to use accurate dates, places and names from verified records. Some of the events were also chronicled in histories written from oral histories, being passed from generation to generation.

My father, Roy Boulter, was five when his Great Grandmother, Phebe, died. I was his youngest child. He was fifty-five when I was born. This made me almost a generation closer to a Great, Great Grandparent than most of my contemporaries. I heard many stories of the olden days in Draper. The fact that the town was named after a Great Uncle caused me to identify with its history and the people who settled it.

In 1949, a few months before my first child was born, my mother asked me to go with her to interview a neighbor who was in her eighties. She was one of the oldest early residents of Draper. As her interesting story unfolded, I realized that Eunice Walbeck, who we called Grandma Walbeck, was one of the younger daughters of Ebenezer Brown and his polygamist wife, Samantha. Grandma Walbeck told us about "Aunt Phebe" helping them when they were children and helping to care for Ebenezer's other family of children when their mother died. She spoke of her with great respect. Phebe had outlived three of Ebenezer's wives and been instrumental in guiding their children to adulthood. She was Ebenezer's wife for thirty-five years.

Realizing that I had known two people who knew this grandmother made me feel closer to her. I had often recounted the stories I knew of her life to my children and my friends. Needless to say, I was proud of this person who had been baptized by Brigham Young, lived in Kirtland and Far West as a widow. Had married Ebenezer, a man promised to her in a blessing, and lived with him in Nauvoo, crossed the plains of Iowa in the dead of winter and then went with him on the Mormon Battalion trek to Mexico and on to California. I knew she had panned gold in California and ridden a mule back to Utah where she and Ebenezer were the first to settle in what is now known as, Draper.

As I felt inspired to review the histories again I found that I could only find two direct quotes. One from each of her husbands. The first husband is reported to have said about her decision to be baptized, "You wouldn't be satisfied until you got your backside wet." The second quote I heard myself from her second husband's daughter. She said that the night before her father died he said to the bishop, "I have always tried to do what the Lords has ask of me and my only sorrow is that I have to leave these little children without anyone to care for them." Comparing the statements I have tried to describe the men as I feel they were in their temperament and devotion.

Almost weekly, as I wrote, I would find evidence in research that verified the direction I was taking in the writing of the novel. Early on in the book I had written of her father as being a religious man who read the Bible to his children. Within the week I read a history describing him as a student of the Bible. In a very unusual way I received a packet of materials containing genealogical records of Phebe's mother, traced back to the fifteenth century' and the reference to a book written about a famous grandfather.

As I described the exodus from Nauvoo across the icy Mississippi River and the imminent death of her mother, Lucy, I left the story line once more to verify in the records the death date of her mother. There on the genealogy sheet my mother had recorded years ago, was the record of the death of Lucy

Lathrop Draper, as occurring on the west bank of the Mississippi River in February 1846.

Comparing historical accounts, I found some instances where hearsay had been no more accurate than fiction. Some histories recorded that she had a large family of young children when she married Ebenezer, but further research and the comparison of birth dates, marriages and locations revealed that she only had three of her seven children still living with her at the time of their marriage and he had three of his four children. Accounts of their days in the gold fields reported them working for wages but upon further investigation it would seem that they panned for gold themselves and brought a sizable amount to Utah with them. To my surprise, I found a book, by accident or inspiration, that showed a receipt to Ebenezer of $100.00 paid for tithing at the gold mint in Salt lake in 1848. $6.00 was paid in cash and the rest in gold dust. It was the first receipted gold dust paid into the mint. Zemira Palmer indicates in his history that he found a rich vein of gold and was able to come to the Salt Lake Valley with $500.00.

I have always loved puzzles and this was very much like solving a puzzle. A little information found in one person's history filled in a gap in another history. Because we know that people don't live in a vacuum, it is easy to make realistic assumptions from the recorded histories of contemporaries. Much of Phebe's life was spent in the close proximity of her younger brothers, William Draper Jr. and Zemira Draper. Gleaning information from excerpts of William Draper's journal helped many pieces of the puzzle fit together.

I have often been asked if I wrote from Phebe's journal, but as far as I know she did not leave a journal. There was not one in the box of treasures my father found. It is my hope that this book will take the place of her journal. To alleviate the curiosity of the readers I will reveal the few fictional characters I wrote into the story.

Okinihah, the Indian. An Indian is referred to in the histories but not by name.

Master John Park and his relationship to the real John R. Park.
The preacher/teacher, Reverend Black
The Milliner, Mrs. Kenny
The Banker, Mr. Green
The storekeeper, Mr. Barnes
Joseph Stewart and family
Emanuel Green of Pleasantville
Elijah Palmer, George's brother.
Jason, Serena and Julia Spencer
Mountain men, Jed and James and the Carson brothers.

Other fictional parts of the story were:
    The tea set
    Grandmother Draper's cake plate
    The Journal Phebe lost in the Bear River

I have found no evidence that Phebe taught school in Canada or Kirtland but several histories of early settlers in Draper refer to her as being well read and teaching the little ones. It would seem that she would have come from an educational background to have taken on that assignment. I admit I may have written some of myself into the book because of my teaching background.

It is my sincere belief that I have been guided to write this book in the present format to help people understand the commitment and dedication of the early saints. Their sacrifices were minimal compared to the degree of joy they found in their conversion to the Gospel.

I would like to add two quotes which I think summarize the spirit of this book. The first is from Ebenezer's Patriarchal blessing given to him in Far West. The second is an excerpt from Zemira Palmers letter to his sister Lovina. These were the two men who Phebe accompanied on the Mormon Battalion trek. The first was her husband and the other her son.

1. "And if oppression awaits thee, it shall only cause thee to smile, for the chains of the oppressor shall not hold thee because if thou are faithful, thou shalt be sanctified and all power shall be handed to thy posterity, to thy companion and thy children and it shall be realized by thy posterity 'til the Savior shall make his second advent, thou shall be caught up with thy posterity to meet him in the air with Abraham, Isaac and Jacob and I seal this blessing upon thee in the name of the Lord for ever and ever, Amen and Amen." (Ebenezer Brown and His Descendants) page 8.

2. "There is one thing which seems to be true however. The Lord is fulfilling His promises. He has said by the mouths of His prophets that He would send judgments on the wicked and trials on the faithful so that every one that can be shaken will be and those who cannot be shaken shall gain the great reward of eternal life and supreme happiness. It would be well I think, for every one to ask themselves the question seriously. "Can I stand?" (The Descendants of George Palmer and Phebe Draper) by Sarah P. Collinwood, page 454b. A photograph of the original letter written by Zemira Palmer in Orderville, Utah, September 19, 1880.

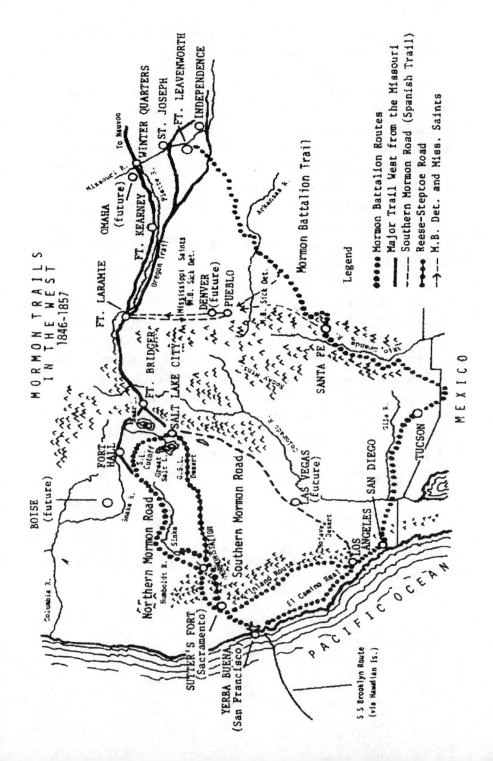

MORMON TRAILS
IN THE WEST
1846-1857

Legend

••••• Mormon Battalion Routes
━━━ Major Trail West from the Missouri
━ ━ ━ Southern Mormon Road (Spanish Trail)
•••• Reese-Steptoe Road
→→→ M.B. Det. and Miss. Saints

A Leaf from Family Bible of Phebe Draper Palmer
(Brown)

(1584) Rev. John Lathrop/Hanna House
Samuel Lathrop/Elizabeth Scudder
Israil Lathrop/Rebecca Bliss
Jabez Lathrop/Delight Otis
Isaac Lathrop/Lucy Pike

Thomas Draper/Jane Braman   Josiah Rogers/Lydia Goodsell   David Byington/Mercy
William Draper   David Rogers/Eunice Byington
            Thomas Draper/Lydia Rogers

William Draper/Lydia Lathrop
            Charles 1795
            PHEBE 1797
            Carson 1799
            Lucritia 1802
            Fannie 1804
            William Jr. 1807
            Zemira 1812

George Palmer/PHEBE DRAPER
            Lovina 1816
            Asahel 1819
            William George 1821
            Eliza 1824
            Lydia Elizabeth 1826
            Zemira 1831
            Rhoda 1834

Ebenezer Brown/Ann Weaver (first wife)
            Joseph Gurnsey 1824
            Harriet 1827
            Norman 1830
            Baby Ann 1842

PHEBE DRAPER PALMER (second wife)
            No children

Elsie Samantha Pulsipher (third wife)
            Ebenezer 1854
            Samantha 1856
            Clarissa 1859
            David 1861
            Joseph*
            Eunice 1865
            Hyrum 1867
            Zina 1869
            Priscilla 1870
            Elisha 1872

Mary Elizabeth Wright (fourth wife)
            William 1856
            George 1858
            Mary Elizabeth 1858
            Franklin*
            Jullietta*
            Alfred*
            Chester*
            James Edward 1870

*Died as children—dates not available